GREEK WINDS OF FURY

Novels by Judith Gould

Sins
Love-Makers
Dazzle
Never Too Rich
Texas Born
Forever
Too Damn Rich
Second Love
Till the End of Time
Rhapsody
Time to Say Good-Bye
A Moment in Time
The Best Is Yet to Come
The Greek Villa
The Parisian Affair
Dreamboat
The Secret Heiress

GREEK WINDS OF FURY

[A Novel of Romantic Suspense]

Judith Gould

Copyright 2008 by Judith Gould. All rights reserved.

Manufactured in the United States of America

This trade paperback original is published by Alyson Books
245 West 17th Street, New York, NY 10011
Distribution in the United Kingdom by Turnaround Publisher Services Ltd.
Unit 3, Olympia Trading Estate, Coburg Road, Wood Green
London N22 6TZ England

First Edition: December 2008

08 09 10 11 12 a 10 9 8 7 6 5 4 3 2 1

ISBN: 1-59350-086-6
ISBN-13: 978-1-59350-086-3

Library of Congress Cataloging-in-Publication data are on file.

Cover design by Victor Mingovits
Interior design by Charles Annis

With Love and eminent respect to my parents, Gunther and Erna Bienes, who plucked a wild child out of the Russian Occupied Zone of Austria, brought it to the United States, adopted it, gave it the gift of American citizenship, and sent it on its way through thick and thin, through understandings and misunderstandings, forgiveness and, above all, for showing their generosity, support, and love over five decades. And hopefully for more decades to come.

Acknowledgments

Special thanks are due to the following:

Arto Penttinen, archeologist and co-director of the "Kalaureia Research Program" on Poros, Greece, who gave me invaluable advice, most of which I have taken, and some of which had to be discarded for the furtherance of the plot. Any errors, or deviations from his sage advice, are the author's, and the author's alone.

Leonard Mosley, whose biography, *The Reich Marshal; A Biography of Herman Goering* and especially Ella Leffland, whose novelized biography of Göring, *The Knight, Death and the Devil: A Novel of a Life Corrupted by Evil* have proved invaluable during the Karinhall scenes.

Constantine N. Ordolis and Marina Kouloumoundra of Bell Harlenic, my Greek publisher, for their generous hospitality and enlightening me on a variety of issues and subjects from a non-touristy and highly urbane viewpoint.

"The Mykonos Gang"—David Gourgourinis, Sandra Clare, and Ivo Stoykova—for providing fertile fodder and inspiration year after year.

Rhea Gallaher, my life partner and co-author of some thirty years. We couldn't have done it without each other.

Dale Cunningham, publisher of Alyson Books, for her patience and forbearance and understanding, extending my deadline to the very last minute.

Paul Florez, Richard Fumosa, and Anthony La Sasso of Alyson Books for putting up with the same.

The late, great Gladys Allison, who sent me on my way. If ever a teacher existed who inspired, it was she. May she rest in heavenly peace.

Joseph Pittman, editor and writer, who believed in this novel from the start.

Maria Carvainis, of the Maria Carvainis Agency, who sniffed early developing talent and gave a not-always-grateful author my initial start. Many, many thanks, great lady.

Elaine Koster, ex-publisher and now literary agent, who pushed "Ms. Gould" along. Believe it or not, you're thoroughly missed, and shall always be respected for knowing exactly where I stood in your graces, whether good or bad.

Sterling Lord, Irving "Swifty" Lazar, and, currently, Alan Nevins of "The Firm" who, at various times, represented and represent me and my writings.

And finally, to Billy and Jeffrey, my canine cohorts, brothers from the same litter who have never been separated for a day in their lives, and who have been lying patiently at my feet, waiting for me to finish. Like their late "Happy" and "Mina," whose graves I personally dug, they're poster children for Humane Societies everywhere!

And above all, to you, my readers, to whom I owe everything. Yes—*you*!

The Meltemi *is one of the legendary Mediterranean winds. Fiercely strong and dangerous, it funnels southward through the Aegean. The ancients called it the* Etesian, *and it creates adverse currents and wind velocities which can range from four to seven on the Beaufort scale. In the region between the Dodecanese and Cycladic islands, the* Meltemi *can reach thirty knots and create wave heights of up to ten feet.*

"Meltemi" *can have various other definitions as well. It can be used to describe the unpredictable moods of a bad-tempered person, for instance, or even be used as the name for a swift vessel whose owner thinks it as strong or fast as the wind.*

[PART I]

What Happened Before

[CHAPTER ONE]

August 12, 522 B.C.

The Northern Aegean island of Samos, formerly an independent island state, now under the rule of the tyrant Polycrates

The eroded cliff face was like an open wound, plunging nakedly from the overhanging crest above to the pebble-beached cove far below. The sky was cloudless, all blue haze throbbing with brutal heat. Relentless, the sun baked the corrugated volcanic rock, schist, and marble that was indigenous to the geological composition of Asia Minor, from which the island had split during a long-ago volcanic eruption. The blazing sun cast every protrusion and scar into deep purple shadow. The sea, a blue so deep it was nearly black, sent low breakers shoreward, where they washed up the incline of smooth gray pebbles and spent themselves in lacy white spume before receding so that the next wave could follow, and then the next, and the next.

The sound of water crashing gently ashore was obscured by the cacophony of man-made noises. Shouted commands and warnings, the creaking of ropes against block and tackle, the sound of hammers and curses rang out from within the towering, inverted V of a defile in the cliff face, which led from the beach into a natural amphitheater of rock open to the sky.

This was the studio of Arion the sculptor, and it was a hive of activity.

Arion was a short, usually quiet man with a fluff of black curly hair on a balding skull, intense lively dark eyes the color of polished obsidian, and sun-browned skin perpetually white with marble dust so that unless he was moving he could almost be mistaken for a statue himself. Bare-chested and extremely broad of shoulder, his arms were knotted with muscle and his hands were large, the skin thick and rough, callused from decades spent chiseling blocks of marble into identifiable shapes.

At the moment, he didn't look so much like a statue as a two-toned creature; such was the effect of the vertical streaks left by rivulets of dripping sweat. Besides having to dash around giving orders, his nerves were strung as tightly as the strings of a lyre.

For there, inside his amphitheater-like studio with its natural skylight, and bathed in golden sunlight, stood his masterpiece.

Hera.

The marble goddess represented the crowning point of his career. She was the culmination of six years spent chiseling a single massive block of pale gray marble with darker, gray-blue striations into a glorious statue nearly forty hand-spans tall—almost four times the height of even the tallest among the army of slaves assigned to help move it.

Transporting any completed statue required complex engineering. But moving this, the largest free-standing statue in the entire world, called for exceptional finesse.

"No, no, no!" Arion shouted up at the slaves on the wooden scaffolding surrounding the giant figure. "That rope is too thin! Someone—" he grabbed the arm of the nearest slave "—get them thicker rope. *Thick*, do you hear!"

For before the blocks and tackles could be used, the wooden cage of thick notched logs, bound together with rope, had to be strong enough to support untold tons. Only then could his vertical masterpiece be lowered horizontally into the giant wooden cradle, where countless bales of hay would provide a protective cushion. Then the cradle would have to be rolled outside on perfectly round logs down the beach, where more blocks and tackles would lift it aboard a raft.

He sighed. Sculpting the goddess was one thing; moving it to its spot at Heraion, where the new temple was being erected, was another.

Arion had been to Heraion only the previous day. As always, he had been awe-struck by the unfinished structure. Far larger than the Temple of Artemis in Ephesus, on the nearby mainland of Asia Minor, it would be the most monumental temple in all Greece. And although it already had one towering statue of Hera, Polycrates had not been satisfied. After all, he believed he owed his success to Hera, the goddess of the Samians, who was said to have been born nearby at the stream called Imbrassos.

In order to please Hera and remain in her good graces, Polycrates, the scourge of the Aegean with his mighty naval fleet of one hundred ships called *Samians,* each of which had five tiers of oarsmen, and whose profitable pirate raids enriched the island state's coffers to the point of bursting, had personally commissioned not only the new temple, but also had ordered Arion to sculpt an even larger and more impressive statue of the goddess.

A statue which, like the temple Polycrates had ordered built at Heraion to her, would overshadow even that of the mighty statue of Artemis at Ephesus.

The statue which Arion had at long last completed.

It had been a Herculean task, one which had never before been conceived, let alone executed, on such a monumental scale. For Polycrates was a man for whom nothing was impossible. His ego was as vast as his power and his plunders. His orders to Arion had been precise: "You shall sculpt the biggest, most beautiful, most impressive statue in the entire Greek world."

Arion had made certain his patron and master would be pleased. He knew what would happen if the tyrant found fault—he, Arion, would be ordered killed on the spot.

So Arion had put all his talent and skill to work. Not only to please and create, but also to ensure his own longevity. Polycrates had yet to see the finished sculpture; he was off on another pirate raid, but was expected back any day with yet more plundered riches.

"Get up, you two! Stop wasting time!" Arion snapped at a pair of sweat-drenched slaves who were resting. "My lord Polycrates expects that statue in place by the time he returns. Or would you rather experience his wrath?"

They needed no further prodding. Everyone in the Aegean feared Polycrates, and that included his own subjects. As for slaves, one or two fewer didn't matter; the tyrant always returned from his raids with a fresh batch.

"Ships! I see ships!" a worker stationed on the clifftop shouted excitedly down into the roofless studio.

Ships! The flurry of electric whispers passed among apprentices and slaves alike.

"Whose ships?" Arion demanded. He hurried outside to the pebble beach to see for himself, where he lifted a hand to shield his eyes from the blinding sun as he scanned the sea. At first, it was impossible to tell where the sea ended and the sky began. The shimmering haze of blue gave the illusion of seamlessness, the illusions that he was staring at a single endless fabric. Behind him, he could hear work slowing, then stopping altogether as the workers came out to join him on the beach.

Then suddenly, when he divined the faraway spot where water met sky, he saw them. The ships were little more than smudges floating on the horizon, but their shapes were unmistakably those of *Samians*.

"They're ours!" someone cried excitedly. "The fleet is returned!"

"Doubtless filled to overflowing with treasures!" marveled a voice from beside Arion with satisfaction. It belonged to Thrasyllus of Paros, who had trained under Eupalinos of Megara, the hydraulics engineer famous for his work on the underground aqueduct, finished several years earlier, which guaranteed an endless supply of pure mountain water from Mount Kastri to the city of Samos in case the mighty stronghold was ever besieged.

"We must not count our catch before we fish," cautioned Arion. "Do you not notice something amiss?"

"Notice? Something amiss?" Thrasyllus of Paros shaded his own eyes and squinted. "By almighty Zeus!" he exclaimed under his breath. "You are right. There are so few! Perhaps the rest of the flotilla follows?"

Arion's voice was quiet. "Follows even more slowly, you mean. Can you not see that those *Samians* are limping home? Whatever happened to the swift oar thrusts of a triumphant return?" He felt a shiver of unease crawl along his spine. "I fear they may have suffered a goodly amount of damage."

His words spread from one man to another. They had the effect of water thrown upon fire, bringing about a total hush. In the absence of work or talk, the sound of waves curling inland and sliding up the beach seemed suddenly amplified.

No one moved; all eyes were focused on the sea. In due time, a handful of other ships eventually appeared, sluggishly heading for the city of Samos. Clearly some mighty misfortune had befallen them. A sudden storm, perhaps? Surely not. No, it was impossible! Not defeat!

Arion turned to the man at his side. "Thrasyllus," he said, "climb the cliff and commandeer the swiftest horse we have. Ride into town like you have the *Etesian* wind at your back. The moment you have news, make haste to bring it."

"Consider me gone," Thrasyllus said, and vanished quietly.

Arion and the others remained rooted where they stood on the beach, watching and waiting. No one spoke. It was unheard of for Arion to let work slow, let alone halt, and that he allowed it underscored the magnitude of his worries.

No one kept track of the passing time. The sun and heat were merciless, beating down upon the men assembled on the pebble beach. Arion's eyes ached from staring out at the glare of water. Yet he never moved unless it was to switch arms and shade his eyes with his other hand.

Every so often, another distant *Samian* would move feebly, sluggishly, toward the city of Samos.

Eventually, when the sun was beginning to set in the west, gilding the face of rock, they heard the sound of hoofs trampling the dried yellow grass atop the cliff like approaching thunder. Everyone turned, heads leaning far back, and looked expectantly up to the edge of the drop-off.

Thrasyllus did not wait to dismount. His chestnut horse danced nervously at the cliff's rim, loosening stones which rattled down to the beach below.

"What news, Thrasyllus?" called out Arion.

"Tragedy!" Thrasyllus shouted back breathlessly. "Our lord Polycrates was captured by the Persians and has been crucified! Our proud fleet is decimated! Decimated!"

Polycrates crucified? There was a collective gasp. Arion's head reeled. His mouth was agape and he was in a state of shock. He, like the others—apprentices, engineers, and slaves alike—could only stare up at Thrasyllus with incredulous disbelief. Then, as the news sank in, they exchanged stupefied looks and sagged like marionettes whose strings had gone slack. A few sank down onto the beach and sat there dumbly, gazing out to sea.

Arion waited until Thrasyllus had dismounted and scrambled down the switchbacks of the narrow path hewn into the cliff face. He was glistening with sweat and out of breath. "Defeated!" he rasped, gripping Arion's arm and shaking it. "Only Hera knows what will happen to us now!"

Arion left him and the others and staggered through the spire-shaped cleft in the cliff that was the entrance to his studio. Inside it was cooler, the air perpetually blurry with marble dust. His eyes began to water, whether from the dust particles after he'd been out in the fresh air for so long or the terrible news.

He stared up at his monumental creation. Although confined to her temporary cage of wooden logs, and attached to blocks and tackles with hawser-like ropes, the goddess looked serene and almost expressionless. Then the setting sun crept in through the giant gash in the rock, tinting part of her in a reddish-orange glow and casting her face in partial shadow.

As the sun moved lower, so did the shadow, and Arion thought he could detect her full lips turning down into a frown.

Arion fell to his knees in front of the statue and held out a beseeching hand in midair. "Almighty Hera," he moaned, "why have you deserted us, your faithful worshipers? Can it be possible that the gods of the Persians wield more power than you?"

Afterwards, Arion would never know what caused it—his blasphemy, Hera's rage at Polycrates' fate, or a reminder to her faithful that she was still in possession of mighty powers. Whatever the reason, he suddenly felt himself trembling.

Is it my fear of the future, he wondered, *the abyss of the looming unknown?* For it was not like him to tremble; he prided himself on having the steadiest nerves and hands on Samos. A sculptor could not, after all, have hands that shook. One wrong slip of the chisel and years of work could be ruined.

There. That was better. His shaking had stopped. He had himself back under control.

"Arion!" Thrasyllus called anxiously from the entrance, his long shadow blocking a portion of Hera's reddish tint.

Arion did not turn around. "Later, Thrasyllus. I need to be alone for a while."

"Yes, but—"

"Later!" The sharpness of Arion's voice brooked no argument.

A pause. And then, as he withdrew, Thrasyllus' shadow shortened, gliding away until it disappeared. Once again, the setting sun bathed the statue completely.

And once again Arion felt himself trembling. It took the accompanying rumble for him to realize that it was not he who was trembling, but the very earth itself! A hail of small stones slid down the rock walls on all sides, and marble dust, which had clung to every surface, was stirred up, clouding his vision.

He jumped to his feet and nearly fell, but managed to retain his footing.

The tremor stopped as suddenly as it had begun.

Arion held his breath and waited, his heart pounding. Had Hera called upon her fellow god, Poseidon the Earth-Shaker, to punish those who dared think she had deserted her faithful? Or was she showing her fury at the loss of Polycrates?

Then came another tremor, more violent than the last, and with a far more powerful rumble. The quarry-like walls rippled and cracked, loosening pieces of once-solid rock, and sending them crashing down all around. And now, as the vibration gathered strength, Arion could feel himself being scooted sideways, despite the fact that he himself hadn't moved a single step!

In front of him, like a ghostly giant seen through a scrim, Hera was not only wobbling unsteadily, but she too was moving sideways. There was a sharp crack, and on her left one log of her cage snapped and came crashing down, weakening the others. Under the strain, the mighty ropes, so thick that Arion's fingers could not encircle them, tore as easily as the flimsiest thread, and suddenly the entire scaffolding of logs and planks collapsed like twigs, sliding down around Hera as though a robe had been loosened and had fallen to gather around her feet, freeing her completely. And despite the thunderous grinding and shrieking of rock against rock, of fissures splitting open, of the catastrophic salvos of the plunging scaffolding, he was dimly aware of the men outside panicking, screaming with fright and shouting out prayers.

"What the—" He let out a cry as a small but pointed shard of rock, only pebble sized, pelted him on the shoulder. The pain was sharp and needle-like and jarred him to the bone. He felt a moist burning sensation and touched himself.

When he looked at his hand, his fingertips came away smeared with blood.

I have to get out of here!

The thought exploded in his head like a bolt of lightning.

While I still can—

—before I'm buried alive!

Yet he was riveted to the spot, unable to move. How *could* he leave? Why, his towering statue looked alive! Almighty Hera was rocking forwards and backwards, as though taking steps toward him! It was too awesome and mesmerizing a sight, this illusion of marble perfection come to life.

I can't leave her.

She's my masterpiece.

The ground gave its most violent shudder yet and the barrage of falling rocks increased; he stared up at her in the increasing murkiness.

Rock dust merged with marble dust, but he could still see her dimly, she was that close . . . leaning over him . . . then leaning back . . . then leaning forward again, teetering—

She really is coming towards me! he thought.

"Arion!" The yell belonged to Thrasyllus of Paros. "Get moving!"

At his colleague's voice, Arion came to with a start, but it was too late. Hera was already directly above him and falling forward, yet he was spellbound.

"*Now!*" Thrasyllus leapt toward Arion, grabbed his arm, and yanked him out of harm's way just as the giant statue toppled right where he had been standing. Another second and he would have been crushed to death.

Luckily, the tons of carved marble missed the men as Hera crashed to the ground with a deafening boom, adding yet more reverberations to the earthquake's rumbling, rattling, and rolling.

It was as if the world was coming to an end.

As the two men raced through the rent in the rock that was the entrance, Arion glanced back over his shoulder and saw that Hera was in two pieces; she had cracked in half at the waist.

Then he and Thrasyllus burst out into the open air, gasping, coughing, and with stinging eyes. A giant, mushrooming cloud of debris and dust billowed out of the entrance behind them, as though giving chase while a second mushrooming cloud bloomed skyward, out of the huge open roof of the cavern.

Thrasyllus had to shout to make himself heard. "Into the sea! Hurry!"

For that was where the clusters of frightened workmen and slaves had gathered, as far out into the churning, leaping water as they could get, for the towering wall of naked rock had become one continuous mass of landslides. Boulders were plunging down and bouncing onto the pebble beach amid untold tons of volcanic rock and earth.

Into the sea Arion and Thrasyllus waded, the resistance of the water slowing their progress, the convulsively shifting sea floor and algae-slimed rocks making it difficult to keep their balance. The water was cold against Arion's sweaty skin; he could feel the salt burn in myriads of cuts he hadn't been aware he'd suffered.

When they were chest deep in the sea, the two men stood, side by side, and stared landward in silent awe as an avalanche of rock and earth totally sealed the natural gash which only moments earlier had led into the studio. Almost simultaneously, the rim of the cliff top—Arion's natural skylight—collapsed and closed in upon itself.

Arion thought: *Had I remained in there, it would have become my tomb.*

"Everything's gone," he whispered in a choked voice, tears streaming down his face. "Everything."

"Don't worry," Thrasyllus told him. "You'll find another studio."

But Arion shook his head. He hadn't been talking about his studio. He said, "The gods have deserted us."

For with Polycrates slain, the naval fleet and army decimated, and now the earthquake's damage, the island state was weak. In one fell swoop, Samos' mighty power was broken, and he knew she would never again recover her former status or glory.

And it was for this loss that he wept.

[CHAPTER TWO]

September 12, 509 B.C.

It was thirteen years after the fall of Polycrates, and the little girl squinted thoughtfully the way children will, her head tilted sideways, her lower lip jutting out as she watched the old man apply thin slips of wet clay to the surface of the big, unfired pottery krater. Despite his age, his large gnarled hands were steady as he deftly employed the ages-old technique, using two pots of clay, each containing a different mineral mixed with iron, which he then incised with details using a sharp instrument of his own making. Once fired, depending upon the temperature, the colors of the clay would turn black or red.

The krater was of common shape but perfectly proportioned. Larger than most, with the two traditional handles between its wide mouth and great, elongated ovoid bowl, it was meant more for ceremonial use rather than for the daily use of mixing wine with water.

The artist, on the other hand, was anything but perfectly proportioned. He possessed a most peculiar physique. A strangely-shaped little man, he had too-wide shoulders and a large chest. His once-muscular arms had shrunken, leaving loose skin dangling from the bones, and he was otherwise gaunt, with almost stick-like legs. His small withered face was a net of wrinkles, with the thinnest fluff of white hair curling from the midst of his balding skull, but his every touch was nimble and sure, surgical in its precision.

"What myth are you depicting, Great-uncle?" The child's voice was high and sweet, but she looked puzzled. "I have never seen anything like it."

He smiled indulgently as he put down his thin metal instrument and covered the two small pots of mineralized clay with a wet cloth to keep their contents moist. Before replying, he paused to appraise his handiwork.

It was masterful, he admitted to himself. The stylized, linked lotus leaves and palmettes encircling the flared top of the rim possessed a mathematical precision. Yet it was the figures themselves that he had etched with such magisterial delicacy that had attracted his great-niece's attention.

For instead of the traditional himation-clad youths, or scenes depicting Theuseus pursuing Aithra, or romping flute-playing donkey-mounted satyrs and Dionysos holding a large *kantharos,* or even perhaps Herakles, wearing the lion skin as he wrestled with Triton, the sea deity, this krater was illustrated with scenes such as she had never before seen.

He patted his knees. "Come here, sit on your great-uncle's lap, and he shall explain it," he told her.

She scampered happily atop his knees. "Well?" she demanded, looking up at him with a mixture of adoration and excitement.

"If you look carefully," he said, "this has no mythological or religious connotation. It tells a story."

"A story!" She clapped her hands in delight. "Oh, do tell, Great-uncle! Please?"

Her eyes shone with pleasure.

He pointed a gnarled finger at a particular spot on the ovoid krater. "The story begins here," he told her.

She twisted around on his lap, eyes eagerly following his moving finger.

"It is a story of something that happened long before you were conceived. You see the top here? Where it shows a man carving a giant statue?" He pointed to a completed portion at the underside of the thick rim.

She frowned prettily. "Yes?"

"Well that, my sweet child, is where the story begins. And as you go around and around, spiraling downward—" he spun the krater very slowly on its wooden turntable and pointed "—it tells of the biggest statue in the world, and the catastrophe that buried it deep inside the ground. It also shows the spot where this happened."

"Why? Is that important?"

He smiled indulgently. "Remember last week when you lost your little clay doll? And we searched and searched until we found it?"

She nodded solemnly. "Yes."

"Well, I'm portraying this just in case someone wants to find it someday."

"But you haven't finished the story," she pointed out. "You've only completed it halfway down."

"That is because I'm doing it slowly and carefully. By the time the bottom is completed, it shall tell the entire tale. You will then be able to read it in pictures."

"But I don't *want* to have to wait until you finish! Can't you tell me the story now? Oh, please, Great-uncle?" she pleaded. "Please?"

He smiled. It was difficult to deny his great-niece anything. "Oh, alright, my impatient little one." He pretended to be grumpy, then laughed and tickled her.

She shrieked happily.

"But I'm only going to tell it now because you are my sweet little nymph. So. Are you ready to listen?"

"Oh, yes!" She wriggled out of his arms and sat down beside him, hugging her knees with her arms, wide eyes sparkling with anticipation.

Arion began, "Well, it goes like this. Once upon a time, there was a man who sculpted marble statues." A half-hidden smile hovered on his lips and his eyes took on the distant look of memory. "His name happened to be Arion."

[CHAPTER THREE]

June 5–June 8, 1942 A.D.

The Northern Aegean island of Samos, now occupied by the Axis powers

He wasn't sure which was worse. The perpetual cloud of gritty dust, the noise of heavy equipment and generators running twenty-four hours a day, or the Wehrmacht encampment which made up the site. If only the digging could be done the careful, scholarly way, who knew what might be unearthed?

But he had to follow orders—they had come from the highest level. And when you make a pact with the devil, you must dance to his tune.

Besides, success was close. Doktor Professor Friedrich Hammerschlag of the Berlin Reichsmuseum could almost smell it. His lifelong obsession and search was about to be realized. He could feel it in his bones.

Outside his tent it was night, but stark floodlights bathed the area where the bulldozers and steam shovels, Wehrmacht corps of engineers, and forced laborers from the island toiled in the glare while armed guards patrolled the barbed-wire perimeter. Inside his tent, he was writing in his journal by a lantern's light. Also on his makeshift table were the cracked and faded sepia photographs which had sparked his obsession.

These photographs.

Putting aside pen and journal, he picked them up and yet again spread them all out in front of himself like cards from a deck. They depicted a krater, discovered nearly seventy years earlier, that had disappeared into a private collection somewhere. Though distorted by the curvature of the krater and the lense of the primitive camera, the decoration on it convinced him that they provided the key to making one of the world's great archeological discoveries.

His colleagues had scoffed, and he had become a laughingstock. After all, it was common knowledge that the motifs on Ancient Greek vases were peopled with mythical figures of gods, goddesses, animals, or highly stylized scenes of daily life. None was known to narrate a complete story.

But Doktor Professor Hammerschlag was convinced otherwise. He had made it his mission in life to prove his colleagues wrong.

But if he was right, one question had always loomed: where *had* the ancient krater come from? Greece obviously, but from which exact location? Which island? Hundreds, if not thousands, were scattered like haphazard coins flung by some benevolent giant into the sparkling wine-dark sea that was the Aegean.

And so he had spent every summer holiday for nearly three decades searching various islands and comparing what was depicted on the krater in the photographs to the seashores along which he wandered.

Finally, at long last, he had it pinned down to this very spot on Samos.

Then came war. There was no money to fund nonsense such as archeological expeditions. Armaments, not art, were the order of the day.

As fate would have it, war became Doktor Hammerschlag's greatest ally, and provided him with a patron—one of history's most notorious plunderers of great art—none other than Field Marshall Hermann Göring.

Thanks to Göring, the professor had everything he could possibly need—and a lot he didn't want, but did not dare refuse:

The Corps of Engineers augmented by Wehrmacht troops.

The camp commandant, SS Sturmbannführer Markus Engelmann, who had been hand-picked by the Field Marshall because he was a task master who shot first and never asked questions later. The matériel (among it dump trucks, tractors, bulldozers and steam shovels), ostensibly bound for Rommel's "Afrika" campaign, which had been diverted to Samos instead.

Slave labor conscripted from among local Samians.

Even the *Kriegsmarine* transport ship standing by offshore.

Suddenly he became aware of the abrupt drop in noise level, the ceasing of activity. Now the only mechanical sound was the ever-present throb and clatter of the gasoline-powered generators.

The rest of the machinery was oddly silent.

Curious, Professor Hammerschlag frowned, carefully placed the precious photographs in their waterproof box, and pushed himself heavily to his feet. He was no longer the spry young man who had first set out on his search—when? He sighed to himself. It seemed a lifetime ago. In fact, it *was* a lifetime ago.

Parting the flap of his tent, he stepped outside to investigate.

The night was cool, the blinding floodlights throwing everything into stark relief. Only the perpetual, choking dust cloud, still hovering and not dissipating, did anything to soften the glare—and irritate the eye. Looking around, he winced inwardly. Upon his arrival, a scrub-covered scree had sloped sharply down to the pebble-beached cove below. Since then, it had become a blight, and had the ugly, mutilated look of a strip-mine.

It's hideous, he thought. *And I'm responsible for destroying the natural beauty.* He could only pray that his discovery would be worth it.

"Herr Doktor!"

His thoughts were interrupted by the young Unterfeldwebel, hardly more than a child, who came running breathlessly, *Feldmütze* in hand.

"Professor Hammerschlag." It was all the young man could do to catch his breath. Now that he wouldn't lose his soft cap while running, he set the *Feldmütze* back on his head. "Sturmbannführer Engelmann —" he took another deep breath "—said to bring you—" and another "—at once!"

"*Zu befehl*," the professor said, not without a touch of irony. "Did he say why?"

A shake of the head. "*Nein*, Herr Doktor. Only that you must come."

Doktor Professor Hammerschlag wasn't about to go dashing out just because the SS officer had summoned him. After all, he, the archeologist, was supposedly in charge, although only nominally. The SS officer could override him at every turn.

So, at a dignified pace which suited both his age and position, and refusing to be rushed, he followed the Unterfeldwebel down the wide, machine-leveled terraces of volcanic rock which angled down to the pebble beach far below. If he shielded his eyes, he could see the lights of the transport ship anchored offshore. He leaned his head back to see the heavens, but the glare from the floodlights made it impossible to see a star. Even on this, the clearest of nights.

The closer they got to the spot where the machinery had recently been stilled, the thicker the air became with grit and dust. It got so bad that Professor Hammerschlag had to hold a handkerchief against his nose and mouth. He noticed that the laborers, guarded by soldiers with rifles at the ready, were now using shovels, sledge hammers, and pick axes.

Surely an auspicious sign!

Although his heart hammered and he felt a surge of excitement flood through him, he kept his face carefully neutral.

Sturmbannführer Engelmann was waiting for him among the giant metal behemoths which, for the time being, had been blessedly silenced. He was smoking a cigarette, holding it between thumb and forefinger, and tapping a riding crop against his dusty boots. As usual, only he, of all the soldiers, was wearing a dress uniform.

Professor Hammerschlag lowered his handkerchief. His nose twitched involuntarily at the stench of gasoline fumes and recent exhaust. He wished Englemann wouldn't smoke in this area; the fumes could be combustible.

But curiosity took precedence. "Do you think we've found it this time?"

"Perhaps, Herr Doktor." Engelmann smiled coldly. "And then again, perhaps not. You are the expert. As you know only too well, this is the third location you've had us dig at within a two kilometer range. I'm beginning to feel—"

A verbal slap, but the professor tuned him out. Right now there were more important things on which to concentrate.

"Yes, yes," he said with an impatient wave, then strode over to where the Samians were digging. He noted, with satisfaction, the men were not digging down, but toiling at unclogging a tall, spire-shaped natural fissure in the exposed rock. Clearly it must have been filled with dirt and rock for centuries.

So the machines had unearthed the original cliff at long last. And that gash in the rock—

He was beside himself with excitement. *Can it be?* he wondered, his eyes aglow. *Can it finally be the natural entrance we've been searching for?* Something—and it was an almost tangible feeling, told him that this *was* the spot. If memory served correctly, the fissure seemed to match the one depicted on the krater. He wished now that he had brought the photographs down from the camp in order to compare.

Well, there was plenty of time for that; he would send the Unterfeldwebel who had fetched him, ask him to bring the box with the pictures.

Meanwhile, it was impossible not to notice that the slave laborers, underfed and weary Samians, required rest. Their movements were sluggish and sloppy. This kind of digging called for finesse.

"Well, Herr Professor?" Sturmbannführer Engelmann had come up beside him, taking a last delicate puff on his cigarette, then tossing it down and grinding it out under his boot. "What is your professional opinion?"

"My professional opinion is that a shift change is in order," he replied dryly. "These men are exhausted."

"So?"

Professor Hammerschlag sighed. How many times did he have to repeat himself? Feeling like a broken gramophone record, he said, "Tired men make mistakes and cause accidents. The rate of injuries here is intolerably high."

Engelmann shrugged. "So? What is one Greek more or one Greek less?"

It was useless. *If only a Wehrmacht officer were in charge, instead of this thick-skulled SS brute!* the professor thought. But Sturmbannführer Engelmann had been personally assigned by the Field Marshall himself. There was no getting rid of this bane of his existence.

"Pontormos!" Professor Hammerschlag called to the foreman of the Greeks.

One of the laborers detached himself from the group, laid down his tool, and approached with dignity, though the wary, uneasy ghosts of apprehension and suspicion showed in his carbon-black eyes. He was tall and lean-faced, had thick black eyebrows, and an upper lip partially curtained by a moustache.

"Yes, Professor?" Kostas Pontormos spoke in his native Greek.

"Tell the men to be careful." Professor Hammerschlag, fluent in Greek, replied in the same language. One good thing about Sturmbannführer Engelmann—about the only good thing, he thought—was that the SS man didn't deign to learn the local tongue. Unless an official interpreter was present, the professor could say things he couldn't otherwise. "I am worried about the men. Tell them not to be in too much of a rush. I will try to have the officer change shifts more often. Also, for the sake of safety, as soon as a section is cleared of rubble, frame it in. The lumber should keep it from caving in. This is for my sake and also makes for safer working conditions."

"Yes, professor."

"That is all."

"What was that all about?" Engelmann snapped.

"I was giving him instructions on how best to clear the opening. Now, if you'll excuse me, I'll return to my tent and update my journal. When the men break through, please summon me at once."

Sturmbannführer Engelmann touched the brim of his cap with his riding crop. "You can be assured I shall," he said, his tone one of smug skepticism.

A day and a half later the men broke through the cleft.

No athlete, Professor Hammerschlag climbed the pile of rubble outside the cliff face awkwardly. "A lantern!" he cried. "Quick!"

The excitement in his voice was infectious. Even the slave laborers, on the point of exhaustion, crowded eagerly around. Only Sturmbannführer Engelmann kept his distance, pacing the pebble beach, his disinterest communicating his thoughts—that this was just another phase in what was surely a wild goose chase.

The lantern was brought forthwith. Professor Hammerschlag held it up inside the opening, which as yet was no bigger than a small, misshapen window with a very deep sill of rocks and stones. Craning his neck forward, he peered inside.

His lantern could barely penetrate the first few feet of what he perceived to be a vast cavern. But he felt a draft; somewhere there had to be another opening, however small, and the air pouring out towards him was stale.

A most auspicious sign.

He instructed Kostas to have the men continue to dig. "But slowly," he warned, "with pick and shovel. No machinery. Too much vibration could result in a cave-in."

After insisting upon a shift change, the professor left and the digging continued.

It took another twenty-four hours for the men to clear an opening big enough for a man to walk through. But first, the dust inside the cavern, thick as a blinding fog, had to settle.

"We'll go in first thing in the morning," Professor Hammerschlag told Sturmbannführer Engelmann. "Meanwhile, I want a guard posted at the entrance at all times. I want to make certain no one goes inside and disturbs anything until after I've inspected it personally."

"Anything else?"

"Yes. I shall need some portable lighting. For now a pair of high-power, hand-held lights on twenty-meter cables should suffice. Telescoping tripods to set them on would be helpful. Also, I don't believe we need all the floodlights blazing tonight. Why don't we shut them off for once so we can all get a good night's rest?"

But that night, Professor Hammerschlag found it difficult to sleep. He was too wound up, and he lay awake for hours, his emotions spiking between exhilaration over what he hoped he would find, and agony over whether or not this was the spot depicted on the krater.

Morning would tell, but as the night dragged on it seemed that morning would never come.

At last it did.

At the crack of dawn, he was dressed and outside. It was nearly five o'clock in the morning, and something struck him as very strange. At first he didn't know what it was. And then it hit him. For once, the floodlights for around-the-clock work had not bathed the camp or work site throughout the night till full daylight. In fact, this was the first time in weeks that he could enjoy seeing the last of the stars fade as the black night receded into gray, and then grew paler and paler until the sky brightened with the molten gold of sunlight spreading from below the horizon of the Turkish coast, gilding land and sea alike.

In the tents surrounded by barbed wire, the slave laborers were awakening to a meager breakfast. From the Wehrmacht tents surrounding the enclosure wafted the aroma of coffee—real coffee, not that repugnant ersatz stuff. But Professor Hammerschlag didn't need caffeine to jolt him awake. Not on this particular morning. He was too fired up, and he hurried, with uncharacteristic speed, down to the site, twisting his ankle in the process. But he ignored the mild pain.

Today was the day!

Today would determine either the crowning point of his career or . . . but no. He must not even consider the possibility of defeat!

Sturmbannführer Engelmann was already at the site, the ever-present riding crop in hand, his dress uniform freshly brushed and his spit-shined boots reflecting the rising sun. An Unterfeldwebel guarded the entrance to the cavern, rifle at the ready. Even as the SS officer showed him the hand-held electric torches which had been rigged to a generator, Professor Hammerschlag could hear the Samian slave laborers being force-marched down the gradient to the beach.

Every laborer and soldier, including the camp cook, turned out for the occasion.

When everyone was in position, one of the Wehrmacht soldiers handed the professor the electric torches, one for each hand, then switched on the generator. It started up with a clatter and thrummed noisily. The bulbs flickered uncertainly, then glowed brightly.

Sturmbannführer Engelmann said, "Herr Professor?" and gestured elegantly toward the entrance with his riding crop. "We are ready when you are."

The professor took a deep breath. He could feel his pulse quickening, the blood rushing through his veins, and a burning sensation in the pit of his stomach. This was it. The moment that would decide his place in the archeological history books. He drew himself up, thrust his shoulders back and stepped through the opening, the electric cords trailing behind him.

First sun, now darkness. Vast silent darkness. The electric bulbs lit the immediate area surrounding him, but his eyes had yet to adjust to the change of light. Slowly he moved further into the cavern, cautious of where he stepped. Rubble was strewn everywhere, centuries of it, and shifted underfoot.

After a few minutes his eyes adjusted to this netherworld and the darkness seemed to lighten. His shadow loomed, swallowed in a void as he moved.

He turned a slow circle, torches held high. His heart began to sink.

Nothing! And he had been so certain this was the spot! Could all these years spent searching have been for nothing?

He could scarcely believe it. Perhaps Engelmann was right? Perhaps he *was* on a wild goose chase—

—no, *not* a wild goose chase. What was it he had caught out of the corner of his eye? And where—?

There! He blinked. Was that it? Or was it merely wishful thinking? A trick of the eye, perhaps? Or elusive shadows thrown by the electric lights?

He inched closer, warning himself against getting too excited, lest he be disappointed.

"*Mein Lieber Gott!*" he whispered.

He stood there, awe-struck, staring at a massive, dust-covered shape showing through the rubble. His heart leapt and thundered within his rib cage. No natural shape, this! Surely nature could not produce what looked like the flowing, vertical folds of a giant garment! Another few centimeters of rubble, and he'd have missed it completely.

His feet propelled him forward, as if on their own accord. Gently he laid down the electric torches and sank heavily to his knees, unconscious of the sting of sharp stones digging into his kneecaps. He felt no pain, only a curious giddiness.

Lovingly he ran his hands over smooth, cool, carved marble, raising fresh clouds of dust. He coughed and his eyes stung, but he barely noticed.

More, more, more! He longed to see more. And now, not later.

Like someone possessed, he suddenly began to scoop away rubble furiously, using bare fingers to dig, heedless of scraping his hands bloody.

So. All these decades of searching hadn't been for nothing after all! He had found it!

It!

The massive statue of Hera as depicted in the photos of the krater.

It truly was the find of a lifetime.

Suddenly overcome with emotion, he began to weep.

[CHAPTER FOUR]

September 13, 1942 A.D.

Inside the floodlit cavern.

At last, the two halves of Hera had been cleared of tons of rubble. The entryway had been widened to accommodate the enormous marble, and was braced with joists and a steel lintel to ensure against cave-ins.

Professor Hammerschlag had ordered everyone out. He wanted to savor some time alone with his phenomenal find. He was both awestruck by the majestic splendor and shaking with fury.

Hera, though broken at the waist and lying prone, seemed to taunt him with her beauty. Dug out and cleaned, she was in all her glory, with one leg advanced and her arms slightly bent at her sides. She was a true masterpiece, one of the finest marbles—if not *the* finest—he had ever seen. Her expression was one of utter serenity, and she had extravagantly plaited shoulder-length hair and wore a tasseled, cross-slung *himaton* over the traditional folds of her chiton.

Every detail spoke of the work of a master carver, and so lifelike was she that it was difficult to believe she was fashioned of stone rather than flesh. The myth of Pygmalian and Galatea sprang to his mind, and he found himself thinking: *Oh, if only I could bring her to life!*

This rousing ecstasy was the very opposite of Professor Hammerschlag's conflicting emotion—fury. That was the result of the telegraph he had received just minutes earlier, and had crumpled into a ball. It had originated from none other than his patron, Field Marshall Hermann Göring, and the orders were explicit. Every last soldier, from

Sturmbannführer Engelmann to the corps of engineers and all the troops down to the lowliest Unterfeldwebel, as well as all the earth-moving equipment, had been reassigned to Rommel's Afrika campaign, from which they had originally been diverted.

Furthermore, if there was no time for both halves of the statue to be crated and transported to the ship waiting offshore, then at least half the statue was to be loaded aboard and shipped to Brescia, in Italy. There it would be transferred to a freight train, and the ship, equipment, and men would continue on to Africa.

With the exception of one man. The Field Marshall insisted that Professor Hammerschlag personally accompany the crated marble to Karinhall, Göring's lavish, art-filled hunting lodge. According to the instructions, until men and matériel could be spared, the other half of the statue was to remain in situ but well hidden. No one else must be able to find it.

While the opportunity to view the trove of some of the world's finest plundered art appealed, Professor Hammerschlag did not want to return to Germany. He had his heart set on remaining in Greece and continuing his search for antiquities.

Of course, it was not to be. Orders were orders.

And then slowly, very slowly, a crafty smile appeared on the professor's usually stern visage. He didn't need to be told which half of the massive statue the Field Marshall preferred—and expected. The same half he himself would choose—the top half, from the head down to the waist.

Not that the telegraph *specified* as much.

So, since his work force was being withdrawn, and only the gods knew when Professor Hammerschlag would return, he came to a daring decision. He would send the bottom half!

Oh, yes! It was a brilliant way to give tit for tat.

"Herr Professor!" The voice startled him and he spun around. It was Sturmbannführer Engelmann.

"Yes, yes," Professor Hammerschlag replied testily.

"We are wasting time. Our orders are to—"

"Then send the men in," the professor snapped. "Have them crate the bottom half of the statue and float it out to the ship."

"Are you certain you want the bottom half first? Not the—"

Professor Hammerschlag raised his chin imperiously. "As you yourself pointed out," he interrupted, "we do not have the luxury of time. Packing a piece as huge and yet as delicate as the top half requires time and patience. I am not about to take responsibility for a rush job which might damage such a masterpiece. I do not believe the Field Marshall would be at all pleased."

There was a pause. "*Ja*, I see. Good thinking." The Sturmbanführer turned smartly on his heel and left.

"*Arschloch*," the professor muttered under his breath.

[CHAPTER FIVE]

September 14–18, 1942 A.D.

It was done.

The bottom half of Hera had been crated in a nest of hay. Then the steam shovels and bulldozers had inched it out of the cavern with pulleys along a track of logs and up the ramp to the raft constructed of barrels and various inflatable rubber craft. On this ungainly but effective contraption, it was floated out to the transport ship. There, the cargo boom swung it effortlessly onboard and Professor Hammerschlag supervised its being lashed in one of the cargo holds.

The bulldozers, steam shovels, and generators were next.

It was amazing, the speed and ingenuity with which an army unit accomplished the seemingly impossible.

Naturally, Sturmbannführer Engelmann was everywhere at once, ensuring that events proceeded with renowned Germanic efficiency. In his pocket he carried the latest encrypted telegraph, which he had personally deciphered. It contained additional orders—orders that were best kept to himself.

The Wehrmacht troops, unusually alert because of the rise in nervousness among the Samian slave laborers, had their weapons unslung and at the ready. It wasn't difficult to guess that some of the Samians were ready to make a run for it. But Sturmbannführer Engelmann was not about to give them the chance. Meanwhile, the laborers were forced to work twice as hard and twice as fast to dismantle their own camp, then the barbed wire fence, and finally the Wehrmacht tents.

All equipment was shuttled out to the transport ship.

Finally it was time for the German demolitions expert to lay small charges so that all signs of the dig would be obliterated. Only thus could the exact location of the top half of Hera be kept secret.

"Careful," Professor Hammerschlag cautioned the demolitions expert. "We want a landslide to hide the entrance, but not a cave-in. That would be disastrous!"

"*Jawohl,* Herr Professor. I shall be as precise as a surgeon."

"*Gut. Gut.*"

With their work completed, the Samians, meanwhile, had been herded into a circle. As Professor Hammerschlag passed by, Kostas Pontormos pushed bravely forward. "*Parakaló —*" he began.

A Wehrmacht trooper growled and jabbed him in the belly with his rifle.

The professor pushed the barrel aside. "*Né*, Kostas?" he replied in Greek.

"The men, they are anxious. They wonder what will happen to them now that they are no longer of use?"

"What did he say?" The voice was Sturmbannführer Engelmann's.

He would have to be just steps away, Professor Hammerschlag thought, as he translated.

"Tell him," the SS officer said, with a grim smile, "tell him that we are not monsters."

The professor's translation in Greek brought relief to a few of the Samians' faces, but others looked skeptical and fearful.

"Countdown in five minutes!" The shout blasted from the demolitions expert's hand-held loudspeaker. "All stand clear, take cover on the ground, and clap your hands over your ears! Four minutes . . . one minute fifty-nine seconds . . . seven seconds . . . three . . . two . . . one . . . *los!*"

Even from where Professor Hammerschlag, the troops, and the Samians lay prone, the string of carefully timed explosions was awesome; flashes of blinding light lit up the crest of the cliff, one after the other, followed by starbursts of rock and dirt spraying upward and out. The professor couldn't help but think of some hellish fireworks celebrating a dark and evil rite.

A split second later, he and the others could feel the shock waves, and the earth shook and bucked beneath them. Massive dark clouds of smoke and dirt rose like sinister blooms. Then, as though in slow motion, the edge of the cliff top went crashing down like an inverted wave of surf.

When the air cleared, the men staggered to their feet and stared dumbfoundedly. No longer was there any evidence of an opening in the cliff. Nor could any of the machine- or man-made rubble be construed as anything but the natural accumulation of erosion.

The explosives expert had been wrong. He was not only as precise as a skilled surgeon; he was truly an artist of destruction.

What a grand finale! the professor marveled. *It was truly worthy of the finest production of the* Götterdämmerung.

Because somehow, miraculously, the silhouette of the cliff itself still retained the exact profile of the paintings on the krater. The landmarks were intact, and Professor Hammerschlag knew for certain he could find the site again without even having to search.

These thoughts were interrupted by Sturmbannführer Engelmann ordering the Samian slave laborers to fall in. Then, tapping his boot with the inevitable riding crop, he strutted up and down the row of suspicious, dark-eyed men and snapped: "I have received special orders. You are to accompany us on the transport ship—"

And that was when all hell broke loose. There was a huge outcry in Greek. Kostas Pontormos, eyes ablaze, lunged at Engelmann.

"Kostas, *óchi!*" the professor shouted.

The Samian never stood a chance. The SS officer's Luger was like a live black snake in his hand. There was an ear-shattering blast, and at point-blank range Kostas was hurled backwards, the top of his skull spraying bone, blood, and viscid custard-like matter in all directions.

He was dead before he hit the ground.

The silence that followed was more deafening than any noise.

Professor Hammerschlag sank to his knees beside the body. Tears streamed down his face as he looked up at Engelmann with loathing. "Did you have to kill him?" he demanded angrily.

"You forget your place, Herr Professor," was the cold reply. "You might be in charge of the antiquities, but I am in charge of the laborers. Or, would you rather join—" with a sneer Engelmann rolled the fallen body over with a boot "—your young olive-skinned friend here?"

Professor Hammerschlag did not reply. Unhurriedly he unbuttoned his shirt, draped it carefully over what little remained of Kostas' head —his jaw and the lower portion of his nose—and rose stiffly to his feet. He crossed himself with his thumb, etching miniature crosses on his forehead, sternum, heart and right side of his chest. Then, staring long and hard at Engelmann, he slowly made his way to the beach where the first tenders were arriving.

An hour later, when the ship hauled anchor and steamed off, he stood on deck, hands clutching the iron railing with such fury that his knuckles shone white as bone. Thus was his departure from the island of what should have been his greatest glory but had turned into his deepest shame. The clifftop, he noticed, was lined with villagers, many of them women in black, like a long row of silent crows watching their husbands, sons, and nephews being deported. Not that the watchers could actually see them. The forty-four slave laborers from Samos had been herded into a sweltering, windowless hold.

Professor Hammerschlag remained on deck until Mount Kerkis and the even more distant Mount Ambelos with its rich vineyards decreased in size and were finally lost under the deep blue horizon. Only then, once Samos was no longer visible, were the sweating and thirsty slave laborers let out and marched to the stern deck.

"Prisoner roll call!" a Wehrmacht officer called out. "Fall in!"

With a shudder, Professor Hammerschlag noted that the soldiers guarding the men were not carrying their standard issue rifles: they were armed with submachine guns.

Something akin to a boa constrictor crushed his entrails. Still trying to swallow the bile that threatened to rise constantly in his throat since watching Kostas' gruesome murder, he was now unable to face what he feared—no, what he *knew* was coming, but was unable to prevent—and scuttled below decks to the ventilated hold where the crated bottom half of Hera was secured. Here he would remain, guarding his treasure.

The space was barely habitable, of course, a monstrous metal box in which he felt mouse-like, but it was preferable to the bunk in the closet of a cabin he'd been assigned, and here were his personal effects, still packed in their steamer trunks, a hammock slung to one side, and several skylit hatches. For ablutions and meals he would have to leave the chosen isolation of this sanctuary, but at least here he was distanced, self-quarantined, as it were, from The Others. As though segregation made him morally superior, or at least less culpable as he impersonated two of the three monkeys, the ones that see and hear no evil.

Above decks, the Samians were lined up along the stern rail. Sturmbannführer Engelmann stood off to one side, left hand tucked in the small of his back, his right gripping his ever-present riding crop. "It is time," he told the Samians, with a steel blade of a smile, "to say *Leb'wohl.*"

And then, raising his crop, he brought it whistling down through the air as he gave the order: "*Schiessen!*"

The soldiers facing the slave laborers let loose with a continuous, thunderous volley of machine gun fire—

—and the Samians screamed and danced jerkily like epileptic puppets while they were mown down, many literally stitched in half.

Engelmann's expression did not change. He neither blinked nor looked repulsed.

He was well used to wholesale slaughter.

In his refuge below decks, Professor Hammerschlag clapped his hands tightly over his ears, his mouth forming a silent scream. But no matter how hard he tried to drown it out, it was impossible to muffle the staccato bursts of the machine guns.

He did not need to see the carnage up on deck; he could envision it all too vividly. And so he wept, finally acknowledging what he had for so long tried to suppress. The whispered rumors and stories that circulated about unspeakable German atrocities, and that he, in the shelter of his academic ivory tower, had categorically denied, were true after all.

We really are monsters, he concluded. And he understood for the very first time his own complicity. For he, who had arrogantly assumed himself to be without sin, was by no means unsullied. His experiences since Engelmann had been assigned as his overseer had taught him that he could no longer shirk his own involvement: he must shoulder his personal burden of guilt. For like it or not, even the insular worlds of academia and archeology were not immune from Germany's madness.

His lifelong search for Hera for example: if he hadn't pursued it for his personal glory with such single-minded determination, then perhaps he might not have petitioned the patronage of the Field Marshall so avidly.

Then there would have been no monstrous Engelmann. No curdled glory.

How many lives might have been spared then?

How many families might still be intact?

Instead, how many lives from that luscious, fertile island had been cut down in their prime, their ghosts now pressing untold tonnage upon his conscience?

"Get rid of these, these Mediterranean *Untermenschen,*" commanded Engelmann sharply. "Throw them overboard and hose down the decks.

And swab them well!" His pale eyes bore into each soldier's like an icy drill. "I won't have a single drop of blood from these *Untermenschen* polluting my ship. Is that understood?"

And from the well-rehearsed Chorus: "*Jawohl,* Herr Sturmbannführer!"

A sloppy salute: "Heil Hitler."

The Chorus, flinging their arms out at smart angles: "Heil Hitler!"

Bored, Engelmann wandered off as the bodies were alternately kicked or heaved overboard. One of the Samians, still clinging to life by a thread, managed a single word before dying. "Hera!" he whispered, and then he, too, was picked up roughly and flung into the sea.

And that was when it happened.

Almost instantly, a fierce and inexplicable wind sprang up, barreling southward and gaining velocity with unusual swiftness. The sea, which had been smooth sailing, suddenly churned and turned into massive troughs topped by foaming crests. The transport ship, an ungainly workhorse of a vessel, wallowed in the sudden onslaught. It heaved and plunged, its bow digging deeply into waves as high as its hull and throwing back lashing showers of water as it rose back up again. As if the constant dip and rise weren't enough, there was also the increasing violence of the sideways rolling motion to contend with.

Sturmbannführer Engelmann's peaked cap was blown off his head and was lost to sea as he staggered to keep his footing on the continuously heaving deck. He clung to the handle of the hatch-like door for dear life, and was drenched before he could finally wrench it open and slam it shut behind him. Throughout the ship, even the most seasoned sailors found themselves bent over and vomiting, and it was all the captain and the first mate could do to meet the towering troughs head-on.

Each wave was higher than the preceding, and the ship was tossed about and battered like a toy in the bathtub of a destructive child.

"Man overboard!" a soldier shouted, but his cry was lost in the shrieking of the wind and the crashing of the waves. Besides, there was no way to turn the ship safely around without the risk of capsizing.

"*Du lieber Himmel!*" the first mate muttered as yet another wall of water thrashed the wheelhouse windows, entirely obscuring the view. That the glass didn't shatter was a miracle. He clung to a handhold even as his feet slid out from under him. "I've never experienced a *meltemi* like this one!"

"This is no *meltemi,*" the captain told him grimly.

"Then what is it?"

The captain was fighting to control the wheel. "How should I know?" he replied. "You'd do better by asking the gods."

In the solitude of his chosen hermitage Doktor Professor Friedrich Hammerschlag of the Berlin Reichsmuseum thought it appropriate that every groan and creak of strained steel, each pop and ricochet of rivets that could no longer bear the pressure exerted upon them, and the leaking skylights above that went dark every few seconds as waves crashed over them, were surely indications that the *Kriegsmarine*'s transport vessel was about to become his watery coffin.

"And Engelmann and his murderers will go down with me," he muttered with the satisfaction of a penitent. "Serves them right. Serves me right, too. It's what we deserve."

As an archeologist and scholar, the professor was not normally superstitious. He had built his reputation upon a bedrock of proven facts, intelligent theories, and the interpretation of ancient myths as they might apply to the realities of everyday life some 2,500 years earlier.

Yet now, clinging for dear life to the ropes securing the crate containing the bottom portion of Hera, he felt a curious kinship with the mythical heroes of times long past.

Had Jason and his Argonauts not endured life-threatening tempests and other seemingly insurmountable dangers in their search for the Golden Fleece?

And had not Ulysses on his Odyssey had to contend with a Cylops, the Sirens, and a multitude of other life-threatening monstrosities?

After all, this was the storied Aegean, that most myth-surrounded of all seas, so was not the suddeness of these brutal conditions somehow appropriate? Perhaps there was more to the ancient gods than mere myth. Could it be possible that Poseidon, god of the sea and shaker of the earth, had whipped up these waters expressly to display his anger at the massacre? Or, to use the Archaic definition, the rape of Hera?

Down here, in the giant metal box of the hold, with the battered ship going pitch and yaw and dip and rise, pitch and yaw and dip and rise, like some crazy carnival ride gone out of control, anything seemed possible.

Or am I losing my mind? he wondered.

It was even conceivable that he was in a state of shock induced by the rat-tat-tat of the submachine guns.

Professor Hammerschlag wasn't sure which was the case.

But of one thing he was absolutely certain: he was not afraid to die. What he *was* ashamed of was living, since living meant that he would be forever haunted by the knowledge that his search for Hera had resulted in wholesale slaughter.

So focused was he on these tumultuous thoughts, so overwhelmed by feelings of guilt, and so loud was the thunderous pounding of relentless tons of water against the creaking hull, that he was unaware of what was happening right in front of him. Secured as the crate was by thick ropes and expert seamen's knots, all attached to fairleads on the steel deck so there would be no chafing, the rope had not been fastened quite tight enough. There was just enough slack for the splintery wooden edge of the crate to rub against hemp, and with every violent motion of the ship, the crate shifted ever so slightly. The effect was rather like that of a blunt saw slowly but surely sawing its way through its bonds.

Pitch and yaw and dip and rise. Pitch and yaw and dip and rise. Slice, slice, slice, slice. Strand by strand, the woven rope was steadily weakening.

And then the rope was sliced beyond its endurance. Thick strands unraveled and—

Snap!

—Professor Hammerschlag let out a cry and tried to scramble out of the crate's way. But the dipping deck made escape impossible and the last thing he ever saw was the loose crate looming swiftly down on him, bigger, bigger, bigger with every second.

Hera, be merciful, he thought, stretching out his arms to break the crate's progress. But Doktor Professor Hammerschlag was no match for a crate weighing untold tons, and any prayers to any god or goddess were too late. The crate slammed into Doktor Professor Hammerschlag of the Berlin Reichsmuseum and pinned him to the starboard hull, crushing every bone in his body before sliding back to the port side and banging into the opposite side of the hull.

But the gods had been kind. Professor Hammerschlag, crushed by the very treasure he had spent a lifetime trying to find, died instantly.

Feeling no pain.

[CHAPTER SIX]

10 October, 1942 A.D.

Karinhall, the hunting lodge of Hermann Göring, Luftwaffe Chief, one-time Führer-in-Waiting, and second-most powerful individual on the European Continent

It was the second shipment of the week, this convoy of six panel vans following a long, elegant black Daimler touring car with its top down and swastika Luftwaffe flags fluttering from both fenders. The rest of the convoy consisted of a flatbed carrying a large steel crane and two truckloads of heavily armed troops, one in the front and one at the rear. Additionally, an escort of four motorcycle outriders with a heavily armed guard in each of the sidecars, two in the lead and another two bringing up the rear, proclaimed the importance of the cargo.

As if anyone would dare waylay this vehicular convoy! Once each week—sometimes even twice—Leutnant Bernd Hohne supervised the arrival of these shipments in Berlin by railroad from points all over Europe. It was his duty to ensure that the priceless cargo, looted art from Europe's finest museums, matched the manifests and that each and every crate was accounted for. It was also his duty to oversee the loading of the crates aboard the panel vans and to personally accompany the treasures to their ultimate destination.

The distance was a mere sixty kilometers—but it might as well have been measured in billions of reichsmarks, gold thalers, Swiss francs, and American dollars.

Leutnant Hohne, aware of Generaloberst Ernst Ulrich Kutner, who was smugly ensconced in the rear seat of the Daimler enjoying a second-rate cigar, glanced nervously at his wristwatch as the convoy made its way across the vast, flat, purplish-blue heather of the Schorfheide and entered the pine and beech forests. He let out a deep breath and relaxed visibly. They were making excellent time today. The weather was perfect, the day clear, crisp, and sunny, with autumn's snap in the air, the beech trees wearing their temporary finery of yellows, golds, and reds.

Before long, the convey stopped at one of the gate houses, the archway carved with Göring's coat of arms, a scroll carved of stone, on which two crossed scabbards made an X above a cluster of three oak leaves.

No mere Wehrmacht troops guarded and patrolled the entry or perimeter of the premises, nor the hunting lodge itself. The troops consisted of elite Fallschirmjäger—paratroopers—hand-picked and heavily armed. They had been sworn to protect the life of the Reichsmarschall with their own.

After the usual ritual of suspicious inspection of papers and personnel, during which Generaloberst Kutner seethed, chomping on his cigar, the convoy was waved through.

From his front seat in the Daimler, Leutnant Hohne watched in fascination as several stags, each with a rack of at least five antlers, eyed the approaching convoy from the roadside before leaping gracefully across the gravel lane and into the game preserve's sun-dappled depths. A quail squawked indignantly and fluttered ungainly into the shelter of the nearest underbrush, of which there was little.

If only Heidi were here to see this! Hohne thought wistfuly. *How she would love it here!* Heidi was his affianced, and adored the outdoors. Above all, she envied her fiancé's access to this most private of private preserves, just as she envied the wives of the cream of Nazi society and industrialists who waltzed in and out of this retreat for feasts, hunts, and parties, about which she had heard so much.

Unfortunately, because of Leutnant Hohne's lowly officer status, Heidi would never set foot near Karinhall, let alone in it, and had to be content with his second-hand tales of the storybook hunting lodge. Each time he returned from one of the convoys, she grilled him in depth, eating up every morsel of details like a gluttinous child indulging in *Berliners,* that great capital's renowned jelly donuts.

The beech forest gradually gave way to the luscious, deep loden green of sap-fragrant pines and clusters of gnarled oaks, those fabled, sacred trees of the German forests.

And finally, in a park-like clearing, there it was.

Karinhall.

Hermann Göring's famed hunting lodge.

Like a monument dedicated to Teutonic dominance, it commanded its setting with all the brawny pomposity of a Wagnerian opera. Constructed of huge blocks of Brandenburg granite as well as half-timbered white plaster, the main building with its steep, thatched roofs sprouted two shorter wings that protruded protectively forward, enclosing a three-sided courtyard.

It was an architectural pastiche, this Germanic pleasure dome: part medieval fortress, part traditional hunting lodge, part baronial hall and part rustic farmhouse. The windows were quaintly bucolic, with wooden shutters painted with blue and white diagonal stripes and topped with rows of multi-racked antlers.

The main entrance, however, was purely fascist, with stupendously towering doors that dwarfed all who passed through its portals, and was flanked by immense wrought-iron torches.

Göring was in residence, out back on the flagstone terrace, living out his fantasy life as some kind of medieval prince. A grotesque figure of corpulence, he lay sprawled on the cushions of a white wicker chaise. As always, he was sweating copiously, and wore a rust-colored leather jerkin over a white shirt with puffy sleeves. His trousers were rolled up above the knees, and he had on high green leather boots. An emerald brooch was pinned near his throat, and around his gargantuan waist was a broad, gem-encrusted belt. Giant diamond solitaires and his prized ruby flashed from sausage-like fingers.

Well-fed industrialists surrounded him like planets revolving around the sun, paying homage to the jovial Reichsmarschall while puffing on fat cigars and laughing dutifully at his jokes, smug in the knowledge that they were at the very epicenter of National Socialist superiority, and unaware of the ridiculous figures they cut in the theatricality of the Teutonic gear Göring insisted they wear in preparation for the afternoon's boar hunt. And there, ensconced in an armchair, was the gaunt-faced Doktor Goebbels, Propaganda Minister for the Reich, attired in his customary suit and tie. Born with a deformed leg, he remained seated, ever conscious of his metal leg brace and limp: a less than perfect specimen of the Hitlerian super race. It was understood that he would not be joining the hunt. Nor would Reichsführer Heinrich Himmler, resplendent in his black, silver-trimmed uniform, peaked cap, and wire-rimmed spectacles which reflected the sunlight like small twin mirrors. He was standing at the edge of the terrace, hands clasped Germanically behind his back as he stared out at the sparkling lake beyond, no doubt contemplating the next group of "subhuman undesirables" on his list for extermination.

Bodyguards and adjutants kept a discreet but vigilant distance.

Emmy Göring, née Sonnemann, held court at the other end of the terrace, where the deep contralto of Zarah Leander warbled scratchily from a gramophone. Emmy, blond, stately and somewhat on the plump side, was Göring's second wife, and was hostess to the weekend's contingent of marcelled wives and mistresses, all of whom were wearing coats draped across their shoulders like capes against the blustery wind as they sipped lavishly dispensed glasses of Sekt and smoked cigarettes. She and her old friend, Rose Korwan, shared anecdotes about their struggling actress days, amusing the others, who basked in the reflected glory of the Reichsmarschall's wife, and tittered like excited schoolgirls. Magda Goebbels, sharp-eyed and humorless, tipped her head to one side, gesturing at Hedwig Potthast, Himmler's very pregnant mistress, to follow her. The two women stood up quietly, and Magda took Hedwig by the arm, leading her away from the chattering group to dispense maternal advice. For Frau Goebbels, as the Third Reich's paragon of a good Aryan wife, had already, like a champion thoroughbred bitch, produced a litter of six perfect little National Socialists, who had not been invited, and were back in Berlin under the supervision of a virtual army of nurses and nannies.

"Ninnies, the bunch of them!" opined Frau Goebbels grimly. "You can never trust hired help. Children need their *mothers,* Fräulein Potthast! It is up to us mothers to ensure the future of the Reich. You must always remember that—"

The wind swished through the flowering hawthorn and young birches bordering the walls of the house. A bee swooped past, hovered over a late blooming flower at terrace's edge, then alighted and crawled inside its petals in search of nectar. Like ghosts, silent servants circulated, refilling glasses. Leander's voice segued from *Kann denn Liebe Sünde Sein* to a rousing if somewhat inappropriate rendition of *Davon Geht die Welt Nicht Unter;* inappropriate because, the way the war was progressing, it appeared that the world *would* indeed soon go under. The Battle of Britain denied Germany its air superiority, and soon another long winter was in the offing at Stalingrad; the lethal Russian counterthrusts on the Second Front were still keeping three million Axis soldiers at bay.

The mounting casualties on both sides were horrendous.

But at Karinhall, life was a perpetual party; reality was a thousand kilometers away. Nero fiddled and Leander sang as Rome burned.

At the table, the ladies shrieked with laughter at one of Rose Korwan's hilariously delivered punch lines. Then the heads of the female contingent turned as an exquisitely mannered youth drifted out of the house: Göring's stepson, Thomas. Hesitantly he eyed the men clustered at one end of the terrace, then the women at the other, undecided about which group to join.

Emmy Göring decided it for him, waving him over. She and Thomas, son of the Reichsmarschall's beloved first wife, the Swede Carin von Kantzow, after whom Karinhall was named and behind which she was entombed in grandeur *and* imported Swedish soil, got on extraordinarily well.

He approached the table and clicked his heels as he bowed courteously at each lady in turn.

"Thomas. You must sit here beside me, *mein lieber Schatz,*" Emmy said fondly, patting the seat of Frau Goebbel's recently vacated chair.

"What the devil is that infernal noise?" inquired Rose in a stage-whisper, eyebrows lifting dramatically at the distant rumble of rolling thunder.

"Oh, *that.*" Emmy waved a languid hand. "Another shipment of art for Hermann, what else?" She shrugged elegantly, carelessly. "You know how he is. He can never have enough art or antiques."

The deep throaty roar of the convoy increased in volume as it drew up to a halt in the circular drive at the front of the house, then grew progressively silent as, one by one, the engines were switched off.

"I *imagine,*" said Rose, "that this means the hunt will be called off?"

"It all depends upon the shipment," replied Emmy, noting that one of the industrialists' wives—or was it mistresses?—it was *so* difficult to keep track of the constant parade of houseguests—had half-emptied her glass of Sekt. Ever the gracious hostess, she would have filled it herself, but no bottle was at hand. She caught the eye of the hovering majordomo, whose lifted eyebrow at one of the servants produced the pop of yet another cork.

The door to the terrace opened once more. As though with perfect timing, Leander's voice faded and the gramophone record fell silent, the thick black disc revolving around and around until a servant lifted the arm. The butler appeared at the door. "Generaloberst Kutner, Herr Reichsmarschall!" he intoned with gravity.

Heels clicked on flagstones as the beer barreled Generaloberst, sans cigar, and accompanied by a slim young ramrod-postured Schutztaffel orderly, nodded at the ladies and headed directly for the Reichsmarschall's chaise, in front of which the men stopped. Two sets of heels clicked sharply, two uniformed arms flew up smartly. "Heil Hitler!" the men chorused.

Göring lifted a lazy bejeweled hand. "Heil Hitler," he acknowledged in a bored voice. The wicker chaise creaked as he shifted his great bulk. His eyes, deep in his bloated ruddy face, squinted up at the Generaloberst. "The Hera?" he inquired. "It is on the manifest?"

"*Jawohl,* Herr Reichsmarschall!" But the Generaloberst's eyes strayed greedily to the side table with its glass of bubbly Sekt, to the china platter piled lavishly with petit fours and slices of torte, then to the self-importance of the visiting industrialists puffing on fragrant cigars, all of whom pretended disinterest.

"And Doktor Hammerschlag's possessions?" Göring demanded. "They have arrived also?"

"*Ja,* Herr Reichsmarschall." A pause as the Generaloberst forced his eyes from the temptations on the table. "Everything he was traveling with. The Herr Doktor's was a most tragic death. Tragic also that the transport ship from Greece was torpedoed on its voyage on to Africa. There were no survivors. Not a one."

Göring nodded indifferently. In his opinion, that was the concern of Grossadmiral Dönitz of the *Kriegsmarine,* not his own. To him, the only real tragedy was the death of Doktor Hammerschlag. "Have you inventoried the good Doktor's possessions?"

"Of course, Herr Reichsmarschall."

"And did it include certain photographs of a Greek vase?"

"I cannot say, Herr Reichsmarschall. There is a metal waterproof box, but it is locked. We did not have the key and were awaiting orders before forcing it open."

"*Gut.*" Göring nodded. "Leave it be." He would make certain it was done under his own supervision. Then: "Well?" Göring clapped his pudgy, beautifully manicured hands. "What are you waiting for? Start uncrating the Hera!" And to the cluster of industrialists, who looked visibly relieved: "Gentlemen. I regret that this afternoon's hunt is called off."

And thus speaking, the Reichsmarschall, former commander of the Richthofen fighter squadron during the first Great War, and current Oberbefehlshaber der Luftwaffe, swung his great thighs over the side of the protesting chaise and pushed himself heavily to his feet, heading inside the house to change outfits for the third time that day.

"*Zu befehl!*" Generaloberst Kutner and his orderly clicked their heels smartly, then followed.

Emmy Sonnenmann, whose reputation in Berlin as a stuck-up bitch was undeserved, and who possessed a kind heart, had not missed Kutner's longing gaze at the confections. "Herr Generaloberst," she called.

He paused in midstep and turned. "*Ja, gnädige Frau?*"

Emmy's smile was like a ray of sunshine. "Let your orderly see to it. It shall take some time for my husband to get changed. Here." She reached for a silver cake server and personally cut him a thick slice of Sachertorte. She held out the plate and handed him a silver fork. "You must have had an arduous day. Please, do have some." And she signaled to the majordomo to fetch the grateful Generaloberst a glass of Sekt and offer him one of Hermann's fragrant Havanas.

"See to the unloading," Kutner commanded his orderly. "You are dismissed."

Emmy, ever conscious of the comfort of others, instructed the majordomo to see that the men of the convoy up front were served refreshments as well. Rose, eyes glued to the departing backside of the handsome young Schutztaffel orderly, nudged Emmy's elbow.

"Now *that* splendid looking specimen of manhood is exactly my type." She sighed theatrically. "Oh, if I were only twenty years younger."

To which Emmy responded with a burst of good-natured laughter. "Rose," she chided playfully, "since when did that ever stop you? As I recall, you've *always* robbed the cradle."

"*Me?*" Rose, ever the consummate actress, feigned virtuous innocence. "I never seduce men only half my age!"

"Oh?" Now it was Emmy's turn to raise her eyebrows. "And when did this turnaround come about?"

"*I,*" declared Rose, with a toss of her head, "insist that my men are at least five years older than half my age!"

To which the other wives and mistresses tittered, and Thomas, ever the young gentleman, blushed bright scarlet.

"Well? What are you waiting for?" hissed Emmy, *sotto voce,* under her breath while jabbing an elbow in Rose's ribs. "If you just sit here and wait, he's liable to slip through your fingers."

She scooted back her chair, looked down at the other women, and suggested, as though they had a choice: "Why don't we all go up front and watch the unpacking? It might prove interesting." This with a wink at Rose.

"And take your drinks and cigarettes with you," she added.

And hooking one arm through Rose's and the other through Thomas', she led the contingent of coat-draped, Sekt-sipping women into the house, through the immense hall echoing with their heels, and out the heroically scaled front doors, where they gathered at the top of the imposing granite steps.

The courtyard was a hive of activity.

Soldiers grunted and poured sweat as they heaved crate after crate from the panel vans. Wood and nails screeched in protest as crowbars wrenched them open. Protective hay, used to cushion fragile treasures, crunched and grew into haystacks. On the front terrace, the ladies had moved to the side as treasure after unloaded treasure was hauled into the great house.

Wives and mistresses eyed the continuous procession with undisguised sighs of envy. The spoils of war. Tapestries, paintings by Rubens and Caravaggio and Mario de' Fiori, priceless Aubusson and Persian carpets, antiquities, furniture, silver, china, bronzes. The spoils of war. From museums. Castles. Chateaux. Private homes. Loot.

And above all, the piece Göring had lusted after more than any other in his shipment.

Hera.

"*Vorsicht. Vorsicht!*" Leutnant Bernd Hohne shouted, gesticulating wildly with his hands to the operator of the crane, as if directing traffic. "*Langsam!*"

The uncrated lower half of Hera, mummified and unrecognizable, wrapped and roped as she was in protective puffy eiderdown and burlap, swung precariously in midair. The reinforced pallet to which she was secured with ropes creaked ominously, twisting slowly on its thick iron chains, first in one direction, then the other. Less than half a meter below her, in the very center of the three-sided courtyard, the white marble plinth with its stepped gray marble base and matching cornice, erected in expectation of her arrival, awaited her presence.

The autumn sun was lowering in the sky; the wind had picked up and long purple shadows crept across the orange-tinted courtyard. Leutnant Hohne was drenched beneath his armpits. Beads of sweat, like translucent pearls, seeded his forehead and trickled down into his eyes. He blinked back the stinging salt, tempted, but not daring, to wipe a forearm across his brow. This maneuver required intense concentration. One second's lack of vigilance, and the Reichsmarshcall's highly anticipated treasure could well end up in bits and pieces. Although why this massive chunk of marble—supposedly not even a complete statue!—should have such importance attached to it was beyond his comprehension.

"*Links!*" he shouted. Left! "*Nein—rechts! Rechts!*" No—Right! Right!

Hohne was aware of, but for the time being dismissed, the presence of Generaloberst Kutner, who strutted around, eyes bright with self-importance as he puffed on one of the Reichsmarschall's fragrant Havanas while pretending supervision. Getting in the way. Every now and then barking an unnecessary order to establish and reestablish his authority.

Hohne also managed to ignore the audience that had multiplied atop the granite steps.

On one side, the women, shivering in the settling chill, several of whom stuck their fingers in their ears against the constant din while the rest clutched their caped coats together at the front. Presiding on the other side was the imposing, bloated Reichsmarschall with his male contingent of guests and underlings.

Göring, freshly talcumed and cologned for the third time that day, had divested himself of his Teutonic hunting gear, and was resplendent in a pale blue uniform, matching peaked cap, and gleaming jackboots that mirrored the setting sun in miniature. A different set of magnificent rings decorated his pudgy fingers and a new set of brooches flashed from beneath his double chin.

Before him, as though kneeling in supplication, a hammer-wielding minion burst the padlock on Professor Hammerschlag's tin box. The lock clattered as it fell. Breathing heavily, Göring leaned eagerly forward while the minion lifted the box ceremoniously with both hands and held it high, as if it were a religious offering.

Göring opened the lid and a sound, like a sigh of pleasure, escaped from his lips. The heavily bejeweled hands quickly riffled the contents and seized upon the sepia photographs the archeologist had used to unearth Hera. "*Gut, gut—*," he muttered, the tip of his greedy tongue moistening his upper lip.

He paused momentarily to flick a glance at the mummified statue still precariously twisting on its pallet, then continued pawing through the contents of the box. A frown of displeasure marred his face and his heavily pouched eyes snapped at the Schutztaffel orderly, who stood off to the side. "These are all? No photographs of work as it progressed on the site?"

The orderly snapped to attention. "*Verzeihung,* Herr Reichsmarschall, but Herr Generaloberst Kutner assured me that other than his clothes, this box constitutes the entirety of the Herr Professor's personal possessions."

"I see." With disappointment, Göring let the lid fall back into place. "Well, have it taken inside to my office. I want it on my desk."

"*Zu befehl,* Herr Reichsmarschall." The orderly clicked his heels and turned smartly, gesturing at the minion to follow him.

Emmy Sonnernmann saw her opportunity. Just before the Schutztaffel orderly passed by, she turned to Rose Korwan, purposely knocking her friend's cigarette out from between her fingers. It fell to the granite in front of the orderly's feet.

"Oh, how utterly clumsy of me." Emmy looked appealingly at the orderly while giving Rose a discreet nudge.

The orderly snapped his heels, bent forward, and swooped up the cigarette. He offered it to Emmy.

"No, no, it's hers, not mine," she said sweetly.

He nodded. "Fräulein?" He held it out to Rose.

"How absolutely lovely of you," said Rose, still an arresting beauty, and at her most seductive. She stared at him intently from under half-lowered eyelids before accepting the cigarette. Their fingers touched for seconds longer than was necessary.

"My pleasure, Fräulein." His clear baby blues held her gaze.

She smiled invitingly. "*Vielen dank.*"

"*Nichts zu danken,*" he replied gallantly.

Her voice was soft. "Perhaps our paths shall cross again?"

He smiled, not unpleasantly. "Yes, Fräulein. Perhaps they shall." Then, clearing his throat, he straightened his shoulders. "Ladies." And executing a semi-bow, he continued on into the house.

Rose sighed wistfully as she watched his departure. "What an utterly gorgeous man. Tall, blond, blue-eyed, handsome, beautifully mannered—"

"—And don't forget the bulge in his breeches," Emmy reminded her in so quiet a whisper that no one else could hear.

Rose pretended ignorance. "I didn't even notice," she said loftily.

"Liar," retorted Emmy, and they both burst into peals of laughter.

Rose's face turned serious as she regarded her retrieved cigarette. "Emmy," she said, "what do you think the chances are of his path and mine ever crossing again?"

Whereupon Emmy, remembering long-forgotten lines from their days as actresses, quoted Shakespeare: "'Beauty provoketh thieves sooner than gold.' Never forget that, Rose."

Rose's eyes brightened. "You think?"

Emmy smiled knowingly. "I *know,*" she replied, secure in the knowledge that a word whispered in her husband's ear would produce instant results. Her Hermann was, after all, one of the most powerful men in the Reich, in many ways second only to the Führer himself. One snap of Göring's fingers, and the Schutztaffel orderly would be reassigned. Not to mention promoted.

"*Jetzt! Runter! RUNTER!*" The frenzied shouts from Leutnant Hohne rose above the other noises, even above the constant din of yet more crates being wrenched open with crowbars, and drew attention away from the continual parade of yet more priceless treasures being lugged into the house. Now the spectators' eyes—none more keenly or hungrily than the Reichsmarschall's—were riveted upon the monumental, bundled statue.

There came a heavy thud and the cracking of wood from the splintering pallet, and the very earth seemed to tremble as the mighty bottom half of Hera settled perfectly onto the marble plinth.

From the terrace came a smattering of polite applause. Leutnant Hohne permitted himself a deep sigh of relief and took a moment to wipe his glistening forehead with his sleeve. And another to glance up at the two groups gathered at the top of the steps. The camera of his eye registered the ladies' fashions, for he knew Heidi would grill him mercilessly upon his return, demanding to know every detail. He made a mental note of the cut of the coats, the lengths of the dresses, the exact shades of their stockings. Shifting his gaze, he caught sight of the Reichsmarschall rubbing his hands in anticipation, as though washing them in air.

Generaloberst Kutner, cigar clenched between his teeth and chest puffed out proudly like a pouter pigeon's, clapped his hands. "*Los! Mach schnell, schnell!*"

Hohne drew his eyes back in, instantly reverted to work mode and snapped out orders: "You heard the Herr Generaloberst! Get the rods! You, you, you—" he pointed at the beefiest of the men "—and you! *Schnell!*"

The selected soldiers trotted dutifully to the vans and returned dragging long heavy iron rods. So thick and heavy it would take two men to maneuver them into position.

"Now carefully lever the statue and push out the wood from underneath. "Carefully . . . just a few centimeters . . . carefully!"

And finally, after much grunting and groaning, when that Herculean labor was completed, came the command everyone had been waiting for: "Cut the ropes! Unwrap the statue!"

When the last of the burlap and eiderdown duvets fell away, a communal gasp rose from the terrace. Even the soldiers laden with loot stopped to gape.

There she was.

Hera.

Majestic in Samian marble splendor, the pale gray, with its darker, vertical grayish-beige striations, bronzed golden by the setting sun, her weight resting on her right leg, and a sandaled foot protruding from beneath the flowing robes of her long *peplos,* the edge of her chiton gathered at her hips, where she had been diagonally guillotined in the earthquake some 2,500 years earlier. Even in half, she was huge. Monumental. Awe-inspiring.

The Reichsmarschall slowly, almost reverently, descended the steps, never once taking his acquisitively gleaming eye off the statue. The spectators, keeping a respectable distance, followed in his wake.

The soldiers fell back, giving Göring and his guests room to circle around and stare upward from all angles.

"Notice," Göring pointed out, voice raised in rapture as he reached high to caress the huge sandaled foot, "how the folds of her robes seem almost transparent! *Ja!* As weightless as thin cotton! What unsung genius her master carver must have been!"

The entourage, like laughers and clappers of old, murmured agreement. On the sidelines, Generaloberst Kutner preened. Leutnant Hohne found he was still shaking from the stress of responsibility.

"And unlike the English poet Shelley's *Ozymandias,*" the Reichsmarschall continued, "with his 'two vast trunkless legs of stone' and who called his statue a 'colossal wreck', well, you can see for yourselves how perfectly she has been preserved!

"Our beloved Führer," he went on, "speaks of a Thousand-Year Reich. Now imagine: this marvel of antiquity has survived for more than two thousand, five hundred years!"

"And may the Thousand-Year Reich last forever!" added Frau

Goebbels staunchly, who was National Socialism's fiercest supporter and who, with Fräulein Potthast, had just joined the group.

There was a muted chorus of "Heil Hitler."

"It's so—*huge,*" murmured Rose to Emmy under her breath, for once nearly at a loss for words.

"Huge, you mean, like the bulge in your young Schutztaffel's breeches?" teased Emmy with a sly wink.

Before Rose could reply, the Reichsmarschall clapped his hands together. "And now, *meine Damen und meine Herren,*" he announced jovially, his good humor restored after the disappointment of Dr. Hammerschlag's lack of photographs, "come. Let us go inside and raise a glass in celebration! This deserves not even the best German Sekt in my cellar. This occasion deserves to be toasted with the finest vintage champagne from France!"

Later, the windows of Karinhall glowed brightly. The convoy had departed, taking with it the detritus of crates, hay, excelsior, and eiderdowns.

From inside the great house, music seeped out into the courtyard. Shadows of movement passed back and forth behind the glazed mullions, accompanied by endless toasts and bursts of laughter. The moon, nearly full, rode slowly across the bowl of the clear, star-speckled sky.

Here, enfolded in the protective embrace of the jutting wings of the courtyard, and bathed in moonglow, reigned the trunkless goddess of a distant shore.

Mute.

Motionless.

As though awaiting the next stage of her journey.

[CHAPTER SEVEN]

6 April, 1945 A.D.

Hera was on the move.

Again.

And again, Karinhall was a hive of activity.

This time of an altogether different sort.

Overhead, formations of flying fortresses, like prehistoric beasts bent upon reducing nearby Berlin from rubble to ashes, darkened the sky. From the east came the distant, steady pounding of the Russian artillery. The Red Army had broken through Poland and was marching westward, preceded by a flood of refugees.

The Allies had crossed the Rhine. Hamburg, Dresden, Nürnberg, Cologne, the once-proud cities had become smoldering ruins. Hitler was in his bunker, deep under Berlin.

At Karinhall, the party was over. The laughter and music had died. Emmy Göring, the children, and the Reichsmarschall's two sisters had fled to safety on a special train to the Görings' chalet on the Obersalzberg, and the hasty evacuation of art works was in full swing.

One after the other, treasure-laden convoys rolled out of the courtyard, some bound for the bunker in Potsdam until the contents could be shipped south, others for the nearby Zinna Forest Railway Station, where the crates were transferred onto boxcars and shipped by train down to Neuhaus, where they would be transferred to yet more convoys and brought to Burg Veldenstein, filling the Reichsmarschall's wind-whipped fortress in Bavaria to the rafters, like some overstocked warehouse.

Inside Karinhall, the rooms were already nearly stripped bare. Now, no groups of finely dressed guests were gathered atop the front steps to envy the procession of treasures. *The spoils of war.* Fine period furnishings, priceless antiques, tapestries, carpets, thousand-piece sets of porcelain. *The spoils of war.* Loot: Now an encumbrance to be kept out of the hands of the approaching Russians. Only the Reichsmarschall's den still remained virtually intact.

Bernd Hohne, since promoted to Hauptmann from Leutnant, was back, once again supervising the movement of the mammoth statue that presided in the center of the courtyard.

But this time he was not there to deliver looted treasures, and there was no satisfaction in carrying out his duties. Instead, he felt an oppressive, overwhelming sense of doom. It weighed down upon him like an ever-darkening, smothering cloud. The other men, working carelessly while smoking ersatz cigarettes, could feel it too.

It was in the air.

The *Götterdämmerung* was at hand. The Twilight of the Gods had come, and the end of the promised Thousand-Year Reich was writ in stone.

Defeat, like a miasma, hung in the air and clung to one and all. There was no denying the inevitable any longer.

Hauptmann Hohne could not shake the peculiar sensation of watching a sloppy rendition of a familiar film being run in reverse. Instead of the creaks of carefully constructed crates being wrenched open and delicately unpacked, he could hear the sloppy, rushed hammering of shabbily constructed new ones. Rather than priceless tapestries and palace-sized carpets being gently maneuvered into the great house, soldiers were dragging them out in rolls, bouncing the ends down the wide granite steps and creating great furrows in the once pristinely raked gravel. One after the other, the waiting convoys of trucks and lorries were overloaded and then roared off. Away from the park-like clearing, through the stands of majestic pine and beech forests, and across the flat heather of the Schorfheide, where spring was making its presence known, as nature is known to do.

Spring. The season of rebirth. But at Karinhall and all over Germany, the sense of futility and panic was contagious.

Orders were orders, and were to be obeyed.

Suddenly, from inside the open windows of the house came a lurid burst of song. One of the soldiers had chanced upon the gramophone, placed a record on the turntable, and dialed the sound up to full volume. Zarah Leander's deep, warbly contralto poured forth from Karinhall for one last time, singing *Ich weiss, es wird einmal ein Wunder geschehen.*

Hohne could only shake his head and sigh. The rendition of *I Know Someday a Miracle Will Occur* struck him as especially morbid and gruesome; added yet another surreal touch to an already surreal situation. And then he heard a crash.

He jumped at the earsplitting sound as a careless Feldwebel tripped on the granite steps. Stacks of priceless Limoges dinner plates, once the property of Napoleon Bonaparte himself, flew out of a box like flying saucers and shattered on the front steps.

The Feldwebel, apple-cheeked and far too young for his ill-fitting uniform, blushed scarlet and looked around sheepishly, expecting punishment.

None was forthcoming.

Hauptmann Hohne, weary and prematurely aged, could only surrender to hopelessness. *Children,* he thought. *We are now sending children out to war.* He was at that point at which nothing mattered, and couldn't care less about some smashed shards of crockery. Besides, there was no Generaloberst to mete out punishment: Kutner had died in just one of many botched, desperate attempts to stop the Russian advance. Dead, too, was Hohne's beloved wife, Heidi.

She and their newborn son had died in Berlin when the air raid shelter they were in suffered a direct hit. When measured against that tragedy, what were a few ruined dinner plates?

An unwanted memory, consciously and constantly suppressed, painfully burrowed its way to the forefront of his mind, and he flashed back upon happier days. How well he remembered Heidi's breathless excitement each time he returned from overseeing a delivery at Karinhall. How she had excavated his memory for every last, remembered detail!

Perhaps, he thought, *she and the baby are better off dead. At least this way they don't have to face the multiple indignities of defeat, desperation, and condemnation.*

For condemnation, he was certain, was soon to come.

"Herr Hauptmann!"

The intrusive voice of the Stabsfeldwebel jerked him back to the present. Startled, he turned around and blinked in momentary confusion.

"*Ja?* What is it?" he asked, his voice unnaturally harsh and irritable.

"Herr Hauptmann, is something wrong?"

Is something wrong? Hohne wanted to repeat in disbelief. *Don't you realize that everything in the world has gone wrong?* he was tempted to bark, but stifled the urge.

"*Nein, nein,*" he snapped. "Nothing is wrong. What is it?"

"The crane is in position, Herr Hauptmann. The operator is awaiting your order."

Hohne nodded curtly and the Stabsfeldwebel scurried away. Hohne turned around slowly. The platform of the crane hovered above the massive, torso-less statue. Overhead, dark gloomy storm clouds scudded across the overcast sky, and a distant fork of lightning added to the sense of doom. Then he looked at the statue, still rakishly amputated at the waist.

He approached it slowly, for the first time truly seeing and understanding the perfection of the pale gray marble and appreciating its beauty. For a long moment he stood and stared. He was gripped by the illusion that the very folds of Hera's marble *peplos* and chiton rippled in the chill April wind.

Or was it his imagination playing tricks on him?

"She's exquisite, isn't she, Herr Hauptmann?" said a voice from beside him.

Hohne's head snapped to one side and glared. He had not been aware of a young Feldwebel coming up and standing beside him, who stared, with mesmerized awe, at the giant statue.

The Hauptmann's face softened. This Feldwebel, too, was just another boy who had been conscripted at far too young an age: cannon fodder for a last-ditch attempt to augment the decimated ranks of the Third Reich.

"And what is it you want?" he asked, his tone gentle.

The Feldwebel was holding a tin box. It looked vaguely familiar. Then Hohne recalled how its padlock had been forced open at the Reichsmarschall's feet.

"Is this worth packing, Herr Hauptmann? If so, with which shipment does it go?"

"What is inside it?"

"I have not looked, Herr Hauptmann."

"Open it."

The Feldwebel lifted the lid. Hohne reached inside, gave the contents a cursory glance. Papers, some bound journals, and old sepia photographs, crackled with age.

"It's her, Herr Hauptmann," the youth replied.

"Her? Who are you talking about?"

"See? The statue." The Feldwebel pointed at the trunkless goddess, then held up one of the photographs. "The paintings depict her, when she was still in one piece."

"Mmm, yes, I do see." Hohne looked from the photographs to the bright, shining face of the youth. At the face of Germany's future . . . if indeed the *Vaterland* had a future. "You are interested in art?" he asked.

The boy drew his shoulders back proudly. "In archeology, Herr Hauptmann!" Then, remembering his station and the duties at hand: "You will notice the box is not tagged. With which shipment is it supposed to go?"

Bernd Hohne shrugged. What did it matter? The war was lost. Did anyone really care where that tin box ended up? Would anyone miss it? He seriously doubted it.

After a moment's thought, he made up his mind. "Why don't you take it?" he suggested.

"Excuse me, but I do not understand the Herr Hauptmann. Take it where?"

"With you. Keep it as a reminder of . . . " Hohne's voice trailed off.

. . . *what might once have been,* he didn't say.

"Me? Truly, Herr Hauptmann?" The blue eyes shone with disbelief. "The Herr Hauptmann is serious?"

"*Ja.* Now go, *go.* I have to get the statue moved."

"*Vielen Dank,* Herr Hauptmann!" The youth's voice was grateful, and he turned away and started to trot off with the box under his arm.

Hohne caught the young man at his sleeve. "One more thing."

The youth turned and looked at him questioningly. "*Ja,* Herr Hauptmann?"

"What is your name, *junger Kerl?*" he asked softly.

The youth snapped to attention. "Waldemar Hirsch, Herr Hauptmann. From Dortmund."

Bernd Hohne nodded and half-smiled for the first time in many months. "Now go about your duties, young Waldemar from Dortmund." Then, turning his attention back to the statue, he whispered: "And you? You have survived for more than two thousand five hundred years. What will happen to you now? Where will you end up?"

But Hera was still and mute, as though guarding her secrets while patiently awaiting reunification with her missing top half.

[PART II]

What Happened After: Present Day

[CHAPTER EIGHT]

New York City

"There. The alarms are set, the awnings retracted, the windows shuttered, the doors locked, and now for the security gate—" Mara dramatically let the steel accordian crash down in front of the double glass doors of the Jan Kofski Galleries before locking it "—and whoo-ee!" She spun around. "Just imagine, guys, five entire weeks of vacation!"

Mara used the word "guys" in the broadest unisex sense, in that it included two males and four females.

Good-byes were said, "Have a great time!" called about, and they went their separate ways. Jörg mounting his ten-speed titanium bike to pedal his way to Park Slope. Phil, openly gay and ever on the prowl, heading to the nearest Islanders bus stop, overnight bag in hand. Rena braving the heat and hoofing it down to the East Village. And Gita stepping out into traffic to hail a cab to the Lower Fifth Avenue loft that came with her marriage to one of Wall Street's bright young coyotes.

That left Mara and Miranda. Best friends as well as colleagues, they lingered in front of the gallery, reluctant to part. July's heat spared no one in Manhattan, not even in the privileged, tree-lined stretch of world-class shopping that is Madison Avenue in the Sixties, and both yearned for air-conditioned comfort. Even so, they found it difficult to say farewell, although it was for only five weeks.

"Dammit! I wish you'd sprung for the Hamptons share," grumped Mara mournfully. "We could have had so much fun. What am I going to do there without you?"

Miranda laughed. "I would only get in the way. Just think! You'll be surrounded by armies of testosterone-exuding, eligible young males with high-paying jobs."

"And an army of estrogen-loaded competition," Mara added darkly. "Let's face it, Miranda. Neither of us is getting any younger, and every year there's a new crop of size-two bimbos snaring the cream of the crop. And there I am, in my tankini, trying to hide those ten pounds I can never seem to shed. Nothing seems to work. Atkins, South Beach, vegan . . . "

"Pizza, Yoo-Hoos, Snickers . . . "

"Oh, do shut up," Mara retorted good-naturedly. "I've got to have *some* vices. Look at Phil. Ever notice what *he* eats?"

Miranda laughed. "I try not to think about it," she said slyly. "Besides, he's a gym bunny. And you hate exercise."

"Tell me about it. Still, I ask you. Is there any justice in the world?"

"There will be," Miranda assured her confidently, "once you hook up with Mr. Right."

Mara snorted. "I wish you'd tell that to Mommy Dearest. I bet you anything that when I get home, there'll be a message from her on my answering machine."

"You should have told her you'd be long gone by now."

Mara pulled a face. "I did. But it won't have made any difference."

Poor Mara, Miranda thought. She's my age, thirty-two, and although she fled the nest when she went to college, she was still badgered by a mother who, when she wasn't playing mah-jong down in Boca, called long-distance to see how her daughter's love life was coming along.

And although Mara did score more than her share of the occasional one-night stands, Miranda didn't need to be told that wasn't exactly the kind of information that would warm the cockles of her Jewish mother's heart.

Mara said, "Well, if we stand out here much longer, I think I'm positively going to wilt. I've got to get indoors and turn up the AC. This heat is killing me."

And so they hugged on the sidewalk and promised to keep in touch before heading in opposite directions to their respective homes.

"I'll phone!" Mara called over her shoulder.

"Well, I'm not going anywhere!" Miranda returned, as yet unaware that fate had other plans in store. They threw air kisses, waggled fingertips, and Mara turned a corner and was lost to sight.

Almost instantly, Miranda's footsteps dragged and her mood plunged. It had nothing to do with the oppressive heat and humidity. It was the prospect of facing nearly five weeks off and having nothing planned and nowhere to go. The Jan Kofski Galleries, one of the most respected purveyors of rare antiquities from ancient times, traditionally closed for the entire month of August, as did the best restaurants and snootiest shops. Everyone who could afford to leave town did so, even if it was only for weekends. Except for working stiffs, people who couldn't afford to escape to the country, tourists and tourist-reliant businesses, Manhattan went into a kind of suspended animation. The city wouldn't switch back into high gear until the beginning of September, and then it was invariably with a turbo-charged vengeance.

Miranda duly trudged north on Madison until she reached Seventy-Second Street, then headed West toward Fifth Avenue and Central Park. Even though she kept to the shady sides of the streets, she was soon wilting from the heat and humidity. She considered catching the crosstown bus, and then switching to the M10 uptown, along Central Park West, but seeing the sweating clusters waiting for an air-conditioned bus—and imagining trying to find a seat amidst some of Manhattan's sweatiest—held little appeal.

The subway held even less. The heat in the stations would be hellacious, and she'd have to switch trains and God alone knew how long she'd be trapped underground. A taxi might have been a providential alternative, but she had to watch her pennies. Besides, she'd ridden in one too many air-conditioned cabs whose plexiglass divider between driver and passenger let scant cool air into the tipper's section. Also, it was shift-changing time, and finding an available taxi would take a miracle. How Gita always managed to find one was a mystery Miranda had yet to solve.

Miranda loathed mysteries. She was one of those people who always had to know the answers.

Waiting to cross Fifth Avenue, she felt vindicated. Fleets of yellow cabs were migrating downtown, OFF-DUTY signs inevitably lit.

So she traversed Central Park on foot and fooled herself into thinking it was a cool and pleasant alternative. The effect of all that green, she supposed. The route she'd picked was a sun-dappled lane with mature trees that was free of cars and lined with green park benches. It more or less followed the north shore of the lake that lay parallel to Central Park West from about Seventy-Second to Eightieth Streets. She paused to watch some rowers in the boats that could be rented from the boathouse, and didn't envy them. It was too hot and muggy. Unfortunately, the walk also gave her ample opportunity for reflection. She was facing five weeks of nothing. Five entire weeks of staying home in her 350-square-foot studio with a window air conditioner that wheezed asthmatically and her cat. Seen in that light, it seemed more like a prison sentence rather than a vacation. Or, if she wanted to be optimistic, she could always pretend she was on probation, and brave the heat to see a movie or visit a museum.

She had to face reality. Being stuck in the city in summer, when her friends were off cavorting somewhere cool, glam, or terribly in, was no holiday.

Too late, she wished she'd listened to Mara and sprung for that share in the Hamptons.

And then there was Harry. She thought of him now.

Harry.

Harris Milford Palmer III, her fiancé whose ring adorned her finger.

Harry, from whom she had reluctantly accepted the ring and the proposal, but to whom she knew she could never actually commit.

Harry, the hedge fund manager who worked twelve- to fourteen-hour days and was constantly flying here, there, and everywhere to woo, snare, and mother his clients.

Harry, who wouldn't take no for an answer, and was out of town more often than not.

Harry, whose Yale drinking buddies she couldn't stand, and whose parents' seaside mansion in Maine she secretly referred to as the WASP's Nest.

An elderly man coming from the opposite direction leered at her, smacked his lips noisily, rasped "Yum-yum!" and actually licked his lips.

Resolutely tucking her chin down into her chest, Miranda pretended to ignore him, quickened her pace, and revised her previous thoughts.

It was just as well that she hadn't let herself get snared into the Hamptons share. She'd done that one year and, as the saying went, once was more than enough. Put eight co-ed singles into one house at any given time, add the neighboring houses rented out similarly, and between the elevated testosterone and estrogen levels, the non-stop sophomoric partying, and being all but physically dragged into the dunes, she'd fled back to the city. Losing the small fortune, nonrefundable, of course, that she'd plunked down for a seasonal share seemed a small price to pay for peace and quiet. Well, considering Manhattan, relative peace and quiet at any rate.

No, that hormone-intensive beach bunny singles scene was not for her. Besides, unlike Mara, Miranda didn't have an overbearing mother in Boca who constantly called, demanding to know when she was getting married, or what man was in her life at any given moment.

That was the one advantage, she supposed, of not having parents to harass her. Miranda had been in her senior year at Berkeley at the time both her parents had died in an automobile crash. It was one of those senseless accidents that could have been avoided had the driver of the other vehicle not been DUI. Losing a loving mom and dad had been the single worst blow she'd ever suffered. Being an only child, she had no siblings to share her grief with, or to draw strength from. For that matter, she had no other family to speak of. Her father, a second-generation Greek-American, who had been raised in the Orthodox Church, was an only child, and her mother had escaped the clutches of a Midwestern cult of radical Christian fundamentalists, the women of which never cut their hair, and the members of which, male and female alike, were expected to speak in tongues and handle poisonous snakes.

She couldn't blame her mother for bolting; if anyone dangled so much as a harmless garter snake in front of her, Miranda's shoes would have left skid marks on the pavement. Guaranteed.

But due to marrying outside their faiths, both her parents had been cruelly disowned by their respective families.

Subsequently Miranda grew up without having any kind of religion drummed into her. She didn't attend church services or Sunday school. There were no prayers before meals. She never had the opportunity to meet her disapproving grandparents on either the maternal or paternal sides, and to this day had no idea whether they were dead or alive.

Nor did she care. Her parents had been the gentlest and most loving of creatures. Having been so close to them, she never felt any desire to make contact with those who had so unfairly cast them out.

Even today, eleven years after her parents' untimely deaths, the void they left in Miranda's life was with her always. She had yet to meet a family as close-knit as the three of them had been. Not a day went by that she didn't think of the happy threesome they had once made.

Psychologists might explain the lack of religion in the Kalli household as being directly responsible for Miranda's choices for higher education. Actually, it was Berkeley's archeology department that cinched it, since she decided to major in archeology and minor in comparative religion.

Her interest in religions was purely academic. Because even the most primitive cultures worshiped some deity or other, religion went hand-in-hand with the study of cultures and peoples, beginning with the goddess of fertility, or the Earth Mother, the study of religion tied in directly with her fascination with archeology. Miranda never once forgot that it was religion that ruled the daily lives of the Mesopotamians and Egyptians, who left behind tombs and treasures. Likewise, the most ancient Greeks worshiped their featureless Cycladic idols, and later fashioned marble gods and goddesses in their own image, no matter how idealized.

Perhaps the imagined psychologists really would have been onto something; if so, it was strictly subliminal and buried deeply in Miranda's subconscious.

The truth was, even when she was a little girl, from the moment she first laid eyes on pictures of the Parthenon, the Pyramids, and the Sphinx, she was hooked. And once hooked, there was no going back. Other kids her age were fascinated by dinosaurs, but Miranda's head was already deep into ancient civilizations. So enchanted was she by the very idea of the Hanging Gardens of Babylon that she conjured mile-high mental images of what, she later realized, were some outrageous follies worthy of Cecil B. DeMille.

But once ignited, a childhood fascination, especially one encouraged by one's parents, could shine the guiding light along the path to one's future.

Fast forward some fourteen or fifteen years. As the sole inheritor of her parents' estate, she managed to use her inheritance to complete her first four years of schooling, and then she furthered her education by getting a master's degree in archeology and doing course work in comparative religion.

But where did a master's degree in archeology leave one? Neither here nor there; at best, in a kind of scholastic limbo.

So, ever practical, Miranda Kalli took stock of what was left of her inheritance. Since she was frugal—she could pinch the proverbial penny till it bled, and fixed everything from loose shoe soles to plumbing leaks to broken taillights on a car with duct tape—she decided that if she was very, very careful she had just enough funds left for further studies, and could thus earn that magical degree that might lead to Great Things. Or at least open the right doors.

The gods were with her. During her course work, her doctoral committee chairman was none other than one Waldemar P. Hirsch, Ph.D., one of the world's most respected, most experienced, and most published archeologists in the field of Archaic and Classical Hellenic Culture.

Thus, over the next four years, she duly finished her course work, her writtens and orals, and had her dissertation idea accepted—"Physical Depictions of the Mother Dia in Early Cycladic Society."

Finally, after eight years on campus, it was time for the oral defense of her dissertation.

Her timing couldn't have been better. Professor Hirsch, itching to get back to the Aegean sites on which he worked summers, was about to retire and devote himself to his digs full-time. Her dissertation defense was held a mere two weeks before his departure.

Talk about finishing in the nick of time.

Although she now cringed at the fatuous title of her dissertation, she was also secretly pleased that it had been published and was still actually in circulation, studied by archeology students in universities the world over.

I have Professor Hirsch to thank for that, she thought gratefully. *Without his wise counsel and guidance, I might never have completed my Ph.D.*

And another thing for which she silently thanked him almost daily: it was Professor Hirsch's contact with Jan Kofski, owner of the Madison Avenue gallery of that name, that had gotten Miranda her job in New York City.

Having become as close as anyone to being the kindly uncle she never had, Professor Hirsch still corresponded with her with irregular regularity—a letter out of the blue every now and then.

Now, exiting the park above Eighty-Sixth Street, Miranda crossed Central Park West and moseyed uptown a few more blocks in the shadows of those grandiose pre-war apartment palaces. From her shoulder bag, her cell phone emitted an electronic rendition of Beethoven's *Fifth*.

Digging it out, she flipped it open and checked the caller ID. Probably Mara already, she thought.

Nope. Wrong.

Harry.

Harris Milford Palmer III, who juggled his off-hours to share her bed between his frenzied hedge fund managing.

Harry, who expected her to be ready, willing, and able whenever *his* schedule permitted.

Harry, who insisted upon calling her Mandy, a diminutive she'd told him over and over she despised.

Harry, who forever harassed her about setting a date for their wedding.

Harry, who would start off with, "Mandy, Mother thinks that now June's past . . ."

Annoyed and sweaty by her trek home, she snapped the phone shut and stuffed it back inside her bag. Right now, she just wasn't in the mood to deal with him. Later, perhaps.

Heading over to Columbus Avenue and her local D'Agostino's, she luxuriated in air-conditioned chill, purchasing a container of cottage cheese, a jar of artichoke hearts in olive oil, and a 6-ounce container of plain yoghurt for herself, as well as two cans of Fancy Feast for Magoo.

Cats, she reflected, made the ultimate roommates. They didn't get drunk, didn't smoke, didn't hang out with unbearable Yalies, and didn't mind it if you were gone all day, so long as they had their litter box and their vittles.

And above all, cats didn't call her on the spur of the moment and expect her to jump with joy—or through hoops.

Hauling her plastic D'Ag bag, she trotted on up Columbus to Magoo's veterinary clinic. You couldn't miss it. The storefront was of frosted white glass. It was printed all over with black paw prints of various sizes. The frosted glass door was emblazoned with gold letters outlined in black:

The Healthy Pet

Beneath it was the legend:

"The Small Animal Hospital That Cares"

And under that, in discreet letters:

Martin Gatsby, DVM
Donna Wang, DACVS

An air-conditioner thrummed above the door, dripping a continuous stream of water onto the sidewalk, promising cool air inside.

When Miranda entered she almost purred with pleasure at the chill. There were several customers sitting in the waiting room. A man's schnauzer tugged at the leash and growled at the intrusion. A couple's small furry mutt wagged furiously, then rolled on his back, all four paws in the air, expecting a belly rub. A grim-faced woman with a lethargic cat in a carrier sat off to the far side, as far from the dogs as possible.

Mitzi Orbach manned the front desk. She was wearing a yellow smock dotted with smiling cats and dogs and her usual toothy, friendly smile. "Hi, Miranda," she greeted cheerfully. "I have your month's supply of Magoo's meds ready. Enough insulin and syringes to last you till September." She reached below the counter and placed a plastic bag on the counter. Its surface was printed with the same black paw prints as the frosted glass window. "How's the big feller doing?"

Miranda smiled ruefully and handed over her MasterCard. "Driving me bankrupt, as usual."

Mitzi barked a laugh as she slid the plastic through the little machine and typed in a code. "Hey—love doesn't come cheap."

"You telling *me?*"

"Going anywhere this month?" Mitzi asked as she waited for the authorization to go through. "It's gonna be one heck of a hot month."

"Nah, I'm staying put," Miranda said. "You know me. Can't stay away from the baking asphalt, the aromas of rotting garbage, gasoline fumes. Smog."

Mitzi brayed laughter. "You're too much." The credit card machine chattered, Miranda scrawled her John Hancock on the receipt, tucked the credit card into her shoulder bag and swung the plastic shopping bag off the counter. "See you next month."

"You have a good one," Mitzi said.

"Yeah. You too, Mitz."

"And look on the bright side, Miranda. You never know what might happen."

"Yeah, I might even win the lottery," Miranda called over her shoulder.

"Hey—don't knock it. You never know."

Leaving the air-conditioned comfort zone, Miranda was back outside in the blast furnace heat and trudged on to her apartment.

Home for Miranda was a Ninety-Fifth Street walk-up. A brownstone on a charming tree-lined block, it had, a century earlier, been an elegant single family dwelling. Since then, a series of real estate-savvy landlords had broken it up into ever smaller and smaller units until there were twenty studio apartments, four to a floor.

You couldn't break it up much further unless you got rid of the tiny bathrooms and turned the whole place into a flophouse.

Which, if it happened, wouldn't have surprised Miranda, already a jaded Manhattanite, one little bit. Not with the way the real estate market in the city kept skyrocketing.

Using one of a handful of keys on her key ring, she unlocked the outer front door and let herself into the vestibule. Dutifully she checked her mailbox. It was crammed full of the usual—junk mail and bills. These she stuffed into the plastic D'Ag bag and unlocked the inner front door.

Four flights of steep airless stairs loomed. She trudged up the metal-edged linoleum slowly. Passing 2E on the second floor landing, she heard a floorboard creak, followed by a click as her landlady peered out of her peephole.

Miranda couldn't help but smile. Eva Shapiro—the tenants called her "Evil Shapiro"—didn't have a clue that anyone was wise to her spying. As always, Miranda was tempted to waggle her fingers in greeting, but stifled the impulse and followed building tradition, pretending not to notice.

Three more flights. She could swear the air got thinner the higher she climbed. Finally, feeling she'd conquered Everest, she set down her shopping bags, caught her breath, and proceeded to unlock the two deadbolts and the snap-lock.

The instant she opened the brown steel door, there was Magoo. Making catbird-like yeowing noises and rubbing himself against the doorjamb, tail straight up in the air, he eeled himself around her shins.

"Hey there, big fella," she said, leaning down and stroking two fingers along the back of his neck.

More unpleasant yeowing greeted her. Magoo, an 18-pound Maine Coon, didn't seem to understand that cats were supposed to purr. On the other hand, he had giant green eyes that Miranda swore made him look like Marlene Dietrich. His favorite position was to sit in sphinx-like splendor on a corner of her bed, and every now and then throw her some unexpected affection. He was higher maintenance than a green plant—especially since he'd developed diabetes—but then a plant didn't lick her hand with a rough tongue, pad around with dignity, or cough up hairballs.

"Ma-goo-*oo!*" she chided as he ignored the open apartment door and rubbed himself against the wooden banister spindles, poking his head forward to stare straight down the stairwell before finally obeying and making a stately entrance.

She was just about to shut the door when she heard lock tumblers turning noisily from the apartment next door. Her neighbor, Ron, was a performance artist who appeared Off-Off Broadway under the name, "Lotta Puss." Unless it was a Wednesday or a Saturday—matinee days when the Bridge-and-Tunnel crowd filled Manhattan's theaters, he didn't have to keep 9 to 5 hours like a lot of the city's working stiffs.

"Yo, Cinderella," he said, lounging against his doorjamb and fanning himself with an oversized cardboard DHL Express envelope.

Miranda glanced over at him and winked. "Hey, Lots. How's tricks?"

"Don't ask," he said with a dramatic sigh.

Ron was in his late twenties, spent mornings keeping buff in the gym, ran marathons, and carried around roughly zero percent body fat. With his fashionably shaved head, black designer tee shirts that showed off his athletic, perfectly proportioned physique to advantage, and his handsome face with its ready smile, he was more than merely attractive. Unfortunately for members of the opposite sex, he was also one hundred percent gay and comfortable with it. In other words, he was the perfect friend when a girl needed a shoulder to cry on or a presentable escort for gallery openings or parties, but hopeless when it came to anything beyond platonic friendship.

Considering her doomed past romances, and her present engagement to Harry, Miranda easily preferred friendship over a good lay. Too many of the straight men she'd met since coming to the city had turned out to be shits. Total shits.

"I *was* hoping that DHL man would be a hunk," Ron mused somewhat dreamily.

"Which DHL man?" she returned.

"The one who brought this." He stopped fanning himself with the envelope long enough to hold it up. "I heard your doorbell ring. You know how thin these walls are—"

She grinned knowingly. "Ah. So that explains why I heard you playing Intruder and Victim so clearly Sunday night."

"Oh, *him.*" Ron flapped the envelope dismissively. "Total dud."

She tilted her head and eyed him slyly. "Didn't sound that way from next door."

"That's because of distortion." Ron always had a quick retort for any comment, something she'd always envied in him. "At any rate, hearing your doorbell, and knowing you were at work, I went over to the intercom. 'Package for a Ms. Miranda Kalli,' a deep macho voice said. So I said, 'Come on up and I'll sign for it.' I was in the middle of testing some new makeup, so I toweled it off in a jiffy, flung off the stocking mask I wear under my wig—"

"Ah. One of which your so-called 'Intruder' wore on Sunday?" she teased.

Ron sniffed. "You know I have tons of them," he said loftily. "For theatrical purposes."

Her reply, an evil grin, spoke louder than words.

"Besides which," said Ron with dignity, "Sunday's trick wore his own wooly balaclava. So *there*."

Her grin widened.

"Oh, will you stop?" he said with feigned exasperation. "To get back to the DHL guy, I answered the door . . . "

" . . . and?"

"And nothing." Ron scowled. "I was hoping, you know, he'd be like some of those cute UPS guys? Wearing those brown short-shorts in summer?"

"Yes?"

"Well, this guy turned out to be a perfect ugh. Probably a breeder from Jersey. Shoulda kept on my makeup. Anyway." With a flourish, Ron handed over the envelope.

Miranda accepted it and frowned. She hadn't been expecting a package. But there it was: her name and address and the usual tracking numbers and requisite bar codes. She had to squint to read the return address, the print was so small:

Albatross
Waterfront
Pythagoria 83103
Samos, Greece

Miranda's brow furrowed as she murmured: "Albatross? What the devil is Albatross?"

"A bird, or a chain around your neck?" Ron suggested helpfully.

She cast him an evil eye. "Fuh-nee," she said, and pulled the tab across the top of the cardboard mailer.

Inside it were two legal sized envelopes. She reached for one. It wasn't sealed; the flap was simply tucked inside the opening. It contained a folded sheet of paper and a color photograph.

She studied the photograph first.

She recognized the man instantly. It was none other than her favorite professor at Berkeley, Dr. Waldemar Hirsch. He was tan as a nut, and wore a loose, long-sleeved shirt of thin white cotton. Seated at a table, he was grinning proudly, one arm draped around the shoulders of a middle-aged, bronze-haired woman with a kindly face and a shy smile. Overhead, a pergola dripped vines and grapes.

She unfolded the accompanying letter, recognizing the inimitable hieroglyphic-like penmanship of a man who does not waste time.

> My dearest Miranda,
>
> I have always been lax when it comes to correspondence, because there is always so much to do. As the enclosed photo obviously shows, I have finally remarried. Eleni is a fine woman, my age, also widowed, with two grown sons. She owns a restaurant here on Samos named Albatross, which has acquired quite the reputation for its seafood.
>
> Of course, you are well aware that I never write without a reason. I well realize that Jan Kofski closes for the entire month of August, and I could use an extra hand on an exciting dig here on Samos. I've procured special permission from the Ministry of Culture for you to join us . . .

Miranda felt the world tilt, then stop turning. She hardly dared breathe. Her hands were shaking, and she had to consciously still them. She was in a daze, a kind of dream-state. For a moment, the possibility of the most dazzling summer of her life lit up her imagination.

An archeological dig! In the Aegean, that wine-dark sea of the ancients, no less!

Her spirits soared into orbit, then plunged as abruptly as Icarus after he flew too close to the sun. It was all she could do to blink back tears of disappointment.

Damn! she thought. *Oh, fucking damn, damn, damn, damn*, damn! She hadn't budgeted for an overseas trip. In fact, her credit cards were all but maxed out.

Suddenly dispirited, she could feel the world once again revolve on its axis, and desultorily continued to read:

> . . . If you fly to Athens, you can take the bus to Rafina, and catch the overnight ferry which shall bring you here. (Sorry, the local flights are all overbooked this time of year.) Unfortunately, I can't offer more than room and board; the facilities at the site are adequate, if a bit primitive. I do hope you haven't made other plans, my dear, and accept my apologies for such short notice, but there have been . . . well, to put it mildly, some rather peculiar goings on. I can't go into details now. Hope to tell you all in person and see you soon.
>
> Yours ever so fondly,
> Wald

She must have worn a strange expression, for Ron had adopted a robotic tone, repeating: "Earth to Miranda. Earth to Miranda . . . "

Earth . . . ?

Her cheeks were quivering and it was difficult to concentrate. She could hear the robotic voice repeating, "Houston, we have a problem." Ron's constant theatrics. Couldn't he shut up! Disappointment possessed her; it was all she could do not to weep.

It was then that the second envelope slipped out of the mailer, distracting her by falling at her feet. The flap of the envelope had come undone, scattering its contents. She looked down and drew a deep breath.

What?

A mirage, surely, manufactured by her mind. She shook her head and blinked. Shut her eyes. Then opened them again.

She could scarce believe what she was seeing. Surely she was dreaming. It had to be her imagination starting to run away with her.

But no. Staring up at her from the stained linoleum of the landing was the unmistakable green and white of a "paper" airline ticket, several stiff, computer-printed copies stapled together. And there was another, thinner ticket, also stapled together and made out in her name. A ferry ticket from Rafina to Samos.

Wide-eyed and not daring to breathe, she slowly stooped down and gathered them up and held them against her breast. "Oh, Ron!" she whispered.

"Taking a trip, sweetie?" Ron asked archly. "Lemme see where you're going." He snatched the airline ticket from her hands and perused it closely. A grin crossed his lips. "Better get a move on, Cinderella, else you're gonna miss the ball."

She frowned. "Why? What do you mean?"

He pointed at the ticket. "See? The flight's this afternoon at four-thirty. On Olympic."

"What!" Her mouth gaped in astonishment. "This afternoon? You mean *today?*"

"Yep. Today."

"Holy Hannah Yarby!" She glanced at her watch in panic. "But there's no time—"

"There's just time. So, girl? I suggest you stuff some clothes into a carry-all super-quick and get moving. You know how long it takes to get out to JFK."

And suddenly she was laughing and crying at the same time, and Ron was picking her up and whirling her effortlessly around and around, and through tears of joy she managed, "Ron? I just picked up a month's worth of insulin from the vet's. Would you . . . would you mind . . . terribly if I asked you to look after Magoo?"

[CHAPTER NINE]

Spada, Greece

Olympic Flight 412 coasted into Eleftherios Venizelos, the shiny new Athens airport, within seventeen minutes of the scheduled arrival—not bad, considering the nine-and-a-half hours of non-stop flying. Miranda was so grateful for the opportunity to stretch her legs that she didn't even mind having to wait in the long, slow, non-EU passport line. Meanwhile, the EU passengers breezed smugly through their gate en masse and disappeared.

The rest of the passengers waited.

Eventually it was her turn. The uniformed bureaucrat in the glass booth seemed to take an awfully long time comparing her face to her passport photo.

Not that Miranda could blame him. Passport photos, like those of driver's licenses, invariably turned out looking like mug shots, and hers was no exception. She didn't know how those photographers managed to do it, and had come to the conclusion that it took a special talent.

He scanned the first two pages through a computer, then asked the inevitable question. "Are you here for business or pleasure?"

The smart-aleck in Miranda was tempted to reply: "Serial killing," but that was no way to gain entry into a foreign country, and this guy didn't look like he had a sense of humor. So she replied truthfully: "Both, I suppose. I'm going to be working on an archeological dig—"

That got his attention. His dark eyes narrowed, his moustache twitched, and she could feel him projecting the full power of his authority upon her. "Do you have the permission?" His voice was full of suspicion.

She stared right back at him. "The person in charge of the excavation does."

"The government does not permit the unauthorized excavations. You must have the approval from the Ministry of Culture. You understand?"

"Yes," she replied solemnly, "fully."

"Your name is Kalli. You are Greek?"

"My father's family was Greek." She nodded. "But I was born in the States."

"Where were they from?"

"Uh, Chicago, originally. Then California."

"I mean, where was his family from in Greece?"

"I don't understand."

He didn't elaborate. A long moment passed. He flipped lazily through her passport pages, which didn't contain much. A budget vacation to Cozumel, a faded stamp from the time she'd accompanied Harry to Grand Cayman. He frowned, and at long last deigned to rubber stamp a page near the back. That was another thing she had never been able to figure out: what criteria did these bureaucrats use to decide which page to stamp?

He slid the passport back at her and indicated that she was free to go on through. No "Welcome to Greece, Ms. Kalli." No "Enjoy your stay."

"Thank you," she said sweetly, and went on through.

She knew it was petty of her, but she resented his lack of a welcome.

Friendly soul, she thought sardonically. But she knew better than to press her luck, and proceeded to the baggage claim area, which could have been in any major airport in the world. She had expected something a little more,well, a little more rustic and *Greek,* rather than a setting so institutionally homogenized. But that was happening the world over, and there was no use harping on the inevitable.

As she'd feared, a wall-to-wall crowd was clustered around the baggage carousel for Flight 412. As she approached, a buzzer went off that sounded suspiciously like the response to the wrong answer on a game show, and presently luggage began to be disgorged.

Luggage carousels are one of those places which bring out the savage beast in otherwise civilized people. No matter where, it was always every man or woman for him or herself, and Miranda could swear it was a lot more aggressive among Greeks, something she had noticed upon boarding the Airbus 340-600 in New York. No matter which row was being called, it had became a sudden free-for-all.

A Greek line, she'd heard one experienced wag call it.

Being only human, she found a tiny break in the crowd around the carousel, wriggled her way sideways toward the front, and then did what any New Yorker worth her salt would do—assertively nudged aside the competition (suffering a few jabs from elbows on both sides of her) until she had enough space to lean forward and, like everyone else in the front, faced the direction from which the luggage was coming.

Before long, the crowd began to thin as one piece after another was heaved off the moving belt. Her two yellow nylon bags appeared sooner than expected, and she trotted off smugly, one in each hand. Neither was particularly heavy. During her hurried packing, she'd only tossed light-weight clothing and a few essential toiletries into her bag, since she knew that summers in the Aegean, especially in July and August, tended to be hellaciously hot and perpetually sunny. Besides, she liked to travel light. Ron had quipped that it was because she had no heart.

She begged to differ, although her behavior at the luggage carousel could be construed otherwise. That was just her Manhattan survival tactics kicking in.

Following the signs that pointed in the direction of taxis and busses, she started toward the nearest exit. That was when an announcement in thickly accented English came over the speakers: "*Would New York passenger Me-rahn-da Kahlee please cahm to the een-formation desk? New York passenger Me-rahn-da Kahlee . . .* "

She stopped in her tracks, causing the crowd behind her to detour to her left and right like a school of fish avoiding an obstacle before merging back into a single entity.

Me-rahn-da Kahlee. Her first thought was, *They couldn't possibly be paging me. Why would they want to?* And on the heels of that thought: *Oh, oh. Don't tell me the guy at passport control had second thoughts.*

She was not certain how long she stood there, blocking the exit through the automatic doors. Dr. Hirsch's instructions had been explicit. She was supposed to take the bus to Rafina to catch the ferry to

Samos. Also, there was a good chance that the name she'd heard was being torturously mispronounced and didn't refer to her at all.

But what if it did?

Executing a 180-degree turn, Miranda found herself colliding with a scowling, heavy-set woman who uttered what were obviously curses in a foreign tongue. Greek? Bulgarian? Romanian? . . . and who, for good measure, maneuvered one wheel of her suitcase over Miranda's foot.

"Ouch!" Miranda blurted, hopping up and down and earning the woman's triumphant sneer. Then, one yellow carry-all clasped tightly in each hand, she fought her way against the human tide and took the escalator to the massive departure hall. It seemed to stretch for miles from one end to another, with more ticket counters than she'd ever seen in any one place.

She was immediately taken aback, thinking: *What the hell?*

For it was bedlam, particularly the area devoted to domestic flights. She had the overpowering premonition that war must have been declared. Or some other state of emergency. Why else would everyone be pushing and shoving to catch the last flights out? And the number of cell phones in use. She'd never seen so many in one place at any one given time. Not even in Manhattan.

The intercom system was working overtime. Various announcements were being broadcast in Greek, beginning with "*Kiría e kírie . . .*" and repeated in English: "*Ladies and gentlemen. We are sorry, but due to the situation, all flights to Rodhos, Crete, Samos, Mykonoy, and Santorini are sold out . . . please be patient, we are trying to add additional flights . . .*"

Situation? What situation? She could only hope the announcement didn't refer to anything she should be aware of.

Further announcements concerned this person or that person, and would they please pick up a courtesy telephone or come to the information desk?

Then she heard it again: "*Would New York passenger Me-rahn-da Kahlee please cahm to the een-formation desk? New York passenger Me-rahn-da Kahlee . . .*"

All fine, well, and dandy, but the information desk was as mobbed as a new Ikea store offering half-price specials. Miranda valiantly attempted to fight her way to the front, but realized it was a losing battle. For one thing, she was schlepping two bags. For another, compared to this lot, the people at the baggage carousel had been downright docile, mere lambs. These passengers, however, were Aggressive—with a capital "A." Tempers were flaring. She saw tickets being waved in the air like weapons and heard shouts in various languages ring out. Two harried, attractive young women behind the desk tried to answer questions and keep order, but it looked like a losing battle.

"Goodness, I *do* hope it doesn't come to blows," clucked a rather short, middle-aged woman beside her as they were both violently jostled from behind.

Miranda looked over at her. The woman had a distinct Midwestern twang and was dressed in a proper pale pink suit with a white blouse and sensible low white heels. She had a gold brooch in the shape of a flower, centered with a faux pearl, pinned to her lapel. The jostling had knocked her wide-brimmed straw hat askew and she was rearranging it on her head.

Eyeing Miranda anxiously, she added, with a significant glance behind her: "You don't suppose it will get *violent,* do you?"

Grateful for the companionship of a fellow American, Miranda said, "I should hope not, but these people don't exactly look like happy campers."

"No, they don't, do they?" The woman sighed. "I wonder what on earth is going on." She cast Miranda a hopeful sideways glance. "You wouldn't happen to know, would you, dear?"

Miranda shook her head. "Sorry. I just arrived and was on my way out, but I think I was paged."

"Oh. I do see. Yes."

Presently two security officers appeared and restored a semblance of order. Airport workers set up chrome stands with velvet ropes. "About time, don't you think, dear?" The Midwestern woman, separated from Miranda by a velvet rope, had to raise her voice above the din. Presently, the shouts all around turned to grumbles as lines were formed.

In due time Miranda found herself at the counter at precisely the same time as the Midwestern woman, who was being helped by one bottled blonde, while Miranda was being taken care of by the other.

"What is happening?" Miranda inquired. "Surely it's not always like this."

The young blonde rolled her eyes and shook her head. "Like this? Not always, no. The problem is, everyone is demanding flights because the ferry service has been temporarily halted."

Miranda blinked, not certain she'd heard correctly. "Did you say ferry service has been halted?" Her voice faltered.

"Yes." The blonde pecked a quick nod. "All over Greece."

"Don't tell me," Miranda moaned, casting her eyes heavenward. "I'm supposed to go to Rafina and catch one!"

She received a blank look. Harried as the information clerk was, Miranda could sense that she was beyond compassion, and that it was a struggle for her to maintain even a modicum of courteousness. If so, Miranda had to give her an A for effort.

"I am sorry," the blonde told her, pronouncing it "sore-ee." "There was a ferry disaster off Crete last night. All ferries have been temporarily grounded, pending inspection." She paused. "If you are inquiring about flights to the islands, it is useless. The waiting list is two days."

Miranda's heart sank. "I'm not here about a flight, though. I believe I was paged? The name is Miranda Kalli. K-A-L-L-I."

From beside her, at that exact same moment, she overheard her Midwestern fellow citizen saying, "I heard an announcement concerning my sister, Miranda Kallas? That's spelled K-A-L-L-A-S."

The woman had obviously overheard Miranda too, because both their heads swivelled simultaneously, and they exchanged astonished glances. Their expressions were identical: *What a coincidence, the similarity in names!*

The young woman helping Miranda stopped scrolling down her computer screen. "Ah, yes. Here it is. Me-rahn-da Kahlee. That is you?"

"That's me," Miranda replied, even as she heard the other blonde telling the Midwestern woman, "I am sorry. There is no Kallas . . . "

But Miranda had her own business to attend to and could sense the growing impatience of those behind her in line. She tuned out what was being said beside her and gave the blonde her full attention.

"There is a message from a Professor Hirsch?" the young woman said, mispronouncing his name, but Miranda didn't waste time correcting her.

"Yes?" she nodded. "That would be for me."

The clerk kept her eyes on the monitor. "His message," she read off, "it says, 'Am aware of the ferry situation. Suggest you take a bus to the Plaka, find an inexpensive hotel, and wait until the ferry system is running again. These things never last more than a couple of days," the blonde paused hesitantly and looked at her questioningly. "Couple . . . that *is* the correct word?"

Miranda nodded. "Yes, absolutely. It means two or three." Then: "The Plaka," she repeated, absolutely clueless. "What is the Plaka?"

"Is simple," the clerk assured her. "You take bus to Syntagma Square. In your language it means Constitution Square. It is near the base of the Acropolis. The Plaka is within a few short blocks of there. An easy walk."

Miranda thanked her for the information, hoisted her bags, and scooted aside so as not to hold up the line any longer.

The Plaka, she repeated to herself, lest she forgot. *Syntagma Square . . .*

What a drag! But then the other thing the young blonde had said registered in her mind, and a mental lightbulb glowed with enough wattage to light up an entire city, and suddenly lemons turned into lemonade.

It is near the base of the Acropolis.

The Acropolis!

Any residual disappointment Miranda might have felt instantly faded and fell away. Suddenly she was filled with the buoyancy of soaring spirits such as she had never before known. It was all she could do not to throw her arms out like Julie Andrews in the opening sequence of *The Sound of Music* and start spinning in place and bursting into song.

The Acropolis!

What more could any archeological buff want? she asked herself deliriously. *I should be* grateful *for this opportunity! Yes, grateful—!*

Indeed, it seemed the gods of the ancients were indeed smiling down upon her.

Her eyes glistened with tears of joy.

The Acropolis! That flat-topped mount from which Greece's eternal symbol, the Parthenon, had presided over Athens for some 2,500 years! That great Panathenic temple commissioned by none other than Pericles himself, and that was dedicated to the goddess, Athena, for whom Athens was named, and that had always headed the list of her childhood fantasies!

And now to be blessed with the opportunity to actually climb up and view it first hand—

Miranda's head was spinning.

—would wonders never cease?

For despite her best intentions, plus early Hellenic culture being her area of expertise, Miranda had never had the opportunity to set foot in Greece, the country from whence her father's ancestors had sprung.

The reasons had always been financial. Her parents' legacy had been modest, and when she wasn't studying, she'd had to support herself by holding down a succession of low-paying, part-time jobs. Then, after she'd moved to New York City and, thanks to Professor Hirsch, had landed her plum job at the Jan Kofski Gallery, she was faced with the exorbitant costs of living and working in Manhattan—not to mention the necessity of keeping up the kind of appearances a Madison Avenue gallery expected of its employees.

As for her salary, in the beginning it hardly covered the bare necessities. She'd kept consoling herself with the mantra that it was a miracle she had even landed the job in the first place. Manhattan, after all, attracted experts in her field like a picnic attracts ants, what with the plethora of museums, galleries, and auction houses.

But luxuries like travel, even for learning purposes, seemed forever out of reach.

Even now, after several years and raises, Miranda's salary still couldn't keep up with inflation and the rising costs of living, and it was all she could do to keep her head above water. Then there was the Presentability Factor. Working in an upscale Madison Avenue Gallery demanded that one always look sharp. You didn't have to be beautiful (though that helped), but you had to be chic and groomed to the nines. Which, of course, required expensive haircuts, perfect manicures, cosmetics, stylish clothes, shoes, and hair-raising dry-cleaning bills. Even thrift shop bargains had evaporated, what with vintage clothes having become all the rage.

Quite simply, there had never been enough money left over for travel, especially not overseas travel with the monetary exchange rate being what it was.

But now—

Newly energized by the prospect of having the time and opportunity to explore the Parthenon, the National Museum, and myriads of ancient sites and cultural institutions she'd only read about, she surged forward to the automatic sliding doors and through the exit, intending to board the next bus to Syntagma Square.

How rejuvenated she felt! As if she'd been reborn. As though jet lag was but a myth!

In retrospect, she should have known better. This was, after all,

Greece, where in ancient times it was believed one's destiny was decided by the Fates, those three goddesses of destiny known to the ancients as the *Moerae,* who were forever spinning the foreordained futures of mere mortals. And although she was in a shiny twenty-first century airport in modern-day Greece, the Fates, it seemed, were still hard at work, and had spun yet other plans for her.

[CHAPTER TEN]

Spada, Greece

"Yoo-hoo, Miranda! *Mi . . . ran . . . da!*" trilled the now-familiar voice from behind.

Miranda had just burst outside from air-conditioned comfort to confront an invisible wall of blast furnace heat. She'd had no idea it would be this hot, and the shock of that scorching intensity left her gasping for breath. It was as if she was inhaling invisible fire.

"Miranda, wait!"

She turned around. Her Midwestern acquaintance from the information counter was rushing out through the automatic sliding doors after her, pulling one of those wheeled, soft-sided suitcases. For an instant, sheer momentum kept the woman going—and then she hit that invisible furnace, came to a dead stop, and drooped before Miranda's eyes. "My goodness!" the woman rasped, and took off her hat and began fanning herself briskly with it. "Goodness me, but it *is* hot."

Miranda backtracked a few steps and set her bags down. "Are you all right?" she asked solicitously. For she was genuinely concerned. Some people, especially those of an older generation, had been known to collapse under such conditions.

"Oh, I'll be fine," the woman assured her, gasping for breath, "once I get used to this." She fanned herself a little quicker. "It's just the initial shock."

Miranda looked around. An approaching tourist coach seemed to shimmer atop a mirage of water. A trick of the heat, she realized, and the pale blue mountains in the distance seemed hazy, as though viewed through a scrim. Then the overhead signs caught her eye.

"Oh, damn," she said softly, but with feeling.

"What's the matter?"

"I wasn't thinking. This is the arrivals area. I suppose we probably should be downstairs?"

They immediately headed back inside. Despite the milling crowds, the cool air made it feel positively luxurious.

"By the way," said Miranda's temporary companion, "my name is Madge Blessing. From Cincinnati."

They stopped again. Miranda momentarily put down one bag and shook the proffered hand. "Miranda Kalli." She smiled.

"I know." The woman returned her smile and placed her hat back atop her head. Miranda picked up her bags again, and they continued negotiating their way through gaps in the clusters of frustrated travelers. "It *is* a coincidence, though, isn't it?" Madge Blessing chattered breathlessly, the wheels of her suitcase making slight clicking sounds, like a railway carriage on rails. "I mean, you being Miranda Kalli, and my baby sister, well, she's not a baby, she's in her forties, also being named Miranda, and having Kallas as her married name?"

"It is." Miranda nodded pleasantly. "Yes."

"Well," continued the chatterbox, "my Miranda was supposed to meet up with me, you see, but Thomas, that's her youngest child, fell ill, and she had to cancel. Then, when I heard *you* being paged, well, I admit I was *hoping* that perhaps it was her, and that she had managed to come at the last minute after all. I confess it was rather a disappointment to find out otherwise. Oh, dear!" She laid her free hand on Miranda's arm. "I hope you're not offended."

"Why should I be?" Miranda said reasonably. "Your disappointment is perfectly understandable."

"You're a very sweet young lady. I like you." Madge Blessing smiled brightly, and Miranda couldn't help liking her. The woman's Chatty Cathy exuberance was infectious, and her outgoing, down-to-earth charm and honesty infused her with a home-spun, Heartland kind of warmth that was hard to resist, rather like that of a lively, fun-loving, take-it-as-it-comes favorite aunt.

"Now, to be perfectly honest—" Madge's voice dropped an octave, as if she was about to impart a momentous secret "—I own up to being what the late Mr. Blessing called 'the world's most dreadful eavesdropper!' And of course, I couldn't help but overhear what your information clerk said about the ferries not running. So do tell. Where are you headed? Some place specific, or were you just planning to island hop?"

"I've been invited to work on an archeological dig on Samos, so that's where I'm supposed to be headed."

"Samos!" exclaimed Madge, and slowed her pace. The clicking wheels of her suitcase slowed down along with her. She pursed her lips thoughtfully, and Miranda could almost hear the gears in the woman's mind turning and clicking, much like the wheels of her suitcase. At last a broad beam brightened the wide lips. "Why, what could be more perfect? And with your name being so similar to my sister's, and since her ticket *is* paid for and I *have* it—"

Miranda blinked in confusion. "I'm afraid I don't follow."

Madge gave a delicious little chuckle. "Oh, dear me. Of course you don't. I'm thinking out loud. You see, my dear, it's like this." She stopped walking completely, set her wheeled suitcase upright, and unslung her white leather shoulder bag. As she unclasped the flap and began to dig around inside it, she said, "I'm going on a cruise. Aboard a yacht."

"Really!" Miranda was impressed. "That sounds terribly fancy."

Madge interrupted her rummaging long enough to flick her a quick glance and flapped a hand dismissively. "Don't be silly, my dear. They *claim* it's a yacht, but that's just a sales tactic, of course. I wouldn't want you to get the wrong impression. Technically, I suppose it ought to be called a mini-cruise ship. One of those converted traditional caiques . . . or is it a gulet? I can't remember which is which. Now, where could I have . . . ah! Here it is!"

She triumphantly brandished a folded color brochure for Miranda's inspection.

Miranda hesitated. She didn't want to be rude, especially since she'd taken such a liking to Madge, but she was in Athens, Greece . . . or rather, she was somewhere far on the outskirts of the birthplace of democracy and cradle of Western civilization as well as the repository of some seven millennia of treasures, all of which the inquisitive archeologist in her couldn't wait to feast her eyes upon. She was itching to get on the first bus and go into the city, find an inexpensive hotel, and begin seeing the sights. First and foremost on her list, naturally, was the Parthenon.

It was as if she could hear the Sirens calling out to her. Using her most diplomatic, Madison Avenue gallery tone, she said, "It was lovely to meet you, er . . . "

"Madge. Madge Blessing, but do call me Madge."

"Madge then. I hate to be impolite, Madge, but I really have to get going—"

"Yes, of course you do. But that's my very point, don't you see?" The hat stopped fanning and she peered up at Miranda with sparkling eyes.

Actually, Miranda didn't see, but since Madge was still holding out the color brochure, she decided to indulge her out of politeness' sake. It was one of those glossies that folded out, accordian-like, making several narrow pages out of one large printed sheet. The cover was headed:

Oracle Yachts
Cycladic and Turkish Jewels 10-Day Cruise

Dominating it was a photograph of what must have once been a good-sized traditional cargo vessel—a caique or a gulet—that had obviously been converted to passenger use. Somewhat aged and ungainly, this classic traditional motor sailor had charm, in that although the hull with its portholes was painted white, the top two decks were entirely of varnished wood. It had two masts with brownish-red sails, a rather rakish bowsprit, and an open deck topsides, half of which was covered by a canvas awning, and the other half of which was completely open for sunbathing. It was hardly the most elegant of vessels, especially since the uppermost deck seemed to have been an afterthought, giving the ship a somewhat top-heavy appearance, but it had obviously been added to maximize precious space.

She unfolded the brochure further. The next "page" showed a map of the itinerary. Pictured within a square was the central Aegean, with each destination marked by a dot, and the name of the island printed beside it. The dots were connected by lines, like a map of a constellation.

Underneath the map, a series of artfully arranged squares and rectangles contained flattering photographs of what Miranda assumed to be the sundeck, a lounge/dining area, and several of the cabins. The "yacht" was called *M/Y Meltemi II,* and there was a list of "Technical Specifications":

Length:	35 m (115 ft)
Passengers:	30 (14 cabins)
Crew:	10–12
Cruising Speed:	11 knots
Engines:	2 × 491 HP GUASCOR
Flag:	Greek

She unfolded the paper accordian further. This page was headed *Itinerary*, and listed the ten-day cruise schedule:

Day 1: PIRAEUS—MYKONOS
Piraeus—Embarkation at 15:30.
Welcome cocktail and Crew Presentation.
Late afternoon departure for Mykonos.
Dinner on board.
Day 2: MYKONOS—DELOS
Morning arrival at Mykonos.
Explore and shop the world-famous "Saint-Tropez" of the Greek islands, made famous by none other than "Jackie O."
Optional tour to Delos.

There was more, but that was as far as Miranda got.

Delos!

She felt the rise and ripple of gooseflesh along her arms and thought: *Surely the gods are smiling down upon me!*

For Delos was the most holy and sacred site of all ancient Greece. A mere rocky speck in the middle of the Aegean, the entire island was one huge archeological treasure trove. In fact, the entire group of islands surrounding it were called the Cyclades, because they encircled Delos like larger, worshiping entities.

Miranda stared at Madge Blessing, who was smiling as widely as a fairy godmother.

"You can't mean—" Miranda began, sputtering.

Madge cut her off. "But of course I can, dear, and I do. The ferries may not be running, but the cruise ships and yachts are. I asked the young lady at the desk, and she checked for me. As I told you, I have the extra ticket, and since it's been paid for in advance, why spend the money on a hotel in Athens and wait around? We'll be in Mykonos tomorrow, Kusadasi the day after, and then Samos, where you can get off."

"Really," Miranda said ruefully, "it's awfully nice of you to offer, but I couldn't. And I can't afford to—"

Madge laughed again, a cheerful gurgling sound. "Oh, but I wouldn't expect you to pay! It's been paid for already, you see, and since this is a last-minute cancellation, they won't give me a refund. I'd hate for my sister's fare to go totally to waste. It won't cost you a thing, dear, and quite frankly, I'd be grateful for the company. You'd be doing *me* a favor, actually. I'm rather shy when it comes to being tossed into the midst of a bunch of strangers."

Miranda had to smile. She sincerely doubted that. Effervescent and outgoing, Madge Blessing was a doppelgänger for the actress, Joan Plowright, the type who never met a person she didn't like.

"Why, even the shuttle bus to Piraeus is included," Madge elucidated, producing two blue coupons from her bag. "See? I have the transfer vouchers right here." She gave a little sigh. "Really, dear, it would be such a waste."

The Sirens were still calling out to Miranda from atop the Acropolis. On the other hand, she could hear the Sirens from Delos trying to drown out the Athenians. Besides, who knew when the ferries would be up and running again? Madge's offer would at least guarantee her an arrival time on Samos. And three days on a yacht, even if it was a mini-cruise ship, would be a welcome respite after playing The Human Pretzel nine-and-a-half hours in the air.

Miranda could feel herself being tugged in one direction and then in the other. Athens. Delos. Delos. Athens. Plus Ephesus thrown into the bargain! What self-respecting lover of archeology could resist?

For a moment she chewed thoughtfully on her lower lip. She shut her eyes. When she opened them again, she met Madge Blessing's vivid smile. Madge really did have the most irresistible smile.

And so, despite the ferries not running, and the Acropolis Sirens' desperate songs, Miranda found herself on the motorcoach with Madge Blessing, heading to Piraeus after all.

[CHAPTER ELEVEN]

New York City

Harris Milford Palmer III opened one sleepy eye, registered the bright light leaking in through the mini-blinds, then swiftly shut it against the glare. Moaning, he gingerly touched his throbbing head. Another bad hangover. What in all hell had he been up to last night? Another microbrewery bust with his Yale buddies? Or was it that steakhouse with the lap dancers who squirted whipped cream into his mouth along with a slug of Kahlua?

"Hey, Big Boy," cooed a feminine voice from beside him, and underneath the sheet, he felt a possessive hand gripping his engorged member tightly.

"Shit!" he said sharply as he sat up too quickly. The speed with which he'd half-risen and opened both eyes seemed to shatter his skull into splinters. The manicured, taloned fingers wrapped around his penis loosened and let go. "Where the fuck—?" he began, trying to get his bearings.

"*Har* . . . ry!" reproached the voice from the other side of the queen-size bed. "What's the matter with you? Is that any way to treat a lady?"

Lady?

Slowly, avoiding any sudden movements, he turned his head sideways. Odalisquing on melon-colored sheets beside him were the slender, pale pink thighs, hard belly, and girlish, roseate-tipped breasts of an athletic woman in her early thirties. She lay there, propped on one elbow, eyeing him from under smoldering, half-lowered lids, a half-curtain of streaked, straight blond hair cascading down one side of her face à la Veronica Lake.

"Oh, Christ," he mumbled, then squinted to take a closer look at her. Recognition took a moment to dawn. "Tiffany?" he said uncertainly. "Tiffany Pfeiffer? What in hell are *you* doing here?"

"What am *I* doing here?" His coworker's laugh sounded more like a bray than a tinkle. "Harry, I think you should ask yourself what *you* are doing *here.* Will you take a look around you? This look like your Tribeca loft?"

Without moving his head, he managed to swivel his eyes partway around the room. Unfamiliar melon-colored bedding, pale rose walls, decorative floral curtains framing rose mini-blinds. He would have shaken his head if even the slightest movement wouldn't have caused splinters of pain to shoot through his skull.

"Where the blazes am I?" he groused, ever-so-gently raking his hair aside from his forehead. "Motel Hell?"

Incensed, Tiffany abruptly shifted on the bed, causing the mattress to move and another stab of pain to shoot through his throbbing skull before grabbing a pillow and flinging it against his head. His move to deflect it only caused yet more shards of agony.

"Harry Palmer!" she accused. "Don't you remember a *thing?* What did I tell you last night?"

"Why don't you tell me?" he mumbled weakly.

"'*Mi casa es su casa.*' Doesn't that ring a bell?" Clever fingers walked spider-like across his muscular, racket-ball developed thigh, once again intent upon imprisoning his penis. Then they stopped and her lips turned into a pout.

"Or don't you remember?"

Actually, he honestly didn't remember. Nor did he really care to, or at least, he wasn't ready to face reality just yet.

Coffee, he thought longingly, *my kingdom for a cup of coffee!* He desperately needed a hit of caffeine, but with Tiffany's mood being what it was, he thought better of suggesting that she get her tush out of bed and brew some.

And suddenly—*boom!*—yesterday's memories came at him like an oncoming train. Now he recalled his repeated attempts to phone Miranda, and her not answering his calls. And now since he remembered that, even more of yesterday's events, or were they non-events, flashed through his head.

Miranda's last-minute call from the airport, for instance, from

J. F. fucking K. International, for crying out loud!, with a hurried message about her flight starting to board. A flight to *Greece,* of all places—

Goddamn Greece! Without so much as a word of warning!

—and when he'd tried to talk her out of it, or at least explain what was going on, she'd instantly severed the connection without uttering so much as a hurried "Love you," or "I'll miss you."

Women! he thought dismally, all too aware of Tiffany Pfeiffer's naked, perfumed proximity. *Hard to live with 'em. Even harder to live without 'em.*

Even tousle-headed and nursing the mother of all hangovers, Harris Milford Palmer III was appealing. He was a tall man with thick light brown hair worn a tad too long, dark penetrating blue eyes, a square jaw with a cleft chin, and a straight thin nose. He was extremely handsome—if you went in for the kind of preppy WASPs who dominated Ralph Lauren ads. He looked as though he'd been born with a silver tennis racket in his hand.

Women tended to agree he was a gorgeous specimen, which he couldn't quite understand. What they saw in him, he himself couldn't see in the reflection of his mirror, which perpetually brought up that age-old quandary: were they after him for his so-called looks, his wealth, his family's social position, or did they like him for his own personable self?

He never could figure that one out, and had long since stopped trying. Besides, there was only one woman to whom he was attracted—Miranda Kalli. Could it be because she was one of the only ones who found him resistible, and was never ready to commit? Even when it came to their engagement, he'd had to practically force his ring onto her reluctant finger, and she still kept postponing the date of their wedding.

And now, for some inexplicable reason, she'd fled the country, God only knew what for. "I'll explain it all later," she'd told him before hanging up.

Later . . .

He clenched his teeth.

. . . when was later? And why later?

In the meantime, he'd somehow ended up in Tiffany Pfeiffer's bed. Worse, he didn't have an inkling of how he got there.

"You shit," said Tiffany, an edge creeping into her voice. "You little shit! You really don't remember anything, do you, Harry?"

"Not really," he admitted sheepishly.

"But you *do* recall talking to your sweetheart on your Blackberry? You know, your so-called fiancée? Miranda What's-It, the one with a last name sounds like a Greek coffee shop?"

There was no need for Tiffany to get ugly, but he ascertained that this wasn't the best time to point that out. For one thing, he wasn't in a position to. This was obviously her apartment. For another, he caught sight of a pink-upholstered Parsons bench squeezed against the wall at the far end of the bed. Its surface was completely covered with a mountain of Teddy bears in various shades of pink and puce plush. They were two rows deep, with smaller ones sitting on the laps of the larger.

His headache increased exponentially. He never could understand grown-ups who collected cuddly cutesy-pie children's toys.

High time to say *adios,* he decided, and gingerly began to swing his legs out over the side of the bed.

"Not so fast, Buster." Tiffany's hand seized his cock again and squeezed the base tightly.

"Piss hard-on," he gasped.

She instantly let go. "Well, just don't pee in my bed," she snapped, shooting him a severe look. "Bathroom's that-a-way." She pointed a pearlized nail at the door.

He made it to his feet, swayed momentarily, and found his way.

"And close the fucking door!" she yelled upon hearing the sound of urine hitting water.

After taking care of his most pressing need, he ran cold water in the sink and doused his face with handfuls. Eyeing her electric toothbrush longingly, he pondered the wisdom of borrowing it, then wisely decided against it. He squeezed a bit of Rembrandt on his finger, rubbed his teeth, and rinsed. Vigorously.

"Time to make tracks," he told his red-eyed reflection in the mirror.

When he came out of the bathroom, Tiffany was standing right outside the door, eyeing him balefully. "Here are your clothes." She tossed him a rumpled armful. "Now get out. *Out!*"

"What did I do?" he asked, assuming a hurt tone.

"It's not what you did," she snapped. "It's what you didn't do, you useless son of a bitch! I spent all night commiserating with you, brought you home, tucked you into bed, and you didn't even have the decency to throw a girl a fuck!"

He looked taken aback. "You're holding my gentlemanly behavior against me?" he made the mistake of saying. "For treating you like a lady?"

"You treated me like shit!" she snarled, raking him up and down with her eyes, and sneering at his now-limp member. "Now either get it up or get out."

He chose the latter, and she propelled a stark naked Harris Milford Palmer III to the front door, unlatched the deadbolt, and shoved him out into the carpeted corridor.

He could feel the rush of air as her door slammed behind him, missing his naked buttocks by mere inches. Almost instantly, he heard the deadbolt being thrown.

So that trite old saying is true, he thought. *Hell really hath no fury like a woman scorned.*

From the apartment across the hall, a middle-aged woman clutching a miniature poodle clipped like a topiary opened her door. Catching sight of him struggling into his Calvins while hopping around on one foot, she displayed the attitude of the true New Yorker who'd seen everything, and squeezed blithely past him on her way to the elevators without raising so much as an eyebrow. Even the canine topiary ignored him completely.

Harry was suddenly all smiles. *Nothing happened!* he thought exultantly, feeling a sudden heady sense of undeserved virtue. *Despite my drunkenness, and aside from a few sloppy kisses and ending up in Tiffany's bed, nothing happened! We didn't have sex!*

Relieved that, at least as far as Tiffany Pfeiffer went, he was still chaste as the driven snow, he proceeded to dress, leave the building, and flag down a providential taxi. Once downtown, he quickly showered, shaved, brushed his teeth and changed into a fresh suit. Then, reasonably presentable, he arrived early for work down on Wall Street for another day's round of managing Other People's Money. Realizing, too late, that his Blackberry must have fallen out of his pocket back at Tiffany Pfeiffer's.

Aw, shit! he thought, before reassuring himself that all was not lost. Surely she'd bring it along to work with her.

But when Tiffany sailed in an hour later, she smiled smugly. "Your Blackberry? Oh. Tell you what, Harry. When I get home tonight, I'll make sure and check. Maybe it fell under the bed."

"Couldn't you go home and get it now?" he inquired, giving her his most appealing look.

"Certainly not," she said loftily. "I have work to do. Later, Harry. After work."

He rubbed his still-throbbing head and groaned.

His Blackberry—other than his desktop computer and laptop, his single most important line of communication with the entire world—was being held hostage.

By Tiffany Pfeiffer, no less!

You bitch! he thought, watching her sashay complacently, buttocks twitching, down the hall to her own corner office. *Why, you mother-fucking bitch!*

Some days . . .

Again he rubbed his face with his hands.

Some days you just couldn't win.

[CHAPTER TWELVE]

Piraeus, Greece

The images in Miranda's head were in grainy black and white and from before her birth: Melina Mercouri and a gaggle of earthy, fun-loving prostitutes sashaying along the docks of Piraeus and jumping into the harbor, and the dockworkers all stopping their work to go jumping in after them.

But the Piraeus where the *Meltemi II* was docked was not the Piraeus of 1960. *Never on Sunday* was many Sundays ago.

Nor was it the big, sheltered, and U-shaped commercial harbor of cinematic fame. Here, at the bottom of the U, and across multiple lanes of traffic, various grounded ferries jammed up the waters. They ranged from old ungainly workhorses to humongous high-speed catamarans built in New Zealand. Rocket-like hydrofoils imported from Russia that looked like something out of those old Saturday matinee episodes of Flash Gordon were packed in like sardines; nor even was it along the sides of the U, the right of which seemed specifically slated for a variety of service vessels, while the left was reserved almost exclusively for cruise ships of all ages, sizes, and budgets, from the intimate to the monstrously huge, which towered so obscenely above everything else that one feared they might actually start taking bites out of the low-rise city.

No, Oracle Cruises' motorcoach from the airport bypassed that giant harbor entirely via a new highway, and let the passengers off at Marina Zea, where *M/Y Meltemi II* was berthed. The marina, crowded with shiny yachts of all sizes, from small sailboats to multi-decked floating palaces, made the *Meltemi II* look like a stray that had limped in from the Aegean by mistake.

That was Miranda's first impression.

Her second was that the vessel had definitely seen better days. In the unforgiving white blaze of the sun, the wooden hull showed every lump from layers upon layers of slapped-on, blistered white paint, and here and there she could see blatant streaks of rust weeping from the metal surrounding the portholes. Teak decking had given way to stained, grass-green Astroturf. The chaises and deck chairs were the same white stackable resin types you could buy at your local hardware store back home. The much-mended reddish-brown sails were temporarily furled, and a gangplank linked its stern with the dock.

Miranda glanced at the line-up of sleek modern motoryachts whose gleaming smooth white hulls reflected moving spotlights of sun sparkling upon water.

Madge Blessing was, predictably, not in the least bit put out. She was the type who would always see the sunny side of things. "Oh, Miranda!" she fluted excitedly. "Doesn't it look exactly like in the brochure?"

Since life had taught Miranda that beggars couldn't be choosers, she kept her personal opinion to herself and her lips firmly zipped. Her reply was a noncommittal, "Mmm." But she did flick Madge a sideways glance, just to make certain her new-found friend wasn't being facetious.

Which she was not. Madge Blessing saw a yacht while Miranda gazed at, well, at what she sincerely prayed was *The Little Top-Heavy Boat That Could.* It made her wonder how different her life might be if she had been born as content as Madge, and been able to experience the world through rose-colored glasses. Madge was, she decided, truly one of the chosen few. She would always embark upon marvelous adventures, never have a bad time anywhere, or even taste a terrible meal.

Hers was the kind of *Weltanschauung* Miranda truly envied.

Around them, the other passengers from the motorcoach gave little cries of oohs and ahs and were murmuring among themselves. Two sweating crew members from the *Meltemi II* were emptying the baggage compartment of the motorcoach and transferring the luggage onto manually pushed trolleys. The driver was removing the sign inside his windshield, which had read *M/Y Meltemi II,* and was replacing it with one that proclaimed *Royal Olympia Triton.* A kind of folding lectern with tripod legs, but a flat top, was set up by the gangplank. Two crew members in white short-sleeved shirts came and set up a laptop computer, an electronic machine the size of an electric pencil sharpener, but with a slot, and a digital camera facing outward. Miranda was aware of the slapping of little wavelets against quay and hulls, the cries of seagulls wheeling overhead, and the gentle motions of superstructures rocking slowly back and forth. The faintest breeze was blowing in off the sea, a welcome respite from the heat, but it tinged the salt air with the sharper fumes of diesel fuel and oil.

A door swinging open and snapping shut drew her attention. A young woman with smooth shiny waist-long black hair had come out onto the aft deck of the *Meltemi II.* She was carrying a tote bag and posed there a moment, as though surveying her audience from a stage. She had the high forehead, patrician nose, and expressionless stare of Bronzino's portrait of Eleanora of Toledo. Even the part in her hair was like Eleanora's.

But that was where she and Bronzino parted company and Estée Lauder took over. She radiated a tawny cosmetic glow, her face smoothed over with amber bronze and blusher highlights, her eyes rimmed with dark liner, and her lips glistening with metallic, wet-look bronze lipstick. She was fashion-model thin and perfectly proportioned, with legs that wouldn't stop. Add the sleeveless, lemon-colored A-line dress which ended a good eight inches above her knees, and which, to Miranda's Madison Avenue-trained eye, must have set her back what a Jan Kofski employee earned in two weeks.

Eleanora's double slipped on a pair of black Gucci sunglasses, strode down the gangplank like it was the catwalk at a fashion show, and busied herself at the laptop atop the lectern. The milling passengers, twenty-seven polyglot heads by Miranda's count, waited for a signal to surge forward.

"Oooh . . . isn't this *thrilling?*" purred Madge, almost beside herself with excitement.

"Yes," Miranda nodded. "It is."

By this time, the luggage trolleys were fully loaded, the motorcoach belched a cloud of black exhaust and drove quietly off. At the lectern, the young woman in the lemon-colored dress fished a small, battery-powered microphone out of her tote and spoke softly into it.

"*Kiría e kírie,* ladies and gentlemen, *meine Damen und Herren.*"

The little microphone was amazing, clearly amplifying her heavily accented, husky voice just enough to be heard above the diesel generators throbbing within the bowels of the *Meltemi II,* the various sounds and noises coming from the restaurants and tavernas lining the quay, and the cries of the gulls circling overhead.

Having captured her audience's attention, she continued: "On behalf of Oracle Yachts and Captain Aris Leonides, I wish to extend a warm welcome to you for our 'Cycladic and Turkish Jewels Ten Day Cruise.' My name is Chara Zouboulakis, and during this cruise I am your purser, cruise director, hostess, and interpreter. As you can see, *Meltemi II* is not the most luxurious vessel in the marina—" this understatement elicited some polite chuckles and a titter from Madge "—but bigger and newer is not necessarily better. Do not let appearances fool you. *Meltemi II,* like her sisterships, *Meltemi* and *Meltemi III,* are of a traditional, age-old design, and are among the most seaworthy of all the yachts you see in this harbor. Also, our yacht-like ambiance, *intime,* size, and crew of twelve ensure that this will be the most memorable cruise of your lifetimes."

Crew of twelve,? Miranda thought, eyeing the *Meltemi II* even more skeptically. *Holy Hannah Yarby! Wherever do they stack them? In the engine room? Plus twenty-seven passengers?*

The already small *Meltemi II* seemed to shrink even further before her eyes, and she took Chara's French pronunciation of *intime,* to be a euphemism for overcrowding. Thirty-nine people on a 115-foot vessel? Perhaps it was cynical, but Miranda had visions of Haitian boat people piled high in a swamped dingy. But she put these negative thoughts on hold and decided she'd best pay attention to the cruise director, lest she miss out on anything of import.

"I have a computerized list of our passenger manifest," Chara Zouboulakis was saying. "Please have your tickets and passports ready. When I call out your names, kindly step forward and I shall give you your cabin "key," which looks like a credit card and also serves as your identification as a passenger. Please carry it on your person at all times. You shall need it each time you leave the ship or get back on. Dimitris is just inside the lounge and shall direct you to your cabins. You may wish to hurry, as the interior is air-conditioned."

This earned her another round of good-natured chuckles.

For her part, Miranda kept silent. Her years in Manhattan had hardened her, had taught her to be ever wary and distrustful. She didn't fall for just any old *schtick.* What was more, she knew a cold fish when she saw one. And despite her professional delivery, Chara Zouboulakis definitely struck her as anything but warm.

While awaiting their turn to be called, Madge was already striking up friendships with a quartet of jolly, bawdy-humored nurses from Down Under who were traveling together. One of them, a tall gangly woman, wore a white T-shirt emblazoned with "Pediatric Oncology Unit" in blue letters across the front.

Miranda was starting to rearrange the letters into more cheerful anagrams when Chara Zouboulakis of the two-thousand-dollar frock paged them. "Mahdge Blahs-ing and Me-rahn-da Kah-las" and Miranda resigned herself to being called "Me-rahn-da" for the remainder of her stay in Greece.

"Ooooh!" Madge visibly thrummed with barely suppressed excitement. "She's paging us, dear!" And to the quartet of nurses: "We'll continue later." Then: "Come on, Miranda. Good. I see you already have your passport out."

And so they presented themselves in front of the lectern, with Miranda hanging a half-step behind.

"Madge Blessing," said her companion, fishing Miranda's passport out of her hand, and proffering both tickets and the two passports over to the fashion plate. "This is my sister, Miranda Kalli." Radiating what could only be construed as sibling pride, Madge clasped Miranda's clammy hand and drew her up beside her.

Madge beamed. Miranda pasted on a smile she hoped hid her tenseness. She felt beads of perspiration breaking out along her hairline, and was aware of too many sensations. Lovely and generous as Madge was, Miranda knew that they were pulling a scam with their pretended sister act. A harmless prank, perhaps, but a prank nevertheless . . . and *was* it really harmless? Illegal, possibly. And would they get away with it?

"Welcome aboard the *Meltemi II*." The reply was rattled automatically by rote, totally devoid of expression, and Chara Zouboulakis didn't so much as glance at them as she uttered it. It was as though singly or together, Madge and Miranda weren't worth the effort she'd expended playing to the entire group.

Miranda watched her tear a copy from each set of tickets, which resembled multiple-copy paper tickets issued by airlines, and place them in her tote. She didn't even look at her or Madge until after she'd flicked open the passports with beautifully manicured, bronze-lacquered nails to make sure their faces matched the photographs. Then she glanced at the screen of the laptop.

A frown abruptly brought expression to her features and she looked sharply at Miranda. "The ticket . . . " she pronounced it "tee-keet" " . . .

was issued . . . " ("ee-should") "to Miranda Kallas. K-A-L-L-A-S. That is the name on the manifest also. No?"

Madge rose to Miranda's defense. "I know, my dear," she told Chara good-naturedly, but with a sigh of exasperation. "These days, no one can spell anymore, can they? It won't surprise me when the day comes that people shan't even be able to read."

Chara Zouboulakis was about to close Miranda's passport when another discrepancy apparently caught her eye. She pushed her black Gucci sunglasses slowly atop her head. Her smooth brow furrowed, forming two unkind vertical lines on her forehead as she checked something else on the passport against the information on the computer screen.

The manifest, she'd called it.

Without her dark glasses Miranda had a clear view of her face. She was even more beautiful close up, but there was a hardness to her features that no amount of make-up could soften. Also, her eyeliner was way too far on this side of black; it should have had more of a bronze tone, and the metallic lipstick cheapened her, taking away from the lemon dress.

From close-up, Miranda also noticed that she hadn't been mistaken. That little A-line number was no designer rip-off. Someone had dished out *mucho dinero,* for it, and she was willing to bet Ms. Zouboulakis hadn't been the one to hand over her own cash or plastic. Naturally, it also occurred to Miranda that if she'd been born with Chara's kind of looks, she might not have to pay for her own wardrobe, either. Yet Miranda didn't begrudge Chara Zouboulakis her looks or her clothes; she didn't feel the least bit of Venus envy. Perhaps it was the young woman's iciness that showed through the surface that she didn't care for. Chara's lips had tightened. "Which of you booked this tour?" she demanded coldly, casting an accusing glance from Madge to Miranda and back.

Miranda thought it best to play the little mouse. After all, if anyone was capable of talking her way in or out of any situation, it was Madge Blessing. She was the one with the gift of gab.

"Why, I booked it, of course!" bubbled Madge, breasts thrust forward as proudly as a pouter pigeon's.

And with a crestfallen look, she added: "Don't tell me I did something wrong!"

"When you booked the tour, you were asked to list—" Chara pronounced it 'least' "—your passport numbers for the manifest. Do you recall that?"

Miranda shifted uneasily. She should have known that pulling the wool over Oracle Cruises' eyes wouldn't be as simple as Madge had anticipated.

"Yes, yes, I clearly remember the passport numbers," Madge was prattling impatiently. "Why, our very own nephew helped book the reservation. He did it entirely online. And?"

"However," declared Chara Zouboulakis, drawing out the syllables and sliding Miranda the kind of suspicious look a cop might give a potential street dealer loaded down with illicit drugs, "the passport number you gave for Me-rahn-da Kalli does not match the number on her passport."

"You don't mean it!" One of Madge's hands flew to her breast and she registered what Miranda could have sworn could only be construed as absolutely genuine shock. With utter amazement, she watched and listened as Madge launched into a performance worthy of an Oscar—or at least a Golden Globe.

"B-But how could such a mistake have been made?" she burbled on, evidently so flustered she even had to take off her hat and begin fanning herself briskly with it. "Surely *I* didn't mix it up with . . . oh, dear me!" She looked at Miranda. "Darling, this is really quite, quite distressing." And turning pleadingly to Chara: "My little sister and I were *so* looking forward to having a good time together and . . . and . . . well, surely you can do something to fix this most unfortunate situation, can't you, my dear?"

She switched on her brights, blinding Chara Zouboulakis with her high beams; then switched them back off, her expression crumbling.

"I mean, this is supposed to be the best cruise we'll ever have had," she added, stifling a little sob. "You said so yourself. And just look at the way it's starting out . . . "

Miranda was ready to start handing out the Kleenex when Madge turned in her direction and sent her a conspiratorial wink.

"One moment, please." Looking put out, Chara Zouboulakis whipped out a tiny cell phone, flipped it open, punched in a pre-programmed code, and pressed the TALK button. While she waited she rolled her eyes expressively skyward while tapping an impatient, expensively-shod foot. A Jimmy Choo-shod foot, if Miranda's eyes didn't deceive her, and she didn't believe they did. Makeup aside, Chara Zouboulakis really did have flawless taste when it came to clothes.

Or, more likely, it was somebody else with deep pockets? Judging from her job and the condition of the *Meltemi II,* that seemed the most plausible explanation.

When the phone was finally answered at the other end, Chara began rattling off a machine gun barrage in Greek. Miranda didn't understand a word, except when she tried to pronounce her and Madge's names. Chara listened without interrupting, rattled off another round of hard-sounding staccato words, which carried the suspicious tone of an argument, and listened some more. Finally she exhaled a long-suffering sigh, said, "*Né,*" and hit what had to be the END button. She took time out to scroll for messages, found none to her liking and, lips curving down into a frown, thrust the phone back into her tote.

Madge and Miranda were looking at her expectantly.

Chara shrugged her bare shoulders and said, "It is approved. I must now change the spelling of your name and enter the correct passport number on the manifest."

At the very least, Miranda expected a perfunctory smile to accompany this happy piece of news, or perhaps even a taste of that famous Greek hospitality one was always hearing about. But it was just as well that she didn't wait around for the cows . . . or in this country was it the goats? . . . to come home. The wait would have been eternal.

So they bided their time as Chara Zouboulakis "corrected" the spelling of Miranda's name and changed the passport number on the computer, careful to use the pads of her fingers rather than risk ruining her expensive manicure.

The hold-up was not taken in stride by all the of the passengers awaiting their turn. Miranda heard a German woman with a high-pitched voice complaining about the delay, and two dour Dutch women grumbling between themselves, but the quartet of jolly pediatric oncology nurses from Down Under were chattering away, happy as magpies.

Meanwhile, a diesel-belching, tarpaulin-covered lorry pulled up alongside the *Meltemi II*'s curvaceous hull, and Chara turned her face away and made a production of wrinkling her nose and fanning a hand against the fumes. A pair of stout, muscled men with black moustaches climbed out of the cab and hopped down, and a crew member up on the vessel's main deck leaned over the varnished wooden balusters and shouted down an order. With an ear-splitting creak, a cargo boom near the bow of the vessel rose at an angle, lifting a pallet of crates high out of a hatch before slowly swinging it over the side and lowering it.

Chara stashed Madge and Miranda's passports in her tote and said, "Now please, one at a time, stand in front of the camera."

Madge stood there first to have her picture taken, and Miranda gathered it was now stored in the laptop's memory. Chara Zouboulakis then fished a blank plastic credit card emblazoned with the legend "*Oracle Cruises*" and the line's logo out of her tote and slid it through the slot of the gadget, which looked like an electic pencil sharpener. A little green light blinked and there was a buzz and she handed the plastic "key" to Madge. "You are in cabin twelve," she said shortly. "Dimitris is inside the salon. He will direct you."

"Cabin twelve," Madge affirmed, and effusively spouted: "I cannot thank you enough for clearing this up."

Chara nodded distractedly, didn't reply, and took Miranda's picture and repeated the plastic "key" routine. She handed it over wordlessly and then consulted her screen for the next names to call out. "Herr und Frau Pleshke," she began.

The German couple pushed forward, and Madge was already halfway up the gangplank. But Miranda hung back. Her business wasn't quite finished.

From the dark look Chara bestowed upon her, Miranda was clearly the thorn in Ms. Zouboulakis' side. "Y-Yessss?" It was more a hiss than a question.

Miranda held out her hand. "My passport," she said.

Chara stared at her blankly. "What about it?"

"I shall be needing it."

"On cruises," Chara snapped impatiently, "it is customary for the purser to collect all the passengers' passports. They shall be kept in the safe onboard, used for dealing with customs formalities, and then be returned to you upon disembarkation."

"Yes," Miranda said, holding her ground, "but you see, I'm not taking the entire cruise."

The heavily mascara-ed eyes widened perceptibly. "Oh?"

"I'm getting off at Samos."

Chara's eyes narrowed. "Three days from now?" she asked in disbelief. "Let me see . . . you are taking our cruise only to leave us on our third stop?"

"That's right. I'm only accompanying my sister as far as Samos."

"But this makes no sense! It is highly irregular! Would not a flight or a fer—" She never completed the sentence, for that was when she had her light bulb moment. Miranda could actually see realization sink in. "Ah." Chara gave her a knowing kind of smirk. "I think I see."

At this point, Miranda couldn't care less whether she did see or not. She was getting a little fed up with their purser-cum-cruise director-cum-hostess-cum-interpreter-cum-fashion plate from whom wafted the unmistakable mixture of jasmine, damask rose, and mimosa. Calèche from Hermès, a scent that the Madison Avenue in Miranda recognized was so highly prized that only a thousand limited editions had ever been marketed.

Well, wild horses weren't going to get her to admit she wasn't the Me-rahn-dah Kallas who'd been expected, or that she and Madge had only just met at the airport. Her lips were sealed, and she was positive that she could count on Madge's silence, too. Madge Blessing was, after all, just the kind of good-natured soul who thrived on harmless little conspiracies to spice up what otherwise might have been a dull life, had she allowed it to be.

So there they were. Chara Zouboulakis and Miranda Kalli squaring off with their eyes. Add the sun beating down upon them and reflecting its hot glare off the concrete quay at Marina Zea, and it might have been the climax in that Gary Cooper film *High Noon.*

"The reason I'm accompanying my sister only as far as Samos," Miranda explained patiently, "is because I'm an archeologist. I've been invited to join a dig there. In fact, I have received special permission from the Ministry of Culture."

"A dig!" Chara's voice was sharp and brittle. "You are to work at an archeological site?"

For some reason, Miranda's little revelation seemed to startle Chara, who seemed to stiffen and draw back, as though confronting something poisonous. Or perhaps it was merely Miranda's imagination fulfilling some wishful thinking?

There was no way to tell, for at that moment Madge Blessing hailed her from atop the aft deck of the *Meltemi II.* "Yoo-hoo! Mi-randa!" she trilled. "Well? Are you coming, or aren't you?"

Miranda signaled that she'd be joining her in a second and turned back to Chara. Their eyes held again, but Miranda no longer had that impending sense of *High Noon.* She could swear Ms. Zouboulakis had decided to back off a bit, as if recognizing a fellow snake. Also, her manner had undergone a slight change. She didn't smile. She didn't actually welcome Miranda aboard, either. But when she spoke, Miranda thought she detected a kind of wary deference in her voice.

She said, "Ms. Kalli, your passport will be returned when you disembark. I shall need it for when we dock in Kusadasi the day after tomorrow. I shall see to its return personally. Yes?"

And Miranda, having gotten away with Madge's little scam, and not wishing to press her luck any further, nor hold up the boarding process any longer, nodded her thanks and began to head towards the gangplank. She breathed deeply. Overhead, the cloudless sky seemed to shimmer with heat, like a piece of porous cloth.

And then the *Meltemi II*'s cargo boom spun out of control and the heavily loaded pallet hit the quay from far too high, crushing the wooden boards and sending a tremor throughout the concrete. The ropes securing the crates flew apart under the impact, and the cargo came loose. The waiting passengers, emitting little cries of distress, jumped back, while as though in slow motion the carefully balanced wooden boxes somersaulted off the crushed surface on which they had been piled and rolled off, end-over-end, one of them breaking open on the quay.

Chara hopped aside just in time as the crushed crate's contents—bubble wrap and Styrofoam peanuts and pieces of pottery and small terra cotta heads and marble figurines—came tumbling out like badly packed, scattered toys. Miranda, too shocked to move, watched a small buffware Oinochoe roll towards her foot and crack in half in front of her, its handle smashed to bits.

The trained archeologist in her immediately took over. Squatting down, she examined the pieces without touching them. Slowly she tilted her head upwards. She stared at Chara Zouboulakis. "My God!" she gasped. "This piece is a genuine antiquity! East Greek, Fikellura class. It's from around 600 to 650 B.C.!"

Chara, brushing off the pesky Styrofoam pellets that clung stubbornly to her legs, produced a hollow laugh and kicked the shards away with one of her Jimmy Choos. Straightening up, she squared her shoulders. "Miss Kalli, I do not doubt your area of expertise, but let me assure you of something. That piece of 'antiquity' as you call it, is nothing but a first-rate reproduction for the tourist trade. There are hundreds of workshops throughout Greece that specialize in the handiwork of creating exact museum copies. Is most excellent workmanship, no? Just like the original?"

Miranda begged to differ. "It *is* the original," she insisted, but that hardness was back on Chara's face.

"Is a copy," Chara reiterated icily. "Hand-made and so perfectly executed it would fool most experts. Surely you, as an archeologist, should be able to recognize that?"

Miranda understood that there was no arguing with her—especially not if she wished to board and join Madge. Slowly she rose to her feet, and Chara gesticulated furiously and shouted something in angry, staccato Greek up to the crew member manning the cargo boom. Then, gesturing at the lorry drivers to pack up the spilled mess, she turned the full force of her gaze upon Miranda, who was still staring around at the broken shards.

"If you wish to accompany us, I think you'd best board, Ms. Kalli," Chara said softly, but with menace. "The other passengers are waiting."

Miranda nodded, took one last look at the smashed pottery, and slowly made her way over to the gangplank. Once onboard, she joined Madge on the aft deck.

"What was *that* all about?" Madge inquired, but instead of replying or going inside to enjoy air-conditioned comfort, Miranda drew her friend aside into the shadows and kept staring down at the quay.

The lorry drivers were tossing the pieces of pottery back into the crate as though they were worthless souvenirs. But Chara Zouboulakis hadn't continued the boarding process just yet. She was back on her cell phone, having what looked like an urgent verbal confab. A slight breeze rippled her frock and she had to loop a stray length of her glossy, waist-long hair over her ear with a fingernail. Miranda wouldn't have been surprised to see a fashion photographer hopping around her, snapping away. Even angry, Chara Zouboulakis looked that picture perfect.

Miranda felt another irrational surge of irritation. The buffware Oinochoe aside, that woman's wardrobe was starting to get to her. Also, her curiosity was piqued. What was anyone who could afford those kinds of clothes doing on a budget boat like the *Meltemi II?* After all, Ms. Zouboulakis was merely an employee of Oracle Cruises—right? Or . . . was it possible she could be something more? After all, there was that outfit. Those feloniously expensive shoes. The even more extravagant scent of Calèche.

Not to mention what Miranda could swear had been a genuine antiquity.

Miranda did not consider herself a latter-day Nancy Drew. Nor did she aspire to be one. But she really hated it when pieces of a puzzle didn't fit.

And what was more, she sensed that there were more puzzles than pieces to this particular riddle.

[CHAPTER THIRTEEN]

Piraeus, Greece

Miranda followed Madge from the aft deck of the *Meltemi II* into what was called the lounge. Actually it was a wood-paneled area the full width of the vessel with banquettes lining large windows, which gave it an airy feeling. Along each side of the center aisle were four tables with wooden ladder-back chairs pushed against the banquettes; the lounge obviously doubled as the dining room. It had blue wall-to-wall carpeting, blue curtains tied neatly back at the windows, and clean blue upholstery on the banquettes and chair seats.

Miranda was pleasantly surprised. She even succumbed to the strum and beat of the bouzouki music playing softly from speakers mounted in the corners. Naturally it would be that inimitable theme from *Zorba the Greek.* She gathered that it would be immediately followed by the theme from *Never on Sunday.* But never mind. Dimitris was waiting right inside the doors to the lounge. He was a handsome man in his fifties, had a receding hairline, and what hair he had was black, unruly, and wispy. But his teeth were as white as his shirt, and he had a most engaging smile. He wore a pin-on name plate with the word *Dimitris* emblazoned upon it.

"*Kaliméra,* ladies. Welcome aboard *Meltemi II,*" he said, and his tone and manner were so genuine and gallant that Miranda instantly took a shine to him. "I am Dimitri." In speaking, he left off the "s" at the end of his name.

Miranda was nearly beside herself with joy. Here at last was some of that famous Greek hospitality she'd been yearning for! But she managed to act cool and sophisticated and exercise extreme restraint, subduing the urge to start clicking her fingers and dancing to the bouzouki beat.

Madge was preening. "Cabin twelve, I believe it is?" she said coyly, showing Dimitris the plastic key card, which Chara's little machine had embossed. She also showed him the two paper tickets, from each of which Chara had torn a copy.

Call it nosy or snooping or chalk it up to mere curiosity, but Miranda's enquiring mind could be utterly without shame. She couldn't help but peek over Madge's shoulder and pry. Their cabin category, she noticed, was listed as "C," and the cruise tickets alone, exclusive of airfare, had cost $1,110 dollars per person. Port charges had added another $30 each.

Not outrageous by travel industry standards, but not exactly chump change, either. Miranda felt a flash of guilt at freeloading, and had to remind herself that it was Madge who had insisted she accompany her.

"And cabin twelve it is." Dimitris inclined his head in a kind of semi bow, and gestured forward with a flourish. "There are two sets of stairs to the lower deck. Yours are the second ones. Your luggage shall be brought to your cabin within a few minutes."

Madge consulted a miniature phrase book, cleared her throat, and hesitantly used phonetics to say, "Ef-cha-ris-to?" You could practically see her giant question mark hovering in midair. She eyed Dimitris a bit anxiously. "That is correct, I hope?"

Dimitris parted his arms and smiled broadly. "Ah! Madame is already learning the Greek!"

Madge purred with pleasure and Miranda liked him all the more for his delightful graciousness. He was probably working twelve or fifteen . . . or perhaps even more . . . of these weekly cruises each season. She didn't even want to think of the number of times he was confronted with the very same well-meaning, mispronounced word. Yet he made it sound as if Madge was the very first passenger to have ever tried it out on him.

"Could I ask you a question?" Madge inquired.

"By all means, *Kyría.*"

"Your name." Madge pointed at the nameplate on his shirt. "It reads *Dimitris,* but you pronounce it *Dimitri.*"

He laughed good-naturedly. "That, *Kyría,*" he explained, "is because in Greece, written names ending in vowels are feminine. However, in conversation, we drop the vowels. If it were written "Dimitri" on a letter, for instance, it would probably be addressed to *Kiría,* meaning Mrs., instead of *Kírie,* which is the masculine form."

"Ah!" Madge was fascinated. "And you speak such excellent English as well!"

He flashed Madge one of his Pepsodent smiles. "That is easily explained. I have cousins in New York, in Astoria, Queens. I spent five years there."

"How lovely! And my . . . my younger sister? She is unmarried. What would you call her?"

"*Despiní.*"

"*Despiní,*" Madge repeated. "How fascinating. Well, we better get going and not hold up the line. You said the second set of stairs forward?"

"That is correct."

Humming *The Good Ship Lollipop,* Madge led the way forward and Miranda followed her to the second flight of steep, stamped-metal stairs down to the lower deck. The stairwell was as narrow as a set of parallel bars, and had handrails affixed to both sides. The only difference between the bars in a gym and these was the sharp, 40-degree angle of descent, and Miranda imagined they came in very handy in choppy seas, when the little ship surely rocked and yawed.

"Oh, Miranda!" exclaimed Madge over her shoulder, "isn't this *too* exciting? Admit it. Finding each other was sheer serendipity."

"Or else we owe it to the Fates," Miranda added, waiting as Madge unlocked the door to cabin twelve by sliding the plastic card into the slot. Which made Miranda wonder. The *Meltemi II* had obviously seen better days—as she knew from seeing the rust bucket from outside—yet she would have expected far less high-tech amenities inside. Like an old-fashioned metal key, for instance.

A green light blinked and Madge opened the door as Miranda looked along the narrow hall. This, too, was equipped with handrails in case of stormy weather. And cabin 12 was one of six lining this section of the lower deck's corridor. The doors were lozenge-shaped and hatch-like, in that they had high sills one had to step over, a safety feature common on smaller vessels and designed to contain water that might otherwise seep under doorways in conditions she thought it best not to anticipate.

"Come, Miranda," Madge trilled.

And with Madge in the lead, they squeezed into the cabin. The air conditioning, while not exactly on a par with refrigerators, nonetheless kept the cabin's temperature at a constant, bearable level—this despite the fact that one bulkhead abutted what was obviously the midship engine room. Madge, naturally, could tune out the constant throb and vibrations of generators running as easily as she could tune out all the unpleasant vagaries life handed out on a regular basis.

She truly was, Miranda decided, one of those chosen few: Mary Poppins and Pollyanna rolled into one.

She watched as Madge surveyed the compact quarters with delight. The cabin measured perhaps eight feet in length by six in width, and the berths, a narrow upper and a narrow lower fitted with thin foam mattresses, snowy sheets and blue blankets, were built in lengthwise along the curvature of the white-painted, riveted metal hull. Each had a small, cylindrical reading light next to the pillow. There was a round porthole with short blue tied-back curtains beside the lower berth. The porthole was sealed—a fact for which Miranda was grateful, seeing as they were barely above water level. The fitted carpet was blue and looked as it had just been vacuumed.

All in all quite basic, but clean and neat and pleasantly, unexpectedly, serviceable.

Separating the bunks from the engine room bulkhead was a two-foot wide, two-foot deep hanging locker with three drawers on the bottom. At the other end of the cabin, there was another hatch-like door with the same high raised sill as the cabin door. Miranda opened it and peered inside. There was a miniature fiberglass cubicle containing a pint-size sink with one of those faucet handles that doubled as a shower, and a small toilet that made her grateful for having a small gluteus maximus. She also noted a small plastic wastebasket that opened with a toe-tap, and a sign in three languages admonishing that all paper products, toilet paper included, were to be deposited there rather than flushed.

All in all, not the lap of luxury, but more than adequate. The cabins were obviously designed for sleeping; one clearly spent most of the time either in the air-conditioned lounge-cum-dining room above, out on deck, or ashore.

"Yes, we probably do owe it to the Fates," Madge chirped. "Oh, look, Miranda. How convenient: we can stow our luggage under the lower bunk."

"Which is yours," Miranda told her firmly, automatically claiming the less desirable upper for herself.

"Oh, you really *are* a dear," Madge bubbled. "Knowing my sister, I was afraid I was going to be stuck sleeping up *there*—" Then, catching herself, she lowered her voice to a conspiratorial whisper. "—what *am* I saying? You *are* my sister, at least for the duration of the time you're aboard!" And she gurgled with the guiltless pleasure of a child who has successfully pulled the wool over many an eye.

A knock on the cabin door announced the arrival of their luggage. Miranda helped Madge unpack, hanging up her things and placing them in drawers. They were done in a jiffy. As for her own bags, she simply unzipped them and scooted them under the lower bunk, but kept them packed. After all, she was only aboard for three days, and it would be insane to take everything out only to have to pack it all up again before she disembarked on Samos.

"Well, dear?" Madge beamed at her. "What do you say we change into tank tops and shorts, go up on deck, and see about wetting our whistles, hmmm?"

Miranda beamed right back at her. "Nobody needs to twist my arm."

"Splendid!" Madge was genuinely thrilled. "I could tell you were a girl after my own heart!"

[CHAPTER FOURTEEN]

New York City

Magoo!

The thought exploded from nowhere. Or rather, from the turmoil of Harris Milford Palmer III's emotions. He was in his enviable corner office downtown in the Financial Center—no bullpen for this firm's golden boy, no siree Bob! Untouched beside him his lunch waited, delivered to the office an hour earlier and still resting in its open Styrofoam container. His favorite, a half-foot-high pastrami on rye, mouthwateringly fragrant, and accompanied by the two halves of a giant old-fashioned kosher dill pickle.

His favorite lunch, preferable to the usual business lunches in Wall Street-area overpriced restaurants.

But today, despite the pastrami on rye at his desk, he had no appetite.

Other, more important matters than food rested heavily on his head and stomach. If only he could focus on preparing the report and sales pitch on a promising new IPO to entice his inner core of investors, all of whom lived charmed lives floating in luxury in the financial stratosphere, high above the hoi polloi. With only a few exceptions, they represented a handful of the top three percent of the world's wealthiest men and women.

But his personal life kept intruding upon his professional concentration, and he found himself checking his e-mails and cell phone every few minutes.

Still no word from Miranda.

Damn that woman all to hell! What was *it with her?*

His mind was so consumed by her sudden departure that he found it impossible to think of anything else. It was intolerable that she'd left so abruptly without discussing it with him beforehand! And during that brief call as she'd boarded the plane, she'd mentioned some island in Greece—he'd forgotten which one—where she was headed.

Greece, for crying out loud. Fucking Greece!

And there hadn't even been time for her to give him an address or telephone number, and he had no idea where she could be reached. All his calls to her cell phone had gone unanswered. Of course, he kept reminding himself, the possibility always existed that she might be out of range. Or that she might even have tried to get in touch with him on his Blackberry, which was their usual mode of communication.

The thought brought a scowl to his handsome, Ralph Lauren ad features. Trouble was, he'd apparently left it uptown, at Tiffany's.

And then he'd remembered Magoo. Miranda's diabetic cat.

She would never leave him behind without seeing to his daily insulin injections!

In fact, there were times when that cat got seriously on his nerves. Like when they went to his place to spend the night and, in the morning, instead of enjoying another round of love-making, Miranda would suddenly leap out of bed, throw on her clothes, and dash uptown to give Magoo his injection.

There were times, Harry brooded reflectively, when he felt as if Mandy was engaged to Magoo instead of to him.

Cats. He wasn't fond of them. He had grown up among slavering, devoted Labrador Retrievers—in his mind, the king of dogs.

But the fact remained. Surely Mandy had seen to it that *someone* was taking care of Magoo. But who? Certainly not man-hungry Mara, who was likely to shack up with a guy and not surface for days on end.

Who then? *Who?*

And that was when it hit him. Of course! Most likely that . . . well, that swishy neighbor of hers, whatever his name was. That buff gym bunny. The fairy who performed in those Off-Off Broadway shows, one of which Miranda had dragged him to see.

Once had been more than enough.

Harris had been appalled; had wanted to escape that little theater as if it had been napalmed. He'd only stayed on till the end for Miranda.

The swishy fairy. That fag neighbor of hers. *Of course!*

Harris decided he'd best lose no time dashing uptown and finding out what he could. Long as the fag didn't hit on him, there wouldn't be any trouble.

Magoo! Once again, the thought of the cat erased everything else from Harris Milford Palmer III's mind. Leaning forward, he hit his intercom button. Told his secretary he'd be unavailable for the next two, three hours and to reschedule any appointments. Chucked the untouched pastrami sandwich into the wastebasket, spun his chair back from his desk and leapt to his feet.

Time to head uptown and face the fairy who did the drag acts.

He was halfway out the door when his private line emitted its signature chirps. For an instant he was undecided. Then he lunged for the phone and snatched up the receiver.

"Mandy—!" he half-shouted, in relief. "I've been trying to reach —"

"Oh. I'm sorry, Mr. Palmer." A woman's voice laughed nervously, and his bubble burst. "This is Bunny Neuman? Your real estate agent at Stribling? You're a very, very lucky man. I believe the perfect co-op apartment you've been searching for has just come on the market. This duplex has everything you've been looking for. Location, renovation, wraparound terrace, chef's kitchen, plenty of large, sunny rooms . . . "

He shut his eyes and massaged his forehead. It was yet another painful reminder. He hadn't told Miranda about his apartment hunting. He'd wanted to surprise her with the perfect Park Avenue nest for the two of them to feather. Not to twist her arm about committing to at least living together before getting married, but to cut down on shuttling back and forth between his bachelor loft and that depressing tiny rental of hers . . .

. . . but no. He wasn't being entirely truthful with himself, he realized. He *was* trying to twist her arm. Not that his intentions weren't good. Hell, he was in love with her. Why else would he have spent seventy grand on that rock for her finger? Okay, so she was playing hard to get. But the truth remained that she was the only woman he'd ever met with whom he wanted to father children.

"Ms. Neuman," he said swiftly, cutting her sales pitch short. "I'm really interested in seeing the place, but I'm in the middle of something urgent at the moment. I'll call you later."

"Of course. Just don't wait too long, Mr. Palmer," she warned. "You know how quickly these high-end apartments get snapped up."

But she was talking to a dead phone. He'd already hung up and was on his way out. Rarin' to get uptown.

In the reception area, he prowled the carpeted bank of elevators like a nervous cat, waiting for one going down instead of up. Impatiently he bopped up and down on the balls of his feet, hands thrust nervously in his pockets.

Ping! The brushed steel door of a down elevator opened without a sound and he rushed toward it.

Who would emerge and bar his way but Tiffany Pfeiffer.

"Harry!" she trilled. "What a pleasure. I was just going to drop by your office."

"Later, Tiffany," he growled. "Later."

He tried to elbow his way past her, but she was immovable. Behind her, the brushed steel door slid silently shut and the elevator continued its descent without him.

"Shit!" he swore softly.

"What's the mad rush, Harry? Late for an appointment?"

He glared wordlessly at her.

She laughed lightly. "What's the matter, Harry?" she asked. "Cat got your tongue?"

When he didn't reply, she clutched his sleeve, fingers digging into his forearm. "Here's what I decided, Harry," she continued, her lips unable to suppress a triumphant, calculating little smile. "Since you want to pick up your Blackberry at my place, I figured I deserve a treat. Here's the skinny. You'll have to wine and dine me first."

"Tiffany—" he began.

But she cut him off. "Say the Gotham Bar and Grill? It's the least you can do. They wouldn't take reservations for weeks, but I got through to the manager and pulled rank. With all the business we throw their way—*voilà*. 'Of course we can fit Madame in,' I was told when I threatened that this firm would boycott them in the future. 'By all means, Madame. I shall personally see to it that you have the best table in the house.'"

Her eyes were hard and unrelenting.

"So I'll expect you to show up at six-thirty, Harry. And don't be late. You *do* want to pick up your Blackberry, don't you?"

His heart sank. Dinner with Tiffany Pfeiffer. Then on to her place.

Those were the last, the very, very last things he either wanted or needed at his point in his life.

On the other hand, she *had* gotten him home and given him shelter after last night's drunken binge, and he owed her.

"Alright," he grumped. "See you there."

She winked and started toward her office. "Six-thirty sharp, Harry," she called over her shoulder, as though he needed reminding. "And don't be late."

"Yeah, yeah." And swift as a cat, he lunged forward and pressed the elevators' down button.

[CHAPTER FIFTEEN]

At Sea

Underway at last.

The reddish-brown sails had been hoisted, but it was not the wind which propelled the *Meltemi II,* but the propulsion generated by powerful diesel engines. The decks vibrated not unpleasantly beneath Miranda's feet, wavelets slapped playfully against the hull, and Piraeus was left behind. Along the shore on the port side, the sprawl of Athens' whitish, low-rise apartment buildings was reduced to Z-scale models against the dramatic backdrop of the mass known as Mount Hymettos. To starboard, she could make out the hazy blue outline of distant Aegina. They were clipping along at a steady ten knots and the sailing was smooth, the waters of the Saronic Gulf the deepest shade of cobalt she'd ever encountered. Not a cloud dared mar the perfection of the clear blue sky, but the gray, low-lying scrim of Athens' smog did.

The sun was hot. Very, very hot.

No matter. She and Madge had staked out the choicest cushioned chaise longues, smack dab in the sun, slathered each other with sun block and slipped on their dark glasses. Being the first to congregate on the Astroturf sundeck, they enjoyed some moments of solitude before the rest of the passengers would inevitably flock up, making the two just part of the crowd.

No matter. Miranda was content to luxuriate on the sunny side under the reddish brown sails and creaking masts, sipping a *caffé freddo* through a straw. Soaking up the rays. Feeling that the sun, sea, and view of the Attic peninsula belonged to her and Madge, and to them alone.

Under these conditions, it was easy to pretend they were onboard their very own private yacht.

Below, the door of the aft deck opened and slammed shut. Miranda heard a man's voice booming in German, and a woman's high-pitched bickering response, and her lovely daydream of a private yacht shattered silently into a million fragments. Soon, two sets of footsteps slowly clomped up the steep, stamped-steel steps, and the couple came into view.

They were a lot older than the noise they made implied. The man was frail and had an emaciated look and wore a snap-brimmed cap and cheap eyeglasses with huge thick black frames. His clothes were far too big for him and his pants were hoisted way up near his chest, practically under his armpits; he'd obviously shed a lot of weight since he'd last updated his wardrobe. It seemed impossible that such a shrunken little man could have such a powerful set of lungs. Miranda wouldn't have been surprised if his voice carried all the way ashore to Glyfada.

The frau was his exact opposite. Strong as the proverbial ox, she was stout and large-breasted, and had the moon face and healthy, apple-red cheeks of a Frans Hals peasant. Neither of them seemed very happy, and for a moment they stood there, looking around to get their bearings. Then she pointed forward and led the way to the shade under the canvas awning. There was an awful lot of clattering and bickering as they moved around the stackable white resin armchairs before finally getting settled.

Miranda silently thanked the gods that they were as far from her and Madge as the deck allowed.

The Germans were barely seated when a very young English couple appeared, both thin, sallow-complected, sullen, and trying hard to be hip.

The girl, barely out of her teens, sported spiky black hair, bluish-black fingernails and lipstick, and had several rings through her eyebrows and a round silver stud in her nose.

The boy, ditto: hardware in both ears, a thong knotted around his neck, and a black tee-shirt with the sleeves ripped off, the better to display skinny arms so covered with tattoos that they looked like he'd pasted on pages from a comic book. Sadly, despite the punk rock togs and in-your-face toughness they tried to project, their faces were too gentle and pasty to pull off that hard, edgy barbarity, and they moved with the hesitant, slouchy shuffle of the exceedingly shy and insecure.

They reminded Miranda of nothing so much as the kids who hung out in shopping malls dressed up as punks.

They certainly were no match for the quartet of pediatric oncology nurses who followed on their heels and swooped around them, the tall, angular one blurting, "Brits, are you? From your accents, I'd say you were from Manchester. Am I right?"

The punk rock couple looked nonplussed and were tongue-tied. Another of the nurses, the shortest and jolliest, piped up and trilled: "Can you guess where *we're* from? I'll give you just one clue. We're antipodean, but we're *not* from Australia!"

And the six of them also headed forward into the shady area afforded by the awning, the punks wearing the bewildered look of earthlings who'd been abruptly abducted by aliens.

"So much for looking tough," Miranda murmured.

Madge placed a gentle hand atop hers. "Now be nice, my dear," she advised softly. "I'm sure they're very nice."

Awfully nice, Miranda thought, but didn't say.

Before long, the rest of the passengers appeared: a smattering of Austrians, Dutch, Poles, and Czechs. Curiously, there was privacy in numbers. A crewman in a short-sleeved white shirt and black trousers circulated, taking orders for drinks.

Madge stretched luxuriously and made little mewling sounds of pleasure, and despite Miranda's daydream yacht having dissipated with the arrival of the others, the combination of sun and sea were intoxicating, and as she traded her empty *caffé freddo* for a melon daiquiri, she all but purred.

And had every reason to. After Manhattan's constant wailing of fire engines and police sirens and paramedics, the never-ending cacophony of multiple car alarms, and the ever-present honking of gridlocked traffic, she realized she was about as close to paradise as she was ever likely to get.

Unfortunately, she'd almost forgotten that even paradise contained its serpent. And there she was, her personal onboard nemesis in the flesh.

Chara Zouboulakis. Posing at the top of the steps, as though allowing everyone to admire the casual clothes she'd changed into.

Casual, my eye, Miranda thought uncharitably. Ms. Zouboulakis was wearing a white cotton-voile shirt, all see-through lace and pom-pom embroidery which was cinched at the waist over a pair of white, form-fitting, cotton faille knee-length shorts. Inwardly Miranda frowned. Hadn't she seen that very outfit in a shop window somewhere? At Bergdorf Goodman perhaps? And on those dainty, perfectly manicured feet . . . weren't those a pair of lowly flip-flops as transformed by Jimmy Choo into $300 white thongs with futuristic, curvy heels?

Indeed they were. The *Meltemi II*'s fashion plate had even gone so far as to switch sunglasses—gone were the Guccis, replaced by frameless oval wrap-arounds of the palest green.

The woman's wardrobe was really starting to get under Miranda's skin. Perhaps, she mused, she should consider dropping her career in archeology, ditching her job at the Jan Kofski gallery where she worked for peanuts, and exchanging it in favor of becoming a cruise director on a rust bucket? For if Chara Zouboulakis could afford clothes like these, then the rest of the passengers were the unwitting cast members of a budget remake of *Ship of Fools.*

Before finishing her pose, Ms. Zouboulakis let her eyes wander in Miranda's direction—without sending out any hateful vibes, at least none that Miranda could detect, and which she took as a positive sign that their unspoken cease fire seemed to be holding. Then her eyes moved on; Miranda gathered that she was counting heads. After ascertaining that most, if not all, of the twenty-seven passengers had congregated, she moved forward and stopped in the middle of the deck. There she lifted her little battery-powered microphone to her lips.

"*Kiría e kírie,* ladies and gentlemen, *meine Damen und Herren,*" she began. "On behalf of Captain Aris Leonides, whom you shall meet personally at dinner—" she paused and her lips formed a practiced smile "—since I believe we would all prefer he remains at the helm for the time being, yes?"

Ha, ha, Miranda thought. *Fuh-nee. A regular stand-up comic, that Chara Zouboulakis.* It was the kind of thought that, when expressed aloud, Mara always called the "chinchilla side" of her coming out.

But a smattering of polite laughter proved that everyone didn't have the alter ego of a spiteful, nasty little rodent, and Miranda felt a stab of shame.

"In the meantime," continued the ship's purser-cum-cruise director-cum-hostess-cum-interpreter-cum-fashion plate, "as you are enjoying your complimentary cocktails, I would like to introduce you to the rest of the crew. You have already met me—" another smattering of polite laughter "—as well as Dimitris, but allow me to introduce him to you formally."

After Dimitris' appearance, which Miranda and Madge both endorsed with enthusiastic applause, Miranda tuned out and lost herself by gazing hypnotically back at the foamy aquamarine and white wake the *Meltemi II* left behind. They passed a handsome sloop coming from the opposite direction with its sails optimistically raised, and she watched as it dipped and rose and dipped and rose when the *Meltemi II*'s wake reached it. Further out to sea, she noticed more tiny white triangles marking the positions of a veritable armada of sailboats. From this far away, they looked as if they were standing still.

Something in Chara Zouboulakis' tone had changed and she decided it might behoove her to tune back in.

"Our first stop," she was saying, "and please to notice that I call it a stop instead of a port of call, is Cape Sounion. It is located at the southernmost tip of the Attic peninsula, where the Saronic Gulf ends, and the open waters of the Aegean begin. It has served as a landmark for sailors since ancient times. We shall stop in the bay below Sounion and drop anchor there for ninety minutes. Those of you who wish to go ashore to visit the temple to Poseidon are welcome to do so. Our Zodiacs shall be at your disposal to shuttle you ashore and back."

She paused to smile that practiced smile.

"However," she continued, "the headland is 195 feet above sea level, and please to be advised that it is a steep and arduous path. If you are not physically able to accomplish the climb, see the temple, and return within the allotted time, please do not attempt to do so. We must keep to our schedule and I would very much dislike leaving any members of this group behind. In the meantime, please to enjoy your complimentary welcome cocktails."

She repeated this information in German, and in what Miranda took to be Czech and Dutch.

Sounion!

The level of Miranda's excitement was almost more than she could bear. After all, every student of Classical Greek antiquity knew that the temple to Poseidon, which dated back to the middle of the fifth century B.C., was considered to be one of the most magnificent, important and, after the Parthenon, perhaps most photographed spots in all of Greece. Even Lord Byron, that forefather of graffiti "artists" had defaced one of the columns by carving his name on its base. It would take a pack of wild dogs—or more likely, a herd of Jurassic flesh eaters—to keep her from making that pilgrimage.

A long-forgotten verse of Byron's filled her head to ecstatic bursting. She turned to Madge and quoted, *sotte voce:*

> Place me on Sunium's marble steep,
> Where nothing but the waves and I
> May hear our mutual murmurs sweep;
> There, swan-like, let me sing and die.
> A land of slaves shall ne'er be mine—
> Dash down yon cup of Samian wine!

Madge was enchanted. "Oh, how lovely, my dear! Goodness, you *are* clever!"

"Not me. Lord Byron. Oh, Madge! We *must* go see it!" Miranda whispered back forcefully. "To miss out on such a wonder would be nothing short of criminal! Who would ever have thought—"

But Chara Zouboulakis had switched back to English, and Miranda's ears perked up.

"Anyone who wishes to go ashore and climb up to the temple, please to raise your hands."

Predictably, Miranda's shot up like a rocket.

"Ah. Ms. Kalli. Yes, of course." Whereupon she added to the passengers at large: "I am proud to announce that we have onboard a distinguished archeologist. May I present Ms. Me-rahn-da Kalli."

Miranda stifled a painful groan. Naturally, Chara gestured right at her. And naturally, twenty-some pairs of eyes snapped in her direction. Everyone's, it seemed, with the exception of the British punk couple, who were obsessed with one another, was eyeing her like some kind of curiosity on display inside a glass-fronted cabinet.

Miranda couldn't help it. Under all that scrutiny, the blood rushed up to her face and she flushed bright red. Was there anything worse than being singled out and put on the spot in front of total strangers? She wanted to blurt out, *No, I am not a distinguished archeologist!* but that would only compound her dilemma. Plus there was Madge to consider. Dear, sweet, well-meaning Madge. Madge, without a mean bone in her body. Madge, who was beaming like a proud mother.

It made Miranda wish the deck would open up and swallow her whole. *I should have kept my trap shut back at the marina*, she realized. *I should never have brought up the subject that the Oinochoe that had spilled from the broken crate was a genuine antiquity.*

But it was too late now. What was done could obviously not be undone.

Chara bestowed the sweetest smile in her arsenal, saying: "Ms. Kalli? Perhaps you could do us the honor of acting as the unofficial tour guide for those wishing to go ashore?" There. She'd thrown down the gauntlet. Not only in public, but sending a message loud and clear. That no cease fire was in effect, after all.

But Mr. and Mrs. Kalli's little girl wasn't a complete idjit. Miranda recognized a challenge when she encountered one. What's more, she had the distinct impression that Chara Zouboulakis was counting upon her surprise tactic—not to mention Miranda's own ego—to walk into her trap. Miranda tried to picture the *Meltemi II*'s fashionista hiking up a steep incline and getting all hot and sweaty and ruining her designer clothes and expensive shoes in the process.

Somehow it was difficult to visualize.

Miranda was all too aware of everyone looking at her with expectation. Madge, bless her good-natured heart, was naively unaware of her predicament, and preened in the vicarious spotlight of Miranda's momentary importance.

But Madge hailed from the Midwest, and was therefore a kinder, gentler soul than Miranda. This was the kind of situation where living in Manhattan definitely gave one the edge. No other place else on earth prepared one to treat the simplest, most mundane daily routine—crossing a street, waiting for a cup of coffee and not letting someone cut in front of one in line—as just battles which must be fought and won.

Returning the cruise director's smile with one just as saturated with saccharine, Miranda smugly replied: "Oh, but I couldn't. I'm not a trained tour guide. Nor is the fifth century B.C. my specialty. You're the expert here, Ms. Zouboulakis. I wouldn't dream of usurping your position. I'll let you lead and gladly follow. Surely I can learn much in the process."

Which just went to prove that two could fling down a gauntlet as easily as one.

Sipping her daiquiri, Miranda silently congratulated herself on having won this round. She'd neatly turned the tables on Chara Zouboulakis. Now the *Meltemi II*'s fashion plate was stuck leading the group ashore—which she needn't have done if she hadn't messed with The Chinchilla.

So I've made an enemy, she thought. *Big deal.* It wasn't as if she and Chara Zouboulakis were going to be seeing much of each other. Once she disembarked on Samos, that would be it.

But Miranda had forgotten her Aesop: *"It is easier to get into the enemy's toils than out again."*

How was she to know that their paths would continue to cross? That the Fates had already decided that her destiny and Chara Zouboulakis' were intertwined?

Somewhere the gods were laughing.

Unfortunately Miranda wasn't able to hear them.

[CHAPTER SIXTEEN]

New York City

Harry Palmer wasn't exactly having the time of his life.

First had been his run-in with Tiffany Pfeiffer at the elevator, during which she'd given him no choice but to meet her for dinner at the Gotham Bar and Grill after work. Holding his Blackberry hostage.

Then, when he'd left the office building, there hadn't been an available taxi in sight. Finally he'd resigned himself to taking the subway uptown. Not his favorite mode of transportation. And with good reason.

The subway station had been sweltering, trapping August's heat wave. To top it off, the air-conditioning on the train had been on the blink. Making matters worse, one of those inexplicable delays occurred in the darkness of one of the subway tunnels, with no explanation given. By the time the train continued, his Brooks Brothers suit was drenched under the armpits.

Finally, almost an hour later, he arrived at Miranda's brownstone. He'd forgotten Ron's last name, and all the nameplates beside the door buzzers only listed last names, without first initials or apartment numbers.

In desperation, he'd jabbed every buzzer in the building. The few responses he'd gotten had been met with typical Manhattan suspicion. "Ron? Ron *Who*?" and "I don't know any Rons. If ya don't know his last name, ya got no business being here. Buzz again, and I'm calling the po-lice."

Inspiration hit when he realized the locked outer front door had a snap lock. So he'd used his American Express card to try and slip the lock open. After several tries, he succeeded, probably damaging the magnetic strip in the process.

The least of his worries at the moment.

Then he was faced with the inner front door to the tiny vestibule where the mailboxes were located.

Luck was with him; a woman in the building was coming down the stairs. Swiftly reaching for his keys, he pretended to open a mailbox, flashed her a friendly smile and received none in return. Not that he expected one. But he did manage to wedge his foot between the inner door and the doorjamb before it snapped shut.

The stairwell, too, was airless, hot, and stifling. The stairs steep and listing. The ocher walls pebbled from dozens of layers of paint, the steel doors the ugliest shade of brown imaginable. Passing the second floor landing, he could hear the sound of someone spying on him through the peephole.

Three more flights.

Depressing. How Miranda could stand living in this hellhole instead of moving into his sprawling, renovated, full-floor loft was beyond him. But then, so were her excuses for postponing their wedding.

He was huffing and puffing by the time he reached the top floor. Her neighbor, Ron, he remembered, lived right next door. He could hear music leaking out from within. A snappy old tune he recognized but couldn't quite place.

Harry steeled himself before knocking. He knew Ron was gay, and prided himself on having nothing against discreet gays in general, so long as they appeared straight, didn't flap their wrists, tap their feet in public toilet stalls, or flaunt their sexuality openly by donning weird Western, latex, or leather outfits. But men who performed on stage as *women* . . . how well he recalled that highly-touted drag show of Ron's that Miranda had once twisted his arm to attend, and that had made him distinctly uncomfortable, to put it mildly. He'd squirmed in his seat throughout the performance. It had been supposed to be funny; the audience had laughed uproariously with appreciation and had applauded thunderously.

All Harry had wanted to do was to get out of there. So he'd done the next best thing. He'd slunk way down in his seat and pretended to be invisibl,silently praying that none of his friends or acquaintances were in the audience.

Now to face that self-same Ron.

Squaring his shoulders to steel himself, Harry heaved a deep breath and knocked briskly.

Nothing. He knocked again, a little harder and louder. Now he heard movement from within, then sensed an eye appraising him from behind the peephole. A safety chain rattled, several lock tumblers turned noisily, and the door swung wide, amplifying the tune he couldn't quite identify, or the singer whose husky voice was anything but musical, and yet stylish and unforgettable.

Harry instinctively took a step back. He was expecting the worst—a mincing transvestite, perhaps. Or—he cringed inwardly at the politically incorrectness of the word that popped unbidden into his head—one of those aberrations in black leather so tight it looked sprayed on.

These days, you never knew what to expect.

Instead, he found himself face-to-face with a buff, barefoot young man with a shaved head. Jade green eyes. Pale skin and a perfectly proportioned, well-developed athletic physique. He was naked save for a pair of the briefest of white briefs and he a sported a stylish Aboriginal tattoo on each shoulder that reached his chest and biceps.

Worse, for Harry, Ron appeared totally at ease, leaning casually against the doorjamb, one muscled arm across his chest, the elbow of the other resting upon it as he held up a syringe in his hand, the needle pointed upward.

"Oooooh," he said. "Miranda's hedge fund stud, if I'm not mistaken?"

Their roles had reversed, and it was Harry, perspiring in his pinstripes, vest, and orange Bulgari tie who was made to feel out of place; the interloper who had crashed a universe where he didn't belong. Hunching his shoulders belligerently, his hands clasped behind his back, he was barely conscious of having taken another step backward, and then another, until his fingers felt the sticky railing of the balustrade, aware that his sweat-glossed face mimicked his nervousness at encountering more gay male flesh than he'd anticipated—or ever cared to face. Nor could he help but register shock and revulsion at the sight of the hypodermic needle.

Anabolic steroids? he wondered.

But Ron's body wasn't bulked up enough for those. At least, not yet. Had he, perhaps, just begun to use them, flaunting the syringe in front of Harry for the very purpose of intimidation and giving offense?

"You are welcome to enter my lair, as the spider said to the fly,"

Ron invited, with more than a touch of amused irony. "I've got the A.C. running, and don't want to let this infernal heat in."

Harry, wondering about the friends Miranda cultivated, hesitated and peered suspiciously past Ron through the door of the compact studio. Fearing a seraglio hung with beaded curtains, lengths of pink chiffon, and lit by red-shaded, tasseled lamps, he was pleasantly surprised.

The walls, painted a medium matt gray, effectively played down the lumpy plaster, and the furniture and lamps were inexpensive, but modern and with it—Target, he guessed. *Style on a shoestring.* The floor was wall-to-wall industrial carpeting, and the bed was covered with what he presumed to be a leather spread. It looked, as he'd heard some wag remark about an interior once, "hotel spotless."

"I don't bite, you know," Ron said easily, with a chuckle. "Besides, you're more preppy than metrosexual, so chill. You're definitely *not* my type, okay? Now that we've gotten that out of the way, you have one of two choices. Either come in and help me, or go away. It's your call."

Help? Harry wondered, fingers fidgeting nervously behind his back. *Help how?*

But he'd come on a mission—specifically to find out what the hell was going on with Miranda, and now wasn't the time to chicken out.

"Well?" Ron stepped aside. "Coming in or not?"

Harry braved the threshold. From a CD player, the song switched from "I've Gotta Get a Man" to "You Do Something to Me."

And that was when recognition of that inimitable voice dawned. "Hey. That's Dietrich, right?"

"Ping, ping, ping, ping, ping." Ron mimicked the sound of a correct game show answer to perfection. "You've won the lottery. Proceed to Go and collect two hundred dollars. Now let me turn this off."

With a foot, he adroitly slammed the door shut, picked up a remote control, aimed it, and shut off the music. "Want something to drink?"

"No, thanks. I only came to find out what's up with Mandy."

Ron cocked one eyebrow. "You mean *Miranda,* don't you?" he said, with emphasis. "She *loathes* being called Mandy. Or didn't you know?"

Harry was momentarily thrown. "I . . . uh . . . I always call her Mandy," he replied, somewhat sheepishly.

Ron rolled his eyes. "In that case, big fella, I'm going to give you some friendly advice. Like you'd better start calling her *Miranda?* It's what she prefers."

"How do you know?"

"Cause we're girlfriends," Ron replied, obviously comfortable in his own skin. "We share secrets. It's what us girlfriends do."

Harry was stumped for a reply and tried to pretend the giant chrome-framed Herb Ritts poster of a male nude on the wall wasn't there. "I . . . I assume Mand . . . I mean, *Miranda*, left a contact number, or maybe a forwarding address with you?"

"Have you tried her cell phone?"

"Yes. She called me from J.F.K. But since then, I haven't heard a word." Harry decided that Ron, being self-confessed "girlfriends" with Miranda, didn't come under "need to know" about his Blackberry. The fewer he told about last night's fiasco with Tiffany Pfeiffer, the better.

"But what gives you the idea that I know more than she told you?" Ron persisted. "I mean, you *are* her fiancé."

Because you're girlfriends? the smart-aleck in Harry was tempted to retort, but he wisely stayed his tongue. Instead he said: "Magoo. I know she'd want to leave him in good hands."

Ron grinned. "Yeah, kinda like Allstate," he quipped. "But you're right. I'm the cat sitter."

"Speaking of which, how is that . . . " Harry stifled the word *damn* " . . . cat doing?"

"Magoo?" Ron laughed. "Ever hear of a cat with 99 lives? He's fat, spoiled, and missing his litter box on purpose, probably to punish Miranda for deserting him, and me for bringing him over here."

"You mean, he's *here?* In your apartment?"

"I thought it would be easier and more sociable than leaving him alone next door. Besides which, if you do get hold of Miranda, remind her that there are dust bunnies galore under her bed? Cat hair is bad enough, but I'm positively *allergic* to dust. Which is why I decided he's better off here with me."

Harry looked around. "But I don't see him."

"That's because he's hiding under the bed. I thought he and I had come to an understanding. If he doesn't bite or claw me when I give him his shot, then he gets fed." Ron laughed. "Unfortunately, it doesn't quite work that way. He knows when his insulin shot's coming, and he goes into hiding. Believe me, it takes a special talent to reach *under* the bed and do it. Miranda's a pro at it. I'm not. In fact, I was just in the process of trying to give him his injection when you knocked."

Harry felt a sudden flash of shame. So that explained the syringe Ron was holding! He wasn't taking steroids; he was merely getting ready to give Magoo his shot.

Talk about thinking the worst of people.

"I'm glad you dropped by," Ron told him, "because as it turns out, I can use some help. Now, what you need to do is get down on all fours, reach out, and hold him. I'll try to make quick work of it. Okay?"

Groaning to himself, Harry reluctantly pinched his trousers, hoisting the legs higher, then knelt down beside the bed and, grimacing, used the tips of two fingers to gingerly lift up the end of the spread. It wasn't leather, he realized, flipping it up, but some form of washable PVC. From his mind he tried to banish whatever hijinks—and too many scenarios flooded his mind—had occurred on it.

Better to concentrate on the cat.

And there, right in the very center underneath the box spring, was Magoo. Sphinx-like and grand, with his front legs tucked under. Big green eyes wary, ears twitching.

Shit! he thought, wondering how he'd managed to get roped into this.

"You're going to have to lie flat on your belly," Ron told him. "If you can, pull him out. Otherwise just hold him where he is."

"Magoo isn't especially fond of me," Harry murmured, seeing, but trying to ignore, the thick steel chains and handcuffs padlocked to each corner of the metal bed frame—obviously part of Ron's Adult Toy chest. Something else best overlooked.

"Magoo," Ron was saying, padding around to the other side of the bed and flipping up the PVC spread at that end, "doesn't need to be fond of you. He just needs his shot."

What I won't do for Miranda, Harry thought, stretching out flat and reaching under the bed with his arms. He tried, unsuccessfully, to ignore Magoo's stare, which had become positively malevolent.

"Here, kitty kitty!" he cooed, inwardly flinching at the sound of his own voice. "Good kitty. That's right, Magoo. *Nice* kitty . . . "

Even in the dimness he could see Magoo's fur standing up straight. The cat showed its teeth and hissed.

Not an auspicious sign by any means.

"There. Nice puddy cat," Harry said softly, not believing he was reverting to baby talk. "Yeah, nice puddy cat." Gritting his teeth, he forced his hands to close in, ostensibly to stroke Nice Puddy's back.

But Magoo wasn't having any of it, and hissed another warning, this time showing sharp fangs.

"Grab him and hold on tight," Ron instructed from carpet level from the other side of the bed.

Harry grabbed hold of Magoo, who struggled violently to get loose. He couldn't believe the cat's amazing strength and agility. It was like clinging onto a miniature bucking bronco.

"Hold tight!" Ron warned. "Whatever you do, don't let him go!"

Sharp claws caught in Harry's suit jacket, then he felt fangs sink into his forearm.

"*Shit!*" he yelled. "Cat fucking *bit* me!"

"Just hold him a couple more seconds," Ron said calmly. "Here goes." And he stabbed Magoo's rear end and depressed the plunger of the syringe. Then: "Done. You can let him go now."

Harry was only too glad to. He scooted back, got to his knees, then raised himself to his feet. He clapped dander off his hands, then surveyed the clawed cuff of his suit jacket, unbuttoned his shirt, and pulled up his sleeve. Drops of blood were welling up from two puncture wounds on his forearm.

Ron leapt lithely to his feet, put down the syringe, and came over to inspect the damage. "The good news is, you don't need to worry about rabies. Miranda's very good about Magoo's inoculations. You might, however, want to see about getting a tetanus shot."

"That damned cat!" Harry swore angrily. "I don't know what Mandy—"

"Tsk tsk!" Ron held up a warning finger.

"—I mean *Miranda,* sees in that . . . that beast."

"Want my advice? Never, ever, broach that subject with her. She loves Magoo."

And seeing Harry's darkening expression, he added, "Don't worry, she loves you, too."

"Sometimes I'm beginning to wonder."

"Let it go. There's people love and animal love, and never the twain shall meet," Ron said wisely. "Don't even try to analyze the two. Now, I'll get you some peroxide, rub on some bacitracin, and we'll put on a couple of bandages. As for your jacket sleeve, it doesn't look too bad. If that's Brooks Brothers, they can easily reweave the shreds. Now come into the bathroom and we'll wash that wound and clean it. You don't want it to get infected."

And with a chuckle, he added, "Don't look at me like that. Unlike Magoo, I don't bite."

Harry hesitated, then followed him. Ron proved competent in first aid. "I were you, I'd still get that tetanus shot," he advised. "You never know."

"I'll see to it right away."

"You do that." Ron led the way out of the bathroom.

"About Mand . . . I mean, *Miranda's* . . . contact information," Harry said as he buttoned his shirt cuff.

"I've got an address and a phone number for her in Greece," Ron supplied.

Which is more than I've got, Harry thought unhappily.

He watched as Ron jotted the information on a notepad and tore the sheet off with a flourish. "Here you are." He held it out.

Harry accepted it and read it. "Albatross? Pythagoria? Samos?" He glanced up. "What's Albatross?"

"Apparently a restaurant or taverna owned by the wife of one of her professors."

"Thanks. I owe you." Harry folded the note and tucked it in his wallet.

Ron laughed. "I think you paid your dues via Magoo. So we're even-Steven. Oh, and before you go . . . "

"Yes?"

"Here. It's the very least I can do for your troubles. Do you want one comp ticket or two?"

Harry looked baffled. "Ticket? To what?"

"My show. I just changed the act. It's a real drag!" Ron gave him a sly wink.

Harry gave a start. Since the drama of dealing with Magoo, he'd all but forgotten about Ron's sexual preference as well as his status as a performance artist. His stage name came back to him now: Lotta Puss. And suddenly he was once more acutely aware of Ron's near-nudity. The giant Herb Ritts photo. The chains and handcuffs he'd seen padlocked to the bed frame.

"S-sorry," Harry stammered, taking a step back toward the front door, "but I won't be able to make it. I've got a dinner engagement tonight."

"Want one or two for tomorrow's show then? I don't lipsynch. I do my own songs, tell my own tasteless jokes." He grinned disarmingly.

"Oh. Right. Ma . . . Miranda . . . took me to one."

"I change them every two months. To keep it fresh and up-to-date."

"I . . . uh . . . no thanks. But it was nice of you to offer. Now I think I'd better run and see about that tetanus shot."

"Yeah, you better do that."

Harry was only too happy to beat it out of there.

Ron followed him out into the stairwell. “Don’t trip on your way down,” he called out after him, and laughed softly. Then, shaking his head he went back inside his apartment. Magoo had come out from under the bed and was sprawled atop the PVC spread. Ron sat down, picked him up, and sat him in his lap. “Magoo,” he mused aloud, scratching the big cat between the ears, “what on earth does Miranda see in such a stuffed shirt from Wall Street? You have any idea?”

But Magoo, his trauma for the day over, only purred softly and half-closed his eyes.

“Girl,” Ron said aloud to the walls in general, and to Miranda who was thousands of miles out of earshot in particular, “you can do a lot better than that. I just hope you keep postponing that wedding.”

[CHAPTER SEVENTEEN]

The Attic Headland

With a massive splash and the rattle of chains being let out, the *Meltemi II* dropped anchor in the bay below Sounion. For a while the ship kept moving. Then the anchor caught, the engines were cut, and the sudden silence was awe-inspiring.

They were by no means alone. An armada of sailboats and white motor yachts rode at anchor, keeping the vessel company. Ashore, the crescent of beach was packed with so many bodies broiling in the sun that one couldn't see the sand for all the human lobsters.

Of course the silence couldn't last. Two rigid inflatables were duly launched and the *Meltemi II*'s passengers were carefully helped down into them and shuttled ashore in relays. It took each launch two trips before the sightseers were assembled on the jetty extending its stone finger from this, the farthest end of the beach.

From there it was all uphill—literally. Needless to say, the chinchilla in Miranda had been hoping their reluctant tour guide would have to hoof it in her Jimmy Choo's. She was sorely disappointed. Ms. Zouboulakis showed up in spanking new sneakers—from Chanel, no less—gold leather with big black C logos and black laces.

Miranda sighed to herself, thinking: *I should have known.*

She was, however, rewarded by such an uncongenial look that had Chara been Medusa, Miranda would have instantly been turned to stone.

But Chara wasn't Medusa, and Miranda reciprocated by projecting her best "Don't tread on me" expression.

It had the desired effect. Chara backed off and so, with Ms. Goldfoot in the lead, they headed uphill at a punishing force-march pace. Miranda predicted the grueling pace couldn't last, and it didn't. Although by now it was late afternoon, the heat was the kind that quickly sapped one of all energy, and expending too much of it too fast was unendurable, even if it was fueled by animosity.

Before long, Ms. Goldfoot slowed considerably. A little later, she faltered and slowed even further. The hardy quartet of oncology nurses, being the outdoorsy types, soon overtook her. So did the apple-cheeked German wife. Others—the German husband and Madge included—started to fall behind and became stragglers.

Miranda, anxious as she was to reach the temple, was among them, since she purposely adjusted her pace to Madge's. One thing was for certain: Ms. Goldfoot hadn't been kidding. It really was wicked going.

The path, meandering through dry thorny scrub which hadn't seen rain in months, was more gully than path. It was much steeper, rougher, and far rockier than anticipated. In most places it was so narrow that they were forced to climb in single file, like school children. Every so often someone ahead would slip or stumble and nearly fall, and either utter a curse in some foreign tongue or laugh good-naturedly. Inevitably, a small rockslide of stones and parched dirt would immediately follow, sending small lizards darting off into the shelter of low green brush, thistles, and parched yellow grass. Seeing them, Miranda fervently prayed that they wouldn't come across any legless reptiles.

As far as she was concerned, Chara Zouboulakis was snake enough.

Behind her, Madge's labored breathing become even more intense. Miranda stopped and turned. Madge, poor thing, was wilting fast. Her blouse and shorts were soaked, and her face glistened with perspiration. She had taken off her hat and was fanning herself furiously with it.

"Oh lordy, lordy," she gasped, between gulping lungfuls of hot air. "Goodness me . . . it really is . . . quite a climb and . . . in this heat . . . " She broke off to take a series of quick deep breaths. "Listen, dear . . . why don't you . . . just go right on . . . and . . . and run ahead while I—"

Miranda would have none of it. "No, Madge," she replied firmly, if a little out of breath herself. "Come on. You can make it. I *know* you can!"

She cast her eye briefly to the summit, which they could no longer see. Then she glanced downhill, back the way they had come. The stragglers behind them were also taking a rest.

Madge heaved a deep sigh. "Really, Miranda, I'm . . . I'm not so *sure* . . ."

"Oh, but *I* am. You're a trooper, Madge, and you know it."

"Well . . . if you *say* so . . ." Her new-found friend looked anything but convinced.

Still, Miranda's cheerleading had the desired effect. Madge Blessing rallied and continued on, and as they progressed on uphill, so did the rest of the stragglers. Along the way, they passed an old water tank, the convex end on which someone had spray-painted the English word "NUDISTS" in large letters, along with an arrow pointing northeast.

Fortunately for the inhibited, their route zigged and zagged uphill in the opposite direction, beside a stretch of chain-link fence. And then, at long last, the path let out on the road from Athens.

That last stretch—on soft, mirage-creating asphalt—seemed the hardest. Motor coaches roared past, nearly running them down and choking them with the stench of diesel exhaust and slipstreams of yet more heat. Not pleasant, to say the least, but they were so close now that they were undeterred and their steps quickened.

And then—magic! The sky seemed to expand as they crested the top, and all their sweat and effort were rewarded a thousandfold. Suddenly they were oblivious to the pitiless sun beating down from westward, the hordes of tourists prowling about. Their minds were emptied of everything but the temple columns which rose majestically from yet more of a rise just beyond.

The breath caught in Miranda's throat as Byron's immortal words once again burst forth from her mental vault:

> Place me on Sunium's marble steep,
> Where nothing save the waves and I
> May hear our mutual murmurs sweep;
> There, swan-like, let me sing and die . . .

Truer words, she reflected, had never been written . . . nor could those unfortunate souls who had arrived by bus rather than making the pilgrimage on foot from below, adequately appreciate the sight which greeted her. To say it was glorious was a pathetic understatement. Only the poets, and not many of these, were able to express the mystery and majesty of what rose before her.

It really was a beautiful place to sing one's swan song and die.

Some of their group split off and headed toward the taverna and souvenir complex to the left for refreshments, but Madge and Miranda followed the example of the New Zealand nurses, waited in line at a small booth, purchased their admission tickets, and entered the temple compound.

Neither of them spoke. Despite the tourists, the silence was churchlike. Sepulchral, as if the intense blue of the sky was a vast protective dome. Other than the temple, only the wind registered in Miranda's consciousness. Thus subdued, they passed the ancient remnants of what had once been the foundation of the *propylon, stoa,* and rooms.

But these they ignored for the time being, because it was the temple itself, rising stalwart from a stepped platform of marble at the very highest point of this acropolis, which drew them as inexorably as a magnet attracts bits of metal.

Cautiously they picked their way around the massive blocks of marble that littered the area, all hewn some twenty-five centuries earlier.

They drew as close as the roped-off area surrounding the temple to Poseidon allowed, and there, at various vantage points, they leaned their heads far back to admire the looming Doric columns crowned with weatherbeaten lengths of entablature that seemed to scrape Apollo's very sky.

Standing there, mouth agape for Miranda knew not how long, she felt tingles of electrical currents thrumming through her, and her eyes moistened with tears. With wonder-struck awe she marveled at the mathematical precision and engineering which had created a masterpiece of such sublimity: strength, beauty, and perfect proportions in equal measure. Too, the knowledge that this landmark had been a sentinel for sailors over a period of some 2,500 years put her own inconsequential and dispensable lifespan into sobering perspective.

Who was she, she wondered silently, but a single ant in the teeming waves of humanity which came and went unnoticed with the passing of every tide?

It was uncanny, the way the great monuments of civilizations long past could so easily humble one, and make one see oneself for what one really was.

And then the inevitable intruded. The babble of voices and the shuffling of a small crowd encroached upon her reflections. A tour guide, holding aloft a yellow umbrella (to distinguish her group from the other guides, who carried blue, black, or striped umbrellas), infringed upon her worshipful silence. Resenting the intrusion, she and Madge moved off and strolled the perimeter of the promontory.

There, another revelation awaited her: the location was as spectacular as the temple itself, and robbed her of all breath. She felt that Poseidon himself could not have chosen a better spot at which to be honored. It was that glorious.

And being a clear day, she could see forever. Or so it seemed.

To the west, across the Saronic Gulf, the hazy bluish silhouette of Aegina rose from the deep cobalt waters and stood out against the even paler, hazier mountains of the Peloponnese. Looking eastward, across a somewhat choppy Aegean, she could just make out the distant island of Kea. And to the south she could actually see all the way to Kythnos and Serifos.

Standing there, at the cliff's sharp drop-off where a brave cousin of the aloe vera managed to flourish and flower, she experienced one of those rare moments of extreme clarity and self-discovery.

She had found her spiritual home. This—not New York—was where she belonged.

The realization stunned her. What was perhaps most ironic was the fact that it should have taken her thirty-two years to come to this conclusion—and this *after* she'd spent years studying archeology!

Ah, the difference between poring over photographs of antiquity's remains and confronting the awesome ruins themselves! Virtual reality was but a poor substitute for the real thing. Now she fully appreciated Professor Hirsch's decision to move to this land where history and myth, and times ancient and modern, merged and became one—

"—*Hul*-lo there!" hailed a chorus of voices.

Inwardly Miranda sighed. Just her bad luck to be interrupted in the midst of the most pleasant of contemplations. But she did her best to hide any irritation and turned to greet the quartet of well-meaning Antipodean nurses.

They were all chattering excitedly:

"*There* you are! Hiding, are you?" This from the plump jolly one the others called "Em," which Miranda gathered was an abbreviation for "Emma."

"We couldn't wait to hear what you'd have to say, your being an archeologist and all." Thus spake Fanny—"call me Fan. All me friends do."

"I couldn't believe my *ears* when that Chara Whatever-Her-Name-Is told us you'd actually be working *and* living on Samos!" exclaimed Donna, with an unashamed touch of envy. The tallest of the nurses, she was a raw-faced, sinewy woman, by far the most athletically built of the foursome.

"We may well run into you on Samos," burbled Em. "You see, once this cruise is over we'll be island-hopping by ferry for another three-and-a-half weeks!"

"*If*, that is," Donna reminded her somberly, "the ferries are up and running by then."

"Oh, Don, of course they shall! Why shouldn't they?" prattled an unruffled Em optimistically. "With all these islands, shipping routes are the roads of Greece." For Em, like Madge, was an irrepressible little bubble of enthusiasm.

And as an aside, the fourth member of the quartet, a mousey, waif-like woman called "Soph" (for Sophie, what else?), stage-whispered: "Don't mind Don, luv. She's a queer bird, she is. Likes to do things the 'ard way. You know . . . camp out with Bedouins in Morocco . . . climb the most difficult face of a mountain. *Those* sorts of things." She pretended to shudder, but it was obvious they all took great pride in their friend's exploits.

"Oh, but how fascinating!" crooned Madge, gazing at Donna with admiration.

"Last winter," Fan added, "when it was summer south of the equator, she kayaked the rapids of some nasty river way high in the Andes. *Imagine!*"

"Anyway," continued Em, "we had some questions about this temple, so we decided to ask Ms. Chara What's-er-Name, and *she* suggested—"

"—blew us off, you mean," grumbled Don.

"—we ask our resident archeologist," completed Em. "Meaning you, of course," she said, looking at Miranda hopefully.

Oh, did she now? Miranda thought to herself darkly, and lifted her sunglasses a few inches off her nose, the better to sweep the area with a squinty gaze.

But Chara Zouboulakis was nowhere to be seen; she'd most likely decamped to the air-conditioned comfort of the nearby taverna. No doubt dusting off her Chanel sneakers.

Replacing her glasses atop her nose, she realized the nurses must have caught her expression, because they took an uncertain step backward and made great pains to look apologetic.

"We didn't mean to be intrusive," Soph said awkwardly.

"Nonsense," Miranda told her brightly. "You just caught me off guard, that's all." Her lips formed a friendly smile. "I don't know how helpful I can be, but I'm honored and delighted to be asked."

"Really?" said Fan doubtfully.

"You mean it?" added Em, with concern.

"Of course I do," Miranda assured them staunchly. And catching Madge's eye, she saw her flash back a look of such pleasure and approval that it made going out of her way to be helpful more than worthwhile. Besides, she owed Madge; if it weren't for her, Miranda well knew, she wouldn't even be standing here. She did feel it important, however, to make one point perfectly clear. She tried to explain that, although she had earned her Ph.D. in the Classical Period of the Hellenistic Arts, she was really nothing more than a glorified salesperson in a high end gallery.

"Calling me an 'archeologist' is really stretching the truth. And as far as Samos is concerned," she confessed, "that will be my very first hands-on experience at a dig. Ever."

Never mind. She could have saved her breath. Why was it that in circumstances such as these, the more you try to be honest about your limited credentials, the more convinced people become of your expertise? Clearly, anything else she could say to try to dissuade them otherwise would be construed as humility on her part—a virtue Miranda was afraid she didn't exactly possess in abundance.

"Bosh!" exclaimed Em.

"Fiddlesticks!" added Fan.

Finally, realizing the futility of further disclaimers, Miranda went with the flow and let her little audience believe what they wanted. But she had to spend some moments speed-searching her mental files to dredge up what she remembered of Poseidon and his temple at Sounion, and collate what she recalled.

Being unprepared, she really didn't remember all that much.

Fine mess you got us into this time, Ollie, Stan Laurel's voice rebuked inside her head.

Miranda's audience was staring at her with such eager expectations that she felt a moment of asphyxiating panic. Then Madge, bless her heart, beamed another of her encouraging I-know-you-can-do-it! smiles. Cheerleading her, just as earlier Miranda had reassured her she could make the climb up.

What's good for the goose is good for the gander, Miranda thought, and felt she had to give it her best shot—if only for Madge.

Moving a few paces toward the temple, with Madge and the nurses trailing along, Miranda plucked up her courage, took a deep breath, and plunged.

"Poseidon," she began, "is always spoken of as the god of the sea. However, from earliest time, it was believed he was the fruitful earth as well as the sea on whose back the ancient mariners sailed. He was the brother of Zeus, and was often referred to as the 'Wave-Gatherer.' Interestingly, it was a widely held belief that he could appear in the guise of either a man or a horse. The horse image makes sense when you put it into context. You see, Poseidon was also called the Earth-Shaker, since he was the god people attributed to making the ground heave and quake through stamping and whinnying. Therefore, as he was supposedly responsible for causing earthquakes, his power was immense . . . "

She couldn't remember when or where she'd learned all this, or how she'd even retained it, but one sentence flowed smoothly into the next, and that one into yet another, each one nudging open yet another mental door she'd forgotten existed. Before long, the floodgates were open, and long-buried information spewed forth.

Madge and the nurses hung on her every word. They were truly fascinated.

"Naturally," Miranda continued, "the Hellenes, being a sea-faring people, inhabited both a mainland and islands that are highly susceptible to earthquakes. So is it any wonder that they should do their utmost to appease a god they believed possessed such awesome powers? Therefore, seeking his protection—"

Here Miranda paused and gestured dramatically at the Doric columns supporting the lengths of architrave.

"—they built mighty temples and altars to worship him and, presumably, remain in his good graces."

Her audience listened raptly. Several more of the *Meltemi II*'s group drifted toward her and tagged along to listen, but Miranda paid them scant attention. She was too caught up in ancient times for the here and now to register.

But how peculiar it felt, to hear such long-shelved knowledge issue forth from her very own lips—especially about a place she'd never before set foot on! To her own surprise, she heard herself saying things like: "It's been a long-held belief that the Parthenon in Athens, which is dedicated to the goddess Athena, the temple of Aphaea on the island of Aegina over there—" she pointed, she hoped, in the correct direction at the craggy, bluish haze rising distantly from the Saronic Gulf "—and this temple to Poseidon were positioned to form a perfect equilateral triangle. Today, however, we know that this is not really true . . ."

By the time Miranda exhausted what her brain had stored, she was greeted by a surprisingly loud round of enthusiastic applause. She blinked and gazed about, only now realizing that as she'd held forth, a veritable crowd—some of them strangers not from the *Meltemi II*—had gathered round to listen.

She could feel her face flush, not out of humility, but because she really didn't know whether or not she deserved such praise. Even more embarrassing was the fact that she actually had to decline several people who attempted to tip her by pressing some Euros in her hand!

She held up both hands. "No, no," she told them. "Thank you, but no. I'm not a professional tour guide."

However, as her audience dispersed, she felt the warm afterglow of satisfaction which came from a job well done; then, as if more validation was needed, the outdoorsy oncology nurse named Don flashed her a wide grin and gave a firm thumbs-up. But what Miranda savored most was Madge's reaction. Puffing out her breast like a proud mother, she beamed broadly out at the world, and purred, "Hurrah, Miranda! *Bravo!*"

Miranda was gratified to have done Madge Blessing proud; it was the very least she could do to repay her generosity.

With the impromptu guided tour finished, the group dispersed, the *Meltemi II*'s passengers starting toward the exit, and from there back downhill through thorn and scrub to the waiting "yacht." Being the visual glutton that she was, Miranda felt the need to linger a bit longer and soak in some solitary contemplation.

"Now you go on ahead and start back," she told Madge "I'll catch up with you in no time."

"Just don't tarry too long," Madge chirped. "Remember, they'll want to cast off as quickly as possible. I wouldn't want you to be left behind."

Miranda smiled. "Not to worry," she assured her blithely. And the instant Madge was gone, she greedily feasted her eyes some more on what Lord Byron had so lyrically waxed—"Sunium's marble steep."

She would have been content to stay there forever; Sounion had that strong an effect on her. However, the height of the day's heat was slackening, and the sun was a giant orange orb beginning to edge over towards the mountains of the Peloponnese, and she knew it was time to high-tail it. To make leaving easier, she made a silent vow to Poseidon that she would return time and again.

Then, not daring to tarry a second longer, she hurried downhill, speed-walking past the remnants of the *stoa*'s walls and what in ancient times had been the *propylaea,* or entrance, to the temple proper, her destination the admissions booth, which also served as the exit.

And that was when four angry women of various ages, who had been standing on either side just beyond the chain link fence, drew together to create a formidable phalanx, effectively barring Miranda's way out, each armed with a furled umbrella of a different color, but all with pointy ferrules, shiny and threatening, jabbing the air in front of her like swords.

A chill rippled along Miranda's spine. The women's hostility was no joke. And four umbrellas can become four highly potent weapons.

She had no idea what this was all about. She looked around for a familiar face. Perhaps someone could clue her in.

But the *Meltemi II*'s group was gone, and Chara Zouboulakis was nowhere to be seen.

"Is . . . is something the matter?" she asked hesitantly, in English.

"Yes, something is the matter!" snapped one of the women in heavily accented English.

She thrust herself forward, which Miranda took to mean she was appointing herself the spokesperson for the group. She was short and stout, with a helmet of carefully coiffed and hennaed hair and lively, inquisitive eyes. They were as large and dark and shiny as oil-cured Kalamata olives, and she had crow's feet which gave her a friendly look, although there was no friendliness in evidence at the moment. Her mouth was wide, her lipstick a shade too bright, but she took obvious pride in her appearance. She looked neat as a pin in her pistachio-colored pantsuit, and seemed what Miranda guessed would normally be the extroverted, rather lively type.

"Did you not see the sign?" the woman demanded ominously.

"Sign?" Miranda frowned. "Which sign?"

"*This* sign!" The woman took a step forward and Miranda instinctively shrank back. But instead of aiming the ferrule at her, the woman tapped it against the plexiglass of the admissions booth.

Miranda looked.

There, above eye level so as not to obstruct the cashier, a printed sign was taped to the inside.

Miranda groaned inwardly. Upon arrival, she had been so anxious to get inside the temple premises that reading posted notices had been the last thing on her mind. Yet there it was in black and white, like an accusation. In large crisp block letters and multiple languages—with English right at the top—sending a clear message:

TOURS BY LICENSED GUIDES ONLY!

"I myself," said the woman darkly, "and these good ladies are professional tour guides."

At that mention, the other three umbrella-wielding women all thrust out their bosoms and raised their chins as one.

"We earn the living by giving multilingual tours of this site. Do you notice the identification cards on our clotheses?" That was the way she pronounced it—"clothes-es"—using the double plural.

Miranda looked. Three of the women had laminated photo ID cards pinned to their blouses; the spokesperson had hers hanging from around her neck on a length of pistachio-colored ribbon.

"These cards are official licenses issued by the Ministry of Culture. The jobs are highly regarded and all applicants are carefully tested and screened. It is a stringent process and requires much classical education and study of languages."

Miranda swallowed, feeling miserable.

"The Ministry of Culture," added the woman grimly, "does not lightly tolerate unlicensed guides. That is most highly not legal and can resolt—" again, her pronunciation: 'resolt' "—in big problems."

"B-But—" Miranda stuttered.

The woman cut her off in mid-sputter. "I already explained to these good ladies that you were surely unaware of stealing their livings . . ."

Good Lord! Stealing their living! Depriving them of their rightful livelihood! At that instant, Miranda felt about two inches tall. What kind of monster was she, taking food out of the mouths of these women's families? Truly, she was the Ugly American, charging around the globe like a bull in a china shop, with nary a thought for how many toes were mashed.

And that was when Miranda had her epiphany. It was as if a sky of dark clouds parted, and the guilt that had been heaped upon her was swept away by a tide of red hot anger which started at the center of her chest and shot outward throughout her entire body.

Because sudden recall flashed in front of her:

. . . Complimentary Welcome Cocktails being served on the sundeck of the *Meltemi II* . . .

. . . Chara Zouboulakis in her curve-heeled Jimmy Choos trying to enlist her as an unofficial tour guide . . .

. . . and her own brilliant (or so Miranda had congratulated herself an hour or two earlier) way of ducking out of that one.

Then, not thirty minutes ago:

. . . The quartet of oncology nurses asking Chara Zouboulakis some questions about the site, only to be referred to . . . whom? One of these "good ladies" carrying their color-identifiable umbrellas?

Not on your life.

No, that scheming ice cold fashionista had sent Em & Co. to none other than Ms. Kalli!

Deliberately setting the trap. Most likely even pointing her out to these women.

And who had walked blindly right into the snare? Why, Mr. and Mrs. Kalli's little idjit, that's who!

But hindsight was always clearer than foresight. And at the moment, there was a situation that needed to be defused.

Two things were for certain. Miranda was damned if she was going to let Ms. Goldfoot set her up and hang her out to dry. Ditto the temptation of shifting the blame to Chara, who was nowhere in sight. Besides, Miranda had a secret weapon of her own. One didn't work at one of the most prestigious and important art galleries in Manhattan, where one had to deal with very, very rich and very, very demanding clients (who were *always* right), without learning a thing or two about soft-shoe diplomacy.

Into Miranda's mind her own voice played back a dozen or more past scenarios:

"Goodness, *Mrs. Villareal. You said it arrived with a* chip*? Of course we'll be only too glad to . . . I'm* so *sorry for having kept you waiting, Mr. de Bellano . . . It* still *hasn't arrived, Mrs. Javora? I'll look into it* straight *away . . .*"

Thus donning her Madison Avenue persona, Miranda faced the phalanx of women squarely. Arranged her face into a friendly and sincere expression and made eye contact with each in turn, reminding herself that these tour guides had been as victimized by Chara Zouboulakis as she herself.

"I'm terribly sorry for this misunderstanding," she told the spokeswoman of the four in a deferential voice. "I really had no idea what was happening. And yes, the fault is entirely mine. Do any of the other ladies speak English?"

Politeness had its desired effect. "Yes," replied one lady.

"I speak the English also," piped up another, with an air of multilingual pride.

"Besides speaking the Greek," the spokeswoman informed her, "one of my other two colleagues speaks the French and the Italian, and the other specializes in the Spanish and the German."

"I see." Miranda nodded. "In that case, I'd be ever so grateful if you could translate what I'm about to say so that they, too, may benefit from it."

There was a rapid-fire exchange in Greek. It was, Miranda thought, not the most musical of languages. The voices are too throaty and the tones too harsh and raspy. Nonetheless, four sets of dark eyes appraised Miranda with varying degrees of interest and . . . was she imagining it? . . . no, she definitely wasn't . . . with the slightest lowering of their sharp ferrules.

An auspicious sign.

Continuing to speak slowly and solemnly, Miranda took care to enunciate clearly. "This is a most unfortunate situation. I had no intention of trying to take any of your places as a tour guide. How could I?"

She paused while her words were translated into Greek: another staccato barrage of harsh sounds.

"I only arrived here this morning," Miranda explained. "This is my first visit to Greece. I came up here like everyone else, to enjoy this splendid sight. I had no desire to infringe upon anyone's livelihood in the process. If I inadvertently did so, I offer you my most sincere apologies."

As this underwent translation, the other women listened intently. One of them had a question, which their spokesperson translated: "My colleague asks where you are from?"

"New York City."

A smile reached the Kalamata eyes, crinkling the crow's feet. "Ah, New York! I have a sister there. In Astoria, Queens. But I am sorry, I did not interpret the question precisely enough. My friend means *here.* Are you with a group? Or are you traveling by yourself?"

"Oh. I'm with that . . . er . . . little cruise ship down there?" Miranda gestured to the bay below.

Four faces craned their necks, four sets of eyes searched the sheltered, vessel-crowded bay. One of the women grumbled something, and Miranda was asked, "Cruise ship? My friend says she does not see a cruise ship."

Miranda put herself in their shoes, looking at it from their points of view: cruise ships were apparently humongous floating cities. Big and white and shiny.

"Um, it's that . . . er . . . that large caique with the reddish-brown sails?" She pointed down. "There. The largest one? With the bright green decks?"

Upon translation, one guide twisted her lips; another murmured something and gestured dismissively. A third looked at Miranda with something approaching pity. "*Panagia mou!*" she spat.

"*Panagia mou?*" Miranda asked, with interest. "What does that mean?"

The leader of the group smiled. "It is not a nice term. "It is better that I do not interpret it. I am certain you shall find out soon enough."

"Yes, but those *Meltemis!*" the other grumped, shaking a fist. "Those three boats come here and never hire a guide. *Never!*"

Miranda could feel the hostility level undergo a dramatic decrease. In fact, she could almost *hear* it deflate, like air hissing out of a punctured balloon.

For the first time since facing the women, she felt herself relax. Apparently she'd been successful in getting her message across: that no matter what they'd been told, she was no threat to them.

To hammer that point home once and for all, she repeated, "Again, I wish to reiterate that I hope you'll pardon my naivité. Apparently some of my fellow passengers had some questions, and someone else from the boat steered them my way. Before I knew what was happening, more people joined us." She shook her head in bewilderment. "I don't know where some of them came from."

"Yes, that happens to us also. People hear someone guiding a tour in their language, and they, how do you say . . . ?"

"Tag along," Miranda supplied dryly.

"Tag along. Yes. They want a tour without paying for it. We find them quite irritating."

One of the non-English speaking guides had another question.

"My colleague tells me you seem to have held the people spellbound. She asks, how it is that you know so much about this site?"

"Actually, I know very little," Miranda confessed, explaining that she had majored in Classical Greek archeology, and had been invited to participate in a dig on Samos.

"This will be my very first experience in the field," she added, lest she sounded too boastful. "But it was an offer I couldn't refuse."

More translating. Any remnants of hostility were gone; all those bad vibes had vanished into thin air. The umbrellas were down, ferrules resting on parched earth, and used like canes to take pressure off weary feet. The foursome was clearly impressed by her destination and credentials. Not only had ruffled feathers been smoothed; the women suddenly became downright friendly.

Miranda glanced at her Swatch watch. "And now, if you'll pardon my rudeness, I'd best be on my way. Before the boat sails off without me."

The spokeswoman was understanding. "Despite our little unpleasantness," she said, "it has been a pleasure meeting you. On behalf of my colleagues, I too wish to apologize for our behavior. And please, do not use judge all Greek women by this unfortunate incident. Yes?" She eyed Miranda anxiously.

Miranda smiled and promised she wouldn't, and while they didn't part with hugs and kisses, the phalanx of women parted and the goodbyes were warm and friendly. She was no longer the Ugly American, and was glad.

When she reached the junction where the treacherous path forked off from the asphalt road, Miranda could see a miniaturized Madge down beyond the water tank on which the word "NUDISTS" and its accompanying arrow had been spray painted. Her friend was looking anxiously uphill, searching for a sign of her. And further below, the rigid inflatables were already ferrying the *Meltemi II*'s group back to the ship.

Miranda waved and hurried on down, half-sliding and sending a small avalanche of dirt and small stones downhill. Once she caught up with her, Madge said, "Goodness me. You had me quite worried, Miranda. For a while there, I was afraid you weren't coming. Whatever kept you?"

Miranda gave a wry smile. "Oh, you know," she said breezily, shrugging off the unpleasantness that had occurred. "Making friends, influencing people . . ."

Madge raised one intrigued eyebrow, but since Miranda didn't elaborate, she let it go. Without further ado, they quickly but carefully picked their way down the rest of that steep, gully-like path in single file.

[CHAPTER EIGHTEEN]

At Sea

The chatter of voices, clinking of glassware and inevitable strum and beat of recorded *bouzouki* billowed out from the ship's lounge as Madge and Miranda made their way up the steep, stamped steel steps. From the galley wafted the aromas of olive oil and basil, fish and pork.

"You're sure I'm presentable?" Madge asked anxiously, stopping at the top of the steps and patting her hair for one last inspection.

Miranda looked her over. Madge Blessing was turned out in a sensible, lightweight, wash-and-wear jacket the color of butterscotch with a matching skirt that reached just below the kneecaps. For contrast, she had on a high-necked blouse the color of terra-cotta, and pinned to one lapel of the jacket was the inevitable costume jewelry brooch, in this case a gold-tone starfish sprinkled with tiny blue aquamarine-colored stones.

"You look very ladylike," Miranda assured her.

"Too dressy, you think?" fretted Madge. "Or too under-dressed for the Captain's welcome dinner?"

Miranda laughed. "Madge! This isn't exactly the *Queen Mary II.* You look *splendid.* Really. I mean, look at me." She pinched the three-quarter-length sleeve of her bold, vertically striped top. "Straight off-the-rack Gap. And you saw how the others dress. Now stop worrying."

"Well, if you say so," Madge said reluctantly.

"I do. Now let's go in and, to use your term, wet our whistles, shall we?"

Madge needed no further encouragement. "You lead the way, dear, why don't you?"

The lounge had been transformed into a festive dining room. The simple glossy pine paneling gleamed richly in the glow of the wall-and-ceiling mounted lights, the tables had been covered with white paper "cloths," and place settings had been neatly laid. The thick, inexpensive white china shone and the stainless flatware could almost have been mistaken for silver. For centerpieces, each of the four large tables held pots of fragrant live basil, and with the blue curtained windows looking out upon the darkening sky and gentle swells, the atmosphere was positively enchanting.

Most of the group was already seated, sipping white wine.

Dimitris, serving double duty as headwaiter, greeted them warmly. "*Kyría* Blessing. *Despiní* Kalli." He inclined his head slightly. "I have reserved a special spot for you by a window. I have placed all the English-speaking people at the same table."

They followed him, Madge nudging Miranda and whispering, "Isn't he attractive? And so *nice!*"

The others were already seated there: the four pediatric oncology nurses, chattering away, and the Goth punk couple, who looked sullen but most likely were, Miranda guessed, for all their tough exterior in truth very shy. Chairs were scooted in and Miranda and Madge squeezed past and took their seats on the banquette. There was still one empty seat at the head of the table.

"Oh, this is so *heavenly!*" Madge purred with pleasure. "Isn't it, Miranda?"

"We're all of the opinion that Miranda is heavenly!" burbled Em as a crew member, making the rounds, filled their wine glasses from a carafe and topped off the glasses of the others. "Don't we, mates?"

There was a chorus of agreement and glasses were raised. "To Miranda!" Fan toasted.

"To Miranda!" the others chorused in unison.

"Your impromptu tour was exceptional," added Don. "I don't know what we would have done without you."

"Oracle Cruises really could have organized a better sight-seeing package," said Soph.

Miranda accepted their praise graciously and dipped her nose into her wineglass and sipped. There was no use bursting their bubbles by recounting the drama that had ensued with the tour guide ladies, and she held her tongue, not wanting to spoil the jolly atmosphere.

Chara Zouboulakis, having changed into a gold top, floppy white linen pants and gold sandals, strolled through, stopping at table after table. Using a fingertip to move aside a stray shaft of her silken hair, she looked at Miranda. "Did you enjoy the temple, Ms. Kalli?" she inquired, her face expressionless.

Miranda smiled, not about to give her the satisfaction of knowing she'd walked into her trap. "It was fantastic!" she waxed enthusiastically. "I'd only seen photographs of it, but in reality . . . well, nothing ever prepares one for the real thing, does it? I can't wait to return."

"Really. How very nice for you."

And Chara continued on.

"For some reason," whispered Em, "I'm really not all that fond of that woman."

Midships in the lounge-cum-dining room, Chara tapped a spoon against a glass to get everyone's attention. The conversations quickly dwindled until only the *bouzouki* soundtrack and the steady thrumming of the diesel engines could be heard.

"*Kiría e Kirie,* Ladies and gentlemen, *meine Damen und Herren.* It is my pleasure to introduce to you the master of this vessel. May I present Captain Aris Leonides."

She stepped aside as he made his appearance.

Miranda craned her neck, as did most of the other diners. She half-expected a bearded sea-dog, or someone befitting the outward appearances of the *Meltemi II:* rotund, grizzled, and Zorba-like.

Instead, she was pleasantly surprised.

He wasn't a particularly tall man: almost boyishly good-looking, somewhere in his mid-forties, and with slightly receding dark hair. His skin was olive, his physique athletic, and he had dark eyes that exuded warmth and confidence. His features were neither soft nor chiseled, but somewhere in-between. Verging on the handsome, though not quite reaching cinematic star status. His starched white uniform was crisp, with gold stripes on black epaulets.

He looked capable and trustworthy and every inch the captain of a ship.

Gallantly, he stopped at each table and exchanged a few words with everyone. Finally he approached Miranda's.

"I hope you do not mind," he said with a wink toward Madge as he pulled out the one remaining chair at the head, "but this is the captain's table."

"Mind!" Madge burbled, clasping her hands to her bosom. "We're thrilled! Aren't we?" She glanced around the table, and everyone was smiling, grinning, and welcoming him. Even the Goth couple couldn't quite keep up their appearance of bored nonchalance.

Small talk ensued. Madge turned to Miranda and said softly, "I don't know if I warned you, dear. The cruise only includes half fare. That means breakfast and dinner. For lunch we have to fend for ourselves."

Miranda smiled. "It's far more than I expected."

And then plates of food began to arrive in quick succession. A multitude of Greek dishes, a feast by any standards was laid out. Kalamata olives, a loaf of crusty, sliced white bread, *tzatziki,* carp roe spread, mashed fava beans, fried smelts, little meatballs, moussaka, lamb-stuffed grape leaves, and octopus salad.

Don, the most adventuresome of the nurses, was the first to dig in, helping herself to a spoonful of everything and attacking the delicacies with gusto. The other nurses followed suit. The Goth punk couple sniffed, and slowly ventured for some moussaka. And Madge sat there, uncharacteristically stiff and pale, staring at the octopus salad.

"Is something the matter?" Miranda asked.

"Oh . . . oh, dear . . . " Madge turned to her in distress. "Goodness. Are those . . . " she pointed tentatively at the small purplish bits of chopped tentacles " . . . those little round things *suckers?*"

"Indeed they are," Miranda said, scooping a spoonful onto her own plate. "It's octopus. Or octopi, if you will. Really, you ought to try some." She tasted a forkful herself and smacked her lips. "Delicious! Really, Madge, you ought to try it."

"I . . . I think I'll start with some bread," Madge said faintly, and broke off a piece.

"Did you know," said Captain Leonides, "that octopi are very gentle creatures? The mothers are very attentive. If their young are in danger of starvation, she will actually bite off one or two of her tentacles to feed them?"

Madge looked even more distressed.

"You needn't worry," he assured her. "The tentacles grow back."

"Aw, come on. At least try some of the smelts," Em urged.

Madge peered at the plate of small fried fish with suspicion. "They . . . they still have their heads on!" She swiftly downed half a glass of wine.

"Madge," Miranda cajoled, "at least try some of the spreads. As they say, 'When in Rome . . . '"

"The *tzatziki* is nothing but yogurt, cucumbers and garlic," Don said briskly, between mouthfuls. "And sometimes contains mint as well. The Turkish influence, I imagine."

"Well . . . yes," Madge demurred. "Alright."

Don reached out, snatched Madge's slice of bread from her hands, spread it liberally with *tzatziki,* and handed it back.

"And the meatballs," Miranda added, "are nothing more than spiced hamburger. Perhaps lamb instead of beef. But honestly, Madge. They're better than meatballs."

She paused and added, "At any rate, better than a Quarter Pounder."

Captain Leonides eyed Miranda with interest. "Ah, you are familiar with Greek cooking?" he asked.

Miranda smiled at him. "My father came from a Greek family."

"Where was he from?"

"California."

He smiled. "In Greece, when we ask where someone is from, we mean what part of Greece the family is from. Or what island."

"Oh." She had to think back hard. "Daddy, that is, my father, didn't talk much about the family history. They were estranged after he married Mom." And then something in her mind clicked. "Oh. I remember now. Lefkas? Am I pronouncing it correctly?"

"Indeed you are. Lefkas is in the Ionian. An island above Kephalonia. A few islands below Corfu."

"And you, Captain? Where are you from?"

"Andros. Just one island above Mykonos." He looked intrigued. "So, your father introduced you to Greek cuisine?"

"Yes. And my Mom? She was from the Midwest. Daddy always accused her of cooking from the *old* Betty Crocker cookbook."

At which Madge, devouring the *tzatziki*-spread bread, cracked up and almost spewed a mouthful.

"And in New York," Miranda continued, "my fiancé, Harry, was always trying out various ethnic cuisines. Oh, shi—" She broke off in mid-word and slapped herself on the forehead.

The others laughed heartily.

"You can say the word, luv," Fran chuckled. "It's nothing we 'aven't 'eard before."

Even the punk rocker nudged the Goth girl, who cracked a tentative smile. The ice between the pierced and the non-pierced had definitely been broken.

"No, it's not that." Miranda grabbed her bag and rummaged furiously through it until she came up with her cell phone. "It's my fiancé. Harry. I promised him I'd call."

"*Panagia mou!*" she added, remembering the word one of the tour guides had used.

Captain Leonides grinned, his teeth straight and white and perfect. "It seems you are picking up some . . . ah . . . rather choice Greek words," he commented, with amusement.

Miranda pulled a face. "Sorry. But I completely forgot to call Harry and explain everything. My departure was rather, well, rather unexpected and abrupt." She consulted her Swatch Watch. "Let me see. The time difference between here and New York is . . . ?"

"Seven hours," Captain Leonides supplied, without hesitation. "It is earlier there."

"That means it's nearly one o'clock in the afternoon. Lunch time." *No better time to catch him.* She started to rise. "Could you all please excuse me for a few minutes? I despise being rude, but I'd better go do this out on deck, where it's private."

She rose and squeezed past the chairs. Captain Leonides rose like a gentleman, then sat back down and she slid open the half-glazed door to the aft deck, went outside, and slid it gently shut behind her.

There was light outside: a string of clear, brightly lit bulbs had been strung from the stern to the topmost mast. The air had cooled considerably, with a breeze coming from the north that tugged at her hair. For some reason, she was more aware of the dips and yaws of the vessel out here than she had been inside, and the steady hum and beat of the diesel engines and the vibrations of the deck were more pronounced. Lulling waves splashed gently against the hull and the air smelled of salt. In the far distance, the sun had disappeared behind the mountains of the Peloponnese, and phosphorescence glowed dimly on the long white wake the *Meltemi II* left behind.

Flipping open her tiny phone, she scanned Harry's various numbers. Home, cell, office, Blackberry—

Aha.

—Blackberry. For like his American Express card, she knew he never left home or office without it. A single press of a tiny key and she dialed.

Ether and static crackled in her ear, then she could hear the faraway tones of a telephone ringing. Once, twice, thrice, then a fourth time and—

"*Hellooo-ooo,*" crooned a woman's unfamiliar voice.

Miranda frowned. Woman? What woman? Obviously she must have pressed the wrong key. Either that, or she'd gotten a crossed connection. It happened sometimes.

"I-I'm sorry," she said, somewhat flustered. "I must have dialed the wrong number."

"Who are you trying to call?" the woman asked.

"I thought it was Harry Palmer's line," Miranda said apologetically. "I've evidently got the wrong number. I'm so sorry."

"Oh, don't be," the voice assured her. "You've got the correct number. Harry . . . " there was a pause " . . . well, Harry is, er, how should I put it? Temporarily indisposed."

Miranda's guard immediately went up. "Who *is* this?" she demanded.

"Sweetheart, I don't think you really want to know. I take it I'm speaking to the much-talked-about Miranda?"

"Y-yes . . . "

"Well, you needn't worry about Harry, sweetheart." There was a pause and a chuckle. "I'm personally making sure he's being *very* well taken care of."

Slowly Miranda lowered the phone. Her hands were trembling badly, and it was all she could do to snap the accursed little cell phone shut, severing the connection. Even above the steady throbbing of the diesels and the splashing of the waves, the strange woman's voice kept reverberating in her ears.

It was as if the snap of a hypnotist's fingers had sent her into a nightmarish trance. Her chest felt tight, so constricted that she could barely breathe. From deep within her, a sob rose to her throat, and her hands twitched, almost dropping the cell phone. Her eyes stung with tears.

Harry.

How could *he?*

Or . . . had he been seeing someone else all along?

She clutched the wooden railing with one hand and shut her eyes. Her body felt, but didn't register, the sudden trough which sent a mist of salt spray across her face.

Harry.

Harris Milford Palmer III.

Harry, her supposed fiancé—

Betrayal stung like salt in an open wound. Savagely, she thrust the cell phone into her pocket, then worried her engagement ring, twisting it back and forth on her finger until she'd worked it loose. She glared at the Tiffany diamond flashing white and blue shards. DeBeers' famous ad line, *A Diamond is Forever,* sprang into her mind.

Forever, my ass! she thought angrily. And lifting her arm she swung it backward to fling the damned bauble into the sea. Only long-ago words of her mother's stayed her throw.

"*A lady* always *returns an engagement ring,*" she remembered her mother once remarking, scandalized after a neighbor broke off her engagement and kept the ring.

Slowly Miranda let her arm fall to her side. She thrust the ring into her pocket along with the cell phone. Told herself to get a grip. Took a series of deep salty breaths tinged with the unmistakable undertone of diesel fuel. Wiped the moisture from her eyes with her fingertips.

Then, squaring her shoulders, she tried to put her best face forward as she went back inside to join the others, but flinched against the laughter and happy chatter and *bouzouki* that assailed her. Numbly she pushed her way past Chara Zouboulakis, who was wearing her invisible professional hat while slowly patrolling the aisle of the lounge, keeping an eye on the level of service.

"Everything alright, sweet'eart?" Em asked as Miranda blundered leadenly past the chairs Don and Em scooted in to let her past to the banquette in front of the window. "Did you get through?"

Get through? Miranda thought dully. *Get through to what?* And then she remembered. Of course. Em meant the telephone call.

"Yes, without any problem," she murmured.

"I've taken the liberty of filling your plate," Fran poined out heartily. "I hope you don't mind?"

"No, of course not. It was terribly kind of you."

But Miranda stared desultorily at her plate which, while she had been outside, had been heaped with a few bites of everything. She had lost her appetite, but for Fan's sake and the others, she lifted her fork and began to push food around, pretending to eat.

"Is something wrong, dear?" Madge inquired softly, with concern.

"Oh. No," Miranda lied, much as the effort cost her. "Not at all." She could not bear to reveal the truth.

But of course, everything was wrong. One phone call, and her world had been turned upside down. The griffon had reared its ugly head. *Betrayal, delusion, false pretenses, deceit.* She flashed back upon all the nights Harry supposedly spent out with his fellow Yalies. Getting pie-eyed. Carousing around? Playing musical beds?

She'd never questioned Harry's nights out with "the boys" before. It had never even occurred to her.

So much for monogamy, she thought dully.

Captain Leonides motioned to Chara and said something in Greek. Chara gave Miranda a quick look, nodded, and went forward. Within a minute, Dimitris appeared with a snifter containing several fingers of brandy.

The captain took it and handed it across the table to Miranda.

She looked at him curiously.

"This is . . . how do you say?" he asked gently. "On the house?"

He had seen through her transparent masquerade and surmised . . . no, *knew* she was in mental and physical agony.

So much for pretenses. *Some poker player I'd make.*

She accepted the snifter gratefully, quaffed half of it in a single swallow. The brandy burned her throat like liquid fire, then radiated warmth outward from her stomach. Liquid courage, they called it, didn't they? Legal morphine for a hollow heart. She drank some more, perked up a bit, even managed to put in a word here and there and eat a bite or two.

But it did nothing to alleviate the deadness within.

"Feeling better?" Captain Leonides asked solicitously.

"Yes, lots. Thank you, Captain. When I was outside, the rolling motions of the vessel seemed . . . well, more pronounced. I'm fine now. Honestly."

He nodded, accepting the fiction with grace. "The next time you travel by sea, might I suggest scopolamine patches? They work far better than Dramamine."

Miranda had to hand it to him. His face was friendly and outwardly guileless, but Miranda could tell by the expression in his eyes that he knew she'd suffered not a bout of sea-sickness, but a severe personal shock.

"Feelin' a bit queasy, are we?" said Em.

"I was. Yes. I'm feeling much better already. But it's been an awfully long day. First the eleven-hour flight, then stopping at Sounion. Plus there's the time difference and jet lag. Quite frankly, I better turn in early. I'm quite exhausted and can use the rest. Now if you'll all be so kind and excuse me, I think I'll call it an early night."

"But we're going to be taught traditional Greek dances up on deck after dinner!" Fan cried. "I'd hate for you to miss out on it."

"So do I, Fan. Unfortunately, this body needs rest."

And to set their minds at rest, she joked weakly: "Besides, a girl needs her beauty sleep."

Miranda got up, the Captain rose politely, and Don and Em scooted their ladder-back chairs back in and hunched forward to let her pass and then scooted them back out again.

"Want me to go with you, dear?" Madge fussed, starting to rise.

"Oh, for heaven's sake, no. I wouldn't hear of it. You stay put, Madge, and enjoy yourself. I'll be fine and you're in very good hands. Really."

"Well, if you're sure . . . " Madge said hesitantly.

"I am." Miranda turned to the master of the ship. "I can't thank you enough for the brandy, Captain Leonides. It's worked wonders. The next time I travel by sea I'll certainly heed your advice and take along some scopolamine patches."

Miranda went forward and down the steel steps to Cabin 12, her plastic key card in hand.

She didn't need it. The cabin door was cracked, emitting bright light from within, and she could hear a scraping sound. Pushing it wider, she found Chara Zouboulakis inside, bent forward over the lowermost bunk.

As though caught in a criminal act, Chara straightened abruptly and turned around. "Oh. Ms. Kalli. You gave me quite a fright. I'm just in the process of turning down the beds. It happens to be one of my many duties."

But a scarlet flush had risen from her neck and suffused her bronzed face. Miranda caught the look of guilt as Chara's eyes slid away and she turned around again, ostensibly to resume what she hadn't yet begun. And it was then, when Miranda noticed the toe of one of Chara's gold stilettos with their multiple ankle straps furtively nudging one of her yellow nylon bags further under the lower bunk that the explanation of that guilty look fell into place.

Admittedly, Ms. Zouboulaki's duties consisted of multi-tasking, but Miranda clearly remembered shoving her two bags as far back under Madge's bunk as possible. And so far, even the open waters of the Aegean were proving rather gentle, Miranda's lie about seasickness notwithstanding; outwardly appearances aside, the *Meltemi II* was demonstrating herself to be a sturdy little ship. Surely those slight motions weren't enough to have caused the bag to slide forward on its own. Besides which, wouldn't the turning down of beds be the task of a lowlier crew member? And wasn't the *Meltemi II*'s resident fashionista supposed to be on the deck above, supervising the serving of dinner and dessert rather than potentially ruining her perfect manicure?

She waited until Chara had turned down the bunks. When she finished, she turned back around to face Miranda. The flush had receded and the perfect snowy white teeth flashed what passed for a smile.

"There. Now you should be comfortable, Ms. Kalli." As soon as Chara closed the door behind her, Miranda squatted on her haunches, pulled out the yellow bag, and unzipped it. She took out her rolled up pajamas. Despite the shock she'd suffered from making the phone call, and the wine and brandy she'd consumed, suspicions lurked deeply in her mind. She ascertained that it might behoove her to give the rest of the bag's contents a cursory check.

Everything appeared undisturbed. Everything, that was, except for Professor Hirsch's letter, which Miranda had tucked into a zipped side pocket. She distinctly remembered . . . or was her imagination playing tricks on her? . . . that she'd tucked the flap of the envelope inside the opening. But the flap was on the outside of the envelope.

Shoving the bag back beneath the bunk, she wondered whether or not she'd been mistaken. Perhaps her memory was too fuzzed and she was seeing a mountain where there wasn't even a mole hill?

She changed into her striped pajamas, brushed her teeth in the little head, and began to climb up into her bunk. She unstrapped her watch and placed it on the little shelf beside the top bunk.

There was a tentative knock on the cabin door. Most likely Madge, she thought, either checking up on her or else calling it a night also.

"Yes?" she called out. "I'm decent."

Another knock.

With a sigh, Miranda climbed back down and opened the door. Chara had returned. She was standing in the doorway, two coin-sized chocolates wrapped in shiny silver foil in one hand, and a snifter of brandy in the other.

"I am so sorry to bother you again, Ms. Kalli, but I forgot to place the mints on the pillows. The brandy is compliments of Captain Leonides."

Miranda accepted the mints and the brandy. "That's very kind of you, Ms. Zouboulakis. Thank you. There's no need to trouble yourself. I'll personally place the mints on the pillows myself." She paused, adding more firmly: "It's been a long two days of travel, and I'm ready to go to sleep now. Please convey my thanks to the good captain for me. And thank you again, Ms. Zouboulakis, and good night."

[CHAPTER NINETEEN]

New York City

The maître d' of the Gotham Bar and Grill greeted Harry with that mixture of obsequiousness and genuine friendliness reserved for a favored customer. "Miss Pfeiffer," he murmured discreetly, "is already here. If you will come this way, please."

Even at this early hour, the high-ceilinged restaurant was packed. Harry followed him past the long rows of banquettes and white-draped tables with little flower arrangements on each.

"Here we are," the captain said, having led him away from the madding crowd to one of the many intimate nooks and crannies reserved for intimate dining.

Harry cursed under his breath. *I should have known,* he thought dismally. *She would ask for the most private table in the house.*

"Harry!" Tiffany greeted brightly. She set down the litchi-lemon cooler she was sipping and held up her cheek for the requisite kiss.

Having no choice, he went through the perfunctory motions as the captain held the table away, then sat down opposite her. She hadn't missed a trick. Tiffany was no longer in her Wall Street business suit; she'd taken the time to sprint uptown, change, and hurry back. Or did she keep a set of evening wear in the office, or at whatever health club she frequented in order to keep up her slender, athletic physique? Her cascade of Bergdorf blond gleamed softly, covering half her face, her makeup was freshly applied and she wore a little black cocktail dress with a plunging neckline. A thin gold necklace with a charm at the end hung from her throat down into the cleft of her bosom, matching her little dangling earrings.

"I see you look-ee," she said, elbows on the table. "You lik-ee?"

Before he could reply, a waiter drifted over at once. "A cocktail?" he suggested.

Harry was tempted to order a vodka neat. A double, in fact. Better yet, a triple. But he was determined to stay stone sober and out of Tiffany's clutches. All he wanted was his Blackberry back. "I'll have a glass of sparkling water."

"Harry!" Tiffany pouted. "Is that any way to start a date?"

You mean, an expensive ransom dinner, he wanted to correct her, but didn't. "You're looking good, Tiffany," he said.

She eyed him over her glass of litchi-lemon cooler. "Only good? Is that all the compliment a girl gets? 'Good' is a weak word, Harry. Same as 'nice.'"

But Harris Milford Palmer III wasn't going to walk into that trap, either. He'd have had to be blind to—or snockered to the gills.

"Aw, Harry," she said in her husky, most seductive tone. "You're not going to hold it against me, my throwing you out stark naked, are you?"

He shaped his lips into a smile. "I never hold grudges, Tiff," he lied smoothly. "They're a waste of time."

"Great." She perked up and her smiled broadened. "Then we understand each other."

The waiter brought his sparkling water and set it on the table with a flourish. Harry lifted the glass. "To you," he told Tiffany.

"To *us*," she corrected, with that meaningful look Cleopatra had invented, but Tiffany had perfected. She clinked her glass against his.

The waiter hovered discreetly and cleared his throat. "Would you care for anything else, Mr. Palmer?"

"Yes. The menu, please. And the wine list."

There was a slight awkward pause. "Ms. Pfeiffer has already ordered for both of you."

"Did she? I see. That will be all for now, then. I'm fine, thank you."

Harry looked inquiringly over at Tiffany, who was gazing at him under half-lowered lashes. "You needn't look at me like that, Harry. I know your tastes." Her voice was transparent, filled with double-entendres.

"Besides," she added lightly, "you owe me, Harry. Nobody shares my bed without satisfying me one way or another."

It didn't take a genius to figure that this was a revenge dinner, even if in this particular case, the revenge was not exactly a dish served cold.

Harry resigned himself to the first course, black bass ceviche, a towering artistic concoction of avocado mousse served with habanero pepper and orange emulsion. The waiter brought an ice bucket on a stand, and the wine steward appeared with a bottle of 2002 Patz & Hall Napa Valley, which Harry was certain would set him back a half-day's earnings.

Tiffany was obviously making him pay for last night's lack of sexual attentions.

Harry covered his wineglass with his hand. "None for me, thank you," he told the steward. "The lady may do the honors."

Tiffany approved the bottle, the steward uncorked it, and poured a splash into her glass. She swirled it around, sniffed the aroma, made a production of tasting it. At last she nodded her approval.

"Yum yum," she said approvingly, and let the waiter fill her glass half-full, before placing the bottle carefully into the cooler. She looked over at Harry. "You really ought to try it. Pure ambrosia, Harry."

"I prefer to be sober," he said.

She tilted her head sideways. "Sure you haven't joined a twelve-step program, Harry?" she teased.

"For tonight," he said without expression, "yes."

"Ah," she teased. "You want to make sure you get it up, Mr. Stiffy, is that it?"

He pushed his ceviche around on his plate, pretending to nibble a piece or two. It was delicious, but he had no appetite. All he could think of was how much it was costing him to retrieve his Blackberry.

"Seafood," Tiffany said suggestively, between taking tiny lady-like bites, "is supposed to be an aphrodisiac. Or should I have ordered you the oysters?" Her pale eyes were bright with a predatory, carnal gleam.

He didn't reply, but kept his expression neutral.

A busboy whisked away the appetizer plates. At this point, Tiffany had consumed half the bottle of Patz & Hall, and was feeling no pain. The wine steward arrived with a bottle of 1953 Haut-Brion, and Harry had to fight to control his rising anger. There went another thousand, seven hundred and fifty dollars down the drain.

Oh, she was out for blood alright.

Tiffany inspected the label and once again the ritual of uncorking the precious bottle was repeated, and once again she went through the motions of swirling and sniffing and tasting. At last she smiled her approval and nodded.

Harry covered his wineglass with his hand. "I'm in best form when I'm not drinking," he whispered across the table at her. *Two,* he decided, *can play this game as well as one.*

"Good for you. And even better for me." She smiled widely. She'd slipped off one shoe, and he felt a stockinged foot slowly crawling, spider-like, up his right leg until it reached his crotch.

With a flourish, the waiter arrived with the main courses. Porcini Crusted Halibut for her, and a steak for him.

Tiffany gestured with her fork. "Notice, Harry. I ordered you the grilled New York steak. Rare, the way you like it. With marrow mustard and Vidalia onion rings and Bordelaise sauce."

She added, with emphasis: *"Manfood.* Plenty of protein there. Natural Viagra. Need to make sure you keep your energy up." She winked lewdly.

"Could you excuse me for a moment?" Harry asked politely. Gently he removed her foot and scooted back his chair as she dipped her nose into thevintage red and drained half the glass. "I have to see a man about a horse."

"Be my guest." She set her glass down and ran the tip of her tongue across her upper lip. "Just don't be too long. You don't want to let your food get cold."

"I won't."

He leaned across at her, brushed her cheek with a Judas kiss, and smiled endearingly. So endearingly that she didn't notice him deftly lifting her little black purse that she'd looped to the back of her chair by its little gold chain.

"Won't be but a jiff," he assured her. And palming her purse and wrapping the little chain around it, he took it with him to the Men's Room downstairs. The beautifully tiled walls escaped his notice; he'd seen them plenty of times on plenty of better occasions. At the moment, one, and only one, thing was on Harry Milford Palmer III's mind.

Locking himself inside a stall, he sat on the closed toilet seat and opened her little bag.

And *Hello!* There it was. His Blackberry.

His.

Either Tiffany had retrieved it when she'd gone home to change, or else she'd had it with her all day long. Neither of which mattered at this point. The important thing was, he had it back. Everything else could wait.

Snatching it, he quickly scrolled for messages and calls. None were from Miranda. A sudden bolt of inspiration hit him, and he accessed the Delete File. And sure enough, there it was. Right at the very top. A call from Miranda . . . a call which Tiffany Pfeiffer had obviously deleted—had in all likelihood even intercepted.

The *bitch!* The fucking *bitch!* A surge of anger, red-hot and suffocating, shot through him like an intravenous injection. But he managed to control it. What was done was done. There was plenty of time to deal with that later. In the meantime, damage control was called for.

Quickly he daubed tiny keys and auto-dialed Miranda's cell number. Instead of an answer, her voice mail clicked in. He listened to the recording and waited until there was a beep. "Mandy, this is Harry," he said. Then, remembering Ron's advice, he was quick to amend his nickname for her: "*Miranda,* sweetheart," he began over, "this is Harry. What's the matter? I'm worried as all hell. Please call me and fill me in on what's going on. I miss you something terrible. Somehow my Blackberry was hijacked, but that's a long story I can't go into right now." He paused, adding softly: "I love you."

Daubing another key, he left his call-back number and pocketed his Blackberry in his suit jacket. But he didn't leave the toilet stall just yet. For long seconds he pondered the matter of ethics. Did two wrongs make a right? And where did a gentleman's behavior end, and a heel's begin?

The men's room door opened as someone else entered, humming a tune. Harry could hear the sound of a zipper, then the splash of urine in ceramic. Finally another zip, the flush of a urinal, footsteps, and the splashing of water as hands were washed.

At long last the door closed again and he was alone.

He had come to a decision. *The hell with ethics and being a gentleman. It was high time Tiffany Pfeiffer had a taste of her own medicine.*

Rummaging through her little purse, he found her wallet. There was plastic galore—gold and platinum, plus credit cards from various high-end retailers. Cash. Driver's license, lipstick . . .

He didn't count the cash. He wasn't a thief. But it was time Tiffany Pfeiffer learned a lesson she wouldn't soon forget. She had it coming.

So he'd make an enemy for life. So what? It wasn't as if they were friends. Their positions at work were identical. Luckily, neither held power over the other, and he didn't need to worry about getting a pink slip at whim. In fact, he knew who was in the driver's seat. His hedge fund was burgeoning with profits, while hers was hemorrhaging money—most likely due to overindulging her overactive libido, not to mention her appetite for expensive wines instead of pulling in the required overtime.

From her wallet he chose an American Express platinum card—making certain it was her personal account rather than the company's. Slipped it into his wallet. Flushed the toilet for good measure, then washed his hands with Pilate water and sprinted up the stairs two at a time.

Feeling better than he had in days.

Returning to the table, he smiled and said, "I'm ba-ack," diverting Tiffany's attention by pecking the nape of her neck with another Judas kiss as he looped the little gold chain of her purse exactly from where he had lifted it. Resuming his seat, he noted that in his absence one of the restaurant's staff had carefully refolded his napkin.

A sure sign of a first-rate establishment.

"Sh-sure you don't want any of thish Brion?" Tiffany asked, her words beginning to slur as she held up her refilled glass and spilled droplets on the tablecloth.

"Positive," Harry said. He turned around in his chair and raised a finger.

Like a magic genie, the waiter instantly popped up at his side.

"The check please," Harry said pleasantly. "I'd appreciate it if you could bring it soonest."

"Harry—!" Tiffany's face began to pale.

"But . . . but you haven't even touched your steak, sir," the waiter pointed out, his expression hovering between the funereal and horror. "Is there a problem?"

"Actually, things couldn't be better," Harry assured him cheerfully. "My compliments to the chef."

The waiter bowed slightly. "As you wish, sir."

Tiffany glowered across the table. "Harry, what the hell kind of game are you playing?" she hissed.

He produced his Blackberry from his jacket pocket and held it up for her to see. She immediately reached for her purse and snapped it open, saw that it was gone.

"You . . . you *bastard!*" she hissed. "You *thief!*"

His voice was soft but dangerous. "*I'm* the thief? You know something, Tiffany? I won't even know what you've been up to until I check all my calls and messages. But want some sage advice? I know you think you're a hot patootie, but let me clue you in. In future? Don't play with the big boys unless you want to get hurt."

"Now what is that sh—" she hiccuped "—shupposed to mean?"

The bill arrived. Harry didn't even glance at it; he simply slipped Tiffany's credit card into the clear plastic slot and handed it to the waiter. Feeling a stab of guilt, he reminded himself that she was, after all, the one who'd made the dinner reservations.

"The lady is authorized to sign it," he said, pushing back his chair and rising to his feet.

He left Tiffany sitting there, red-faced and stewing.

It wasn't until he was halfway across the dining room, discreetly palming the waiter, the captain, and the maître d' large cash tips each when a female scream, issuing forth from one of the alcoves, rent the air.

"You *shit!* Harry Palmer, you sh-shon-of-a-bitch! You're a total *turd!* A low-down rotten scumbag!"

Shock stilled the voices in the dining room. Suddenly you could have heard a pin drop. Not even the sounds of cutlery on china and the clinking of glasses could be heard.

Tiffany Pfeiffer had obviously looked at the credit card bill and realized it was hers.

Harry glanced around the dining room. "My sincerest apologies for my colleague's behavior," he told the diners at large, and the staff in particular.

And to the maître d', *sotto voce:* "I believe Ms. Pfeiffer has imbibed more of your excellent wine than she can handle." He peeled another hundred dollar bill off his money clip. "Could you please be so kind as to see to it that she is put safely into a taxi?"

"Of course, Mr. Palmer."

"I really appreciate it," Harry said. "And again, my apologies."

And as the conversations in the restaurant picked back up, he strolled out casually into the hot, humid night, hands in his pockets, jingling his loose change.

Whistling while he walked.

[CHAPTER TWENTY]

Mykonos, Greece

Miranda was awakened by the sounds of the shower and the gargling of mouthwash coming through the closed narrow door of the head. She struggled up through layers of sleep. Then Madge emerged, one towel wrapped around her like a sarong, the other around her wet hair like a turban. "Rise and shine!" she crooned.

The lights of the compact cabin were lit and Madge had pulled aside the curtains of the porthole next to the lower bunk. Sunlight flooded in through the round of thick fixed glass and reflected blindingly off the wall-mounted mirror and varnished wooden paneling opposite.

In the upper bunk, Miranda blinked and covered her face with her pillow. "What time is it?" she murmured groggily.

"It's eight-forty-five, sleepy head," Madge sang cheerfully, unwrapping her turban and briskly drying her wet hair. "We're on Mykonos, dear."

Mykonos!

That got Miranda's attention. She flung her pillow aside and sat up abruptly. Too abruptly; her head hit the low ceiling of the top bunk. "Ouch." She rubbed the top of her head. "What time is breakfast?"

"They stop serving at nine-thirty. The bus into town leaves at ten o'clock sharp. That Chara woman made the announcement last night, after you'd come down and gone to bed."

Suddenly wide awake, Miranda swung her legs out over the edge of the bunk and hopped down. "Give me ten minutes," she said, padding barefoot into the head. She did her ablutions, turned on the water and swiftly showered with the hand-held attachment. When she came back out, Madge was already dressed. She was wearing a bright yellow dress with a matching belt and had tied a yellow chiffon scarf around the crown of her broad-brimmed straw hat.

"I'm a daffodil," Madge giggled infectiously. "I'll go on up and reserve a seat for you."

"Meet you there in five."

Miranda pulled out one of her yellow bags, dug out a sleeveless white tee-shirt, tan shorts, and a sturdy pair of low hiking boots. White baseball cap to protect her from the sun. Her digital camera, which in her excitement she'd forgotten to take along on the trek up to Sounion.

Stupid, stupid, she chided herself, looping the camera around her neck by its long strap. *Won't make that mistake again.* She was halfway out the door when she remembered her watch. She'd taken it off when she'd gone to bed and placed it on the shelf beside her bunk.

Hoisting herself back up, she switched on the reading lamp and felt around the little shelf. There was her untouched mint, still in its foil wrapper. No watch, however. It must have dropped down into the bunk. She pulled back the sheet. Felt between the mattress and the bunk frame. Lifted the mattress and felt under that.

Still no watch.

Where in all of Hades could it be? Miranda could have sworn she'd placed it on the shelf. Or had she been that exhausted, that slightly tipsy, or that agitated after calling Harry's Blackberry that she'd only *thought* she'd taken it off? But if she hadn't, it would surely still be on her wrist?

She grabbed her sunglasses. No time for that now; Madge would be waiting. After breakfast she would search more thoroughly.

"*There* you are," Madge said, putting down her little Greek phrase book and waving from the same table where they'd sat during dinner.

The lounge-cum-dining room was filled with bright sunshine, and the tables were half empty. The others—the quartet of Antipodean nurses included—had presumably finished eating and were already up on deck. The loud German couple was blessedly quiet, too busy tanking up on food to talk. The two Dutch women, eschewing the buffet, had a packet of thin, dry, grain-filled slivers of Wasa bread that they obviously traveled with.

"It's a self-service buffet," Madge pointed out. "The food is over there, on that counter, and there's a pot of coffee and tea. It's what I believe is called a Continental breakfast?"

But it was more, much more; besides the basket of large toasted buns, little squares of foil-wrapped butter and a bowl of apricot jam, there were thin slices of ham and cheese, some hard-boiled eggs, fresh figs, and a dish of oil-cured olives.

A veritable feast by Miranda's standards; her usual breakfast was a bagel and cream cheese grabbed on the run. The food on board *Meltemi II* definitely outclassed the vessel's shabby, outward appearance.

A pleasant surprise.

Miranda carefully balanced her filled tray to the table, then paused to take a moment to bend down and look out the large wood-framed windows. The *Meltemi II* was anchored inside the sheltering arm of a breakwater, among a small armada of various sized yachts and even small commercial vessels, all tied sideways to sturdy bollards bedded in cement. Beyond a wide quay and outside the breakwater, two gargantuan cruise ships were docked, one behind the other, like monstrosities from another planet with their towering decks. Through the opposite windows, the view was more promising. White cubist houses climbed and clung to naked brown cliffs. In cloudless sunshine, the view was nothing short of magical.

She couldn't wait to set foot ashore.

"Madge," Miranda said, peeling the skin off a fig, "you didn't happen to run across my wristwatch, did you?"

"Your watch?" Madge set down the coffee cup she was holding. "No. Why? Is it missing?"

"Well, I can't find it, is all. Last night, before I went to sleep, I took it off and placed it on the little shelf beside my bunk."

"Perhaps it fell into your bed."

Miranda shook her head. "I checked the sheets and even under the mattress. That's what kept me."

Madge looked distressed. "Oh, dear me. That is most upsetting. We should ask that Chara woman whether they have a lost-and-found aboard. They surely must."

"It isn't any big deal," Miranda assured her. "It's not an expensive watch, nor does it hold any sentimental value. It's just that I'm so used to strapping it on in the morning."

"Yes, but still . . . " Madge frowned. "I absolutely *hate* it when I can't find something."

"I know. It's irritating. But let's drop that subject for now, shall we? What time is it?"

Madge consulted her own little gold wristwatch. "Time enough to finish our breakfast and then search the cabin and see if we can't locate it."

"No." Miranda shook her head. "Let's finish our breakfast nice and leisurely and then go up on deck. I'm dying to see what Mykonos looks like from up there. I'll ask Chara, so don't worry about it." She eyed her friend's plate which was scattered with toasted crumbs and the shell of a hard-boiled egg. "Madge!"

"What, dear?"

"You haven't even tried a fresh fig, have you? They're succulent!"

"I've tried dried figs, of course, but they're not really to my liking. As you've probably noticed, I'm not very adventurous when it comes to food."

"I'm not crazy about dried figs, either. But these . . . " Miranda bit off another small mouthful and rolled her eyes ecstatically. "Come on, Madge. Be a sport."

"Well . . . "

Miranda sliced off a sliver and handed it to Madge, who nibbled a tiny end suspiciously. Her face brightened. "Oh, it *is* delicious!"

"Here, I'll go get you one. And I'm fetching another for myself. Oh, and give me your cup. You could use a refill of coffee."

After they finished their breakfasts, they went out onto the aft deck. The wind had picked up perceptibly, tugging at their hair, and beyond the breakwater, where the waves broke and sent up showers of white spray, that inimitable blue-black sea was topped with whitecaps. On the road opposite the port, a veritable caravan of motorcoaches was already shuttling thousands of passengers from the two cruise ships into Mykonos town. Miranda noticed another, single motorcoach idling just beyond the chain-link fence separating the cruise ship quay from the long, narrow yacht harbor.

Awaiting the *Meltemi II*'s passengers, no doubt.

With Miranda in the lead, she and Madge climbed the steps up to the sundeck. Most of the passengers were already assembled on the bright grass-green Astroturf that clashed against the primitive beauty of the rocky island and the white cubist villas, and the air veritably thrummed with palpable excitement. Everyone, apparently, was at least minimally acquainted with Mykonos—the Cinderella, crown jewel, or whore—depending upon one's point of view, of that group of islands called the Cyclades. The quartet of oncology nurses from Down Under waved as they prowled the deck, all geared up in cargo shorts and sturdy hiking boots.

Chara Zouboulakis was standing just beneath the shady canvas awning, waist-long hair gleaming like black silk as the wind whipped it to one side. She was perfectly made up, had on big round Jackie O. sunglasses pushed up on her forehead, and was decked out in yet another expensive shore outfit. She had a large designer handbag slung over one arm, the hand of which held a tiny cell phone to her ear. In her other hand she held a clipboard and her miniature hand microphone.

After completing her call, she scanned the passengers, obviously counting heads. Then she made another quick call, uttered something in Greek, snapped the phone shut, and waited, impatiently tapping an expensively shod foot.

"Go and ask her about your watch," Madge prodded.

"I shall, later," Miranda promised. "I don't think this is a good time."

The German couple and the black-clad punks, who had obviously still been asleep and were bleary-eyed and yawning, were led up on deck by Dimitris.

Chara nodded curtly and launched into her usual multilingual greeting. "Welcome to Mykonos," she said into her little microphone. "It is called the 'Windy Island,' and I supposed you can understand why, no?"

There was a smatter of chuckles, and she continued.

"The motorcoach there—" she pointed to the other side of the chain-link fence "—will drop us off at the Old Harbor, at the edge of Mykonos Town. From there it is a very short walk. With a few certain exceptions, motor vehicles are not permitted in the town, so it is very pedestrian-friendly. Please to have your room key cards ready. As we disembark, they will be scanned. That way we will know who is ashore and who is aboard. The same process needs to be repeated once you board the ship again. Now please to follow me."

She led the way down to the aft deck, where the inclined gangplank connected ship and shore. There the lectern, laptop, and the little card scanner had been set up. Dimitris slid each person's card through before letting them pass. When it was Miranda's turn, she saw her face and vital information pop up on the screen of the laptop. She cringed at her mug shot; it was certainly not her best picture.

Once they were shepherded aboard the motorcoach, Chara stood beside the driver, holding onto the upright chrome bar and once again speaking into the microphone as the bus began to move smoothly.

"Oh, Miranda!" Madge whispered, quivering with anticipation. "Imagine! I've always dreamt of coming here, but never thought I'd live to see the day!"

"But you have," Miranda whispered back, with a gentle smile. "It just goes to prove that wishes can come true."

Madge gave her hand a fond squeeze. "You are so right. I shall remember that."

Then they listened as Chara continued. "As you can see, we are leaving what is called the New Port. This area is named Agios Stefanos, which means Saint Stefanos, and the bay we are driving along is called Tourlos. I will tell you more when we arrive at our destination."

She took a seat behind the driver and necks craned or heads ducked as the passengers stared out the windows. The road was two-laned and paved, but narrow, with a low stone wall protecting the drop-off to the bay below, and cliffs crowding the other side.

Madge drew a sharp breath and shuddered as a couple walking single-file had to hug the knee-high wall to keep from being run down. "Goodness," she exclaimed, "I would hate to walk along this road! Talk about taking your life in your hands!"

Minutes later, the motorcoach made a sharp right turn downhill, and then a left. It parked by the Old Port, at the far end of a veritable car pool of motorcoaches, all with cards in the windshields identifying to which cruise ship they temporarily belonged.

With Chara in the lead, the bus emptied quickly. Miranda stared, transfixed, around the Old Harbor with its open small craft bobbing at anchor, at an intrepid windsurfer skimming the waves and playing chicken by virtually flying circles around a tour boat bound for Delos.

She felt like the worst kind of tourist, but it was irresistible: she instinctively reached for her camera and clicked off a number of shots.

For nothing, but nothing on earth had prepared her for the stunning reality of this extraordinary little town, a cubist village of dazzling whiteness climbing, helter-skelter, up the steep rocky slopes as it had spread and grown—and was still spreading and growing—and everywhere there was evidence of the tiny cupolas of little churches, the rectangular towers of dovecotes with their dark, multitudinous triangular openings, and those signature cylindrical windmills with their giant wooden spokes lacking canvas. Lining the other side of the harbor were row after row of cafés and tavernas with their brilliant, welcoming awnings sheltering masses of tables and chairs.

But overall, there was something austerely organic about it all, a simple purity that reached deep into Miranda's primordial soul. Even the droves of cruise ship passengers heading into town in a never-ending conga line were unable to ruin the magic: the labyrinthine little streets and alleys seemed to swallow their multitudes.

Chara gathered the little group from the *Meltemi II* around her.

"As you can see, Mykonos is one of the most picturesque and famous towns in all of Greece, perhaps even the world. It is a shopper's paradise, especially for jewelry and souvenirs, a labyrinth of narrow streets and alleys in which it is very easy to get lost. It was purposely built that way in order to deter invading pirates and confuse them."

A pause as she translated her little speech into various tongues.

"Those of you who wish to wander around the town may do so at will. There is no set tour. But try not to miss 'Little Venice,' which is built right along the seafront a little to the left, and behind, the end of the harbor. If you follow the alleys, you will surely come across it. It is an unforgettable place to eat, have leisurely drinks, or simply enjoy a cup of coffee.

"That is one of the choices you have."

Another slight pause. Then: "You have a second choice. For those of you who wish to visit the neighboring island of Delos, tour boats leave regularly every half hour or so from the far end of the jetty." She pointed across to the end of the harbor. "Besides being the Wall Street of its time, Delos was also the holiest of these islands during antiquity, and is, in effect, one enormous archeological site."

Her eyes sought out Miranda's. "As you, better than any among us should know, Ms. Kalli, the entire island is covered with ruins and is one of the most spectacular wonders of the ancient world."

"Yes. I know." Miranda nodded, wondering whether or not Chara was setting her up again as an unofficial tour guide. If she hoped to do so, it wouldn't work. She had learned her lesson the hard way at Sounion.

"There is also quite a marvelous museum on Delos," Chara went on, "as well as a gift shop and a small shop that sells canned and bottled soft drinks and a few items of food. My advice is that you might wish to buy some large bottles of water along the waterfront before boarding one of the tour boats."

Judging from Chara's footwear, Miranda gathered that the *Melte-*

mi II's fashionista was going to stay in town. She also assumed, correctly, from the impatient quartet of boot-shod nurses that they were headed straight to Delos, and were anxious to get going.

"You also have a third choice," Chara went on. "You can do a quick tour of the town as well as pay a quick visit to Delos. However, this is most important, so please to listen carefully."

Another quick switch of languages.

"The last tour boat from Delos departs at three o'clock sharp. There is no other way back, and there are no facilities on Delos to stay the night. In fact, it is quite illegal to do so, just as it is to pick up any object, however insignificant a shard of broken pottery it might be. The Ministry of Culture has very strict rules concerning antiquities, however minor they might be."

Another quick glance at Miranda.

"The only persons permitted to remain on Delos overnight are the archeologists who live there in a few tiny, scattered houses. So I must warn you: please to make sure that you return to this bus by fifteen minutes *before* four o'clock at the very latest. To keep to our schedule, Captain Leonides has informed me that we must sail at four-thirty sharp. It is a very long haul from here to Kusadasi, so we must leave on time. We cannot wait for anyone who is late. If you are not onboard, we shall have no choice but to sail on without you. I have made myself clear, yes?"

She looked around and was evidently satisfied that everyone had understood.

"Now please. Explore the town, Delos, or both. You are free to do as you will."

The *Meltemi II*'s group scattered, and the restive oncology nurses strode off in quick time. Madge, however, hung back for a few moments.

"Miranda, dear," she said, with that fussy solicitude of hers, "I do hope you don't mind. I know you're anxious to be off to Delos. And as for me . . . " she gurgled a delicious little laugh " . . . well, I know I'm being *awfully* touristy, but I simply *must* see all those jewelry shops I've read about. According to my guidebook, it's supposed to be a jewelry wonderland, and I think I shall be extravagant and splurge on a little something *good*. The late Mr. Blessing, may he rest in peace, was a darling, but he didn't approve of spending money on trinkets and baubles. 'A waste of good money,' was the way he always put it. So you won't take it the wrong way if I made up for lost time and we split up? I do so want to mosey around town and shop. And I know you're dying to spend all your time on Delos."

Miranda laughed. "Oh, for heaven's sake, Madge, why should I mind?"

"I just want to assure you that I'm not deserting you."

"That never even entered my mind. Really, Madge, you are too much!"

Arm in arm, they began to stroll slowly around the harbor, heading into town.

"Oh, and before I forget," Madge said. "Here. I'll lend you my watch." She stopped to fiddle with the bracelet of her little Hamilton wristwatch.

Miranda shook her head. "No, Madge. Absolutely not."

"It's just an old watch from the forties, dear. I had it appraised, and it really isn't worth all that much. It might be fourteen karat gold, but it's light and the bracelet is hollow. It used to belong to the late Mr. Blessing's mother and, if truth be told . . . " she lowered her voice " . . . I know it's not a very nice thing to say, but I never was very fond of the old battle ax. Nor she of me."

Miranda laughed but was adamant. "Yes, but it's a family heirloom and I refuse. End of subject."

"But . . . but Miranda, I *know* how lost one can be without a timepiece. I'd feel so much better if I knew you could keep track of the time and not miss the boat."

There was laughter in Miranda's voice. "With all those shops to entice you? No, Madge, I think *you'd* best keep track of the time and not miss the boat. Don't forget, I'm a big girl. You needn't worry about me. I'm not afraid to ask strangers for the time. In fact, I've got my cell phone in my bag, and it tells me what time it is. So stop being a worry wart."

"Well, if you're sure . . . " Madge didn't look all that convinced.

"Absotively posilutely! Now, you put that watch right back on your wrist, where it belongs. And don't forget, I know what shopping is like. That's when it's all too easy to lose all track of time."

"You think?"

"Madge, I *know.* Now off you go. It sounds like you've got an awful lot of shopping to catch up on. Oh, look! Here's a jewelry shop already. See you later."

While Madge stared, entranced, at a glittering display of jewels, Miranda gave a cheerful wave and strode purposefully off towards the jetty where the tour boats left for Delos.

[CHAPTER TWENTY ONE]

Delos, Greece

It is small and stark, this granite island in the middle of the Central Aegean. On the eastern side, two tiny rocky islets and the much larger and longer island of Rheneia held back the choppy, blue-black Aegean, stirred up by the prevailing, cooling winds of a rather gentle *meltemi,* and once inside that strait the whitecaps had disappeared and the shallows were calm, showing clear aquamarine depths and darting small fish. Overhead, Zeus' sky was a blazing wheel of the purest azure that burnished the rocky moonscape and burnt yellow grasses in a miraculous, golden light.

Approaching through the strait between the islands, Miranda leaned eagerly over the railing on the top deck of the *Delos Express,* visually gorging herself on the reality of what sprawled ashore.

Never, never once before in her entire life had she felt so intense a thrill as filled her to bursting as she stared raptly at the wonders of antiquity closing in. For as far as the eye could see, up to where the slope of Mount Kynthos began, it was a staggering archeological dream, a wonderland of such profuse antiquity that it boggled the mind. Everywhere, amid miles of ancient walls and the remains of once-grand villas dating back some three thousand years, the flatness and slopes were littered with marble statuary and punctuated by stately columns rising to various heights.

Though lacking a proper bay or harbor, and possessing virtually no natural resources, an obviously man-made finger of granite thrust out like a miniature promontory, and that was where the *Delos Express* docked, quickly and efficiently, stern to the quay.

Miranda, armed with two bottles of water, waited in line to disembark. Wearing her visored baseball cap with her hair pulled through the opening at the back, the dazzling brilliance of the sun didn't faze her a bit. Nor did the baking heat, which even the mild *meltemi* was unable to alleviate.

Once onshore, she lingered a bit while the hordes from the tour boat crowded the stone kiosk to purchase their entrance tickets. She was giving them time to get a head start and disperse. Meanwhile she stood there, admiring the glittering water, breathing deeply of the fresh clean salt air and savoring the silence, so different from the perpetually smoggy, smelly, and cacophonous brash blare of Manhattan.

But New York seemed a million miles away, part of another planet; a different universe altogether. Manhattan, complete with Harris Milford Palmer III, seemed for a moment not to exist at all, and she was glad.

With the crowd at the kiosk thinning, she went and purchased her ticket. Just beyond, licensed tour guides with their ubiquitous varicolored umbrellas offered their services. Miranda politely declined. "*Efcharistó. Óchi,*" she managed in a firm but friendly tone, using the rudimentary Greek learned from Madge, who perpetually repeated words from her ever-present little phrase book.

One of the ladies twitched her nose, but the others took Miranda's weak attempt at speaking Greek in good stride, and actually smiled.

Delos, Miranda was gratified to see, was large, and so sprawling that it seemed to swallow up the hordes.

She started up the wide, well-worn dirt path to the large, unadorned building that obviously housed the museum, and the smaller, separate structure, which consisted of a small refreshment area and a gift shop. She paced herself, stopping here and there to admire the tip of the iceberg. Massive chunks of marble, all carefully numbered with black paint, various pedestals carved with reliefs, marble well heads, and multitudinous capitals, both Doric and Ionic, waiting to be reconstructed once the correct columns had been unearthed or assembled.

Unable to help herself, she took copious photographs.

She was glad to be by herself. Unlike at Sounion, she was determined to strike out on her own and explore the treasures at leisure.

Alone, without company.

It was almost not to be. She stopped to click some photos of two high square pedestals atop each of which, resting in shameless splendor, were giant marble phalluses, scrotums intact, but with the ends missing. She knew these were characteristic symbols of the cult of Dionysus, and just as she was getting the best shot of one, she heard her name being called.

"*Yoo*-hoo! Miranda!" she heard Em's unmistakable voice call out, and before she knew it, three of the four nurses from Down Under converged upon her.

"You were *so* marvelous at Sounion we thought—" began Soph.

"—well, we were rather hoping we might tag along with you and *learn* something," added Fan.

"Where's Don?" Miranda asked.

"Oh, she's the 'ardiest and most athletic of us all," Em said cheerfully. "She's probably already 'eading up that mountain over there." She nodded toward Mount Kynthos, the highest point of the island, and its only real mountain. "She can out-'ike us all."

Miranda smiled. "I don't doubt it. She seems the outdoorsy type."

"Oh, we all are," declared Em staunchly, "but when Don's 'ead's in a certain mood, it can be quite impossible to keep up with 'er."

Miranda nodded. She understood Don perfectly. She herself wanted to be unencumbered and savor the sights in solitude, without a lot of chatter. Yet she didn't wish to offend, but sometimes white lies were called for, and this was one of those instances.

"Actually," she said tactfully, "I'm quite unfamiliar with Delos. This certainly isn't like Sounion, with one single temple. Quite frankly, I'm overwhelmed. I think I'm going to take Don's lead, but first I have to head for that little shop by the museum and get myself a guidebook and a map before I wander around on my own."

"Oh, we quite understand," Fan said quickly, almost, but not quite, managing to hide her disappointment. "Don't we, mates?"

Soph and Em did their best to agree, although their faces had fallen a bit.

"You might," Miranda suggested, "consider hiring one of the English-speaking tour guides. That way you'll hit the highlights and no doubt see the most important sights. And learn a lot in the process."

"Yes," Fan said. "Perhaps we shall. Well, we won't keep you then. Toodle-doo!"

And flapping little waves of their hands, the sturdily booted threesome marched off, each pointing in a different direction, deciding which way to head.

"And don't forget, the last boat leaves 'ere at three!" Em called over her shoulder to Miranda, who smiled and mouthed her thanks.

And they were off, their chatter thankfully dissipating into desolate silence, which Delos somehow magically managed to absorb. Miranda made her way past reconstructed stone walls and hundreds upon hundreds of more pieces of broken statuary, relics of civilizations long past. The light dazzled, the brown scrub and burned grass whispered in the wind and reeled in the sun, and on the hard, packed ground her feet raised little clouds of dust. Lizards watched her approach and scattered, flashing like emerald sequins. Already her throat felt parched, and she sipped water from one of the bottles. Chara's advice to take along bottled water, she had to admit, had proven wise and useful.

At the little refreshment counter and larger gift shop, she purchased a glossy paperback filled with color photographs and maps of various areas, and she sprang for a large fold-out map as well. Lacking her trusty watch, Miranda dug into her shoulder bag and checked her cell phone for the time. It was still set to Eastern Standard, and adding seven hours, she realized it was already past noon. She only had three hours remaining until the last tour boat departed for Mykonos.

Not much time given the myriad treasures scattered about like marble litter from benevolent gods. To do any kind of in-depth justice to this place would take weeks . . . more likely months!

Meanwhile, she had to make every minute count.

So . . . where to begin.

Consulting the map, she saw that the museum was closest, but Miranda decided its air-conditioned interior could wait until she needed a place to seriously cool off. Instead, she would explore the northern end of the island first, where the Sacred Lake was located.

It seemed only appropriate as the place to start, not least since her years of studying ancient history and myths came back in a flash, as if some long-suppressed mental floodgates had suddenly been flung open, unleashing a torrent of long-stored information.

Not only was the area of the Sacred Lake the closest place to begin, but more importantly it jogged Homer's famous "Hymn to Apollo" in her memory.

Starting off at a brisk pace, she reviewed what she remembered.

According to mythology, Zeus had secretly impregnated Leto, to the fury of his deceived consort, the goddess Hera. And Leto, relentlessly pursued by a vengeful Hera, had desperately searched the ends of the earth for a spot in which to give birth to Zeus' son. But islands, cities, and nations, fearful of the wrath of powerful Hera, refused to give Leto sanctuary. Only Delos, a bare rock in the middle of a tempestuous sea, dared to defy Hera and provide a safe shelter, and here Leto had given birth to Apollo, god of the sun. With his birth, or so went the myth, the island shone like gold in a blaze of glory, flowering blossoms burst forth from the ground, and singing swans glided majestically upon the lake.

And ever since, Apollo drove the chariot of the sun daily across the skies from sunup till sundown.

She reached the lake, a wheel-shaped pool of not great size surrounded by a low wall of granite. Centuries ago, it had been filled with water, and now in summer's heat it had dried up completely. Instead of water it was filled with parched yellow rushes and jackstraw and a single slender palm, which grew tall and proud, its fronds rustling and rattling in the mild *meltemi.*

It wasn't a lake actually, nor could it even qualify as a pond. It was just a medium size circular pool.

But Miranda kept myth and fact in perspective, reminding herself that to the Ancients, who had to deal with the scarcity of that most precious of commodities—fresh water—on this island as on so many of the Cyclades, it had indeed been a lake imbued with magical powers.

Not only a lake, but it was *the* Sacred Lake. The Lake where swans had burst into song upon Apollo's birth . . .

Once again, she lifted her camera and clicked off a few more digital photographs when she heard something. Something odd and disquieting.

Was that the skittering of a dislodged pebble she heard and . . . was she imagining it? . . . furtive footsteps coming from a stone wall directly behind her? Startled, she spun around, imagined she saw the fleeting shape of a disappearing shadow.

She listened carefully, but there were no more sounds, and as she scanned the surrounding area she could see tourists roaming here and there in the distance, little sun-drenched figures casting purple shadows as they picked their way along narrow, stone-strewn paths.

She laughed to herself. How ridiculous to have felt a sudden flash of fear! she told herself. The dislodged pebble had probably been caused by nothing more than the darting movement of a lizard. And the fleeting shadow she'd seen—or had it been her overactive imagination at work? Still . . .

But nothing.

Calming back down, she gazed further to the northeast. There, built on the incline of a hill were a few tiny square houses, none much bigger than a single room, and obviously the abode of the archeologists who worked this site. She'd noticed the places where they'd been excavating, each marked by straw or canvas roofs supported on tall poles to protect the workers from the relentlessly blazing sun.

But at this hour there was no digging going on. It was mid-day, siesta time, and once the tourists had departed, she imagined that the archeologists would surely be out and about and hard at their tasks, ever so carefully and patiently sifting through layers upon layers of artifacts from hundreds of centuries past.

At any rate, enough loitering, Miranda told herself firmly. Time was fleeting. She had to get a move on. There was so much to see, and so little time.

She walked back the way she had come. Something moved stealthily nearby, and once again she had that peculiar sensation of her neck hairs standing up, and she was unable to cast off the disquieting feeling that she was being followed . . . or watched.

A ridiculous notion, she told herself, passing a maze of high stone walls as she hurried past the remains of some temple or other. She couldn't help glancing over her shoulder from time to time but saw nothing, and absurdly wondered whether the ghosts of yesterday's gods were still secretly in residence, haunting and protecting their once holy shrines . . . and dismissed her fanciful, irrational notions, mocking herself for the absurdity, and quelling her unease by heading to the wide open spaces of the main avenue.

Here was the line-up of the famous Archaic lions of Delos, crouching regally on granite bases. If memory served her correctly, Miranda remembered that there had once been eighteen of the great, silently roaring beasts, but their number had dwindled, like an endangered species, down to only five. Some had survived, weathered but virtually intact; others were fragmentary, with steel struts where their front legs had long ago been destroyed.

But these weren't the real McCoy; they were recent casts, and the originals had finally been moved indoors, reposing in the protective bosom of the museum. But they made a breathtaking sight all the same.

She snapped off more photographs from various angles and took a long swig of water from one of her bottles. It was no longer chilled and rather tepid, but refreshing nonetheless. To put her mind at rest once and for all, she took the opportunity to gaze around in all directions.

Everywhere she looked, her eye fell upon rank upon scattered rank of white marble—columns and portions of columns, plinths, portal jambs, benches, and all matter of carved remnants glaring in the sun and casting blackish-blue shadows. The surrounding area was filled with scattered pockets of tourists, either singly, in pairs, or in groups, but their voices were hushed, as though in a church, and the silence was a blessing. There was nothing mysterious about any of them. Nobody lurked in the shadows.

There was nothing to fear. Nothing to raise her fear.

Why she'd had that odd feeling back at the Sacred Lake was beyond her.

Consulting her map and guide book, she ascertained that there were still three major areas which were a must to explore, and she'd just have time if she didn't dawdle. But with Apollo's sun blazing like white fire, she determined it was as good a time as any to head into the cavernous, air-conditioned cool of the museum and scout out its treasures.

From outside, the building was a factory-like rectangle, small by the standards of those grandiose palaces of culture found in major cities the world over, and had no distinguishing architectural features whatsoever. But inside . . .

The breath caught in Miranda's throat.

. . . the instant she stepped over the threshold, she was overwhelmed. The archeologist's heart within her was hammering against her rib cage with such force that its noise surely carried throughout the building like the quickening beat of an anvil. For everywhere, the various galleries of divers periods were spacious and loft-like, lined with Naxian *kouoi* and *korai,* ensembles of marble sculptures, torsos of armless, headless, and penisless athletes. It seemed that over the hundreds of decades, the first defacement of male statuary had been the phallus, followed by the head and arms. But there were nymphs and gods and goddesses galore, a magnificent Diana slaying a deer, giant carved heads, horsemen and horse heads, doves and sirens and sphinxes, luminous marbles of generals and kings and even later Roman Proconsuls, vases and ex-votos from the various sanctuaries on the island, including black-figured pottery brought from the Heraion on Samos.

And of course, here were the glorious, famed Archaic lions, brought in from outdoors to protect them from further deterioration from the elements, which were the centerpiece of attraction.

The museum, so small and yet so rich in antiquities, was a storehouse of priceless treasures, and contained pieces the likes of which never passed through the exclusive portals of even such an elite emporium of antiquities as the Jan Kofski Gallery.

It was overwhelming, too much to absorb all at once. Far, far too much for the eye and brain to register in detail. Miranda could easily have studied each single piece for days on end, but she literally had to waltz through it in quick time.

If she had her druthers, she'd pitch a cot and live right here, contentedly among this trove, for the remainder of her natural life.

A noble if impossible sentiment.

But time was of the essence. Like Cinderella, she was all too aware of the clock ticking—only in her case it was not the stroke of midnight when her coach turned back into a pumpkin, but three o'clock sharp—when the last tour boat departed and all visitors had to be off the island.

Ah, the cruelty of Cinderella's well-meaning fairy godmother, and in Miranda's own case, of her very own fairy godmother, Madge Blessing, who with the very best of intentions had made visiting this magical isle possible.

It took enormous willpower to tear herself away from the treasure trove of the museum and head back outside. There was so much to see. And so little time.

After the cool, sunless interior, going outside was like walking into a blasting furnace. The sun blazed so brightly that Miranda was momentarily blinded, and had to wait several minutes for her eyes to adjust. Having breezed through the highlights of the museum as swiftly as she believed she had—she was certain less than half an hour had passed—she surely didn't need to bother consulting her cell phone to check the time?

Instead, she once again perused the map and guidebook, and her feet led her to the Theater Quarter. Set among a literal maze of yet more remnants of Delian houses and workshops—hundreds of them, each delineated by high granite walls taller than herself, and every block bisected by a bewildering confusion of narrow alleys—she discovered it was as easy to get lost here as in mythology's famed labyrinth of King Minos and the Minotaur. Yet she managed to stumble across a house which her guidebook identified as the House of Dionysos. It had an impressive peristyle entrance to a courtyard that was surrounded by huge, slender gray marble columns. Amid it was a portion of a mosaic floor, incredibly intact, with a dolphin curving elegantly around an anchor.

Opposite it was the House of Kleopatra, a Greek lady of note, where the statuary were modern replicas, but the fluted Doric columns rising majestically from the marble floor were original and ancient.

The shadows had lengthened, but she was unaware of the fact; the dry-laid granite walls kept reality at bay, and sheltered her from the mild *meltemi* blowing from the north.

Then on she marched to the House of Dolphins, with some of the most magnificent mosaics she had ever laid eyes upon. They depicted pairs of dolphins leaping around a large rosette of vegetal motifs. And on and on she was drawn, as though by some invisible hand. The House of the Masks, with its large cistern filled with green brackish water, and the most wonderful mosaics by far: Dionysos sitting atop a fierce panther.

Here and there she ran across a tourist or two coming from either direction, intent upon discovering the same delights which held her so spellbound.

And that was when she heard footsteps just around a granite corner; that and the stealthy crunch of a thorny branch.

Again, she felt that frisson of irrational fear which had come over her at the Sacred Lake. But this time she decided to take the bull by the horns and confront her unseen nemesis.

She turned the corner.

Only a middle-aged matron trying to find her way out of the maze. Half-bent over and picking dried burrs off her skirt. She smiled apologetically up at Miranda, who returned a friendly smile.

An innocent tourist. Nothing to fear.

"*Nothing but fear itself,*" Miranda told herself firmly, Churchill's famous line resonating in her head, and she wondered why she should have had that uneasy feeling to begin with. That vague sense of being threatened. There was no rational reason for the sensation that she had of being watched or followed.

Absolutely no reason on earth.

Why anyone would even want to was beyond her.

Feeling foolish, Miranda continued on, leaving the woman to her burrs. Before long, lo and behold—the maze opened and she came across the theater. Built from flat land into the western side of the hillside, the first marble rows of semi-circular orchestra seats were mainly intact. The rest, which had, thousands of years previously once seated an audience of five thousand, were scattered chunks of marble that mimicked the upper tiers of seats.

Climbing the stepped incline, she stopped at the top and gazed down. The *meltemi* blew warm but strong, and the view was nothing short of glorious. It encompassed the protective harbor, that man-made protrusion that extended outwards like a curved finger, inside of which the distant, shrunken tourist boats docked safely, tiny as toys from this vantage point. Beyond that, she could clearly make out the small rocky islands that protected the channel from the pounding sea, and a little further on, but not far, the large violet hazy contours of Rheneia spread its rocky mounds across the strait. To either side stretched the deep, blue Aegean, frosted with whitecaps, that only the poets could accurately describe.

As though through no free will of her own, Miranda found herself inexorably drawn onwards and upwards, to the haunting Sanctuary of the Egyptian gods. There a headless statue of flowing marble garments reigned from the precise center of an impressive Doric portico.

Yet another photo opportunity; yet more pictures to take. And from there, the scrubby, parched yellow hillside rose sharply towards the peak of Mount Kynthos, the steep granite steps along the boulder-strewn path beckoning like the Sirens of Odysseus.

It was irresistible. She had to climb to the top.

The rocky ramps and steps were uneven and of various shapes and sizes, and were covered with dried lichen. None was of the same height, and she was glad she was wearing her comfortable hiking boots. Huge vivid lizards stared, strutted and scuttled among the stones and scrub. The sun glared and burned her bare arms, but Miranda took little notice. Nor did she take notice of the constant file of hikers *descending,* and having to shrink against the low rock wall and stand aside to let them pass. Nor did it occur to her that she was the only person making the *ascent,* or that the shadows had lengthened even more, casting their dark purpling hues further and further westwards as Apollo's chariot moved across the clear, painfully throbbing blue of the sky.

Surely there was ample time to climb to the top; it was a mountain, yes, but not all that tall, just a prehistoric granite crag 112 meters high. The steps, though irregular, ancient, and arduous, could not deter her strong legs. She had youth and an athletic bent on her side, not to mention the thrill of this island, repository of most every god in the ancient pantheon, brought here by traders and mariners of the entire middle Orient. Besides, in Manhattan she was used to trudging on hard surfaces—concrete and asphalt—and though the city's sidewalks and streets were relatively smooth, there was something exhilarating about scrambling up this haphazard gradient which had been climbed by pilgrims for thousands of years.

More stepping aside for the descending files. But up she went, breaking a sweat and taking regular swigs from the second bottle of water she carried in the large pockets of her cargo shorts.

At last she crested the peak. She was breathless with an almost drug-like high (were these the highly touted endorphins that she'd never managed to experience now kicking in?) or was it the magic of Delos that filled her with such intense elation and accomplishment that it defied explanation?

Delos, she decided. Definitely Delos, which was spread below her, the ruins and mazes looking far away and small.

Best of all, she was blessedly alone, without the distractions of other tourists, which pleased her immensely. The *meltemi* was much stronger this high up, and tugged at her with inconsequential violence, raising puffs and swirls of dust, sand, and grit that lashed her legs. Yet she was unaware of any pain or discomfort. Her lips were parched, she took yet another slug of water, and noticed that visitors had made shrine-like little piles of stones all over the small top of that rocky peak.

And then she looked around and gasped in awe.

This, Miranda thought . . . this was what the gods and goddesses must have viewed from their thrones high atop Mount Olympus—this and the entire world beyond. She felt a burgeoning sense of privilege. Being up here by herself, it took little imagination to feel like a minor goddess surveying her own ancient kingdom, and a romantic flight of fancy dressed herself in wind-whipped white *peplos* and chiton, coiffed her hair elaborately in braids, like those of the statues in the museum.

Standing in place, she made a leisurely, 360-degree turn. The breath caught in her throat. It was impossible to see where the shimmering sea met the shimmering sky. And from up here, too, she had an unparalleled view of all the distant surrounding islands, and fully understood why this group was called the Cyclades. For in Greek, *kyklos* meant "circle," and with sacred little Delos, birthplace of Apollo at their epicenter, the other islands surrounded this barren rock like a distant ring of worshippers not daring to get too close to the source.

To the south, she could see all the way to Paros and Naxos; to the east, Sifnos and Siros; to the north, Mykonos and Tinos. And other distant rocky isles she couldn't identify.

It was too good to last.

The wind found a crevasse somewhere in the granite and inveigled itself, whistling mournfully. It was a melancholy sound, like that of a ship in the night or in thick fog, and it found too empty a place in her heart. Unbidden, her goddess fantasy vanished in a flash. Tears sprang to her eyes and stung as a sudden pang of loneliness overwhelmed her. This was a place and a moment to be savored and shared, whether with a friend or a loved one.

A loved one! She sneered down at her finger, where the engagement ring she'd furiously yanked off had left a pale band, like a despised white tattoo, around the tanned skin. A loved one indeed!

Bitter memories assaulted her like a smothering dark cloud, killing off her euphoria. Again, last night's disastrous telephone call from the *Meltemi II*'s aft deck to Harry's Blackberry reverberated in her head like an evil echo. How could she ever forget that woman's teasing, taunting voice, cooing, " . . . you needn't worry about Harry, sweetheart . . . I'm personally making sure he's being *very* well taken care of . . . "

She clutched her middle and doubled over in pain, the words stabbing her as surely, and painfully, as Brutus' dagger had helped strike down Caesar.

Damn and blast Harris Milford Palmer to hell! she thought furiously.

Harris Milford Palmer, the *shit!*

Harry, her so-called fiancé, who obviously couldn't wait for the cat to be away so that the mouse could play.

Harry, who insulated himself from reality in the ivory towers of his hedge fund office, the very finest and highest-rated restaurants, his massive, multi-million-dollar loft.

Harry, who traveled the world on business, insisting upon flying first class and never straying from boardrooms, mansions, and penthouses, and refusing to set foot in any but the very best and most expensive hotels.

Harry, who would have chartered a luxury yacht or booked a penthouse suite on a luxury liner rather than deign to set foot aboard the *Meltemi II.*

Harry, who had no appreciation whatsoever for the beauty of antiquities and art, aside from their financial investment value. Harry, who never understood why she worked at the Jan Kofski Gallery instead of settling down with him, or at least getting what he called "a decent paying job."

Harry, whose idea of adventure and recreation was riding his four-thousand-dollar ten-speed bicycle along the Hudson River esplanade, cutting a ridiculous, hornet-like figure in his black-and-yellow Spandex, wrap-around sunglasses, and silly black-and-yellow helmet.

Harry. Who was obviously seeing another woman.

What on earth, Miranda wondered, *had* she ever seen in him? What did they have in common? *Anything?*

How did that line go? Something about washing that man right out of her hair?

Indeed it seemed time to wash Harris Milford Palmer out of her hair. High time, in fact.

And as for friends to share the marvels of Delos with, who was there? Mara? Her best girlfriend, who cruised the singles scene in Manhattan and the Hamptons like a female shark forever on the prowl for the right Mr. Rich? No, this wasn't Mara's scene.

Madge?

Miranda thought of her now. Gentle, huge-hearted, adventurous Madge Blessing, whom she'd only just met the day before, but whose physical stamina could never have permitted her to make this climb, and who wisely preferred the glittering boutiques of Mykonos. No, this wasn't Madge's scene, either.

Bits of yet another song lyric popped into Miranda's head, something about being "*Alone again, naturally.*"

Her shoulders drooped. She felt weary and depressed. Hungry, angry, lonely, tired. Even the delights of encountering Madge, of being able to immerse herself in the splendor and magical realities of Sounion and now Delos—all had somehow evaporated, leaving her with a peculiarly empty feeling in the pit of her stomach.

She knew the reason, of course. She was alone atop this mount. And at this particular moment, there was nothing worse for her, despite her pride in self-sufficiency and that streak of independence she could never entirely subdue, that could detract her from the ghost of yesterday's telephone call.

The anodyne, of course, was to join up with people. To be surrounded by life instead of ruins.

People.

She did a quarter turn and her eyes roamed downhill towards the northwest and the sprawling acres of excavation, searching for the nearest cluster of tourists.

There was no one nearby. Even the steep rocky steps back down the mountain were devoid of descending tourists. Specks of human shapes and shadows no longer poked among the maze of ruins below.

Expanding her visual horizons, she gazed further afield. The hordes of tourists had diminished to a trickle during her ascent and all seemed clustered, in a veritable mass of humanity, on that man-made jetty where the *Delos Express* and a second tour boat were docked. A smattering of a few more dark, miniaturized figures were rushing along the yellow grass, packed brown earth, and marble pavers from the direction of the Sacred Lake and the museum. Obviously running to catch the tour boats.

It was clearly an exodus.

Miranda's head snapped up, as though searching the skies for an answer. And there she received her reply. Apollo's golden chariot blazed on is westward journey, far from where she had last seen it—*oh, Christ . . .*

. . . how long had she spent climbing this peak? Standing up here like a solitary goddess, gorging herself upon the near symmetry of the surrounding Cyclades in that wine dark sea. Surely it could not be approaching three o'clock just yet!

Through habit, she glanced at her wrist, then remembered her missing Swatch Watch. But her cell phone would show the time. She dug frantically through her shoulder bag, grabbed the little phone with shaking fingers, and flipped it open.

8:46 a.m. An instant of fool's relief flooded through her—before she remembered that it was still set to Eastern Standard Time. A swift mental addition of seven hours jolted her like an electrical shock.

No, it was *not* 8:46 a.m. Here in Greece it was 2:46 p.m.! Fourteen minutes from Cinderella's toll of the midnight clock.

Chara's warning hammered inside her skull like the pounding of a migraine: three o'clock sharp. No other way back.

Damnation!

One last glance down to the tour boats. The mass of people were already boarding, distant ants filling the benches on the open top decks, others disappearing inside the enclosed cabins. She had been so caught up in the plethora of antiquities that she had forgotten all about the passage of time.

Stupid, stupid, stupid!

Fourteen minutes.

She had *to reach one of the boats before they sailed.*

Miranda struggled to consciously still her hands in order to thrust her cell phone back into her shoulder bag. Then she ran, the bag flapping against her side as she began her mad dash—half-jumping and half-sliding down the slippery, listing granite steps of uneven, time-worn stones. The rushed descent downhill was far more treacherous than the careful uphill climb had been. A thin, thorny branch lashed her right calf, but she was oblivious to the pain.

Have to get down—

—have to!

A third of the way down, a stone gave way underfoot and Miranda felt herself teetering. Down she went, breaking her fall by landing hard on her buttocks, the fingers of one hand desperately grasping hold of a mound of prickly, brittle orange shrub for purchase. She cringed against the tiny thorns embedding themselves in the fleshy softness of her palm and fingers, could hear the delicate, scorched little branches snap like dry twigs, could sense the shallow roots of the plant give way.

Miraculously, the roots continued to cling tenaciously to the parched dirt beneath the rocks. A jagged, flinty shard of granite had gashed her thigh, and a small coiled viper, roused from basking in the sun, reared its head and showed its fangs, but she noticed neither serpent nor the blood trickling down her leg.

All Miranda was aware of was that precious seconds had been lost.

Struggling breathlessly back to her feet, she stole a longing glance down at the tour boats. They seemed to have grown larger now, and were still docked, stern to the jetty, like distant promises emitting small black puffs of diesel. She tried to take comfort from the fact that they were still in place, but was all too aware of the sudden stillness that pervaded the entire scene. From her vantage point, Delos looked, for all the world, like a deserted graveyard whose visitors were departing. Already, the last stragglers were hurrying along the finger of the jetty. If they hadn't boarded yet, and the boats were still docked—

Hope flared and gave her the impetus to continue on down, leaping three steps at a time. It was suicidal—an almost Olympian feat—this 112-meter diagonal dash down the rocky steps and sharply sloping ramps, but she had no choice.

Hurry, hurry, hurry! The Furies seemed to egg her on like mental cheerleaders; Cinderella's coach was still in the harbor. *Faster, faster, faster—*

Too fast. Again the runner stumbled, tripped, and stifled a cry as she felt the razor edge of another rock graze her shin. She clenched her teeth against the pain. The wind had lessened considerably now that she was near the base of Mount Kynthos. But she wasn't home yet.

Pausing atop a sloping ridge, she had to remind herself to breathe. She was barely aware of her drenched tee-shirt clinging to her skin, of sweat seeping from beneath her arms, leaking past the band of her baseball cap and trickling down her forehead, stinging her eyes with salty perspiration.

In desperation, she searched for a short cut. At least she now had a good idea of where she was. Still uphill, but off the mountain at long last, in that area called the Sanctuaries of the Foreign Gods. She was heartened to see that the tour boats were still at the jetty, and that they had definitely increased exponentially in size.

Wiping the sweat from her eyes, swift glances to the left and right informed her that before reaching the flat areas for her final sprint, she still had to negotiate the granite walled mazes of buildings and alleys below.

Damn! But if she hurried, she might still be in time to catch one of the two boats.

Down the slope she scrambled, arms windmilling, sliding between rocks and mounds of topiary-like bracken, realizing too late that the short cut had been a bad mistake. Like Theseus in mythology, she was lost in a maze. And not a flat maze, either. There were too many-stepped, built-up levels to this slope, the alleys at the bottom always seemingly unreachable from above.

Then she thought she saw a way. Ahead, a two-story building, its top sprouting slender, priapic white columns, promised a way down.

A mournful horn rent the silence, signaling the imminent departure of one of the boats.

No!

She flew down a flight of even, reconstructed steps, then crashed down a slope of weeds. Bracken and dried flowers rustled slightly in the breeze, scenting the air with an herbal sweetness. Behind her, she thought she heard another flurry of footsteps, the snap of yet another small dry branch breaking.

Stealing a look over her shoulder as she ran, she thought she caught the movement of a fleeting shadow darting swiftly around a corner.

Forget it! she scolded herself. This was no time to allow her runaway imagination to get the better of her. No one was following her. She was alone, and time was her enemy. Time was running out.

She had to get to one of the tour boats, whichever one it was.

A bleating sound close by stopped her short, one frightened hand scrabbling against her thumping chest. Waist-high to her right was a window-like opening, permitting access to the building's second floor. Inside, a small shelf lacking a balcony railing or balustrade dropped off abruptly to an intricately laid mosaic courtyard far below. Above her rose the columns, their shadows leaning drunkenly eastward.

A skinny goat with large, dark, almost human eyes was looking at her pleadingly from the far corner. Standing very still. Obviously afraid and trapped.

Miranda flashed upon Magoo, whom she'd rescued from the pound. If Magoo were ever trapped, she would certainly hope somebody would rescue him, and wished she could do the same for the goat.

Another mournful blast from one of the tour boats shattered the silence.

Barely time for self—

—let alone a stray goat.

Surely, she consoled herself, it would eventually edge toward the window-like aperture and escape on its own. "Sorry," she murmured, and turned away to continue her mad dash for the jetty. That was when a large shadow loomed from behind, one arm raised. She started to let out a scream, but it never left her throat.

She saw stars and the world went dark.

[CHAPTER TWENTY TWO]

Mykonos, Greece

"But we *can't* leave without Miranda!" fretted Madge Blessing, wringing her hands anxiously. "Why, it, it would be unconscionable!"

She was just outside the open door of the air-conditioned wheelhouse of the *Meltemi II,* pleading with Captain Leonides and a stony-faced Chara Zouboulakis, who was leaning casually back against the varnished wood paneling, slender arms crossed intractably in front of her. The ship's engines were throbbing, the instrument panels surrounding the large old-fashioned ship's wheel glowed, the GPS map was switched on, and the green radar screen swept constant circles, bleeping at every obstruction it encountered, which was constant. At the stern the gangplank was being raised with a winch and hauled aboard.

A few feet behind Madge, Dimitris, hands clasped behind his back, kept his eyes studiously on the Astroturf, an unwilling spectator awaiting instructions.

Chara's oval face was devoid of emotion. "I am sorry, Mrs. Blessing, but we have already waited for half an hour. We should have sailed —" she glanced at her diamond-encrusted gold wristwatch "—thirty minutes ago. We have a schedule to adhere to. I believe I have made that perfectly clear when we first got off the motorcoach in town. Yes?"

"I know, I *know!"* fussed Madge. Her usually cheerful face was a mask of agitation, the chic shopping bags from various boutiques and gift shops that surrounded her as forgotten as the thrill of acquisition. "Perhaps Miranda got lost in town?"

Chara's expression did not change.

Madge turned to Captain Leonides. "Please, Captain," she pleaded. "Can't we just wait a *few* more minutes? Miranda might be here at any moment."

The captain's handsome face registered concern and grave solicitousness, but his voice was firm. "I am afraid we cannot." He shook his head sadly. "Ms. Zouboulakis is correct. Please understand our predicament, Mrs. Blessing. We have a schedule we are required to adhere to."

"This is *not,*" stressed Chara coldly, inspecting the perfectly manicured fingernails of one hand, "a private yacht, where the owner or charter party can decide to cruise or stay in one spot at whim. We have the other passengers to consider. Besides which—" she tossed back her long glossy mane in that manner of hers "—we have Oracle Cruises to answer to. I have already contacted the main office by telephone and reported a missing passenger. Our orders are to sail."

"But, but what's if something happened to poor Miranda? Perhaps —" Madge's face abruptly brightened. "Perhaps we could swing by Delos!" she suggested. "Perhaps Miranda's still there!"

"Mrs. Blessing." Chara's voice was icy. "It is out of the question. For one thing, we are not permitted to dock at Delos. Also, it is illegal for tourists to remain on the island after three o'clock. I believe I have made that perfectly clear also. Yes?"

"Yes. Yes, I *know.*" Madge wrung her hands as though washing them like an obsessive compulsive. "But I can't just leave her behind. Perhaps if I left the ship and waited . . . "

"That is your choice," Chara said without sympathy, "but you would have to leave the ship, surrender your boarding card, take your passport, and be on your own."

"And if we caught up with you in Turkey tomorrow?" Madge persisted. "That's always a possibility, isn't it?"

Chara shook her head. "But you would already have disembarked."

"Mrs. Blessing," Captain Leonides reminded Madge gently, "how would you even get there? The ferries are still not running. And I can assure you that the airlines are overbooked for days."

"Oh. Oh, dear. Yes, of course. Oh, Lordy, this is a fine mettle! I really don't know *what* to do. I do believe I feel rather faint."

"Might I make a suggestion?" the captain said kindly.

"Why, why of *course,* Captain. I would welcome it."

"I suggest you remain onboard. Ms. Kalli is a grown woman and obviously intelligent. Surely she is capable of catching up with us."

"You think so?" Madge looked at him for reassurance. "Oh, I do hope and I pray you're right," she said fervently. "But how would she catch up with us, if the ferries aren't running yet, and the airlines are overbooked?"

He smiled. "Mykonos is a very tourist-friendly island, and very safe. Crime is almost non-existent. Also, the police on this island are very efficient, and can arrange for a seat on an airplane in case of an emergency. In all likelihood, when you were in town today you did not see a policeman or a police car, did you?"

"Hmmm." Madge looked thoughtful. "Well, now that you mention it, no. I haven't." She sounded surprised. "And with all those jewelry shops—"

He smiled. "That is because they do not announce their presence. They are everywhere though, in plainclothes. Sitting outside shops or cafés, strolling the streets like locals or tourists rather than patrolling them in uniform. Rest assured that they will do everything in their power to assist Ms. Kalli. Now what I suggest you do is sit in the lounge and try not to worry." He looked over Madge's shoulder. "Dimitris!"

"Yes, Captain?" Dimitris snapped to attention.

"Escort Mrs. Blessing to the lounge. I think a bottle of sparkling water and perhaps a glass of good cognac will do her wonders. And carry her shopping bags to her cabin."

"*Kyría* Blessing?" Dimitris looked at Madge gently.

Still undecided, Madge waffled, then sighed, her bosom heaving. "Well, if you think that's for the best, Captain."

"I do, Mrs. Blessing. And please, try not to worry. I understand your predicament, and assure you we shall stay in touch with the local police by telephone. As soon as we hear anything, I shall personally see to it that you are informed of any developments. You have my word." He paused. "And now, if you will be so kind as to forgive me, I have my duties to carry out."

"Yes, yes, of course. How thoughtless of me! I quite understand, and I do apologize for putting you through so much bother."

"You need not apologize. In fact, it is we who owe you an apology if we failed to make this holiday anything but perfect for you."

Dimitris picked up Madge's shopping bags with one hand and placed the other gently on her arm. "Come, *Kyría.* You will see. Everything will turn out fine."

Madge forced a smile. "That's very kind of you, Dimitris. Yes. I do hope you are right," she said, allowing him to lead her from the wheelhouse toward the stern, and from there down the metal steps to the lounge below.

Chara stirred like an angry cat the moment Madge was out of earshot. "*Sto diavolo!*" she swore, adding in rapid-fire Greek: "*We* should apologize? For what? That woman and her so-called *sister* have been nothing but trouble from the start. Aris, you should have suggested she disembark. Then we would have a lot less to worry about!"

"Down, Chara, down," he advised her grimly. "The head office has ordered us to behave in a normal, caring manner. Or have you forgotten that we are supposed to conduct just another normal pleasure cruise?"

"Normal!" Chara's dark eyes flashed angrily. "None of these cruises are normal! You mark my words, Aris, those two women are nothing but trouble. We missed a good opportunity by not encouraging the Blessing woman to disembark."

Aris Leonides stared at her. When he spoke, it was as if to a recalcitrant child. "We both know what is at stake, Chara. Or have you forgotten? The less suspicions we arouse, the better. Now wipe that angry look off your face and circulate among the passengers. Assure them that despite Ms. Kalli's absence, everything is normal and being taken care of. Or would you rather raise everyone's suspicions?"

She drew a deep breath and composed herself. "Aye, aye, Captain," she said, her voice heavy with sarcasm, her sardonic salute nothing short of insubordination.

When she was gone, he went and stood behind the big ship's wheel. He surveyed the surrounding vessels in the protected harbor by eye, then checked each of the instrument panels. Finally determining that the coast was clear, he called out in a firm voice: "Cast off!"

The anchor chain rattled and clanked noisily upward, the hawsers tying the vessel to the dock were loosened and tugged onboard. Gradually, the *Meltemi II* began to inch away from the jetty, swung slowly around ninety degrees until the bowsprit was lined up with the entrance to the narrow harbor, and headed sedately out to sea.

From the banquette in the lounge, Madge watched Mykonos slip by, growing smaller and smaller, the whitewashed houses dwindling in size, Little Venice and the windmills at Kato Myli diminishing and then disappearing as the *Meltemi II* rounded the bulging southern tip of the island and sped up, heading east.

The cognac on the table in front of her was untouched.

Em came down from the sundeck, checking up on her. "You all right, luv?" she asked, genuinely concerned.

Madge put up a brave front. "Yes, dear," she said, forcing a smile. "I'm fine."

But Mykonos and Delos were already far behind, giving the illusion of sinking into the sea along with the giant, fiery ball of the sun.

No, Madge was thinking, everything is not fine. Not fine at all.

[CHAPTER TWENTY THREE]

Delos, Greece

Miranda drifted up from total blackness through varying, ever lighter shades of cloudy gray. When she moved her head, the spiky edge of a stone pressed against her cheekbone, and the abrasive discomfort brought her to full consciousness. Her eyes fluttered open. At first it was like seeing everything through a golden scrim. Then, as her vision slowly cleared, she was aware of the unblinking stare of a reptilian eye regarding her with interest.

"And who invited you to my wedding, cutie?" she murmured. "Oh. You must be from Harry's side of the family."

But it was a sage green lizard, and when she raised her head, it darted away.

"So you're the shy sort, huh? Not going to ask me to dance?"

She struggled to sit up, but her head pounded and the world seemed to tilt and spin dizzily, as if she were on some wildly twirling carousel. She felt overwhelmingly nauseated, and quickly shut her eyes and leaned back against a wall. After a few minutes the mad spinning seemed to slow. Opening her eyes again, she frowned at her surroundings. Stone walls, tinted golden by a setting sun, were spread out below her. Moving her head to one side, she found herself staring into a windowless aperture. Inside, the ledge of a floor fell away to a mosaic courtyard. She was alone.

But where?

She climbed halfway to her feet, but the effort intensified the brutal hammering in her head, and caused another bout of nausea and the world once again started to spin madly round. Shutting her eyes, she leaned back against the wall, fought down the bile that threatened to rise, and waited.

This time the twirling and nausea seemed to subside more quickly, although her head continued to pound mercilessly.

And this time, when she opened her eyes, the floodgates of memory flung open and rushed at her like a tsunami, and Miranda suddenly realized where she was.

On Delos, and she had a tour boat to catch!

Suppressing her pounding headache, Miranda stood up straighter, propping herself against the stone wall for support, and looked down toward the jetty. But there were no tour boats to be seen, and to the west the fiery red sun was melting into the sea until it became a thin liquid sliver before disappearing completely.

She recalled climbing Mount Kynthos, her mad dash downhill. But *then* what had happened? Had she fainted, or stumbled and hit her head? She searched her mind for recall, but couldn't remember a thing. Only that she'd been literally flying to catch the three o'clock boats, which were no longer there. Everything else, until she'd come to, was a total blank. As for the passage of time, the sun had obviously set.

What time *was* it?

She instinctively glanced at her wrist and remembered her missing wristwatch. Then it came to her—the cell phone! It would tell her the time.

Her eyes, vision still fuzzy, searched the ground around her while she gingerly examined a large bump on her head with one hand. It felt like the size of an egg, and her hair around it was matted, obviously with dried blood. Then, uttering a small cry of triumph, she noticed her shoulder bag lying on the ground, part of its contents scattered like litter. Slowly, very slowly in order to keep the nausea and dizziness at bay, she knelt down and began to gather up her possessions in the dimness of a pink, silken sky. Delos map and guidebook . . . pens, wallet, notepad, address book, *Meltemi II* boarding card, lipstick.

She widened her visual search. There! A short distance away, her brushed metal cell phone gleamed in the jackgrass like a prize. Hopefully it hadn't been crushed.

She snatched at it with trembling fingers, fumbled it open, and breathed a sigh of relief as the tiny screen glowed bright blue. Not crushed, praise Almighty Zeus. It was still working. And it registered 12:46.

12:46 Eastern Standard Time . . . she forced her mind to count forward. That made it 7:46 p.m. here in Greece.

Holy Moley! Almost eight o'clock?

Carefully she stood up, avoiding any abrupt movements that might set off her dizziness and nausea, and exacerbate her still pounding head. She was all too aware of hours having passed. Again, she looked downhill. Except for the soft soughing of the wind, Delos was silent as a tomb. And almost deserted.

Almost, but not quite. She could see a few tiny squares of scattered dim lights far away, glowing from beyond the area of the Sacred Lake. The archeologists' tiny houses! Now to get down there before it got *too* dark and she couldn't see a thing.

Carefully shouldering her bag, Miranda moved at a snail's pace, holding onto the walls of the maze of stone houses, then struck off toward the tantalizing lights she had seen. As evening dimmed, she was cautious to avoid the multiplicity of antiquities, each one a potential obstacle she might trip over, or walk right into, and there were thousands. No, there were tens of thousands.

Antiquities, her beloved antiquities, had suddenly become her enemies in the darkling of the night. The new moon was a mere sliver, and shed scant light.

She felt like a ghost feeling her way cautiously past the Sanctuary of Apollo and the dark, locked museum and gift shop. Then on to the area of the Sacred Lake. She heard no stealthy footsteps now, nothing but the skimming wind rustling the fronds of the palm and making faint skittering sounds as it whispered through the dried rushes and jackstraw. Except for the squares of light emanating from the archeologists' houses, she couldn't help but feel like a trespasser in some mysterious necropolis.

Foreign voices—human voices—coming from the present and not the ghostly past, wafted on the wind from one of the scattered houses. She headed toward it, feet stumbling on marble pavers and stones. Approaching it, she was about to knock on the wooden door when it opened from within, trapping her in a trapezoid of blinding electric light.

She froze like a rabbit caught in oncoming, speeding headlights and threw up an arm against the glare, which set her diminishing headache pounding back full force. Silhouetted against the bright rectangle was a tall powerfully built man. "*Né?*" His voice hovered somewhere between that of a tenor and a baritone.

"I'm sorry to intrude." She gestured helplessly. "I don't speak Greek, I'm afraid. Do you speak English, by any chance?"

In the room beyond, the babble of impassioned voices fell silent.

"Yes. As a matter of fact, I do." His English, despite his Greek accent, was colored with the unmistakable upper crust modulation that could only come from expensive British boarding schools. His glance was at once inquisitive and provocative, and his perfect white teeth gleamed. "Can I be of assistance?"

Then, aware of the smudges, scrapes, and scabs on her face, arms, and legs, he invited her in. "I think you had best come inside." He stepped back to let her enter and reached out, touching her arm gently to draw her in as she squeezed past him

At first, she was aware of only him. His head nearly touched the low, varnished wooden ceiling, and aside from his white shirt and black trousers, he reminded her of certain Greek statues she had seen in museums and art books.

He was cleanly shaven, and whether by accident or design, his hair was rather short and curly. His eyes were dark, penetrating, and mesmerizing, and he had the strong chin, square-jawed face, full lips, and noble nose like those of a classical Hellenic sculpture brought to life. Only instead of being chiseled from white marble, he was deeply tanned.

He was, she thought, one of the most handsome men she had ever seen, and it was all she could do to tear her eyes off him and look around.

She was in a small room, crowded with a cluster of some fourteen men and women, all who twisted around to stare at her. A cheap, flowered curtain, dividing the space into a narrow bedroom area containing a bunk bed built into the wall, had been pushed aside and held in place by a piece of rope. A hodgepodge of folding chairs had been arranged to form a kind of semicircular cluster around a rickety table so that the three people sitting on the bottom bunk were included.

Miranda realized she had obviously interrupted some kind of meeting or discussion. The air was blue with cigarette smoke that stung her eyes and made them water, but this was Greece, where old habits died hard and she, as the intruder, was in no position to complain.

Keeping the door open to help air out the room, her host said, "My name is Apostolos Malinakis, but my friends all call me "Apos." He left off the 's' in speech, making it Apo. "I am an overseer of archeological sites from the Ministry of Culture in Athens. And you are?"

"Miranda Kalli." The words spilled out of her in a rush. "I don't know what happened, but I must have stumbled and fallen. When I came to, the last of the tour boats was already long gone, and now I'm afraid the ship I was on has probably sailed off without me!" She realized she was prattling nervously like a clumsy, fidgeting goat, but couldn't help herself. "I don't know what I'm supposed to do. I know I shouldn't even *be* here."

A thin, red-haired woman in a lime green top pushed back her chair and jumped to her feet. One look at Miranda and she exclaimed, "*La pauvre nécessité premier secours!*"

"Yes," said another, in French-accented English, also scraping back her chair. "I will fetch the first aid kit at once."

"No, please!" Miranda's hand twitched on her thigh and she looked pleadingly at Apostolos Malinakis. "I somehow have to get back to the ship. If I don't, I'll be stranded!"

"When did your ship leave?"

"It was supposed to sail at four-thirty. If I don't reach it, it'll be in Kusadasi tomorrow!"

"I believe the cruise ships are still in port," he said reasonably. "They leave much later. I can get you back to Mykonos in time."

"No, no! It isn't one of those big ships. It's a small one. You most likely haven't even heard of it. The *Meltemi II.*"

She glimpsed something . . . a dark shadow? . . . a fleeting flicker of interest? . . . momentarily deep within his eyes. Then it was gone.

"Ah. One of the *Meltemi*s," he said dryly. "I see."

There wasn't time to delve into what he meant. "It's really urgent that I catch up with it," she blurted. "The reason I'm on that ship—well, it's a long story, but as you probably know, the ferries are still grounded and all the flights are overbooked. I'm supposed to be working on an archeological dig on Samos even as we speak."

"Samos!" He raised one eyebrow. "You are an archeologist?"

Miranda made a deprecatory gesture. "Well, kind of. I was trained in archeology, but I work in a gallery in New York. I never had the opportunity to work on a site, so when Professor Hirsch sent for me, I immediately said yes."

"Professor Hirsch?" His ears perked up. "You mean, Professor Waldemar Hirsch?"

"Yes! Why, do you know him?"

He smiled, and she found herself drawn to him; there was something charismatic about him, a quality rare among most men she met.

"Indeed," he replied, with an enigmatic nod. "The professor and I are quite well acquainted."

"What a coincidence!" she cried. "Professor Hirsch was my major advisor plus the head of my doctoral committee!"

"Perhaps it is not such a coincidence. Greek archeology is a small world. I help oversee various archeological sites for the ministry, to make certain that all the correct protocols are observed. These include Ancient Asprodavos, which is Professor Hirsch's site. Like this site, which is French, I visit his, which is German, on a regular basis."

"So you are friends!"

He smiled again. "A better description might be that we are friendly acquaintances. It is possible that he might even consider me a thorn in his side. I'm afraid the heads of the various archeological teams do not appreciate my interference."

"But why?"

"We can discuss that another time."

The Frenchwoman in the lime green top had appeared with a green metal box with a white cross containing the first aid kit.

"Is this really necessary?" asked Miranda, in desperation. "I simply *have* to catch up with the *Meltemi II*. Surely they'll see to my surface scratches once I'm onboard."

"But you have a large knot on your head! And there is matted blood in your hair. Not to mention all those scrapes and scratches."

"I appreciate your concern, but that can surely wait," Miranda said anxiously. "I've got to get back on that boat."

Apostolos Malinakis frowned thoughtfully for a moment, assessing her physical condition. "The *Meltemi* left around five o'clock. I saw those unmistakable red sails with my own eyes. Now it is—" He consulted his black scuba wristwatch. "—a little past eight o'clock. The *Meltemi* generally sails at eight knots, which means it is likely to be twenty-four nautical miles distant."

Miranda's face fell. "Damn!" she whispered under her breath.

"On the other hand, if we do not see to your first aid treatment, we could reach the vessel within the hour. I have the Ministry of Culture's boat here, and if we go fast—" he looked at her solemnly "—we could reach it within the hour. It would be a very uncomfortable ride. Are you certain you are up to it?"

"Yes!" Her eyes glowed. "Please. I'd be forever so grateful. I'll do anything to repay you."

"Anything?" He smiled.

"Well, within reason."

He rattled off something in French, and one of the men around the table got up and produced a heavy woolen sweater and a rain slicker out of a chest. He held them out to Miranda.

"*Merci,*" she said fervently. "I'm most indebted. It will be returned forthwith. You will return it for me, Mr. Malinakis?"

He favored her with that charismatic smile. "So long as you call me Apo," he said. "Now we'd better hurry if we want to catch up with your, er, ship. And yes, Ms. Kalli, I shall see to it that these clothes are returned."

"It's Miranda," she told him.

"Miranda," he repeated. "Like the character in *The Tempest.*"

"Yes." She nodded.

"Then follow me." He grabbed a halogen flashlight from beside the open door and, playing its powerful beam back and forth, led her hurriedly but safely past antiquity's obstacle course towards the jetty.

It was nothing if not a wild ride.

The boat belonging to the Ministry of Culture was a rigid inflatable with a tiny, three-sided fiberglass cabin forward. It was equipped with a chrome radar arch mounted with electronics, searchlights, and running lights, and was powered by massive twin outboards.

Once they'd cleared the strait between Rheneia and Delos and were in open waters, Apostolos opened it up to full throttle. The wind was strong, the sea choppy and white-capped, and the rounded bow of the small boat rose up thirty degrees, bouncing—almost flying—from one watery trough to the next.

Huddled in the shelter at the front of the three-sided cabin, Miranda was grateful for the sweater and rain slicker. The huge outboard engines crescendoed to a deafening roar, making conversation impossible, and with each wave they rammed, a torrent of chill saltwater lashed the plexiglass windshield like a blast of hailstones. Despite being protected from the worst of it, Miranda was soon drenched. In other circumstances it might have been adventurous, even exhilarating, but each wave they thudded into was bone jarring and sent fresh splinters of pain shooting through her still-pounding head. Salt spray flew past in a blur, sheets of water streamed down the open rear of the tiny cabin and inevitably trickled into her borrowed slicker, stinging every scrape and scab like sharp needles.

Apostolos was like a madman behind the wheel, a modern-day

Odysseus out-running the Furies, a Formula One racer on water. He was clearly in his element, meeting every trough head-on, throwing back his salt-lashed face and laughing at the challenge.

"Are you all right?" he yelled every now and then down into the little cabin, the sides to which Miranda clung to for dear life.

"Yes!" She shouted back the lie, which was lost to the roaring engines and torn away by the wind.

And on he raced, his lips drawn across his teeth, his eyelids narrowed.

The rugged inflatable was obviously designed to take a lot of punishment, and he clearly relished every moment of it. He was English-schooled, very much the gentleman and overseer of archeological sites, but deep inside him was a daredevil screaming to be let out.

Miranda's stomach lurched, and she desperately fought down the bile, masking her churning insides by concentrating on the pain shooting through her skull and the salt spray torturing her every scratch and scrape. Like a participant on a wild carnival ride, it was too late to wish she hadn't gone on it, too late to turn back. Her only choice was to clench her teeth and ride it out. Every second felt like an excruciating, drawn-out minute. The blazing beam of a searchlight atop the radar arch pierced the darkness ahead, backlighting her from beyond the streaming plexiglass windshield.

How much longer, she wondered, until this insane ride would end? Surely they would soon reach the *Meltemi II?* She fervently hoped so.

Apostolo ducked down again. "I've got her on the radar screen!" he shouted. "Only about six more miles to go. Hang in there!"

She nodded, her face white as a sheet. *Only* six more miles? At this point, "*only*" seemed like forever.

Then finally, after what seemed like hours, the roar of the powerful engines diminished and the rigid inflatable slowed perceptibly. Apostolos ducked down again and grinned, his face and hair soaked.

"We're almost there. We already have visual contact. See for yourself if you like. I'm radioing them to cut their engines." His head quickly disappeared topside.

Bruised and battered, and despite the inflatable's increased heaving, pitching and yawing now that they were slowing down instead of flying across the troughs, Miranda's spirits rose like a balloon. Clinging onto the built-in fiberglass handles to either side of her she cautiously maneuvered herself around, careful not to hit her head on the low roof of the cabin. Looking through the streaming and splattered windshield, she could make out the beam of the inflatable's high-powered searchlights glinting silvery off the black swells with their foamy crests.

Her heart gave a leap.

Not a quarter of a mile distant, the searchlights caught blurry strings of festive lights swaying from the *Meltemi II*'s aft deck and angling up to the rear mast, and from there swagging to the one forward. Even from a quarter mile away, with the sails furled as she motored sedately, *Meltemi II*'s profile was unmistakable.

The water-blurred view of the lit lounge windows beckoned gaily.

As they closed in on the vessel, it seemed to grow in size and had obviously cut its engines to an idle. Miranda crawled out from inside the cabin and clung to the radar arch with one hand, her legs spread in a wide stance in order to keep her balance, shifting her weight from one leg to another.

Minutes later they pulled alongside. The *Meltemi II*'s dark hull, brightened with a sprinkling of lit portholes, loomed like a curvaceous cliff.

Apostolos was on his loudspeaker, rattling off orders in Greek. On the deck high above, there was a sudden flurry of activity. A stepped gangplank was lowered and Apostolos threw up two lines for crewmen to catch.

Miranda blinked back the salt runnels from her face and slipped off the slicker and borrowed sweater. Her eyes shone like luminous pools as they met his. "I don't know how to thank you enough."

He held her gaze, and even in half-shadow, she was once again aware of his extraordinary classic features, the tanned face and hungry mouth. Despite her aches and pains and discomforts, she felt all her senses aflame. This cultured daredevil brought out the woman from deep inside her, and she could feel a redness creep from her bosom to her throat and up into her face. Quickly she averted her eyes, but she couldn't hide her excitement.

"It was my pleasure," he replied softly. "Do not forget your bag." He reached past her into the cabin, and she felt his arm brush against hers. He slipped the straps of the bag over her shoulder, his fingers lingering a little longer than necessary. "I shall be on Samos in a few days," he said. "It appears the Fates have brought us together."

Miranda found it difficult to speak. "Yes." Her voice was husky, almost hoarse.

He held her hand and helped steady her in her awkward leap across the wide gunwale of the inflatable to the gently heaving gangplank, where Dimitris caught her. The instant Apostolos let go of her hand, she felt curiously bereft, as though she had lost touch with a peculiar kind of reality.

Dimitris had a blanket ready that he draped over her shoulders. "Come, *despiní,*" he said gently, leading her up the steps of the gangplank.

Miranda nodded but hung back a moment as the lines were tossed down to the inflatable. She watched as Apostolos put the big throbbing outboards in gear and then, with a wave, expertly turned the little boat around on its axis and opened up, heading back to Delos at full speed. The last thing Miranda saw in the glow of the *Meltemi II*'s lights was the name on the inflatable's transom:

"*Hera.*"

Then Apostolos switched off the searchlights and save for the ever-distant running lights, was lost to the night.

Chara Zouboulakis was waiting at the head of the gangplank. "How good of you to have made it back, Ms. Kalli. And how fortuitous to already have met Mr. Malinakis." Her smile was suggestive, but there was something hard and unreadable in the depths of her eyes. "You do realize that he is among the most eligible bachelors in Greece?"

Miranda didn't know what to reply, but Dimitris filled the silence. "We best get *Despiní* Kalli inside," he said. "It appears she could use some first aid. Also, she must get out of her wet clothes before she catches cold." So saying, he steered Miranda aft toward the lounge.

"I shall see to checking her in with her boarding card," he called over his shoulder to Chara, who stood there, that inscrutable sphinx-like stare on her face.

Meanwhile the gangplank was hoisted aboard, the *Meltemi II*'s diesels throbbed anew, the vibrations of the decks increased and the ship sailed on, headed for the Turkish mainland.

[CHAPTER TWENTY FOUR]

At Sea

The nurses from New Zealand hovered about Miranda like a quartet of clucking hens.

First Fan insisted that Miranda take a good long shower to wash off the salt spray which was already encrusting her, and personally pushed up her sleeves and helped sponge her ever-so-gently.

Then, once Fan had helped Miranda change into dry clothes, she brought her back up to the lounge, where the four-some from Down Under made her lie back on one of the banquettes, requisitioning several pillows and clean white towels. All the while, Madge was at the periphery, at once delighted and relieved, but constantly fussing. She was especially worried about the knot on Miranda's head, which had begun to bleed again as it had gotten soaked, first with salt water and now with fresh.

"Not to worry, luv," Em assured Madge cheerfully. "She's in most capable hands."

"Give us that!" Don commanded brusquely, as Dimitris brought forth a first aid kit, which she instantly snatched from his hands and opened. "We *are* registered nurses, you know." She sniffed in that mannish way of hers.

"You *were* lucky you were wearing that baseball cap of yours, luv," Em added. "When you fell it must 'ave softened the blow. Otherwise . . . well, never mind. We've seen worse. Much worse."

"Thank goodness you're safe and sound and back onboard,"

Madge interjected as she paced back and forth. "You had me worried to tears!"

"You've 'ad us *all* worried," Em emphasized.

"My cap," Miranda murmured as Soph soaked a pad in alcohol and gently dabbed the knot on her head. "I must have lost it. Oh! *Ouch!*"

The alcohol, despite Soph's gentle ministrations, stung as she swabbed the wound.

"It'll be over in a second," Soph assured her matter-of-factly. "Then we'll smear on some bacitracin to avoid possible infection, and that doesn't hurt a bit."

"But you don't remember *anything?*" insisted Madge, fretting with maternal concern from the sidelines, to which she had been temporarily relegated. "Did you slip, or hit your head on anything in particular?"

"I really don't know. I can't recall a thing. It's as if it's all, well, a total blank."

The nurses paused to exchange meaningful glances, then continued about the business at hand.

"And then," Miranda continued, "when I came to—*Ouch!*" Em was dabbing a peroxide-moistened Q-tip along a deep scratch on her forearm.

"Sorry, luv. It won't 'urt but a second. Nasty scratch, that. We'll wrap it up in bandages, since this first aid kit lacks the proper needles for stitchin' it up. Might leave a slight scar, though."

Don spiked a glare over at Chara, who watched from a distance and added, in a voice that carried: "This really is the most basic kind of first aid kit! Quite shameful, if you ask me. I'll suggest to Captain Leonides that it be upgraded in the future. Not quite up to standard, I'd say. Oracle Cruises should equip their boats with something better."

Chara stared back stonily, then tossed her silken mane and with deliberate slowness disappeared forward.

"Good. Ghastly woman," Soph muttered. "Who does she think she is? Queen of the Aegean?"

"Forget *'er,*" Em said. "We have Miranda to concern ourselves with."

"But you really don't remember *anything?*" Fan asked Miranda gently. "How's your head? Is it pounding?"

Miranda smiled weakly, but refrained from nodding, lest the pounding in her skull increased. "Does Thor have a hammer?" she quipped.

Don ignored her attempt at humor. "Any vision impairment?" she demanded briskly.

"Well, things *were* blurry for a while. I really can't say for how long. And now and then they still get a little fuzzy, and I feel a bit queasy, but not nearly as much."

At a signal from Fan, the nurses withdrew toward the door to the aft deck and held a whispered confab. Madge took the opportunity to sit beside Miranda and held her hand. Miranda gave Madge's a squeeze. "You really are a sweetheart," she said softly.

"Oh, balderdash! But I do feel rather, well, rather responsible, my dear."

"Don't. I went off on my own. Plus, now I'm back. All's well that ends well. Right?"

Madge smiled. "You're a very brave young lady," she said, *sotto voce,* making certain no one was within earshot. "I've really come to feel that we *are* sisters."

Then the flock of nurses descended around Miranda once more. "We don't mean to alarm you, Luv," Em said in her best bedside manner, "but we're of the opinion that you might be suffering from a concussion."

"Concussion! Oh. Oh, *dear!* Oh, dear me!" Madge's hand flew to her breast and she looked crestfallen. "Oh, Miranda, I'm *so* sorry!"

Miranda forced a smile. "Don't be. Besides, haven't you noticed? I'm in very good hands. Better than Allstate's."

And she added to the quartet of nurses: "I really regret having put you all through so much bother."

"Bosh!" declared Em.

"'Tis no bother at all," added Fan.

"It's the very least we could do," added Soph.

"Us being nurses and all." Don wasn't about to be left out.

"You've all been angels," Miranda told them. Despite sitting up slowly, her head began spinning once more. "Now I think I'd better go down to the cabin and sleep. It's been a long day. Is there any aspirin?"

"Yes," Don said, eyeing the first aid kit's bottle suspiciously and checking the sell-by date. With a sour expression she dropped it back into the box. "I think I'd better give you some of our own."

"You've missed dinner," Em said, "and I bet you 'aven't had a thing for lunch, 'ave you?"

Miranda's lack of a reply spoke for itself.

"I'll see to it that Dimitris sends some broth down to your cabin," Soph declared.

"And I'll help get her downstairs," Madge said firmly. "Now come on, dear. Upsie daisy." Holding out both hands, she helped Miranda gently to her feet. She swayed unsteadily. Madge grabbed the shoulder bag to take down.

"I think I'd best come along," Em said, brooking no argument.

"I'm not exactly an invalid," Miranda protested.

"I never said you were," Em replied. "But those steps down can be lethal."

"All I need is a good night's sleep," Miranda told her.

"And I'm sure you'll get it," Em assured her.

It was only after they reached the cabin that Miranda realized how dead tired she was.

"Look, Miranda!" Madge burbled, pointing to the top bunk. Miranda looked. There, in the middle of her neatly made bunk, was her missing Swatch watch.

"They must have found it when they were making up the beds."

"I could swear I checked high and low for it," Miranda murmured.

"Never mind, my dear. Now, don't you think you should take the bottom bunk? At least for tonight?"

"No, Madge. And don't worry about me. You go on up and try to enjoy yourself. Once my head hits the pillow I'll be out like a light."

But Miranda was wrong. The sheets and pillow felt good and crisp and clean. Like a cradle, the ship rocked gently to and fro. Fresh air soughed softly through the vent.

She made herself comfortable, drank Dimitris' broth, and shut her eyes.

But she lay awake for far longer than she expected. Each time she shut her eyes, images of Apostolos Malinakis kept intruding. It seemed as though thoughts of him would keep her awake all night long.

Eventually she fell into a deep and restful sleep, but even then it was he who inhabited her dreams.

Apostolos. Apos. "Apo."

Now there was a man. One, she suspected, she would never want to wash right out of her hair.

She couldn't wait to see him again.

[CHAPTER TWENTY FIVE]

Kusadasi, Turkey

For Miranda there were too many sensations in the ship's lounge. Too much bright sunlight striking the gentle waters on the port side of the harbor and shooting silver dollar reflections that renewed the stabbing in her head. Too much multilingual chatter issuing forth from the passengers raiding the breakfast buffet, which groaned under the strain of the *Meltemi II*'s usual morning fare.

The aroma of freshly brewed coffee, usually her wake-up call, caused a mild resurgence of nausea.

The loud, ever-bickering German couple turned up the volume of their voices while the two Dutch women, munching their thin wafers of Wasa bread, seemed to send out unnaturally loud crunches.

And billowing in through the open rear door, the quartet of nurses, already outside on the aft deck, sounded like a happy aviary.

Sounds, even natural ones that ordinarily passed her by, assailed Miranda from all sides. But despite her queasiness, she was determined to put up a brave front. Holding onto handrails and the backs of chairs, she maneuvered her unsteady way behind Madge. It was too late now to wish she'd stayed in her bunk and kept on sleeping.

Dimitris greeted the two women with a smile whiter than Mykonos.

"*Kaliméra, Kiría* Blessing. *Despiní* Kalli. Welcome to Turkey. As you can see, we are docked at Scala Nuova. He gestured round at the windows of the lounge.

"Out there, beyond the docks, is Kusadasi."

Madge lowered her head and gazed out the starboard windows at row after row of dark portholes looming uncountably high from the sides of a giant cruise ship, like the dots of a gargantuan canvas by Lichtenstein. She darted swiftly over to the port side to enjoy a less obstructed view.

Dimitris took Miranda aside. "And how are you feeling this morning, *despiní?*" he inquired solicitously. "Did you enjoy a good night's sleep?"

"Yes, thank you Dimitris." Miranda still felt a little wobbly on her feet, and held onto a chair back. "And thank you also for last night's broth. It was, as we say in English, just what the doctor ordered."

He waved away her thanks. "It was nothing. The very least we could do under the circumstances. Also, your salt-soaked clothing of yesterday should be in your cabin soon. We saw to it that it was laundered."

Miranda couldn't thank him enough. "You are too kind," she said.

"Look, Miranda!" Madge burbled, gesturing impatiently with one hand for her to hurry to her side. "Tell me, dear. Am I dreaming, or seeing double, or what?" She had her nose pressed against the glass of one of the port side windows and was pointing directly forward.

Miranda gave Dimitris an apologetic smile. "I'm sorry, duty calls. I better see what Madge is up to."

"In the meantime, I shall prepare a breakfast plate for you," he told her gallantly. "It will be at your usual place by the banquette."

"That is very kind of you."

Joining Madge, Miranda shielded her eyes with her hand against the sun's glare and peered forward. For a moment, she too thought she was either dreaming or seeing double.

For docked directly in front of the *Meltemi II* along the right finger of the long dock was the ship's twin, identical in every way. It was yet another vessel which had obviously seen better days, with its blistered layers of paint and runnels of rust seeping from the portholes.

But that wasn't all. Everything else was exactly the same too: the seaworthy curvaceous hull built for whatever seas the unpredictable Aegean might throw up. The exact same size and shape as the *Meltemi II.* Those twin masts with much-mended, reddish-brown sails. The rakish bowsprit and obvious top-heavy additions to a once-sturdy cargo vessel that had been converted for maximum space for passenger usage.

Only the ship's name, mounted on a board at the stern, differentiated between the two vessels.

The other was christened *Meltemi III.*

"That is one of our three sisterships," explained an all-too-familiar voice from behind them, pronouncing the word 'seester-sheeps.'

Madge and Miranda turned in unison. There stood Chara Zouboulakis, glossy and fresh as the proverbial daisy. Fashionable as ever in a short, off-white lace mini dress with wide long sleeves and a silk bow tied, Empire-style, beneath her breasts.

Michael Kors, if the Manhattanite in Miranda was any judge.

"There are three sisterships, all built at the very same time and at the very same shipyard on Spetses," an unusually talkative Chara volunteered. "All three were eventually purchased by Oracle Cruises, and for frugality's sake, were converted into passenger vessels simultaneously. Hence their similarity."

She paused, then went on: "So we now have the *Meltemi,* the *Meltemi II,* and the *Meltemi III.* Simple, no? Also, you may inquire of yourselves why the *Meltemi III* is in port at the same time as we are. Yes?"

"I was going to ask you that," Miranda concurred.

"That is simple. We alternate round-trip routes. While the *Meltemi II*'s schedule is Athens, Mykonos, Kusadasi, Samos, Patmos, Kos, Amorgos, Ios, and Athens, the *Meltemi III* does the exact same alternate route. Athens, Ios, Amorgos, Kos, Patmos, Samos, Kusadasi, Mykonos, and Athens."

Chara favored them with a small smile of little warmth, then eyed Miranda closely.

"Ms. Kalli. Today is our all-day tour of Ephesus, including the Holy Shrine of the Virgin Mary and other attractions."

"Y-yes?" Miranda said slowly.

"Captain Leonides is very concerned about your health. The tour is a very long and exhausting journey. And due to yesterday's . . . well, unfortunate incident on Delos . . . and your injuries . . . "

Chara's English was good, but it wasn't perfect by a long shot. Yet even in Miranda's possibly concussed mind, the choice of words held a note that rang false.

"Incident?" she said. "You mean, accident, don't you?"

Chara shrugged and held up her hands. "Pardon my English. I realize it is not so perfect."

Miranda nodded. Incident. Accident. Yes, they certainly could possibly be interchangeable, she thought. But had it perhaps been a slip of the tongue? Those two words were, after all, not quite one and the same.

"As I was saying," Chara continued, neatly changing the subject back, "we are quite worried about your health."

Miranda forced a smile. "Yes. But I'll be fine, really I will." Seized by another round of vertigo, she gripped the back of the chair she was holding onto so tightly that her knuckles shone white. "I'm simply *dying* to see Ephesus. I've wanted to, ever since I was a child."

"And I've prebooked our tours," Madge added staunchly, backing her up.

"Yes, I quite understand," Chara replied.

She added, obviously by rote, "Ephesus is one of the world's great archeological sites and a major city of the ancient world."

"I really do want to see it," Miranda insisted. "Perhaps after I've had a bite for breakfast . . . "

Once again the sounds of voices and laughter, the aromas of ham and cheese, bacon and toast and coffee, assaulted her senses. She felt herself swaying as another wave of nausea threatened to overwhelm.

"Miranda?" Madge inquired anxiously, gripping her by the arm. "Are you certain you're up to it?"

Miranda's shoulders slumped and she sighed deeply. "Oh, *damn*! Well, perhaps Ms. Zouboulakis is right. I'm really not sure I'm in much of a condition to taking such a long tour."

"But, my dear!" Madge chided. "Why didn't you *tell* me you were still feeling so out of sorts?"

Miranda looked at her with a compassionate smile. "I didn't want to worry you or let you down. Besides, I thought that once I was up and about I'd be feeling so much better. What I need is, well, just to lie back down and get some more sleep. I think I'll return to our cabin. Really, Madge, don't look so worried! All I require is some more shut eye."

A gesture from Chara brushed that aside. "On the contrary, Ms. Kalli. You might be suffering from a serious concussion. I insist you are taken to see a doctor—"

"But I just want to go and lie down!"

"I am sorry, but I must insist." Chara's voice brooked no argument. "It is Oracle Cruise Line's policy, as this vessel is not large enough to warrant a full-time onboard physician. Please understand that we could otherwise be held, how do you say? Legally liable?"

Miranda drew a deep breath and shut her eyes.

"Don't worry, dear," Madge clucked kindly. "I'll go with you."

Miranda opened her eyes and shook her head. "No, Madge," she said adamantly. "When I'm on Samos, I can always pop over here, and I shall. But this is probably the only chance in your lifetime that you'll ever get to see Ephesus. So let's make a deal, okay?"

Madge sniffed. "I don't like making deals, my dear."

"Yes, but this one's for both our sakes. You go see the sights and I'll be a good girl and see the doctor. What do you say?"

It was Madge's turn to sigh. "You're not giving me much choice," she said pointedly.

And so it was settled.

"As Scala Nuova is an international port," Chara told them, "there is an extensive security system. They even perform under-vehicle inspections for any busses and automobiles that enter the area. You shall be needing your plastic boarding card to disembark, and also to get back inside the complex."

"Oh. It's down in the cabin," Miranda murmured. "In my shoulder bag. I'll go get it—"

"You will not!" Madge said firmly. "You will stay right where you are and conserve your energy. *I'll* fetch it." And she headed forward and went below.

"I will have Dimitris set up the computer at the gangplank now rather than later," Chara said, managing to sound put out. "The tour bus leaves at nine, but I would prefer you saw the doctor sooner. He will be awaiting you. Adonis, one of our crew members who speaks both the fluent Turkish and the Greek, but unfortunately not the English, is familiar with the city. He will escort you there, and pick you up again and bring you back later. Yes?"

"You're sure I couldn't find my way there and back on my own?"

"No, Ms. Kalli. Absolutely not. Kusadasi is a large city, and the doctor is in the Old Town, past the bazaar. It is . . . what is the word? A warren?"

"A rabbit warren. Yes."

"I insist you are accompanied." Chara paused and flashed her a significant look. "After all, we already lost you once, Ms. Kalli. It would not do to lose you again, would it?"

[CHAPTER TWENTY SIX]

Kusadasi, Turkey

Later, Miranda was glad Chara Zouboulakis had insisted she not go unaccompanied. After guiding her through the maze of Scala Nuova's glossy arcade of expensive shops, pubs, outdoor café, duty free shop, and even a Starbuck's, Adonis (who resembled anything but his namesake) hailed a canopied, three-wheeled rickshaw with a double seat up front and a bicyclist in the back. Despite the early hour, August's heat was already brutal, and Miranda was grateful for the canopy's shade. Everything seemed to glare or pass by in a blur. She barely registered the fleets of luxurious motorcoaches parked outside the gated complex, or the park-like open area beyond the stands of palms, with the marina on the far side where pleasure craft of all sizes bobbed slowly to and fro and masts swayed gently. Nor was she aware of the dizzying traffic on the streets.

When they reached the edge of the bazaar, Adonis helped her out. She started to reach for her shoulder bag, but he shook his head and paid the cyclist. Then, gesturing for her to hold tight to her shoulder bag and stay close, he led the way.

At any other time, and under different circumstances, she might have found it all picturesque. Fascinating. Even exciting. In her current state, however, there was a nightmarish quality to it all. The already crowded bazaar's dim alleys were a confusion, an obstacle course of bright shiny goods, carpets, and designer rip-offs spilling out into their path, and there was the constant seige by merchants, the haranguing of insistent shills of all ages following them for several yards before giving up.

Then came a series of narrow, shop-lined alleys slanting sharply uphill, with flight after endless flight of vertiginous, never-ending stone steps bisected by yet more alleys. They turned left, climbed some more, turned right, trudged up yet another steep flight.

To either side, rows of crumbling, once-grand old houses seemed to tilt drunkenly inward, as though purposely blotting out the sky, or intent upon fulfilling some age-old prophecy to eventually merge roofs. Many had glass-enclosed wooden balconies, like oriel windows, jutting out from the floors above. The higher they climbed, the larger and grander the dilapidated houses seemed to become, though their walls still abutted each other like rows of dominoes, and gave the impression that if you removed one, the rest of the row would tumble downhill, all the way to sea level.

Finally, near the crest, Adonis stopped at a wide house. Consisting of several stories with long, elegant barred windows on the ground floor, it was obviously a city mansion from a bygone era, and had an oversized peeling wooden door set symmetrically into a wall of peeling stucco. Leaning her head back and looking up, Miranda could see several of those balcony-like oriel windows.

To the right of the door was a tarnished bronze plaque that looked like it hadn't seen polish in years. It was engraved in exotic Turkish script:

Dr. Bedir Zeki Babutcu

Permitting herself a major breath of relief, Miranda wiped the glisten of perspiration off her forehead with the back of her hand. Her head was reeling, she was totally disoriented, and from her strenuous breathing felt as if she'd climbed Mount Everest. Above all, she was grateful for Adonis. It seemed nothing short of a miracle that he'd managed to deliver her unerringly to the doctor's door: safely, unharmed, and with her shoulder bag and its contents intact.

Adonis pushed a buzzer beside the plaque and they waited. After a minute or two, Miranda was about to ring it again, but Adonis' gentle hand on her arm stayed her finger.

Eventually, she heard the sound of a big old-fashioned key turning in the big old-fashioned lock, and the great door creaked open.

She hadn't known what to expect, certainly not this Ghandi-thin, lively little man wearing wire-rimmed spectacles and a striped, floor-length djellaba. He must have been eighty, if a day. He had a white skull cap on his shiny pate and longish, thin white hair combed down the sides, giving him the appearance of a spry and thinner Benjamin Franklin. Unlike Franklin, however, he had a neatly trimmed white goatee and despite his advanced years there was something gentlemanly about his demeanor. Miranda was immediately taken by the twinkle in his gently inquisitive dark eyes.

"Come in, come in, *effendi,*" he told Miranda in halting English, and stood aside, inviting her inside with a courtly gesture from a tremulous hand.

She looked hesitantly at Adonis, who cracked a gap-toothed smile and nodded encouragingly and signaled that he would be back. After a moment she decided that if you couldn't trust an old man who looked like a relative of the guy whose mug was on every hundred-dollar bill, who could you?

Smiling shyly, she stepped across the threshold. Behind her, she could hear the heavy door creak shut and slam; the giant key grating in the giant lock.

"For safety," the old man assured her. "Here, at crossroads of East and West, are many thieves and bad peoples. You understand?"

"Yes."

He drew himself up with pride and held out a brittle hand. "I am Dr. Bedir Zeki Babutcu."

She shook the proffered hand. His grip was surprisingly strong and warm, a fact she found oddly comforting. "Miranda Kalli," she said.

"A beautiful name." He beamed up at her. "Please, come. Come . . ."

And carpet slippers flapping, he led the way down an airless, dim, high-ceilinged hall. Overhead, an aged chandelier, reminiscent of the antebellum South, dripped dirty icicles of crystal, too dulled by neglect to tinkle. Tall doors, some open, some half-shut, lined both walls. Glancing inside them as she passed, it was clear to Miranda that these once-palatial rooms, with closed and shuttered windows, hadn't been used for years, perhaps decades. The salmon and *eau de nil* walls of yesteryear had long since faded to a dull gray, with only the barest tones of color struggling through.

She sneezed. Then sneezed again.

Dust. A thick fuzz of it blanketed everything. Upholstered Victorian settees and delicate French chairs long since leached of color. Once bright brass trays on stands which had turned an ugly ashy brown; octagonal tables from Syria whose intricately inlaid patterns were no longer discernable. And on the floors, palace-size carpets that once upon a time had glowed like opulent stained glass, and now lay dead and spiritless, like faded beauties begging to be brought back to life.

Pinching her nostrils to avoid yet a third sneeze, Miranda was reminded of Miss Haversham's house in *Great Expectations.*

The only thing missing seemed to be the decayed wedding cake.

"This way, *effendi.*"

She had to hurry to keep up with the spry little doctor.

Up a once-grandiose staircase he led her, beside a wall of glass panels set into tall graceful Moorish arches. Through the yellowed glass she caught glimpses of a large overgrown courtyard. On the second floor, surrounding it on all four sides, was a roofed verandah supported by a colonnade of ogee-topped arches.

The small room to which he showed her was on the second floor, but faced one of the outside walls. After the dust-choked ground floor, Miranda found it amazingly neat and clean and reassuring. With its old-fashioned equipment it looked like a time capsule, a Norman Rockwell of an examination room.

The walls were glossy white, the glass-fronted enameled cabinets sparkled, and the vintage stainless steel examination table gleamed. Along one wall was a narrow hospital bed with a white enamel frame; cater-cornered to it, a tall window looked out across a sea of red tiled roofs. Its panes were spotless and it was thrown open to the fresh air. The light was so bright that Miranda was momentarily blinded, and had to shield her eyes.

Seeing her expression, Dr. Babutcu smiled indulgently. "*Effendi* is surprised?" he asked gently.

"Yes," she replied honestly.

He nodded. "I am old man and only practice medicine on special occasion. My wife is dead over thirty years, and the children and grandchildren—" he shrugged and sighed philosophically "—have scattered like sand in the wind to places where they earn what they call 'real money.' London, New York, Shanghai. They have no use for the Turkish tree from which they stem. And I?" He laughed softly. "I am too old to move. That is the reason for the condition of the house, yes?"

"It must have been very beautiful once," Miranda said quietly.

"Beautiful? Oh, yes!" He moved aside, perhaps purposely so that his spectacles refracted the light from the window and she was unable to see the expression in his eyes. "Long ago there was music and laughter and much dancing. Then." He shrugged once more and waved away the memories as though they were a swarm of pesky flies. "But enough of that. I notice that the light, it hurts the eyes. Yes?"

Miranda nodded, and he hurried over to the window. He pulled the shutters to and tilted the slats to minimalize the light. The room was cast into dimness and shadows, with only the barest, thread-thin ladders of light leaking through the slats and across the floor and up one wall, lending the clean white space a mysterious air of chiaroscuro.

"Is that better?" he asked.

"Much." Miranda nodded her thanks.

"Good." Dr. Babutcu gestured to the examination table. "Please. Have a seat. Meanwhile I go wash the hands and disinfect. Yes?"

While he went next door, she hopped up on tiptoe and scooted up onto the edge of the table, sitting there and swinging her legs, feeling like a child. As she waited, she could hear the sound of running water in the other room. An old-fashioned dial-tone telephone rang, and the splashing of water abruptly ceased. She tilted her head to listen. First there was only what had to be the usual short greeting, but that quickly dropped to a sibilant whisper in a tongue she couldn't catch or make out. Turkish, most likely, or perhaps Greek or Kurdish? She had no idea. Then suddenly his voice turned sharp and argumentative, then reluctant, and finally resigned. When the conversation was over, the splashing of running water resumed.

Miranda breathed deeply.

With the shutters closed against the fresh air breezing in through the window, she became aware of something else. Various strange aromas.

These were not the usual hospital odors of disinfectants, astringents, and unguents, though she recognized those too, but underneath them, her olfactory senses detected other, more primitive and unidentifiable smells. There was about them the various sharp tang and musty pungence of herbs and distillates.

Something about it unlatched a long-forgotten mental lockbox and drew her inexorably back to her childhood. Back to when she had been six years old. It was 1983.

It had to have been a Saturday or a Sunday, because she wasn't at school, and her mother had taken her into San Francisco to a dress rehearsal of visiting *cancíon* singers who were scheduled to give an important performance that evening. It was about two o'clock in the afternoon and everything was going well. Until, that is, La Perla, one of the lead female singers, suddenly developed a soreness in her throat. Miranda could hear the raspy hoarseness in the performer's voice even before it gave out completely and she began to cough uncontrollably.

Her mother immediately took charge and insisted upon taking the woman to a specialist. But La Perla kept shaking her head and spoke vehemently in hoarse, rapid-fire Spanish. She was gesticulating wildly and kept using the words *maldición* and *bruja* and *diablo,* and refused to listen to her mother's reasoning.

Finally Mrs. Kalli gave in and, with Miranda in the back seat, drove the woman to a *Botanica* in the Mission District.

To little Miranda, it was an adventure.

The *Botanica* was located in a rundown storefront between a Mexican *bodega* and a shop dealing in cheap second-hand furniture. Miranda was fascinated by the *Botanica*'s window display. In front of a purple velvet curtain stood a large painted plaster statue of a man in a turban and harem pants yielding an ax. And arranged all around was an assortment of strung beads and trinkets, talismans and candles, and various smaller statues.

Stepping inside was like crossing over into another world, a world presided over by a fat but stately *curandera* who wore a voluminous robe shot through with silver threads representing arcane symbols. She had giant dangle earrings and multitudes of long strung beads that cascaded down her huge bosom and dropped off to dangle in midair, as if from the face of a jutting cliff.

The interior was airless and stifling. Shelves held garish plaster saints in all sizes. Instead of electricity, the entire place was lit by multitudes of candles in tall glass cylinders, and their flickering flames filled her with a sudden dread. She nearly choked on the miasma of smoky wax and incense intermingling with the earthy, musty smells of dried leaves, fungi, herbs, and roots. One wall was devoted to loops of beads with talismans dangling off the ends, and the entire back wall was devoted to jars containing what looked like powders and dried greens and brittle bones. Some were filled with liquids, and had squeamish things floating inside them that she had rather not look at.

Quickly she looked away. What she had at first found fascinating had turned repellent.

"You have come because of your voice," the *curandera* told La Perla in a somber tone before she could even open her mouth.

"*Sí,*" replied the singer raspily. "How . . . how did you know?"

"Because I see the aura of a *maldición* surrounding you," was the reply.

"Can you cure it?" Mrs. Kalli inquired, with a mixture of hope and suspicion.

The *curandera* turned to her. "For a time, *sí, Señora.* But *el Diablo* cannot be rid of in an instant. It takes time. Many prayers, offerings, blessings, and devotions."

"In other words," said Mrs. Kalli, ever practical where financial matters were concerned, "by the word 'offerings,' you mean money."

The *curandera* gestured helplessly, as though she had no choice. "You do not understand, *Señora.* God and his saints require sacrifice. In olden times it might have been a sheep or a goat. But this is today. The currency of sacrifices has changed."

"La Perla has a performance tonight." Miranda's mother emphasized.

The *curandera* nodded. "Then we shall best begin at once and do what we can."

Miranda clung to the back of her mother's skirt, peering around it every now and then before burying her face back into the folds of fabric.

First came a multitude of chants in languages she couldn't understand. That was followed by a sprinkling of water from a bottle.

"This is Holy Water from the sacred well of the Virgin of Guadalupe," the *curandera* explained.

To Miranda, it looked like ordinary water that had come out of a tap.

More prayers and mumbled incantations followed. As in a trance, the *curandera* began to dance around the singer, shaking castanets on which saints' pictures had been garishly painted. Several jars of dried herbs and weeds were opened and sprinkled upon La Perla. A smelly brew of some sort was heated on a hotplate, which the singer sipped, grimacing with every swallow. Finally the *curandera* solemnly looped a string of beads around the singer's neck.

"You must never take them off, even when you sleep," she cautioned La Perla severely. She then pressed a crucifix to the woman's forehead, breasts, and throat.

At last the ceremony was finished.

"You are temporarily cured," the *curandera* told the singer. "You shall sing beautifully tonight. But do not expect the spells of the saints to last. You must undergo regular ritual cleansings."

"*Sí,*" La Perla said sincerely. "*Gracias.*"

"Mommy!" Miranda whispered once they left the storefront. "It smelled *awful* in there!" She hoped never to have to smell the malodors of those strange herbs and weeds ever again.

"Hush honey," Mrs. Kalli told her gently. "Now be a good girl and get in the car and enjoy the ride back."

That night, the show went on, and La Perla enraptured the audience. Miranda watched the performance from backstage.

Was the singer cured, even temporarily? Or had she suffered some kind of psychosomatic symptoms that regular visits to a *Botanica* cured?

Miranda never did figure that one out, nor did she have any inclination to. She preferred the miracles of modern medicine, and hoped she would never have to smell those vile herbalistic odors ever again.

Until now, in Kusadasi, at Dr. Babutcu's.

Trying to discover the source of the smell, she scooted around on the examination table and eyed the medicine cabinet. The top three shelves held the usual array of medical equipment and medications. But below them, the two lower shelves were devoted to an array of glass jars, bottles, and boxes carefully labeled in indecipherable Turkish. Some were filled with dried leaves and what she presumed were crushed herbs and powders; others with what appeared to be the roots or stems of unrecognizable plants.

To stay . . . or make tracks? That was the question. The little girl inside her wanted to flee. But Miranda wasn't a child anymore. And the gracious little doctor certainly wasn't a *curandera.* There were no garish plaster figurines or talismans or beads or castanets.

Nor was she feeling well. Her headache had lessened somewhat in intensity, but her head still throbbed painfully, and bright light hurt her eyes. Off and on a bout of nausea would grip her and the dizziness would return.

To top it all off, how in all Hades was she supposed to find her way back downhill to Scala Nuova alone, without Adonis to guide her?

In the next room, the water tap squeaked as it was turned off. The splashing ceased. A moment later, Dr. Babutcu returned.

"My sincere apologies for the interruption. An unexpected telephone call. Now, let us discover what ails you, yes? From the plaster on your head and the bandage on your arm and the sticky plasters, I assume you suffered an accident? Perhaps a fall?"

"Yes." Miranda frowned. "Well, actually I can't recall *what* happened. I have no memory of it at all. None."

He nodded and listened gravely, his head tilted thoughtfully to one side. "Hmmm. We have already established that you are sensitive to light. Your head, it hurts? Yes?"

"Not as badly as yesterday, but yes. It does."

He nodded again. "Do you feel nausea?"

"That too. It comes and goes."

"Those are the typical effects of a concussion. Now let me examine you. Yes?"

He produced a ring of keys, unlocked the glazed cabinet and took out a small light. Gently lifting her eyelids one at a time, he shone the light into them. Despite the tremor in his hands, his touch was surprisingly gentle. Then he shone it in her ears. Finally he unwrapped the bandage from her arm and removed the band-aids from her arms and legs.

He nodded approvingly. "It appears these were applied with some skill. No?"

"I was fortunate. There are some nurses on the tour."

He smiled. "Ah. So that explains it. Now I shall examine the, how do you say, 'egg?' atop your head. I will be gentle."

With his fingertips he probed around the nasty lump. "Not very nice," he murmured. "However, it could be worse."

"I was wearing a hat."

"Then you were very fortunate indeed, *effendi.* I shall now cleanse this wound and your scratches. Nothing appears in danger of infection. The long cut on your arm is healing well. I do not believe it requires sewing. Now, this may sting a little."

From the cabinet he took some swabs and a bottle of hydrogen peroxide and applied it to her various wounds. Then he daubed an antibiotic ointment on them and replaced the bandage on her arm with a fresh one, and the band-aids with new ones. He smiled.

"I believe you will survive," he said in a kindly voice. "What you need most is rest. I shall prepare you a special draught, and then you may lie down on the bed for a time. When Adonis returns for you, I believe you should feel much more yourself. Yes?"

She nodded and watched as he selected three of the herbal jars from one of the bottom shelves.

"Is that really necessary?" she asked, with a trace of child-like suspicion.

He looked at her. "It is a medicine passed down through many centuries. You shall find it quite effective. Never dismiss the healing properties of certain herbs. Remember, even aspirin is derived from the bark of a tree. You may sit on the bed now if you wish."

"Yes, doctor."

She slid obediently off the examination table and sat down on the edge of the narrow hospital bed while he took the jars into the adjoining room. Once again she heard the splashing of water. A short while later, she heard the steamy whistle of a kettle, the stirring of a spoon. When he returned, he handed her a small ceramic cup without handles set into a shiny brass holder.

She wrinkled her nose at the disgusting pungency rising from the hot brew. She glanced up at him. "Does it taste as terrible as it smells?"

He made a helpless gesture and smiled. "If anything, *effendi,* perhaps worse."

He remained standing there, making sure that she drank every drop.

She blew on the hot liquid to cool it and grimaced at every sip. The taste was vile and bitter, and she shuddered with every swallow.

"You were right, doctor," she told him when she was finished and handed back the empty cup. "The taste is even worse than its smell."

He allowed himself a small laugh. "Unfortunately, that is the case with many medicines. Now you must lie down, make yourself comfortable, and close your eyes. I shall fetch you when Adonis arrives."

He set down the cup and helped tuck her in, then tiptoed silently from the room, taking the cup with him.

Her head barely touched the pillow when her eyelids drooped shut and she fell into a deep, sound sleep.

[CHAPTER TWENTY SEVEN]

Kusadasi, Turkey

It seemed mere minutes before she awakened, but some time must have passed, for instead of bright light leaking through the slats of the shutters in thin slivers, it was obviously sunshine throwing even more dazzling patterns across the floor.

Miranda felt amazingly rejuvenated and alive. Even more amazing, her head no longer pounded when she sat up, nor did she feel the least bit nauseated or dizzy. Her vision was crystal clear—clearer than she had ever known it to be—but there was a dreamlike quality about it all, and yet she was not dreaming.

She was wide awake.

Feeling renewed, she stretched luxuriously. Her hearing seemed exceptionally acute, and she caught the faint sounds of faraway voices drifting from somewhere inside the house. Looking over at the door of the examination room, she noticed it had been left partially cracked, and she felt irresistibly drawn toward it.

Swinging her legs out over the bed, Miranda got up and headed over, feeling that she wasn't walking so much as skimming, almost floating, supernaturally across the cool inlaid tiles of the floor, her bare feet making absolutely no sound.

The door seemed to open of its own accord, so feather light was her touch.

Only now did she begin to realize the true enormity of the house. It had been designed so that the rooms on the two sides facing the outside world did so, while the ones abutting the adjoining buildings had multitudes of windows that faced the tall hallway which was built, four-square, around the central courtyard. French doors, many with cracked panes set into the Moorish-style tracery, led at regular intervals from the hall out to the covered verandah that surrounded the courtyard.

Stopping to look down, her newly crystalline vision registered the neglected tangle of the cloistered garden. Semi-tropical plants, left to their own devices, had carnivorously taken over, strangling the quatrefoil tiers of a once grand central fountain, its splashing waters long silent, its bowls brackish and murky with algae. Nature had asserted itself, and what must once have been a magical oasis had become a crowded and choked wilderness, with nary a bloom or blossom in sight.

Everywhere there was evidence of crumbling splendor, and even the filigree of the verdegried verandah posts themselves were not immune, and had become prey to creeping, lanky vines that snaked up and clung, tightening their evil grip like serpents intent upon bending them to their will.

From somewhere below the grand staircase, like phantom whispers, wafted the zephyrs of murmurs. And from somewhere overhead, she heard a girlish giggle, followed by the light patter of running feet. A lonely child playing a pretend game of hide and seek?

It was that, rather than the voices, which beckoned her.

On Miranda glided, down that ghostly hall and past unlit gaslight globes dripping dusty icicles of glass. It was as though she was under some kind of hypnotic spell and had no will of her own.

But she hadn't been hypnotized. She was up on her feet and wide awake. And there was a seductive mystery among these decaying walls which begged investigation.

Presently she reached a spiral staircase. She paused at its base and looked upward, her eyes following the whorl of concentric steps that wound up to the topmost floor above which a dirty skylight, splattered with pigeon droppings, leaked in weakened daylight.

Again she heard that girlish giggle, like some ghost leading her onward and upward.

Irresistible, it was.

With one hand on the cool banister, her feet barely touched the steps as she floated upward as though in slow motion. Around and around, up, up . . .

Atop the landing she paused to get her bearings. The ceilings up here were lower, and despite the thick walls, it was much warmer, the roof tiles absorbing the heat of the sun. But again, although the hall was narrower up here, it too surrounded the courtyard completely.

The muted giggles and sound of bare feet seemed to come from the far side, and she began to move in that direction. Then an open door attracted her attention. It was obviously a study, with book-lined walls crammed with volumes covered in cracked Morocco. A large mahogany desk of uncertain vintage, with an electrified brass Argand lamp, was centered to catch the light from one of those oriel-type windows that jutted out onto one of those glass-enclosed wooden balconies.

But that was not what had drawn her. The culprit stood temptingly in that enclosed balcony that opened out from the study: an old-fashioned brass telescope on a tripod. It was aimed at a downhill slant.

Curiosity, it is said, killed the cat. But she was not a cat, and her feet guided her effortlessly inside, across a thick Persian carpet, the faint giggles temporarily forgotten.

From the enclosed balcony, the view was breath taking. It encompassed square, rectangular, and hexagonally-tiled roofs descending the steep hill all the way to its base. There was a fine view of the sea stretching to the horizon, and closer in, the entirety of Scala Nuova, with its modern shopping arcades and long quays reaching out into the harbor like concrete runways. The giant white cruise ship was on one side, and another was arriving behind it. From here, the two *Meltemi*s, docked on the opposite, more protected side of the quay, looked smaller than a child's bathtub toys. A flock of pigeons fluttered past the window, so close Miranda felt she could have reached out and caught one, before they altered course and angled off in another direction. Hazy in the distance, she could make out the causeway leading out to picturesque Bird Island and its ancient fort.

Of course, looking through that telescope was as impossible to resist as it was to peer through a large keyhole lit from within, to where a violent argument was taking place. Shutting one eye, she pressed the other against the lens. For a moment she felt a deep sense of disappointment. All she could see was a cloudy blur.

Of course! How silly of her! She needed to adjust it, just as one needed to adjust a pair of binoculars. She found a brass dial and moved it clockwise and counter clockwise. Made minute adjustments until—

—zoom! The *Meltemi*s sprang into focus. So sharply and powerfully that Miranda felt as if she had been shot downhill at supersonic speed. More minor adjustments, more magnification, then the slightest sideways movement and she was scanning the aft deck of the *Meltemi II* and—

—she unconsciously jerked her eye back from the lens. Chara Zouboulakis seemed to loom in front of her, larger than life, striding purposefully down the gangplank, clipboard in hand.

But wasn't she supposed to be at Ephesus?

Miranda took a deep breath, consciously having to still her hands, and then refocus the lens. Suppressing the guilt of voyeurism, she couldn't help herself and zoomed back a bit, following Chara's brisk pace until she was lost among the buildings of the shopping arcade.

Steady.

Slowly Miranda scanned the entrance to Scala Nuova and waited. *There!* Chara emerged with a uniformed official, those Bronzino eyes sweeping the ever-present fleet of motorcoaches, then finding one and gesturing impatiently.

Miranda inched the telescope in the direction Chara had indicated. She watched the door of a motorcoach open and its occupants spill out.

The tour group? Back from Ephesus and the Shrine of the Virgin Mary?

No, it couldn't be. Not this motley crowd. Men, women, children. But *Meltemi II's* passengers hadn't included a single child. Nor did she recognize one face among this group . . . not a one. And why were all the adults weighed down with bulging shopping bags from various high-end shops—Coach, Silk & Cashmere, The Body Shop, Lacoste, and others—in each hand, with the exception for some of the women who were carrying infants? Was this, perhaps, the group from the *Meltemi III?*

But no, they couldn't be tourists. They didn't fit the mold of people with the discretionary income who could afford the luxury of a round-trip Aegean cruise, even aboard a budget vessel like one of the *Meltemi*s. Nor was there a single Western European face among them. They were olive-skinned and dark-haired, and there was a ragamuffin quality about them . . . a kind of refugee-like furtiveness. Kurds? Iraqis? There was no way to tell. And as for those shopping bags . . . surely none of these people had ever seen the inside of any of those plush stores. The bags couldn't have come from a shopping expedition. They most likely were luggage.

No. Had to be!

Yes! Luggage filled with personal belongings in lieu of tell-tale suitcases! And meanwhile, Chara was waving an arm for them to hurry, *hurry!* Not so much directing the human traffic into the guarded, video camera-equipped sanctum of Scala Nuova, but *hustling* them inside and *out of sight!* Constantly looking over her shoulder.

Swiftly magnifying the scene further, Miranda noticed the adults of this shoddily dressed group clutching something else. What appeared to be credit cards. No, not credit cards—*boarding cards!*

Miranda zoomed in the high-powered telescope further, and her heart skipped a beat before kicking back in.

Oracle Cruises boarding cards, no less!

As soon as the group was inside the compound, Chara tossed her mane of waist-long hair back in that way of hers and briskly followed. It was all the uniformed Customs officer could do to match her determined, long-legged stride. A latecomer came rushing to catch up with them—a crew member Miranda had seen aboard the *Meltemi II*, but one she hadn't had the opportunity to interact with. He had a laptop tucked under his arm and carried what looked like a futuristic pencil sharpener.

Miranda flashed back to the boarding process at Marina Zea in Piraeus. The snapping of computerized pictures. The gadget that looked like a pencil sharpener issuing the boarding passes which did double duty as a cabin key, and through which you had to slide that little rectangle of plastic each time you embarked or disembarked the vessel.

Swinging the telescope a few degrees to the right, she waited for the group to emerge from the hidden, shadowy buildings of the shopping arcade and onto the dock. Or were they possibly passing through Customs? Surely not, unless her eyes were deceiving her. For it wasn't necessary if those were indeed boarding passes.

But still, why such a rush, why such *furtiveness?*

The famous line from *Hamlet* sprang to Miranda's mind: "*Something is rotten in the state of Denmark.*" She'd had that intuition ever since the moment before she'd boarded, when the crate being transferred from the *Meltemi II* to shore had burst at Marina Zea, spilling the contents and that buffware *Oinochoe*—East Greek, Fikellura class—at Miranda's very feet. The piece of antiquity her expertly trained eye instantly identified as genuine, and which Chara Zouboulakis had claimed was a first-rate tourist copy.

Something rotten had been going on there, too.

Just as it was here.

But how was this motley band of migrants in Kusadasi and that

Oinochoe connected? Miranda's mouth formed an involuntary frown. Or weren't they connected? Whatever the case, Chara Zouboulakis was clearly at the center of it, or at least a major player in whatever rotten proceedings were going on.

Meanwhile, the newly arrived cruise ship had docked and was already disgorging its passengers, who swarmed the concrete pier like an endless plague of camera-toting locusts.

Steady, ole gal, Miranda kept telling herself. *Keep the lens focused on the spot where Chara's group will emerge.*

If it emerged.

Every passing second dragged by like minutes, a single minute seemed to stretch into hours.

"Patience," Miranda murmured like a mantra. "Patience."

Her heart was thudding out of sync, threatening to explode through her rib cage. It was all she could do to force herself to breathe.

There!

The little group materialized from the arcade, Chara shepherding them with outstretched arms. Miranda had the impression of a school teacher spurring on a class of confused pupils on an outing, or a tiny school of drab smelts fighting its way through an oncoming, rushing tide of a more colorful species, which threatened to engulf it and carry it back in the direction from which it had come.

Panicked individuals among the shopping bag contingent darted this way and that, were jostled and elbowed by the cruise ship's swarm, became separated, then coalesced into a cohesive whole again as the Bad Shepherdess dashed about madly, snatching her lost charges by the arm and steering them swiftly, roughly forward.

Time. Time was, apparently, of the essence.

Guiltily the insecure little party hesitated at the *Meltemi III,* only to be shouted at and prodded on further, to her identical sistership docked directly behind.

To Madge Blessing's *Good Ship Lollipop,* the *Meltemi II.*

Miranda noted that the flat-topped lectern was in place at the foot of the gangplank, and that the crew member with the laptop had somehow managed, like Dickens' Artful Dodger, to eel his way ahead, and was already setting up his equipment. Connecting the computer to that pencil sharpener-like gadget through which the boarding cards had to be slid.

With her index finger, Chara did a quick dockside headcount. Convinced that all strays were accounted for, she berated the crew member to get a move on even as she simultaneously kept glancing around, consulting her wristwatch, and looking nervously out to sea.

The tension was palpable. Miranda could practically hear Chara snapping commands in that cold, husky, and impatient voice.

Then the computer set-up was complete and a flurried boarding process began. Cards were slid through the gadget, but apparently not quickly enough. Chara literally shoved people ahead or, if they were too slow, snatched the cards out of their hands and personally slid them through before thrusting them back into their owners' trembling hands.

Treating them like a herd of animals, cracking an invisible whip.

Hurry, hurry, hurry! seemed the order of the day. And quick was obviously not quick enough.

Shifting the lens's focus, Miranda aimed it upon a stony-faced Dimitris. He was outside on the aft deck. But this was a different Dimitris, for he was somber, and that ever-present white smile of his was nowhere in evidence. Yet it was the selfsame Dimitris, for he helped the batch of passengers into the lounge with a far gentler hand, and accorded them infinitely more respect than Chara had.

Two crew men squeezed past the boarding passengers and, once ashore, took up positions, one each at the bollard by the bow, and the other at the stern.

Barely had the last boarding pass been swiped than the laptop was snapped shut, the electronic equipment shut down and disconnected. The crew member and Chara made haste up the gangway. Another rushed ashore, deftly folded the collapsible lectern, and carried it on up.

Instantly the hawsers at both bow and stern were cast off the bollard and hauled aboard. Smudges of diesel exhaust smeared the air. The two crew men sprang from the dock across the widening watery gap with the practiced ease of born sailors and landed lightly on the gangway. Once on deck, they raised the gangway, and the *Meltemi II*'s side thrusters pushed her further and further away from the concrete quay. At the stern the water thrashed and boiled as the twin screws began to turn. Then, as if swiveling 180-degrees on the axis of its hull, *Meltemi II* motored out of the harbor at a slow but stately speed, prow aimed out to the open sea.

It took a moment for Miranda's mind to actually register what she was witnessing. The *Meltemi II* sailing off without *her.*

Again!

"No," she moaned as a sudden panic seized her, and she let out a miserable little cry.

It couldn't be happening!

But it was.

"Ouch!" Something stung her left forearm. *Damn mosquito!* she thought, and started to swat it, but her hand moved too sluggishly, then fell heavily, uselessly, to her side. Her eyelids drifted shut and she heard voices that sounded far away, uttering words in strange tongues. She felt her feet leave the ground and she experienced that floating sensation again, of drifting downward in a hypnotic spiral, and then she was aware of nothing at all.

"*Effendi,* it is time to wake up." Dr. Babutcu's hands shook her gently awake. "Did you sleep well?"

She sat up in the narrow hospital bed and blinked. It was late afternoon, judging from the narrow rungs of golden light that had crept across the floor and now glowed high on the wall opposite the window. She shook her head, trying to shake off the aftereffects of the dream. It was still so vivid in her head.

"Adonis," he said kindly, "is waiting to take you back to the boat."

Miranda frowned. "But how can Adonis *be* here? The *Meltemi* sailed off without me!"

He smiled indulgently. "I assure you that your *Meltemi* is still here, and that Adonis is waiting downstairs."

"But . . . I *saw* it leave!"

He nodded sagely. "A dream, surely, *effendi.* The draught I prepared for you sometimes has the tendency of making one dream. It has been known to, how do you say? Dredge up memories?"

She nodded.

"And as with all dreams, they seldom make sense once you are awake. Yes?"

She looked at him. His expression was sincere and she saw no guile in his gentle, caring face. After a moment, he crossed the little examination room and threw open the shutters. Bright afternoon daylight poured in, dispelling the shadows. He returned to her bedside.

Yes, Miranda told herself, common sense asserting itself, Dr. Babutcu was invariably right. Now that she was awake, the disparate components of her dream fell into place and made perfect sense. The *Meltemi II* had, after all, sailed off without her from Mykonos. Why should a dream not contain a variant of that ingredient? And she *had* glimpsed the neglected garden in the courtyard on her way up the grand staircase to this room, hadn't she? It also made perfect sense that the jumble of her dream should be peopled with characters who had figured so prominently in her life during the past few days. Chara Zouboulakis and Dimitris, for instance.

Besides, if she *hadn't* been dreaming—or having a nightmare—how was it possible that she had floated like a ghost along hallways and up a spiral staircase, drawn by those girlish giggles and that pattering of light footsteps? Hadn't her dream dug those up from her childhood days when she'd played hide-and-seek with friends?

Yes, her subconscious had let imagination, that great instigator and imitator of all things real and unreal, past and present, run away with her.

She felt suddenly foolish, having spun mountains out of thin air.

Dr. Babutcu reached out with both thin, trembly arms and helped her up from the bed. She felt surprisingly steady on her feet. Her vision was clear and any residual headaches had disappeared. In fact, Miranda felt better than she had in days.

Whatever draught he had prepared for her had evidently worked wonders, and she was grateful.

Now it was time to get a move on.

Dr. Babutcu escorted her downstairs, made sure she had her shoulder bag, and delivered her into Adonis' capable hands. The doctor accompanied them to the immense front door and unlocked it.

"I can't thank you enough, doctor," Miranda told him sincerely, and reached into her shoulder bag. "How much do I owe you?"

He smiled and waved away any monetary concerns. "Let Oracle Cruises take care of that," he said, with a conspiratorial wink.

Miranda held her hand out to him. "It was a pleasure meeting you, Dr. Babutcu. I'm ever so grateful."

His hand was brittle, but firm and warm. "The pleasure was all mine, *effendi.* It is not every day a lovely young lady appears on an old man's doorstep. Good-bye and have a safe journey always."

She flashed him a smile. "Whatever that was you gave me to drink should be patented," she said. "You're a miracle worker. Good-bye, and thank you again, Dr. Babutcu."

When Adonis delivered her safely back to Scala Nuova, there was the *Meltemi II,* docked at the exact same spot where it had first arrived. The tour group from Ephesus had returned. Chara Zouboulakis was at the lectern, cool as the proverbial cucumber. "Are you feeling better, Ms. Kalli?" she inquired tonelessly.

"Tons, thank you," Miranda said as she dug out her boarding pass and slid it through the little gadget. "Dr. Babutcu was a jewel."

"How nice." Chara nodded inanely and busied herself. Dimitris, all smiles, greeted her with his usual friendliness. Then the welcoming committee descended, with Madge, boarding card still in hand, in the lead. She was closely followed by the quartet of nurses.

"Oh, Miranda!" Madge burbled, engulfing her in a warm embrace. "I fear you missed out on the most wonderful outing. Right up your alley." Then, drawing back, she gazed at her apprehensively. "How are you feeling, dear?"

Miranda grinned. "Right as rain. Couldn't be better."

"No vision problems?" Don inquired briskly.

"None at all," Miranda replied cheerfully.

"No blurring? No headaches?"

"Nope. I'm back to my old self."

"Amazing!" Em exclaimed.

"We missed you something awful," Soph chimed in.

"I think this calls for a little drinkie-poo," Madge declared. "It'll be my treat."

"Just give me a sec or two to park my bag and change," Miranda said. "I'll only be a moment."

"We'll be waiting up on the sundeck," added Fan.

Miranda started to leave when Don reached out and pulled her back by the arm. "What's this bruise?" she asked with a concerned frown, inspecting Miranda's forearm closely with a professional eye. "Looks like a puncture."

Miranda glanced down at it. "Oh, I don't know." She shrugged casually. "Probably a mosquito bite? Now let me go and get changed. Be right back."

Of course it was a mosquito bite. Miranda had a vague memory of trying to slap her arm but . . . but wasn't that part of the dream? But if it *was* part of the dream, then why the puncture?

She shook her head as she headed forward through the lounge. Really, she thought, she had to get hold of herself and separate the dream from reality.

She stopped short.

If the *puncture* was reality, then *had* it really been a dream?

"Enough!" she growled to herself under her breath as she continued on. "If I'm not careful, I'm going to end up becoming a card-carrying member of the Conspiracy Theory Club."

Letting herself into the cabin with her boarding pass-cum-cabin key, she slung her shoulder bag onto her top bunk, almost purring with pleasure as she noted that the cabin had been dusted and vacuumed and that there were fresh sheets on the beds.

Oh, the luxury of maid service. If only it could be like this at home. How easy it was to get spoiled.

Squatting down, she pulled one of her two yellow bags out from beneath Madge's lower bunk. She settled upon a clean Wedgwood blue T-shirt with long sleeves and a pair of indigo clam diggers. She was about to push the bag back when something caught her eye.

Lying on the carpet under the bunk was a rectangular piece of plastic, like a credit card, its magnetic strip facing up. Shaking her head at Madge's folly, she retrieved it, and decided to gently caution her new friend about being more careful with her plastic. Luckily, whoever had vacuumed hadn't been all that thorough and had cleaned around the bags without moving them.

But it wasn't a credit card. When Miranda turned it over, she realized it was a boarding pass. It hadn't been there when she'd shoved her bags under there, or even yesterday. Or this morning. And mere minutes ago she'd distinctly seen Madge still clutching hers.

The front had a familiar logo, and beneath it, in large letters, were two words.

ORACLE CRUISES

And embossed in the lower left hand corner in raised letters was a name she recognized.

MIRANDA KALLI

Miranda compared her own card, which she'd just used to unlock the cabin door, with the one she'd found under the bunk.

Interesting. Both were identical in every way. But strange: she'd only been issued the one upon boarding.

So. From where had this one appeared? And furthermore, how and why?

Before joining Madge and the nurses up on deck, she slipped her own card into the right pocket of her clam diggers, and then went outside into the narrow corridor. She snap-locked the cabin door behind her and proceeded to test the boarding pass she'd found.

No sooner had she swiped it through the slot of the lock that the little light glowed bright green. She pushed down on the door handle.

The cabin door opened.

Snapping it shut again, she stood there thoughtfully, tapping the plastic against her lips. Once more, the Conspiracy Theory reared its ugly head.

Was it possible that what Dr. Babutcu had attributed to be a dream *hadn't* been one? That what she'd witnessed through the telescope, or believed she'd witnessed, had actually *happened?* That a group of total strangers, toting shopping bags and accompanied by ragamuffins, had boarded the *Meltemi II*, which had then sailed off somewhere? And had, afterwards, ostensibly then returned to dock at the very same spot?

Another memory surfaced. She recalled how, that very morning, she'd wanted to go back to the cabin and just sleep. But Chara Zouboulakis had insisted she leave and see the doctor. She had, in fact, been adamant about it.

Out of concern? *If so, certainly not for me,* Miranda decided. *Most likely for Oracle Cruises' sake. For "legal liabilities."*

Or.

Something else occurred to her.

Had Chara insisted upon it in order to hustle one Miranda Kalli off the boat?

And, now that Miranda thought about it, why had the beds been made up with fresh linen after only two nights onboard? This was, after all, hardly a luxury cruise.

Yes. Curious, that.

"Miranda? What's keeping you, dear? Are you quite alright?"

It was Madge, and she was coming down the steep, stamped metal steps. Careful not to mix up the two cards, Miranda swiftly tucked the one she'd discovered under the bunk into the left pocket of her clam diggers. Then, forcing a sunny cheer into her voice which she didn't feel, she called out, "I'm on my way, Madge!"

But Madge Blessing had already reached the bottom of the steps and was approaching. "I was just worried and wanted to check up on you, dear, that's all. I do *so* hate to be a pest. I realize that nobody likes a busybody."

Pasting on a smile, Miranda turned to her. "Really, Madge. *You* a *pest?* I don't think so. I only wish I didn't have to leave you tomorrow."

Madge's face fell. "I know. I know. It won't be the same without you."

And then, her effervescent optimism resurfacing, she added: "But I *am* so glad we met."

Miranda's smile turned genuine. "Even though I turned out to be a major pain in the tush?"

Madge gurgled that delicious laughter of hers. "Especially so! I don't want to sound old-fashioned, but you add a sense of adventure and spice. You know, the way travel was always supposed to be? Plus you really are the most delightful traveling companion. I truly mean it."

Taking Madge's hands in hers, Miranda gave them a gentle squeeze. "I think the same can be said for you."

"Really? Oh, *good!* I'm *so* glad you think so!" And Madge's natural enthusiasm and *joie de vivre* kicked back in and she was brimming with pleasure. "Did you know that tonight is 'Turkish Delight'?"

Miranda looked at her blankly. She didn't have a clue what Madge was referring to.

"That Chara What's-Her-Name sprang it upon us on the way to Ephesus," Madge explained. "They'll be serving local Turkish delicacies at dinner, and a group of costumed dancers and musicians are coming onboard. We won't be leaving port until morning. We're sailing, or I suppose I should say *motoring,* from here to a place on Samos called Vathi, I believe. Apparently it's just a twenty-mile hop, skip, and a jump from here. But doesn't 'Turkish Delight' sound simply *enchanting?*"

Miranda agreed that it did.

"Between us and the nurses, we'll have tons of fun! Oh, Miranda, just imagine! It'll be like girls' night out! Besides, as it'll be our last night together, I do so want you to enjoy yourself."

Miranda stifled a sigh. She needed to be by herself and have time to evaluate the day's events. She was tempted to ask Madge whether Chara had been with the Ephesus tour the entire time, but didn't want to have to explain why.

Least of all, she wasn't about to spoil the evening or put a damper on it for Madge's sake.

Besides, she would have plenty of time to ponder events once she reached Samos.

[CHAPTER TWENTY EIGHT]

New York City

Harry Palmer did his best to steer clear of meeting Mara Jankowicz alone. They'd once shared a brief history, though in actuality their affair, confined mostly to the bedroom, had lasted a day or two shy of three weeks. A man-hunting shark prowling the singles scene for a well-off husband, she'd scared him off.

To her credit, she let bygones be bygones, harbored no hard feelings, and cruised on to richer man-infested waters. To her even greater credit, she had hooked him up with her best friend, Miranda, who was her exact opposite in that she was forever reluctant to commit.

"Dammit, Mara! I don't know what's with Miranda," Harry now confided. "She's driving me crazy!"

"Uh-huh. So *that's* why you invited me to lunch," she said slyly. "I knew there was an ulterior motive. Usually it's Miranda, you, and me, unless we're double-dating."

They were scanning the menu and sipping drinks, Pinot Grigio for her and a bottle of Cuzqueña beer for him in a restaurant called Lima's Taste at the corner of Christopher and Bedford—a stone's throw from her rent-stabilized West Village studio.

"The shrimp soup's to die for," Mara told him.

"I'm ready to slit my wrists."

Mara smiled. "Have some shrimp soup first."

He'd forgotten how easy it was to get along with her, and he appreciated her dark sense of humor. Also, now that he was engaged to Miranda, they shared an unspoken hands-off policy. The only thing that still made him uncomfortable was their history, brief as it had been.

But that was his baggage. Mara had gotten over him and moved on long ago.

A tiny waitress in a dark sun visor came and Mara ordered for both of them. He took another slug of beer, but Mara nursed her wine. As of yet there was no ring on her finger, and she wasn't about to overindulge in calories. Manhattan was full of beautiful single women, plenty of them younger than Mara, and she was obviously determined to stay in fighting shape.

He had to hand it to her.

Another point in her favor: unlike Tiffany Pfeiffer, who'd coerced him into having her revenge dinner at one of Manhattan's most exorbitant restaurants, when he'd called Mara she'd suggested they lunch at a convenient, inexpensive, but, as she'd put it, "marvelously good place where they serve the best food I've ever eaten." And she'd laughed and added, "Not that I dare eat much."

Now, from their table by the big picture window across from the Lucille Lortel Theater, he asked, "Have you heard from Mandy?"

"Jeez, Harry, how dense can you be? Haven't you learned by now how she *despises* that nickname? She prefers to be called 'Miranda,' even by me."

"Yeah," he said, giving a short bark of a laugh. "This is the second time in two days that I've been reprimanded for that."

She raised her eyebrows.

"But *have* you heard from her?" he wanted to know.

Mara frowned. "No, as a matter of fact, now that you mention it, I haven't. I've left a couple of messages on her answering machine and on her cell phone's voice mail. So far, she hasn't called me back."

She paused, adding, "Why? Is she ill? Or has something happened to that horrid cat of hers?"

He pulled the glass of beer towards him and frowned down at it, but toyed with it instead of taking a drink.

"No, Magoo is fine and getting his insulin shots regularly." He laughed humorlessly. "I have the scratches to prove it."

"Harry, what the hell is going on between the two of you?"

"You're asking *me?* Who knows? That's why I called you. She took off for Greece."

Mara nearly knocked her wineglass over. "Ex-*cuse* me? Harry, did I hear you say 'Greece,' as in Europe? *That* Greece?"

"Only Greece I know of."

He smiled tightly and stared out the picture window over to the Lucille Lortel and the assortment of pedestrians passing by: Young couples with baby strollers, straight singles, gays in various fetish outfits, and so many young people that he suddenly felt old and out of it. He turned back to Mara.

"The last time Mand—I mean, Miranda—called me she was at the airport and her flight was boarding. Before hanging up, she told me she'd call again and explain. Only, she hasn't. That was four days ago, and I'm getting worried. I was hoping you'd know something I didn't."

"Well, you apparently know a lot more than I do." She shook her head in disbelief. "Why, that little *minx!* And here she told *me,* her very best friend, that she couldn't afford a share in the Hamptons! And now she's gallivanted off to Greece? I sure wish *I* could afford to have done that."

"Don't feel bad. It came at me out of left field too."

"Did she say *why* she was going?"

"Not to me. But I did pop uptown yesterday, and talked to that fairy who's her next-door neighbor."

"Shit." Mara rolled her eyes heavenward. "Harry," she chided, drilling him with a hard look, "when are you ever going to learn?"

He squinted at her. "Learn what?"

"That's exactly what I mean. For a smart guy, you really are dense, you know that?"

"Like how?" He looked offended.

"Like, her neighbor has a name? It's Ron, okay? He's really a sweetheart, and very, very talented to boot. Plus one doesn't use terms like 'fairy' or 'fag' anymore. That is totally inappropriate, let alone politically incorrect. For God's sake, Harry Palmer, are you ever going to wake up and open your eyes? Ron's one of Miranda's closest friends, and what do you do? Disparage him by calling him names. Is that what you guys down on Wall Street are in the habit of doing?"

Harry finished his beer in one long swallow. "I stand corrected," he said weakly.

It suddenly occurred to him that he'd been standing corrected quite a lot these last few days. Was he losing his touch? It seemed like he was getting hammered left and right by members of the opposite sex. If you could call Ron "opposite sex."

He decided that what he needed right now was another nice, ice cold beer. He held up the empty bottle of Cuzqueña to the little Peruvian waitress.

She came over, eyed Mara's glass of barely touched wine, then took the bottle of beer and his empty glass and went and brought him another.

"So what did you find out from Ron?" Mara asked.

He was relieved to change the subject. "Apparently an old professor of hers is working on an archeological dig. Someplace called Samos."

"Uh-huh. An island in the northern Aegean. His name wouldn't be Waldemar Hirsch, would it?"

He shrugged. "How would I know?"

You should, her accusatory look told him.

"Anyway, according to the—er, to *Ron,* it seems this professor knew she had the entire month of August off, and invited her to join him. Ron said he'd sent her the airline tickets via FedEx. They arrived the very day she was to leave. And she left."

"I see." Mara nodded and took a tiny sip of Pinot Grigio. "Knowing Miranda's passion for antiquities, I gather it was an offer she couldn't refuse. I can envy her, but I can't say I blame her one little bit. I'd have jumped at the opportunity myself."

"Maybe. But she could at least have *told* me," he groused.

"Perhaps she didn't have a chance to. Look, Harry, I'm going to tell you something. Miranda's one of the best antiquities experts Jan Kofski's got. She has a passion for ancient Greek art. I know you never understood that."

He slid her a narrow look. "She tell you that?"

"She didn't have to. It's written all over you. Besides, I know you well enough, Harry. You're like all those hedge fund boys. The only things you understand are about selling short or what something's worth in dollars and cents. You can't grasp things in terms of historic value or beauty. And you don't need to look like I just kicked you in the *cojones.* I'm not trying to put you down."

She added, gently: "I hate to admit it, but Miranda's a thousand times more dedicated to what she does than I am. She's a pro through and through. That's the key to learning what makes her tick. Once you accept that, then you'll understand her completely."

The waitress came and set down two plates of shrimp soup. For a moment he stared desultorily down at his food.

"There's something else," he began.

Mara smiled. "After we've eaten. Come on, Harry. Be a good boy, pick up your spoon, and dig in. As soon as you taste this, I guarantee you'll feel a hundred percent better."

He picked up his spoon, stirred the pink concoction, then lifted a spoonful to his lips. He tasted it tentatively and his face suddenly brightened.

"Hey! This is fantastic!"

"Why do you think I suggested this place? Wait until you try the rest of what I ordered."

Mara had about two tiny spoonfuls of her soup, then pushed it aside. He finished his, showed great restraint by not licking the plate or attacking Mara's leftovers, and drank some more beer. She was still on her first glass of wine.

"Have to watch my weight," she said.

He chuckled. "Come on, Mara. You still look great. And I'm not kidding."

Mara Jankowicz smiled. "Thanks," she said. "But try being a single girl in this town."

"Try being a single guy," he retorted.

"No go," she pointed out, with a shake of her head. "You're officially engaged. To Miranda, remember? That takes you off the eligible list and makes you off limits."

"Yeah, but she keeps putting off the wedding."

"That's only because she wants to make sure the marriage will work. Miranda's not a gold-digger, Harry. She believes in true love and 'till death do us part.' You have to hand it to her."

The waitress came and cleared away the soup plates and came back with two platters. One was in a deep dish, the other held a long wooden skewer of grilled meat.

"What's this?" He pointed at the deeper platter.

"It's called *Causa,*" Mara said, pronouncing it 'Cow-sa.' "You have to eat it to believe it. I might steal a bite or two, but it's all yours. It's got potatoes in it, and I don't dare carb myself up. It's a jungle out there."

She reached for a tiny forkful and nibbled slowly.

"Heavenly," she declared, with a wistful sigh.

He dug in, finished half of it, then slid a piece of meat off the skewer on the other platter and chewed happily.

"The way to a man's heart," he said.

She laughed. "Yeah. Right through his stomach."

"You know, I'm going to have to come back here. This place is great."

"Peruvians are supposed to be the best cooks in South America."

"What *is* this?" he asked, holding up another piece of grilled meat.

"*Anticucho.*"

"Which is . . . ?"

"Grilled chunks of beef heart."

Taken aback, he stopped eating for a moment. "You're pulling my leg."

"I kid you not. Now, as the Italians say, *mange,* Harry. *Mange!*"

He swallowed some more beer, licked it off his lips, and courageously polished off the *anticucho* along with the *causa.*

"You want some dessert?" Mara Jankowicz asked. "Nellie's flan is to die for."

"You going to have some?"

She laughed. "No way, José! You trying to fatten me up? What about you?"

Harry rubbed his stomach. "Maybe next time. Why don't we walk some of this off?"

"Good idea."

He motioned to the waitress for the check and paid it. After the air-conditioned restaurant, August's heat was brutal and the asphalt shimmered. Staying on the shady side of the street, they walked east along Christopher, then moseyed up the shady side of Bleecker, with its outposts of high-end, big name designer boutiques.

"When I was a kid," Mara said, "this street was all antique shops. But the sky-high rents have chased them all away. Now all you see is fashion, fashion, fashion."

"And here I was always under the impression you were a clotheshorse."

"Oh, I am," Mara admitted, "but these shops are way too pricey for my pocketbook. What I do, I'll window shop and maybe go in and check out the latest styles. Then I head straight over to H&M or buy designer rip-offs. The most important things for a girl to never, ever skimp on are very good purses and very good shoes. They'll give you away every single time."

"Gee. It just goes to show that I learn something new every day."

"Don't be facetious," Mara said sternly. "Now, about that something else you mentioned earlier. I take it it's got something to do with Miranda?"

Harry nodded. *Here goes,* he thought, feeling as though he was facing a firing squad. With a grimace, he filled her in on getting smashed with Tiffany Pfeiffer, ending up in her bed, and leaving his Blackberry behind.

Mara stopped short in her tracks and turned to him slowly. Her eyes were huge with disbelief.

"You did *what?* Oh, Harry. Harry. Say it ain't so."

He winced. "It isn't what you think, Mara," he said stiffly. "Nothing happened. And that's what made Tiffany hopping mad. So she held my Blackberry hostage."

She blew out a deep breath that lifted the bangs off her forehead. "Let me make a wild guess. And Miranda called? While your Blackberry was—how did you put it? Being held hostage?"

He nodded miserably. "It appears so."

"And this Tiffany Pfeiffer answered? And talked to Miranda?"

"I have to presume so. Otherwise why would she have switched the call from my line-up to my call delete file?" He shook his head. "God only knows what Tiffany told her."

"Oh boy," Mara said. "Oh boy, oh boy. Knowing Miranda, you're neck-high in shit."

"That's why I called you," he said.

"Me? What do you expect me to do, other than listen to your woes?"

"Well, I was hoping that maybe you could call her, and when you got through, explain the situation? Clear up the misunderstanding?" He looked at her hopefully.

"No way. Unh-unh. No fucking way. Harris Milford Palmer III, listen to me. I am not a relationship counselor."

"But you're her best friend."

She made a kind of growling sound deep in her throat. "Harry, you obviously know nothing about women, so let me clue you in. Do you know what happens when one woman informs another that her husband is having an affair? She's dropped like a hot potato. For good. It's a case of killing the messenger."

"But that's just it. Don't you see? You wouldn't be ratting on me. You'd be trying to explain the situation rationally. You'd be pouring oil on troubled waters."

"You mean, I'd be pouring oil on the *fire,* Harry." She eyed him sadly. "You're the only one who can straighten this mess out. Want my advice?"

"Yes," he said in a small voice.

"If I were you? I'd take a few days off, book the next flight to Greece, and be on it. Plead your case to Miranda in person. These kinds of issues can't be resolved via long distance. And Miranda's not a monster, Harry. Aside from being my best friend, she's also about the most understanding *mensch* in this town."

"Are you crazy?" he said. "I can't afford to take time off. I have responsibilities. The way the market's been fluctuating, it was all I could do to sneak up here for lunch. I ought to be downtown as we speak. My career's at stake, Mara. When you work where I do, personal problems have to take a back seat."

"So take your laptop. Work from wherever. It's a wireless world."

"It's not that simple, Mara."

"Look, Harry. I can't decide this for you. But wake up and smell the coffee, will you? It's up to you to make the decision of what's most important to you. Miranda? Or your career? Either way, Wall Street will survive."

"You don't understand. If I'm not on top of things, my clients could lose millions. Tens of millions. Maybe more."

"No, Harry," Mara said wearily, "it's you who doesn't understand. You could lose Miranda. The choice is up to you."

"But I love Miranda," he said.

"Then show it, Harry. Talk's cheap. In love and war, it's action that counts."

[CHAPTER TWENTY NINE]

Samos, Greece

It was soon time to say good-bye.

Breakfast was over, and the *Meltemi II* was back in Greek waters, rounding the bend of the Samian mountain range called Psili Vigla. On the port side, the bristling verdure of pines and greenery plunged steeply from towering crevassed cliffs that nosedived into the sea; to starboard, the coast of mainland Turkey, from which a prehistoric volcanic eruption had separated the island from Asia Minor, seemed close enough to touch.

Miranda's yellow nylon bags were packed and zipped, and she had already brought them up onto the sundeck in preparation of disembarking. She was wearing a sleeveless khaki tank top, matching cargo shorts, and sturdy hiking boots. In her right pocket was her own boarding pass; in the left was the one she'd found under Madge's bunk.

Clustered around her on the stackable white resin chairs were her five new friends: Madge and the nurses, Em, Don, Soph, and Fan.

Despite the spectacular scenery with a few fluffy clouds touching the higher peaks, the mood was subdued. Madge was despondent, the nurses were muted, and Miranda wavered between the excitement that lay ahead and the sadness of departure.

They had already exchanged their contact information, and had vowed to stay in touch.

"Oh, Miranda, I'm going to miss you something terrible," sniffled Madge, dabbing moist eyes with a lace-edged handkerchief.

"And I'll miss you too," Miranda returned fondly, and included the nurses, adding, "All of you. You've been wonderful."

"You 'aven't 'eard the last of us!" Em assured her.

"That's a promise *and* a threat," added Soph.

"Count on it," declared Don, with a characteristic brisk nod.

Fan nodded silent agreement.

Presently the *Meltemi II* rounded the amoeba-shaped headlands and promontories of the eastern tip of the island and changed course, heading south-east as they began to motor into Vathi harbor from the north. It was a large and very long, watery peninsula, vaguely shaped like a slanting Florida without the panhandle. Vathi, also known as Samos town, was clustered at the very far end, spread out along the eastern shore of the waterfront, from whence it climbed uphill. With its pastel houses with their gently sloping clay-tile roofs and European architecture, it looked more Mediterranean than Aegean, and was a far cry from tiny, parched Mykonos with its organic, blinding white Cycladic cubes and breast-domed churches.

"Look!" Miranda cried, pointing fore and aft. "The ferries are up and running again!"

They all looked round, and sure enough, they were. An old-fashioned ship with the profile of an ocean liner from a by-gone era was nosing out from the still-distant breakwater. Even from a great distance it was impossible to miss the giant red letters emblazoned on its white hull: "CA FERRIES." Small, rocket-shaped hydrofoils, noses raised arrogantly in the air, droned past on wing-like foils. Approaching from far out in the sea lane, a giant, red-hulled catamaran on steroids, with as many decks as it was wide, was fast approaching, rocking tiny but sturdy fishing boats in its churning wake.

"Isn't it always the way?" Miranda murmured to Madge. "The day I arrive here, the ferries would be back in action."

"Yes, dear," Madge acknowledged in a near-whisper, keeping their sister act a secret, "but just think. If they'd been running when we first arrived, we'd never have had the opportunity to meet. Right?"

Miranda smiled. "There is that. You know, somehow the beginning of our little subterfuge seems like only yesterday."

Madge blew her nose. "It *was* practically yesterday. Just four short days ago. But it *was* a happy accident, don't you think?"

"A very happy accident, Madge," Miranda agreed.

"I never realized this island would be so *huge,*" declared Don, the adventurous conquerer of deserts and peaks. She was studying the silver, tawny backbones of a mountain range rising high beyond the sloping green hills. "After the cruise is over and we return here, I intend to climb those."

"Well, I won't be accompanying you on *that* trek," Em told her, lightening the mood. "Some of those must be . . . what? Four, five thousand feet high?"

"Bah! Mere hillocks to me," shrugged Don, and the others laughed.

Below, on the aft deck, the inevitable lectern, laptop, and its accompanying gadget were already being brought out.

"Oh, Miranda," Madge fretted, "they're getting prepared to set up once we dock."

"It's not the end of the world, Madge. Look at it as the beginning of a beautiful friendship."

Still downcast, Madge mulled that over before breaking into a smile sunnier than that of Apollo's chariot riding high in that scintillating blue Aegean sky. "You know, you're right, dear," she said. Her ebullient optimism had returned, rising like a helium-filled balloon.

The giant catamaran caught up with them and surged past, slowing as it reached the breakwater ahead. The much smaller *Meltemi II* swung from side to side in its powerful wake.

"Built where we come from," Don remarked darkly as she eyed the sleek, modern monster in distaste. "Those jet-style engines tear up the sea floor. It's criminal."

Inside the sheltered breakwater, a cacophonous warning claxon rent the air as the giant twin-hulled monstrosity swung swiftly on its axis, backed in, and docked. There was a thunderous crash as the opening garage door at its stern slammed down upon the concrete quay.

Instantly, a mob of tourists surged ashore, followed by a veritable fleet of mopeds, motorcycles, small cars, and cargo vans. As soon as the last vehicle sped off, the line of vehicles waiting to drive on board disappeared into the maw at its stern while a rush of suitcase-laden tourists and a smattering of locals followed.

The *Meltemi II* had barely entered the shelter of the breakwater when the blaring claxons once again ripped the air, the great hydraulic stern doors banged shut, the hawsers were thrown off the bollards, and the mighty cat immediately headed back out into the harbor and sped off.

The speed and efficiency of its arrival and departure was nothing short of astonishing.

"So what the guidebooks say really is true," observed Madge. "The sea lanes are the highways of Greece."

The *Meltemi II* duly docked and the aft gangway was lowered. Dimitris carried the lectern down to the quay. Miranda rose from her chair and lifted her two yellow bags just as Chara Zouboulakis emerged from the lounge.

As always, she was fashion-runway perfect, wearing a white sun dress splattered with a pattern of giant red poppies, sleek dark designer frames, and large gold hoop earrings. All business, she didn't so much as glance around, but strode directly down the gangway to supervise the setting up of the laptop and its accouterments. In one hand she was holding a dark blue passport.

An American passport.

Mine, Miranda thought.

"Damn!" she swore under her breath and set her bags back down.

"What is it, dear?" asked Madge.

"I was hoping someone else would be doing the disembarkation process. I should have known better."

"That Chara woman generally sees to that."

"I *know.* But in this case . . . " Miranda's voice trailed off and she expelled an explosive sigh. "Damn!"

That received a sharp, inquisitive little sideways glance from Madge, but their attention was diverted by a black Mercedes SUV, shiny as an antlered stag beetle, which swung onto the quay. Behind it, as though pulling a trailer, rumbled a small, exhaust-belching lorry laden with wooden crates.

The exact same kind of crates that had been unloaded in Piraeus, one of which had dropped, landed with a crash, and spilled its contents, including the *Oinochoe.*

The genuine Oinochoe.

Miranda was willing to swear to that.

Just beyond the gangway, the SUV stopped with an ostentatious squeal of its brakes, as though needing to announce its arrival. The driver, a lean, narrow-faced young man in his twenties, jumped out and held the rear passenger door open.

The man who emerged was an immense pasha of a gent, but despite his corpulence, he was exceptionally light on his feet. Of indeterminate age—he could pass for anywhere in his mid-thirties to his mid-fifties, he nonetheless exuded wealth and confidence in equal proportions.

He had dark eyes set deep in a puffy, scrubbed, clean-shaven, pink face. Short graying black hair cut into straight bangs across his brow. More chins than the Chinatown Yellow Pages, and was casually, immaculately, expensively dressed. Starched lilac shirt of the palest hue. Crocodile belt with a gold buckle. Big gold watch with a thick gold band. Black suede Gucci loafers.

Even standing still, he gave Miranda the impression of a Spanish treasure galleon under full sail.

Eyeing the *Meltemi II,* he reached for a cigarette, and his driver instantly jumped to and flicked a light. The huge man inhaled, tilted his head back, and exhaled a plume of smoke skyward. Chara immediately left Dimitris in charge and hurried down to greet the newcomer.

They embraced.

He pecked her on both cheeks.

And it was Dimitris who now manned the lectern!

Quick. Miranda calculated her chances and seized the moment. Swiftly she drew Madge aside. "Could you do me a great favor?" she asked in a rush of a whisper.

"Why . . . why yes. Of course. Anything, dear."

Miranda glanced down at the quay. Chara and the huge man were walking towards the end of the breakwater. They were deep in conversation and didn't stop until they were well out of earshot. Meanwhile, two burly men climbed down from the lorry's cab and went to the rear, where they dropped the tailgate and began unloading the crates.

Miranda's voice was hushed. "Madge, when I get off, I'm only going to be carrying one of my bags."

She reached down and lifted it with her left hand and held it by its Velcroed carrying straps.

"Yes?"

"Then, as soon as my boarding pass is swiped through, could you possibly distract Dimitris? Maybe call down that I forgot my other bag? Try to lift it and say something like, 'My, it's so *heavy*. Dimitris, would you be so kind . . . ?' Anyway, something to that effect? Just use your imagination."

"But whatever for?" Then Madge's eyes crinkled at the corners and she smiled mischievously. "Oh, *I* know! You're off on another one of your adventures!"

"Really, Madge. It's very important. This is my only opportunity. We have to hurry to make this work, before Chara's finished chatting."

Wriggling her shoulders, Madge trilled with delight. "Don't worry, dear. I'll do my best. You know how I do so *love* intrigue!"

They glanced in the direction of Chara and the fat man.

The two were in the midst of an animated discussion, both of them gesturing dramatically. He with his cigarette. She with Miranda's passport, the stamped gold seal of the United States of America on the cover catching the sunlight and flashing like a semaphore.

The coast was clear.

Placing a hand on Miranda's arm, Madge added, "But do take care, dear. I sometimes worry about you. Now go, *go!*" She made shooing motions with her hands.

Miranda gave her a swift hug with her free arm and hurried down the metal steps. "I'll fill you in on everything the next time we talk," she called up when she reached the aft deck below. "That's a promise, okay?"

Madge, elbows resting on the railing above, held up both hands, crossed her fingers, and blew her a kiss. Her eyes were glowing with barely suppressed excitement.

Miranda slipped her boarding pass out of her right pocket and danced casually down the gangplank. Swinging her bag nonchalantly. Or so she hoped it appeared.

Quick.

Speed was the key. It was all a matter of timing . . . and luck. More luck than she cared to admit.

Hearing her footsteps on the gangway, Dimitris turned around. "*Despiní* Kalli!" he greeted warmly.

"*Kaliméra,* Dimitris."

His face instantly assumed a melancholy expression. "It is a sad day. I hear you are leaving us."

She nodded morosely. "Yes, it's a sad day for me too, Dimitris. You've been so kind. I cannot thank you enough."

So saying, she set down her bag between her feet and sidled alongside him, intentionally positioning herself to have a full view of the laptop screen and the boarding pass gadget. And, more specifically, to quick-study the keyboard. Until now, she hadn't given it a glance, and wasn't sure how it was programmed.

Please, she prayed to the gods of the ancients, *please let it be in the Western alphabet!*

If it wasn't, her subterfuge would be for nothing.

Careful not to let her eyes stray down at the keyboard too soon, lest she aroused suspicion, she looked all around. She scanned the handsome esplanade with its palm trees and benches and streetlights along the waterfront. The rows of parked cars by the curb. The fishermen, beside their tiny, wide-hulled, little boats, grappling with their nets and spreading them out to dry. The trio of jugglers—one woman and two men—held a small assembly of tourists enraptured by tossing a multitude of objects in the air and tossing them at one another, faultlessly catching and juggling balls, pots and pans, and even terra cotta flowerpots, and keeping them airborne without dropping a one.

"Why, what a lovely esplanade!" she enthused, and in the process of turning back to Dimitris, her eyes managed to register the laptop's screen saver. On it, three cartoon *Meltemi*s sailed this way and that in predetermined loops.

She cast a glance in the opposite direction, ostensibly to admire the hills, but actually to make certain that Chara and the fat man were still preoccupied—*they were!*—and held out her boarding pass, hoping against hope that Madge would wait for her cue and not jump the gun.

"And these hills! Dimitris, I never dreamed Samos would have so much vegetation!"

"Yes," Dimitris said. "This is one of what we call our green islands."

Her hand was still extended, holding out her boarding pass for him to accept.

"The islands of the Dodecanese," he told her, "are much more—what is the word? Verdant—?"

"Yes, that means green."

"—than those of the Cyclades," he completed, apparently not noticing the boarding pass she still held out toward him.

Hurry! she wanted to scream. *Take it!*

Her fingers gripped the plastic card tightly, while she struggled to keep an interested look on her face and simultaneously subdued the urge to thrust it at him and wave it in front of his face.

Why did he have to be so friendly and so *awfully* nice? Was there any way to rush him, without appearing rude? If she'd only called ahead and let Professor Hirsch know how she was arriving, and when and *where*—at Vathi, rather than Pythagoria—and there had been a welcoming committee waiting for her on the dock.

But she hadn't called ahead, and there was no one to meet her and speed the process along.

"Did you know that Samos boasts the highest mountains of any of the Greek islands?" Dimitris volunteered, apparently oblivious to her heart palpitating erratically against her rib cage, her nerves strung so tautly that her palm and fingers, gripping her boarding pass, were moist from perspiration.

"Really?" Miranda feigned interest. "Well, I hope I shall have enough time to really explore the island. Unfortunately, I've come here to work, rather than on holiday."

Another swift, admiring scan of the green hills on the opposite side of the harbor; another opportunity to regard Chara and the fat man. Their tempers appeared to have cooled; whatever they had been discussing so heatedly was concluded. They were gesticulating less, and he was offering her a cigarette and lighting it for her.

"Ah, you must forgive me, *despiní,*" Dimitris said contritely. "How thoughtless of me. For a moment I had quite forgotten. Please accept my most sincere apologies. We Greeks are a proud people and tend to get carried away by the beauty of our islands and our historical heritage. Surely you must be eager to meet your colleagues."

"Yes, I'm quite anxious to. This is most exciting."

"Please." He extended his hand for her boarding pass. If he noticed it was moist from her sweating palm, he didn't appear to notice.

She watched him closely as he swiped her plastic rectangle through the little gadget. He hit ENTER on the keyboard, and the fact that the laptop's keyboard *was* in the Western alphabet, rather than the Greek, filled her with relief. There was a blink and the three little cartoon *Meltemi*s disappeared from the screen. Almost instantly, her mug shot popped up, along with her personal information.

ENTER, she remembered. That was easy enough.

"Good heavens!" she exclaimed, relying on feminine vanity to detract him from her keen interest in the laptop. She leaned into the picture. "What a terrible photograph of me!"

Dimitris smiled. "You are a very beautiful young woman, *despiní.* I think it is a lovely picture."

"If you say so," she said, with a doubtful shake of her head. "I still think you're being overly diplomatic and flattering."

Keep him at ease, she told herself. *Keep him distracted. Small talk can open all doors.*

"You know what they say in English, don't you, Dimitris?" He raised his dark eyebrows questioningly.

"'Flattery will get you everywhere.'"

He laughed. "If only that were true! In that case, the ladies would be—how do you say? Falling all over me?"

"They *do,* Dimitris. You are quite the ladies' man. Or are you blind, like those three old spinsters in mythology? You know, the Graiai? The ones who shared only one eye and one tooth and passed it back and forth between them? The eye that Perseus snatched from them, in order to get them to reveal the location of their twin sister, Gorgones?"

Dimitris looked at her almost sadly. "You, *despiní,* are obviously better versed in our culture than most of us Greeks. A sad commentary, no?"

"That's not the point. What I'm trying to get at is that if *my* eyes serve me correctly, you have two eyes of your own, Dimitris, and I think you should open them."

But not too much, she thought, cautioning herself: *Don't overdo it! Don't arouse suspicion!*

"Now," he said, "I think it is you who are being overly diplomatic and flattering, *despiní.*"

But flattery and charm had served its distracting effect. He didn't notice her watching him depress the CONTROL key with one finger and hit HOME with the other.

Blink! Like magic, the three little cartoon *Meltemi*s continued their endless loops around the screen.

Swipe, ENTER, then depress CONTROL and hit HOME to wipe the screen clear.

Simple as pie, if the opportunity presented itself.

Dimitris handed back her boarding pass with a flourish. "A souvenir," he said.

"Really? How lovely! *Efcharistó.*" She accepted it graciously, smiled with pleasure, and placed it in her right pocket.

"I shall treasure it always, and think of you whenever I look at it," she told him.

Picking up her yellow bag in her right hand, she reached her free hand into the left pocket of her cargo pants. With fingers clammy and trembling from nerves, she gripped the boarding pass she'd discovered underneath Madge's bunk, prepared to whip it out.

Another sneak peek toward the end of the breakwater.

Damn!

Chara and the fat man had obviously concluded their conversation. Both tossed down their cigarette butts and ground them underfoot.

Worse, they were starting to head back to the *Meltemi II!*

Miranda calculated that she had a minute left at most—more likely half a minute—or less.

It was now or never.

Time for Madge's diversionary tactic, and her own skullduggery.

Madge, now! she projected. *Now!"*

"Miranda! *Miranda!*" It was Madge, calling down in a louder version of her cooing voice. "You forgot this, dear!"

Miranda and Dimitris both turned and looked up. Madge, bless her Blessing heart, was leaning over the rear railing of the sundeck, holding up Miranda's second yellow bag in both hands.

"Oh, I am hopeless!" Miranda murmured. "I don't know what it is with me. I'm always so flustered when it comes to departures. I won't be but a moment."

She half-turned to go and retrieve it.

"Just stay where you are," Madge called. "I'll bring it down, dear."

And that was when Madge came through with flying colors. She took a step backward, managed to trip on the Astroturf, and dropped the bag with a thud. Crying out, "Ow!" she hopped about on her right foot, lifted her left leg, and began massaging the left.

Dimitris looked appalled. Miranda's spirits soared.

"Oh, heavens," Madge called down. "Miranda, I hope you didn't have any breakables packed? Dimitris, dear, could I possibly impose on you?"

Of course it was a request he couldn't refuse.

"I am coming, *Kiría,*" he called up, and quick as a wink he left Miranda, hurried up the gangway, crossed the short aft deck, and took the steps up two at a time.

Miranda's pulse was racing.

Now! If only Madge could detain him for a few moments longer.

Miranda didn't waste a second. She whipped out the boarding pass from her left pocket. Her palm was so slippery that she nearly dropped it.

Steady, old girl, she told herself. *What's required now are nerves of steel.*

Which was easier thought than done. Chara and the fat man were already halfway to the boat. Madge was burbling away up on the sundeck, assuring Dimitris that no, she didn't believe she was hurt.

Miranda zoned them out. She had more important things on her mind:

Swipe, ENTER, then depress CONTROL and hit ENTER to wipe the screen clear.

With fumbling fingers, she slid the card through the gadget and hit the HOME key on the laptop.

Nothing. The three cartoon *Meltemi*s on the screen saver circled happily about, each leaving behind a wake of dotted white lines.

What in all hell?

Then it occurred to her what she'd done wrong. She'd swiped the card through the wrong way around, just as she'd done a zillion times with her credit and debit cards. Magnetic strip *down,* she told herself. Not up.

Flipping it around, she slid it through again.

Still nothing. And now she could hear Chara and the fat man's guttural, strangely accented voice clearly, but couldn't make out the barrage of Greek. She caught Madge saying something about her foot. And she couldn't help but get an earful of the ministering quartet of oncology nurses fussing around Madge, urging her to flex her toes.

Miranda was aware of herself only as a bumbling bundle of nerves. The tension was getting to her, slowing down her reflexes. She had to consciously still her quivering hands, they were shaking so badly. And she was losing precious seconds . . .

Concentrate, she railed to herself. *Concentrate!*

She turned the card around so that the magnetic strip faced in the opposite direction. Mentally crossing her fingers, she pressed the ENTER key once again.

Bingo!

Lo and behold, the three *Meltemi*s on the laptop's screen disappeared—

—and up popped a photograph of a gaunt, black-haired woman with olive skin and haunted black eyes. A total stranger whom she'd never met. Yet the name and typed information on the sceen was Miranda's own. Birth date. Nationality. Passport number.

For a fleeting moment, she flashed back upon her stay in Kusadasi.

So, what she'd thought she'd seen through the telescope in Dr. Babutcu's study hadn't been a dream after all. The *Meltemi II* really *had* sailed off somewhere, and had then returned. All while one inconvenient Miranda Kalli had been hustled ashore when all she'd wanted to do was crawl back into her bunk and sleep while the rest of the passengers spent the day touring Ephesus and the Shrine of the Virgin Mary.

Hustled to Dr. Babutcu's. For Oracle Cruises' potential legal liabilities? *Or to clear the vessel for other purposes?* And as for the kindly old doctor, he *had* to be involved in whatever was going on in some way or other. His vile herbal potion, which had reminded her of that nasty smell in the *Botanica* in San Francisco, and then that mosquito sting—or *hadn't* it been a mosquito?—and the resulting bruise on her arm that Don had frowned over . . .

Had he purposely drugged her?

It seemed more and more likely. And yet, Dr. Babutcu had been so *nice.* So gentlemanly. So courtly. Even sweet.

Well, she'd read that Hitler could supposedly be charming. Probably Dr. Mengele could, too. That is, if you weren't one of his human guinea pigs.

But this was no time to ponder probabilities and possibilities. The grandiose, pasha-like fat man and Chara were already strolling past the Mercedes SUV, and Chara's sharp voice cut the air like a knife, apparently rebuking the lorry driver and his sidekick, who were taking a smoke, to get on with unloading those crates. From the sundeck behind and above, Miranda could hear Madge's inimitable gurgle as she thanked Dimitris profusely for his concern, then heard his heavy tread as he hurried down the steps from the sun deck and loped down the gangway.

Swiftly she pressed CONTROL and HOME and the three happy little *Meltemi*s sailed round and round and round again.

When he reached Miranda, Dimitris flicked a glance in Chara and the fat man's direction. "Here is your bag," he said, his voice less than warm.

Miranda turned and glued a smile on her face, all too aware that she was still holding the boarding pass in her left hand. "Why, thank you, Dimitris. You are too kind."

Without a word, he thrust the yellow bag at her and gave her an expressionless look. Gone was his blinding white smile, the friendly crinkles at the corners of his eyes.

Oh-oh, she thought, feeling the heat and color of guilt rising to her face. *Caught in the act.* Now the sixty-four thousand dollar question was, would he rat on her? Or keep his silence?

As she fumbled to grab the nylon handles with her left hand, the boarding pass slipped from between her fingers and landed face-up on the quay.

Directly in front of Chara Zouboulakis' Jimmy Choos.

"Oh, how utterly clumsy of me," Miranda said, beginning to stoop.

To her surprise, Chara actually bent down, scooped it up with one manicured nail, and gave it to her. "A souvenir," she said crisply, repeating Dimitris' exact words—obviously Oracle Cruises' parting line.

"*Efcharistó.*" Miranda smiled, hoping Chara didn't notice the stiffness of her lips, the clamminess of her hand, or the nerves tingling in her fingertips.

Chara handed over Miranda's passport as well. "And this is yours also, Ms. Kalli. As I told you in Piraeus, it would be returned upon disembarkation. Yes? There should be a taxi by the esplanade."

No "Enjoy your stay," no "I hope you enjoyed your time on board," no traditional "*Yá sas.*" Not from Chara Zouboulakis. She simply tossed back that straight glossy mane of hers and breezed back on board to go about her business, whatever that business was.

And a good day to you, too, Miranda thought uncharitably.

Awkwardly clutching a bag in each hand, and the passport and boarding pass between thumb and forefinger, she trotted off a few steps. Then she set her bags down, slipped the passport and the boarding pass into the left pocket of her cargo pants, and turned around. She waved a last farewell up to Madge, who blew her kisses and winked conspiratorially, and the nurses who were leaning over the railing and who waved back enthusiastically. And, just to test the waters, Miranda waved to Dimitris as well.

He stood there, stiff as a board, and returned her wave with a flat stare before turning away.

But no, it hadn't been a flat stare. She had been close enough to detect something flicker deep within his eyes. Not an accusation, exactly. A wary expression. Guilt, perhaps? Or was it fear?

Yes, that was it: fear. But fear of what?

But there was time to speculate about that later. For the time being, Miranda felt a stab of deep shame for having duped a very nice man who, giving him the benefit of the doubt, had somehow, most likely innocently, gotten sucked into something way over his head. On the other hand, except for him, Captain Leonides, and especially Madge and the New Zealand nurses, she was glad to be off that boat. The cruise, short as it had been, hadn't exactly been a picnic.

Heading toward the esplanade, various incidents flashed through her mind with lightning speed.

Granted, she and Madge had pulled, or had at least tried to pull, the wool over Chara Zouboulakis' eyes. Pretending they were sisters and that, upon booking the cruise, Miranda's name had been misspelt and that there had been a mix-up with her passport number.

But Chara was no fool. On the contrary, despite her weakness for expensive designer fashions and accessories, there was a sharp, calculating brain constantly at work behind that facade of cold beauty. She had suspected . . . probably had *known* exactly what they were up to.

Yet despite the discrepancies, Miranda had been permitted to board.

Why? Because an extra passenger meant an extra passport, which translated into an extra boarding pass for the authorities at Kusadasi?

That was something to think about. Whatever the case, it would be a mistake to underestimate Chara Zouboulakis. Miranda had learned that much.

Then there had been the confrontation with the lady tour guides at Sounion. Though she couldn't prove it, there was little doubt in Miranda's mind that Chara had set her up for that unpleasant encounter.

Next had been the episode of her missing Swatch watch, which had miraculously reappeared. She had searched the cabin thoroughly for it. High and lo as it were. Had someone, Chara perhaps, crept into her cabin and lifted it while she'd slept soundly, thanks to Captain Leonides' generous glasses of complimentary brandies? With the express intention that the late Mr. and Mrs. Kalli's little girl wouldn't be able to tell the time on Delos—in the hopes that she'd miss the boat?

Which brought her to the episode on Delos. Had she *really* tripped and fallen during her rush downhill? Or had she been attacked? She had no memory of it whatsoever, but given all the other strange occurrences, she now began to seriously wonder.

And, last but certainly not least, there was the issue of her—what? Stolen . . . or if not stolen, at least borrowed identity?

Oh, yes, there was a whole lot more going on with the *Meltemi II* than met the eye.

Picking up her bags again, she made for the gray taxi parked at the esplanade's curb. The driver climbed out, released the trunk, and deposited her bags inside it before slamming it shut. He held open the rear door for her. She climbed in and he shut it and seated himself in the driver's seat.

"*Parakaló?*" he said, glancing at her through the rear-view mirror. "Where to, Miss?"

Miranda was suddenly tired and overwhelmed by what Madge referred to as her "adventures." Too many odd events had happened in too short a period of time. She needed time to digest them all.

She leaned back against the padded headrest and shut her eyes.

"Pythagoria," she said wearily, "the Albatross Restaurant."

[CHAPTER THIRTY]

Pythagoria, Samos

It wasn't such a long, but it was certainly a winding road. It lifted its two-lane length steep and high above Vathi, at first offering a splendid view of the town, harbor, and massive long bay, and then it cut through the valleys of the Bairaktari Mountains. Close up, the shrubbery and trees looked dusty and thirsty, and the scenery consisted mostly of gas stations and scattered commercial structures. The road was congested. August is, after all, Europe's penultimate vacation month, and Samos was bursting at the seams.

Suddenly the valley opened and there to the south stretched that wine dark sea sequined by the sun, and eastward, just across the strait, the dim, brooding, gray peaks of Asia Minor brushed the sky. Then the curving ribbon of road rounded a bend and dipped sharply. And miraculously, far below, was Pythagoria, picturesque as a glossy postcard.

Blinding white houses with red tile roofs seemed to tumble steeply down to the loveliest small harbor. The water inside was of a paler blue spotted with aquamarine in its shallows, the natural crescent was further protected by a long breakwater extending its long arm far out along one length, while a shorter, triangular esplanade jutted out at a right angle, providing further defense for when Poseidon's whim whipped up the sea. From this height, the colorful fishing caiques of varied sizes, the lineup of visiting sailing yachts bristling with masts, and the sleek shiny motor yachts, all berthed stern to the quay, were like a child's collection of small, bright toys.

Miranda's mood lifted like a buoyant balloon, and any residual weariness was replaced by a burgeoning excitement.

This, not Vathi, was the quintessential Greek island village with its waterfront crowded check-to-jowl with tavernas and coffee shops and tables set out under jutting awnings and beneath the shade of trees.

The taxi negotiated narrow streets crowded with small rental cars and lined with little shops, then turned and crept along the waterfront and its strolling tourists. There was an air of festivity, much like a medieval fair, and the cafés and tavernas were filled to capacity, their patrons sipping drinks or iced *café freddos,* or having lunch, or enjoying very late breakfasts. The smell wafting through the taxi's open windows was rich and aromatic, a mingling of olive oil, basil, thyme, and fresh salt air. Gulls wheeled and cried overhead while pigeons bravely strutted about, pecking the ground, and lithe cats eeled their way under the tables, waiting for handouts.

Spellbound, Miranda leaned out, elbow resting on the car door's sill, taking in the scene. She noted that, without fail, every stuccoed building along the quay sprouted peak-roofed sun awnings like tents jutting far out, every one the exact width of its charming structure, each of which abutted the other, higgledy-piggledy. Most of the establishments could only be differentiated by the colors of their awnings or the varied styles of their chairs and tables—with the exception of one, which with pretensions of Classical grandeur had Corinthian columns supporting a wooden pergola, and had a row of rather gaudy, life-size white plaster caryatids up front.

On the taxi crept and made a sharp left where the buildings petered out and the long arm of the breakwater began. Here, separate from the maddening crowd and adjacent to a repair yard where caiques on trestles were overhauled, their lines hung with freshly caught pink octopuses like so many Christmas ornaments, was a crenelated whitewashed wall, roughly plastered and in dire need of renovation. To Miranda's right it merged into a rugged, and very long and rather disreputable-looking, one-story building. It was L-shaped, and the windows cut into the thick masonry facing outward were high and spare and almost prison-like in their austerity. From what she could see, the walled-in compound was a mass of neglected olive trees, palms in desperate need of trimming, and tired, sagging pergolas dripping heavy clusters of grapes from vines.

The taxi halted. "Albatross," the driver announced.

Miranda's face fell. "Are you sure?" she asked uncertainly, her eyes searching in vain for a marquee, or at least some sign announcing commercial activity. But none was in evidence.

"Albatross," the driver repeated with finality, pointing at a rectangular opening in the crenelated wall that was obviously the entrance, each end surmounted by large milky glass globes. Climbing out, he chucked open her door, and popped the trunk. He lifted out her two yellow bags and set them down on a surface of rough cement.

Emerging from her back seat, Miranda looked apprehensively at what appeared to be a shabby and derelict complex. Then she heard a sound of life from within. It was not the noisy chatter of holiday diners and drinkers, but the banging of a solitary hammer. Between the gap-toothed crenelations, she spied its source: a workman balanced atop a rickety ladder who was adding a diagonal strut to one of the pergolas that seemed in imminent danger of collapse.

After the jam-packed tavernas and cafés, it was hardly a promising sight. And from reading and re-reading Professor Hirsch's letter, Miranda had practically memorized it by heart.

Eleni owns a restaurant here on Samos called Albatross, which has acquired quite the reputation for its seafood—

Her frown deepened. If this was indeed Professor Hirsch's highly touted Albatross—and she knew him well enough to know that he never lied or stretched the truth—this surely could not be it.

There had to be some mistake. Well, if there was, she would have to lug her bags and ask around until she found it.

The driver was hovering at her side. "Twenty-five Euros," he said.

A monstrous price by any standards for an eight mile drive, but then, this *was* the height of the tourist season. Soon, all too soon, Miranda reminded herself, she would have to hit an ATM, and that depressing thought made her all too aware of her alarmingly shrinking bank balance. Greece, which had always been famously renowned as a bargain basement for travelers was, unfortunately, that no more. Especially not with the way the once-almighty dollar was plunging against the Euro.

Dollar, my butt, she thought. *Peso's more like it these days.*

She duly paid the fare without complaint, the Manhattanite in her adding what was probably an overly generous tip for these parts, and off he drove. Then, squaring her shoulders, she hoisted her bags and approached the lamp-flanked entrance with trepidation. There was no gate or buzzer or bell to be seen, so she entered the property in the hopes that she wasn't trespassing.

It took a moment for her eyes to adjust, so sharp was the contrast from the dazzling, vibrant light and heat beating down mercilessly outside the crenelated walls, and the sudden cooler environ of variegated, sun-dappled shade that suddenly surrounded her. From atop the ladder, the workman, with a mouth full of thick, long nails, gave her a cursory glance downward and promptly resumed his jerry-rigging of the pergola.

Miranda set down her bags and looked around. Whatever this place was, she was pleasantly surprised. If dilapidation had been her first impression from outside the property's perimeter, she realized that inside it was ruled by a charming, intentionally benign neglect. Cicadas shrilled from the greenery, and she recognized the ubiquitous olive trees with their gnarled trunks and silvery green leaves, and the locusts, and above all she was enchanted by the fig and orange trees heavily weighed with fruit as rich and glossy as the grapes dripping from the sagging arbors. All these grew and thrived from the surrounding paving of *krokalia,* a huge expanse of terrace fashioned of black and very pale gray round pebbles set into cement in a lovely geometric pattern. Where cracks had appeared in the paving, lemon thyme had been permitted to spread profusely, so that when you stepped upon it up drifted the heavenly scent of herbs.

Oh, yes. Her initial impression had been entirely wrong, for there was a spellbinding magic to this informality, with planters overflowing with aromatic basil and rosemary and drifts of lavender and sage. Giant terra cotta pots from Crete literally bursting with veritable bushes of geraniums, bright as luscious tomatoes, while cascades of bougainvillea, fushsia, and jasmine threatened to overburden strategically placed trellises. A butterfly, fluttering undecidedly in front of her, showed off papery wings of iridescence and a tiny lizard skittered across the *krokalia* just inches from her feet. Despite the continued hammering of the workman atop the ladder, bees buzzed indolently, hovering from one flower to the next, collecting nectar while pollinating the blooms.

So powerful was the enchanting magic of this informal Eden that it took Miranda several moments to realize how prime a spot it occupied, the terrace ending directly at the breakwater's edge. And it took several moments longer yet for her to register the mismatched dining tables and chairs separated by vines and trellises. No cramming of table beside table here, without elbow-room, like at the teeming, awning-lined curve of the establishments crowded, one beside the other, along the crescent of the yacht-lined quay directly across the harbor.

This was no tourist trap, that much was clear, and the view was out of this world, as picturesque as it could get. The harbor, the yachts, the commercial stretch of tavernas and cafés, and rising behind it all the dun-colored, scrub-dotted hillocks, like small mountains.

A long-forgotten verse of the Mogul Inscription in the Red Fort at Delhi sprang to mind:

> If there is a paradise on the face of the earth,
> It is this, oh! it is this, oh! it is this.

But it was time she stopped dawdling.

"Hello?" she called out tentatively. "*Kaliméra?* Is there anybody here?"

There was a light slapping of sandaled feet, two flashes of movement, a rustling of jasmine that disturbed the bees, and a whispered conversation. Then two small heads peeked shyly out from around the nearest jasmine-laden trellis. The boy was ten or so and the girl was a couple of years younger. Both were thin and tanned, with huge urchin-like dark eyes and black hair.

"*Kaliméra.*" Miranda smiled.

Without speaking, they stared at her a little longer, and then the girl pushed the boy forward.

"Good morning," he said politely, if somewhat bashfully. He spoke fluent American-accented English, while the girl hid behind him, sneaking peeks before ducking back out of sight again.

"You're American?" Miranda guessed.

He began to grin and thrust out his chest proudly. "Yes, but I speak Greek also. Plus a little German."

Miranda held out a hand and he gave it a surprisingly solemn shake. A proper little gentleman. Someone had apparently drilled him in decorum.

"And your name is . . . ?" Miranda asked.

"Mike," he replied, raising his head. "Mike Savides. Actually they call me 'Little Mike.' That's because my dad's name is Mike too, and they call him 'Big Mike.'

"To avoid confusion," he added.

"Pleased to make your acquaintance, Mike. And I'm Miranda. Now, what is the name of your shy little friend?"

He pulled the reluctant girl forward by the hand. "This is Penelope. She's my best friend here."

Miranda extended her hand and the girl took it and gave it a quick, limp shake before taking a quick step back.

"Mike,"—Miranda didn't wish to insult him by calling him "Little Mike" just yet; children, she knew from her own childhood experiences, possessed more pride than most people gave them credit for, and hated to be talked down to—"could you tell me if this is the place called Albatross?"

"Oh, yes." His had bobbed up and down. "This is Albatross." He gestured around the compound. "It's named after one of those large sea birds that can fly for long periods of time."

"Then I take it the taxi driver was right? This *is* Eleni's establishment?"

He grinned disarmingly, his teeth showing snow white against his tan. "Yes. But if it's lunch you want, I'm afraid you're too early. Aunt Eleni only serves dinners."

"Don't worry," Miranda assured him. "I didn't come to eat. I do believe I'm expected? Professor Hirsch sent for me."

"Oh!" Realization dawned, and his eyes sparkled with interest. "You're that Miranda? Miranda Kalli? Uncle Wald's friend from New York?"

She smiled. "The one and only."

He turned to Penelope and rattled off something in rapid-fire Greek. The girl's dark eyes got huge, then she turned and raced off toward the far end of the long, L-shaped building.

"She's going to tell Aunt Eleni that you've arrived," Mike said. "Aunt Eleni will be very excited. Uncle Wald told her all about you."

He indicated Miranda's two yellow bags which she'd set down.

"These are yours?"

"Yes."

"I shall carry them," he announced, and before she could protest, he leaned down and lifted them carefully by the straps. "This way, Ms. Kalli."

"Mike," she said, "do me a favor?"

He stopped and looked at her.

"I hope we'll be friends, and if we are, you can skip the formalities. Okay? If I can call you Mike, you can call me Miranda. Deal?"

His smile was sunnier than Apollo's chariot. "Really?"

"Really."

He was bursting with pride. "Deal," he said, shifting the bags from one hand to another, then turning to lead the way, skirting around trellises, trees, planters, and tables of various sizes. They were halfway to the L-shaped end of the building when his pace slowed noticeably, still pretending to lug the bags with ease.

Miranda wasn't about to burst his macho bubble by suggesting she carry one, and anyway, just then she saw a woman striding purposefully out from the building towards them.

She was all smiles and her large half-moon eyes sparkled.

"That's Aunt Eleni," Mike confided in a near-whisper. "Mrs. Vlachos. She kept her last name even after she married Professor Hirsch."

Miranda eyed the woman with sharp interest as they converged.

Eleni Vlachos looked to be in her mid-forties. She was short but not plump, and handsome rather than pretty. She had a somewhat wide nose and a head of tinted reddish-brown hair streaked with highlights and combed off to one side. She had matching, perfectly reddish-brown eyebrows.

In fact, everything about her matched. Her spotless white, lightweight wash-and-wear blouse with its modest curved neckline. Her unlined summer jacket. Her tailored pants. She wore modest white heels and was groomed to perfection. Her recently manicured nails were cut very short and showed clear polish. Her lipstick was red, her teeth white and even. A long chain of gold links, with larger gold cabochons spaced in between, hung to below her bosom, which was thrust out with pride.

Greeks, as Miranda was learning, set great store by outward appearances. It was a matter of pride, and made her own touristy, casual outfit feel shabby by comparison. Penelope, any shyness now gone, skipped happily alongside her aunt, gazing up at her adoringly and chattering away a mile a minute.

Eleni cried, "So *you* are the famous Miranda Kalli! Wald told me all about you!" Her accent was pronounced, but her English was excellent. "Now hush, Penelope," she admonished the little chatterbox at her side. Then, flinging her arms wide, she embraced Miranda in the kind of hearty hug reserved for a long-lost daughter. After a moment, she took a step back, held Miranda at arms' length, and inspected her closely. "I see that Wald's description of you did not do you justice."

"I'm sure he was much too kind."

"On the contrary. Now, let me welcome you officially to Samos and the Albatross. And never, ever forget—" here Eleni let go of Miranda's hands and wagged an admonishing finger "—that you are family. *Yes?*" She beamed with genuine delight.

And to Little Mike, she added: "Take Ms. Kalli's luggage to the little guest room. You know the one I had prepared."

"I think you'd best refer to me by my first name from now on," Miranda interjected. "I told him not to call me Ms. Kalli. Mike and I struck up a friendship already, and I told him to drop the formality."

"Really!" Eleni cast a quick, questioning glance at Little Mike, who was grinning from ear to ear and nodding vigorously.

Eleni laughed. "You see?" she cried. "I was correct. You already *are* a member of the family!"

Not about to be relegated to the sidelines, Penelope looked up at her aunt and piped up, "Can I call her 'Miranda' too?"

"You shall have to ask her for yourself," came the reply.

"Of course you may," Miranda told the girl with a laugh and, happy as a lark, Penelope yanked one of the yellow bags from Mike and insisted upon lugging it personally, even though she had to lean almost drunkenly sideways to compensate for its weight. Her cohort pretended to scowl upon this intrusion upon his machismo, but listening to their chatter, the two went off cheerfully enough together.

"Penelope is my brother's daughter," Eleni explained, the pride in her voice evident. "They live on the Peloponnese, in a little village called Ermioni, but spend most of their summers here on Samos."

"And Little Mike?"

"He is my honorary nephew. His father, Big Mike, as we call him, works at the archeological site. That is over at Asprodavos." She gestured vaguely westward. "But Little Mike and Penelope both look forward to the summers they spend together. They have become the best of friends over the past several years."

"They're both absolutely delightful. *And* well-mannered," Miranda remarked.

Eleni beamed. "They are, aren't they? And they can be quite a handful at times. But I adore them both."

"Which," Miranda pointed out, "is obviously reciprocated. It's always refreshing to see two children getting along so well together."

Eleni gave a hearty laugh. "*Né,* but wait until two or three years from now. They are still young and innocent. But by then Little Mike will have reached puberty and have other girls on his mind. And when

Penelope reaches that point, she will seek companionship among other females of her age—not to mention boys."

She gave a wistful sigh and added, "At that point, I fear, they will not be so innocent or attached to each other anymore. But such is life." She gave a philosophical shrug typical of Greeks. "It's only natural, of course."

As they followed the children, Eleni reached up into the shady arbor and plucked a bunch of luscious green grapes. She handed half to Miranda.

Following Eleni's example, Miranda popped the green fruit, fresh from the vine, one at a time, into her mouth. She was in seventh heaven. Not only did the grapes burst fruity juice each time she bit into one, but here—at long, long last—was some of that famous Greek hospitality she'd found lacking aboard the *Meltemi II.* She felt instantly at home, especially as Eleni hooked her arm through Miranda's as they strolled.

Again, Miranda gazed around the compound with appreciation.

"You have no idea how wonderful it is to be here," she told Eleni. "And this place! It wasn't at all what I expected. It's sheer magic! Not like all those tourist traps across the harbor."

Eleni feigned a serious look. "Please, do not . . . how do you say? Shoot me?"

"Why would I want to do that?" Miranda raised her eyebrows.

"Because I also own a taverna/pizza parlor in Vathi," Eleni confessed. She nodded across the small harbor. "In summer it caters to exactly those kinds of tourists. It is called Porphyry and is located directly on the esplanade."

"I'll have to check it out. If I get the time."

"Not if," Eleni said flatly, "you *will.* Over at Porphyry I have one cook who is a specialist at creating traditional Greek *yia-yia* fare. You know . . . souvlaki, gyros, metzes, mountain greens, grilled octopus, Greek salad . . . those kinds of dishes."

"Sounds delicious."

"Oh, it is. Better than any of the other tavernas, but then, of course I am prejudiced. Also I have a Neapolitan there who makes the most marvelous pizzas. We have two young motorcyclists who, when people call in an order, deliver them door-to-door, just like in New York City!"

"Nothing beats take-out," Miranda agreed. "Smart idea."

"Actually, the credit belongs to Wald. It was his idea, from the years he spent as a professor in Berkeley. Also, Porphyry remains open year-round, because of the large local population at Vathi. Thank God they love Luigi's pizzas. He resisted me at first, but I created a 'Greek' pizza which has become quite popular. First the crust is heated, then when it is cooled it is spread with *tzatziki* and topped with calamari salad, fried eggplant, artichokes, grilled red peppers, Kalamata olives, anchovies and, of course, garnished liberally with basil."

Miranda grinned. "I've just had breakfast and you're making me hungry already!"

"That is as it should be. A delicious meal is food for the soul. Unfortunately, here at Albatross, we are only open from May until the end of October. That is because almost everything in Pythagoria closes once the tourists leave. The entire village practically shuts down. Like one of your Western film ghost towns. So you see?" Eleni laughed heartily. "I am as mercenary as any café or taverna owner! But here at Albatross—"

Eleni spat out some grape seeds, made a circle of her thumb and forefinger, and kissed it.

"—here is where you get the finest Greek cuisine."

"Yes. Wald . . . Professor Hirsch . . . wrote something to the effect that you've made quite a name for yourself for your seafood."

Eleni's brights beamed. "Did he?"

"Oh, yes. But Little Mike said you don't serve lunch. Why is that?"

"Because Greek feasts take an entire day to prepare. Right now, my twenty-one-year-old, Stelios, and his brother, Manos, are out harvesting shellfish for tonight. We have two shellfish farms, one west of here on the island of Icaria—"

"Named for Icarus, I take it, who flew too close to the sun, and the wax melted from his wings?"

"—exactly. You *do* know your mythology." Eleni sounded pleased. "Since he supposedly fell to earth there, the area directly around Icaria is called the Icarian Sea. Our second shellfish farm is on the island of Fournoi, located between Icaria and Samos. There is a small, unspoiled fishing village there called Chrysomilia, which you must visit if you have the time. There are no cars on the island, and very few tourists, so it is very pleasant. But all in good time. Ah. Here we are."

"Here" was the shorter right angle of the L-shaped structure, the end jutting directly onto the quay of the breakwater. And, what from outside had looked like two forbidding, ugly, long boxes were, when viewed from inside the compound, pierced by a series of large arches with sliding glass doors which could be opened or closed, depending upon the weather, and commanded a magnificent view of the arbor, the tree-shaded garden, and the sparkling yacht-brimmed curve of Pythagoria's harbor. Through open doors and windows, Miranda glimpsed a large commercial kitchen from which a hive of activity emanated: the clanging of pots and pans, the sounds of chopping and dicing and slicing, the babble of male and female voices laughing, shouting, or cursing good-naturedly in Greek. A row of octopuses, freshly caught and beaten tender against rocks, festooned a line between two poles, drying in the sun and looking like festive pink Christmas ornaments. A big outdoor grill of stone, topped with metal grating, stood nearby, waiting to be fired up.

This was, Miranda thought, truly a magical place, as close to heaven as you could get.

Eleni led her to the farthest end of the short "L", right beside the breakwater and its cement quay. Little Mike and Penelope were already there, pretending not to be out of breath and waiting beside a door painted that inimitable Aegean blue. They had deposited Miranda's two yellow bags on either side of it, grinned, and scampered off.

"This is one of our two guest rooms," Eleni told Miranda. "It is small and shares a bath. I am sorry, but it is very simple and basic. Also, Wald told me you would be spending most of your nights in one of the little shared houses over at Asprodavos."

She opened the door, gestured for Miranda to enter first, and followed her inside. The room was small and spare, a perfect cube with white stuccoed walls, an unstained pine floor that had been scrubbed to within an inch of its life, and a connecting door to the shared bathroom. A single bed with low, hand-turned, wooden balusters for bedposts, was pushed against one wall. The sheets were as white as newly fallen snow, there was a small, locally woven blue-and-white striped area rug, and a window cut into the thick wall that faced the harbor directly. Its shutters were open and there were no curtains, but a grapevine growing across it filtered the bright sunlight and a slight breeze ruffled the leaves, creating a shifting, monochromatic pattern on the walls. Completing the décor were a small rustic chair, a narrow, carved chest of drawers with a single electric lamp, and an icon of Christ the Pantokrator. A little vase of freshly plucked flowers added a note of welcome.

"I regret that it is not luxurious," Eleni said rather apologetically.

"On the contrary!" Miranda cried. "It's lovely and charming. So clean and neat, and I love the simplicity. And that lacquered pine ceiling! Eleni, it's so much more than I ever dared expect."

Eleni laughed throatily. "The accommodations at the dig are much more primitive, I'm afraid. Also . . . " she opened the bathroom door " . . . as you can see there is a simple shower, sink, and toilet. That covered container there is for depositing used toilet paper and tissues. Please do not flush any paper. We are not exactly up-to-date with septic systems yet."

Miranda smiled. "Don't worry. I find it all absolutely charming."

"I am so glad." Eleni produced a little cell phone. "Now I shall telephone Wald and leave him a message that you have arrived. I know he is busy at the moment with some authority or other from the Ministry of Culture." She rolled her eyes expressively. "You would not believe the bureaucracy involved with archeological digs. And now I had best oversee what is happening in the kitchen. You may freshen up if you like and then sit outside. Little Mike will bring you a glass of our famous Samian wine. Not the tourist house wine. The kind which has made Samos famous, and is controlled by a very few rich families."

"I can't thank you enough," Miranda said gratefully.

Eleni flapped a hand. "Nonsense. It's Wald and I who should thank you for coming. He is so excited at the prospect of your joining us. It is all he talks about.

"Also," she added, "there have been some disturbing occurrences at the dig. But I will let Wald tell you all about those. He did tell me that you are one of the few people in the world he trusts with his whole heart."

And before Miranda could reply, Eleni gave her another warm, welcoming embrace.

And she was gone.

Alone, Miranda sat down on the edge of the bed and frowned. There it was again. Another mention of problems at the dig. She remembered what Professor Hirsch had written in his letter:

. . . there have been,well, to put it mildly, some rather peculiar goings on . . .

What in all of Hades could these mysterious allusions refer to? she wondered.

Well, she would find out soon enough.

She found herself wryly remembering a line from somewhere . . .

Carrie Fisher, she believed . . . something about the only problem with instant gratification being that it was never instant enough.

Well, for the late Mr. and Mrs. Kalli's little girl, the same held true for mysteries.

Meanwhile, all she could do was wait.

Biting her lip, Miranda took Eleni's advice. She freshened up, went out, and sat under one of the shady, scented arbors sagging with grapes, where she sipped a glass of that famous Samian wine and waited for Professor Hirsch.

[CHAPTER THIRTY ONE]

Pythagoria, Samos

Miranda was on her second glass of wine when a small, traditional fishing craft puttered past the docked yachts, let out its anchor chain, and backed in at the quay beside Albatross with a minimum of maneuvering. It was no longer than twenty feet, with wide, low gunwales, a steadying mast in the shape of a cross just forward of a tall, ungainly cabin just roomy enough for one man to stand in, and a long-handled manual tiller at the stern. Within two minutes, it was expertly tied to one of the stanchions and the engines were cut.

Her heart gave a leap. *Professor Hirsch!* she thought with excitement. *At last!*

Pushing back her chair, she started to rise, nearly toppling the little café table with its glass of wine and plate of Kalamata olives in the process. She had to duck to avoid a thick bough hanging heavily with grapes.

But Eleni, rushing past from the direction of the kitchen, waved her back into her seat. "It is only Stelios and Manos, my sons. Returning from the shellfish farms. You shall meet them shortly."

Masking her disappointment, Miranda sat back down under the fruit-laden arbor and nursed her wine as she watched Eleni greet her two sons. Both were strapping young men, bare-chested, olive-skinned, and bronze. She had to admire the way they scampered balletically along the narrow, gently shifting deck like sailors born to the sea.

Which, obviously, they were.

Speckled with shifting sunlight and shadow, Miranda sat and watched as they hauled heavily-laden nets from the hold and deposited them on the quay. Eleni, hands on her hips, gave the haul an efficient, cursory inspection, nodded her approval, and led the way back to the kitchen. Her sons, nets of shellfish slung over their sun-baked backs, followed in quick succession, then returned with the empty nets to the quay. They made three more round trips, then lugged a heavy woven basket, one gripping the handle at each end, through the garden and into the kitchen beyond.

"Sea urchins!" announced Little Mike, startling Miranda by climbing, monkey-like, down from the arbor post beside her. "Yuck!"

"You just don't like them because you stepped on some," retorted Penelope, popping up beside Miranda.

"I hate them because they taste awful," he replied indignantly.

"That," said Penelope with a superior toss of her head, "is because you're not Greek."

"I'm Greek-American. So *there*."

"Anyway, you're just not used to them," came the lofty reply. "They're a delicacy. What Aunt Eleni calls 'an acquired taste'."

"Yeah," he scoffed. "Like beer and wine."

Penelope stuck her tongue out at him, and Miranda had to laugh. Then, their playful bickering over, Penelope raced off to the kitchen to inspect the harvest. Little Mike, rolling his eyes for Miranda's benefit, lingered for a moment and then ran after his playmate.

Miranda savored another sip of wine and nibbled some olives and smiled to herself, marveling at the innocence and energy of children, and remembering her own childhood friends and hijinks.

How much simpler life had been back then! How a year seemed a lifetime in those days, when you thought it took forever to grow up, and life had the illusion it would stretch to eternity!

Before long, Eleni shepherded her two sons to Miranda's table.

"My children from my previous husband," she introduced proudly.

Miranda twisted around in her chair. Eleni had every reason to be proud. Both her sons were barefoot, bare-chested, deeply tanned, and clad in white shorts. And both were exceedingly handsome and slim, with the kind of hard-bodied, classically proportioned physiques of ancient Greek athletes. Their morning's exertion showed in the salt and sweat on their arms and chests.

"This is Stelios." Eleni pushed the elder one forward. "He is affianced to the daughter of a hotel owner."

Stelios Vlachos topped out at over six feet and seemed to tower over his mother. He possessed startlingly virile good looks, had a head of thick, curly black hair, and the chiseled features of a model. He would have been a gold mine for any modeling agency.

Surprisingly, he seemed unaware—even embarrassed—by his effect on members of the opposite sex, and was extremely shy. He shook Miranda's hand and quickly let go of it and looked away.

Eleni introduced the other: "And this is my baby. Manos. He is a year and a day younger than Stelios. Also, he is the clown of the family."

Which, naturally, he had to go ahead and prove.

Manos Vlachos was the exact opposite of his brother. Two inches shorter, he shared the same chiseled looks, but they were softer and less dramatic, and he was obviously the extrovert—a young man with a wide grin and features in perpetual motion. He took Miranda's hand, bent low over it, and gave it the merest whisper of a continental kiss.

"A charming lady makes a charming morning even more charming," he paraphrased from a movie, and pretended to click his bare heels. "What a pleasant surprise!"

He turned to his mother. "*Manoula mou,* you didn't tell me we would have such a pretty visitor. I was expecting another one of those dreadful, grim archeologists with thick spectacles and frizzy hair!"

"Manos!" his mother chided him good-naturedly, giving him a punch on the arm. "Now be nice and mind your manners."

Feigning a put-upon air, she shook her head at Miranda. "I fear he shall always be an embarrassment," she said, even as she affectionately ruffled his hair.

Then, in a sharper tone, she told her sons: "Now you go shower and put on some decent clothes. *After* you have finished spreading the nets to dry."

Stelios strode off gladly, but Manos hung behind and sent Miranda a sly, conspiratorial wink over his shoulder, and she knew at once that despite the discrepancies in their ages they would be friends.

"What marvelous sons you have," she told Eleni once they were gone. "And so good-looking!"

"Yes. They take after their late father."

"Oh? I believe I detected a bit of you in them too."

"Really?" Eleni smiled. "Ah!" She cocked her head to one side and lifted a finger for silence. "Listen."

Miranda did, and frowned. "All I hear is another boat coming in."

"Yes, but not any boat. Every engine has its own distinctive sound. That is Big Mike and Wald arriving." She unconsciously touched her coif. "I had best go and make myself presentable."

Miranda laughed as she pushed back her chair and rose. "But Eleni!" she protested. "You *are* presentable. More than presentable."

"Perhaps. But I am no longer twenty or thirty years of age."

"And neither is Professor Hirsch," Miranda pointed out.

Now it was Eleni who winked, and it was obvious that Manos had inherited his sense of humor from his mother. "A woman," she declared, "can never be presentable enough. I only hope . . . " Her voice trailed off uncertainly and she paused, unsure of how to proceed with diplomacy.

"Yes—?" Miranda said encouragingly.

Eleni held up her hands and sighed. "It is about Big Mike. He . . . well, *before* you meet him, I should warn you." Her fingers fluttered nervously in midair. "He does not take well to newcomers to the dig. Especially not to the women. Why, I do not know."

"Really? I see."

"In fact, he tends to be quite rude to them at times. I hope he will not be uncivil to you, but if he is, please do not take it personally."

"There's no need to worry about me," Miranda assured her. "I can take care of myself."

"Do not get me wrong. I do not mean to disparage him. He has his good qualities also."

"I understand," Miranda said warmly, "and I appreciate your warning."

"They shall be mooring there, beside Stelios' and Manos' fishing boat." Eleni pointed to where her sons were spreading out the nets on the quay to dry. "I will join you there momentarily."

That said, she hurried off to make herself "presentable," and Miranda strolled thoughtfully around the arbor and its scattered tables and chairs to the spot where Professor Hirsch and Big Mike would be docking.

Returning to the full force of August's sun after the cool shade of the arbor, she shielded her eyes with one hand and watched a big rigid inflatable approaching. It reminded her of the *Hera,* aboard which Apostolos Malinakis had shuttled her from Delos to the *Meltemi II.*

What Eleni had warned her about "Big Mike" was that he was a chauvinist. That perhaps he even fit that old adage, "Male Chauvinist Pig."

Interesting.

She smiled tightly. Big deal. Big fucking deal. She was a grown woman accustomed to dealing with some of the world's most powerful and difficult men.

"Big Mike," did they call him?

Well, we'll see about that soon enough, she thought grimly. For if need be, he was going to learn *her* version of the Miranda Rights.

It wasn't exactly love at first sight. Nor was it hate. It was something less and yet something worse. One look at Miranda, and Big Mike dismissed her out of hand as just another Madison Avenue shop girl biding her time while searching for a rich husband.

But two could play that game. Miranda returned his icy reception with a good dose of her own, something he obviously wasn't used to. He seemed relieved when Little Mike came dashing toward him, squealing, "Daddy! Daddy!" while launching himself at his father.

Big Mike scooped up his son and held him easily saying, "Hey-a, Big Guy," and proceeded to give Little Mike his full attention.

The boy's eyes shone happily, and Miranda gave the father a discreet once-over.

Big Mike Savides—assistant director of the dig at Ancient Asprodavos (and answerable only to Professor Hirsch and the officials at the Greek Ministry of Culture) obviously considered himself a hotshot—able to lord it over everyone else and seemed full of himself—which raised Miranda's dander to dangerous levels. Unlike Stelios and Manos, who were magazine model material, he possessed a machismo all his own.

He was stocky, with a compact, beefy build and a low center of gravity. Was five feet nine inches. Handsome in his own way, but not movie star material by a long shot. His face was pitted and scarred from long-ago acne. His eyes were carbon black, with the beginnings of crow's feet from sun damage. His hair was dark and cropped and his body was over-muscled and sunburnt.

"Built like a brick shithouse," Mara would have said. "Not my type by any means."

Mine neither, Miranda would have replied, and focused her full attention on the second man getting off the boat.

"Professor Hirsch!" she cried, as Manos held out an arm to help his stepfather onto the quay.

Not that the spry, elderly gent seemed to need assistance.

"Miranda!" he returned with delight, and they collided and hugged each other fondly for a full half minute. Then they held each other at arms' length, each taking stock of the other. "And what is it with this 'Professor Hirsch' business?" he asked with mock gruffness. "I thought we had dropped that formality years ago."

"Oh. Sorry, *Wald.* It's an old habit. I imagine it comes from respect."

He laughed. "Better that than from old age. Now. How long has it been since we saw each other last?" His English, she noted, still retained an unmistakable German accent that was now tinged with undertones of Greek. "Two years?"

She smiled. "Two and a *half* years. When you were last in New York and gave that lecture at the Met. 'The Representation of the Goddess Hera.' Remember?"

"Yes. And I put half the audience to sleep."

"That's not true. They were all antiquity buffs and you held them spellbound. But what I find so amazing is that you haven't changed a bit. *Wald,*" she emphasized.

He made a face. "I have grown older, but not necessarily wiser. One's body slows down with time, you know." He smiled wryly. "One's hair recedes and grays . . . "

She wasn't having any of it. "Not you! I'd have recognized you anywhere," she exclaimed staunchly.

Granted, Waldemar Hirsch, at sixty-two, had matured somewhat since her doctoral thesis days at Berkeley, but then, as she well knew, so had she.

But that was ancient history.

In fact, Wald was still one of the youngest people, at least in spirit, who she'd ever encountered. His complexion had turned nut brown from the sun, and his silver hair lent him an additionally distinguished air. His pale blue eyes were the same: small, probing, and ever bright with excitement, and they hadn't lost that mischievous glint and sparkle she'd always loved. Field work evidently agreed with him, and had done its physical magic. Gone was his academic pallor, and if he was thinner, it was because he was wirier and more sinewy.

In a word, he glowed.

"Life," she noted, "seems to agree with you. "You look trimmer and more fit than ever."

He laughed. "I have to stay in fighting shape, now that I am a happily married man. You have met Eleni, I take it?"

"Oh, yes. She's an absolute marvel. I adored her from the moment we met."

"And you?" he asked, as they began to stroll arm in arm from the relentless sun into the shady arbor, where they took a seat at one of the tables.

Cautiously, as though handling a treasure, Little Mike came bearing a tray with another carafe of white wine, two glasses, and a plate of cantaloupe, each flesh-colored piece sliced at regular intervals like a row of perfect teeth.

"Aunt Eleni will be out soon," he announced, and, quite the little waiter, he filled their glasses with care.

"*Efcharistó,*" Miranda told him, which earned her a huge grin, and off he disappeared to join Penelope.

Professor Hirsch lifted his glass in a toast. "*Giá sas!*" he said.

"*Giá sas!*" returned Miranda, clinking her glass against his.

They each took a tiny sip.

"Eleni's wine is exceptionally good," Miranda said. "If I'm not careful, she'll turn me into an alcoholic."

He chuckled. "That I sincerely doubt. You possess too much self-control for that to happen. But yes, my Eleni does serve the best wine on the island. She has sources everyone else envies. But then, her uncle owns the finest vineyard. She comes from one of the oldest families on Samos. And as for her cooking—" he kissed his thumb and forefinger noisily "—it's divine."

"No more sauerbraten and potatoes?" Miranda teased.

"No more sauerkraut and bratwurst either." He pretended to shudder.

Miranda laughed and glanced out toward the quay. Stelios and Manos were still carefully spreading the precious nets, inspecting them for spots that needed mending.

Eleni came sailing out to join her husband. Miranda noticed that she had carefully touched up her lipstick and had powdered her face. A sullen Big Mike, hands thrust in the pockets of his tan cargo shorts, followed reluctantly, apparently the result of Eleni's arm-twisting.

Professor Hirsch started to rise, but Eleni gestured him to stay put. From behind, she bent forward, wrapped her arms affectionately around him, and gave his half-turned cheek a peck. Then, pulling out the chair beside his, she sat down, scooted close to her husband, and proprietorially clasped his hand. The table being one for four, Big Mike was forced to sit beside Miranda. He literally plopped himself down, elbows on the table, making no bones that he'd rather be elsewhere—

maybe in Philadelphia. Little Mike brought another tray with chilled bottled water, a second carafe of white wine, and two more glasses.

Professor Hirsch poured Eleni water. Big Mike grabbed the carafe and filled his glass to overflowing and scowled. He seemed to take up an awful lot of space, not so much with his bulky muscular body, but with his brooding. Throwing back his head, he downed half his wine in one swallow, disregarding the etiquette of making a toast.

Eleni shot him a sharp look of rebuke, but it bounced off him as if off Teflon.

Miranda decided to ignore him. Whatever chip Big Mike carried around on his shoulder was his problem, not hers.

Throwing oil upon troubled waters, Professor Hirsch looked at Miranda and said gently, "Now then. The ferries have just begun running again. We did not expect you until at least tomorrow. How on earth did you manage to get here a day earlier?"

In a nutshell, Miranda began by filling him in on her chance meeting with Madge at the airport, the similarities between her own name and that of Madge's sibling, and the subsequent, harmless-seeming stunt they'd pulled on the *Meltemi II* by pretending to be sisters. Nor did she leave out the crate that had been dropped during unloading in Piraeus, scattering its contents, including the *Oinochoe.* "It rolled right to my feet and broke in half."

"She-*it!*" Big Mike cursed explosively under his breath. "And I take it you also told those *Meltemi* crooks you were coming here to work on the Asprodavos site, huh?"

"Yes, I did." She raised her head with dignity. "And why shouldn't I have? It's the truth."

He slid Miranda a look of disgust. "Because you've obviously aroused their suspicions!" His voice was savage. "They most likely thought you were a plant. You know—like in spy?"

"But why should they have thought that?" Miranda asked.

"Because," Mike said brusquely, "like I just got through saying, they're a bunch of crooks."

"I gathered that. But would someone here please clue me in on what the hell is going on?"

"Everything," Mike snarled, spiking her with a dark look.

Professor Hirsch's expression was grave. "Mike, please," he said pacifically. "Control yourself. Perhaps Miranda has learned something useful."

"Yeah, right." He sounded anything but convinced.

The professor looked at Miranda searchingly. "First of all, the *Oinochoe*. You're convinced it was genuine and not a tourist copy?"

Despite Wald's gentle tone, she couldn't help but feel as if she was being subjected to a military debriefing.

"Absolutely," she replied. "The clay was ancient. Where it broke, it wasn't pink like newly thrown clay that had been antiqued. It *was* the genuine article."

Big Mike shook his head and poured himself some more wine and took a slug. He banged his glass back down. "Of all the boats to pick, it would have to have been one of those damn *Meltemis!*" he grumbled.

"Which," Professor Hirsch ruminated, "might be a stroke of good luck for us." He made a Norman steeple with his fingertips. "Now Miranda, dear, please continue. Try to remember everything, no matter how minor or inconsequential it might seem."

"Okay," she said slowly, and proceeded to relate her experience at Sounion with the umbrella ladies. "I can't prove it, but I'm almost certain Chara Zouboulakis set me up," she concluded.

Big Mike's eyes glinted narrowly. "*That* nasty piece of work!" he burst out. "She's more poisonous than a viper!"

"So I've gathered," Miranda murmured, and from Big Mike's vehemence, and the knowing glances Professor Hirsch exchanged with his wife, it was apparent that somewhere along the line Big Mike had shared more than a passing acquaintance with Chara, and had fluttered, moth-like, too close to the flame. Clearly there were still definitely very deep, and very hard, residual feelings.

She continued on, her voice level, describing her missing Swatch watch when they'd docked on Mykonos, and her subsequent experience on Delos.

"You were physically attacked?" Eleni looked shocked.

Miranda frowned. "The thing is, I don't *know.* I have absolutely no memory of what happened, except that the *Meltemi II* sailed off without me. If it hadn't been for Apostolos Malinakas—"

"Apostolos *Malakas* is more like it!" Big Mike grunted. "Another snake in the grass." He shook his head. "Lady, you sure do know how to find them."

Miranda took exception and rose to Apostolos' defense. "Actually," she said, tossing her head and giving a slight smile that might easily be construed as a taunt, "he was quite charming and went far beyond the call of duty." Her eyes took on a dreamy, faraway look as she remembered her physical attraction to him. "If it weren't for him, I'd have been stuck on Delos."

"Charming, my butt!" Big Mike grumbled. "What are you? Catnip for crooks?"

"He was quite the gentleman," Miranda sniffed. And, unable to help herself, the Chinchilla side of her came out and she added pointedly: "Unlike *some* of the men I've recently had the opportunity of meeting."

"I don't need to listen to this!" Angrily, Big Mike pushed back his chair and started to get up.

"Sit down." Professor Hirsch's voice was soft, but there was no mistaking the authority in his tone.

Nostrils flaring like an angry bull, Big Mike breathed deeply two or three times. Then, reluctantly, he obeyed and sat back down.

"Thank you," the professor told him. And to Miranda: "And then what?"

"Then," she said, "came Kusadasi." She related everything that had occurred—and also that which she believed had occurred—in minute detail.

"Probably a result of the doctor's drugs," Big Mike said dismissively.

"That's what I thought," Miranda said. "And that's what Dr. Babutcu had me believe." She paused for emphasis. "However, I have proof to the contrary."

Three sets of eyes stared intently at her.

Miranda reached into her right pocket, produced her own boarding pass, and slapped it down on the table.

Big Mike picked it up, gave it a cursory glance, then tossed it back down and shrugged. "Typical cruise ship I.D."

"As I understand it, yes. It is," Miranda said patiently. "When they slide it through that gadget, my picture pops up on the laptop, along with my pertinent information."

"And that's your proof?" he scoffed.

"No. That's my proof that I was aboard the *Meltemi II,*" Miranda corrected him levelly.

She aligned her boarding pass carefully on the table to her right and reached into her left pocket. She took out the second boarding pass.

"I found this one in the cabin I shared with Madge. Someone must have lost it, and the cleaners missed it when they made up the bunks. It was wedged between my two pieces of baggage."

"Looks identical," Big Mike commented after examining it closely, and he passed it around. "It has your name embossed on it."

"Yes," Miranda said wryly. "It does, doesn't it? But upon disembarkation at Vathi, I had the opportunity to swipe it through that gadget. On the sly. And guess what? The photograph on the magnetic strip on the back of that card? It's definitely not me. It's a total stranger. But the information is exactly the same as mine."

"Identity theft," Big Mike mumbled.

"More like identity borrowing."

"Unh-unh. Make no bones about it. They're one and the same."

Everyone stared at her trembling hands as she placed the second boarding pass to the left of her own in order to avoid mixing them up.

"What I saw through Dr. Babutcu's telescope," she said thickly, "was no drug-induced dream."

Professor Hirsch's voice was hushed. "Obviously not. My God! So they are using those *Meltemi*s to smuggle illegal immigrants into the E.U.! Refugees, terrorists, who knows who—so long as they can pay an exorbitant fee. And all along we only suspected them of smuggling antiquities."

Miranda sat still as a statue, only now beginning to realize the enormity of what she had stumbled across.

"What you have discovered is highly dangerous information." Wald Hirsch's pale blue eyes seemed to change into the color of a cloudy gray sky. "Do you have any idea how high the stakes are for smuggling immigrants across international borders? A boatload of the size you mentioned can mean hundreds of thousands of Euros. Think of it: ten thousand per person, perhaps more. And with three *Meltemi*s . . . in one summer alone that can amount to millions. *Millions!*"

Pausing, he added softly: "People have been known to kill for less. For much less."

Miranda shut her eyes as his words sank in. She sat limply back in her chair and took a series of deep breaths to steady her jumpy nerves.

"Now think back carefully, Miranda," he said gently. "Did anyone see you swipe that card through the gadget?"

"Did anyone see me?" A breeze rippled the vines overhead, the great bunches of ripe grapes swung gently like green chandeliers, light and shadows shifted and dappled, and the voices of happy holiday goers drifted across the water from the taverna-lined side of the harbor.

"Yes," he said again. "*Were* you seen?"

For the first time since arriving in Greece Miranda felt fear, true fear, as though scorpions were crawling along her spine. What had begun as her and Madge's seemingly harmless pretense had inadvertently plunged her into an unimaginable conspiracy.

She had to clear her throat and swallow, and her voice shook as she spoke. "I believe one of the crew members caught me at it."

Professor Hirsch shut his eyes. Eleni reached across the table and patted Miranda's hand in a maternal fashion, as if conveying that everything would turn out all right. Big Mike scowled. "Do you have any idea of the danger you've put us all in?" he snapped.

"It was Dimitris who I think saw me," Miranda said penitently, in a very small voice. "He's a very nice man."

Big Mike gave a mirthless laugh. "Jesus H. Christ, lady! Don't fool yourself. Nobody on any of those *Meltemi*s is *nice*."

"Dimitris is," Miranda said stubbornly, her voice gaining strength. "I don't think he'll tell."

But would he? she now wondered, remembering the cold shoulder he'd given her upon departure. He'd looked hurt—wounded, was more like it—and patently disappointed in her. He hadn't even acknowledged her good-bye wave.

But Big Mike wasn't finished grilling her. "And where was that viper Chara when you did this? She's usually the one at the computer."

"Not when I swiped the card through. She was at the end of the dock. A chauffeured Mercedes had pulled up, followed by a lorry full of crates. There was this huge man, very fat and expensively dressed, that she had some kind of private conversation with. In fact, for a while it looked like they were having an argument."

"Describe him." This from Big Mike.

Miranda did, in detail.

"Nikos Mitropoulos!" Eleni swore softly under her breath. "I should have guessed!"

"You mean, 'The Witch of Samos' don't you," Big Mike muttered sourly, and told Miranda: "That's what we call him behind his back."

Miranda looked from one of them to the other. "And who is he?"

"Probably one of the richest and most powerful men on this island," Eleni told her. "He owns businesses throughout the Aegean—in Athens, on Lesbos, Mykonos, Santorini, Ios, Paros, Hydra, Aegina—wherever there is the most tourist traffic. These include high-end boutiques, expensive jewelry shops, pottery factories making tourist reproductions of antiquities which he transports and sells in cheap souvenir shops, vineyards, olive groves, several big luxury resorts, that sort of thing. It would not surprise me if he traffics in drugs—"

"—and don't forget the three *Meltemis*!" Big Mike added gruffly. "The Witch *owns* Oracle Cruises."

"But if he's so rich," Miranda asked naively, "why would he involve himself with smuggling illegal immigrants?"

"Because, *sweetheart* —" Big Mike's voice dripped sarcasm as he talked down to her "— when you're very, very rich, you're never rich enough. There's always someone richer than you who you need to bypass in wealth."

"Yes," Wald added, nodding sagely, "accumulating great wealth can be an incurable disease. And when the rich are as sleazy and crooked as Mitropoulos, there's nothing they'll stop at to get even richer. They never have enough. And nothing can stop them."

"So you're saying that nobody's caught on to him? He can just go ahead and do as he likes?"

"Put it this way," Big Mike remarked bitterly. "As far as we know, nobody's lived to tell."

It was Eleni who now picked up the thread of the conversation. "Miranda, what you must understand," she said softly, "is that Mr. Mitropoulos has powerful friends in Athens, as well as highly placed individuals overseas. He enjoys protection from important officials of various governments."

Miranda reached out and tapped the left-hand boarding pass. "So what you're saying is, even with this proof, there's nothing we can do? No authorities we can go to?"

"None that we dare trust," Professor Hirsch said quietly.

"In other words, we just forget it?"

"For the moment, yes, the best thing we can do is nothing. We have to go about our normal business as though you never found that boarding pass. In fact, it would not surprise me if the argument you witnessed between Mitropoulos and Chara was about it being missing. Whatever the case, we *must* act as if it does not exist."

Miranda was suddenly angry. "And let them get away with—"

"Murder?" Big Mike supplied. "For now, yeah. The prof is right. Plus, for all our safety, we never had this conversation."

"One more thing I should mention," Eleni announced, quietly dropping the bombshell. "Mr. Mitropoulos' secretary called. He has dinner reservations for tonight. A table for ten. Here at Albatross."

"Oh, Christ!" Big Mike massaged his sunburned face with meaty fingers. "Just what we need. So what do we do with our loose cannon here?" He indicated Miranda with a sideways tip of his head. "Spirit her over to Asprodavos right away?"

"No," Professor Hirsch said after a pause. "That would arouse even more suspicion. For tonight she shall stay here as planned. She'll join the Asprodavos team tomorrow morning. We will act like everything is business as usual."

His pale eyes regarded Miranda solemnly.

"I don't know about your acting abilities, my dear, but we will be counting upon them. Just be your charming self. And remember: think of the three monkeys."

"You mean, 'See no evil, hear no evil, say no evil'?"

Professor Hirsch smiled grimly. "Exactly. Stick to the truth as closely as possible. And as for *that*—" he shoved the boarding pass on her left toward her as if it had burned his skin "—put it away and hide it in a safe spot. Do not even tell any of us where it is. And beware. The Witch of Samos, as Big Mike calls him, will undoubtedly attempt to pry information out of you. Most likely not tonight, but he will eventually try."

"Count on it," Big Mike added, picking up the carafe for a refill and grunting when he found it empty.

Eleni scooted back her chair and took the carafe. "I have to get back to the kitchen. I will send Little Mike out with more wine. And Miranda?"

"Yes?"

"Try not to worry. Just—" Words failing her, Eleni gestured helplessly without finishing the sentence and hurried off.

Miranda's head spun, her chest constricted. All along, she'd gathered that things aboard the *Meltemi II* were not what they should have been. But she'd never imagined *this!*

Mentally Miranda finished Eleni's sentence.

—Just stay alive!

[CHAPTER THIRTY TWO]

New York City

Some wag had once told Harris Palmer that it was too bad the sun had to set over New Jersey. And that reminded him of a line he'd read some time ago in the *New York Times* in which a woman was quoted as saying the sun setting over the Hudson reminded her of sunsets in the Mediterranean.

Now, seated in one of the sleek leather chairs in the penthouse suite of his boss, Walter Kirkland, looking out the floor-to-ceiling windows at the millions of vertical lights gleaming in the windows of the financial district's skyscrapers, he watched the huge red orb disappear behind the glittering towers, creating a theatrical backdrop worthy of a production at the Metropolitan Opera (not that he ever went), and he found himself wondering how this sunset differed from those in the Aegean.

Miranda could tell him.

Miranda. Her very name made him grind his teeth in frustration. She had been occupying a lot of space in his head lately. So much space, in fact, that it took twice as much concentration as usual just to keep his mind on his work. So far, none of his calls to her cell phone, nor a single one of a slew of text messages, had yielded a reply.

Mara's advice that he book the first flight to Greece seemed to make more and more sense.

Across the acre-size office, Walter Kirkland was still on the phone, shoes with no wear on the soles propped on the lake-size, mirror-like surface of his macassar and ebony desk.

Walter Kirkland was a legend in financial circles, and one of the founders of hedge funds. A single share in his Hartford-Kirkland Group cost a cool half a million bucks—and required a minimum purchase of 200 shares. Nor did his select group of shareholders ever utter a complaint. Why should they? They were members of that most exclusive of clubs—the happiest bunch of investors in the world, and reaped record profits year in and year out.

Walter Kirkland truly had the Midas touch.

Now approaching eighty, he also possessed the stamina of men a quarter of his age. He was a grand seigneur, the kind of man who drew every eye the instant he stepped into a room. With his thick mane of white hair and still erect posture, he emanated power, had a certain sex appeal (power and wealth being, after all, the greatest of all aphrodisiacs), was famous for his razor sharp wit, could charm the scales off a snake, and controlled more money than the gross national product of 120 countries combined.

In short, he had the financial world by the balls.

It was also reputed that he was an insatiable sex maniac. One of his most oft-repeated lines was: "If it flies, floats, or fucks—rent it."

Not that he heeded his own advice. He owned a fleet of corporate jets, kept one mega-yacht in the Mediterranean, another in the Caribbean, and was on his fifth trophy wife.

This, then, was the man Harry Palmer had to answer to. The head honcho. The high lama of the financial lamasery.

His phone conversation finished, Kirkland scanned the data on his computer screen—perpetually tuned in to the world's various financial markets, which never slept—and which gave his face a bluish tint. "Palmer!" he barked, and gestured Harry over to the desk.

Putting thoughts of Miranda on hold, Harry leapt up and strode across the acre of carpeting, consciously straightening his tie. "Sir?"

"Sit down, Palmer." With his pen, Kirkland gestured to one of the brushed steel-and-leather chairs facing him.

There was no, "How's it going?" No, "How's tricks?" No, "How's your hammer hanging?" With Kirkland, there was no small talk whatsoever.

"I'm sending you on the road, Palmer," he said without preamble. "Three of our top clients need to be coddled one-on-one. Here's your itinerary."

Kirkland tossed him a printout which slid smoothly across the huge, glossy desk. "Moscow, Brunei, Bahrain. You're leaving in the morning."

Harry glanced at the schedule. Air France. Singapore Air. Royal Brunei Airlines. His heart sank. Three commercial flights. Three encounters with hell on the ground, no matter how pampered you were in your full-length sleeper pod at the front of a plane.

"One of our corporate jets will whisk you from Bahrain back home. Five days, Palmer. Zip, zip, zip."

Harry cleared his throat. "Sir, any chance I can stop off in Greece on the way back?"

Kirkland's expression darkened. "We don't do vacations, Palmer. You know that."

Harry smiled grimly. "I know that, sir."

Kirkland tapped a few computer keys. "I'm reviewing your performance, Palmer. For the past week it's been satisfactory. Not exemplary. Not great. Not even good. Just satisfactory. Which is simply not good enough. Not for pulling your weight around here at H-K." He spiked Harry with his eyes. "Time you got back up to snuff, boy."

Harry swallowed, his face reddening under the rebuke. "Yes, sir."

"Bad timing to ask for time off, Palmer."

"I know that, sir. But it's personal business, not a vacation. Two days, that's all I need. I'll work like a dog while I'm there. The whole world's wi-fi these days. And Greece isn't a third world country anymore."

"Greece. Hmmm." Kirkland tilted his chair further back and tapped his pen thoughtfully against pursed lips. "Come to think of it, I guess it wouldn't hurt if you stopped off in Greece and stroked old Yannis Liapsis. He's considering the purchase of two thousand additional shares, but can't seem to make up his mind."

Harry waited.

Kirkland swung his feet off the landing strip of his desk and leaned forward. "Tell you what, Palmer." He pointed the pen at Harry with little stabs. "Set up a meet with Liapsis and give him a nudge. Help him make up his mind, you get your two days."

"Yes, sir. Thank you, sir."

"Two days, Palmer," Kirkland warned, his eyes narrowing. "Two days, max."

"Understood, sir."

"Now go watch the Asian markets. May be time to sell a company or two short in Singapore."

Walter Kirkland was all business—24/7 business. If he'd had the power, he'd probably outlaw time zones altogether.

"The financial markets of the world never sleep," he growled, as if Harry had forgotten. "Remember that, Palmer."

"I do, sir. All the time."

"Now get outta my sight." Kirkland made sweeping motions with a hand. "And bring me results."

One thing about Walter Kirkland. With him there was no mistaking a dismissal.

Glove leather sighed as Harry Palmer swiftly rose from his chair. "Yes, sir. Thank you, sir," he said, and hurriedly left.

In the high-speed elevator shooting halfway down the building to his own spacious corner office, he loosened his tie and consulted his gold wristwatch. Baume and Mercier, thirty-five thousand bucks at Tourneau. It showed what any cheap Timex or Casio would have: that it was after seven.

As if his body clock couldn't tell.

Unfortunately, he still had several more hours to put in before he could head home. It occurred to him that in the meantime, most of the Westchester commuters were already in their steroid MacMansions, kissing their wives, eating dinner, bouncing little ones in their laps. Leading the good life.

He consoled himself with the fact that he always had a fully packed suitcase ready and waiting in case he had to skedaddle off to some far-flung corner of the world at a moment's notice. At least he wouldn't have to pack before heading to the airport in the morning.

Yannis Liapsis.

He thought of him now. Liapsis, the third-generation Greek zillionaire.

Liapsis, his key for squirting off to Samos for two days. The big question now was, where would he *find* Liapsis? In Athens? London? God only knew. It being August, hopefully on his family's private island. All those super-rich Greek families seemed to own one.

That would be the most convenient.

Two thousand shares of Hartford-Kirkland at half a million bucks per.

One hundred million dollars.

If he could pull this one off, he would be back in Walter Kirkland's good graces—for a week, maybe two if he was lucky.

Most importantly, he'd get to see Mandy. Have a good face-to-face and explain about Tiffany Pfeiffer. Show her how much he really cared. Promise to settle down, quit the rat race, even invest in art.

It wasn't as if he needed his Wall Street bonuses. Hell, he had plenty socked away. Between his trust fund, his parents' blue chip fortune, and his own savvy investments, he was sitting on a shit pile of moolah.

What more did he need? Other than love?

[CHAPTER THIRTY THREE]

Pythagoria, Samos

Darkness had just begun to fall, dinner at Albatross was well underway, and Miranda lingered in the darkened doorway of her room, grateful that the big round table reserved for the Mitropoulos party was unoccupied, conspicuous by its plastic, tent-like "RESERVED" sign. Perhaps they weren't coming after all, and her worries had been for naught? Meanwhile, she enjoyed the visual enchantment of tiny electric lights shimmering in the arbors, and the trees whose foliage was discreetly lit from below. Every table except the one was occupied, the flames of votive candles dancing gaily in their little glass jars and flickering on the faces of diners, including a surprising number of Greeks who knew genuine local cuisine when they tasted it. A trio of musicians, tucked in a corner, strummed soft *bouzouki,* accompanied by a lovely-voiced local songstress. There was the tinkle of glasses and the sounds of cutlery and muted conversations and laughter.

Magic was in the air.

From across the harbor drifted the more raucous sounds of hard partying, but that seemed a world away. The yachts glittered. The bronze statue of Pythagoras, elongated and robed atop his pedestal on the protective jetty, pointed one arm skywards at the broken triangle towering above while holding a smaller triangle at his side, softening the blinking beacons indicating the harbor's entrance.

Octopus sizzled on the grill. Olive oil and spices—fennel, oregano, rosemary, mint, and more—perfumed the night. Stelios and Manos, smartly turned out in crisp white shirts and black trousers, proved themselves efficient waiters. Eleni, ever groomed, cheerful, and lively, made the rounds and welcomed her regulars and newcomers as if they were family, all the while keeping a discreet sergeant major's eye peeled, to make certain everything was running smoothly.

Without the Mitropoulos party present, Miranda felt secure and safe, and slipped out of her room to join Professor Hirsch. He and Big Mike were seated at a small, out-of-the-way café table sheltered behind a cascade of bougainvillea.

"Do sit down," Professor Hirsch invited, obviously pleased by her presence.

Miranda did, still looking around with bright-eyed wonder. "This is like something out of a fairy tale!" she enthused. "Now I understand why Eleni doesn't bother with lunch, and only concentrates on dinner."

"Yes," Wald agreed, proud affection evident in his voice. He poured her a glass of white wine and pushed it toward her.

"Eleni has been written up in newspapers and magazines the world over," he continued. "Even in the *New York Times* and all the important travel books. *Fodor's, Frommer's, Baedecker* . . . did you notice all the people at the bar, hoping to snare a table?"

But Miranda didn't reply. She was distracted by a huge white yacht, ablaze with three decks of lights that slowly, grandly, entered the harbor, passing the Coast Guard patrol boats berthed at the end. It proceeded to dock lengthwise along the breakwater at a very long and obviously reserved spot. Conversation stilled as diners watched the expert maneuvers of its white-uniformed crew.

"What is *that?*" Miranda gasped.

"The Liapsis yacht," the professor replied.

"Yeah. They own a private island between here and Patmos," Big Mike growled. "It's called Samosapoulo. It's virtually impregnable. You name it, it's got it. Radar. Underwater sonar. Just try getting within five hundred yards of it. I guarantee you'll be turned back by their own private little navy." He paused.

"At gunpoint," he added.

"They must be rolling in it," Miranda said.

Professor Hirsch laughed. "That is an understatement. They are one of the richest families in Greece, perhaps among the wealthiest one hundred in the world. Only recently they endowed a museum in Athens that is open to the public. It is a few blocks up from Syntagma Square, on Vasilissis Sofias. 'The Liapsis Collection of Ancient Art' it is called."

"'The Liapsis Collection of Vanities' is more like it!" Big Mike sneered unpleasantly. "Money and vanity." He shook his head and barked a laugh. "They go together like a marriage without prenups. Or love."

"You forget yourself, Michalis Savides!" the professor rebuked sharply. "Give credit where credit is due. The Liapsis family has been most generous. They are also the major contributors to our Ancient Site at Asprodavos. Without them, we'd have to shut down. We should be grateful."

"I presume," mused Miranda, "that this means we have to be very nice to them."

"Nice!" Big Mike muttered under his breath, and flashed her an ugly look. His hand shook as he poured himself another glassful of wine, spilling a good portion in his anger. "We're constantly kissing their stuck-up asses!"

Wald flinched at the accusation, and he was breathing heavily. It didn't take a blood pressure monitor to tell that he was struggling to keep his temper in check. How, and especially *why,* he put up with Big Mike was beyond Miranda. She'd have thrown him his walking papers long ago.

"If you've noticed," the professor murmured to her, "Mr. Savides, senior, is no fan of the rich."

"And why should I be?" Big Mike demanded, glowering at him. "They plunder."

"That's quite enough!" Wald Hirsch thundered quietly. "We have no proof of that! Besides, they have given the cream of their collection to the public."

But Big Mike wasn't finished quite yet. "You mean, they gave what they *claim* is the cream. What we're told to *believe* is the cream. Nobody has ever laid eyes on the entire collection. Come on, Wald. Admit it. Even you've only seen the tip of the iceberg."

The professor soughed a deep, calming breath and rubbed his forehead. For her part, Miranda was beginning to dislike Big Mike more and more. His constant hectoring and bickering were grating on her nerves, and jarred against the blissful, carefree atmosphere around her, robbing it of its carefully constructed magic.

"Aha! And lookie here! 'By the prickling of my thumbs, something wicked this way comes,'" Big Mike quoted grimly. Hand still wrapped around his wineglass, he pointed his index finger like a gun.

Miranda followed the direction he indicated and sat perfectly still, as if that would render her invisible. Though some yards distant, the immense, pasha-like figure was unmistakable. Nikos Mitropoulos, a.k.a. The Witch of Samos (despite herself, even Miranda was beginning to think of him by Mike's highly unflattering nickname), was on foot and under full sail. Puffed up with self-importance and grandly making a beeline along the breakwater towards the yacht.

He was closely followed by a very thin, stork-legged woman with a beak of a nose and wavy, shoulder-length black hair. She was all emerald. From the short, iridescent designer shift with spaghetti straps to the matching slingbacks and the necklace of startlingly big emeralds—even from this distance each stone looked the size of a scuba weight.

"Ever notice," Big Mike observed, "how you can always tell the Greeks from the foreign tourists by the way they're far better dressed?"

"As a matter of fact, yes," Miranda replied, "I have. The Greeks seem to put great store in appearances."

"*Outward* appearances, you mean," he corrected contrarily, with a growl.

Miranda let that one go. "Who's the woman?"

It was Professor Hirsch who replied. "That," he said, "is Despina Mitropoulos. His wife. She is Brazilian by birth, but of Greek descent and holds dual citizenship. She is also the only person he cannot control."

"Oh? And how's that?"

Big Mike chortled. "Yeah, she keeps him on a short leash. He gets out of hand? She only has to threaten to move back to Brazil and take their two kids with her." He drank some more wine. "Makes you wonder, man his size, how they ever managed to make babies. Think they used a bulb baster?"

Despite herself, Miranda burst out laughing. Then, catching Professor Hirsch's censorious frown, she said, "Sorry," and swiftly covered her mouth with her hand to stifle her continued giggles.

At the yacht, a hydraulic gangway had come down and a group descended, four men and four ladies of varying ages. The ladies were all holding their high-heeled shoes in their hands and were being helped ashore by gallant crew members—or, more likely, crew members who'd learned how to act gallant. Once on the dock, the shoes came on and there was a flurry of handshakes, embraces, and air kisses.

Miranda noticed that she wasn't the only person who followed the proceedings; half the restaurant's diners were craning their necks, also gawking at the glamourous assemblage.

Finally, the greetings were over and The Witch led what looked like a stately procession (*or a conga line*—Miranda couldn't quite quash the mental image) into Albatross proper.

Manos swiftly whisked the "RESERVED" sign off the empty table. Eleni, all smiles, greeted the new arrivals with a mixture of deference and familiarity.

Miranda, not ready for a confrontation with The Witch, willed herself small and invisible, and scooted further back into the shadows as The Witch made a production of pointing at various chairs and deciding who should sit where.

"Which one's Liapsis?" she asked Professor Hirsch from behind her hand.

"The short, balding, old man with the thick, black-rimmed spectacles. That is Yannis—Johnny to his friends. He inherited the family fortune from *his* father and multiplied it exponentially. The handsome dark-haired man in the open-necked shirt and blazer is his son, Leonides. He is being groomed to take over the family interests."

"And that very tall and thin el Greco of a man? The one with the van Dyke?"

"That is Theodoros Vassilakis. He is the Foreign Ministry's general secretary in Washington, D.C."

The professor's face took on a somewhat concerned expression as he added slowly: "He is also in charge of stamping out the smuggling of human cargo into this country. I gather he is on holiday and staying with the Liapsises on Samosapoulo."

"Yeah, and get *this*." Big Mike grinned sardonically, showing teeth. "He's also Despina's half brother. Makes you wonder, doesn't it, about a conflict of interests?"

"And the fourth man—" the professor began, then blinked and looked visibly taken aback.

"—is, oh, my God!" Miranda finished for him in a choked voice. "Why that's my own boss! That's Jan Kofski!" She couldn't believe her eyes. "You don't think . . . ?"

She stared wildly at the professor, too shaken to say anything more.

" . . . that he traffics in stolen artifacts?" Big Mike snarled softly but brutally. "Where do you think your fancy Madison Avenue gallery gets its inventory?"

"But we're *respectable!*" she sputtered. "We buy at auction, and from estates and various private dealers."

"And from where, Miss High and Mighty, do you think all those Egyptian, Greek, and Roman antiquities originated? Digs in *California?* In *Nevada? South Dakota,* perhaps?"

Every blunt, sarcastic word hit its mark like a sharp blade being thrust and twisted in a fresh wound.

"Of course not!" Miranda retorted, feeling a surge of red-hot anger at his insinuations. "Or have you forgotten that antiquities have been collected over the centuries? Or that a lot of them have passed from one owner to another, or from one collector to this museum, and from another to that? The Met, the Louvre, the British Museum, the Pergamon, to mention just a few, all have first class collections. No, don't interrupt, I'm not finished yet. I know what you're going to say. But despite the recent scandals at the Getty, and repatriation of pieces from the Met, it doesn't mean everything has been stolen and spirited clandestinely from current digs!"

She shook her head defiantly, then lifted it high in a show of dignity. "We're highly respected and above reproach."

"Come on, Miranda." Big Mike's voice softened somewhat. "Open your eyes. Isn't that table over there circumstantial evidence enough? Oh, and that *Oinochoe* you described? The one that fell out of the crate in Piraeus?"

"What about it?"

"From your description of it, I'll wager it came from our dig. No, don't look at me like that. Too many of our pieces have been going missing lately—including an *Oinochoe* that exactly—and I mean exactly!—matches the one you mentioned."

To keep her temper under control, Miranda shut her eyes and slowly counted to ten. From The Witch's table burst the sounds of multiple conversations, of laughter, and Champagne corks popping and gold lighters clicking expensive Cartier flames. When she opened her eyes again, Miranda glanced over. The Witch held center stage, and was gesturing dramatically with a cigarette, the glowing tip sketching orange loops in the air, his throaty, frog-croak of a voice, thick with multiple accents, overriding that of the others at his table as he recounted some anecdote or other.

There were shrieks of laughter from the bejeweled ladies, guffaws from the men.

"Look, Mike," Miranda said levelly, "I understand what you're saying. But you can't prove that the *Oinochoe* was headed to the Jan Kofski gallery."

"No, I can't. But it *was* headed somewhere."

He leaned across the table at her, and she flinched at the sour smell of wine on his breath. He wasn't drunk, that was the worst of it.

If only he were, she thought.

"Miranda," he said, "let me put it this way. The Ministry of Culture requires us to keep scrupulous records of any antiquities we uncover. And when I say any, I mean *any.* Every last shard of broken roof tile. What I'm saying is, each individual piece, every single *fragment,* is carefully numbered and catalogued. It's also photographed. Tomorrow, at Asprodavos, I'll show you our files. It wouldn't surprise me if you recognized some of the pieces from your *reproachless* gallery."

She sat there stiffly, silently taking the verbal punches as they came. Too overwhelmed to continue responding. Desperately trying to zone out.

It was impossible.

"You see," Big Mike went on relentlessly, "we've had a lot of problems at the site recently. More than our fair share."

He flicked a glance at Professor Hirsch.

"Care to fill her in on them, Prof?"

"Tomorrow," Professor Hirsch told Big Mike firmly. "I think Miranda's been hit with enough shocks for one day."

"Yes." Miranda's voice was trembly and she gripped the edge of the table with white-knuckled fingers. "Wald is right. Tomorrow is soon enough. Now, if you gentlemen will excuse me, I'm tired. It's been a long and wearying day, and I'm ready to hit the sack."

"But you haven't eaten yet!" Professor Hirsch exclaimed. "I shall have a tray sent to your room."

Miranda shook her head. Despite the mouth-watering aromas, she had lost her appetite. Only good manners prevented her from saying so.

"That's very kind of you, Wald," she replied, "but I'm really more tired than hungry. I'll see you in the morning."

And to Big Mike, her tone sardonic, verging on the caustic: "You needn't worry. I'll be up early." And more savagely: "All bright-eyed and bushy-tailed!"

She nearly knocked her chair over in her haste to escape. She felt trounced, Big Mike's implications swirling in her head like a dense flock of rabid bats, and she needed to get away, needed to flee to her room and shut the door. Not only on Big Mike, but on the entire world. She felt beaten down. K.O.-ed once too often even before the starting bell began to ring. And here she'd expected—

She all but brayed humorless laughter.

—not only the excitement of actually working on an archeological dig, but to savor the land she'd always dreamed of visiting. Dreamed of, yes—but not to find herself spinning ever deeper and faster into the vortex of a waking nightmare. Certainly not to have her world turned completely upside down.

Rest. She needed rest.

She started for her room, blundering her way around the tables, trees, and shrubbery that best shielded her from The Witch's table.

But escape proved impossible. Before she'd taken ten steps, a voice rang out, calling, "Miranda? Miranda!"

She stopped in her tracks and slumped. The voice was smooth, Dutch-accented, and all-too-familiar.

Before she knew it, Jan Kofski had jumped up from his place at The Witch's table and was beside her. Slender and elegant and all in chic Madison Avenue black. Silk trousers. Long-sleeved silk shirt. A Barry Kisselstein-Cord belt of lizard with chunks of sterling hardware. His blond pageboy hair was a tad long, his Botoxed face unnaturally boyish, his veneered teeth whiter than chalk. With his angular cheekbones and pale eyes, he was a dead ringer for a young Klaus Kinski.

"What a delightful surprise!" he enthused. "For goodness sake, Miranda, what brings you here? And why on earth didn't you tell me you'd be on Samos? Now then. You must come and join us. There are some very interesting people you should meet." And *sotto voce:* "Very important clients."

She began to protest, but it was useless. He wouldn't take no for an answer.

"I insist," he told her. "Boss' orders. Besides," he chuckled, "we don't bite, and our table's big enough to squeeze in an extra chair."

It was useless to argue. He had his hand on her arm and was already steering her to the last spot on earth where she wanted to be at the moment. Right to The Witch's table.

Straight into the hornet's nest she had been trying so desperately to avoid.

[CHAPTER THIRTY FOUR]

Pythagoria, Samos

From the frying pan into the fire.

Jan Kofski made the introductions. "This is my associate from New York, Ms. Miranda Kalli. She's my top resident expert in classical Greek antiquities."

"Welcome, welcome! Any friend of Jan Kofski is a friend of mine!" The Witch rose ponderously and greeted Miranda with oily charm, open arms, and air-kissed her cheeks with tiny, cherubic, pursed lips. Then he raised an arm and snapped fat fingers, on one of which glowed a great ruby cabochon.

Stelios rushed over with an extra chair and Eleni seemed to appear out of thin air and pitched in, expertly helping to rearrange the place settings in record time. Chairs were scooted closer together, and before leaving, Eleni shot Miranda a discreet warning look.

Miranda replied with a knowing look and turned from Jan Kofski to The Witch. "Really, this isn't necessary," she begged off. "I hate to intrude. Plus, I was actually just turning in. I have an early start tomorrow."

"*What?*" The Witch pretended wide-eyed shock, as though World War III had been declared, and threw up his pudgy hands. The cabochon caught the fire from the votive candles and the lights strung in the pergola and shone like pigeon's blood. "You were going to *bed?* At *this* early hour?"

It was all Miranda could do to make sense of that thick, garbled frog's croak of an accent, further distorted from chain-smoking and indulgence in rich foods. What was it? A mixture of Greek and some form of Arabic? Or perhaps Greek and Hebrew? She didn't have a clue, and wasn't about to ask. That would have been considered downright rude.

"Nonsense! In Greece we traditionally dine late!" The Witch huffed and puffed and gestured dramatically around the table. "For us, the night is young, and the fun is yet to begin. Is that not so, my friends?"

Agreement was voiced from all around, ranging from discreet murmurs and tacit concurrence to a half-drunken shriek, and the members of the Mitropoulos party eyed Miranda with varying degrees of interest.

Miranda felt underdressed and out of place among all the couture and jewels. She, better than anyone, was only too aware that she was, so to speak, from the wrong side of the sales counter and, although she dealt daily with wealthy collectors from all corners of the world, she knew when she was out of her social league.

Which did little to add to her comfort.

"You shall sit on my left!" announced The Witch, making it sound like a royal decree.

Old Yannis Liapsis eyed her through thick lenses with the keen interest of a lepidopterist studying a newly discovered species of butterfly. His terrifying-looking wife, weighed down with sapphires and diamonds and fighting every inch to keep age at bay, nodded curtly. Despina gave Miranda a quick once-over, a condescending smile, and smoothed a possessive hand over her necklace of emerald bricks. Theodoros Vassilakis gave Miranda's hand a courtly kiss. Dolly Vassilakis, veteran of years spent in diplomatic circles, was perfectly charming. Leonides Liapsis, the heir, waved a hand casually while his anorexic wife flashed a shy hello. Jan Kofski winked at her from across the table. He was on his third wife, whose lips formed a Restilayne smile.

With a flourish, The Witch pulled out a chair and unctuously helped Miranda get seated. Another Champagne cork popped, and her flute overflowed with bubbly.

The Witch held up his glass and made a toast. "To Miranda!"

Glasses were lifted all around. "To Miranda," was echoed in various tones of sincerity and insincerity.

Over the rim of her flute, Miranda caught Big Mike and Professor Hirsch shooting her warning glances from beyond the cascade of bougainvillea.

Careful, she told herself. *Don't forget. You're Daniel, and you're in the lion's den. Drink slowly, very little, and watch every single word.*

Clever conversations in a variety of languages were lobbed back and forth between various couples like shuttlecocks. Miranda tried, but failed, to follow the various anecdotes, morsels of gossip, and business talk. Bits and pieces flew into one ear and out the other.

"Over eighty million dollars for one of Monet's *Water Lilies!"* Old man Liapsis sounded scandalized. "It's all that Russian new money, I tell you! Fifty million—I drew the line on bidding at that," and he proceeded to launch into a discussion of high finance with his son, Leonides.

"Judith Lieber," announced a proud Dolly Vassilakis, passing around her minaudière for inspection. "Isn't it gorgeous? It's encrusted with genuine stones. It was designed exclusively for me. Judith herself assured me it was one of a kind. Now I'm on the waiting list at Vuitton for my 'Pegasus' suitcase."

"I already have mine," piped up Jan Kofsi's third wife in a smug little girl's voice. "I'm at the top of their list. My Jan saw to that. Everyone adores my snakeskin bag."

"And I thought *I* was on the top of their list!" Dolly Vassilakis all but wailed, with patent jealousy. "I'm still waiting for *both!*"

"*This* thing?" Despina Mitropoulos was saying to old Liapsis' wife. "It's straight off the runway. It's why I fight to stay a size four. I always buy the runway prototypes. Saves my dear Nikos a *fortune.* Isn't that right, Nikos *mou?*"

"Of course you're right, Despina *mou,*" came The Witch's response.

In this ear and out that one. There was no way Miranda could hold her own on any of these subjects. She was truly a fish out of water. Besides, she was on the alert for The Witch's interrogation, which couldn't be long in coming.

And sure enough, it wasn't. Like a cross between a bloated jellyfish and a tarantula, The Witch waited for a lull in the conversation. As he was owner and operator of Oracle Cruises, Miranda was expecting a gentle interrogation at the very least.

And then the inevitable subject was raised.

"So." The Witch patted her hand in an avuncular fashion that made Miranda's skin crawl, and it was all she could do not to snatch it away. "I assume you are the young lady from the *Meltemi II?*"

He spoke in that indefinable, raspy-husky accent of his as he stubbed out one cigarette and immediately lit another with a gold lighter, blowing the smoke away from her.

"Yes," replied Miranda, on her guard and cautioning herself: *Stay as close to the truth as possible, but don't give too much away.*

"And how did you find the cruise? Pleasant, I hope? Your honest opinion, please. Do not try to spare me."

Miranda frowned into her barely touched Champagne. "Well, I do miss my sister, whom I accompanied this far," she said carefully.

"Of course!" He was all false jovial cheer, with his pursed little lips and his twinkly little eyes, set deep in the fatty tissue of their pouches, widening dramatically. "One always misses one's family when one is separated! Brothers, sisters, parents, cousins, nieces, nephews . . . " He sketched another series of orange loops in the air with the tip of his cigarette. "I quite understand. Here in Greece, families are very close-knit. Relatives are what holds the fabric of our society together. I take it you come from a large family, yes? Greek, judging from your last name?"

"Yes. My father's family background is Greek. I've always yearned to come here. I only wish I hadn't had to wait this long."

Nodding sagely, he drew deeply on his cigarette, tilted his head skyward, and exhaled a stream of smoke. "One's ante . . . what is the word?"

"Antecedents?" she suggested.

"Yes. That is it exactly! They are most important. We Greeks always put family first and foremost."

Miranda knew precisely what he was up to. Diverting her attention to the subject of family and putting her at ease. But it wouldn't work, not if she could help it. She took the tiniest sip of Champagne. She had to watch her alcohol intake; this was no time to drink too much. It was imperative that she tiptoe through this verbal minefield with infinite care. One wrong step, and she was likely to give away . . . how had Professor Hirsch put it?

What you have discovered is highly dangerous. People have been known to kill for less.

Well, she was damned if it was going to cost her her life.

"So tell me," The Witch was saying. "What did you think of Oracle Cruises?"

"Well . . . " *Stick as close to the truth as possible.* "Well, let me see. The *Meltemi II* is not exactly a *yacht*."

He coughed a laugh and waved his cigarette dismissively. "But what *is* a yacht, but a pleasure craft? That is its definition, yes?"

"Nor was it exactly the *QM2*."

He nearly sprayed Champagne. "True. True," he said, once he'd recovered from snorting laughter. "It is a budget cruise, priced within reason so almost anyone can afford it."

"Which is why Madge and I chose it," she returned, smiling into The Witch's face. "Because it fit our budget."

"Ah. There, you see? Now then—"

He drained his glass and clicked his fingers preemptively for a refill. Eleni happened to be closest and was quick to do the honors.

"*Efcharistó,* my dear Eleni," he rumbled, half-twisting around and looking up at her with an intentionally sheepish expression. "My apologies. If I had known it was you, I would not have summoned you so rudely."

Eleni was nothing if not a pro. She gave him her widest smile, and if it was forced, this was undetectable. "Anything for you, Nikos, you know that. You only have to ask. Miranda?"

Eleni was holding up the bottle, raising her eyebrows questioningly. Miranda instinctively understood that she wasn't referring to a refill, but querying her on how she was surviving The Witch's deadly game of verbal chess.

"I'm fine, Eleni." And: "Good grief! Do you have any idea how *much* wine I've had just today? More than I usually drink in weeks!"

Eleni managed a sincere-sounding laugh. "That is the Greek side of you coming out. If you want more, you have only to snap your fingers. Like my best customer here." She gave The Witch's shoulder what was intended—and likely construed—as an affectionate squeeze.

"I think I prefer to clap my hands," Miranda spoke up gamely. "That might get even faster attention."

The Witch wheezed laughter. "I like this young lady," he told Eleni. "She not only has spirit, but she shares my sense of humor."

"You had best not like her too much, Nikos Mitropoulos," Eleni, ever the charming proprietor, cautioned playfully. She wagged an admonishing finger. "You do not want Despina on your bad side."

"Heaven forbid!" he brayed, glancing over at his wife and rolling his eyes.

Eleni laughed again and went around the table refilling flutes. Another Champagne cork popped. Another dead soldier was whisked off. Manos came and added ice to the sweating buckets. Miranda sneaked a glance toward the tumble of bougainvillea. Professor Hirsch and Big Mike had subtly moved their chairs, the better to keep her in their line of sight, pretending to be in deep discussion. Meanwhile, snatches of conversation swirled around, louder than the cicadas shrilling from the trees, louder than the soft strum of *bouzouki* and song:

"—India. India is economically becoming the new China . . ." Old man Liapsis.

"—always used to be faithful to Yves St. Laurent. Until, well, you know—" Dolly Vassilakis.

"—just diamonds, *always* diamonds. Jan says colored stones are a drug on the market, especially in New York—" Lolita Kofski.

"—but Nikos always insists I wear colored stones . . ." Despina Mitropoulos.

"—the E.U.'s tougher measures on illegal migrants has to be implemented. It has nothing to do with the erosion of human rights—" Theodoros Vassilakis.

Miranda was dying to keep an ear tuned to listen in on what Theodoros was saying, but The Witch continued craftily: "Miranda, darling . . . may I call you darling?" He didn't wait for a reply. "I have been made aware that you, very unlike your sister, are quite the adventuress."

He knows, Miranda thought, treading carefully in the minefield. *Or rather, he suspects Madge is not my sister. Careful, now. Careful.*

She sighed and shrugged. "Madge is quite a bit older than I am. Plus we were born under different astrological signs. She's actually my half-sister, but don't tell anyone. And yes, it *is* strange how she's always been quite the Midwestern homemaker while I've always been the rebel."

"Ah, that explains so much. Yes, no two family members are ever alike. It is what makes life interesting, if complicated. And you, my darling Miranda, must now accept *my* sincerest apologies. Please."

"But, whatever for?"

"On behalf of Oracle Cruises. I was informed that the *Meltemi II* had sailed from Mykonos without you. That was unforgivable."

Pursing his tiny lips, The Witch made a moue and pounded the table with a fist. Plates, cutlery, and glasses jumped and clinked, and everyone went silent for a few seconds and glanced over at him before resuming their conversations where they'd left off.

"Totally unforgivable!" he repeated, as though scandalized.

With his acting abilities, he'd be a hit on Broadway, Miranda thought. Surely he was the one Chara had called from the dock in Piraeus about allowing her to board? And most likely also about leaving her stranded on Delos?

However, the late Mr. and Mrs. Kalli's little girl wasn't Sarah Bernhardt, but she wasn't entirely without acting abilities of her own.

"No, it's not unforgivable," Miranda replied staunchly. "It was my fault entirely. I wasn't watching the time—" she did not mention her missing watch "—and in my rush down from Mount Kynthos to catch the last boat from Delos, I must have tripped and fallen and hit my head."

And it was at that very instant that a sudden flashback clicked in her mind. The clouds parted, and revelation shone clearly. Memory had resurfaced. Now she remembered looking at the trapped goat, and how she had turned around and been confronted by a large, looming shadow the moment before she'd blacked out.

So her memory *was* returning! And she hadn't tripped and fallen. It *hadn't* been an accident, after all! She'd been attacked.

She was certain of it now.

The Witch leaned inquisitively toward her. "And you have no memory of it?" he prodded, suspicion coloring his thick accent. He held her gaze directly. "No memory at all?"

She stared, seemingly at the distance, but actually at Professor Hirsch and Big Mike.

She drew her eyes back in. "None," she lied emphatically, hoping she wasn't giving herself away by the blush she felt rising warmly from her neck to her face, and she was grateful for the star-spangled night and the tiny lights in the arbor and the flickering of the votive candles. "I wish I did, but—" She shrugged. "Luckily for me, a gentleman named Apostolos Malinakas was on the site. Do you know him?"

The Witch grunted, which she took to mean yes.

"Well, he went above and beyond the call of duty, and personally took me on his high-speed boat to catch up with the *Meltemi*. And here I am!"

She beamed radiantly.

The Witch's eyes looked at her unblinkingly, lizard-like. "Ah. So you have met our august overseer from the Ministry of Culture," he said contemptuously.

From his voice, Miranda gathered there was little love lost between the Witch and "Apo."

"To tell you the truth, he was very kind. He didn't have to rescue a damsel in distress. But he did."

"Humph!"

She paused and couldn't help adding, "He's also a most attractive man."

That, at least, was no lie.

"And then?" The Witch ground out his cigarette and feigned disinterest.

"Once back onboard, Ms. Zouboulakis and some passengers, nurses from New Zealand, were afraid I'd suffered a concussion. The problem is," Miranda made a production of frowning . . . "I have absolutely no recollection of what had happened. One moment I was rushing down from Mount Kynthos, and the next thing I knew, the sun was setting."

"And you have absolutely no memory of what happened?"

"None at all. The nurses and Ms. Zouboulakis attributed it to a concussion. They told me I might never remember anything at all! Isn't that frightening?"

"Indeed," The Witch murmured, settling back and sipping his Champagne contentedly. Although he tried to hide it, Miranda could swear he looked relieved. Then Stelios and Manos arrived with huge platters piled high with a king's ransom of delicacies. Eleni followed with a tray on which rested a mind-boggling assortment of condiments in bowls. Salt and pepper shakers and glasses had to be moved aside to create room for it all.

"What are those?" Miranda asked, pointing a finger.

"That," said The Witch, "is *Kreas se Fetes Melintzana.* And that other one is called *Arni me Aginares Avgolemono.*"

Miranda gave him a blank look and added a small laugh. "Mr. Mitropoulos, now you're losing me! It's like hearing a doctor talking!"

"I apologize. And please, call me Nikos. All my friends do. Now, that there," he said, pointing at the first dish, "is veal in eggplant slices. Succulent! Only Eleni knows how to prepare it correctly, but she refuses to share her recipe. Not that I blame her." His features had taken on a crestfallen look, but his nostrils flared greedily. "The other is lamb and artichokes in egg-lemon sauce. And this one is lamb roasted in oiled parchment, and that is rabbit and pearl onion stew—"

The list went on and on.

"Which would you like?" he asked, switching from the role of gentle interrogator to that of the gracious host.

"I'm a great believer of 'When in Greece, do like the Greeks,'" Miranda paraphrased staunchly. "I'll try a bite of everything. But just a tiny bite, mind you."

"Good! Good! I shall prepare for you what I believe is called 'a tasting menu.'"

The Witch took her plate and heaped it lavishly. Although her appetite hadn't returned, Miranda forced herself to take a tiny nibble of everything.

"Well?" The Witch demanded, his eyebrows arched.

Until now, Miranda hadn't noticed how carefully they had been plucked. Gargantuan weight aside, he was groomed to perfection, right down to the clear polish on his fingernails.

Miranda swallowed a mouthful of lamb and artichokes before replying. The egg-lemon sauce was divine. "This food is out of this world!"

The Witch looked pleased. He had tucked his napkin into his open shirt collar and was digging into his own Matterhorn of a plate, shoveling down food into those little pursed lips like there was no tomorrow.

"Do you know how many times I offered to finance a restaurant in Athens for Eleni?" he asked.

"And?"

His lips turned down into a sad frown, his fatty jowls wobbling. "Unfortunately, she continues to refuse."

"I can well understand why. She has her hands full as it is."

He half-smiled. "Yes, Eleni has all the makings of a great kitchen general. But she could have become the Napoleon Bonaparte of Greek cooking!"

"Yes, but remember where Napoleon ended up. On Elba."

"Which," The Witch responded, "is like remaining on Samos, no?"

Naturally, his interrogation of Miranda wasn't finished quite yet. Nor had she suspected it had.

And here it came.

"Chara," he said, speaking as he chewed, "informed me that she had you consult Dr. Babutcu in Kusadasi."

"Yes," Miranda said, all but purring as she tasted the rabbit and pearl onion stew. "Ms. Zouboulakis was quite insistent, although I would rather have preferred to remain on board and sleep."

"She was worried." The Witch waved a forkful of lamb in midair. "It is company policy to consult a doctor when there has been an accident. Ms. Zouboulakis might give you the impression of—how do you say it in English? Something about an icy fish?"

"A cold fish. Yes. I gathered she wasn't particularly fond of me."

"You have to understand her." The Witch spoke while chewing a mouthful of onion pie. "She comes from a very poor family in Epirus and has risen far above it. She takes her duties very seriously."

"Yes," Miranda said dryly, "I'm quite well aware of the way she carries them out."

He coughed more laughter, covered his mouth with the end of his napkin, and delicately dabbed his gluttonous, tiny pursed lips. "However, she is my most trusted employee. My second-in-command, so to speak. Right now she is in Vathi."

"But I was under the impression she was the cruise director aboard the *Meltemi II!*"

"She is that, and much more. I own some pottery factories here. Their recent output has been—" he swallowed a mouthful of veal and eggplant and washed it down with more Champagne "—let me say, less than perfect. We supply many shops and even the national museum with copies. Unless someone has a watchful eye out, the workers tend to be sloppy. That is unacceptable. I always expect perfection. In fact, I shall have to give you a tour of the factories. With your background in archeology, you should find it quite fascinating. I might even ask for your help."

"*Mine?* What could I do?"

"We have been trying to emulate the ancients by firing clay with various minerals and iron to make exact copies of the originals, rather than to merely paint them. Unfortunately, to date no one has discovered the secret formula."

"I take it you have tried?"

"Over and over," he sighed, "year after year. I have had scientists working on it. Archeologists. To date, it has cost me a fortune. Unfortunately, the formula is a long-lost secret. Perhaps lost forever, although I fervently pray not."

He shook his head, and his jowls and chins wobbled, reminding her of a dog shaking itself. Then he dabbed his lips most delicately with his napkin, sipped some more Champagne, and switched the subject back into that exceedingly clever . . . and exceedingly devious . . . interrogation mode of his.

"I take it Dr. Babutcu treated you well?" he inquired.

She dazzled him with a smile. "Oh, yes! He was quite the gentleman. Whatever brew he gave me to drink, some herbal concoction that tasted horrible—horrible, I tell you!—seemed to have worked wonders! My headache and weariness were gone! I wish I knew what he put in it." She gave a little laugh. "No, scratch that. It's probably better that I don't know! But he also set my mind at ease about a dream I had."

The Witch's eyes blinked lazily, and beyond the folds of fat she detected the keen, hard look of a reptile. "And what dream was that?"

Whoa! she cautioned herself. *Careful. Careful. You see? You've already given away too much. Remember, kiddo, you're skating on paper-thin ice here. Beware the traps he sets. Don't let those interludes of joviality fool you. You're way in over your head.*

"I wish," she murmured slowly, "that I could remember."

She frowned at her barely touched Champagne, idly dipped her finger into the flute, and began to trace circles around its rim, causing it to chime.

"You know what dreams are like," she told him. "When you wake up, you think you'll remember them forever, but a minute or two after that—*poof!* They're gone. Just like *that.*"

She snapped her fingers, then swiftly looked around and let out a breath of relief. "Thank goodness Eleni didn't take that as a summons for a refill!" she said lightly.

He grinned widely, a gold tooth gleaming. "You told her you would clap your hands. Remember?"

"Now that you've reminded me, yes. I did, didn't I?"

Then, elbow on the table and resting her chin on her fist, she mused seriously: "I always wonder about dreams. They seem so real when you wake up, but vanish almost instantly. Or, perhaps in my case in Kusadasi, it was that terrible-tasting brew Dr. Babutcu had me drink? Which do you think it was?"

She stared straight into his eyes.

"So you really remember nothing?"

"About what happened on Delos? Or at Kusadasi, after Dr. Babutcu gave me that . . . that whatever it was . . . to drink?"

"Both." He stared intently back at her through slitted eyes.

Like a human lie detector, she thought.

"I'm afraid I can't. However, I will say one thing for Dr. Babutcu, though. He was absolutely one of the most charming old gentlemen I've ever met."

The Witch nodded agreement. "Yes, he was."

There was a finality in his tone that made her sit up straighter. "What do you mean, he *was?*"

The Witch made another moue. "It is sad what has happened."

"What are you talking about?" She was genuinely flustered. "What happened? I saw him only yesterday—"

"Miranda, darling." Once again, The Witch patted her hand. "Oracle Cruises have been using him for many years, several decades in fact, since his official retirement."

"And?"

"I only received the telephone call this afternoon. It appears that he suffered an accident."

"An accident! But I gathered he hardly ever left that big house of his."

The Witch shrugged. Layers of fat throughout his body jiggled. "Oh, dear. I should not have opened my mouth."

Again: "What *happened?*" she demanded. "Is he all right?"

"Oh no, my dear. He is anything but all right. From what I was told, he suffered a fall. On the staircase of that old house of his."

"No!" she blurted. "No!" She shut her eyes and shook her head violently, oblivious to the stares of the others at the table.

"If it is of any consolation, my darling Miranda," The Witch said softly, "he most likely died instantly. His neck had been broken."

Miranda could only stare at him in horror.

"But he was *alive* only yesterday!" she insisted stubbornly.

"These things happen, Miranda darling. Do not distress yourself so. He was very old and lived alone. He had a good, long life. His housekeeper, who came in several days a week, was the one who found him and called to tell me."

Miranda sat there in shock, her mind a blazing whirlwind of confusion. Dr. Babutcu—*dead?* But he'd been so alive! He'd let her out that huge front door less than a day and a half ago . . .

And then the conspiracy worm burrowed its ugly way back into her thoughts.

Had Dr. Babutcu perhaps told Chara or The Witch or whoever about herself and what she might have witnessed through the telescope?

Am I perhaps the one responsible for his death?

She did not want to believe it, but her nagging conscience refused the simple explanation of an accident.

Ever since her arrival in Athens, there had been too many coincidences, too many strange occurrences.

A shudder passed through her and she pushed her plate away with a violent clatter. "I have to go."

She stood and swayed unsteadily on her feet. The Witch rose and helped support her. Eleni, ever alert, came rushing over.

"I-I'm sorry, Mr. Mit—I mean, Nikos," Miranda said dully. "Please forgive me, but—"

"I quite understand."

"Oh, *God!*" Miranda cried out, and then she felt Eleni's maternal arms around her, forcing her to walk, insisting she put one foot in front of the other as they negotiated her through the leafy bower to her room.

Miranda was unaware of other diners watching her with curiosity, of the conversation and sounds of party talk and laughter and popping corks resuming at The Witch's table. For her, the little lights strung in the arbor had disappeared. The clusters of grapes hung threateningly, and her ears were deaf to the strum of the *bouzouki* and the singer.

In one fell swoop, the magic had vanished.

[CHAPTER THIRTY FIVE]

The Site at Ancient Asprodavos

It was the following day. "Here we are," Professor Hirsch announced from the backseat as Big Mike stomped on the brakes so hard that Miranda's head all but hit the windshield. "I realize it does not look very prepossessing."

Which was an understatement. The meltemi had kicked up and was blowing strongly from the north, so they had chosen a battered surplus Jeep rather than one of the swift, rigid inflatables. The land route took them along the main road from Pythagoria, which petered out into a smaller coast road to the village of Ireo, and finally along what was little more than a tooth-rattling, rutted, rock-strewn, dirt path south along the edge of the plunging cliffs of schist and volcanic rock. Below and beyond, the Aegean was frothy and angry, and on land, the meltemi whipped up sand and dirt and small pebbles, pelting the Jeep relentlessly.

"Not the finest of days, eh?" the professor continued mildly from the backseat, "At least we are on the more protected south coast. Now is not the time to be at Vathi. There the meltemi whips up a storm coming down from that great open bay."

"But it's so sunny out!" Miranda exclaimed. "There's barely a cloud in the sky. Except for the meltemi, it would be a beautiful day."

"Indeed, it otherwise is. Also, and this may be of some interest to you, according to local lore—and you must bear in mind that by this I mean the fishermen of the Aegean—claim they used to be able to predict the meltemi accurately, but that since the nuclear reactor disaster at Chernobyl, it has been impossible. Whether or not this is true, I cannot attest."

It hadn't been the most scenic of drives, to say the least. This wild section of coastline did not hold the allure of the postcards and tourist brochures of the Greek isles. The rugged, crumbling cliffs, to which shrubs, briars, and brambles clung tenaciously here and there among the stacked layers of jutting schist, reminded Miranda of the less—far less—scenic portions of California's famous Highway 101. Nor had the wild firs and pines, many of their thick trunks scorched black, added a bucolic touch.

"Samos suffered severe wildfires several years back," Big Mike growled. "About a third of the island encountered major fire damage."

"Yes," Professor Hirsch sighed. "Many of the pines and firs exploded. Like unattended Christmas trees lit with real candles. Others were scarred but survived, like those you saw with the charred trunks. But happily, nature is slowly reasserting itself. As it usually will."

He added, with a wry smile, "This is something the tourist brochures do not like to mention."

Miranda chucked open her door and climbed out. She was wearing a pair of heavy, lace-up, work boots and olive cargo shorts, and her unprotected calves immediately stung from the lashings of sharp pebbles and rock dust. Too late, she wished she'd worn long pants.

After Professor Hirsch flipped down the front seat and stretched his long legs on terra firma, Miranda reached inside and grabbed her two yellow nylon bags.

"So what do you think?" Big Mike asked, giving a sarcastically theatrical wave. "Welcome to Asprodavos. Pretty, huh?"

Miranda wasn't particularly put off. She knew enough from studying photographs of archeological digs not to expect a place of beauty. However, she hadn't expected Big Mike to park outside an ugly chain-link fence that had warnings, in several languages, posted at regular intervals.

"Why did you park outside?" she asked Big Mike curiously.

"You tell me," he growled, as usual in a surly mood. "We'd probably have unearthed that damned Hera by now if we were permitted to use heavy machinery, like the Germans did during the Occupation. As it is, vehicles aren't permitted inside. We're supposed to count ourselves lucky that the Ministry of Culture allows us the *luxury* of having a generator! There should be barbed wire strung atop the length of chain-link, but our budget's stretched to the limit as it is."

Miranda nodded. The six-foot-high fence enclosed three sides of the large area comprising the site proper, and was easily climbable. Nature herself protected the fourth, or sea side, with a sheer cliff plunging down to the sea a hundred feet below. However, a switchback of rickety wooden steps led down to a crescent of pebble beach, although a short length of locked chain-link made unauthorized access impossible . . . unless you couldn't climb six feet of chain-link.

Which, she silently thought, any child or ambulatory adult could quite easily accomplish.

The stark, sun-drenched setting was alleviated by a few surviving, wind-whipped pines with scorched trunks which afforded a few shady spots, and there were spots with spiky clumps of high, sun-yellowed grasses. She noticed five ugly, prefabricated huts clustered at the far end, and nearby there stood a large metal shed. As on Delos, small areas under excavation were shielded from the sun by flat-topped tarpaulins mounted on metal poles. With the meltemi blowing hard, they billowed and flapped noisily in the wind, like horizontal sails threatening to break loose.

With their arrival, a lone guard, embroidered scarf wrapped protectively around the bottom half of his face against the swirling grit, came hurrying to unlock a padlock and let them into the chain-link compound.

As soon as they were inside, the guard clicked the hasp back on the padlock and carefully tested it to make certain it was locked.

Professor Hirsch introduced Miranda to the guard. "This is Nikitas Tatoulis. His family guards the premises. He has two brothers, and they take turns. They all speak some English. They and their sister, Maria, used to tour with a small provincial circus that has since closed down. They are quite accomplished jugglers. Amazing, in fact. They perform at festivals and for tourists. Hopefully there is an occasion when you can see them perform."

Miranda smiled. "Yes. I would enjoy that. I believe I saw your brothers and sister performing at the esplanade at Vathi when I disembarked. They were quite impressive."

"Kyría is most kind," he said, and the embroidered scarf came down. Polite greetings were exchanged and then Nikitas raised the scarf back over his nose and mouth.

"I should also warn you," Professor Hirsch said as they headed toward the cluster of five huts, "that the Tatoulis brothers take their duties very seriously. You must not take it personally, but as we have had some thefts in the past, they check the bags and pockets of everyone who leaves the compound. Even mine. I gave the order, and insist I be treated the same as everyone else."

"Nothing like democracy at work," Big Mike murmured sourly.

"I notice that no one's at the dig," Miranda observed, nodding in the direction of the wind-thrashed, tented little stations.

"That," Wald Hirsch replied, "is because we must wait until the meltemi abates. For the protection of the eyes, and also because anything that we might uncover and carefully begin to dig up is likely to be covered up again before we finish. Like everyone else the world over we are, unfortunately, martyrs to the weather."

Squinting against the flying dust and grit, Miranda surveyed the surroundings. "You know," she said slowly, "this area does have a certain wild kind of beauty."

"A vile kind, you mean," grumped Big Mike, but she and the professor let it go.

"Ah. This is it."

They had passed one hut and Professor Hirsch stopped at the entrance to the second. Like the others, it was small, boxy, and had been hastily erected of concrete blocks between which long-dried cement had oozed, and was unadorned by whitewash. Laundry, what were obviously women's clothes, flapped violently in the meltemi from a jerry-rigged line. The door and windows were wide open and hung with sheers.

To keep bugs out and let air in, Miranda guessed, although at the moment the wind puffed and twisted them this way and that.

"This is our ladies' dormitory."

"Also known as the hen house," Big Mike added, under his breath.

The professor chose to ignore him. "I believe I warned you, Miranda my dear,or at least I should have, that the facilities are very crude. Primitive, in fact. That fifth and smallest outbuilding over there?" He pointed to the furthest one away. "That is the privy. It also has an outdoor shower of sorts."

Big Mike laughed. "A bucket with holes drilled in the bottom."

"Well, I didn't exactly expect the Ritz," Miranda retorted with a sniff.

A woman's voice called out from the hut, "Is that the professor?" and then three women appeared one by one in the doorway, and came down the concrete steps.

"You must be the famous Miranda Professor Hirsch was telling us about!" the first one bubbled excitedly in a British accent. "I'm Rosalie Hobhouse, but my friends all call me Rosie. And this—" she pulled a tall, attractive brunette in her early thirties forward, "is Verena. She's one of the professor's protégées from Berlin. And this is Pernilla. She's from Stockholm. We call her our 'Swedish bombshell.'"

Of course she wasn't one. Pernilla was petite, with elfin features, dark hair worn pulled straight back, and she certainly wasn't stacked. But good humor shone from her eyes and there was a quality about her that made her instantly likeable.

Only after greeting each one was Miranda aware of a fourth young woman who had moseyed out just as far as the doorway and was leaning lazily against the jamb, a lit cigarette dangling from the corner of her mouth, a bored expression on her face. The term "Sex Kitten" sprang to mind.

"Welcome to hell," she drawled to Miranda in heavily-accented French, not bothering to introduce herself.

"And that," sighed Rosalie, "is Yvette."

"Hello, Yvette," Miranda greeted.

Yvette ignored her and, from under half-lowered lids, was eyeing Big Mike above the heads of the others. "And you, *mon homme?*" she called out. "Where have you been hiding? Or is it a case of *le chat parti, les souris dansent?*"

Big Mike colored and glared at her. Muttering "God save us," he strode off, hands thrust in the pockets of his shorts.

"What did she say?" Miranda whispered to Rosalie. "I'm afraid French isn't my strong point."

But it was Yvette who answered. "The literal translation," she said in a voice loud enough to carry, is "When the cat is gone, the mice dance."

Cigarette still glued to her lower lip, smoke curling into one squinted eye, she looked Miranda up and down appraisingly. Then she shrugged, her mouth twisting in a crooked smile. "Not bad looking for an *Américaine.* But not Big Mike's type, either."

"*Yvette!*" Professor Hirsch's voice was sharp and critical and could have cut the air like a knife. "Can you not ever be civil?"

"Civil? Or civilized?" she purred.

He threw up his hands in despair. "As Big Mike would have said," he told Miranda grimly, "welcome to the Hen House."

Then, taking her aside by the arm, out of earshot of the others, he whispered, "Take care. And if you have that boarding pass with you, I suggest you hide it well. Also, watch what you say. Here, even the hills have eyes and the walls have ears."

She stared at him. "Why? Do you think—?"

"I think and assume nothing, my dear. But I am trusting you to be *my* eyes and ears. Now then, after you have unpacked and settled in, come to the large shed. We have much to catch up on. And some serious things to discuss."

Not the most auspicious of words, but Miranda was intrigued. It was apparently his version of "I'll see you in my office."

"I won't be long," she promised. And, holding up her two yellow bags, she added, quoting one of Ron's favorite lines, "If you've noticed, 'I travel light. No heart.'"

A line, she thought, which her favorite New York neighbor had obviously copped from one of the slew of old, classic, black-and-white movies he was addicted to.

Which one, she couldn't for the life of her remember. But it did add a note of levity.

"Welcome to the Grand Hotel!" announced Rosalie, with ironic laughter in her voice and a majestic sweep of her hand as she led Miranda inside the Ladies' Dormitory.

The meltemi was not a cool wind by a long shot, but the thick concrete walls and cross breezes from the open door and windows cut the blazing outdoor temperature by a good twenty degrees, which Miranda found a relief. Even more of a relief was the absence of wind-borne, stinging pebbles and grit.

The quarters were cramped. By Miranda's reckoning, the building couldn't have been more than twenty-two feet by ten, and five low cots, fashioned of rough wooden frames with thin foam mattresses, lined the walls. Personal storage space, she noted, consisted of two coat hooks per cot for hanging up clothes, plus whatever could be shoved beneath the cots, each of which had a narrow wooden shelf affixed next to the wall for personal items—a photograph of parents or a boyfriend and a few essential toiletries. Privacy consisted of very thin, and very cheap, unmatched fabric—remainders, from the looks of the various lengths —which were tacked up around each cot.

"I know it looks grim," Rosalie said lightly, "but it's . . . well, let's just say it's functional, shall we? Now, why don't you get unpacked?

This first cot, by the door, is for newcomers, since it affords the most fresh air and helps acclimatize them. It's yours."

She held aside a length of garish fabric, displaying an unmade cot with a rumpled tangle of sheets.

"*Excuse moi?*"

They turned around in unison. The cold voice belonged to Yvette, who stood behind them, one hand poised on a hip, half-smoked cigarette in the other.

"That cot is *mine,*" Yvette snapped in no uncertain terms at Rosalie, "and you well know it."

Rosalie heaved an angry sigh. As the senior-most member of the women's group, she had inherited the position of the Hen House's den mother, and took her position seriously.

"Look, Yvette," she said flatly. "The only reason this cot is yours is that until now you *were* the newest person in here. If you'll recall, when you first arrived I explained how it works. The newbies always get the first cot, since it's the closest to the door, and is the airiest and therefore most comfortable. Then, when a newer person arrives, you get moved to the back."

"I'm not giving it up." Yvette drew on her cigarette and deliberately exhaled a plume of blue smoke directly into Rosalie's face.

"You also know we have a rule of no smoking in here," Rosalie said sharply, fanning the air in front of her with her hand.

Miranda frowned at the unappealingly messy cot and quick-scanned the narrow shelf. It virtually groaned under a collection of high-end cosmetics, packets of Assos brand cigarettes, and some framed photographs of very young and, from the looks of them, very virile young men. No fan of messiness, let alone conflicts, she attempted to defuse the situation before it went any further.

"Rosie, I didn't come here to cause trouble. I don't *care* where I sleep."

She glanced around.

"What about back there?"

She pointed to the far wall, where a curtain was pulled aside from an empty cot. At its foot rested a rather flat pillow, two clean, neatly folded sheets, a pillowcase, and an embroidered blanket. It certainly looked far more appealing than the tobacco-impregnated mess in front of her.

"I'd be a lot happier back there, Rosie. Truly."

"But rules are rules!" Rosalie persisted. "Without them, we'd have chaos."

"I understand that. But Yvette smokes."

"It's against house rules," Rosalie said darkly. "She shouldn't. Not in here."

"But she does," Miranda pointed out mildly, "and since she does, I'd rather she occupied the better-aired space. For all our benefit. Really, I'd be much happier in the back. Plus it's right under that window."

Rosalie hesitated, torn between asserting her position and acceding to Miranda's wishes. "Oh, alright," she said finally, with a toss of her head. "But only since you insist. But not because of mam'selle there's wishes. You give her an inch, and she takes a yard. She's impossible."

"I'm not insisting upon anything, but admit it, Rosie. It certainly looks awfully nice and clean and tidy in back. Plus I know I'll sleep better there. I'd much rather be where there's less traffic in and out."

Which was hard to argue with.

"I suppose you're right," Rosalie agreed reluctantly. She led the way to the back, but not without shooting a smirking, triumphant Yvette a hard, resentful look over her shoulder. "If you like, I'll help you make up the bed and unpack," she told Miranda.

"Oh, Rosie. That's really not necessary."

"I'd like to. Besides, with this meltemi blowing, there's nothing much else to do around here, is there?"

"In that case," Miranda smiled, "I'd welcome your help."

Together, they made up the cot in no time.

"Nasty piece of work, that Yvette," Rosalie mumbled under her breath to Miranda while making a valiant attempt, but failing, to tuck hospital corners on a piece of foam. "Thinks she's God's gift to men, she does."

"Oh, just ignore her." Miranda placed her yellow bags on the newly made cot, unzipped them, and arranged her meager toiletries on the shelf. She propped up an unframed photograph of Magoo, which she'd shoved into her luggage at the very last minute, and the irony that she'd taken along a picture of her cat rather than one of her so-called fiancé occurred to her.

Which, she thought, said tons about her and Harry's relationship.

"Who is that?" Yvette had wandered over curiously and was pointing cattily at the photograph of Magoo. "Your boyfriend?"

"Ever hear of privacy?" Rosalie demanded, snatching the curtain and drawing it swiftly around the cot to block out Yvette. She shook her head despairingly. "Is it any wonder why Big Mike calls this 'the Hen House'? Oh, what's that?"

Miranda was in the process of placing the Oracle Cruises boarding pass beside Magoo's photo. "Oh, just a souvenir from the boat I arrived on," she said casually. "They use these as boarding passes."

"May I see it?"

Miranda handed it over for inspection.

"Goodness! You arrived on a cruise ship!" Rosalie looked impressed. "I've always been dying to take a cruise!" she said dreamily. "Deck lounges, swimming pools, ballroom dancing, discos, all-you-can-eat buffets, movies, casinos, floor shows . . ."

Miranda laughed as Rosalie handed the boarding pass back.

"What's so funny?"

"Well, if that's your idea of a cruise, Rosie, I certainly don't recommend Oracle Cruises. They actually have the nerve to call their little rust buckets 'yachts.' They're just old converted caiques. No swimming pools. No fancy buffets. No Vegas or Broadway-style shows. Add a rather nasty bitch of a 'cruise director' who thinks she belongs in *Vogue,* and makes Yvette look like a saint, and there you have it—Oracle Cruises!"

"You mean, there's *worse* than our Miss Hoity Toity?" Rosalie, molding her features to an expression of disbelief, jerked her head towards the front of the small building.

"Oh, *yes,*" Miranda reflected. "Trust me, Rosie. Yvette's no match for Chara Zouboulakis. On the other hand . . ."

"Yes?"

"Well, I really oughtn't complain. The boat did get me here, despite the ferries not running."

"Right, I forgot about that!" Rosalie said, slapping her forehead, as if realizing how out of touch she'd become with the world at large. "That's what happens when you live in our insular little environment."

Miranda prominently propped the boarding pass beside Magoo's photo. "Well, that's it for my personal items." She stood back, crossed her arms, and shook her head. Her breath escaped in a sigh. "Rather pathetic, isn't it?"

"Better a cat than a budgie, but that's my personal opinion. Of course, I'm a pussycat person myself." Rosalie pointed at Miranda's two yellow nylon bags. "What about the rest of this stuff? Aren't you at least going to hang anything on the hooks?"

"Why bother?" Miranda asked. "That can all get shoved under the cot. And now that I've *unpacked,* so to speak, I'm supposed to see Professor Hirsch at the big shed. Tell me, Rosie. Do you think I should change and wear long pants? Protect my legs from all those sharp little flying rocks and stinging debris?"

Rosalie blinked. "You have *got* to be kidding! Long pants in *this* inferno? I prefer my legs to be bruised and scratched and shredded to pieces. In my opinion, all those women who worry about varicose veins? They should be required to work at an archeological dig like this one. That would cure them. Would save their husbands a bundle on laser surgery, too. Not to mention manicures."

Despite herself, Miranda burst out laughing. "In that case, I'll just go as I am." Then her voice turned serious. "I can't thank you enough for the hearty welcome, Rosie." She sought the other woman's hands and gave them a gentle squeeze. "I mean it. Sincerely. And now I'd better be off and see what Professor Hirsch wants to discuss."

She paused and added: "Oh. One last thing. Maybe you can clue me in on something?"

"Ask away," Rosalie said cheerfully.

"What *is* it with Big Mike? Is he surly *all* the time? Or is it just with me?"

Rosalie essayed a hopeless, almost despairing look. "Oh, he's that way always, I'm afraid. Especially with women."

"But *why?* What's his problem?"

"You tell me. If you ever find out, that is. My best guess is, he's come out of some kind of bad relationship. Or perhaps something tragic happened? If so, I have no idea what. And him being that brooding, silent, Heathcliff type? All close-mouthed? Don't expect him to open the mental floodgates and spill whatever monkeys he's carrying on his shoulder. I've often wondered myself what it is. A wife? A divorce? A death? Something tragic?" She shook her head. "Whatever it is, it's a total mystery."

"Hmmm." Miranda's face clouded. "I realize he's an angry young man. I was just wondering *why.*"

"But you know what's so strange?" Once started, Rosalie chattered on. "Women are attracted to him like flies. If you had any idea how many chippies have tried to put the make on him, convinced they could penetrate that stony armor of his? Just to be rebuffed? You'd be amazed. I mean, with that face of his pocked by teenage acne, he's admittedly not the sexiest man alive. Yet let's face it. He does possess this macho quality that's exceedingly rare. I mean, the bloke *exudes* testosterone. Just look at his muscles. His body is hard as a *rock*."

"Do you think it's possible that he might be gay?"

Rosalie shook her head vehemently. "No way."

"I didn't think so. One just never knows."

"What it is, he just has no use for women. At least for the time being, and I've known him for several summers now. Nor does he have any use for men, period. He's strictly a loner."

"Luckily," Miranda said lightly, "I've never been attracted to that type. So you needn't worry your pretty little head about me, Rosie."

Her eyes were suddenly several miles distant, at Albatross. "But what I can't understand is how such a cold, jaded fish could have such a delightful child like Little Mike," she murmured thoughtfully. "He's a marvel! So clever and open and refreshingly unrepressed. He really is the most loveable bundle of warm, wonderful energy!"

"Isn't he just?" Rosalie's face brightened momentarily, then flickered into a worried frown that reminded Miranda of a dying candle. "I only pray his father's attitude doesn't rub off on him. You know that old saying, 'The apple never falls far from the tree?'"

"Personally," Miranda responded optimistically, "I think it's safe to throw that adage out the window. At least in Little Mike's case."

"Granted, Big Mike dotes on him like the sun, the moon, and the stars. And it's all he can do to keep Little Mike in Pythagoria. They're very close, I'll give our Heathcliff that. It's just—"

"Just what?"

Rosalie seemed to realize that she'd already gossiped too much. She shook her head, looking sheepish and slightly embarrassed. "I know it's none of my business, and I should keep my big trap shut. But if you want my advice?"

She leaned confidentially closer and lowered her voice. "They say the way to a man's heart is through his stomach. Well, the way to Big Mike's ice cold heart is definitely *not* through his son. You wouldn't believe the number of women who've made that mistake."

"But . . . how awful! Using an innocent child—"

"I know, I know." Rosalie lowered her voice even further. "Just beware, that's all."

She cast an almost furtive look frontwards, as if she could see straining ears through the thin curtain.

"Little Mike's a smart kid. Smarter at reading people than most. Probably even wiser than his dad."

"As I said, you needn't worry about me, Rosie. I'm not into the cold silent types. Besides, I have enough problems of my own."

Miranda held up her hand, where despite days in the sun, the paler band of skin on her finger still showed where she'd taken off her engagement ring.

Rosalie raised her eyebrows.

"I've been postponing the marriage for a couple of years already. And right now, I have no use for another man in my life. In fact," Miranda couldn't keep the trace of bitterness out of her voice "—at this point in time, a man, *any* man, is the last complication in the world I want. *Or need.*"

She glanced at the shelf, at Magoo staring down at her with wise feline superiority, and then drew the curtain aside.

"Believe me, the last," she told Rosie emphatically over her shoulder, and left to meet with Professor Hirsch and Big Mike at the shed.

[CHAPTER THIRTY SIX]

The Site at Ancient Asprodavos

When she got to the shed, Professor Hirsch was in the process of flipping his little cell phone shut.

"That was Eleni," he said. "She's been receiving calls at Albatross from someone named Harry Palmer. It seems, my dear Miranda, that he is desperate to get in touch with you, and that your voice mailbox is full."

Miranda, clapping dust off her shorts and legs, stopped and stared over at him.

Just what I need, she thought, swallowing the heavy groan that rose in her throat. *Harry tracking me down.*

He'd obviously been to see Ron—*no Holmesian deduction needed there, Watson!* she was thinking sourly—since Ron was the only person she'd given the Albatross number and address. Just in case an emergency arose with Magoo. It also indicated that Harry really was, as the professor had put it, desperate to get in touch with her.

She bit her lip to keep any sound from emerging. The trouble was, she was anything *but* keen to speak with Harry. Too, she was only too well aware of what Harry thought about Ron, whom he did his best to avoid. But for him to go and seek out Ron . . . especially after she'd dragged him to see one of "Lotta Puss's" Off-Off Broadway shows, proved persistence. And resoluteness. But how well she'd remembered how he'd been less than amused at Ron's performance, which was putting it mildly. More bluntly, he'd been patently ashamed, mortified, and disgraced by merely sitting in the audience. Even away from the shabby small theater Harry was, pure and simple, highly uncomfortable in Ron's presence—as if he was afraid that Ron would try to jump his bones!

Was Harry homophobic? Or just embarrassed, prudish, ill-at-ease, intolerant, and out of his element?

More importantly, at this point, did she really give a hoot?

She sincerely thought not.

Ditto the young Wall Street sharks Harry hung around with. She, certainly, could gladly do without *them.* Without their unceasing jabber of money, female conquests, and off-color jokes. Plus there were his oh-so-politically correct parents at the Wasps' Nest.

Them. Harry's cronies and family.

Involuntarily, she glanced again at the pale band on her ring finger.

It was over. Definitely over between Harris Milford Palmer III and herself. She'd have to inject herself with a massive dose of confidence, call him, and tell him straight out. Make him understand, in no uncertain terms, that she was breaking their engagement. That whatever they had shared was over. *Kaput. Fini.* And the sooner she did that, the better. Then maybe, just maybe, she could feel more at peace with herself? Rid herself, once and for all, of the uncertain future dangling over her head like Damocles' sword?

"Also," Professor Hirsch went on, his hands steepled in the circle of light thrown by his desk lamp, his tone gentle but grave, "Harry Palmer told Eleni that he will be here in three days' time."

Miranda's head jerked, as though she'd been slapped. She stared at him.

"Here?" she found herself echoing stupidly, her voice a squeak.

"Yes," he nodded. "Here. On Samos."

Shit! she thought to herself. *Shit, shit, shit, shit, shit, shit* shit!

Slowly, like some somnambulist, she shuffled her way over to Professor Hirsch's desk, ugly in its battered, utilitarian gray metal, and obviously a piece of donated surplus. Only now did she become aware of the intense heat . . . no, the *broiling* heat, the *inferno* inside this windowless shed, and of Big Mike lurking discreetly back in the shadows, several large, thick portfolios tucked under one arm. Cheap metal shelving ran around three of the walls. On them, carefully aligned, were unearthed artifacts, each piece of which had been carefully inventoried and coded on its undersides with an indelible marker. The fourth wall acted as a bulletin board, and was a collage of maps, schematics, photographs, sketches, and notes, all tacked hastily, inartistically, upon it.

Say it ain't so! she wanted to beg Professor Hirsch as she groped blindly for the nearest of the two swivel chairs, both duct-taped where the vinyl was torn, also obviously donated pieces of surplus that reeked of a stringent budget.

Slumping heavily down onto the nearest, she clutched her belly with one arm and pressed the thumb and forefinger of the other against her throbbing temples. She shut her eyes.

Harry here.

Here. On Samos.

At her Great Escape. At her temporary bolt hole.

It seemed an outrage that he should set foot here, a sacrilege.

"Miranda, Miranda." The professor's voice was softly sympathetic. "Listen to me. You first wrote me of your engagement to Harry Palmer . . . when was it? Two years ago now?"

Still pressing her forehead with her fingertips, she nodded mutely. "Something like that," she murmured.

"And during all that time, I have not received an announcement of a wedding. Yes, of course I noticed your hand, where until very recently you wore a ring. But you are still single? Correct?"

"Yes," she whispered miserably, thinking: *Because I'm a coward. Because I was afraid to make a mistake by rushing into marriage, and also because I was afraid of making a mistake by breaking off the engagement. I wanted my cake and to eat it too.*

"Not to pry, my dear, but I assume the reason you have not yet exchanged vows is because you were not prepared to take the . . . what is the word? Plunge?"

She nodded again. "I only decided to break it off a couple of days ago," she said, without going into details. She gave her shoulders a birdlike little shrug. "I suppose what I was doing all this time was trying to avoid a commitment and a confrontation. I finally realized it was inevitable."

"In that case, his visit could prove to be a godsend. Look at it from this perspective. Perhaps you were wise not to answer his calls. Emotional situations are always best settled face-to-face. If he were not coming, you would otherwise have waited until you returned to New York at the end of the month. And even then, you might have been tempted to delay the inevitable. Am I correct?"

She drew a deep breath and nodded. He was right. *I really am a chickenshit.*

"You see? This way you can get it over and done with. Sometimes procrastination is one's worst enemy. Also, you must not forget that you are still young and very attractive. If Harry Palmer is not the right man for you, that is hardly the end of the world. I realize that this is a painful time for you, my dear. But try to view it as a new beginning."

He paused to chuckle. "Take myself, for example. Look how long it has taken me to find Eleni! A lifetime! *Me,* an old man!"

"But you found love," she said softly.

"Yes, and when least expected. Your finding the right man may take time also. Hopefully not as long as it took me. However, I am glad you did not rush into marriage. Too many young people do that blindly these days, and the result can be disastrous and emotionally damaging. I believe you were wise to wait."

Wise, she thought dully. *Dumb is more like it.*

He looked at her solicitously and added, "I hope I am not depressing you?"

Her fingers left her temples and the faintest of smiles touched her lips. She shook her head. "On the contrary, Wald. I'm grateful for your insight. You're absolutely right, I dread what I have to face, but you've made me feel better already."

From the shadows, there came the sounds of an impatient rustling and Big Mike clearing his throat.

"There is nothing like work," Wald said, "to keep one's mind off personal problems. And I can tell that Big Mike is anxious to break you in."

Miranda squared her shoulders. "And I'm anxious to get to work," she said. But she was thinking: *Big Mike. Of all the people in the world to have to deal with, why him?*

But she kept these thoughts to herself.

Work. The ultimate antidote for personal problems.

Work. The straightest route to spinsterhood. Manhattan was full of single women who'd had to substitute jobs and careers for the love and family that had eluded them. She'd seen it all too often, and wondered whether she was ultimately doomed to join their ranks.

But there was nothing to be gained through negative thinking.

"Alright," she said, pushing back her chair and rising purposefully to her feet. "I'm ready."

She looked from Professor Hirsch, bathed golden by his desk lamp, to Big Mike, standing in the shadows beyond. Outside, the meltemi buffeted the shed, pelted its metal sides with pebbles, sounding like gravel hitting the undercarriage of a car.

"Well?" she asked. "So what are we waiting for? Let's get cracking."

It wasn't just Big Mike who proceeded with Miranda's initial orientation. She was grateful that Professor Hirsch joined them for the first half hour.

He began at the bulletin board.

"This is the current excavation." He sketched the air around a carefully-drawn, apparently professionally-surveyed map. "As you can see, it covers quite a large area."

"Too large, if you ask me," Big Mike groused.

"That cannot be helped," the professor said calmly. "We are at the whims and mercy of the Greek Ministry of Culture. As it is, we are highly fortunate that they gave us permission to proceed with this dig in the first place."

"Yeah," Big Mike said crankily, aiming a caustic look at Miranda. "Have you ever noticed how the Greeks rely on foreign archeological expeditions? Take Delos. It's basically a French site. Knossos, on Crete, was due to Sir Arthur Evans in the early part of the nineteenth century. The Kalaureia Research Program on Poros? That one is being undertaken by the Swedish Archeological Institute at Athens, and is funded by—thank you, the National Bank of Sweden. Not to put the professor down, but Samos has somehow ended up basically German. And as for the Acropolis in Athens? Don't even get me started. When the Greeks finally had the sense to bring the caryatids from the Erechtheion indoors and behind protective glass? *Who* did they have to go begging to in order to provide the best replica casts of the ones that you now see outdoors? The British. Because Elgin brought one back. And as for the Elgin . . . " he produced an ironic cough into his cupped hand and his tone became downright sarcastic " . . . I mean, the recently-renamed *Acropolis Marbles,* pray tell what condition they'd be in if the Turks hadn't sold them to Lord Elgin, and they'd been left outside to deteriorate in Athens' ghastly pollution?"

"That's quite enough." Professor Hirsch sighed painfully and pinched his nose; Big Mike was obviously voicing his pet peeves, and not for the first time.

"According to my research," Miranda spoke up, shooting Big Mike a withering look, "you forget yourself. During Elgin's time, Greece did not exist as it does today. It was part of the Ottoman Empire, and Athens was a mere village. There was no pollution back then, so strike that argument."

She'd been tempted to add, "Buster," but decided it was best to keep it professional and take the high road.

"Also," she continued, "if memory serves me correctly, the British managed a lot of screw-ups. For one thing, they used everything from chisels to acid—*acid,* mind you, to clean them up. And why? Because they thought they were supposed to be white, not realizing they're of Pentelic marble, which turns honey-colored when exposed to any kind of weather."

And in an even frostier tone, she added: "Not to mention that Elgin had them cut up. Yes, *cut up.* And why? To make shipping them easier!"

"Okay, okay, you've made your point," Big Mike growled, but he wasn't finished yet. "Granted, it's not just the Greeks who rely on foreigners to save their ancient sites," he went on. "Look at the Egyptians. *Who* saved Abu Simbal and moved that *entire temple* to higher ground when *Egypt* had the Russians build the Aswan Dam? And the Italians. *Who* helped begin the excavations at Pompeii and Herculaneum, and built one of the finest collections of antiquities, now in the British Museum? Including tons of some of the best preserved Attic wares?"

"Sir William Hamilton," Miranda murmured, "envoy to the British Embassy in Naples. Along with Pierre-Francois Hugues D'Hancarville."

Big Mike grunted with what she took to be approval and gave her an ironic round of silent applause. "At least you're not a total dilettante," he remarked waspishly. "Like too many among our small, bored, ever-rotating staff."

Miranda caught Professor Hirsch shooting her a surprised look. Apparently, Big Mike had grudgingly conceded what, for him, amounted to high praise indeed. Not that she cared what Big Mike thought about her. In fact, as far as she was concerned, Big Mike could take his Big Attitude and shove it where the moon never shone.

Except—

She had to credit him one thing.

—his passion *was* genuine.

Forget it, she told herself harshly. Forget him. Pretend he doesn't exist.

"We're fortunate," the professor said, trying for a note of levity, "that Big Mike did not join the diplomatic corps. He tends to forget that this is neither my country, nor his. We are guests here. We must remember that at all times."

Miranda nodded.

"Now *this,*" the professor said in a hushed voice, pointing to several scanned photographs tacked up to one side, "is what we are searching for. Oh, do not get me wrong. We are carefully sifting the site at various locations, trying to uncover evidence of what life at Ancient Asprodavos was like. In that sense, this is just like any other archeological excavation. Except for one thing! What I have devoted the better part of my lifetime trying to find!"

His eyes lit up, shining like twin dental mirrors even before he switched on a gooseneck lamp that seemed to raise the already sweltering temperature a good ten degrees and aimed the light directly at a quartet of very old photographs.

"These are computer-enhanced copies," he said. "I have stored the originals in a climatized facility in Athens."

Miranda stepped closer. Despite the enhancements, they were sepia-toned, and she could tell they had suffered severe craquelure, but her breath caught in her throat and she could swear her heart stopped beating for a full half minute.

Concentrating on the first photograph, she could scarcely believe her eyes. It had obviously been taken from high atop a ladder and showed the bottom half of a female marble statue, cracked diagonally at the waist and lying prone but face up in what looked like a cavern. There was a breathtaking beauty about her, an innate elegance rarely seen.

Such perfection! Miranda thought. Why, the marble garments seemed to flow like liquid folds of fabric, they had been rendered with such realistic perfection.

"Hera!" Professor Hirsch breathed reverently.

Miranda nodded mutely, unable to tear her eyes away from the photograph. She knew a masterpiece when she saw one, and to think that this statue had been lovingly chiseled from stone so many thousands of years earlier by some long-forgotten master of the art filled her with awe. Even more awesome was that from the human figure in uniform lying beside it to give a sense of scale, she was—*massive!* Undoubtedly half of one of the largest Greek statues Miranda would ever encounter—if not the largest.

Then she felt something oddly familiar stirring in her memory bank. She had seen pictures of this bottom half! From some museum . . .

And then it hit her.

"Why, it's the one in the Pergamon in Berlin!" she exclaimed.

"That is correct." Professor Hirsch nodded. "She was discovered by Professor Hammerschlag of the Reichsmuseum in 1942. I was a young conscript of sixteen at the time, and was personally at Karinhall when the Russians advanced and she was moved to safety. That is when the originals of these photographs fell into my possession."

Miranda inched sideways to the second photograph. It had been taken at the same time, also from atop a high ladder.

Professor Hirsch's voice was hushed. "And that, my dear, is the lost top half."

Miranda studied it so closely that her nose practically touched it. If her heart had stopped beating earlier, it was now thundering up a storm, threatening to burst through her rib cage. This was her first opportunity to ever lay eyes on the top half, and she was floored. Never once—not once!—during her long years of study, her haunting of major American museum collections, her perusals of antiquities auctions, her tenure at the Jan Kofski Gallery, even her close inspection of photographs in hundreds of tomes, had she ever encountered an early work of such ethereal, unearthly beauty and dexterity. Hera's expression was serene as the Buddha's, and her extravagantly plaited, shoulder-length hair was, from what Miranda could see, among the finest carving of any ancient Greek era.

Slowly, she turned to face Professor Hirsch. She wanted to express in words what she felt, but was rendered speechless.

He was watching her closely. "And to think that she is lying somewhere beneath our very feet, Miranda!" he whispered. "One of the greatest, if not *the* greatest, treasures of ancient Greece."

"My God!" She had finally found her voice, but it came out as a hoarse whisper. "But . . . but if both halves were found, why didn't the top ever see the light of day?"

"War." He sighed wearily. "You see, it was Hermann Göring, perhaps the most notorious art thief of all time, who financed the dig—if using stolen money is the right term for financing anything. Apparently, Dr. Hammerschlag convinced the Reichsmarschall where it could be found."

"But how could Dr. Hammerschlag be so sure of where to dig in the first place?"

"Ah." He held up an index finger. "Remember how Schliemann found Troy?"

"Of course. Every child knows that. By using Homer as an historical guide rather than pigeonholing him as a mere storyteller."

"Exactly! Now come. Take a look at these photographs, here on the left." He gestured to another set, tacked up on the far side of the carefully drawn map.

She went over to them, and he followed with the lamp, flooding the pictures with light.

These photographs were much older, perhaps late nineteenth century. Also sepia-toned and computer-enhanced and enlarged.

She didn't hesitate. "They're views of various sides of the same krater," she said at once.

"And?"

Miranda knew he was testing her.

"Take your time," he advised. "There is absolutely no rush."

Several minutes ticked by, and at first she could practically feel Big Mike breathing down her neck and smirking from behind, waiting for her to stumble. But the feeling didn't last long; she was too intrigued by the photographs, each of which she studied closely in turn, one after the other, and then studied each over and over again.

"Hmmm. How odd," she murmured at last. "The photos are not in color, so I must assume the pictorial sequence has been fired in black and some lighter tone on a terra cotta background. At first glance it would appear to be Attic, but it definitely is not. Echinus mouth, disk-footed, the coloring . . . that all generally also points toward Attic. Or even Apulian, for that matter. Yet it's neither. Oh, it has the usual chain of palmettes around the top, and the band of lotus leaves decorating the base. But what strikes me as so *strange*—"

"What does?"

"Well, for one thing, there's the matter of *style*. The pictorial scene's characters are too individualistic. Too realistic."

She glanced at Professor Hirsch.

"Go on, my dear," he encouraged, his expression neutral, showing neither agreement nor disagreement, only intense interest.

"Okay." She took a deep breath and plunged ahead, but cautiously. "The other thing is, it doesn't show the usual scenes of satyrs or Dionysos or panthers or gazelles or warriors. No Theseus pursuing Aithra. No horsemen or those precursors of angels, the winged goddesses."

The longer she studied it, the deeper her frown became. "You'll both probably think I've lost my Elgins . . . " she expected laughter or, at the very least, tolerant smiles at her weak attempt at humor, but none were forthcoming " . . . but in my opinion it evidently tells a story. It starts at the top right here and continues downward in these three separate bands to its conclusion here."

She traced her finger along both the front and the back views of the krater.

"It's incredible, really," she said. "I've never run across anything remotely like it."

"In what way?" the professor asked.

"In almost all ways. I realize that the krater is round, so I have to figure in the camera's distortion factor. But if you ask me—"

"Yes?"

"It tells the story of the Hera statue's beginning to its burial during a calamity. And notice the tattered ships."

"Samians. Yes."

"And that crucified figure. Almost Christlike in its depiction."

"That would be Polycrates, the Samian tyrant. Slain by the Persians."

"But what I *can't* for the life of me figure out from just these pictures is whether or not this krater really is ancient. If so, it would be among the most valuable in the world! Priceless, in fact. But *is* it genuine? That's what I keep asking myself."

"Dr. Hammerschlag believed it was, and managed to convince Göring. And you must keep in mind, my dear Miranda, that he did find her, using the pictures of this krater as a historical record to do so."

"Unbelievable! No one during that era—it would have been,what? Five, six hundred B.C.?"

"522 B.C., to be exact. Or at least, history has recorded the fall of Polycrates thus."

"In other words, the krater could have been created some time after the fact."

"True." Professor Hirsch allowed himself a modest smile. "Just as the New Testament was recorded several hundred years after Christ's crucifixion. However, as for the krater, I tend to believe it could not have been created long after the calamity, or calamities, occurred. From the accuracy of the pictorial story, and the uncanny depiction of Hera, my guess is that it dates no more than twenty, perhaps thirty, years after Samos fell. We must never forget that Professor Hammerschlag used these very photographs to actually locate her."

Miranda stared at him. "So where *is* this mysterious krater?"

He sighed deeply and shrugged. "If we only knew! In his copious diaries, which he kept scrupulously, Professor Hammerschlag never mentioned how he came across these photographs. Indeed, if we had the actual krater to go by, it would certainly make our progress so much easier. As you yourself have noted, the distortion factor makes it difficult to pinpoint the accurate position. My assumption is that it exists in some private collection."

"But whose?"

"If only we knew the answer to that, our jobs would be that much easier. However, other than these photographs, there is absolutely no record of its existence. None whatsoever. I have spent years searching for the answer. Still, the fact remains that Professor Hammerschlag did unearth our Hera. So from that, we must deduce that the krater is genuine, that it truly exists—or existed when those photographs were taken—and that the krater does not lie."

"So we cannot just use these pictures as Professor Hammerschlag did to pinpoint the exact location?"

"I'm afraid not, my dear. You see, he was forced to stop the excavation. He did manage to get the bottom half shipped to Karinhall, the part for which the Greeks are already rattling their sabers, making Elgin-type noises for its return. Meanwhile, the top half remains here, somewhere below us."

"But why couldn't the top half be shipped also?"

"The men and materiel were diverted to the North African campaign, on Hitler's orders. So Dr. Hammerschlag dynamited the site, intending to return. That, and subsequent earthquakes . . . you know, of course, that Samos was once part of Asia Minor, and was broken off from the continent during a terrible geological upheaval. And these subsequent ones have changed the landscape immensely. Between the dynamiting and the earthquakes, the exact location of the site was lost."

"But surely some of the old locals must remember where—"

He shook his head sadly. "Unfortunately, there are no survivors of the original dig to help guide us. The locals only know it was this general area." A sweep of his hand indicated the map of the entire site. "Unfortunately, Professor Hammerschlag was killed in a storm while the bottom half of Hera was transported. To make matters worse, the ship carrying the entire corps of engineers was bombed on its return trip to Africa and sank without survivors. A fitting end, perhaps, since they first killed all the local slave laborers before they left."

"It almost sounds as if there is a curse on the statue!" Miranda murmured.

"A curse?" Big Mike brayed a laugh. "You mean like that Englishman, Lord Carnavon?"

Miranda nodded.

"That's all hogwash. Carnavon, or should I say George Herbert, Sixth Earl of Carnavon, was the guy who financed Howard Carter, the Egyptologist who discovered Tutankhamun's tomb. And yeah, they opened the tomb together, and Carnavon died several months later in the Continental-Savoy Hotel in Cairo. But if there was a curse, why did Carter live on for another sixteen years? Try to explain that."

They glowered at one another, but before Professor Hirsch could intercede, his cell phone emitted a mechanical tune. He opened it, looked at the caller I.D., pressed the TALK key, said, "*Parakaló,*" and listened for a moment. He shut his eyes and wearily snapped the phone shut. His expression was blank and he suddenly looked old and fragile. A vein throbbed in his neck and his hands were shaking.

"What is it?" Miranda asked anxiously. "Why, your face is white as a sheet!"

"That was Philippos Tatoulis," he said in a shaky voice. "The shift has changed and it is his turn to guard the gate."

"One of the jugglers. The other one's brother."

"Yes," he said, staring at her as though through a void, his voice dull as lead. "Nikitas' brother. It appears we have visitors."

"Is that so unusual?" Miranda asked naively.

"From the police, yes."

"The police!" She stared at him, but he didn't seem to notice. "What would they want?"

"Mike—" Professor Hirsch murmured in a shaky monotone. "Mike, show Miranda around. Introduce her to the other members of the team. Fill her in on the problems we've been experiencing. It appears that my presence is required at the hospital in Vathi." He shut his eyes momentarily, his face a mask.

"The hospital!" Miranda exclaimed. "But why? Has there been an accident? Has one of the team been hurt?"

He shook his head, his mouth working loosely. "Worse," he sighed, his body shuddering as he lurched toward the door.

"Are you alright?" she asked.

"I am, yes. Or perhaps not. It appears that a body washed ashore at Potami. They need help identifying it. I-I must go. I am needed at the morgue."

[CHAPTER THIRTY SEVEN]

The Site at Ancient Asprodavos

"What the *devil,*" demanded Miranda, "is that all about? Why would the police need Professor Hirsch, of all people, to identify a body?"

Big Mike, slumped in the chair behind the Professor's battered desk, raked his large hands through the stubble of his cropped black hair, his beefy elbows weighing on the stack of oversize, thick albums he had slammed down upon the surface. The clitter-clatter of pebbles and gravel strewn by the wind against the sides of the metal shed had diminished; outside, the meltemi was dying down. A generator throbbed from somewhere nearby, the oscillating Chinese-manufactured fan making a pretense of cooling the stifling heat.

"In his letter summoning me," she said tartly, "Wald mentioned that there were problems here that he would explain once I arrived. Well, he hasn't had a chance to yet, has he? And now *this!* Come on, Big Mike, you heard him. You can tell me. What gives?"

"What *gives?*" he mimicked in a blast of exasperation, expelling tension, which only flooded right back into him as if the levee that was supposed to contain it had ruptured under his own outburst. "I'll tell you what *gives!* This whole damn dig is cursed, that's what gives!"

She sat primly opposite him, hands folded in her lap.

"Yeah, cursed," he repeated, rasping a sharp laugh. "And here I just got through needling you about Carnavon and curses."

He shook his head violently, then rubbed his sun-damaged face with his meaty hands and breathed deeply. "Look, I'm sorry. I was out of line. It's just—"

"Just what?" she asked calmly.

"Things. Everything. This whole place." He punched the air around him angrily, as if in accusation of every shelf and object. "The pressure just keeps building up."

"If there's anything I can do—"

Her calm appeared to have a taming effect on him. "Actually, yeah. You can. Come on, let's get outta here. Go outside and take a walk. That damn wind's died down and I'm starting to feel like a caged tiger."

"Hey," she said brightly, "great idea! It is getting to feel rather claustrophobic. Not to mention sweltering."

She made the first move getting to her feet, and he grabbed his baseball cap and stomped out after her into the blinding sunlight. They both immediately popped on their sunglasses. The waning wind, warm as it was, combined with the fresh salt air, felt exceptionally good, despite the blazing temperature and the puffs of grit and dust still being stirred up. But the pebbles had settled and no longer stung, the pale blue sky shimmered and seemed endlessly high, and the Aegean dazzled, shining like crinkled aluminum foil. Small, swift, battleship-gray coast guard cutters, none much longer than sixty feet, patrolled the narrow Greek waters, searching for rafts of illegal migrants from the hazy, mountainous coast of Turkey. Far out to sea, miniaturized by distance, an oil tanker rounded the strait of Steno Samou.

Without either of them choosing a destination, she and Big Mike themselves patrolled the inside perimeter of the chain link fence, away from the dorms, shed, and privy; away from the laughter, chatter, and muted techno-beat of somebody's CD player drifting out from the men's dorm. Big Mike, with his strong, stocky build and thickly muscled calves and thighs, adjusted his pace to match hers, their heads even. Until now, she hadn't realized they were both exactly the same height.

The worst of his anger seemed to have abated, but his expression was solemn as he looked sideways at her. "What I'm about to tell you stays between the two of us and the Prof. Okay? Even Eleni doesn't know the half of it."

"Of course!" she said.

Big Mike closed his hand around her arm and turned her to face him. She expected his fingers to dig into the soft flesh and leave bruises, but calluses aside, his grip was surprisingly gentle.

"Miranda, I've been on this dig with Professor Hirsch from the very beginning. That was five summers ago. From the start we've had, as he so delicately puts it, problems. But the really serious ones started occurring during the last two years. Lately, though, they've been coming at us faster and faster, like curveballs from the outfield."

"Problems such as what?"

He let go of her and she continued walking, without conscious direction, slowly southwest along the rock and scrub along what was obviously a well-worn dirt path. To her immediate right rambled the ugly, industrial length of the chain-link fence which ran along the dirt road outside. Beyond that, a small cluster of hardy parched pines rose to a long-untended, terraced hillside. And to her immediate left, a knee-high, carefully excavated stone wall, from antiquity, outlined a surprisingly perfect geometric square.

"Problems such as that foundation right there," he pointed at the low wall, "where besides uncovering what used to be a house, we started to find more than just the ordinary bits and pieces of shattered pottery. A Lekythos, several Skyphos in remarkably good condition, even a tiny bronze figurine of a warrior."

"I'd love to see them!"

"So would I," he responded dryly. "But the Lekythos and the warrior disappeared."

She stopped walking, turned to him, and whipped off her sunglasses. She stared at him. "What do you mean, disappeared?"

Big Mike took off his own Ray-Bans, his onyx eyes blazing even as he squinted against the blinding sun behind her. "That's exactly what I mean. They vanished into thin air. Poof! Like that!" He snapped his fingers. "One day we inventoried them, took pictures, numbered them, and shelved them. A week or so later, they were gone."

Her eyes grew huge. "Stolen, you mean?"

"What other word could there be for it? That was when the Prof decided we needed to secure the area." He drew a deep breath and expelled it in frustration. "Believe it or not, it took nearly a full year of lobbying before the Ministry of Culture finally broke down, gave us permission, and released the funds to put up these useless playground fences."

He gestured savagely at the chain-link undulating along their right, following the contours of the land.

"A six-foot chain-link without concertina wire!" he muttered in disgust. "I ask you, who can't climb that?" His voice dripped disgust. "In fact, it's one of Little Mike's favorite pastimes when he's here, clambering up and down it like a monkey. You call that *secure?*"

Miranda said, "Point well taken. It could use razor wire. But go on. I take it there's more."

"Oh, lots. Tons." He stuck his Ray-Bans back on just as an approaching rumble of rolling thunder came from the direction of Ireo. "What on *earth?*" she said, turning in the direction of the noise, "is that infernal racket?"

"*Panagia mou!*" he cursed, and spat in annoyance. "Those bastards are back at it!"

"Who is?"

Instead of replying, he whipped his baseball cap off his head and thrust it at her. "Here. Take my cap."

She grabbed it and looked at him in confusion. "What's this for?"

"You'll see soon enough. Just hold it over your face when they go by. Your tank top's too skimpy to do much good. My T- shirt's thicker, and I can pull it up to cover my nose and mouth. And whatever you do, when they pass by for God's sake, turn your head away from the fence and face towards the sea."

The decibels increased to ear-splitting volume; the barbarous roar of heavy engines and grinding, downshifting gears that already drowned out the faint sounds of the techno beat emitting from the men's dorm. From here, Miranda could see the women's dorm, and Rosalie and Pernilla darting outside to the makeshift laundry line, unclipping the clothes as if in a sped-up film, then sprinting back inside carrying armfuls of freshly laundered garments. At both dormitories, shutters, doors, and windows were being tightly slammed tight.

Then the source of the mounting din turned a curve in the dirt road and she saw it approach just along the outside of the chain-link. A convoy of heavy construction vehicles, the first few of which raised huge ugly brown cumulus clouds of dust that almost, but not quite, obscured the vehicles in the very rear. The slow-moving parade was a succession of eight huge dump trucks, all outfitted with giant, heavy-treaded tires. Through the scrim of dust and belching exhaust she could just make out the last two, which laboriously pulled one laden flatbed each.

Strapped down atop the second to the last, like some monstrous, insectile mechanical beast, was what she recognized as a giant yellow steam shovel. And riding piggyback atop the last lurked a bulldozer, which brought to mind a metallic prehistoric beast slumbering after having gorged itself on a feast of earth and rock, the maw of its enormous shovel lowered.

Big Mike pulled the rounded neck of his T-shirt up over his nose. Following his lead, Miranda held his baseball cap against her nose and mouth and turned away.

The heavy throb and whine of eight dissonant engines swelled to a barbaric crescendo. Miranda felt the earth beneath her feet vibrate, and she made a face behind the makeshift mask of Big Mike's baseball cap. An incredible blast of heat mixed with the stench of diesel exhaust assaulted her senses as the mechanized procession passed by, raising a spreading, A-bomb-like cloud of dust that hovered and threatened to blot out the sun. She quickly did as Big Mike said, turned her face towards the sea, and shut her eyes.

The vehicles lumbered along, then eventually the noise level and vibrations decreased. Just as slowly, the mushroom cloud began to settle.

Miranda removed the baseball cap from her face and coughed up a mouthful of dust.

"Can you explain that?" she rasped. Her throat felt dry and gritty, and her voice sounded hoarse to her own ears.

Lowering his T-shirt from his nose and mouth, Big Mike thumped his chest, turned his head aside, hawked noisily, and spat out a lungful of dusty saliva.

"Yeah. The explanation's simple." His lips formed a rictus of a smile; his voice sounded like sandpaper. "Just another in the endless series of problems that've been plaguing us."

"Where are they headed?"

"You'll see soon enough. It's just beyond the perimeter of this site."

"But the vibrations! Surely they can't be good for the dig."

"You're telling me? And that's the least of it."

"What do you mean?"

"You'll experience it for yourself soon enough. Believe me."

She didn't press him, and they continued walking the perimeter along the well-worn track. Here and there she could see cordoned-off little areas, some of them tented with flat tarpaulins affixed to long iron poles to shade the dig's workers from the worst of the blazing sun. Taut ropes, slanting downward to anchored pegs, turned them into trapezoidal sculptures.

"Those are spots we believe are promising," Big Mike explained. "Only, they'll have to wait."

She shot him a quizzical sideways look. "But why wait?"

Instead of replying, he answered her question with a question. "Haven't you ever wondered why the Prof sent for you?"

"I take it because he knew I had the entire month of August off. Most likely because he knows that gallery assistants aren't well paid, and that I couldn't afford a holiday, so he took pity upon me."

"Is that what you think?"

She raised her chin stubbornly. "And why shouldn't I?"

He stopped walking, took off his Ray-Bans, and turned to her, his bituminous eyes showing a gleam of amusement. "You really are naive, aren't you?"

"Well, if I am, then why don't you clue me in," she retorted sharply, "rather than uttering mysterious sentences like, 'You'll see soon enough'? Do I look like Sylvia Browne?"

His lips twitched sardonically. "You ask me, you look a hair better."

She threw up her hands in frustration. "Talk to me, Mike Savides. Get to the freaking *point!*"

He regarded her hesitantly, pondering her as if calculating what, or how much, to divulge. After a moment he seemed to make up his mind. When he spoke, his voice was solemn. "Okay. But what I say stays between the two of us. Understood?"

She nodded. "Understood."

"Alright . . . I think you're already aware that our budget's stretched to the outer limits, and that we can't afford to hire the required amount of experienced helpers."

She nodded wordlessly.

"Don't ever quote me, 'cause I'll deny it, but whenever we run short of funds, the Prof and Eleni both pump money from their personal savings into this place. Which explains why we depend so heavily upon volunteers."

He paused and added, "Though even if we *could* afford to hire the required pros, it's doubtful they'd stay on for very long."

"But that still doesn't explain anything. For heaven's sake, Mike! Will you drop your sphinx act and stop talking in riddles?"

He shifted his weight from one foot to the other. "Well, let me see. For starters, one of our crew suffered a fatal fall down a ravine last year. He knew the terrain backwards and forwards. Besides, what was he doing out in the middle of the night? Another had to be medevacked out after he and his moped were run off the road."

Miranda's forehead crinkled into a frown. "Why is it I have the feeling that there's more?"

"Because there is. Take this season, starting back in April. Three of our best volunteers just up and disappeared."

"There's a rational explanation for everything. Maybe they simply got tired and wanted out," Miranda suggested.

"Without giving notice or saying so much as a good-bye? Nah. That doesn't wash. I'm telling you, they were *dedicated.*"

Miranda's frown deepened. "I would think anyone fascinated with this particular period in history would jump at the opportunity to work here. What I can't understand is your having trouble finding replacements."

"Yeah. You'd think." Big Mike's chest heaved, followed by a massive exhalation. "I don't need to tell you that the world's archeological community is tiny. Or that the Greek Antiquities community is an even tinier subset."

"Nor that those specializing in the particular period circa 500 B.C. is tinier yet," said Miranda. "So? I know all that."

"You'll probably think I'm losing it, but for want of a better word, this site is considered cursed. Like your Lord Carnavon. There's even a rumor circulating that it's haunted." He shook his head briskly, like a dog shaking off water. "Hell, even I'm starting to half-believe it! *Me!* The eternal skeptic."

"I presume you must have a reason."

"A reason? Yeah. An explanation? No." He continued walking, but at a slow pace. "Then there's the case of Angelica Veloso, from L.A. Young, but smart as a whip and dedicated like all hell. One of the most beautiful women you've ever laid eyes on. Why she didn't go into modeling is beyond me. I mean, take Jerry Hall and Salma Hayek and put them in a blender. Legs that went on forever, long, shiny black hair down to here." He made a karate motion across his waist. "She worked this site for two consecutive summers. This was her third. And when I say worked, I mean, she slaved like there's no tomorrow. Archeology was her *life.* It's what she lived for."

"And?"

His expression was bleak. "She disappeared four weeks ago. Never even said good-bye. Didn't leave so much as a note. Knowing her, she'd never have left like that. Not Angelica. And the weird thing is, no one even *saw* her leave."

"But the guards . . . they would have had to let her out, wouldn't they?"

"Guards?" he sputtered. "*Guards?* Is that what you call that second-rate, has-been circus act?"

"But Wald hired them."

"Unh-unh. Wrong. Someone at the Ministry of Culture hired them and shoved them upon us when the fence was constructed. See, they *came* with the fence. I'd hate to burst the Prof's bubble, but I don't trust those Tatoulis Brothers and their sister as far as they can throw their juggling equipment."

Miranda digested that in silence.

"What alerted us," Big Mike said, "is that her family's worried as all hell and have been calling us daily, pestering the Prof about her whereabouts. You've got to understand, Angelica was as dutiful a daughter as they come. She and her family were close. Like that." He held up his hand and crossed two fingers. "She always called them every Sunday. I mean religiously, without fail. So when two Sundays went by and she didn't call, her parents started panicking."

Miranda's voice was a near-whisper. "Go on."

"Finally, the Prof had the police and the Ministry of Culture look into it. They dragged their feet, so to get results he had to pressure the American ambassador at the embassy in Athens."

"And?"

He trudged on in silence for a minute. The remnants of the meltemi had died down completely and the dust of the construction vehicles had settled. Their shadows followed them unevenly at their sides, the patterns thrown by the chain-link like black netting thrown upon the ground.

"According to Immigration and Passport Control," he continued grimly, "their records show Angelica left the country four weeks ago. According to Aegean Airlines, she flew from here to Athens. Delta confirms that she flew on to New York and caught a connecting flight to L.A."

"Perhaps she just got fed up with the dig," Miranda murmured thoughtfully.

He whirled at her, glaring so sharply that she flinched. "No way, José. Angelica's mysterious departure was totally out of character. She loved working here. And she wasn't the type to just take off without saying good-bye to her friends. Not Angelica." He shook his head violently and kicked a small stone, sending it skittering.

"Could she have just up and left? Gone off somewhere with a boyfriend?"

"According to her, she didn't have one. All we know for certain is that, according to her family, she's missing."

"But if she got to L.A.—"

"Well, *someone* flew to L.A. Someone *with her passport* was on that plane. You'd think, wouldn't you, that she'd at least have informed her family to meet her there?"

Miranda gripped his arm, her fingers pressing rock-hard muscle. "Mike?" Her voice quavered. "Do you think this is why Wald was called upon to identify a body at the morgue?"

"*Christ!* I sure as hell hope not!" He clenched his fists at his side, his arms rigid as steel.

"But if she flew back to the States—"

"*If,*" he emphasized with a snarl, startling her. "These days, with identity theft . . . "

He shut his mouth with a snap of his jaw and quickened his pace, as if to vent his frustration through sheer expenditure of energy. Miranda had to hurry to keep up with him.

"Look," he said, "what you witnessed in Kusadasi. From what you've told us, your passport, which Oracle Cruises was holding, was obviously used to create a boarding pass for what had to be the smuggling of illegal immigrants. Right?"

She nodded soberly.

"And doesn't it strike you as odd that we've had three workers simply disappear, or suffer fatal, or paralyzing, accidents over the past two years?"

Her voice was small. "Yes."

"So now you know what I mean when I say this site is cursed. Cursed by *man,* not the supernatural. Here, let's make a left."

They had reached the end of the length of chain-link fence, which abruptly angled sharply out to the direction of the sea. Several yards beyond the clumps of dried grass and weeds, the ground plunged a dizzying hundred feet down a sheer precipice where nature, and winter's run-off, had cut a wide ravine. It was as wide, or more, than it was deep, both sides consisting of stark, bare cliffs of raw, striated fangs of rock with deep vertical cracks. And here, incredibly, hundreds—perhaps thousands—of years of winter runoff and buffeting winds had created a narrow natural bridge, an arch of crumbling rock spanning the two cliffs. It was, Miranda guessed, at most two feet in breadth at the widest spot, and time and weather had eroded it to a shallow span. If it lasted for another ten years, she would have been surprised.

She shivered unexpectedly, and turned to Big Mike. "Is this the ravine where the fatal fall you were telling me about occurred?"

He nodded. "It happened somewhere outside this fenced-in area near that natural bridge. What Yves was doing here in the middle of the night is beyond me. He can't have been on that span. That would have been sheer madness. It crumbles more every year, and he knew that. Maybe he just climbed the fence, wanted to walk along it." He shrugged, gesturing futility. "There's just no rational explanation. As for me, I wouldn't be caught dead walking near that drop-off in daylight, let alone at night. And as for that natural bridge, if it lasts another two years, I'll be surprised. Yves was rash and intrepid, yeah. But he'd never have tried to cross it. He *knew* better."

A shrill whistle suddenly rent the air from somewhere beyond the ravine, sending a small flock of birds skyward and streaking inland.

"*Sto diavolo!*" he cursed under his breath. "Better take a wide stance, balance yourself, and hold your hands tightly over your ears. There's going to be noise."

"But—"

"Just *do* it!" he ordered sharply.

The ferocity of his tone compelled obedience and she spread her legs wide, clapped both hands over her ears, and waited, she knew not what for. One second passed, then two, then three.

Before the count of four the earth beneath her feet convulsed drunkenly, the fence heaved, and a second later there was a concussive sound wave, like a sonic boom, that all but knocked her off her feet. It loosened the built-up scree along the stratification on both sides of the ravine, and a sleet of pebbles and loose rocks rained brutally down to the wide gully far below. She watched a tilted boulder on the far side break loose and tumble down, crashing into rocky outcrops, the impact sending them hurtling downward like a secondary wave of missiles. Was it her imagination, she wondered, or did she actually see the thin span of that natural bridge rise before slowly settling back into place? The explosion had loosened pieces of it from the edges, too, and they showered down into the ravine like a rocky hailstorm. From somewhere beyond, a massive cloud, like great, ugly curds of brown and gray rose up, staining the pristine porcelain sky.

Big Mike uncovered his ears and gently pried her hands loose from hers.

She stared at him, her expression and eyes wild with confusion.

"It's okay now, for the time being," he was saying.

Her ears were ringing so badly that it was difficult to hear him. His voice sounded far away, or as if he was speaking through the far end of a long tin barrel.

"What in all Hades *was* that?" she demanded, all too aware of her own voice sounding as far away to her own ears as his had.

"Oh, just another one of our endless string of problems."

"But, Mike! That was an *explosion!*"

"Yeah." He smiled grimly. "Tell me about it. A charge of dynamite, to be exact."

"But I thought we weren't permitted to dynamite!"

"*We* aren't. Not within our so-called protected perimeter."

"But others can?"

"Outside of this site itself? Yeah. Our fine neighbors have *permission.* Our fine neighbors have gotten *dispensation* from the authorities. Our fine neighbors can do as they damn well *please.*"

Miranda ignored the blunt sarcasm. "But this is criminal!" she stammered. "It's terrible for the excavation. Antiquities are fragile! If I think of the pieces that might be waiting to be found, but meanwhile get shattered by these explosions I—"

"Get sick?"

"Yes," Miranda nodded. "To my stomach."

His smile was anything but pretty. "Then welcome to the club."

"What I want to know is, how did they get permission to blast over there in the first place? Especially since it so obviously affects this site."

"How? Come on, Miranda! Where've you been? Money talks. Especially if it's bribes to the right officials."

"But surely the Ministry of Culture is—"

"—'above reproach'?" he mimicked her cruelly from the night before. "Well, think again. It's as riddled with corrupt officials as any other government organization anywhere. In case you didn't realize it, there's a burgeoning underground economy in this country. Greeks worship money."

"Aren't you being just a wee bit cynical?" she retorted, but without passion. "Not to mention guilty of generalization? This is a socialist country."

"Take off the blinders, sweetheart. You been up to the Acropolis in Athens recently? Ever seen it before the Olympics and the Euro?"

"Actually, no," she replied stiffly. "I never had the opportunity to see it before or after."

"Well, then let me clue you in. How do you explain that since the Olympics, when you go up there, you can suddenly see all these illegal swimming pools that popped up in small backyards all over the place? Like an epidemic of blues and aquas? Small fortunes were *skimmed,* sweetheart, and make no mistake about it. With all the frenzied building and modernization suddenly going on, from the new German-designed airport to the tram, Greece's first toll highway, the subway extensions, the *infrastructure,* the stadiums, the sudden *surge* in shiny new cars and SUV's that can't even negotiate some of the streets in the Plaka—where do you think all this new money came from?"

She was silent, unable to answer, his every word a sharp barb that stung and poisoned the wound of her innocent preconceptions of the Greek ideal she had always worshiped and yearned to experience.

"And how do you explain that a lot—and I mean, a *lot* of hotels keep two sets of books? Some even *three?* Take late last January, when my folks decided to visit. They stayed at a small hotel in Vathi. I was going to find them decent lodgings, but my dad had already reserved a room online. When it came time to check out? The hotel owner claimed his credit card machine was on the blink, and *said* he had a history of customers being charged twice through his charge machine, and refused to use it? So my parents had to go to an ATM and pay in cash—in this day and age, mind you—the hotel thereby bypassing the on-line commission in the process. Sweet, huh?"

The clean, clear Aegean air seemed suddenly hotter, filled with the stench of dust and deceit and dead fish that in her imagination were washed up upon the pebble beach beyond and far below.

Miranda was nearly shocked into silence. "I can't believe I'm hearing this," she said, her voice sounding hollow and weak.

"Oh, believe it." Big Mike obviously wasn't one to dilute his opinions or sugar-coat what he believed to be the truth. Or at least the truths as he saw them. "And don't get me wrong. I'm not knocking this country. I love it. I could stay and live here happily ever after. First time I set foot on Greek soil? I never wanted to leave. Hell, I have the greatest respect for the Greeks. They're among the most warm-hearted and generous people you're ever likely to meet. The most ruthless, too, once you get past the guide-book façade. What you've got to remember is that before you put people on a pedestal, never forget that the shiniest apple has its worms. That's a universal fact."

Her crash initiation to Big Mike's version of Greek reality shook her, to say the least. But then, she *had* experienced the chilliness of Chara Zouboulakis, the false bonhomie of The Witch, just as she'd been drawn to Eleni's irresistible heart-felt warmth, instant acceptance, and hospitality. The modern Greeks were a people of contradictions, the same as people the world over: the good, the bad, and the ugly.

Why she should have expected anything different was sheer naïveté.

Still, her emotions had undergone a sea change in the heat of Big Mike's monologue. She had anticipated the fervor of dedicated archeologists working hand in hand toward a common goal, had expected the Site at Ancient Asprodavos to be a peaceable kingdom of serenity, devotion, and the occasional excitement of shared discovery. Instead, she found herself embroiled in turmoil, deception, immigrant smuggling, nearby dynamiting that shook the site to its foundations, and only the gods of the ancients knew what else lay in store.

Comedy and tragedy, she reminded herself. Weren't those among the two greatest gifts the ancients had given to Western literature?

Somewhere, she thought, the ghosts of Aristophanes and Euripides were surely laughing.

"Come along this way."

Big Mike semaphored impatiently for her to follow, and without waiting for a reply he led the way single-file, tromping boy scout-like along the inside of the fence, adroitly avoiding obstacles of parched thorny brush and rock.

"We're going to the far end of this length of fencing," he said over his shoulder. "Right where it stops and the cliff drops down to the sea. From there you'll be able to see first-hand what our *highly favored* neighbors across the ravine are up to."

For a few moments Miranda savored the sound of waves spending themselves along a pebbled shore, the cries of gulls circling overhead, the bright flash of small emerald lizards, like living Harry Winston jewels, darting out of their way. Then the machine gun-like racket of jackhammers and drills abruptly drowned out the songs of surf and bird.

Big Mike had stopped just this side of the cliff's edge, where nature's precipice made fencing along the sea side unnecessary. Miranda picked her way carefully over loose stones and scree toward the dizzying edge of the cliff.

She drew alongside him. The ravine had widened to nearly double its width at this point. Just beyond the chain-link and far below, the sun sparkled sequins on an inlet of pristine water, ranging from dark blue at its depths to lighter shades of blue and aquamarine and pale green at its shallows, the edges along the pebbly beach scalloped with frothy collars of white lace.

"How beautiful!" she breathed.

"Yeah, but look over there," Big Mike grumbled, jabbing a thick, callused thumb in the direction of the noise.

Miranda followed his finger with her eyes and gasped.

Beyond the inlet, at the far side facing the sea, a wide ramp of stone and gravel, zig-zagging with switchbacks, and capable of supporting a lumbering front-end loader with a claw bucket and steel treads, scarred the cliff from top to bottom. It looked for all the world like an ugly, diagonal strip mine. A crew of laborers, dwarfed by distance and assisted by explosives and heavy machinery, had already gouged what looked like an immense cavern out of the schist and volcanic rock.

It was a hideous blight as only such a construction site could be.

"It's horrible!" she cried. "Criminal!"

"And that," Big Mike informed her grimly, unnecessarily, "is where they're dynamiting. Not to mention that that piece of real estate should technically be part of our excavation site. Yes, *ours!*" he emphasized. "Only a lot of very powerful and very influential people paid off a lot of very powerful and very influential politicians."

She kept staring at the construction site, her brow furrowed. "But what in blazes is the purpose of that? What am I looking at?"

"Sweetheart," he said acidly, "you are looking at 'progress'."

"*That* . . . is progress?"

"They are constructing—rooms, banqueting halls, swimming pools. They are constructing a 'genuine Greek village,' as I understand it."

"I don't get it. What would be genuine about it?"

"Nothing, of course." Big Mike's eyes burned with fury and he flung his arms about. "They're creating what might as well be a '*Disney World of what is already being touted as a world-class resort,* an entire *village* of faux villas and hotels and condominiums!'" His words hissed. "Imagine! All quaint, red-tiled roofs and pastel stucco tumbling down the cliffside! A new five-star playground for attracting yet more tourists with deep pockets, as if we're not inundated with enough of them already!"

"Surely they must have encountered some obstacles?"

"Yeah." He coughed a laugh. "From the Prof and fellow academics. But you know what they say—'Money talks, bullshit walks.' Well, the latter's us—*we're* the bullshit!"

"But who's behind it?"

"A giant corporation, what else? GlobaLux International, to be precise. They apparently own a chain of—" his voice was sour "—so-called *indiginous* vacation villages the world over, from Mexico to Thailand, from the Maldives to the Seychelles, from Crete and Rhodes to 'safari camps' in Africa. Christ, but they make me want to vomit!"

"Calm down, Mike, you're working yourself up into a lather." Her voice was gentle. "Sometimes there's only so much one can do."

"Oh, don't I know it! What you're seeing is Big Business and Big Investors' money at work. Jesus, but greed just kills me! As if there aren't enough resorts all around this island as it is! They're like a cancer that keeps spreading—"

"Yes," she said patiently, "I understand. But who *owns* GlobaLux?"

"Who? Who knows? It's a Swiss-based hotel consortium, that's all we've been able to find out. Oh, and that it's financed through smaller, privately-held corporations that keep their owners and shareholders top secret. But just who are the faces behind those corporate walls?" He laughed harshly once more. "Try to find out, and you'll hit a brick wall every time. Holding companies in Liechtenstein, on Bermuda, Grand Cayman, Barbados—all sorts of off-shore tax havens keep popping up. But the individuals behind them? Rich people, obviously. Fancy ass people. People who can afford that true final frontier, ultimate privacy. People with private jets and obscene yachts the size of ocean liners. People who hang Picassos and Braques instead of wallpaper—that's who!"

"GlobaLux," Miranda repeated to herself under her breath. "GlobaLux."

She stood there in silence for a long moment, chewing thoughtfully on her lower lip. Her eyes followed the progress of a distant front loader, its claw bucket gouging more rock out of the cliff face and depositing its contents into the back of a dump truck, but her brain barely registered it. Her concentration lay elsewhere.

There must be a way to crack the corporate shields, she was thinking, convinced that nothing was impenetrable, not in this day and age. *There* has *to be a way to trace the owners of the corporations behind GlobaLux. The only question is how?* How?

"Come on." She felt Big Mike tap her on the arm. "Let's go," he said. "Every time I look over there my blood pressure goes through the roof! I need a change of scenery. What do you say we take the Jeep over to Vathi?"

"But don't we have to start work?"

"This *is* about work. I need to go over an album of my own I created on the sly. It contains pictures of all the missing pieces we've unearthed."

"But I'm all caked with dust!" Miranda protested.

"So take a quick shower and change. Forget drying your hair, the sun will do that. Meet you at the gate in five."

They started back, heading towards the little cluster of buildings: the shed, the privy, the men's and women's dorms.

Halfway there, she had a revelatory moment and stopped in her tracks. "Mike?"

"Now what?" he demanded, a testy undertone in his voice.

She hesitated, inwardly shrinking from the emotionally charged path she knew she might be embarking upon, the deception and procrastination it required. On the one hand, it was possible she might be of immense help to Big Mike and Professor Hirsch, and especially the Site at Ancient Asprodavos . . . on the other, the process would require guile and duplicity on her part, not to mention exploitation of affections.

To plunge, or not to plunge; that was the question. And did she have it in her to take advantage of a romantic involvement that was over, at least for her?

She drew a deep, oxygenating breath for courage. Let it out slowly. Then took the plunge.

"Mike, let's meet up in, say, half an hour? I've got a call to make."

His smirk wasn't exactly pleasant. "And here I thought you were anxious to get to work. I should've known."

He turned his back and continued on, but she caught his arm and forced him to face her.

"Not so fast, *Mister* Savides," she snapped, her voice dripping sarcasm. "Can't you, for once in your life, ditch that 'Angry Young Man' attitude and get off that high horse of yours? You're not the only person in the world weighed down with baggage, you know. Only we don't all take it out on others."

He lowered his Ray-Bans and squinted over them at her with something approaching puzzled amazement. The fact that she could match his own tone and mood seemed to have thrown him. Evidently he wasn't used to being on the receiving end of the medicine he dished out.

"Well?" he said.

"Something's just occurred to me. I *believe,*" she enunciated slowly, carefully, "that I just might, and I stress the word *might,* have a contact who may be able to help uncover who's behind those corporate brick walls you were talking about."

"*You?*" he said with evident irony, reverting to unpleasantness.

"Yes, *me,* dammit!" she shot back in a flare of anger so fierce and passionate he was taken aback. "And believe me, this isn't exactly an easy begging mission for me. For your information, it's goddamn *hard!*"

Blinking back tears, she flicked an unconscious glance at her finger where the pale band of skin, like a pallid tattoo, glowered like an accusation where Harry's engagement ring had encircled it. It aroused a wave of shame and self-loathing.

Big Mike followed her eyes and she quickly curled her fingers and lowered her hand to her side. But not quickly enough. He had the savvy to put two and two together in a flash. But at least he respected her privacy and didn't question her. Or even raise his eyebrows.

"Sure," he said, thumbing his shades back up on his nose. "Why not? Half an hour, then."

They walked on in silence for the rest of the way. When they reached the buildings, he lifted a hand in a half-wave and headed for the shed while a handful of archeologists and volunteers began to spill out of both dorms—spades, shovels, rakes, and brooms propped over their shoulders, sifts in hand, ready to pair off and scatter to their respective tarpaulin-shaded digs.

Rosalie Hobhouse flashed Miranda a grin as she passed. "Hi ho, hi ho," she sang merrily, "off to work we go."

"Rosie?" Miranda said hesitantly.

Rosalie stopped and turned. "Yes, dear?"

"Could I ask you for a favor? I need to take a quick shower and change. Mind showing me how the facilities work?"

"*Avec plaisir!*" came Rosalie's sly reply, with a sharp, rebuking glance aimed at Yvette, inevitable cigarette glued to her lower lip and her bubble butt twitching in her too-tight shorts as she made her leisurely way past.

"I really ought to be ashamed of myself," Rosalie added with a touch of guilt as she propped her tools against the wall. "It's just . . ." she sketched a futile gesture " . . . I don't know why, but that girl really knows how to get on my nerves. Always acting like a latter-day Brigitte Bardot."

Miranda couldn't help but laugh. "I think you mean a present-day Britney Spears or Paris Hilton, don't you?"

"Whoever." Rosalie flapped a hand. "Little tramp. Won't last the season, you mark my words. Why she's even here is beyond me. Doesn't even have a degree! Someone's pulled strings, you can count on that. Probably got her sent here to keep her out of trouble. As if that's possible. And, of course, there's Bruno."

Miranda blinked. "Bruno?"

"Our German. The handsome blond with curly hair and what they call a 'swimmer's build'? Well, since our mam'selle's gotten the arctic treatment from Big Mike, she's set out to seduce him.

"Until," she added dryly, "someone sexier comes along, no doubt."

"I haven't met any of the guys yet," Miranda reminded her.

"Oh, right." Rosalie chuckled. "Silly me. Well, you will, dear. Soon enough. Now let's go inside and get you a towel and that change of clothing."

They headed through the dorm to Miranda's bunk at the very rear. Rosalie produced a towel that had seen better days. "But it's freshly laundered, that's the best I can say," she apologized with a laugh as she flapped it.

"I've got worse at home, I'm sure," Miranda murmured. She was on her knees, rummaging through one of her yellow nylon bags, flinging clothes up onto the bunk. A clean set of undies. A short-sleeved lilac top with a bias-cut, single-button flap. Purple shorts and a matching pair of purple and white Pumas and a white sun visor. Plus her sleek little cell phone. The latest state-of-the-art gadget that did everything except vacuum your house.

This phone.

A gift from Harry. Electronics-minded Harry, whose mind was always on the gadgetry of the future while hers was on the art treasures from the long distant past. What *did* they have in common?

How well she remembered the day, several months earlier, when he'd given it to her.

"It's got world-wide range," he'd told her.

"So I can reach out and touch someone?" she'd quipped, recalling a television ad her mother used to like to quote.

He hadn't a clue what she was referring to. "So you can reach out and touch me," *he'd replied.*

Now it seemed to scald her hand, as though punishing her for the the betrayal she had yet to perform. Too late, she wished she'd kept her big trap shut. It was all she could do to steel herself for the call she despised herself for having to make.

"Ready, dear?" Rosalie asked as Miranda pushed herself to her feet.

"Yes." She was grateful that Rosalie had the grace not to ask where she was going.

Miranda collected her clothes from the bunk and held them against her breast when something occurred to her.

"Rosie," she asked, "who occupied this bunk before me?"

The question earned her a peculiar look, and she felt a chill and shivered, guessing the answer before she even heard it spoken aloud.

"Angelica Veloso."

[CHAPTER THIRTY EIGHT]

Moscow, Russia

Alexandr Grinkov gestured for Harry Palmer to put his wallet away, extracted a diamond-encrusted gold money clip from his bespoke suit, and peeled off not one, not two, but several large bills from the thick wad of rubles.

The porter, overcome by the lavishness of the tip, bowed deeply and departed, walking backwards, as if from royalty, and shut the door to the suite with barely a whisper. Grinkov's assistant, a slim, sharp-eyed Asiatic beauty named Galina, turned out in a low-cut, black Prada shift and spiky Gucci stilettos, stalked stork-like from room to room, inspecting the suite for possible shortcomings.

Alexandr Grinkov was in his early forties. He was six feet tall, trim, and fighting fit. He had Tatar cheekbones like cliffs, blue eyes as pale as a glacier, and lips as thin as a knife blade. He could almost have been handsome in a cold-blooded way, save for the disfiguring scar that slashed from his right eye down to the corner of his mouth. Without the expensive trappings of his tailored suit, orange Bulgari tie, and Rolex watch, he would, Harry thought, have looked equally at home as a leather-jacketed thug, and exuded an air of pent-up violence and danger.

Harry's take wasn't far off the mark. Before *perestroika* and *glasnost* and the reinvention of the Soviet Union from its leaden history to its wealthy oligarchic present, Grinkov had been in the 12th Spetznaz Brigade operating out of Sverdlovsk, with Special Forces training and parachuting skills. After the fall of the U.S.S.R. came a stint as a loan shark's heavy, until he saved Nikolai Kosichkin's life during a mugging. As a reward, he was invited to join the oligarch's private security force, in whose ranks he swiftly rose.

"This is the Ritz-Carlton Suite," Grinkov informed Harry with pride. "2,250 of your American square feet. Mr. Kosichkin insisted upon the finest accommodations in all of Moscow, and has upgraded you from an Executive Suite to this one. Only the best for Mr. Walter Kirkland's representative." He smiled thinly. "That was his order. He admires your Mr. Kirkland very much."

As well he should, Harry thought cynically. As one of Hartford-Kirkland Group's major shareholders, Nikolai Kosichkin raked in millions every year in dividends.

"A private dining room has been reserved for you and Mr. Kosichkin at the Turandot Restaurant," Grinkov continued. "A limousine shall pick you up at eight o'clock. You and Mr. Kosichkin will discuss business over dinner. Afterwards, you are cordially invited to accompany him to the Dyagilev Project nightclub, where a V.I.P. box has been reserved."

Harry stifled a groan. He knew what "cordially invited" meant—an offer he didn't dare refuse. From experience he also knew only too well what lay ahead. A vodka-fueled, multi-course feast at a 50-million-dollar restaurant that out-Versailles-ed Versailles, followed by a champagne-fueled night at Moscow's most elite nightclub—both outrageous fantasylands of such over-the-top opulence that it made your eyes ache for days afterwards.

"Please relay to Mr. Kosichkin that I am highly honored," he replied.

Grinkov nodded curtly. "I shall be glad to."

Galina, her inspection over, nodded at Grinkov. Apparently Moscow's most opulent and expensive hotel suite met with her approval.

"And now," Grinkov said, pretending reluctance, "we must unfortunately leave you. Please enjoy your stay."

"I am already enjoying it," Harry lied diplomatically. "And thank you for picking me up at the airport and having the formalities dispensed with."

"It was our pleasure."

The moment they were gone he took his Blackberry out of his pocket, shrugged off his suit jacket, flung it over the back of the nearest sofa by the marble mantel, loosened his tie, and heaved a sigh of relief. God, but he was glad Grinkov had left. The man never failed to unnerve him. And it wasn't just that blasted scar running down the side of his face. It was the quiet violence he projected.

Definitely not the type of man you ever wanted to turn your back on.

He lifted one of the bottles of champagne out of the two sweating silver buckets. How typical. Cristal. But not just any Cristal. *Vintage,* of course.

He shoved the dripping bottle savagely back into its bath of shaved ice. Christ, but he could use a drink! Grinkov always had that effect on him, but he needed to keep a clear head. This was no time to indulge in a single glass of anything alcoholic. From previous experience, Harry knew that Kosichkin would expect him to match vodka for vodka, champagne for champagne—and then roar sonic booms of delighted laughter at puny Westerners who couldn't hold their booze.

But who could, other than fellow Russians who were weaned at the teat of bottled vodka?

Idly he wondered whether they had bugged the suite before his arrival. *Probably,* he thought, then instantly revised that thought as sheer naiveté. *Of course they had.* Back in the old days, hadn't the younger, blunt-headed and peasant-faced Nikolai Kosichkin practically tangoed with the K.G.B.? Wasn't that how he'd managed to grab a huge share of gas and oil refineries in Siberia?

And old habits never died. They merely adjusted themselves to a new era, to new electronic devices, to *new money.* For these days, Moscow rocked to the beat of piles of hard currency, just as in London, New York, or Shanghai. Money here spelled *new power. Showy power.*

Blackberry in hand, his anger at having to dance to Kosichkin's tune in order to sell him yet more H-K shares fermented inside Harry, just as the 200-year-old bottle of Heritage Marie Domain Cognac, presiding over cut-crystal glasses that refracted scintillating rainbows of light from atop the gilded sideboard added to his revulsion.

Growing up amid WASP stealth wealth, the swank gaudery and sheer gaucheness grated. Enough was enough, and too much was too much. The secure rich knew when to soft-shoe it.

To calm himself, Harry crossed the plush living room to the corner walls of picture windows and looked out. Situated next to the Kremlin and Red Square, the view from the Ritz-Carlton with its palatial façade was as priceless as the suite was pricy: gilded onion domes blinding in the sunshine; masses of elaborately carved stone spires reaching heavenward to Mammon, as if praying for yet more infusions of cold hard cash. A Czarist view for the new czars: the moneyed elite, the oligarchs and billionaires, pockets flush with crisp new bills, overseas bank accounts barely able to contain their wealth. Platinum cards, bottomless checking accounts, shiny Western automobiles clogging the streets, glittering Western boutiques everywhere, the new rich switching new girls like they switched socks and stocks.

Disgusted by the overkill of ostentatious luxury—Russians had yet to learn the value of quiet WASP wealth—Harry switched on his Blackberry and started to scroll through messages, when the device emitted a bleep. He punched the telephone key, glanced at the caller ID, and gave a start.

Miranda?

Could it be? Mandy, who'd dropped out of his life like the Dow Jones Industrials upon particularly bad economic reports?

He turned his back on the whorish spectacle and nearly missed the TALK key, heard the hiss of static.

"Mandy!" he half-shouted. "Doll cakes, is that you? Jesus H. Christ, I've been trying to get hold of you for *days!*"

"Harry, yes. It *is* me."

"—been worried like *hell!* God, but it's great to hear your voice. Listen, about Tiffany. I want to explain. Sweetheart, *nothing happened!* You understand? The bitch hijacked my goddamn Blackberry—"

"Harry, that's not why I'm calling. I need your *help!*"

It was as if he hadn't heard her plea or the urgency in her tone. "I miss you something awful, babe. It's like you've left a black hole in my life. Look, right now I'm in Moscow. But I'm going to be on Samos in a couple of days. Well, damn near Samos, anyway. Did that woman —"

"Eleni? Yes. She told me you were coming."

"Isn't it great? I have some clients I've got to meet up with who have a place nearby. A goddamn private island. Christ, but it'll be good to see you."

"Clients?" she asked, above the hiss and crackle of static.

"Yeah. Some rich-as-the-SeeBees Greeks."

Something he recognized as caution crept into her voice: "Would I happen to know them?"

He laughed and began to pace the huge suite aimlessly, his mood suddenly buoyant as he traced a path from living room to the bedrooms with gilded cherubs for headboards and king-size baths tarted up in Italian and domestic marble and luxury toiletries from Bulgari. "Doubt that, sweetie," he said. "They travel in stratospheric circles. I mean, they inhabit a different universe altogether. Hell, if it weren't for my job, *I'd* never even get past first base."

"Near here," he heard her murmur, then pause. "Harry? They wouldn't happen to be named Liapsis, would they?"

He caught his surprised reflection in a beveled mirror. "How'd you guess?"

"I've met them."

"*You?*" he said in disbelief.

He couldn't realize that he'd echoed the very word in the very same tone that Big Mike had used when she'd told him she might be able to help uncover who was behind GlobaLux's backers.

"Yes, *me.*" Miranda's voice came across as snappish and acerbic. Then it gentled. "Harry, I need your help."

"Run out of cash? No problem. I'll wire you some."

"It's not *cash* I need. It's information. Harry, this is important. You're the only person I know who I can ask—"

"Wait. Hold on. I think there's someone at the door," he said irritably. "For God's sake, Mandy, whatever you do, don't hang up. Stay on the line. If we get cut off, I'll call you right back." He pressed the HOLD key, silently cursing the interruption, and went to answer the door.

Not Grinkov and his sidekick again, he wished devoutly. Couldn't they just leave him alone? They'd let themselves out, he remembered, and noticed, too late, that he'd forgotten to hang the "Do Not Disturb" sign outside the door. Stupid, *stupid!* Now he snatched it so he wouldn't forget to post it prominently.

But it wasn't Grinkov or Galina, but a frock-coated management representative. Or was it the manager himself? Harry wasn't certain, but the man wore a professional smile and an unctuous, apologetic expression. Behind him, in a massive crystal urn, stood a Mafia-size bouquet of tiger lilies, orchids, and fat roses in full bloom attached to a pair of trousered legs.

A floral arrangement more suitable for a state funeral, or some commemorative monument, he thought sourly.

"Yes?" he asked.

"I hope we're not disturbing you, Mr. Palmer," the man apologized in a smooth, British-schooled voice, "but these have just arrived for you."

Not now! Harry wanted to shout. *Take that obscene floral arrangement and shove it! Send it to a hospital, for Christ's sake. Or give it to one of the underpaid, green-uniformed policemen, or maybe to one of the unshaven cabbies driving those decades-old rattletrap Ladas to take home to their wives. Or better yet, make one of the gray, scuttling old* babushka's *day, give it to her to break down into two dozen smaller bouquets to sell on the street.*

But good manners prevailed and he stood politely aside. The legs belonged to a porter, who carried the too large floral tribute inside with an air of self-importance, and placed it carefully on the round center table of the suite's entrance hall.

The management representative or manager, whichever he was, suddenly noticed the "Do Not Disturb" sign in Harry's hand and looked appalled. "We're terribly sorry for the intrusion," he said contritely, wringing his hands in agitation. And looking past Harry, he called out something in Russian.

The porter stopped rearranging some loose blooms and hurried outside; more sincere apologies wasted yet more precious moments, and Harry hung the sign on the door handle and snap-locked the door shut in annoyance. Swiftly he pressed the TALK key again and lifted the Blackberry eagerly to his ear.

"Mandy? You still there?"

"Yes, Harry. Now *please* listen, I beg of you!"

"Are you in some sort of trouble?"

"*No!* But we need your assistance, damn it!" He could hear the passion in her voice rise, a passion he wished were directed at him. "*You* might not think it's important, but it *is!* You're the only person I know of in a position to help."

The potent scent of the floral arrangement assaulted his senses, reminded him too much of funerals, and he moved out of the hall and back into the living room.

"Can't this wait until I get to Samos?" he asked.

There was a pause, and even over the ether he could hear her take a deep breath and expel it. "Look, I've never asked you for anything, have I, Harry?" He recognized that her voice was colored with a defensive, almost desperate note.

He didn't even have to think about it. Miranda was right. Unlike most women who chased after him, she alone had never asked for a single thing—which was one of the reasons he'd been attracted to her.

Even her infuriating streak of independence, pride, and self-sufficiency was unlike that of any woman he'd ever met. She preferred bistros and inexpensive restaurants to the latest celebrity chef's culinary haunts, and resisted—even refused—most of the luxuries he wanted to bestow upon her. She was at her most comfortable in shorts and T-shirts or jeans and a sweater rather than the latest collections of high-end designers, and was as satisfied with seeing a movie on DVD and munching on popcorn at home as going out to some exclusive club. Visiting museums and listening to music ranging from opera to Cesária Évora to early madrigals was her idea of entertainment. As were the free Concerts in the Park, for which she prepared their picnics. Nor did she sleep around. She had been a virgin—a goddamn *virgin* for Christ's sake!—before she'd finally consented to sleep with him.

She was one in a million, and he knew it.

"No," he said slowly. "I don't believe you ever asked for a thing. Why? What can I do?"

"Are you familiar with a hotel chain called GlobaLux?"

"Who isn't? They specialize in building and managing resorts the world over. Huge outfit. Very secretive, too." He frowned. "This wouldn't, by any chance, have anything to do with the Liapsises," he asked, with a dark inkling of suspicion, "would it?"

Miranda's faraway voice sounded offended. "Harry, the Liapsis Foundation is the major contributor to the archeological project we're working on! They help fund us, for Chrissake! But right next to us, GlobaLux is building a giant resort. They're using *explosives,* Harry! Explosives that shake this site like an earthquake and are liable to cause irreparable damage to any possible antiquities we might unearth. The cultural damage is incalculable!"

He rubbed back his hair from his forehead. That was his Mandy . . . his *Miranda* . . . out on a white charger without a jousting stick. Still, his relief was audible. The last, the very last, thing he needed was to get on the Liapsis' shit list. But if they helped fund whatever project she was working on during her summer vacation, he figured they had to be clean. Surely there couldn't be any conflicts of interest.

"Okay, Mandy," he sighed. "So what, exactly, do you want me to do?"

"We need to find out who GlobaLux's investors are. As far as we can determine, they're all private off-shore corporations. Corporations *within* corporations. Surely you can understand how that works?"

"Only too well," he murmured, feeling a headache coming on. "You're talking about a virtually impenetrable organization. No, scratch that. You're talking about a multi-headed hydra that's invisible."

"I know, I *know!* But we need to find out who, exactly, owns those offshore corporations. The individuals. The people with names. The people with faces!"

"Mandy, for God's sake, do you have any idea what you're asking? We're a hedge fund, not a detective agency! This is the kind of setup that would drive government agencies of God only knows how many countries off the wall! Offshore investors who hide behind corporations *pay* to be anonymous! They pay dearly."

"I understand that, Harry," she concurred, but stubbornly. He could imagine the way her chin was thrust upwards.

"That's why we're stymied!" she added.

He puffed out his cheeks, then exhaled slowly, deflating them like a punctured balloon. "Then how the hell am *I* supposed to find out who they are? The whole point is that they don't want to be identified! They set it up so they wouldn't be."

There was silence at the other end. But she was still there. He could hear the quickened, frustrated soughs of her breathing, sensed her intractability. At other times, he might have admired it. Then he shook his head. No, he thought, he may as well admit it, if only to himself: he still admired it, conjuring up a mental image of a female David attempting to slay an invisible, multi-headed Goliath. Without so much as a slingshot in hand.

What utter folly, however admirable.

He glanced across the room to where his laptop waited on the ornate desk. "Alright, alright," he said reluctantly, shutting his eyes. "Tell you what. I'll call in favors, talk to certain people, see what I can find out. But Mandy?"

"Yes. I'm still here."

"I can't guarantee anything," he warned. "Don't count on success."

"I won't," she promised huskily. "And I appreciate your efforts, Harry. Really I do. Sometimes I . . ."

"You what?"

Her voice was so soft it almost didn't carry. "I sometimes think I don't deserve you."

He pinched the bridge of his nose. *Anything to win your heart, sweetheart, darling, honey bunch. Anything for love and a triumphant march up to the altar,* he thought wearily, but didn't voice.

"I'm looking forward to your visit," she added hesitantly.

"So am I. Love you," he said, signing off.

"Yes," she replied, severing the connection.

He stared at his Blackberry and inhaled deeply. "*Yes.*" Now what the hell kind of a reply was that?

[CHAPTER THIRTY NINE]

Vathi, Samos

Miranda watched Big Mike as he expertly maneuvered the Jeep into a tiny parking space on the right side of the esplanade, just down from the Tourist Police headquarters. It was a miracle that someone had just pulled out from in front of them; both sides of the two-way street lining the esplanade were bumper-to-bumper with parked cars, most of them compact, and the lanes themselves were clogged with traffic. Cars, taxis, and lorries crept by in both directions; daredevils on mopeds and rented scooters wove alarmingly in and out with suicidal dexterity and bursts of speed.

"Here we are," Mike said unnecessarily, cutting the engine and carefully chucking open the driver's side door before sidling out.

Miranda opened her door just as carefully and squeezed out to avoid hitting a pedestrian. She stood on the sidewalk and gazed about her.

It was, she thought, as if a swarm of colorful, multilingual locusts had descended. It was noisy, but there was an air of carefree festivity, and she was aware of the lack of honking horns and sirens, that ever-present cacophony of New York. Across the street, beyond the palm-lined esplanade with its lampposts and benches, the bay scintillated, silvery as fishes' scales. Children squealed and shouted and chased each other and licked ice cream cones. Elderly couples sat contentedly on the benches, watching the youngsters with tolerant smiles.

In this holiday atmosphere it was almost easy to forget Professor Hirsch's summons to the morgue, the problems plaguing the excavation, her telephone call to Harry, pleading for his help. That had been the hardest thing of all, letting Harry believe their engagement was still on.

Big Mike tapped her on the arm, scattering her guilty thoughts.

"Let's head up this way," he said, and together they strolled up the street, carried along by the current of Europeans in summer shirts and bright dresses and designer sunglasses. They passed banks and ATMs, the odd boutique, and row after row of cafés and *tavernas* whose tables and chairs spilled out onto the sidewalk from under deep, shady awnings. Nearly every table was taken. Iced *café freddos,* tiny cups of Greek coffee, and larger cups of Nescafé seemed to be the order of the day.

"Is it my imagination," Miranda murmured as they threaded their way through the throng going in both directions, "or does Greece run on caffeine?"

Big Mike laughed, teeth gleaming in the sun, and it occurred to her that it was the first time she'd heard him utter a laugh that was neither bitter nor sardonic, and it made him attractive in a way she couldn't quite put her finger on. "And don't forget Coke, ouzo, beer, and bottled water," he pointed out.

Music throbbed from the deep recesses of the cafés—techno beat from one, traditional songs from the next, DJ remixes from yet another. She glimpsed sleek designer interiors with giant, flat-screen TVs tuned in to fashion runway shows rubbing elbows with traditional Greek island decor with paper tablecloths. There was an exuberance about the mixture of the old and the ultra modern being mutually embraced, of the past and the present coexisting so seamlessly while Greece had leapt into the 21st Century. She had expected a third world, or perhaps a second world country, but she had obviously been way off base.

"Just a sec," Big Mike said. "Here's the newsstand. I want to pop in for an *International Herald Tribune.* Since we don't have a TV at the site, it's practically the only way to keep up with what's going on in the world."

He guided her into the air-conditioned comfort of what amounted to little more than a kiosk jam-packed with newspapers, magazines, and paperbacks from dozens of countries and in as many languages. Most of the Greek magazines, she noted, were shrink-wrapped, and included an inducement to buy, like a CD or a pen or some kind of gewgaw. Competition in the Greek publishing industry was obviously fierce.

Mike fished a copy of the *International Herald Tribune* from a revolving rack and paid for it. Then they were back out in the sun and heat of the esplanade.

"There's a café a couple of blocks up," Big Mike said. "We could sit in the shade and look at the paper. Or we could just people-watch."

"There are cafés everywhere," she pointed out. "I've never seen anything like it. Hey, doesn't Eleni have an outpost here?"

"Yeah, but I hate going there."

"It's that bad?" She couldn't believe it.

He chuckled. "No, it's that *good.* The trouble is, they all know me, and since Professor Hirsch and Eleni have practically adopted me and Little Mike, they refuse to let me pay. Makes me feel like a freeloader. The place I tend to frequent is up here."

He stopped in front of a rather grand waterfront building, the legend "Bank of Greece" displayed prominently on its façade. "I have to pop in here for a few minutes."

"Why not just use the ATM?"

"I've got enough cash on me. Plus credit and debit cards."

"Cashing your paycheck?"

He shook his head. "I have a safe deposit box here. There's something I have to get out of it. You want to wait inside or out here?"

"Out here's fine. I can do some window shopping at that boutique two doors down. Maybe go inside and check out the latest fashions."

"I'll be quick," he promised. "Mind holding this?" He handed her the newspaper.

"Sure. No problem."

While he went inside, she moseyed down the block and looked into the boutique window, then went inside. By the time Big Mike returned with what appeared to be a photo album, she was paying for a silky, deep red sarong bordered by a yellow Greek key design.

"Women and shops," he murmured.

"It's not for me. It's for my friend Mara, the beach bunny. If I don't bring her back a souvenir, she'll be very disappointed. Besides, the price is right."

He placed his album atop the glass counter and waited while the shop girl slipped the folded sarong into a chic little black shopping bag.

Once back outside, they continued walking northward. She glanced at the album he'd taken out of his safe deposit box.

It looked like any ordinary dime store photo album with a padded green faux-leather cover decorated in faux gold trim and, she was willing to bet, it held pages of sticky cardboard backing to hold photos in place, and clear plastic sheets that folded over them to protect the contents from dust and scratches.

She didn't ask what it contained, secure in the knowledge that it contained pictures of the missing antiquities.

A couple of blocks further up, they came to a sizeable open square. It had a large paved area open to the seaside and was enclosed on three sides by various cheek-by-jowl buildings painted in pale yellows, ochre, dusty rose, and creams. A majestic stone lion presided from atop a high gray marble plinth in the center, and four mature palms, perfectly trimmed and set back four-square, towered far above it. Around the edges, more cafés, some with awnings, some with umbrellas, did a brisk, if leisurely business. Pigeons strutted bravely all about, pecking at the cement.

"Oh, how lovely!" Miranda began. Then she gripped his arm as she glanced toward the bay. "Mike! Isn't that—"

For there it was, docked sideways along the esplanade.

The Liapsis yacht.

Three decks of gleaming Dutch shipbuilding and Italian artistry. One hundred and sixty feet of conspicuous consumption, with not a single rivet visible on the sleek white aluminum hull. Its hydraulic gangway was lowered to the quay, a thick velvet rope strung across it to deter unwanted visitors. Crew members in pristine white were squeegeeing the windows on the main deck, others were rinsing down portions of the superstructure and scrubbing the decks, still others were setting a table under the blue awning on the sundeck, supervised by a gesticulating majordomo. Sterling and crystal flashed in the sunlight.

"Yeah," Big Mike said. "It's the *Olympia II* alright. Seems like they're setting up for lunch. Wonder who they're expecting. Guess Samosapoulo gets to be a bore. Remember your Donne?"

"'No man is an island'," Miranda quoted.

"Right. Same goes for the *Olympia II* out there. Otherwise she'd be at sea."

"Speaking of Samosapoulo," Miranda said slowly, "I didn't tell you, did I, that my—" she swallowed "—my friend who's looking into GlobaLux's investors? The reason he's coming here is for a meeting with the Liapsises about their hedge fund."

Big Mike raised one eyebrow, but didn't pry. Instead, he did a swift visual sweep of the cafés and cocktail bars.

"C'mon," he said, "let's dash. See those people at that table over there?" He pointed. "They're starting to leave. Let's snag it before someone else does."

"Why?" Miranda hurried to keep up with him. "Because it's the closest to the yacht?"

"Because you never know what you might discover. It'll be interesting to see who comes and goes. Whatever you do, keep your sunglasses on."

"To avoid being recognized?"

"You got it."

The café table had four sleek rattan and chrome chairs and was shielded by a hexagonal, oyster-colored umbrella. It hadn't been cleared yet, but no matter. Big Mike indicated that they should sit facing the yacht. Miranda deposited her little shopping bag on the empty chair beside her, and he set his album on the one next to him. He started to unfold the *International Herald Tribune* when the waitress sashayed over and began clearing the table.

Miranda smiled up at her. She was a small, sexy young thing with see-saw hips, spiky maroon-dyed hair, a silver stud in one nostril and several silver rings at the top edge of each earlobe. She was wearing skin-tight, low-rise jeans and a skimpy, sleeveless T-shirt that showed off her pierced navel and the butterfly tattooed on one shoulder. Her fingernails were lacquered black and she had on high-soled wedgies, a throwback to the seventies, which were coming back in style. She kept looking over at the Liapsis yacht.

"I'll return with menus," she murmured in near-perfect English, gathering up the cups, saucers, tall V-shaped glasses and used napkins and piling them on her round tray. She wiped the table clean and went back inside the long way around, tray held high on one hand, hips twitching like they were attached to a fulcrum. Taking her time. Working hard to get attention. Eyes constantly flickering over toward the big yacht.

"Poor little trolley dolly," Big Mike said.

"Er, translation, please?"

"Trolley dollies," he explained, "are pretty young girls who pull their little wheelie suitcases along the quays, trolling places where big yachts are docked, hoping to get invited aboard. You know, to spend a few days living like the rich and famous before they're kicked back off. There're armies of 'em on the Riviera and in Sardinia, places like that. Anywhere the rich park their floating palaces. Unfortunately, Samos isn't exactly wall-to-wall mega-yachts."

"In other words, these are bad hunting grounds for trolley dollies."

"You could say that." He nodded. "And then there's Olympia Liapsis to contend with. She'd never allow one on board."

"The old man's wife? That terrifying looking woman with the Lady Bird Johnson bouffant?"

"That's the one."

The waitress returned, making a show of snapping her hips this way and that, her pierced navel winking in the sun. She set down two menus. "Would you like something to drink?"

Miranda glanced inquiringly at Big Mike. "I could use a glass of wine. Think it's too early?"

"Nah. In Beijing, it's cocktail hour."

"What are you going to have?"

"Me? A good, ice-cold, blue-collar beer. You ought to order a half carafe, though."

Miranda smiled up at the waitress. "A Samian white wine?"

The little sexpot bobbed her head. "Of course."

"A small carafe, then."

She scribbled it down on a pad. "And you?" She raised her maroon eyebrows at Big Mike.

"An Amstel." He handed back the menus and she wiggled off in slow motion, still stealing longing glances over at the Liapsis yacht.

"Back in the States," Miranda mused thoughtfully, "that girl would be jailbait. She'd also be carded any place she went. I swear she can't be a day over seventeen."

"It's different over here." Big Mike cracked a crooked grin. "You got any tatts or piercings?" He waggled his eyebrows.

Again, she was struck that he did, indeed, possess a sense of humor.

"I hope you won't be disappointed," Miranda replied primly, "but the answer's no. I don't."

"Neither do I. Tatts, piercings, and graffiti." He shook his head. "America's three greatest gifts to the world."

He unfolded the *Interntional Herald Tribune,* snapped it flat, and handed Miranda the insert.

"That section is *Kathimerini,* an Athens newspaper that's translated into English. You should find it interesting. It primarily covers headlines and stories concerning Greece and the EU. It's essential for providing local information to the foreign community."

Miranda took it and began leafing through. After a few moments, she stared at him. "But this is fascinating! Look, besides the news, they even post pharmacy hours and ferry schedules, lists of archeological sites to visit, and the hours they're open. Plus the news seems a lot more direct, say, than in the *New York Times.*"

"Yeah, it's a lot more to the point. But the *International Herald Tribune* is *owned* by the *New York Times.* It used to be a joint venture with the *Washington Post,* but they were bought out. Another thing you'll discover here is that the news on local Greek television doesn't pull any punches, either."

She tilted her head. "In what way?"

"Well, for one thing, they don't hesitate to show violence. Let's say they cover a car crash. I hope you have a strong stomach. Expect to see blood and gore. That sort of thing. All the unpleasantness they won't show on TV stateside." His tone became cynical. "Protecting us from the ugliness of life, no doubt."

They both scanned some articles. Then the waitress returned with his beer bottle and a frosted mug and Miranda's carafe of white wine. She set the beer and mug in front of Big Mike, the wineglass and carafe by Miranda, and added a cooled, sealed liter bottle of water and two extra glasses on the table, along with a tiny bowl of mixed nuts. She stuffed a thin, printed cash register receipt into a shot glass and placed it on the table, then did a kind of pirouette and sauntered around, checking on other customers.

"If we order anything else," Big Mike said, indicating the shot glass, "another little receipt goes into that glass. Want something else still? Another little receipt is stuck in. Way they keep track of orders around here."

"Sounds sensible to me," Miranda said.

"They do it all over Greece, except in the really upscale places."

Ignoring his frosted mug, he pulled at the beer bottle, his Adam's apple expanding and contracting as he chug-a-lugged. He set the bottle down heavily and wiped his mouth with a thick forearm. Then he pinched a fingerful of nuts delicately out of the little bowl and scattered them on the concrete around the table.

Almost instantly, a small army of intrepid pigeons strutted over from all directions and began to peck at them.

Here was yet another side of Big Mike that surprised her. If it had been Harry, he'd have chased the pigeons off, calling them "flying rats."

Telling herself not to compare the two men, Miranda closed the *Kathimerini* section and folded it in half and put it aside. Carefully she poured herself half a glass of white wine from the carafe. "I didn't take you for St. Francis of Assisi," she said.

"That's the best news I've heard in years. Talk about a real looney." Big Mike fingered loops around one ear with an index finger. "That guy went around preaching to *birds,* for cryin' out loud! I ask you. *Birds?* And that made him a saint? These days they'd institutionalize him."

Miranda took a tiny sip of wine, selected a nut, and popped it into her mouth, chewing slowly. Through her sunglasses, she held his Ray-Ban gaze. "I wasn't aware that you knew so much about religion."

He tossed the pigeons another fingerful of nuts. "There are lots of things you don't know."

He looked over at the yacht and she followed his eyes. Nothing unusual was happening aboard just yet, except for some waiters on the sundeck carrying out silver platters heaped with what were obviously delicacies.

"Ready to face the album?" Big Mike asked.

"No." Miranda sighed in honest reply. "But I have to. I need to know what's going on. I need to know the *truth!*"

She half-expected him to mock her, saying something smart ass like, "And the truth shall set you free." Instead, he simply nodded, folded his *International Herald Tribune,* and put it aside. He took the green album he'd collected from his safety deposit box and placed it on the table.

His voice was strangely quiet. "For the record, this is my personal album. I began keeping it after the first few pieces went missing and disappeared from the site, along with the pictures from the Prof's albums."

She was shocked. "You mean, records of discoveries and their photographs just vanished?"

He shook his head. "No, not the records themselves. Just the photographs. The register in which we list all of our finds hasn't been touched. But what good is a description and its number if an item's gone, along with its photograph? There are ways to burn away the indelible numbers with acid, or else to chip them off. Without the pictorial record, it's virtually impossible to trace what's been taken. These antiquities can easily pop up at an auction or a gallery or in a private collection with a fake provenance, and then what? We're sunk. What other proof do we have that they were unearthed here?"

"So you've resorted to keeping your own secret set of books." She nodded at the unopened album.

"That's right. It's the only way I can think of to keep track of the missing pieces. I've got several other albums, but this one's exclusively devoted to all the missing inventory, except for the first few. After those vanished, I started taking my own secret set of pictures. Which is why I keep this album locked away in a safe deposit box."

Despite the heat, she felt icy fingers, like something that had crept out from a grave, crawling up her spine. Her voice trembled. "Mike, you're continuing to frighten me."

He'd scratched half the label off his bottle of Amstel and was working to scrape it off completely. "Hell, sometimes I even frighten myself. I don't trust anyone except for Wald," he confided. "And even he doesn't know I've been taking my own set of pictures behind his back and compiling this record. For his sake. The way I figure it, it's in his best interest that he doesn't know it exists. At least not yet, or else until something can be done. If the Prof should even hint the wrong words into the wrong ears, who knows what might happen to him?"

Her face became a rigid mask. "You're afraid for his safety!" she whispered.

Big Mike shook his head. "Not for his safety." He took off his Ray-Bans and stared intently at her, his voice a near-whisper. "Miranda, don't you see? I'm afraid for his *life!*"

Miranda searched his eyes, hoping this was some sort of mischievous prank, a melodramatic joke, perhaps. But the dead seriousness of his expression told her otherwise.

He leaned close toward her, his voice so low that no one passing by could hear. "You've got to understand. Whoever's been stealing the antiquities is certainly not afraid of violence. Take the so-called 'accidents' and 'disappearances' we've had either at the site, or not far from it. The hit-and-run. Yves' 'fall' into the ravine—*outside* the fence! And now there's Angelica—"

He clenched a fist so tightly around the neck of his beer bottle that his knuckles shone white, and she was afraid the thick, dark glass might shatter.

"I hope to God that's not her in the morgue."

She sat there, immobile, shocked into silence and feeling weighed down by the freight of his words. She couldn't believe what she was hearing; she didn't *want* to give it credence. But her thought processes had slowed, creeping sluggishly like a steam locomotive pulling a too-heavy load up a too-steep incline. Her head ached and her throat felt parched. Even the trembling glass of wine that she lifted and from which she sipped, spilling droplets, seemed to have lost its flavor.

"Miranda, look," he said quietly. "We've barely met. I know I've ridden roughshod over you and that we got off on the wrong foot. I also realize saying 'sorry' is not enough."

His eyes held hers, his reflection in her tinted gray sunglasses dark images of himself.

"But for some peculiar reason," he said, "I trust you." He shrugged. "Don't ask me why. Call it instinct, intuition, or whatever. And now I'm trusting you not to tell a soul—and I mean *nobody,* not even Wald —that this album exists."

"I take it you're not just being paranoid," she said hoarsely.

"I'm certainly no conspiracy theorist, if that's what you're saying. But don't you see? I have no idea *who* to trust anymore. Am I being paranoid and imagining schemes and subterfuges? I honestly don't believe so. I just don't dare take the chance that I might be wrong. Not if innocent lives are at stake!" His breathing quickened, became difficult gulps. "If you want to know the *truth*—oh, *damn* me for my stupidity! Damn me, damn me, *damn me!*" He pounded his fist on the table so hard that the album jumped and Miranda had to grab her wineglass and his bottle to rescue them from toppling.

"Why? What did you do? You can't go around wearing a hair shirt all the time, Mike."

"Oh, can't I?" he blurted, but quietly. "Then try this on for size. The last person who saw this album—?"

He shook his head miserably, and Miranda had a queasy feeling that she knew what was coming.

"Was Angelica?" she guessed gently, feeling nausea rise at the back of her throat.

He nodded, slipped his Ray-Bans back on, and took another slug of beer from the mouth of the bottle, then let out a noisy lungful of air.

"Yeah. She didn't know it was mine, or that I kept it locked in the vault at the bank. I was sitting at my usual table up a ways." He gestured. "Sorting pictures I'd downloaded from my camera a few minutes earlier at an Internet café. I didn't even know she was in Vathi when she ran into me, gave me a hug, and pulled out a chair. Before I could stop her, she grabbed the album and started leafing through it.

She'd worked here enough summers to know what those pictures represented, and apparently she assumed the album was the Prof's. And I didn't let on otherwise."

Holding the bottle by the neck with one hand, he clawed at the rest of the moist beer label with his fingernails.

"Before I could warn her to keep silent, off she flitted to meet some friends. God only knows where, or who she ran into. That night we had a break-in at the shed, but the Prof's albums with the missing pictures weren't taken. This one, of course, was safely locked away at the bank."

He paused. "That was also the night she disappeared," he added.

"Oh, Mike! And you're still blaming yourself?"

"Who else can I blame?" he hissed savagely. "I'm assuming she must have told somebody about this album. See, Angelica was a special kind of girl. The kind who never met a person she didn't like. She had this personality that made her popular everywhere. Don't get me wrong. She wasn't like Yvette. Not a chica-chica-boom-boom party girl, but just very outgoing and genuine."

"And you never told Wald any of this?"

He shook his head. "Maybe I should have. Who knows?" He shrugged again. "The Prof's another one of those people who doesn't seem to have an enemy in the world. He always thinks the best of everybody. Meanwhile, Angelica's disappearance has been burning a hole inside me."

"Mike, it's not your fault. Stop beating yourself up. Besides, we don't know where Angelica is. For all we know she's safe and sound."

"Without sending a letter or a note or calling? No way. She was the type who was brought up to write old-fashioned thank you notes by hand. No quickie e-mails. Same with birthday and Christmas cards. She never missed sending one to everyone she knew. *Ever!*"

Miranda digested his words in silence, barely aware she was flicking away the nuts that had scattered on the table when he'd thumped it, and brushing them off with her hand for the pigeons. All around them, there was laughter and chatter, women showing each other purchases, men deep in conversation, a baby crying for attention in a stroller, lovers holding hands, people signaling to the waitress. But all that was part of another, normal world, a parallel universe neither she nor Big Mike inhabited any longer. Their world had shrunk; nothing seemed to exist outside the perimeter of their table.

"Okay," she said, taking a deep breath. "You've forewarned me. I understand the implications, but I'm not one to shirk, Mike." There was no ignoring the finality in her voice. "So let's go through this album and get it over with."

"You're sure?"

"Absolutely," she nodded. "Remember what Winston Churchill said?"

"'We have nothing to fear but fear itself'."

"Exactly. And you needn't worry. I won't tell a soul it exists. You have my solemn word."

"So you *are* aware of the dangers involved?"

"For heaven's sake, *yes!* Fully. You've spelled that out quite clearly." She lifted her chin pugnaciously. "And for your information, *Mister* Savides, I am not afraid."

His voice was soft. "You should be. Remember what you witnessed in Kusadasi. I sure hope you hid that phony boarding pass where it can't be found."

Her expression did not change. "I have, and I'm not letting anyone know where I've buried it. Not even you. Satisfied?"

He nodded.

"Now let's get on with it, shall we?"

He looked at her with a kind of admiration. "If you say so."

"I do."

Big Mike flipped the album over on its reverse side. "Let's start at the back and work our way to the front. That way you'll see the missing artifacts from the latest pictures to the earliest, when I started to keep track. You'll also notice that I've numbered and described every item, just as it was first inventoried."

She nodded soberly. "Will you stop procrastinating? I already told you. I trust Professor Hirsch with my life, and I wouldn't dream of putting him into any kind of danger.

"If it weren't for him," she added quietly, "I'd never have landed my job at Jan Kofski's, perhaps not even earned my Ph.D. I *owe* him, Mike. I owe him big time."

"Then that makes two of us."

She looked surprised. "You studied under him too?"

Big Mike nodded. "He was my mentor." He waited a moment, then said, "Okay, let's get started."

He turned the album on its back and flipped halfway through, past the blank pages. Then they came upon the first photographs. Several views showed both the front and the back sides, as well as the base, the top, and close-ups of the decoration on the vessel.

Miranda gasped, grabbed the album, and smacked the page with the flat of her hand. She didn't need to study the pictures closely, nor to read the description. "Mike! That's the *Oinochoe* from the *Meltemi II!*" Her voice broke. "The one that tumbled out of the crate they dropped in Piraeus and broke apart at my feet!"

"You're positive?" She could feel him staring at her intently from behind his sunglasses.

"I have a near-photographic memory for these things. I recognized it at once. Buffware, East Greek, Fikellura class."

He rubbed his chin as though it had developed a severe itch. "We unearthed it about a month ago," he said grimly. "What was so unusual is that it was in perfect condition. Didn't have so much as a single crack or split! It was stored in the shed for a little over a week. Then, about three weeks ago, it simply vanished."

Miranda felt a vise tightening around her temples and sought to ease it by rubbing her forehead. "And fool that I was, I pointed out to Chara Zouboulakis that it was a genuine antiquity. She claimed it was a hand-crafted museum copy. I begged to differ, but didn't pursue it because the ferries weren't running, Chara already suspected Madge and I were pulling a fast one on her by pretending to be sisters, and I was desperate to find a way to get here. If only I'd kept my big trap shut!"

"Small wonder you've run into, ah, problems," he said dryly, "eh? But it explains a lot, particularly your experience on Delos. It's obvious Chara and her cohorts were hoping to lose you."

"Yes, but what they hadn't counted upon was Apostolos Malinakis. If he hadn't been there, I'd never have caught up with the *Meltemi.*"

"So where does this put your knight in shining armor?" Big Mike wondered aloud. "On the side of the angels? Or up to his neck in smuggling . . . even choosing what items are worth stealing? Tell me. Was he aware of your expertise in antiquities?"

She knit her brow as she tried to remember. "Well, I *did* tell him I was coming here to work at Asprodavos for Wald. That much I do recall. And he said something to the effect that we'd surely run into each other again. He claims he comes here regularly."

Big Mike made a face. "Which, unfortunately, he does. But did you tell him about the *Oinochoe?*" he pressed.

Miranda's frown deepened as she thought back. "I don't think so. In fact, no. I didn't. I mean, I never got the chance. I was the stranded damsel in distress and sought his help. And he provided it."

"So it's obvious he hadn't been told about the *Oinochoe.* Someone left him out of the loop."

Big Mike was silent for some moments, looking thoughtfully into the distance, seeing the Liapsis yacht but not registering it. She could sense the wheels turning inside his head.

"So this still doesn't prove we can trust him," he said. "Personally, I never have. One thing is obvious, though. If this *Oinochoe* is the one you said it was, and I believe you, The Witch is up to his ears in smuggling. Antiquities *and* immigrants and God only knows what else. At Eleni's, you saw for yourself what friends and relatives he enjoys in high places. Friends and relatives who can help him, or at least who can close their eyes to his activities. For Chrissake, his wife's half-brother, the esteemed Dr. Theodoros Vassilakis—" he rolled the title and name on his tongue with a sneering edge "—is supposed to be in charge of *stamping out* the smuggling of illegal immigrants into this country!"

He snatched his beer off the table, lifted it to his lips to take another sip, and discovered it was empty. He held the bottle high for the waitress to see, and refilled Miranda's wine from the carafe.

"Know what I think?" he said, waiting for the waitress to bring him another.

Miranda rolled her eyes. "I distinctly remember telling you that I wasn't Sylvia Browne."

"Yeah, and you can't see dead relatives hovering like forgiving angels, or tell people they're suffering from a disease before they know it! Miranda, do not be so goddamn flippant. And don't get me wrong. I'm not trying to spook you."

"Then go ahead. Spell it out. Tell me—" she mimicked his voice as best she could. "'I think you should get on the next flight out of here.'" She glared at him. "That *is* what you were going to say, isn't it?"

He nodded and said quietly, urgently: "Yes. And I'll tell you why. You've witnessed way too much. One." He folded back his index finger. "You recognized the *Oinochoe* for what it was.

"Two." He folded back his middle finger. "Then you were hustled off the boat in Kusadasi, but you saw what you shouldn't have at Dr. What's-His-Name's."

"Dr. Babutcu," she said quietly.

"Right. And he spun you that fairy tale about your having 'dreamt' what you saw."

She watched him fold back the finger next to his pinkie.

"Plus there's that crew member—"

"Dimitris."

"Right. Who you think might have caught you red-handed swiping that boarding pass through that electronic gadget."

She sat there in silence, like a penitent listening to her sins being added up.

Next, Big Mike folded back his pinkie. "And that, of course, brings us to the *small,*" he said sarcastically, "*small* matter of the fake boarding pass with your identity that you discovered. Don't discount that. They surely must suspect you of having found it. You can't for a minute believe they didn't collect them from all those illegals when they were transferred to another boat or nearby island from that *Meltemi.*" He shook his head. "Unh-unh, no way, kiddo. Even if your Dimitris didn't say a peep, they know exactly from which cabin it was missing, and whose identity was on it. Make no mistake about it."

They fell silent as the waitress brought him another Amstel and stuck another little bill into the shot glass before wriggling off.

"Mike?" Miranda's voice was husky. "There's one last thing you should know."

He was in the process of lifting the bottle to his lips, and paused.

She took a deep, shuddery breath. "I didn't tell you what The Witch told me at Eleni's last night. Which was the reason I departed that table so suddenly."

"No, come to think of it, you didn't."

Slowly he set his untouched beer bottle back down.

"And what, might I ask, was the reason? Other than being in the company of snakes?"

Her voice quavered, but was so quiet he almost had to read her lips. "Because of what Mr. Mit . . . I mean, The Witch, told me."

He waited for her to continue.

She swallowed hard and stared down into her wineglass. Despite her sunglasses masking her eyes, there was no mistaking the misery of her expression, or the paleness of her face.

"Well?"

"He told me that Dr. Babutcu died shortly after I'd seen him." She looked up at Big Mike, her lips tight but twitching. "From a fall, he claimed. Broke his neck. Granted, Dr. Babutcu was very old. But he certainly was as spry as they come."

Big Mike set his untouched beer down and inhaled very deeply. "Shit," he swore under his breath. "Aw, *shit!* If that wasn't a warning, I don't know what is. Look, Miranda, just listen to me and don't argue."

He plucked the little receipts out of the shot glass, added up the bill, and scraped his chair back to reach into his pocket for his wallet.

"And just where do you think you're going?" she snapped stiffly.

"I'm not going anywhere. But you are."

She remained seated. "And where to?"

"The nearest travel agency, that's where. And from there straight back to the Big Apple. You're in way over your head, Miranda, whether you want to admit it or not."

Her face was pinched, but a belligerent pugnacity and strong-jawed determination shone through. She shook her head.

"No way, Mike. I refuse to let them scare me off. If you believe for one instant that I'm going to just up and leave unfinished business behind, you've got another think coming. I'm not a quitter. Get that through that thick noggin of yours. I intend to see this thing through to the finish!"

"Girl, can't you open your eyes? You wouldn't be quitting. You'd be saving that pretty skin of yours."

He might as well have saved his breath.

"First of all," she said tartly, "I'm not a *girl.* I'm a grown woman and I make my own decisions. Got that, *boy?* And second, do you think I'd be able to get a moment's rest if I just up and left?"

The sun hitting her opaque glasses echoed her flash of anger.

"Yes, Mike, I admit they frighten me. But they also piss me the fuck *off,* if you'll pardon my French. If I leave, then what? They win, goddamnit! Now drink your beer like a good boy and let's go through the rest of the album. We're wasting time."

Despite her shaking fingers, she made a show of lifting her wine-glass and taking a calm sip.

He gnashed his teeth in frustration. "Miranda, are you always this damn stubborn?"

She pasted on a sweet smile. "Always, just as you're always one ornery bastard," she retorted, putting down her wine and continuing to flip slowly frontwards through the album.

Page after page fascinated Miranda. Despite the knowledge that these items had gone missing, each one gave her a view, however limited, into the lives of the ancients:

. . . the wafer thin, tiny marble idol, almost modernistic, and obviously from Asia Minor . . .

. . . the seven-inch tall limestone figure of a Maenad, as timeless as she was graceful, her hair bound in a fillet and falling in long braided tresses as she played castanets . . .

. . . the fragment of a marble grave stele, the high relief of a boy holding an *aryballos* and gazing up, a portion of an athlete's leg just visible at the break on his right—

"Oh my God!" she croaked in a whisper and recoiled, as if from a serpent. "I know this piece!"

"You're certain?" Big Mike asked.

She nodded mutely, incapable of speech. Physically, she felt assaulted and pummeled like a prize fighter going down for the count. Something inside her had gone dead and her shoulders seemed to collapse. She knew now, with utter certainty, that she could no longer retain her pride and arrogance. She had been robbed of her dignity, her feeling of being above reproach. The photographs in front of her stared back like accusations, knocking her off her high horse.

"Where did you see it?" he prompted, his voice gentle.

She moaned aloud, still rocked by the discovery, and it was some moments before she managed to recover her power of speech. "That . . . that stele is currently in the inventory at the Jan Kofski Gallery," she whispered dully, unwilling to believe it, but knowing it to be the truth.

"You're sure?" His eyes seemed to penetrate both their sunglasses. "A hundred percent sure?"

She pecked a series of tiny, birdlike nods. "I'd know it anywhere," she murmured in a tight little voice. "It stands a hair over twenty-five inches tall."

"That's right. We uncovered it the April before last. By the following May it had disappeared."

"And it entered our inventory last September." She shook her head in disbelief. "I just can't believe Jan Kofski could be involved in the purchase of looted antiquities. It had to have come from a private collector or another dealer along with a fake provenance. Perhaps from one of the auction houses? We keep records of all our purchases, so that can be checked out. But for Jan to deal *knowingly* in looted objects is . . . well, it's absurd! Totally ludicrous!"

Yet her words sounded hollow to her own ears, and Big Mike's lack of a reply spoke for itself. Miranda shrank from what was left unsaid. It was not recognition of any voiced beliefs, mockery, or knowledge of the underground antiquities market that affected her. Rather, it was the silence in which he projected those matters; they were evident in his posture, his bland expression, his confidence, his patience.

Abruptly she thrust the album viciously sideways toward him, as though its pages contained contaminants. "Here, you leaf through it," she snapped, knowing her anger towards him was unreasonable and misdirected. "Just touching it makes me feel so . . . so *dirty!*"

"You're certain you're up to it?" There was patent concern in his tone. "Sure you want to?"

Her face flickered with pain. "No, I don't *want* to. But want and need are two entirely different things. I *need* to, Mike. I *have* to know!"

"If you say so." He flipped forward through the thick pages slowly. One, two, three—

She was beginning to feel the stirring of relief.

—four.

"Hold it! That *Skyphos!*" Her hand flew to her mouth.

"You recognize it?"

"Yes. Only too well." Her voice was small and muffled behind her fingers. "Granted, it's traditional and not all that unusual as far as *Skyphos* go, but the youths wearing himations and carrying staffs? What made such an impression on me were the traces of original red pigment that indicate their diadems. The diameter at the rim is—" she leaned sideways toward him to read the description "—12.6 centimeters. And that's exactly—and Mike, I mean *exactly*—what the one at the gallery measures! It's Attic, if I recall correctly, from around 470 B.C."

"I must say, you know your stuff."

She rejected the compliment. "Attic," she murmured, half to herself, "and yet you found it here. At Asprodavos."

"Don't forget, there was a brisk trade between the mainland and the islands, even back in those days."

She nodded, gesturing for him to keep flipping pages. His pace picked up considerably, until Miranda's hand slammed down on yet another plastic-protected sheet. "This red-figure *Lekythos! It's* in the gallery too!" She stared at Big Mike in a daze, as though the hushed, insular walls of the art galleries as she knew them were crumbling down all around. "I just can't believe this!"

"It was the best find of this early season," he said softly.

"And it's unmistakable," she replied, suddenly weary. "I remember trying so hard to identify the motif to the left of the woman, but I never could quite figure it out. I finally concluded she's approaching an altar, but I can't be certain of that."

He nodded. "That's the same conclusion I came to. Of course, we might both be wrong—"

They went flying through the rest of the pages. Miranda recognized four more pieces of pottery and a bronze figurine. Then Big Mike slammed the album shut.

"That's it," he said with finality, "at least for the missing pieces from this site. Excluding the earlier ones, before I decided to keep my own record. But you've got to remember, these particular eight pieces are from Asprodavos alone. In other words, how many other *objets* from sites all over the Aegean—hell, from all over the Med and the Middle East—might be in the Jan Kofski Gallery, not to mention all the other galleries the world over?"

His insinuation was contagious, and she sat there, numb with cold despite the stifling heat, barely able to digest completely the enormity of the ghastly discovery.

Eight pieces from Asprodavos alone resided in the rarefied, luxurious atmosphere of the Jan Kofski Gallery on Madison Avenue. Eight patrimonial treasures that she herself had studied so closely, innocent and oblivious to the fact they'd been stolen.

Eight ancient artifacts she had handled like the sacred objects they were, lifting them ever-so-gently out of the locked, carefully spot-lit glass showcases and setting them carefully down upon the revolving, suede-cushioned tables for the greedy inspection of well-fed men in bespoke suits with limitless pockets and their glossy, bejeweled, and sable-clad trophy wives.

Eight . . . *eight!*

"What I'm wondering," Big Mike murmured, "is, now that we know where those eight pieces are, how we can find out who sold or consigned them?"

Even as Miranda tried to reject Jan Kofski from collusion, even as she desperately clung to the belief that he was a duped, injured party, one of the men in white hats, she wanted—no, she *needed*—to prove him innocent.

And if he wasn't *innocent? If he turned out to be one of the men wearing black hats?*

She tried, but couldn't quash the old black-and-white Western movie image.

But this wasn't the time for speculation.

Innocent until proven guilty. Wasn't that the Great American Mantra, even if too rarely held true? But it was a thread, however thin, fragile, and temporary, tethering the fragments of her own sanity. She also had to find a way to justify, if only to herself, her own years of showing and unsuspectingly peddling items whose provenances she unquestioningly took for granted; her own guilt through ignorance. Through wearing blinders and trusting blindly.

Whatever the consequences, it was time to face them. And she, not Big Mike, was in the position of getting hold of the stolen items' alleged provenances, however faked they may be.

Time to call in another favor.

She stared into her wine, aware she was gripping the stem of the glass too tightly. Aware too that her stomach was in knots, her nerves on edge.

Another favor.

It was the last thing she wanted to ask. Assistance, obligation, an unsuspecting accomplice . . . how much could you ask of even your closest friend?

She quailed at her indebtedness adding up. Yet, for her own peace of mind, she saw no other choice.

She looked over at Big Mike. "I'll find out where they came from," she said in a haunted whisper. "I know how. I'll need to borrow that—" she indicated the album, almost knocking over her glass in the process "—and I'll need to find an Internet café. It's still early in New York. I could possibly get hold of their provenances as early as today, perhaps as late as tomorrow."

Seeing her drawn expression and tight lips, Big Mike said, "You're sure you want to do this?"

Miranda sighed. She felt young and bruised and frightened, a reluctant Pandora apprehensive of lifting the lid off the accursed box. "Of course I don't want to."

"Then?"

"I *need* to know! And I need to borrow this book of filthy crimes so I can scan those pictures and send them."

She snatched the green faux leather album from in front of him and shoved it vehemently into her shopping bag.

"Where's the nearest Internet café?" She pushed back her chair and began to get to her feet.

"Whoa!" Big Mike's hand gripped her wrist. "Not so fast."

Half standing, hands clutching the chrome and rattan arms of her chair, she shot him an odd look. "I'm not going to run off with your precious album, Mike, if that's what you're worried about."

"I'm not." He pulled her gently back down. "Remember why we chose this ringside seat?"

She stared at him, then slapped herself across the forehead and lowered herself back into the chair. "Of course. How stupid of me. The Liapsis yacht!"

She glanced over at it just as a small blue SUV with an orange dome light and a yellow stripe painted along its sides jumped the curb and pulled up alongside it, scattering tourists strolling along the quay.

"See?" Big Mike said. "A police car. So before you go traipsing off, let's finish our drinks, hang onto our front row seats, and continue our little stakeout. There seems to be some sort of activity going on over there that it might behoove us to watch. Who knows? We might learn a thing or two."

He shrugged his powerful shoulders and took another swig from his long-necked bottle.

"And then again," he added, "maybe we won't."

[CHAPTER FORTY]

Moscow, Russia

In the living room of the Ritz-Carlton Suite overlooking the Kremlin.

Eschewing the study with its massive, Imperial-style mahogany desk topped with a bouillotte lamp and world globe, Harry Palmer had opted for the corner living room where he sprawled lengthwise on the sofa with its big rolled arms, impervious to the Zhivagoesque view of cupolas and turrets and multiplicity of onion domes stacked like so many giant gilded snowmen surmounted by Russian Orthodox crosses. He had chucked his suit, and sent it down to be pressed, along with his shoes for a polish. He had then stripped down to a white T-shirt and a pair of boxer shorts that were printed with a pattern of enormous red fire ants—a gift from Miranda, who was always on the lookout for "amusing" items (like the silk tie you had to look at very, very closely in order to make out the pattern of what were actually minuscule jockstraps). Now, using one of the sofa pillows as a headrest, and his chest as a surface for his laptop, he was scrolling through his e-mail, his Blackberry on the coffee table beside him.

He opened a message from his boss:

From: T. Walter Kirkland
To: Harris Palmer
Sent: Friday, August 8, 2008 6:20 AM
Subject: Itinerary Change

Sultan's brother switched Brunei meeting to 12th. Bahrain expects you the 14th. Liapsis rescheduled for the 10th. Fly to Greece tomorrow AM.

6:20 a.m? Doesn't the old man ever sleep? he wondered with irritation, mentally echoing office lore. Christ, but he hated last-minute changes! So much for a well-planned, if sudden, business trip. Well, the front desk could rearrange his flights and lodgings.

Only then did his stroke of good luck overcome his annoyance, and he perked up, feeling a pleasurable jolt of excitement. Why, he'd be heading to Samos the very next morning instead of several days' hence! Tomorrow was the ninth, which meant he'd be seeing Miranda then—days sooner than expected!

Unlike Archimedes, Harry didn't jump up, yell, "Eureka!" and go racing naked through the streets. Instead, he contained himself and decided to message Ziggy Holmes.

Holmes, the Rastafarian computer hacker *extraordinaire* who, like Walter Kirkland, also never seemed to sleep. Who lived and hacked his free-wheeling way through life, crisscrossing the country in an RV stacked floor-to-ceiling with more hand-built computers, electronic equipment, and self-designed programs than any mobile operational headquarters of the FBI or the CIA.

If Ziggy had managed to make any progress infiltrating at least one or two of GlobaLux Hotels and Resorts' secretive investors, or was at least well on his way, it would certainly put him, Harris Milford Palmer III, in a shining light as far as Miranda was concerned.

What better gift could he come bearing?

Knowing Miranda: none.

Logging off, Harry accessed one of his several Yahoo accounts, typed in his User Name and Password, logged on, and clicked on "Mail." He entered Ziggy's e-mail address, which he knew would be forwarded through a dozen or more virtually untraceable accounts, and hit "Compose."

Harry's message was concise and to the point:

> Subject: Previous Message
> Any knowledge re: progress appreciated. Know it's putting u on the spot. Time is of the essence. Thanx.

He clicked "Send," and the hotel's WiFi sent the message out into the ether. Now to wait for a response. Knowing Ziggy's gypsy-like habit of being constantly on the move, it might take some time. Heaven knew whether he was manning one of the countless computer consoles in his rolling computermobile, or on the road in some remote spot. With Ziggy, you never could tell.

Logging off, Harry picked up the house phone and called the concierge.

"Yes, Mr. Palmer?" came an unctuous voice playing the humble servant.

"I need to change my travel arrangements for tomorrow. I realize all flights might be booked—"

"Oh, that shall be no problem, Mr. Palmer," the English-accented voice assured him smoothly, "no problem at all. If you would be so kind as to give me your choice of time, and the itinerary . . . "

Harry supplied the necessary information and hung up, secure in the knowledge that the concierge would move heaven and earth to accommodate the occupant of the Ritz-Carlton Suite and, more importantly, pull all the necessary strings for a guest of Mr. Nikolai Kosichkin. Even if flights were overbooked, Harry could rest assured that a First Class passenger of lesser importance would be bumped.

If he felt a twinge of guilt, it didn't take up much space in his mind. Experience had taught him that a handful of select few at the pinnacle of the global financial pyramid, representing a thousandth of the one percent of the world's wealthiest men and women, wielded enormous power and privilege—and always got their way.

Clearly in Mother Russia, and other parts of Europe, Asia, and the Americas, Nikolai Kosichkin ranked among the few, the proud, and the extremely pampered who inhabited the very, very tip of the moneyed iceberg.

Money talks, bullshit walks. Apparently here in Russia, money did not talk. It shouted, screamed, no, *blared* as if from megaphones mounted on rooftops.

An ormolu clock softly chimed the half-hour. Snapping his laptop shut, Harry left it on the sofa, swung his legs over the edge, got up, and stretched mightily. He idly scratched his crotch, as if the fire ants on his boxer shorts were alive and biting with their sharp, stinging mandibles.

It was time to decide whether or not to call Miranda. Inform her that he'd be seeing her on the morrow—

As if he didn't have enough on his mind as it was!

—or perhaps not to call? That was the question. To simply show up and surprise her?

Decisions, decisions.

Nervously, restlessly, Harry pondered his choices and prowled the suite. *Accommodations for the new czars with their plundered wealth, and their honored guests.* Living room, master suite the size of a typical American ranch house, but with a panoramic view overlooking Red Square where, eleven stories below, a crowd of Burberryied, Cartiered, and Vuittoned army of tourists, toting video cameras and photography-equipped cell phones were oblivious to the inevitable Communist-era pensioners and stooped gray *babushka*s scuttling about unnoticed. Master bath the size of a Manhattan studio, complete with sauna. Powder room, music room with a goddamn grand piano in case, he thought sourly, a pianist and a fat lady showed up to sing. Study with its ormolu-mounted furnishings and white, Louis XVI-style marble mantel. Dining room-cum-conference room; several connected hallways skirting the outside perimeter of the L-shaped suite to ensure ultimate privacy. *Accommodations for the new czars with their plundered wealth and their honored guests.*

The overkill of the New Russia grated. He half expected to see a collection of priceless Fabergé eggs. Where was Lenin? Still in his tomb, on view behind his glass coffin, below in Red Square?

Not that he knew, or cared.

A discreet knock on one of the hallway doors interrupted his aggravation. Opening it, he found himself face-to-face with an impeccably uniformed porter holding aloft his freshly pressed suit, sheathed in shiny plastic in one hand, and his gleaming black shoes in the other.

Harry instinctively felt for his wallet, encountered his ridiculous boxer shorts, and gestured the man towards the master suite while he went to get his wallet from the living room.

If the porter noticed his strange boxer shorts, he gave no indication, though Harry was certain it would inspire some below-the-stairs gossip and hee-haws.

Well screw 'em, he thought, handing over a handsome tip.

After the porter let himself out, Harry deliberated the wisdom of uncorking a bottle of Cristal . . . or better yet, hitting up one of the refrigerators for an ice cold Stoli. Then he decided that either choice was a very bad idea. An evening with Nikolai Kosichkin, with the ever-present Alexandr Grinkov and whatever function Galina served—not to mention a small army of burly, impeccably clad, and armed-to-the-teeth bodyguards, stayed his hand.

He had enough to deal with concerning Miranda, not to mention the alcohol-fueled evening ahead. How the Russkies managed to mix booze and business was beyond him.

For his own part, the more sober he remained, the better.

So he headed back to his laptop to see if Ziggy had squirted him a reply.

[CHAPTER FORTY ONE]

Vathi, Samos

"That," Big Mike said, hand wrapped around the neck of the beer bottle and pointing with an index finger, "is Captain Pispas." He pronounced it "Pea-pa."

Miranda's eyes registered a rather short, plump man with a thick black moustache and a uniformed chest thrust out in self-importance as he slammed the driver's side door of the police SUV and stood on the quay, hands clasped behind his back as he surveyed the gleaming white yacht with evident longing.

"And, unless my eyes deceive me," added Miranda in a surprised voice as she watched the passenger emerge stiffly from the other side, "that's Professor Hirsch!"

"They must have come from the morgue. The hospital's just north a little ways, up beyond the breakwater and the Customs building." He nodded at the concrete arm extending into the bay, where the *Meltemi II* had docked and she had disembarked. "It's maybe a ten-, fifteen-minute uphill walk, where the road narrows and curves."

"But it's been several hours, surely, hasn't it? Mike, if they went to the morgue directly from the site, surely Wald would be back at Asprodavos, wouldn't you think?"

"Perhaps there was paperwork to fill out," Big Mike said bleakly, rubbing his face with a meaty hand. "The police station's between here and the hospital."

She looked at him sharply. "That's assuming it *was* Angelica, you mean. What other reason would they have? Why don't we just pop across the street and ask?"

Once again, she began to push her chair back, disturbing a pigeon that had been pecking the cement near her feet. It rose with an indignant flutter of wings, swooped a semi-circle over some umbrellas, and landed nearby. And once again, Big Mike stayed her hand.

"Not so fast, Wonderwoman," he breathed.

She tried to read his expression behind the Ray-Bans, but his face had turned into an impenetrable mask.

As if, she thought, he regretted having let down his guard and was covering his emotions with macho posturing, or regretted permitting Miranda a glimpse of his personal feelings toward Angelica—dedicated, work-consumed, beautiful, missing Angelica. Head tilted, the pigeon eyed her warily from a few yards away, then strutted forward with dignified purpose.

"Don't get me wrong," Big Mike muttered almost angrily, his work-roughened thumb scraping at the moist Amstel label. "I admire your gumption. Nothing like a get-up-and-go attitude. But if there's one thing you learn at an archeological dig, it's patience. Hardly a virtue, but a little more surveillance can't hurt. But let's become a little more invisible, huh? Although with these crowds I doubt we'd be noticed."

She disliked the idea of spying and possibly being spied upon. "Come on, Mike! It's not like we've got anything to hide! We're not committing any crime by sitting here, are we?"

He didn't reply, but snatched up the *International Herald Tribune* from the chair beside him, the snapping of the paper like a rustling caution as he held it up and peered around it with one eye. Following his lead, Miranda ducked forward over the table, as if inspecting her wine for a speck of cork, her eyes raised and alert as she gazed over the frames of her sunglasses.

At the Liapsis yacht, a broad-shouldered security guard in a lightweight blazer came bounding down the hydraulic gangway to unclip the heavy velvet rope. He held it aside like the doorman of an exclusive club while the promenading tourists on the esplanade skirted the parked police car and slowed down, like the traffic on the clogged two-way street, to rubberneck.

Captain Pispas sketched a magnanimous, almost mocking, flourish for Professor Hirsch to board first. There was a short verbal exchange and some gesticulating on both men's part. As Miranda watched, her frown deepened. The professor seemed reluctant, and looked about furtively, scanning both lengths of the esplanade with what appeared to be discomfort, nervousness, even guilt.

"For some reason," she murmured slowly, "I get the feeling it's almost as though he'd rather not be seen. I can't imagine this is the first time he was on board, the Liapsises helping fund the dig and all."

"No. But he only socializes with them when the occasion requires it. Like that dinner at Eleni's? If you recall, he stayed carefully in the background and didn't mix."

Her eyes slid sideways. "Do you think he's acting this oddly because he's not anxious to be seen with Captain What's-His-Name?"

"Pispas?" Big Mike shook his head. "I seriously doubt it. The guy's a fawning, unlikeable little bantam, and it's no secret he's got his sights on becoming prefect. But the Prof gets along well enough with him. He has to. Being foreigners, we're in no position to make enemies with the local cops."

For one long moment, Professor Hirsch turned his gaze toward the crowded square. Miranda froze like a rabbit caught in a set of oncoming brights, and had the distinct impression that he was looking directly at her and Big Mike.

She held her breath, feeling a flush of shame at being caught spying. "Do you think he made us?" she mumbled penitently, barely moving her lips.

Just then a gaggle of giggling, miniskirted and halter-topped girls from Prague or Kiev or somewhere in that region skipped by on sandaled feet, shielding them from sight.

"I doubt it," Big Mike replied out of the side of his mouth.

Then Captain Pispas was placing a proprietorial hand on the small of the professor's back, obviously urging him aboard.

"He looks resigned," Miranda observed, watching him ascend the incline of the gangway, Captain Pispas strutting pompously behind, like one of the pigeons in the square, both becoming black shadows against the great porthole-studded hull. The security guard clipped the velvet rope back in place and remained just outside it, presumably awaiting other arrivals.

On the main deck, a pretty hostess in a white blouse welcomed the guests aboard and led the way aft, then showed them up an elegantly curved, teak-and-chrome set of stairs to the awning-shaded sundeck. There, both men remained standing, Professor Hirsch gazing northwest at the spines of mountains on the other side of the bay, each distinct range decreasing in color, from green to olive to gray and on to lighter, bleached shades of blue as the mountains sloped into the water. Captain Pispas strode around a large round table, inspecting the place settings, lifting a piece of silver cutlery and squinting closely to read the brand name stamped on the back.

"Tacky, tacky, tacky," Miranda whispered in reproof. "Is he the type you have to hide the silver from if he visits?"

Big Mike gave her a crooked grin. "Maybe. But not if you're a guest of the Liapsises, you don't."

Captain Pispas was just replacing it when a small group burst out on deck from inside an air-conditioned lounge.

"Here come the usual suspects," murmured Big Mike.

The group was led by Yannis Liapsis, wearing big black Onassis-era glasses, with Olympia, his Ladybird Johnson clone of a wife at his side.

"Word has it the old man's suffering from macular degeneration," Big Mike told Miranda. "Flies to Paris several times a month for eye injections. That's why he has to wear those big, ugly glasses in bright light."

The senior Liapsises were followed by Leonides, the handsome heir, and his anorexic wife, who wore what looked like a sprayed-on little designer number that emphasized her painfully skeletal frame. Then, strolling arm in arm, came Dolly Vassilakis and Jan Kofski's third, but possibly not last, wife. And making up the rear were Theodoros Vassilakis and Jan Kofski, deep in conversation.

"What I wouldn't give to be a fly on the wall," Miranda murmured.

"Count your lucky stars you aren't," Big Mike murmured back. "Flies aren't tolerated aboard the *Olympia II.* Candles, spray, crew members with swatters—you wouldn't last half a minute."

Miranda pulled a face. "In that case, I'm glad I don't have wings." She changed position, raising her head but holding her wine glass in front of her. Big Mike turned a page of the newspaper and folded it in half so he could peer over the top. Both kept their eyes on the mimed skit being enacted atop the sundeck.

Old Liapsis had detached himself from his wife and was greeting Professor Hirsch with a Zorba-worthy hug, then acknowledged Captain Pispas with a curt, dismissive nod. The heir shook the professor's hand. The women exchanged air kisses with him and permitted Captain Pispas to shake their limp fingers.

With one exception. The senior Mrs. Liapsis, who sent him a cutting look and made a point of realigning the piece of cutlery he had been examining. That done, she stalked to the railing, glanced up and down the esplanade with irritation, and consulted her bejeweled wrist.

Someone who was expected was obviously tardy.

Turning around, she rejoined the group, said something, and gestured elegantly at some lounge chairs. The men waited until the ladies were seated. The majordomo hovered. A small army of stewards produced bottles and poured glassfuls.

"Ah, here comes the missing party," observed Big Mike tartly, as the security guard adopted the mantle of traffic warden, shooing pedestrians aside so that the familiar, beetle-black Mercedes SUV could jump the esplanade's curb and park smack dab behind the police car.

"The rolling broomstick has arrived," he added dryly.

Miranda recognized the lean, narrow-faced driver from when The Witch had arrived at the *Meltemi II.* Jumping out, he opened the rear door. From within, a thin, elongated hand imperiously sought his. Then one stiletto-heeled leg emerged from the interior, followed by the other, and the driver helped beaky, rail-thin, stork-legged Despina Mitropoulou out onto the esplanade.

Oblivious to the staring pedestrians—or playing to them, it was difficult to tell which—she tossed her hair, pulled on the hem of her tight, 60's-style Pucci shift, made minor adjustments, and headed to the gangway like a shark slicing through water. Diamonds at throat, ears, and wrist flashed in the bright sun.

Now it was the security guard's turn to help her as she clutched his shoulder while doing a balancing act first on one foot and then the other as she took off her slingbacks before boarding.

Spiked heels, like trolley dollies and flies, were evidently *verboten* aboard the *Olympia II.*

The velvet rope was whipped aside for Despina, then clipped back into place. The security guard remained at his station.

"Despina *without* The Witch?" There was mockery in Big Mike's voice. "Remarkable."

But Miranda, whose peripheral vision had caught half a dozen of the square's incensed pigeons suddenly bursting skyward, quickly averted her head and elbowed him sharply in the ribs.

"Don't look now!" she hissed. "Turn your head to the left."

For despite his dark sunglasses, she had glimpsed the unmistakable Farouk-like figure of The Witch, wreathed in blue cigarette smoke, angling across the square. Not so much walking, nor huffing and puffing, as floating grandly, swift as a gondola, on light, small feet. Corpulence defying all laws of gravity. Tiny lips pursed, pink face newly shaven, multiple chins overlapping the starched, pale lemon collar and key lime silk tie.

Miranda held her breath as Nikos Mitropoulos sailed past within arm's length, overlooking them as he carelessly tossed away his cigarette and made a beeline for the yacht.

"And now," muttered Big Mike, "the coven's complete."

Miranda finished off her wine.

"Perhaps this explains Professor Hirsch's reluctance to board? Because he was forewarned that The Witch would be there?" she suggested.

"It's no secret that the Prof avoids him like the plague," Big Mike agreed.

"There you have it."

"Only—"

She glanced at him sharply. "Only what?"

"The damn thing is, the Liapsises *know* how the Prof feels about The Witch, and they've always respected that. So why, and more to the point, *how,* could Pispas have hustled him on board?"

"Maybe because the captain has clout?"

Big Mike stifled a laugh. "That bumbling operatic fool? I doubt that. Not with the Liapsis crowd, he doesn't. They could squash him like a bug and have him transferred to the Bulgarian border with a snap of their fingers. He's only tolerated, you could see that from the way they greeted him. Hardly with open arms. More like a pesky fly."

Meanwhile, under the canopy of the sundeck, the comedy of manners continued to be played out. Big Mike watched it with obvious contempt; for Miranda, who only dealt with this set of people on a professional basis, it was like viewing an updated parody of a Noël Coward play.

The men stood and exchanged air kisses with the newly arrived Despina, slingbacks in hand, who smiled widely, made apologetic gestures, and sparkled under the attention. Professor Hirsch accepted his kisses stoically, but did not bother to return them. Then Despina made the rounds, bending down to blow extravagant kisses past the seated ladies' cheeks. A steward pulled up a lounge chair and she sat and accepted a flute of Champagne, raised it in a toast, and sipped, chatting animatedly.

The men duly took their seats.

Definitely a social animal, that Despina, Miranda thought to herself. *Unquestionably in her element.*

Below, on the esplanade, the strollers, and now The Witch himself, had yet another obstacle to contend with. Two of the three Tatoulis Brothers—Miranda recognized Philippos and Nikitas, two of the three supposedly Cerbereans taking turns guarding the gate into the Site at Ancient Asprodavos—along with a short but rather pretty middle-aged woman with orange dyed hair who Miranda took to be their sister, had staked out an area directly in front of the small police SUV, effectively barring the gangway to the yacht, where one of them had flung down a straw hat, primed with bills and coins, on the paved sidewalk. There they had begun their act of juggling yellow tennis balls, first two each, then four, then six, then eight apiece. Bouncing them off their elbows, shoulders, hands and knees, before tossing them with effortless dexterity back and forth amongst each other. Never dropping a one, as though their vertical and diagonally elliptical orbits were governed by a planetary theorem.

Miranda found their mastery of the act mesmerizing, the balls like multiple hypnotists' charms swinging back and forth before her eyes.

A small crowd of onlookers had gathered round the performers, creating a further bottleneck. There was a smattering of applause, and from between the spaces of passing cars, Miranda could see the glint of occasional coins being tossed into the basket, the clinking sounds obliterated by the noises of traffic, voices, and distant music.

From on high, Olympia Liapsis investigated the commotion, rising from her seat and coming forward to lean over the sundeck railing.

At the edge of the curb below, The Witch waved two lemon-sleeved arms up at her and did a helpless pantomime. She shouted something down to the guard, and he elbowed a path to the gangway, but not before The Witch produced a crumpled handful of paper currency from a pocket and tossed it, with *noblesse oblige,* into the hat.

"Generous," Miranda said, "don't you think?"

Big Mike grunted in reply. Then, like the sea responding to an ocean liner displacing thousands of tons of water, the crowd parted and The Witch cruised on through, waiting for the guard to catch up and remove the velvet rope. That done, he sailed up the gangway, exuding the dignity and grandeur of a pasha. Reaching the sundeck, he took both of Olympia Liapsis' hands in his and flattered her with effusive air kisses.

She accepted them as her due, but eyed him severely, ready to rebuff him. But he had come prepared, and produced a tiny box from his pocket and handed it to her with an air of contrite solemnity.

Instilled manners precluded outright rejection of his gift. Miranda watched as Olympia lifted the lid, then she saw one perfectly manicured hand fly up to cover Mrs. Liapsis' mouth. There was no mistaking the wide-eyed surprise and pleasure, the attempt to put up a weak argument. Miranda could almost read her lips: "For *me?* You really shouldn't have! Really, I cannot accept this!"

But of course she could, and he indicated so by pressing a finger to her lips and shushing her. Currying favor, *earning* favor.

Or Brownie Points, thought Miranda.

Slowly, almost reverently, Olympia Liapsis lifted out a small object and held it up to the light. Something gold and sapphire glinted expensively in the sunlight.

The Witch said something, took it from her and, like a prospective bridegroom, slipped it smoothly onto one of her fingers.

A ring.

He stood back proudly, tiny pursed lips smiling. From where she was seated, Despina emanated equal pride and largesse, like a male peacock trapped in a female peacock's body, spreading its invisible fan of multi-hued feathers.

Despite herself, Olympia Liapsis was not without feminine vanity. She stretched out her hand to admire the bijoux at arm's length. Moved her hand this way and that. Again, but even more half-heartedly, she tried to deny the gift, but The Witch was adamant, and she finally gave in. She held his big pink baby face in both hands and kissed him warmly on each cheek.

No mere social air kiss, this: the kiss between friends. Close acquaintances. Or perhaps coconspirators?

Any further, ever-weakening protests earned deprecatory gestures from The Witch: *It is nothing. A mere bagatelle, just a throwaway trinket . . .* and in the blink of an eye he and Despina had shot from near the bottom rungs of the Liapsis social pile half a ladder higher. Tardiness was instantly forgiven; blessings bestowed.

Leading The Witch by the hand, Olympia pulled him toward the seated others to show off her bounty. The ladies leaned forward to examine her finger and cluck over it, their expressions a mixture of surprise, awe, and patent envy. Captain Pispas' eyes shone with greed.

"Diamonds," Miranda mused, "are not necessarily a girl's best friend." She slid Big Mike a swift sideways glance. "Was that an aquamarine or a sapphire?"

He shrugged. "How would I know? All I caught was a flash of blue. Dark blue."

"A sapphire, then," she said thoughtfully. "It looked awfully big, even from here. Quite a gift, don't you think?"

He shrugged. "For the likes of you and me, yeah. Among that circle? I really couldn't say."

On the esplanade, the Tatoulis trio had exchanged their tennis balls for more dramatic props: domestic pots, pans, and skillets. The cluster of onlookers had grown. Children stared in wide-eyed wonder or shrieked with joy. On the street, cars headed in both directions had crept to a crawl, the drivers' attention diverted by the circus act.

Miranda turned to Big Mike. "Do you," she asked in a hushed tone, "see what I see?"

He cast his eyes out upon the esplanade. "What? That third-rate circus act scrounging for Euros?"

"Mike!" She couldn't keep the irritation from creeping into her voice. "Will you please, *please,* drop your cynicism for once and open your damn eyes?"

He took her sharp voice as sufficiently reprimanding. "They *are* open!" he objected.

"Then tell me what you see."

"I see jugglers," he said wearily. "And they're not exactly top-of-the-line, are they? Otherwise they'd be tossing chainsaws or some other sort of lethal devices."

Miranda sighed in despair and blew stray strands of hair out of her eyes. She massaged her temples, as if ridding her forehead of frustration. "In that case, I'll let you in on what *I* see."

"Which is?"

"Two or three juggling brothers and their sister doing their act. And if they're that good—and admit it, Mike—they *are* good. Not one of them has dropped so much as a single ball or a skillet—"

"—which would *hurt,*" he said, in a vain effort at humor.

Miranda ignored his attempt at levity. "Well, the brothers take turns guarding the gate at Asprodavos. Right?"

"Right," he said slowly, keeping his eyes on the juggling act: pots, pans, and skillets flying ever higher and faster.

"So how do *you* think the missing items are smuggled out? If everyone, including Professor Hirsch, is thoroughly searched at the gate? In shopping bags? *Laundry bags? Garbage?* Come *on!*"

He drew a long, deep, whistling breath. "Well, I'll be damned! They've got to be tossed over the chain-link. Probably at night, by whichever brother is on duty, and one of the others, maybe even the sister, catches it outside."

"Bravo, Watson!" she said, applauding softly. "And they were foisted upon you by the Ministry of Culture. You told me so yourself."

He dropped the newspaper on the table, put his head in his hands, and shook it. "God, I must be dense. Or blind. Or both! And here I've seen them perform their *innocent little act—*" he used an ironic tone as he gestured accusingly toward the jugglers "—on and off, and never even made the connection!"

"Mike, will you stop beating yourself over the head?" Miranda said kindly, giving his arm a gentle squeeze. "You're neither dense nor blind. Remember, you've been here from the very start. Maybe it's just a case of not being able to see the trees for the forest. Sometimes it just takes a fresh eye."

He turned his head sideways and looked at her with respect—or was it admiration? With his Ray-Bans on, she couldn't quite be sure which.

"Say, Doc," he cracked, only half in jest, "are you always this smart?"

"Oh, yeah," Miranda said sarcastically, unconsciously glancing at the pale band on her ring finger. "That's why my personal life is in a shambles."

She scooted back her chair.

"I think we've seen enough of that *farce* being enacted on the boat," she declared. "Besides, it's time I went to that Internet café. I need to scan the photos of the missing pieces I know are at the gallery and e-mail them to Mara in New York. Besides Jan Kofski, she's got the only sets of keys to the place, not to mention the alarm code and the combination to the safe. It's practically a bank vault, and that's where all the inventory is stored over the summer. It's also where all the paperwork is. Then I'll call her, and after she's checked out the provenances, I'll have her e-mail them to me. Even if they are faked."

Miranda gave him a significant look.

"Which," she continued, "I'm willing to bet my life on they are. Now, where did you say this Internet place is?"

"In the narrow street behind this square. On Kapetan Lachnia, which runs into Kapetan Strati. They run parallel to the esplanade. That's where all the shops are. Butcher, baker, appliance stores, opticians, jewelers, antique dealers." His lips formed a humorless little smile. "Who knows? Maybe even a candlestick maker."

She waited as he totaled up the scrunched-up little bills from the shot glass, stuck a twenty Euro note under it, got up, and tossed down some extra coins from his pocket.

Miranda rose too, shouldering her leather bag and snatching the shopping bag containing Mara's sarong and the green album off the chair beside her.

"I'll take you there," Mike offered.

"You don't have to do that. I'm sure I can find it myself."

"It's no problem," he assured her. "Especially since I'd rather avoid this stretch of the waterfront."

"Because you don't want to risk being seen from the yacht, is that it?"

"That's right. And besides, it's not exactly out of my way. A few blocks further up, I'll cut back out to the esplanade."

"So where are you off to?" she asked as he guided her away from the waterfront, turning their backs on the circus act and the huge yacht, and heading diagonally towards the back of the square.

"I'm going to the morgue," he said grimly as they passed in the shadow of the majestic white lion atop its gray marble pedestal.

"The *morgue?*" She stopped short, her eyes, behind her sunglasses, enormous. "But why? Wald's already been there. He'll tell us whether or not it was Angelica."

"Because," Big Mike said softly, looking away, "I need to see for myself whether or not it's her. Don't ask me why. Call it morbid, but I have to satisfy my own curiosity. If it *is* her, it's the very least I can do. The very least she deserves."

"Does this mean you don't even trust Wald anymore?"

He was silent for a moment. "Sometimes, only seeing is believing," he said.

She inhaled a deep breath and studied her shoes as he stood opposite her. She took off her sunglasses with her left hand, held them by the stem, and looked up at him. "But why put yourself through extra heartache? Aren't there enough problems to deal with?"

"I'll say. But there are some things one can't shirk."

She shook her head. "You seem to have a strange sense of duty, Michalis Savides, as well as your own honor-bound set of values," she said.

A faint kind of smile touched his lips. "I believe the same can be said of you."

She looked up at the lion. From this close, standing at the base of the pedestal, she could only see the top half. Then she looked back at him. "Don't you trust anybody?" she asked directly.

"Myself," he said quietly. "And for some weird reason, I trust you. Don't ask me why."

She was silent.

"We both have something in common with him." He nodded up at the stone lion and she followed his gaze. "Call it instinct, intuition, or whatever. But neither of us are mice."

She looked away, not wanting to meet his eyes. "You flatter me. Not that it'll get you anywhere."

He shook his head. "One thing about me, Miranda. I never flatter. Nor do I expect flattery to get me anywhere. I just call it as it is."

She was silent for a moment, uncomfortable with the turn the conversation had taken. Things were getting too heavy, too personal, and too fast, for her liking.

Her voice was brusque. "Mike, we both have things to do. Me at the Internet café and you at the morgue."

She began walking briskly, and he fell into step beside her. They didn't speak until they had reached the narrow, shady shopping street.

He'd been right, she noticed. Unlike the cafés and *tavernas* cramming the waterfront, this was the commercial heart of Vathi. Greengrocers, boutiques, shoe stores, and yes: the butcher, the baker, but no candlestick maker. A few blocks further on, he stopped.

"This is it." He indicated the INTERNET sign jutting out above their heads. "I'll leave you off here and meet up with you later in the square. Unless you need help."

She allowed herself a small smile. "I think I can fend for myself."

He shrugged and she watched as he continued on, his tread suddenly heavy, his hands thrust inside his trouser pockets, his shoulders hunched forward. Something inside her told her to let him go; yet something else compelled her to catch up with him and clutch his arm.

"Mike!"

He turned to her in surprise.

Her voice was soft. "Mike, are you certain you don't want me to go to the morgue with you? Nobody should have to endure that alone. I'll be glad to accompany you."

He chucked a gentle finger under her chin. "Don't worry about me. I'll be fine." And added, with bravado: "Hey—I'm 'Big Mike.' Remember?"

"But how will you get in? You can't just waltz into a hospital and ask to see a body."

"I know someone who works there. I broke my arm last summer, and made friends with the doc who set it. We meet for a beer every now and then. On occasion, he and his wife invite me to dinner. You don't need to worry about me."

And yet, she *did* worry. For beneath his tough guy exterior she sensed a vulnerability he worked hard to suppress and keep hidden. It was his armor against the world; the force field from which the zircon in the rough let the hurtful arrows of life bounce off.

"Just . . . well, take care."

She didn't know where her next words sprang from.

"And remember," she said throatily, meaning it. "I'm here for you. Anytime. Okay?"

He nodded gruffly. "And you take care too," he said abruptly, and continued on.

Miranda stared after him for a few moments, then retraced her steps and entered the air-conditioned chill of the Internet café. The room smelled strongly of ether and was long and narrow and silent except for the hum and buzz of multiple computers and the tap-tap-tap of keyboards. It was elbow-to-elbow with young people, foreigners and locals alike, all hunched over rows of work stations. Checking their e-mail. Logging onto various Internet sites.

A thin, vivid, green-eyed young woman was behind the counter.

"A scanner?" she replied to Miranda's question. "I am afraid we only have one, and it is currently being used by one of the local students. Many Greeks cannot afford their own computers, you see. It should be available in twenty or thirty minutes if you do not mind waiting. If you wish to take a seat, I can get you a coffee." She smiled. "At no charge."

"I don't mind waiting," Miranda said, not that she had much choice. "And a coffee would be lovely, thank you."

"I shall get it from next door. Which would you rather? Nescafé or an iced *café freddo?*"

Miranda chose the *freddo* and settled in to wait.

[CHAPTER FORTY TWO]

Westhampton, New York

If her mother could see her now.

Fortunately for Mara, the widowed Mrs. Jankowicz was safely ensconced some twelve hundred miles south in her Miami Beach highrise, oblivious to her daughter's sleek tanned hips arching up to meet her latest conquest's pelvic thrusts.

"Oooooooh, *yeah,* baby!" Mara cried out. "Harder! Give it to me! Faster! Come on! *Faster! Harder!*"

Stu, the muscled young lifeguard astride her, scissored her legs further apart with his knees, took a deep breath, and determined to make yet another home run.

The curved white wooden headboard hammered a quickening drumbeat against the wall while Mara whipped her head ecstatically from side to side on the sweat-drenched pillow, both hands forcing Stu's head even further down, the better to suck and nibble on her right nipple even as his fingers kneaded her bruised left one.

If there was one thing Mara excelled at, it was sex.

"Yeah, big guy!" she cried. "Oh, *yeah!* That's more like it! Come on, plunge! *Plunge!*"

As his thrusts sped up, the headboard slammed faster and faster against the wall, banging up a storm.

Somebody in the bedroom next door—Tami most likely ("that's Tami with an '*i*'" as everyone was told upon meeting her)—began to pound on the other side of the sheet-rocked wall with her fists. "Keep it down, willya?" the muffled voice yelled. "Some of us are still trying to get some goddamn sleep!"

This beach rental, like so many of the Hamptons shares, had paper-thin walls. Cheap, like everything else in the house: its construction, its finishing details, its furnishings—except that it *was* on the beach in Westhampton.

Stu stilled his movements for a moment. "Think we're making too much of a racket?"

Mara's eyes narrowed into dangerous slits. "No fucking way, José. You nuts or something?"

"But—"

"Aw, forget Tami. She's just a jealous bitch. Probably cranky since she didn't get any nookie last night." She attempted, but failed, to suppress a wicked giggle.

Only now did it vaguely occur to Mara that, judging from the sunlight leaking in through the closed vertical blinds, it had to be around eight in the morning. And this was what? The third—no, the *fourth* time since she and Stu had hit her mattress. The guy was a maniac, a fucking sex machine!

Dismissing Tami's jealousy, she got back to the business at hand.

Stu continued pounding away with abandon, his breath now coming in short, noisy bursts, his sweat raining down from his over-exerted body.

"Ahhhhh!" he growled. "I'm so close to comin'! Oh, babe! I can't hold back much longer!"

Mara gripped her steely thighs tighter around his firm buttocks. "Oh, oh, you sly thing!" she exclaimed, feeling a ticklish buzz in the small of her back. "You devil you! Why didn't you tell me you stuck a vibrator under my back? Oooooh!"

Stu suddenly stopped thrusting, raised himself up on his elbows, and frowned at her with genuine confusion.

"Hey!" she pouted, feeling his engorged member twitching inside her. "Why did you stop?"

He elbowed aside the sweat dripping from his forehead. "'Cause I don't know what the hell you're talkin' about, babe. What vibrator? Think I need fuckin' sex toys to function? Yo—" he held both arms stretched out sideways while slowly continuing to thrust, giving her an eyeful of his buff pecs and convex six-pack. "You got yourself a livin', breathin', fuckin' sex machine!"

"Indeed I do." Mara smiled up at him and ran an admiring finger from his breast bone down to his navel and yet further down to his nest of honey-colored pubic hair, all the while wriggling her back, the tingling vibrations feeling so good and *nice.* So *sexy.*

With a snarl he dug a hand under her, groped around, and slid her tiny cell phone from beneath her.

She stared at it. "God *damn!*" she murmured, then burst into peals of laughter. "You mean I was lying on my phone all this time? Jeez, I've probably got Motorola tattooed all over my back!"

He scowled, not amused. "Look, babe," he grumbled darkly, "I sure as hell hope you're not gonna answer that."

In reply, she snatched the phone from his fingers. Self-centered young stud that he was, *she* knew—and more importantly, *he* well knew that sex headed her list of hobbies—and sublime youth that he was, she could still broaden his limited carnal horizons from here to Timbuktu.

With a flick of her wrist, she flipped the phone open and checked the caller ID.

Miranda. *Miranda?* she thought, instantly revising the carnal horizon from Timbuktu to Athens and exotic points beyond.

"C'mon, Mara," Stu cajoled. "Johnson here is all hot to trot. You're not gonna actually—"

"I have to," she said, "but *you* don't have to stop."

She punched the TALK button and held the phone to her ear. "Miranda?" she said in disbelief. "Miranda—is that really you?"

"Mara? Mara—thank God I caught you! Look, I know it's still early there. I'm not catching you in the middle of anything, am I?"

"Of course you are! Girl, interrupted, so to speak." Mara giggled, raising her pelvis to Olympic heights so that she was balanced on mere shoulders and toes—take that, all you Bulgarians and Chinese gymnasts! "Why do you think I—oh, oh that's so *good!*—come out to the Hamptons? For a *tan?* There are parlors all over Manhattan for *that.*"

"Mara, *stop it!*" Miranda's voice was peremptory and high-strung, taut and pleading despite the vast distance, the hiss and crackle of constant static. "Will you please *listen to me?* I wouldn't be calling if it weren't an emergency! I need your *help!*"

"What kind of emergency?"

Stu tuned out, keeping up slow, steady thrusts, though at his age, when he couldn't go into a liquor store without getting carded, a hard-on was never much further than just a handshake away.

"Mara, this is *serious!*" Miranda blurted into her ear. "I need you to do something. You're the only person who can help!"

"Miranda, what *is* it? Are you in trouble?"

"Look, if you don't help we're *all* in deep shit. You, me, Jörg, Phil, Rena, Gita—all our careers will be down the drain."

Her voice faded in and out. "Mara—don't you *understand?* We'll be *ruined!* We'll have become *pariahs!*"

Something in Miranda's urgency made Mara take notice. She flattened a moist palm over the mouthpiece. "Take a break, Stu. This is important."

She pushed him gently aside, and nearly moaning with agonized, unrequited orgasm he slid out of her and slumped sulkily down beside her. The mattress bounced with seismic aftershocks under the impact of exasperated weight. Now she sat up straight, alert.

"What kind of deep shit are you referring to? Miranda, do you need money?"

"No, I do *not* need money! I need *help!* Do you have your laptop with you?"

"Since when do popes shit in the woods? Come on, Miranda, you know I never leave home without it."

"Good. As soon as I hang up, check your e-mail right away. I've scanned some photos and—"

"Dirty pictures, I trust?" Mara teased hopefully.

"Mara, Mara—*please!* This is no time for humor! This is *not* a lark!" Miranda's desperate voice drifted in and out over the airwaves. "Now listen, Mara. Please, *please* listen carefully. First, check your message and the pictures. I even cc-ed myself as well as several others, just in case they didn't come across or—" The voice at the other end trailed off.

"—or what? Miranda, has all that Greek sunshine and heat gotten to you?"

"No! It hasn't! But there's a serious situation here that's too complicated to explain over the phone, or even in e-mails. Believe me, Mara, if there were anyone else I could call or trust, I wouldn't be bothering my best friend. Damn it! You have *got* to do this!"

"You still haven't explained what I'm getting myself into," Mara persisted. "What the hell is going on over there?"

"I can't get into that now. But you'll need to print out the photos. If you can't do it from your laptop, head to the nearest Kinko's. *Then* go to the gallery."

"Please tell me you don't mean Kofski's?"

"Yes! Of course I mean Kofski's!"

"Oh, *shit!*"

Mara leaned wearily back against the headboard and shut her eyes. She saw Catherine wheels spinning round and round, planets orbiting far too fast around a blue, cloud-covered planet, Betty Boop doing a cartoon dance while holding down her poppy-red skirt demurely in a sped-up film. Her head was starting to throb from drinking too much the night before. Plus smoking those joints they'd passed around at the party. They *had* to have been laced with something. How else to explain the endless sunflowers bending this way and that in opposing winds, the Pacific breakers curling to spend themselves crashing upon a distant rocky shore, or having the sensation of a space shuttle docking at the International Space Station while Stu had been thrusting in and out?

She shook her head to clear it of the images and opened her eyes, then regretted it the instant she squinted against the blinding slivers of sunshine sneaking in through the vertical blinds like a Bertoia sculpture composed of pure light.

"Mara! *Mara*—are you still there?"

"Yes. Look, Miranda, is this some kind of practical joke? You've got to be pulling my leg. I mean, leave Paradise and my stud to go all the way into *Manhattan?*"

"No, this is *not* a joke, Mara!" It was a desperate, demanding wail. Then softer, her voice quickening, Miranda continued: "I'm dead serious. You're the only one who has the keys to Kofski's and knows the security code for the vault. I explained what you have to do in the e-mail. Once in the vault, check the pictures carefully against our current inventory. Make certain the items at hand are the real McCoy, not just first class fakes. And if they are the genuine article, which I believe them to be, compare them with the pictures I sent, jot down their provenances—this is *essential!*—and e-mail that information back to me. Do not, I repeat, do *not* phone. I might be out of range. Or God only knows who might be within earshot!"

"Miranda, aren't you're starting to sound just a bit paranoid? Like you've discovered who assassinated J.F.K.? Or where the Lindbergh baby is?"

"Believe me, Mara, I am not paranoid. Just do as I say. *Please!*"

"And just when I'm in the middle of hot sex!" sighed Mara heavily. "Girl, you really know how to make my day. And you know what these Hamptons shares are like. You have to take advantage of every second. Do you have any idea what this is costing me?"

"I have a very good idea," Miranda added, with a touch of asperity, "since you've told me a thousand times. That's why I didn't join you. But you can't put a price tag on what I'm asking you to do. Our reputations are at stake!"

"I still can't imagine why this is so important," Mara mumbled. "Is all of this really necessary, Miranda?"

"I already *told* you—*yes!* It's extremely important!"

Despite her aching head and the remnants of whatever she had ingested, Mara knew that Miranda wasn't one to blow things out of proportion. What she was saying had to be true. Of all the people she knew, Miranda Kalli was the last person on earth to qualify as a drama queen. She never cried wolf. Nor was it in her best friend's nature to ask for a favor—even the smallest favor—unless it was vitally important.

At last Mara exhaled a long-suffering sigh. "Hold on a sec, Miranda, will you?"

Mara covered the mouthpiece of the receiver once again and turned to Stu. "Hey, Big Boy. How'd we get back here from that party in East Hampton last night?"

"I borrowed my friend's Boxter. The silver one with the top down and your mouth in my crotch the whole time?" He looked hurt. "Don't tell me you can't remember?"

"How could I forget?" Mara murmured, and found that she did remember, now that he'd jogged her memory. They'd sped recklessly along curving back roads, the radar detector on, the trees flashing phosphorescently past in a psychedelic blur while—well, while she'd done things which would have made her mother's hair stand up straight.

Now, tracing a strategic finger down his chiseled body to the nest of crinkly hair surrounding his extremely well-hung member, she murmured, "Stu?"

He lifted his head a few inches off the pillow and looked at her. "Yeah?"

"One good turn deserves another. Right?"

"Yeah?" he frowned. Stu wasn't the brightest star in the firmament, but when it came to sex, Mara inevitably chose brawn over brains—her major shortcoming.

"Well, it seems I'm in need of a good turn," she said softly.

"Then just spread your legs, babe."

"I'm talking about a different sort of good turn."

"Like what?"

"Like, I need a lift into the city. Just in and out. It won't take but a few minutes, and then we can be back out here and pick up where we left off. What do you say, stud? Hmmm?"

He stared at her as if she'd lost her mind, and she noticed his pupils were still dilated.

"Drive into the *city?*" he echoed. "In this summer traffic jam? You got any idea how many hours each way'll take?"

She put the phone down beside her, tightened her grip on the base of his cock with one hand, licked the palm of her other hand, and rubbed the wet hand in slow circles around the bulbous head.

He groaned with a mixture of agony and ecstasy.

"So what do you say, Big Boy?" she said sweetly.

"Why *now?*" Stu asked hoarsely, back to full arousal, his engorged cock straining and twitching under her expert ministrations. "Can't it wait until we finish?"

"Oh, we won't be finished for a long time." She gave his thick, reddish-purple shaft an extra squeeze. "Do you think I'm ever satisfied? Besides, when's the last time you met a girl who'll do the things I do?"

"Uh, well—"

"*Plus,* I'll be extra nice to you once we get back. Show you some things you never even dreamed of."

Stu's eyes lit up momentarily. Mara was one hot chick, that was for sure. Probably the hottest he'd ever had the good fortune to encounter. He expelled a long-suffering sigh. "Oh, alright!" he said. "But you better make it worth my while. And be extra nice for sure."

"Don't you worry, Big Boy. Mama will take real good care of you. Besides, what we did tonight?"

"Yeah?"

"As they say on Broadway, that was just the preview. Wait until the premiere! Now, the sooner you're ready to roll, the sooner we'll be back."

He started to swing off the bed and she gave him a resounding smack on his cute bubble buns.

"And ditch your boxer shorts," she added. "You never know how we may have to pass the time in traffic."

Picking up the phone, Mara said, "Miranda? You still there?"

"Yes."

"Okay. Gotta dash. I'll e-mail you as soon as I have the skinny."
"Mara?"
"What?"
"I caught some of that. You really are shameless, you know that?"
"Absolutely!" Mara said cheerfully, "anything for a friend!"
And that said, she snapped the phone shut.

[CHAPTER FORTY THREE]

Vathi, Samos

Time is the scientific measurement of the earth's revolutions.

But *tempis* does not always *fugit.*

There are occasions when it seems to slow down completely, such as when a driver sees an oncoming vehicle on an obvious head-on collision course.

So it seemed to Miranda, who had stopped watching the red second hand creep sluggishly, rather than sweep grandly in circles inside the casing of the black and white wall clock in the Internet café. Too, she had ceased to register the ever-so-tiny, jerky shivers of the black minute hand that also seemed to sneak almost furtively forward at an excruciating snail's pace. She had even stopped consulting the Swatch watch on her wrist.

"The watched pot never boils," had been one of her mother's favorite axioms, and as Miranda waited for the student to finish scanning his material, and then, after almost an hour, to sort his file, print out hard copies, and tap out some messages, it seemed that a lifetime had passed.

The girl at the counter had been extremely apologetic, explaining that there used to be two scanners, but that the other was in the shop. Anxious as Miranda was, she'd lied and assured her that yes, of course she would wait and that it was no problem and yes, another *café freddo* would be most welcome, and thanks so much for the magazines.

Finally the student was finished and it was Miranda's turn. The process proved slow and tedious, requiring the careful removal of each photograph and description of every missing item from the album, scanning them individually, sending them all to her own personal computer back in New York as well as to Mara and, for good measure, another copy to her next-door neighbor, Ron aka Lotta Puss, and yet a fourth one (she wasn't quite sure what possessed her) to Harry—not to mention the tedium of placing each and every photograph and description back into its exact spot in the green album.

Now, leaving the Internet café a good two hours and three *café freddos* (on the house) later, a glance at the wall clock proved that *tempis* had indeed *fugit*ed.

Outside the Internet café, with Big Mike's album tucked safely back inside the boutique's chic paper shopping bag along with Mara's sarong, and with the strap of her leather bag slung over one shoulder, Miranda turned right on the narrow, shady street and quickened her pace. Big Mike would be waiting, no doubt impatiently, at one of the cafés on the square. She knew he would be anxious to retrieve his album so he could return it to the security of his safety deposit box in the bank. Plus, *she* needed to hear, hopefully, that the body at the morgue hadn't been Angelica's, after all.

Heaven alone knew how long he'd been waiting for her to show up by this point.

She hadn't gone five steps when—

"Miranda!" she heard her name called out. "Miranda! My friend!" Pronounced, of course, "Me-rahn-dah!"

That inimitable frog-croak of a voice was instantly recognizable and could only belong to one person, and she froze. And there he was —the very last person on the planet she wanted to see—effectively blocking her path and looming gargantuanly in front of her. She noticed he'd loosened his lime-green tie and unbuttoned the top two buttons of his starched, lemon-yellow shirt, which looked the worse from wear and heat, the armpits stained dark with perspiration.

Her heart sank. Just her rotten luck to run into Nikos Mitropoulos, known behind his back as The Witch of Samos!

The ends of his tiny, pouty, cherubic lips were curled upwards in a smile indicative of surprise and sheer delight, and before she knew it, he tossed down his cigarette and engulfed her with toad-like arms, smacking little nicotine-tinged air kisses past both her cheeks.

Fighting to resist her revulsion, and stifling a sigh, Miranda subtly rearranged her features into a semblance of the friendliest smile she could muster.

"Why, hello!" she greeted him with the falsest cheer she could summon. "Or should I say *Kalispéra?*"

"A 'hello' from a beautiful young lady is quite sufficient," he assured her with oily smoothness. "But what are you doing in town, Miranda? Are you not supposed to be sifting through dirt, rubble, ancient ruins? Are you not supposed to discover something grand and great and worthy?"

It was all she could do to make out that garbled Greek accent, mingled with another Middle Eastern language that she still couldn't for the life of her place. She also noticed that within the fatty pouches, his sharp, dark eyes registered exactly from which storefront she had emerged.

Stick as close to the truth as possible, she warned herself. *Don't give away more than absolutely necessary.*

"I should be at Asprodavos, yes," she found herself babbling nervously. "But this morning the *meltemi* was kicking up a fuss, so a colleague insisted I should see some of Vathi. So I took the opportunity to check my e-mail and do some shopping. I was anxious to get some souvenirs for friends back home while I had the opportunity."

"The meltemi, yes. It was blowing quite strong."

Get moving! she told herself. The green album in her shopping back seemed to emanate heat, and she had the sensation that the string handles were burning stigmata into her fingers.

Keeping the album from him was imperative.

Politely disengage yourself. Big Mike is waiting, and the last thing you need is to be trapped by The Witch, that conscienceless trafficker in humans and stolen antiquities.

"I fear it is too late to take you on a tour of the pottery factories where we make museum copies, which I had promised you," he was saying, with a little pout. "Well, another day. However, you must visit my shop. I insist. It is just a few doors down."

"I . . . I'd love to," she protested, "but I really must join my friends." She cast a worried glance at her watch, aware of its economical plastic while his wrist gleamed richly with heavy gold. "The way I've been loitering and getting distracted, I'm certain they'll be anxious about my whereabouts by now."

He gave a throaty croak of a laugh and gestured, the ruby cabochon on his finger shining like a great bubble of blood. "But you are on *Greek* time! Surely they will understand."

Before she realized what was happening, he had taken her arm, turned her effortlessly around, and was steering her skillfully through the pedestrian-choked traffic and back in the direction from which she had come. Shoppers and tourists alike gave them a wide berth, such was his air of self-assurance and belonging as a man of substance—as well as his substantial girth.

"You see?" He pointed a nicotine-stained finger. "There it is, only eight shops down on the left. The one with the yellow awning? I promise you that you will be dazzled."

And so she permitted herself to be led reluctantly forward, too weary, and too aware of the futility of uttering further protests. As they approached the scalloped awning, she noticed that the lettering was in English:

The Midas Touch Fine Jewelry

And he *had* been right. She *was* dazzled. Floored. Rendered absolutely speechless. For here were no discreet Cartier or Harry Winston windows displaying a solitary breathtaking gem. On the contrary. Here the exact opposite held true. At The Midas Touch, discretion was obviously not the better part of value.

Behind the thick, polished plate glass on both sides of the open door, from which the chill of a high-powered air conditioner blasted luxurious cool air out into the narrow street, there lay a king's ransom: diamond and emerald necklaces on headless velvet busts, hundreds of bracelets dangling from horizontal velvet cylinders. Gold bangles. Jewel-encrusted Byzantine crosses. Earrings and ear studs. Stepped velvet row after row of rings set with precious stones of all sizes. Rubies. Sapphires. Diamonds. Emeralds. Cluster rings. Dinner rings. Wedding bands of all widths. Jewels fit for a maharajah and a maharani . . .

Miranda had the feeling that Ali Baba's cave had been emptied and was spilling forth to tempt the vanities and greed of one and all.

"Oh, that is nothing," rasped The Witch, gesturing unctuously toward the open door. "There is much more inside. And directly across the way is my wife's shop. Despina specializes in museum copies of Ancient pottery."

Miranda turned to look. "Oh, but I'd love to see them!"

"And so you shall, once Despina returns," he lied smoothly. "She will be only too happy to show you. Unfortunately, at the moment she is out inspecting the pottery factories."

You mean, she's still sipping Champagne aboard the Liapsis yacht, Miranda thought, keeping her lips zipped.

And then his pudgy hand in the small of her back was already propelling her inside the jewelry shop. It had several burled walnut counters of Rolls Royce quality topped in glass; the walls were lined with burled walnut wall cases with glass fronts and mirrored sides and backs bursting with yet more treasures. And everything, everywhere was multiplied by mirrors.

Mirrors.

They covered every surface save the glass tops and fronts of the cabinets and the white marble floor and had, Miranda gathered, been installed not just to propagate the sheer vastness of the hoard, but for security purposes. In each direction she turned, she caught multitudinous reflections of herself, and reflections of her reflection decreasing incrementally in size, to infinity. It was almost dizzying, this jewel box-cum fairground atmosphere, this blinding, glittering bazaar where everything was indeed truly gold.

The furniture, on the other hand, was minimal. This was, after all, a shop, and the furniture consisted of a mirrored desk in an alcove topped with nothing but a velvet blotter, a magnifying mirror, and a jeweler's loupe. There were two delicate white French chairs for clients —the various styles of Louis the This and Louis the That having escaped Miranda's education. A third, and currently unoccupied high-backed throne, obviously reserved for the proprietor, presided from the far side of the desk.

"As you can see, it is only a small shop," said The Witch with false modesty.

Indeed, it became apparent to Miranda that it *looked* much larger than it actually was, with all those mirrors expanding the space.

"I have several other such shops," he continued, his huge chest bursting with pride. "Two on Santorini, one each in Fira and another in Oia, and a large . . . how do you say, flagship—?"

He raised his plucked eyebrows inquiringly at Miranda.

"Yes, flagship store." Miranda nodded, her eyes here, there, everywhere, unable to resist looking at all these riches.

"Yes, the flagship store. It is in Kolonaki, in Athens. Then there is my most successful one on Mykonos, several minor ones on various cruise ships of a certain quality."

"I'm dumbstruck!" Miranda said truthfully, staring around. "I didn't know there were this many jewels in the world!"

"*Ach,* this is nothing!" A gold tooth at the back of his mouth flashed as he laughed. "My shops are mere fleas, not even specks, compared to most others, although my prices are much better. You must remember, Me-rahn-dah, that men and women have been adorning their bodies since time immemorial. First with flowers, then with metals and stones. Now, if you will be so kind as to take a seat for a moment, and I can relieve you of your burdens—"

He reached for her shoulder bag, but she held on to it.

"I really do have to meet my friends," she protested. "I'll be glad to return another time. I'm fascinated, truly I am. I never had any interest in jewels before, but the vast array of colors and tonalities is enthralling!"

"Oh, come now." He tilted his head, his little mouth forming a moue of vast distress. "Just five minutes is all I ask. Besides, I desperately require your help!"

She didn't think she was hearing correctly. "*My* help?"

"Yes. You see, there is a certain necklace I designed, and I simply must see how it looks against a person of your complexion. It is a small favor, surely?"

"But you must have plenty of beautiful women to test it on!"

"No, no, *no!* You do not understand." He shook his head and his multiple chins wobbled as he slid out one of the client chairs and held it for her to sit. "I see I must explain. What you do not understand, my dear—I may call you 'my dear?'"

He waited for her nod and a tiny smile.

"You see, jewels, especially colored stones, reflect their wearer's personalities. What looks dazzling on one skin tone and works with a certain coloring of hair and eyes can look *terrifying*—" his eyes grew wide with horror and he threw up his hands and shuddered dramatically "—and ghoulish, or washed out, on another. I simply do not dare test it on a potential client. She, or she and her husband both, would be speechless and go running, and I would lose a sale and they would never return. I pride myself on my repeat clientele. Please?" He placed his hands in a prayerful position against his tiny lips.

"As a small personal favor?" he pleaded.

Hearing it put that way, she found it difficult to resist. Besides, the jewels beguiled and conjured up long-forgotten Cinderella fantasies from her earliest childhood. And, she rationalized, since she'd kept Big Mike waiting this long, what was five minutes more?

She sighed. "Alright," she said, perching on the edge of the chair and letting him relieve her of her shoulder bag. She set the shopping bag containing the album down between her legs, protecting it tightly with her ankles and knees. "Five minutes."

He smiled his gratitude, produced his cell phone with a flourish, flipped it open, spoke a few words in Greek, then snapped it shut.

"I was calling for the necklace to be taken out of the safe and brought here. It is only a minute or two away. Meanwhile, the least I can do for your troubles is offer you some refreshment. One moment."

Before she could demur, he touched a wall and a cleverly concealed mirrored door to what she assumed was a tiny washroom equipped with an under-the-counter refrigerator slid smoothly, soundlessly aside. He bent down, breathing heavily, and produced a chilled bottle of Champagne and two stylish, nubby goblets of thick ruby glass.

"Really, you mustn't open it," Miranda said. "It would be such a waste."

"On a beautiful young woman like yourself? Besides, I need to fortify myself. If the necklace does not go with your skin tone . . . I have tried it on various ladies, you know . . . and it was a disaster. A disaster! Yes, I need some Champagne to calm my nervousness."

"Well, just a tiny bit, then."

He peeled off the foil, untwisted the wire, and expertly thumbed out the cork. It didn't go flying, nor did the Champagne gush out. He half-filled her goblet, then his, and took a seat on his throne-like chair behind the desk.

"To the necklace, I pray," he said, raising his Champagne in a toast.

She lifted hers and sipped. "Delicious!" she pronounced.

He started to lift his to his lips, then set it back down and leaned across the blotter as though something had just occurred to him. "Oh, I was meaning to ask you the other night, Me-rahn-da. On your short Oracle cruise. You *did* receive two souvenirs before leaving the *Meltemi,* I hope?"

Careful, she cautioned herself, seeing a potential minefield stretching in front of her, and with herself in the middle. *This has got to do with the second boarding pass I discovered.*

"Well, I still have my boarding pass, if that's what you're referring to. Ms. Zouboulakis kindly told me I might keep it as a souvenir. Why? Should I return it?"

"Oh, no, no, no! Of course not!" Another shake of his fleshy head.

"It is a traditional parting gift on all our cruises. But that is *all* you have as a souvenir? Just that *one* boarding pass? Nothing else?"

She was, Miranda realized, being gently, but nonetheless seriously, interrogated.

"No," she said, "that's it. And it's plenty. You'll be happy to hear that as soon as I settled in at Asprodavos, the first thing I did was to prop it up prominently on the shelf beside my bunk in the women's dormitory. Rosie, who's our unofficial den mother, was quite impressed and envious."

"Really?"

"And I'll treasure it always as a reminder of Sounion and Delos and that blue-black sea."

"Just the *one* item?" he murmured, as if to himself, and shook his head once again.

His face had assumed that distressed expression he seemed able to summon up at will, but his eyes were focused inward, and were unfathomable.

"Just your boarding pass?" he repeated. "That is all?"

"Isn't it enough?" she countered, wishing she'd resisted his efforts to bring her into this Ali Baba cave of riches. Wishing she hadn't let herself be so easily trapped.

She took another sip of Champagne. It was more than delicious. The bubbles tickled her nose and burst on her palate. It tasted out of this world. And he hadn't had a sip of his yet.

"Aren't you having any?" she asked.

"In a moment." Then his face abruptly brightened. "*Ach!* Of course!" He clapped himself on the forehead. "You disembarked early! How thoughtless of me. The T-shirts had not yet arrived at that point."

"T-shirts?" she blinked.

"Yes. I personally designed them and had them specially ordered for our passengers. Blue, with the Oracle Cruises logo on the front and with "Oracle Cruises" printed prominently across the back. I intended them to be distributed before the cruise. A small marketing ploy, to be sure."

He produced a slightly shameful smile, which instantly faded.

"Unfortunately," he went on, "they had not arrived from the manufacturer in time. The other passengers shall receive theirs when they disembark in Piraeus." Again, he assumed that look she remembered so well from the dinner at Eleni's, as though war had been declared. "But you do not have yours!"

"Please. There is no need to concern yourself."

"But of course I must! Why, yes! How could I have forgotten? I have several here somewhere."

He pushed back his throne, touched the mirrored wall panel again, rummaged through a box atop the small refrigerator, and uttered a little cry of triumph. "*Ach!* Here they are! You shall now get your second souvenir of the cruise. Your size?"

"If they're unisex, I'd say a small. Or better yet, an extra small."

"Yes. Here is one!"

Holding the shirt in its plastic sheath, he closed the mirrored door, returned to the far side of the desk, and slid the T-shirt out of its protective cover. Remaining standing, he unfolded it on the blotter, carefully smoothing the folds along the front with his manicured, sausage-like fingers.

"What do you think?" he asked. "Too garish?"

"Not at all. I love the color. True Aegean blue, is it?"

"You noticed!"

"And it's quite tasteful. Not at all what I'd have feared."

He beamed, then his little lips turned down in a frown. "Alas, the back," he sighed, "is not quite as tasteful. Tell me your honest opinion, Me-rahn-dah. Do you think it is too garish?"

He flipped it around and again smoothed out the folds.

"Well," she said truthfully, "there's no mistaking it's an advertisement for Oracle Cruises."

"Too blatant, do you think?"

"Well, quite honestly it does shout a bit. But on the other hand, I'm certain the passengers will be delighted. I know Madge and the New Zealand nurses shall wear theirs until they fade. If they wear them at all, that is."

He looked perplexed. "But why shouldn't they?"

"Because some people would put them away as keepsakes. But if you hand them out at the *beginning* of the cruise, I'm willing to bet they'll wear them everywhere they go."

"Blatant . . . hmmm . . . I must make a note of that. Decrease the size of the lettering, you think?"

"That all depends upon when you hand them out. I'd say keep it as it is and use it as a boarding gift."

"You see?" he trumpeted. "I knew from the start that you were a lady of extremely good taste. And more importantly, a very clever one."

She took another sip of bubbly while he carefully refolded the shirt, slipped it back into its plastic sheath, and proffered it to Miranda with both hands.

"Now," he smiled, "you have your second souvenir. "It should fit into your shopping bag."

She accepted it graciously. "I'm flattered. Really, you needn't have. But thank you ever so much."

She parted her knees and calves and hoisted the shopping bag onto her lap, pressing the album and sarong to one side to make room for the T-shirt. There wasn't much space, but if she was careful, there could be just enough.

And that was when two things happened simultaneously.

Someone entered the store carrying a slim, rectangular, silk-covered box. And as Miranda tried to add the T-shirt to the chic little shopping bag, the paper ripped apart diagonally with an angry tearing sound, spilling its contents onto the white marble. Miranda let out a little cry of distress. The Witch hurried around from behind the desk to help gather up the items. And yet another female visage joined the multitudes of Miranda's, fracturing her own infinity-mirrored face. Before she could even absorb the true extent of her calamity, she did a startled double-take. The other face had the high forehead and the patrician nose, but definitely not the expressionless stare of Bronzino's famous portrait of Eleanora of Toledo.

There was only one other face like it, and it belonged to none other than Miranda's nemesis, her very own *bête noir.*

Chara Zouboulakis in the flesh, bringing along with her an invisible cloud of Hermès' Calèche.

"Ms. Kalli!" The heavily accented voice was unmistakable. So too was the smooth, shiny, waist-length black hair, perfectly parted in the center; the impeccably proportioned model's body with legs that went on forever; the flawless, radiantly bronzed and expertly made-up face, and the short, Dolce & Gabbana, ruffled, one-piece dress. And, as Chara's gaze eyed the three items from the torn shopping bag scattered on the marble, even more unmistakable was the flash of sheer horror that crossed her face and killed off the last resemblance to Bronzino's famous portrait as she actually recoiled.

For, most damning of all, Big Mike's green album had fallen open to the very page of the *Oinochoe* that had shattered at Miranda's feet in Piraeus.

Chara Zouboulakis stared down at it in white-faced panic.

Miranda felt her heart stop beating and the universe collapse.

The Witch seemed to take it all in stride and squatted to retrieve the open album. He closed it, in the process managing to flip through some of its pages.

He seemed unperturbed and handed it back to Miranda. "*Ach!* Some of my potter's best work! Despina will be well pleased. You must show her these."

Miranda, glued motionless to her chair, was too speechless and appalled to respond. She accepted the album, the sarong, the T-shirt, and the fiction without a word. How The Witch could be nothing but the very picture of unruffled calm was beyond her.

He turned to Chara as he rose heavily to his feet. "Oh, do put the necklace on the desk, Chara, will you?" he said in English. "And please find Ms. Kalli a larger shopping bag. It's the very least we can do."

Chara, still pale despite her bronzer, was startled into action. She slid the silk box guiltily on the desk, and squeezed between the desk and The Witch and opened the concealed mirrored door.

From inside came the riffling sound of fingers sorting through a pyramid of shopping bags.

"Now, for the necklace," The Witch said in that smooth oily voice. "You must tell me what you think, Me-rahn-dah. Truthfully. Is it too pale for someone of your complexion?"

And so saying, he pressed the latch of the exquisite silk box and the lid sprang open.

Miranda gasped. So too might Marie Antoinette have. Nestled inside on a concave curve of black silk was the most magnificent necklace she had ever seen. A single row of perfectly matched, pale yellow diamonds descended into a row of slightly larger stones, and that row into one of larger stones still. There were ten rows in all, ending in a pear-shaped pendant the size of a thumbnail.

"Canary diamonds!" The Witch whispered reverently into her ear, each word a nicotine-tinged puff of warm air. "Each one flawless and GIA-graded by the four C's. Carat, color, clarity, and cut. One hundred and seventy-two carats in all! The pendant alone weighs twenty-two carats."

"I gather it must be worth a fortune!"

"Oh, it is. But that is not the point."

He lifted it gently from its nest of silk with both hands and held it up for her inspection. "Exquisite, is it not?"

She nodded speechlessly, at a total loss for words.

"Now turn around, face me, and bend backward. Then we shall see how it works with your complexion."

She did as he asked and he held it against her and frowned.

"Perhaps," he said, "and again, perhaps not. There is only one way to tell. If you look away from me and bend slightly forward, we shall see."

He went around behind her and clasped the ends together. For something that looked so warm and fiery, the diamonds and their settings felt cool and heavy against her flesh. Slowly she raised her head.

"There!" he said. "Now we shall see!"

He moved the magnifying mirror from the side of the desk so that it rested directly in front of her and tilted it just so in order for her to see herself. Then he himself stepped back, crossed his arms, and tilted his head to one side to observe the effect.

"What do you think?" he inquired thoughtfully, rubbing his uppermost chin.

Miranda's hand moved up to the necklace as though of its own volition. "I don't know what to think," she whispered. "It's beautiful! And the staggered effect of the rows—I'm really at a loss for words!"

"What concerns me," he said gravely, as though nothing of consequence had occurred only a minute before, "is how it blends in with your complexion. The stones are radiant, but yellow is such a difficult color. What we must judge is, do they enhance your beautiful complexion, or do they overwhelm it? Do they need a more swan-like neck, or not? Fine jewels, you understand, must always enhance and never detract. If a piece of jewelry is not exactly right for a person, I refuse to sell it. It is a matter of honor."

Miranda didn't know why he was telling her all this. Or why it was so necessary for him to judge the diamonds' color against her complexion. But then, what did she know about jewelry? With the exception of Harry's engagement ring, she'd never worn anything fancier than a discreet gold necklace or bracelet, and then only to the gallery or to one of Harry's favorite expensive restaurants or parties, when he asked her to dress up.

"Well, Me-rahn-dah? What do you think?"

Miranda raised her head, looked away from the magnifying mirror to the mirrored wall at the far end of the desk, and turned her head this way and that. She fingered the precious ice and then let her hand drop into her lap. It was easy to imagine, she suddenly realized, how wearing such a necklace could make one feel ultimately superior, and could give the wearer a feeling of power, lifting her high above the ordinary masses.

And something else, a fact she had never before considered. Fine jewels were a *drug*. They altered one's perception of oneself much as she imagined cocaine must. It was something she hadn't understood until now, and it came as a revelation, making her want to rip the necklace from around her throat. But for politeness' sake, and propriety, and long experience understanding the difficulty in being behind the sales counter, she stifled her feelings.

"And you?" she asked him, her eyes drifting from the mirror over to him. "You are the expert. What is your professional opinion?"

"I am still not certain," he murmured. "Perhaps with a low-cut gown of a certain shade of blue . . . yellow and blue go incredibly well together." He shook his head, his multitudinous chins and jowl wobbling. "I am still not sure."

He reached for his goblet and took a sip of Champagne. His pursed lips suddenly puckered. "But this Champagne is horrible!" he declared. "Horrible!" He set his glass down heavily.

"On the contrary," Miranda assured him, taking another sip of hers, "it's delicious."

He scowled. "It is *sour!*" He turned slightly. "Chara!" he called.

The Eleanor of Toledo face appeared from behind the half-open door.

"This Champagne is garbage!" he scowled. "Bring the other bottle!"

Chara's face appeared perplexed. "But it's—"

"Never mind what it is! Chara, the *other* bottle! Thi—" he gestured with disgust "—this is undrinkable!" And in a gentler voice, to Miranda: "My most sincere apologies, my dear. I should have tasted it first."

"I know I'm no expert when it comes to fine wines. Or diamonds," Miranda admitted, knowing it was useless to try to placate him.

"Nor," she added, with a laugh, "a food snob. I'm in no position to be one."

Once again her eyes roamed back upon the magnifying mirror, upon the yellow fire scintillating around her throat. For some reason, she suddenly had visions of dog collars and leashes, and was only half-aware of Chara slipping out from behind the mirrored door, bottle and napkin in hand. The Witch paced, bulky in the confines of the shop. Then he came closer from behind, his arm reaching around her, fat fingers lightly, lovingly touching the stones suspended from her neck.

"It is difficult," he whispered, his face beside hers, "to resist their allure, is it not? They say that diamonds are a girl's best friend."

She started to turn around but his elbow suddenly tightened around her throat and held her fast.

For one incredulous moment she was unsure what was happening. And then it sank in, too late, as he held her captive. "What do you think, Me-rahn-dah?" he hissed. "*Are* they *your* best friend?"

She heard Chara slam the door shut and bolt it; then came the metallic rattle of mini-blinds as they crashed down over the plate glass windows.

Miranda's fingers clawed desperately at his arm, and she caught sight of his face in the magnifying mirror. His pink skin looked pimpled and his pursed lips were open, his bared teeth stained and yellow, except for the gold one in the back, his breath stank of nicotine, and his arm reeked of sweat.

She put up a struggle, gasping, heaving, and twisting, but his strength was ferocious. Her fingers clawed desperately at his arm, and she kicked her legs furiously against the underside of the desk, her shoes thumping, but her efforts were futile. And then Calèche clashed with chloroform as Chara pressed the soaked napkin over her mouth and nose and held it down.

"It is useless to struggle," The Witch hissed, with an obscene grin. "And forget the diamonds. They certainly are not *your* best friend!"

Miranda felt nausea rise and dizziness overcome her. Her eyelids fluttered and she felt herself weakening, sinking, until her struggles ceased altogether and she went limp as she lost consciousness.

"Send for the car," The Witch snapped at Chara. "You know where to take her." He slammed Miranda forward, her forehead banging the desk blotter. "But first take the necklace off this stupid, meddling bitch!"

[CHAPTER FORTY FOUR]

Somewhere on Samos

Darkness.

Darkness pitch and black.

Miranda came to in stages.

The first time she awakened, it was as if from a deep sleep. She felt queasy, and retched. She tried to lift her eyelids, but they felt heavy, too heavy and too much of an effort to lift, and she drifted back into unconsciousness.

The second time she woke, some of the queasiness had left her, and she managed to open her eyes. Blackness surrounded her. True blackness: a total absence of light. A sharp ridge of rock was pressing against her spine and she tried to move, but her body felt leaden and refused to move. Her head pounded and she was cold. It was a relief to just close her eyes and drift back off.

The third time she woke her head was clearer. She even managed to move aside from the sharp, spiky rock pressing into her spine, only to find herself moving from one razor-sharp rock onto another. Memory flooded back at her in an overwhelming rush: the Internet café, The Witch, the diamonds, Chara—

Oh, how easily, how *stupidly* and senselessly she had allowed herself to be lured into their trap! What *had* she been thinking? And where, in all of heaven's name, was she?

Distantly, she heard the plop of a drop of water. She waited, counted off thirty seconds, waited a few more. There! Another droplet hit a puddle.

A cave, she thought, with a shudder, feeling unseen walls closing in on her from all sides. They had buried her alive somewhere, in some spot where she could never be found.

Miranda Kalli, neatly wiped off the face of the earth without a trace.

Suffocation threatened to choke her, and she struggled to fend off an impending sense of panic. If only she could *see* . . . if only she could see *anything*.

But the darkness was absolute.

Buried alive. Alone. No one knew where—

It was all she could do not to succumb to hysteria and scream. But screaming would require excess energy and air, and how much air was there left in this, which had to be a cave or cavern, and had surely had any entrance sealed off?

Then, from somewhere very nearby, she heard a rustle of movement. The first thought to hit her mind was: *rats!* Her second was: *bats!* Neither of them her favorite creatures. In fact, Miranda had a phobia of rodents.

There! She heard that rustle again, this time accompanied by a skittering, scrabbling sound of pebbles being moved about, and it was followed by what sounded, to her hopeful ears, like a very human moan.

"Hello?" she called out, but the bleak black walls, obviously high and deep, mocked her with her own echo: "*Hello . . . hello . . . hello . . .* "

Ignoring the jagged daggers of rock digging into her palms and fingers, she used her hands and arms to lever herself gingerly up into a sitting position.

"Is anybody there?" she called again, her ears sharply attuned to any sounds.

Miranda waited, but her only reply was, once again, her own hollow, futile echo: " . . . *body there . . . body there . . . body there* . . " Only that and nothing more, save for yet another distant plop as a droplet of water fell into a puddle or pool or whatever it was. She was aware of moisture and dead air, and for once in her life she wished she smoked—at least then she might be carrying a lighter. She felt around for her shoulder bag, but if it was there, it was not within reach. Besides, she didn't *own* a lighter, didn't even collect matchbooks.

"Mi . . . randa?" croaked a weak voice, so quietly that at first she thought it was her imagination running away with her. But then it came again, from very close by: "Mi . . . randa."

Her heart gave a leap. How desperately she wanted to believe that the voice was real, and not in her head, and that she wasn't already going stark, raving mad.

"Mike?" she stuttered hesitantly. "That you?"

"Y-yeah. Over here."

"Over *where?* I can't see a thing."

"Neither can I. A . . . coupla feet to your left. I think." His voice sounded groggy and slurred, almost drunken.

"Wait." She took a deep breath, then crawled in his direction, scraping open hands and knees, but not caring. This was no time to worry about surface scrapes and scratches. Not in the pickle they were in.

She came across him so quickly and suddenly, barely just out of reach, that when she touched him she gave a little yelp of terror.

"Is okay," he whispered.

"Oh, Mike! Mike!" she cried. "Am I ever glad to see you!"

"Likewise," he said with grim humor. "Even if we both ended up in hell."

She felt around, laid a hand flat against his forehead. It was moist and cool, but not feverish. "I think you'll live," she said. "At least for the time being."

"Nurse Miranda," he murmured, but there was warmth in his sardonic tone.

"Are you alright otherwise?"

"I think so. Let me move and see."

She could hear a click as he manfully clenched his teeth to stifle his grunts and groans. Then he tried to sit up, gave it a minute, and lay back down. "Don't believe anything's broken. Give me a few minutes. I need to clear my head."

"But what happened? How did you get here?"

"Same way you did, apparently. 'Twas the Witching Hour," he said with gallows humor. "I was at a café at the far end of the square waiting for you when my cell phone rang. It was Captain Pispas, or at least someone who claimed to be Pispas. Garbled something about how you'd had an accident in a taxi just outside Mesokampos."

"But we were supposed to meet at the square!"

"Yeah, like Judy Garland under the big clock."

"Don't tell me! *You're* one of those old movie buffs?"

"Promise you won't tell anyone? It's a sworn secret between me and Little Mike."

"You have my solemn word," she promised. "Besides, who's there to tell?"

A weak laugh escaped him. "You've got a point there. Anyway, fool that I am, I fell for the trap."

"You're not a fool, Mike," she reproved sternly. "Under that macho carapace, I detect a very caring human. Or *mensch,* as we say back in New York."

"If you say so," he sighed. "Anyway, there was a taxi on the verge of the road just outside Mesokampos, where that drop off is. It didn't look dented, now that I think about it, just parked askew on the side of the road with the rear passenger door wide open. Now that it's all coming together, I realize there wasn't even a police car in sight. But someone, a stranger, pointed down the slope a ways to where a woman lay splayed face down in the scrub, as though flung there. I couldn't even remember what you were wearing. But I saw the woman and skidded my way downhill."

"My hero," she murmured.

"Hero, hell! Your idiot, you mean! When I rolled her over, it turned out to be that bitch."

"Chara Zouboulakis, I take it," Miranda said softly.

"Yeah, wearing a light-colored wig. Lying in wait. You should have seen her eyes. She was like a madwoman possessed. I tried to back away, but I was struck over the head from behind. I wasn't quite out, and put up a bit of a struggle, but that maniac of a she-devil jumped up. She had a syringe in her hand. Then, when whoever it was finally managed to grab me from behind, she jabbed that needle into my arm. Obviously drugging me. Next thing I knew, I was here." The anger in his voice gentled. "Beside my very own ministering angel."

He paused, adding, "And you? What's the story there?"

Miranda filled him in on what had happened.

"*Malakas!*" he spat. "The Witch deserves everything he has coming to him."

She heard and felt, rather than saw, him sitting up again.

"Good. The drug is starting to wear off. You wouldn't happen to know what time it is, would you?"

"Sorry. My watch is an old cheapie. It doesn't light up in the dark."

"Mine glows, but the crystal's cracked and the whole face is smashed in."

"If I only hadn't been so damn stupid!" she swore. "They got hold of your album, Mike! The goddamn bag tore—"

"Sssh." He reached out, felt for her face, and put a finger to her lips. "I scanned a copy of the whole thing for my Hotmail site. So all is not lost."

"And if it's any consolation, I did manage to scan the Kofski photos and e-mail them to Mara," she said rather meekly. "I also lucked out and managed to catch her on the phone. She's out in the Hamptons but she's going in to the gallery to check on the provenances. I managed to catch her on the phone, and she's promised she's going to check them out and e-mail them to me. As a back-up, I also e-mailed a copy of the pictures to myself, my neighbor, Ron, and heaven only knows why, but another set to Harry as well."

"Ah, the famous Harry."

She could imagine Big Mike's snide expression.

"By 'Harry,'" he said, "I take it you mean the Harry who called Eleni's, and is on his way to see you?"

She was getting tired of kneeling on sharp objects or squatting on her haunches, and her feminine instinct sought a more comfortable position. She started shoving aside splintery rocks and pebbles with wide sweeps of her bare arms in order to avoid those jagged spikes of stone. Several layers down, with a small area of debris swept clear, she found smoothness, and gratefully sat down cross-legged upon it.

"Yes, Mike," she informed him slowly. "Harry. The Harry who used to be my fiancé, but hasn't realized yet that he's since become my *ex*-fiancé. I haven't told him that yet. I was waiting to impart the news to him in person."

She sighed heavily, folded her arms across her knees, and cradled her head miserably. Somehow, it was easier to talk about her relationship with Harry in the pitch blackness.

"Poor Harry," she murmured. "I suppose I'll never have the opportunity to tell him now."

"Not so fast, sweetheart. Like John Paul Jones so famously said, 'I will not give up the ship'!"

"Which means . . . ?" She looked, uselessly, in the direction of his voice.

She could hear knuckles, elbows, and knees crackle as he got to his feet. She felt him sway, then take a wider stance for retaining his balance.

"Which means," he said, his voice somewhere above her now, "I aim to get us outta this mess."

She all but laughed out loud. "But how? Mike! We're trapped in some sort of cave or cavern. No doubt sealed in. Don't you get it? This is our *tomb!*"

"Then start thinking of the glass being half-full instead of half-empty, sweetheart," he said. "Better yet, start thinking Indiana Jones."

"Oh. So now I suppose you're going to turn into Superman or Spidey?"

"Neither. First, lemme check my pockets."

She heard the unmistakable ripping sound of Velcro opening.

"Aha! They didn't relieve me of my penlight, the fools! Tells you something about who we're dealing with. I take it with me wherever I go. Along with matches, since here in Greece everyone seems to smoke, and needs a light. Now, lemme see if this dang thing works. Or if it's broken, like my watch."

She waited, and suddenly a very bright, if very narrow, beam of light shone directly into her eyes, momentarily blinding her.

Quickly she blinked and raised an arm against its glare. "It works," she said, with a mixture of disdain, annoyance, and amazement.

"And you've certainly found yourself a very comfortable place to park your tush, I'll give you that. In fact—"

He swept the beam of light up and down the rubble, past where she was seated. "Ho-ly Mo-ses!" he exclaimed, switching the light back off. "Miranda, do you have any *idea* what you're sitting on?"

"No. Why should I? I cleared a small area to be comfortable, that's all."

"No. Listen to me, Miranda. We do this my way, okay?"

"Like the song says? But, Mike! Why don't we go and explore the cave, or caves, or caverns, or wherever it is we're sealed in and find a way out?"

"Cavern, sweetheart, cavern. It's got to be huge; why else are we always hearing our echos? And there's no need to waste my batteries unnecessarily, because I sense a way out, even if our enemies don't realize it. Now, you're going to have to take your top off."

"What?" She sounded incensed, and realized the ridiculousness, the *idiocy* of her prudishness under the circumstances. "Now you've become a Peeping Tom?"

"If I'd wanted to be a voyeur, I'd have become one long ago. I've seen enough titties in my lifetime that I don't need to see another pair. I'm just trying to save you from becoming more of a scraped, scratched, bloody mess."

"I look *that* bad?"

"Nothing a good bath and a little ointment and band-aids won't cure."

She heard him feel his way around, curse as he slid on some loose scree, and then he was standing beside her.

"I'm taking my shirt off," he said. "And I strongly suggest you do the same. Or do you want to sweep this thing clear with bare arms and get even more cut up?"

"What thing?"

"The thing you're sitting on, sweetheart. The thing you have no idea you've discovered. Look, I'm not going to switch on the light again until you're decent. Deal?"

"Okay. Okay. But why?"

"Will you," he growled, "for once, just trust me? Like I trusted you with my album?"

That was a hard one to reply to, even if it was below the belt, and she obediently slipped out of her top.

"Now, what I saw," he said, his voice slightly muffled as he pulled off his shirt, "was a whole lot of rubble. Except for the spot where you're sitting."

She heard him rip off his top. A perfectly good, pale apricot Polo, she remembered, that set off his deep tan nicely. Ralph Lauren, with the logo of the polo player embroidered on it—but this was no time to worry about ruining their clothes. Not when their very survival was at stake.

"I'm wrapping mine tightly around my right arm," he said brusquely as she slid down from her small, rubble-free seat, "and I suggest you do the same with yours. Then start clearing the area around where you've been sitting. You take the left, and I'll take the right. What we can't do singly, we'll do together. Ready?"

"You want the truth?"

"No," he grunted.

"Right. So let's get started."

And so they began. She wound her top, skimpy armor against nature's rocky fangs, around her forearm for protection and helped clear an accumulation of inches, sometimes even a foot or so, of schist and marble chunks that had dislodged themselves from the cavern roof and had rained down from above.

Stones, rocks, and pebbles clattered as they dislodged the debris with great, savage, semi-circular sweeps of their arms. At times he needed her help to lift a particularly large chunk and heave it, with great grunts and groans, to go crashing off into the darkness. The largest they managed to roll and shove off to the side. The dust they raised all but threatened to choke them, and they both coughed constantly against the rawness in their throats.

It would have been nice, she thought, if they'd had extra pieces of fabric to wrap around their mouths and noses. It would have been even nicer if they'd had goggles to protect their eyes from the smothering, stinging clouds of invisible grit they raised. And it would have been nicer yet to have had at least a bottle or two of water to ease their parched throats.

"We sure could use some tools and light," he croaked hoarsely, clearing his throat and spitting out gritty phlegm.

But wishes were dreams, impossible dreams for the time being, and she was willing to do anything, anything at all, in order to escape this inky, claustrophobic blackness.

"Mike?" she said at one point.

He was in the process of rocking a particularly large boulder back and forth. He let out a massive grunt, and sent it crashing aside. "What?" he gasped, his breathing labored.

"Angelica," she said quietly. "You never did tell me. Was it her?"

Silence, and she had the sensation of swirling rock dust suspended motionlessly in the air before slowly settling back down all around. Just when she was certain he wouldn't reply, he said, "C'mon, let's sit back. We need to take a short break. I sure could use one."

Miranda could too. Her right arm felt like it was about to fall off, but she couldn't help a humorous jibe. "Big guy like you?"

"Yeah. And little girl like you too."

They sat side by side on the section they had cleared, and she waited wordlessly for him to catch his breath. From his movements, she gathered that he had folded his arms across his legs and had lowered his head. From somewhere in the distance, she once again heard another droplet of moisture loosen itself from the vast roof and plop down into water.

When he spoke, his voice was a near-whisper. "The body, what there was left of it, was bloated, and the fish had gotten to it, so it was hard to tell. But the size and proportions and hair color were hers. And Angelica always wore this little gold ankh around her neck."

"The Egyptian kind."

"Yeah, that cross with the looped top. Symbol of enduring life. What everyone used to wear back in the Flower Power days. She never took it off. Ever. It was her, alright."

There was a long pause, and Miranda wondered whether he was going to say anything more. If not, she wasn't going to push. Not now. Not here.

"It was still around her neck!" he moaned miserably, and she heard him stifle a sob, sniffle, and wipe his nose.

"Oh, Mike!" She reached instinctively sideways, curled an arm around his shoulders, and held him. "I am sorry," she said gently, but the words seemed so inadequate.

"Yeah. So am I." He sniffled again. "You'd have liked her. Angelica had this special spark of life and energy. She didn't even realize how beautiful she was. And popular and likeable as she was, she didn't take shit off of anybody. Not even me." Miranda sensed a fond little smile in the dark. "In that way she reminded me somehow of . . . "

She knew better than to ask.

"Never mind," he said gruffly, but she knew what he was going to say: *Of you.*

After a moment he shrugged off her arm. "She never left this goddamn island, Miranda!" he blurted. "She never flew to Athens and on to New York and from there back to L.A.! She never left goddamn *Samos!*"

"But you said passport control here and in New York and the airlines show that she did."

"No. What they show is that someone of her description—someone with her passport, *someone who could pass for her!*—flew that route. Someone with long, black, waist-length hair!"

Miranda felt a chill rippling along her spine. "You don't think—?"

"Oh, yes, I *think.* No, scratch that. In my bones, I *know.* There's only one other person who could have passed for her, so long as she wasn't slathered with makeup like a painted monkey!"

"Chara!" Miranda whispered.

"Yeah, the very bitch who attacked us both."

"If only we had some sort of proof."

He snarled a laugh as he heaved himself to his feet. "Proof? Look around you, Miranda!" She could feel currents of stale air moving as he flung his arms around. "How do you think we both ended up in here in Hell's Hilton? Through that *bitch,* that's how. I swear, if I ever get my hands on her, and I *will*—"

"Chill, Mike," she said more calmly than she felt. "Chill. Let it go for the time being. Let's expend our energy on trying to find a way out of here."

He fought down his anger and expelled a massive breath. The currents of air he'd stirred up stilled.

"You're right," he sighed finally. "No use expending our energy uselessly. But before we continue, let's see what we uncovered. If anything."

"It had better be good," she said waspishly, "or you owe me a new top."

"And if it's good, *you* owe me a new polo shirt. Deal?"

"Deal. Now dig that penlight out of your pocket and let's have a look-see."

While she waited for him to produce it, she idly let her fingers drift along the spot where she'd been sitting. The stone was cool. Smooth. No, not only smooth, she realized as she felt a raised fold and followed its elegantly sweeping curve.

It had been carved.

Then Mike flicked on the penlight and slowly swept it along the cleared area. Marble, smooth folds of perfectly chiseled and sanded marble, so realistic and masterfully carved they looked like actual folds of cloth. She recognized it instantly as part of a chiton with open sleeves.

"Mike." She was on her feet now, her voice a trembly whisper. "Tell me I'm not dreaming. Here. Shine the light *here.*" She started furiously brushing away a layer of resettled grit with her bare hands, then bent forward, puffed out her cheeks, and blew away any remnants.

"Can it be?" she whispered, taking a step backward and not daring to trust her eyes. "Or am I hallucinating?"

He directed the beam further up and down, outlining the entire, eight-foot, rubble-strewn length. Despite the portions still covered with deep debris, the top half of a giant human form was unmistakable.

"Oh, *baby!!*" he whispered, then turned to Miranda. "It's *her!* It's the top half of Hera! We've found her! We've fucking found her!"

And switching the light back off to conserve the battery, he thrust the penlight into his pocket, abruptly grabbed hold of Miranda, and swung her around and around in an impromptu, musicless waltz in the pitch blackness, both of them tripping and sliding on rocks and laughing and crying at the same time.

"Oh, those *fools!*" he crowed jubilantly. "They didn't have a clue where they brought us and sealed us in!"

She made him put her down. "Mike! What are you babbling on about?"

"Don't you see?" he said excitedly. "Miranda! This cavern has got to be Arion's workshop! That was the sculptor's name, by the way; he actually signed the krater 'Arion of Samos,' which is highly unusual for that time. Which means—"

He began pacing tiny circles, rocks crunching beneath his feet as he thought aloud, and she imagined him gnawing on a knuckle.

"Well, it means several things. First of all, it has got to be nighttime out."

"How can you be so sure?"

"Because we've both been knocked out a helluva lot longer than you thought. I mean, we were really *heavily* drugged, Miranda. You too. I mean, chloroform doesn't knock you out for hours on end or for half a day or more. I'm willing to bet that once you passed out, that murderous bitch probably injected you with the same thing she used on me."

He added, dryly: "Let's just hope she used clean needles, though I wouldn't put anything past her."

Miranda cringed at the thought, but there were more important things to concentrate on at the moment. "But, Mike! Why do you say nighttime? Where do you get that?"

"From those old photos of the krater. You haven't had the chance to study them like I have, Miranda."

"I've barely just arrived. And hardly had the chance to glance at them. Or anything much else, for that matter."

"For which you're forgiven and I apologize. But I've studied them for several years and can picture the illustrations backwards and forwards, even in my sleep. Now get this, Miranda. The first two depictions—*the first two!*—show Arion sculpting in his studio. Inside a cavern *open to the sky!*"

"Yes?"

"Call it a natural skylight, if you will. Which, thanks to Hera here, gives me a very good inkling of where we are."

"And where's that," she asked sardonically, "other than the inner circle of Hell?"

"Cheer up, willya? Asprodavos—where else?"

"So what do we do? Shout our gritty lungs out for help?"

"On the contrary. We'll be quiet little mice. The way I figure it, we've got to be on the wrong side of the natural bridge. Not at the official site itself, but on GlobaLux's side. How else could they have just bulldozed or blasted the entrance to the cavern shut, sealing us in? Or so they thought. And that also explains why Hera's all covered with this rubble. The detonations they've been setting off must have loosened a lot of the rock above us."

He began talking faster now, piecing his theory together, like finally fitting the last little amoeba-shaped bit of a jigsaw puzzle in place.

"I'm willing to bet my boxer shorts that the natural skylight is still up there. In fact, it's probably bigger than ever, taking into account subsequent erosion and tremors from their damn blasting. Also, it's probably so overgrown they never even noticed it."

"Mike? You're sure?" she asked cautiously.

"Ninety-nine point ninety-nine point nine percent. Yeah. So, Ms. Watson, if it were daylight, some light, however slight, would surely be leaking in."

"Okay, that's all very well and good," said Miranda with her typical practicality. "Now all we have to do is find a way out of here."

"Leave that to your super hero."

"You mean, to you?"

"Yeah. Me, myself, and I."

"Why? Don't tell me you can suddenly fly?"

"Nope. But I used to be ace at climbing cliffs as a hobby. Barehanded. No ropes, no pitons. It's been a while, though. Vivica made me stop after Little Mike was born."

"Vivica?"

"Yeah, my ex. She decided to take off for greener pastures before Little Mike turned two. Married some multi-millionaire who could keep her in the style to which she wanted to become accustomed." His voice grew bitter. "She didn't want joint custody of Little Mike. Hell, she didn't even want visitation rights. Still doesn't want him cluttering her cushy life. You believe that?"

Miranda was shocked. "Actually, I can't. But from the little I saw of him, you needn't worry. Little Mike's turning out just fine. A small spitting image of his daddy. He's adorable. And he worships you."

"Yeah, he's quite a li'l fella, if I say so myself. Everything a father could want. But what do you tell a kid like that when he asks about his mother? That she's dead? That she's disowned him? And he's at that age now where he's starting to ask questions."

"I'd think his mother should be very proud of him. But who am I to talk?"

"Or me." His voice thickened, then turned gruff.

"Anyway," he said, "I didn't mean to get into that. Sorry. And it's high time I hit the road, so to speak. Time for showing off my prowess. Show what 'Big Mike' can do with his own two grubby paws and a good pair of boots."

"But it's pitch black in here!" Miranda protested. "How will you see?"

"Don't need to. I climb by feel. Find a crack here, a crevasse there, a protruding rock. Not to worry. I intend to get us outta here."

He paused and added, "Besides, I've got real impetus."

"To save our skins. And especially to be there for Little Mike."

"Those too. But I've got an extra impetus. I'm a Savides, and when a Savides has a score to settle—watch out! He settles it. I'll be taking the penlight cause I'll probably need it when I reach the top. But here."

There was that ripping sound of Velcro again, then he pressed some stiff cardboard into her hand.

"Take these," he instructed her. "They're matches. When you hear me call down, light a few. That way, once I'm up there and can see where you're at, I'll have scrounged a rope and I'll lower it. The end'll be knotted. You're to step on that with both feet. Keep 'em crossed. And whatever you do, be sure you wrap a few strands around both your forearms so I can hoist you up. All you've got to do is hang on."

"Is that all?" She couldn't help the mockery in her tone. "Sounds like a circus act in Hell."

"We *are* in Hell right now, sweetheart, remember?" he said gently. "So it's only appropriate. Besides, if I can do it, then you can, too."

She heard him thump his chest mightily.

"Hey—me Tarzan," he bluffed, "you Jane."

"I wish," she said wistfully, never having had the urge to swing on a vine, let alone dangle in midair from a rope suspended above jagged fangs of schist and marble that might as well have been a sea of glass shards. Laura Croft, she wasn't. Nor did she want to be.

Then in a serious tone, she whispered: "Mike, are you *sure* you're up to this? If anything happens—"

He cut her off in mid-sentence. "I'm positive. Plus I got two kids to take care of, remember? You and Little Mike." He chucked her under the chin.

"You will be careful, won't you?" she asked anxiously.

"Hey," he blustered, full of testosterone-fueled bravado. "I gotta be. How else am I gonna save that pretty little ass of yours?"

"'Pretty little ass'! Jeez, but you really know how to be romantic!" she scoffed, but despite herself, she could feel a warm blush rising from her bare breasts up into her face, and was grateful for the pitch blackness all around. "If anyone could see me right now, they'd take off for the hills. I don't know when I've looked and smelled this skanky. Luckily you can't see me, or my bones would be bleached before you'd even think of rescuing this damsel—no, better make that hag—in distress. 'Pretty little ass' indeed!" she huffed.

"Hey, I call it as I see it. Now then." He had the penlight in his hand. "You stay exactly where you are, and don't use those matches needlessly. I'm going to wander about and play this light around the walls, not that it reaches very far. Just to see where I can get my best start."

"Mike?"

"What now?" He pretended to be put out.

"Just take care."

"Same goes for you. And stay away from the walls, in case I dislodge some rocks and stuff. Now, how about giving your tough guy a good luck kiss to send him on his way?"

She placed a hand on each of his sweaty, gritty shoulders and pecked him chastely on the cheek.

"Hey, that's not a good luck kiss!" he protested.

"Then what is?"

"This." And he engulfed her in his thick, muscular arms, pressed her bare breasts firmly against his own bare massive chest, and covered her mouth with his.

For a moment she kept her lips shut, but the gentleness of his mouth disarmed her. Slowly she parted her lips, raised her hands to the back of his head, and pressed his face closer to hers. His embrace tightened in response, and she moaned as he gently nibbled her lips, then closed his mouth fully over hers and kissed her deeply and urgently.

And she was lost. Although there was no light, she shut her eyes and her inner vision conjured up images not of pornographic carnality, but of a strange, wild kind of beauty. She saw a peony opening in stop-motion, comets streaking across a star-spangled night, untamed horses galloping carefree over unspoiled terrain, brightly colored fish swimming smoothly through live, swaying sea anemones. She could feel the quickening beating of his heart against hers, the delicious moisture of his tongue exploring the landscape inside her mouth, his tongue caressing the smoothness of her teeth, encircling her own soft tongue. She was everywhere and nowhere, poised on the very precipice of the universe, the edge of present and future, and felt herself melt completely.

But then his lips slowly, reluctantly, left hers, and she gave an urgent little cry as he gently took her hands and lowered them.

"Now that," he said, his breath warm puffs of air against her face, "is what I call a good luck kiss. To be continued."

And then he was out of her arms and slipping away, swallowed by the pitch blackness all around.

From the ceiling overhead, a droplet of water dislodged itself and plopped down into the puddle, its musical sound like that of a dropping tear.

[CHAPTER FORTY FIVE]

Asprodavos, Samos

The song says that time's on your side.

Miranda begged to differ. Time was definitely not on her or Mike's side. Time had, in essence, become The Enemy. As had the vast chill blackness surrounding her.

There was also that song about climbing the stairway to heaven.

Miranda begged to differ on that one, too. And in a major way. This was no stairway to heaven. It was, at its most optimistic, the climb up a lethal, vertical wall of rock ascending out of sheer Hell itself.

In the beginning, from far beyond where she was tensely seated against Hera, Miranda saw occasional pinpoints of light flicker here and there as Big Mike scouted out the most promising spot to begin his climb. That alone seemed to take forever, the little bursts of winking light getting fainter and fainter as he wandered farther and farther back into the recesses of the cavern as he sought the foothold he needed to begin his climb.

And that reminded her of the stage production of *Peter Pan,* which her mother had once taken her to see. During the play, when Tinkerbell's glow began to fade, the audience members were exhorted to clap if they believed in fairies. And as the applause grew stronger and louder, sure enough, Tinkerbell's dimming light brightened and the dying fairy was brought back to life. The only trouble was that Miranda was now far too old to believe in fairies. Nor did she dare clap or make any unnecessary sounds. The noise, and its subsequent, inevitable echoes, would only have distracted Big Mike.

Which, under the circumstances, was the very last thing he needed.

When his pinpoint of light went out completely, she knew he had begun his climb.

Miranda thought, *If only I could see!* But she was just as glad that she couldn't. Being able to watch his painful progress up the sheer walls of the cavern, a human fly without wings clinging to a mere crack, inching upwards, sideways, perhaps backwards at times, with only bare hands and booted feet for purchase, would surely have driven her over the edge and thrown her into madness.

As it was, each time she heard rubble clatter and loose rocks go crashing down to the ground, it was all she could do not to jump or let out a scream. She was terrified for Big Mike and she was terrified for herself, grateful for one fact alone: that so far she hadn't heard the thud of a falling body. If she had, she knew she'd never be able to stifle her screams. Or ever stop herself from screaming until her voice finally gave out.

Stay quiet.

Keep still.

Try to remain calm and collected.

Above all, don't distract him.

Those were her mantras, prayers offered up to whatever gods might be listening.

Because, for Miranda, time hadn't only slowed to a crawl. It seemed to have stopped completely, replaced by a river of blood rushing through her veins and arteries with the speed of light; time had become reduced to a single heartbeat, a mere breath, a throbbing pulse in her throat and wrist.

How high was *this cavern? How long would it take him if—*

But her mind refused to finish the thought.

If what?

Because it was as if some unseen finger had pressed a perpetual HOLD button on her mind itself. She lost all concept of seconds, minutes, and hours. Perhaps even days. Every moment stretched into an eternity, an endless highway growing wider, deeper, and longer, a highway without warning signs or markers, which kept spreading like the universe itself, ever self-perpetuating, expanding, lengthening, and gobbling up space before there was such a thing as space, and time, before there was such a thing as time, world without end, amen.

It had to be hours later when she thought she heard a voice reach down into the depths of her darkest despair, a voice that sent painful echoes bouncing back and forth inside her head. She blinked her eyes, and still all her gaze met was the bleak, black lack of light itself. Of nothingness.

"*. . . randa . . . randa . . . randa . . .*"

She came out of her semi-conscious state slowly, lethargically, the echo splintering from one side of her skull to the other.

"Miranda . . . *randa . . . randa . . . randa . . .*"

"Mike?" she whispered, lifting her head. Daring not to hope, barely daring to breathe as she slowly straightened her spine in disbelief.

Could it be?

Was it possible?

She forced herself to stand up, her legs as weak and wobbly as a newborn foal's, trembling so badly she wasn't certain they could support her weight. But then, she was weightless, wasn't she? She was floating out far beyond the oncoming universe—

—and then again, perhaps not?

Was it insanity? Or reality? Or were they one and the same?

But now wasn't the time to question that.

"Mike?" she called out hesitantly, her voice weak and parched and raspy. She produced saliva to moisten her vocal cords. Then: "Mike!" Her voice stronger and louder now, almost immediately bouncing back and forth from the cavern's rocky walls and the insides of her skull— "*ike . . . ike . . . ike . . . !*"

"The matches! Miranda! Use them to find the rope . . . *ope . . . ope . . . ope . . .*"

So it *wasn't* her imagination after all! It was him—*him,* Big Mike!—come to rescue her as promised. He'd made it! *He'd actually made it!*

Her heart surged with jubilation and once again time kicked in and the world's clocks were back at work. She felt like a drowning swimmer suddenly surfacing from the depths and finding renewed strength.

Matches. Yes, he'd handed her some. She reached into a pocket and found one, in her hurry fumbling and letting it drop.

"Shit!" With a cry, she fell to her knees, ignoring the knife-like shards of stone digging painfully into her kneecaps and drawing blood as she felt around in desperation. Where in all Hades—?

There! She seized upon it, snatched it, opened it, and tore out a match. It rasped as she struck it once against the striker with trembling fingers. Nothing. She emitted a little mewl of distress, and struck it again, and then once again.

Third time was the charm. The bluish-red flame was almost blinding, but her heart soared up through the stagnant air and past whatever natural skylight there was, but that remained out of her sight, and to the unseen galaxies far beyond.

Light! Some semblance of light at long last!

"Come towards the back of the cavern!" Big Mike was shouting directions downward, his voice amplified by cupped hands.

It was the heat of the match singeing her fingers that gave Miranda the impetus to move. She quickly let it drop and lit another, this time on the second strike. Then, shielding the precious flame with one hand, she stumbled deeper, step by careful step, into the enormity of the cavern, stunned by its size. Then she scratched another match, and another, and finally there it was, just as promised—

Her very own stairway to heaven!

A length of thick hemp, like an Indian rope trick, but real, and with just a large enough knot on the bottom for her to balance her feet upon. She stepped on it and wrapped her arms around the rough, lashed braid as Big Mike had instructed her, gave it a few swift tugs, and yelled up: "Ready when you are!"

And then slowly, miraculously if somewhat jerkily, he pulled her up, sometimes mere inches, at other times a foot or two at once.

Strangely, the dark was no longer her enemy, but had become her friend. In this lack of light, with nothing to measure how far in space she dangled, or how far the deadly drop to the ground would be, or how much further she had yet to be pulled before reaching terra firma up above, she felt—well, certainly not comfortable, but neither was she clutched with the fear she'd expected. It was, she thought, rather like clinging to some primitive elevator dangling in a vacuum—slowly rising up, up, up, twisting and turning as the rope was hauled until, at long last, she burst through a painful thicket of particularly nasty barbed brambles.

"Ouch!" she moaned. "Ow, ow, ow, ow, *ow!*"

"Sorry about that," Big Mike gasped from the edge, tugging more tightly on the rope. "Now hold on. Lemme secure this end to that olive tree over there. Then I'll swing you back and forth until you're close enough to the edge so I can reach you and pull you over. Steady now, and have patience. And whatever you do, *don't let go!*"

Oh, she wouldn't. Not for the life of her. Not in a million years. Not even if her hands were raw and bleeding and blistered—which she had an idea they were, judging from the slipperiness of her palms and fingers.

But that was not what she concentrated on. Instead, tilting her head back, she looked up high, at the moon glowing behind a hidden cloud, lighting it as if from within, at the vast constellations of stars so bright she felt she could reach out and pluck them.

Her eyes filled with tears. "Oh, Mike! Mike! You did it! You really did it!"

And at long last he hauled her over the edge and she fell into his arms, unconcerned about the thorns embedded in her skin, or her bruises and scratches and scrapes and abrasions. There was time to see to those later.

"My hero!" she whispered, holding his face in her hands and peppering him with kisses.

Although out of breath and clearly exhausted, he laughed softly. "I've always wanted to hear that, y'know? Just like I always wanted to jump into a cab and yell, 'Follow that car'!"

"You big galoof," she said fondly.

"And now we'd better hurry up and get moving," he warned. We're still not out of hot water. We have to get over to that goddamn fence on this side, climb it, and then cross that natural bridge and climb over the other side. We're not home free yet."

"Oh, Mike. Why is it that with you around I feel so safe?"

"Maybe 'cause I like protecting a sweet, pretty, young piece of ass?"

"Male chauvinist pig!" she retorted happily, giving his butt a resounding smack, but he deserved a kiss even more, and she bestowed it, gratefully and hungrily. Overhead, the cloud sailed past, bathing them in bright moonlight.

"We'd better make tracks," he observed, extricating himself from her embrace.

"Yes."

They had hoofed it halfway to the fence enclosing the GlobaLux perimeter when the floodlights clicked on.

Miranda froze and looked over her shoulder. In the garish yellow of the sodium lamps she saw them. Two hundred yards away. Guards armed with rifles, barely able to control the barking German shepherds straining on their leashes, and the thin, all-too-recognizable figure of Chara Zouboulakis.

"Run!" Big Mike yelled, giving Miranda a massive shove to get going.

"But the guns—" she gasped as she ran.

"Never mind the guns! They don't dare shoot," Big Mike wheezed as they continued their Olympic dash to freedom. "Too much noise drawing too much attention. It's the canines—four-legged and *two,* that I'm worried about!"

The words were barely out of her mouth when Chara snarled an order.

And the dogs were set loose.

[CHAPTER FORTY SIX]

Asprodavos

They reached the fence at breakneck speed, just feet ahead of the lunging dogs. Miranda and Big Mike launched themselves at the chain links and started to climb. Behind and below them, the big dogs growled and snapped their huge, bared jaws as they leapt savagely upward. Miranda felt one sinking its teeth into the hem of her shorts, holding her captive, its weight inexorably pulling her down, and she could feel her grip on the chain-link weakening.

"Mike!" she screamed.

He didn't hesitate. Letting go of the fence with one hand and clinging to the links with the other, he whirled sideways and executed a brutal kick with his heavy, steel-toed boot. There was a sickening crunch as it connected with the fanged jaw. Splinters of canine teeth were dislodged and went flying in all directions.

In an instant, the dog let go of Miranda's shorts and, howling and whimpering in pain, slunk away to lick its wounds.

Miranda swiftly scrambled higher, just beyond reach of the other leaping beasts. There were four more, and they smelled blood, their lupine fangs and crazed eyes flashing demonically in the moonlight.

Big Mike whirled back around, gripped the chain links with both hands, flipped neatly over the top of the fence, and dropped down to the ground on the other side.

"I'll catch you!" he shouted, arms outstretched. "Miranda, trust me! Just fling yourself over. I'll catch you. Quick!"

Gritting her teeth, Miranda carefully maneuvered first one leg, and then the other, cautiously over the top. She shut her eyes, let go, and allowed herself to fall.

She would have fallen, and badly, had Big Mike not caught her in both outstretched arms. He set her gently upright and steadied her on trembling feet.

"Now I really owe you," she said, with a shudder. "I didn't know they had dogs!"

"That was a new one on me, too. And not just guard dogs, Miranda. Trained attack dogs. You don't suppose they're getting a little paranoid over there, do you?"

At the far side of the chain-link, the four remaining German shepherds barked madly, flung themselves uselessly against the diamond-shaped mesh of steel, then fell back, howling and whining and running back and forth in frustration.

"Uh-oh," Big Mike muttered. "I shoulda known it was too easy. Here comes the Queen Bitch herself!"

Miranda stiffened and looked through the diagonal links, beyond the baying dogs toward the distant, flood-lit cluster of armed guards, rifles held uselessly in the air, not sure how to proceed. But a fleeting thin shadow had detached itself from them, waist-long hair flying behind her as an obviously female figure made a three-hundred-meter dash for the fence.

"*Chara!*" Miranda half-wailed. "*Now* what?"

"Now we hurry!" Big Mike urged. "The fence won't stop that half-human hyena. We've got to get over the bridge and safely to the other side. Not that that's going to stop *her!*"

On this side of GlobaLux's fence, they still had thirty or forty yards to go before reaching the natural bridge, that frighteningly narrow, crumbling, arched span glowing in the moonlight like an elusive ribbon of promise. The ground here was uneven, all tumbled rock, jutting schist, and deep fissures. In her haste, Miranda misjudged a step, stumbled, and fell, her foot wedged in the split of a rock. She tried frantically to rise and Big Mike had to worry her foot loose and pull her back up onto her feet.

"Ouch!" she exclaimed as an excruciating stab of pain shot through her ankle. "Oh, damn! Fine time to have twisted or sprained it."

"Don't worry about it," he said calmly—how he could remain so coolheaded under these conditions was beyond her. "Just hang onto me," he said, "and we'll be fine."

She almost burst into hysterical peals of laughter. *No, we won't be fine!* she thought. *We'll be anything* but *fine. Because there's something he doesn't know about me yet.*

And she couldn't think of a worse time to tell him.

With one arm supporting his shoulder, she limped valiantly on, casting swift, anxious glances over her shoulder.

Chara Zouboulakis had already reached the fence, the dogs scattering as she leapt up the chain-link like a rabid quadruped, vaulting over it with Olympian ease and landing perfectly on both feet.

"Here comes trouble," Miranda sighed.

They had, at last, come to the beginning of the bridge. "I'll fend her off," Big Mike assured her as he put her down gently. "With your limp, I suggest you crawl across on your hands and knees."

Oh, God. She glanced dubiously down into the rock-filled gorge far below. Teeth, fangs, molars of rocks rose up jaggedly, intensified by the lengthy shadows cast by the moon. The world seemed to tilt, her head began spinning dizzily, and her stomach lurched.

Quickly she averted her gaze and clutched Mike's calf frantically. "Mike?" she whimpered miserably. "Did I ever tell you I suffer from acrophobia?"

"Fear of heights? Well, no. As a matter of fact, I don't believe you did."

He didn't look down as he spoke, but kept his eye on the steadily advancing, lithe figure in form-fitting leggings and dark turtleneck.

"I'd say now's as good a time as any to conquer that fear," he told Miranda grimly. "No choice, babe. Matter of life and death. 'Sides, you did fine on the rope."

"That," Miranda moaned weakly, "is because it was *dark!* I couldn't *see!*"

"Sweetheart, then crawl on your belly. The bridge is narrow, only a foot or two. If you have to, just shut your eyes. Hold on to the edges. Better yet, use your elbows so you don't scrape your ta-tas. Now start crawling. *Crawl! NOW!*"

She lay there, frozen, at the foot of that crumbling span, inert and stiff, clutching the rocks at either side in a death-hold. Strangely, her fear of heights did not extend to the insides of tall buildings (unless there were floor to ceiling windows), nor of airplanes, nor other safely enclosed spaces—but her fear was confined to ledges, steep drop-offs, ravines, aerial tramways, and the edges of cliffs.

And now having to cross that crumbling span.

She quailed at the very thought.

Big Mike's voice roughened. "Get your ass moving! Go! *Now!*" There was no mistaking the command in his voice.

From close by, Miranda heard a wild, derisive, demented laugh, and she turned her head.

Chara Zouboulakis was nearly at the foot of the bridge. A wind had sprung up and whipped her long hair sideways, toward the sea. Her eyes were no longer Bronzino's blank stare, but gleamed murderously. Her face, for once without makeup, was rendered almost white and mask-like in the moonlight. Her lips showed a dark, scimitar smile.

That did it. Shutting her eyes, Miranda released her clutch on the boulders on either side, dug her elbows into the rocky, narrow ribbon spanning the gorge, and began her desperate crawl.

Behind her, Big Mike had assumed a fighting stance. "Hey, nice ninja outfit, Chara," he called out tauntingly. "What's the matter? Forgot to order the hood to go with it? Or did you leave it at home?"

"You cannot insult me, you big, ugly foreigner!" Her mouth looked black in the pale face. "Do you need a moment to say *Yá sas* to your meddling sweetheart?"

Miranda didn't look back, just kept her eyes shut and continued crawling up that arched, uneven incline, using her legs to push her along like a frog. With every movement, she could hear a hail of rocks crumbling from the edges of the fragile, cracked, natural bridge, then eventually heard them land with crashes and clatters far below.

"Why give me a chance to say *Yá sas* to Miranda?" Big Mike said in a dangerously soft voice. "You never gave me that chance with Angelica."

"Ah. So you did identify her." Chara seemed taken by surprise. "Strange. Captain Pispas told me your Professor Hirsch could not be certain."

Miranda didn't want to believe what she'd just heard, and bit down a cry. *Please,* she prayed silently, as she continued to crawl. *Don't let Wald be part of this! It's a lie! It's got to be!*

"C'mon, Chara," Big Mike growled. "Enough of your cheap talk. You want to get this over with, you bony, self-centered smuggler?"

"Smuggler!"

"Yeah, smuggler. Miranda's got proof of you and those *Meltemi*s being used for smuggling antiquities and illegals. You got a little sloppy there, didn't you, Chara? Thought you had it made, did you?"

She spat. "Proof! What proof?"

"Fact is, we've got enough to put you and that fat pig you work for away to rot for the rest of your lives. And where you're headed, you won't be able to take your makeup case and designer outfits. But there'll be lots of nice butch lesbians just waiting to get their hands on you."

No laughter now, just a snarl as Chara hurled herself forward onto the bridge. Miranda could feel the tenuous arch tremble dangerously beneath her as the two bodies collided and fought. Chara went for his eyes with her talons, but Big Mike threw back his head and slugged her across the face with his fist.

There was the sickening sound of crushed bone as his knuckles connected with her nose, and the arch shook again as Chara lost her balance and went down.

Despite her phobia, Miranda forced her eyes open and half-twisted around. Chara had fallen halfway across the narrow bridge, her fingers desperately clutching one side, her legs dangling in midair from the other.

"Had enough?" Big Mike sneered. "Or want me to stomp on your hands?"

But Chara wasn't down and out. Not yet. Somehow, with superhuman strength, she managed to swing her legs over the precipice and leap back up onto her feet. Blood—black in the moonlight—was pouring from her crushed nose and split lip, and she wiped a forearm across her face, smearing it blacker yet.

"*Sto diavolo!*" she spat, and came at him again. She was a whirling dervish, a meltemi, a sirocco, a tornado, and a hurricane of sheer frightening fury all rolled into one. And this time, metal reflected the moonlight as a sharp and shiny switchblade sprang into Chara's hand, its metal point raised high as she lunged toward Big Mike for the kill.

"Mike!" Miranda shrieked. "She's got a knife!"

But he'd already seen. No sooner had Chara's arm arced in midair towards him than his own came up to grasp her wrist. But madness lent her the advantage. Miranda let out a shriek as the switchblade buried itself deep into his shoulder, and he slumped down onto one knee.

Again, the fragile bridge shuddered under the impact.

With a cry of triumph, Chara wrenched the bloodied blade out of his shoulder and raised her arm to strike once more.

Just as she was about to plunge it downward, the wind gusting through the gully changed direction, blowing Chara's waist-long hair across her face and blinding her. Nor had she realized that Big Mike had rolled aside, and that her foot slipped on a pebble as the momentum of stabbing downward threw her off balance.

For one long, awful moment, she tried to stay her momentum and straighten, but it was too late. Blinded by her own silken hair, and unwilling to let go of the switchblade and break her fall with one hand, she reared back instead and teetered at the very brink. Then, like a diver bending back off the high board to do a backward flip, only to discover, too late, that the pool below is empty, she let out a terrible, high-pitched scream and plunged down amid a hailstorm of loosened rock into the void below, where nature's impaling fangs of vampiric rock awaited.

The thud and crunching of human bone as the body hit was a sound Miranda knew she would never forget.

Shaking his head as though shrugging off the pain, Big Mike grunted, got to his feet, and stumbled toward Miranda. His breathing was rapid.

"There's been too much weight and stress on this thing," he said between gasps. "The bridge is not going to last. Miranda, quick! Get up before it collapses!"

Already, behind him, she could see a jagged black crack appear in the bridge of grayish stone and grow longer and thicker, then saw it widen still, and widen even further as chunks of rock and debris began to break away and go crashing down, raising great clouds of grit and dust.

Miranda was too horrified and shocked to move. First Chara's plunge, and now this: the very warp and weft of her most terrible nightmares.

Only she was awake. This was no bad dream from which to wake up.

"Hell and damnation, woman!" Big Mike roared.

Before she could respond or protest, she felt him grab her rigid arms and, expelling a massive grunt, heave her over his damaged shoulder in a fireman's carry. Then he began to run as fast as his legs could carry them both.

She kept her eyes squeezed shut, hearing ever greater chunks of rock disintegrate and fall in great thundering slabs. From the sound of it, she knew all was lost. It was impossible to outrun. She did not have to open her eyes to know the bridge collapse was gaining upon them. Racing towards them.

She felt him leap over a wide gap, and then another, and finally, miraculously, he'd managed to outrun disaster by mere seconds.

He laid her down gently. "We're safe now," he gasped.

When Miranda finally dared open her eyes, the entire arch spanning the chasm was gone, as if it had never existed. In its place was a massive, rising mushroom of airborne detritus. For long minutes they did not speak, and could only look and stare.

"How many lives do you think we've already used up?" she murmured.

"Who cares? We're not cats. I figure humans got to have more'n nine."

"You're hurt." She examined his bloody shoulder with gentle fingers.

"Aw. That's barely a scratch."

"Maybe for you, macho man, but you've got to get it seen to."

"I will," he said. "And for crying out loud, keep your voice and head down."

"But why?"

He poked a thumb upwards and backwards. "By now everyone at the site will soon be clinging to the fence at this side to see what's happened. Luckily they can't see us because of this overhang." He pointed up to the protruding ledge above them.

He was right, of course. She could already hear the babble of excited voices approaching from both dorms at the archeological site.

"And what's wrong with being seen?" she demanded in a low voice.

"Maybe nothing."

Big Mike shrugged, and she knew he hurt more than he was willing to admit by the face he made when he moved his muscled shoulder.

"And then again," he said, "maybe everything. For now, we're both best off being neither seen nor heard. First, though, I've got to stash you somewhere safe, and then go and buy us some insurance."

"Insurance?" She gave him a startled look. "I don't get it."

"What I mean is, we have to protect both our precious, pretty little asses. Don't you understand? We *know* too much, Miranda!"

His words made her shiver, her heart lurch. "Now you're frightening me again."

"As well you should be. For God's sake, Miranda, they tried to *kill* us! *Twice!*"

"So while you go about getting this insurance, as you call it, just where am I supposed to be sequestered?"

"The last place anyone would look for you. A monastery. It's not far from here, no more than half an hour on foot."

"But Greek Orthodox monasteries don't permit women inside, do they?"

"Especially," he said with an irresistibly sly wink, "not topless ones. Father Thanos would be shocked out of his gourd."

"Oh!" She flushed slightly and instinctively crossed both arms over her breasts.

He had to contain his laughter. "No need to be shy. I'm already becoming quite familiar with them. And not to worry. We'll find something to cover Eve's nakedness with."

"Father Thanos, huh?"

"Yep. I think he'll be amenable to you remaining in the chapel, so long as your bodily parts are all appropriately covered."

"Then it had better be more than a fig leaf."

"It's sure to be a robe or a sheet or something. Greeks get very offended by tourists who tromp around in their churches and chapels in sleeveless shirts, shorts, and skimpy skirts. They consider it disrespectful."

"So my next stop is a chapel. And a pew shall be my bed."

"There's worse, believe me. And you'll like Father Thanos. He's a real character."

"Lemme see. Black robes, long gray beard, that funny hat?"

"Yep. And he drives an ancient, beat-up little Fiat. Likes to pull over on the side of the road around here and have a leisurely cigarette." Big Mike grinned. "I once saw him at the airport, taking a puddle jumper to Athens, one of those old ATRs? When they began boarding and calling the rows, what did he do? Barged right to the head of the line, blessing everybody as he cut in, as though to absolve *them of his* offense. Funny little country, this."

He paused and added ruminatively, "And I'm going to have to borrow his car. *If* it starts."

"Where are you headed while I sleep with the saints?"

"To my doctor friend's house. He lives in Agia Zoni. Don't worry, he'll stitch me up. More importantly, he's got an Internet hookup and I need to use his computer. Plus I have a shitload of calls to make. If I use the isp control panel and you trust me enough to give me your server, e-mail address, and password, I can access your computer. In case your friend at the gallery—what's her name?"

"Mara."

"Right. Mara. If there's a message with the so-called provenances of the stolen items, I'll print them out."

"Sure. Got paper and pen?"

Velcro rasped again and he produced them. After she gave him the information, he gave her specific instructions. "You're not to leave the chapel, okay? Not for any reason. I'll ask Father Thanos to get you some food. Then be at Eleni's in Pythagoria at four p.m. But not *before* then. That's crucial."

"Yes, but—"

"Unh-unh. No buts. Four p.m. *No* exceptions. And if anyone from the site happens into the chapel, make yourself scarce. Don't talk to anyone. Got that?"

"Yes, sir!" She gave a mock salute.

"Kiss?" he asked.

She tilted her head. "Perhaps a little one. Wouldn't want to distract you too much."

"Yeah," he grinned. "There's plenty of time for that later. Now let's sneak away from here before the sun comes up."

[CHAPTER FORTY SEVEN]

Pythagoria, Samos

It was four o'clock in the afternoon of that same day. Miranda showed up at the Site at Ancient Asprodavos, where the entire team was abuzz with speculation about her arrival in a priest's black robes, and dirty, bruised, and covered with scabs.

"Later," had been her reply to curiosity about the natural bridge collapse and her physical condition. Rosalie had helped her shower and change into clean clothes, and also had to be content with Miranda's "Later, Rosie," before Rosie drove her in one of the site's Jeeps over to Albatross.

Here, behind the crenelated walls and beneath the peaceful, grape-laden arbors, the silvery green leaves of gnarled olive trees and fruit-laden figs and oranges, hidden amid the aromatic herbs and cascades of bougainvillea and fuchsia and jasmine, the final act of the drama was to be played out. But instead of surrounding Miranda with magic, as it first had upon her arrival, Albatross had taken on the air and look of a stage setting constructed specifically for a conference of major importance.

She was, of course, met by those perpetual lookouts, Little Mike and Penelope. The boy threw himself at her, and then backed away, expressing wide-eyed alarm as he pointed at her various bandages and band-aids. Penelope, still shy, hung back a few feet.

"Not to worry," Miranda assured them warmly. "They're just surface scratches. Like *you—*" she smiled at Little Mike and ruffled his hair affectionately "—no doubt get when you climb trees and rocks and arbors."

Eleni Vlachos, tailored and groomed to perfection, hair freshly hennaed and set, came hurrying upon hearing the children's voices raised in excitement. She expressed visible shock at Miranda's appearance and embraced her carefully, so as not to inflict additional pain.

"*Christe mou!*" she exclaimed, placing one hand dramatically over her heart. "What on earth has happened?"

Then, clapping her hands sharply and making shooing motions, she sent the young ones scurrying, admonishing them in Greek to make themselves neither seen nor heard.

"I'll tell you all about it later," Miranda promised, but it was an empty promise, she knew. She and Big Mike had some major conferring to do, and some major decisions to come to first.

And there he was. Big Mike. Shoving back his chair from the very same big, round table where the Mitropoulos group had only so recently partied, and where he had now been conferring with Professor Hirsch, Apostolos Malinakis (whom she instantly recognized from a distance as her rescuer from Delos), and two strangers she had yet to meet. Captain Pispas was also there—she assumed by virtue of a gesture, though nobody seemed to pay him much attention. She noticed that Big Mike was waving a sheaf of printout at her, and was favoring his right shoulder, where Chara had stabbed him.

And, to Miranda's immense surprise, even shock, there was Harry—yes, none other than Harris Milford Palmer III, who still believed her to be his fiancée—even closer, seated at a separate small table under heavy clusters of grapes. The instant he spied her he sprang to his feet, papers in hand, and outdistanced Big Mike by several yards.

I'm not ready for this, Miranda thought dismally. *He wasn't supposed to have arrived here yet.*

But he obviously was. Several days earlier than expected.

"I believe," Eleni told her wisely, "I had best leave you alone for now. We will talk later. Yes?"

There was a twinkle in her eye as she gave Miranda a conspiratorial wink before diplomatically making herself scarce.

Harry reached her first.

"Mandy! Oh, Mandy. I mean—" he swallowed awkwardly, obviously out of his element "—I mean, *Miranda!* Ron told me in no uncertain terms how you hated being called Mandy. Oh, God. You've had me worried sick. *Sick!*"

Miranda gestured for Big Mike, never one to hold his horses, to give them space. "I need ten or fifteen minutes alone, Mike," she said softly. "Okay?"

She could see him sizing up Harry with narrowed eyes, who in turn sized Mike up. Harry in his Brooks Brothers suit, tie loosened and top collar of his Wall Street-acceptable shirt open, jacket slung over his shoulder. And Big Mike in a lightweight shirt and cargo shorts and boots.

Then Big Mike gave a grudging nod and returned to the big round table.

"Hello, Harry," Miranda said softly, with affection, and accepted the peck on her lips.

It was then that Harry took a good long look at her. "Jesus H. Christ!" he exclaimed. "What happened to you? Were you in a battle?"

If he only knew, she thought, *only he never will.*

"Harry," she said gently, "it's a long story, and I'll fill you in on it later."

Later. That delaying adverb had, she realized, suddenly shot to the top of her vocabulary.

"Harry," she suggested, "let's take a walk." She hooked her arm through his and led him back out, limping slightly, along the *krokalia*—paved, dappled walk and past the lanterns at the crenelated entry.

"God!" he said, "have I ever missed you! You have no idea!"

She smiled slightly. "And I've missed your ugly mug too," she murmured, but without either humor or passion. "What do you say we stroll this way, past the boat repair yard and along the waterfront."

"But your foot—"

"It's just a sprained ankle, and I'll lean on you if I have to."

"You're welcome to," he said.

I'll try my best not to, she thought. *I've left him hanging long enough.*

"I've brought you these," he said, proffering the papers in his hand with the eagerness of a student bringing home a straight-A report card. "This computer hacker I know managed to compile quite a list of the people who own some of the offshore corporations that have invested heavily in GlobaLux."

And when she didn't take the papers right away, he added, with a hurt expression: "What's the matter? I thought you needed these."

"I *do,*" she said, ducking her head guiltily, "but I can't accept them under false pretenses. Harry—" she forced herself to look him straight in the eye "—we really need to talk. And I could use a nice stiff drink. Let's find a table at one of these places over *there*—"

She was steering him towards the tourist-jammed crescent of cafés, tavernas, and bars with their various awnings jutting jauntily out onto the quay, where the tables were filled with high-spirited merry-makers from all over Europe intent upon holiday cheer and over-imbibing food and drink. Mainly drink.

"Why can't we just sit at a quiet table at Albatross?" he asked. "It seems a helluva lot more pleasant."

She sighed to herself. How could she explain to him that she needed to be away from Eleni's and the cast of characters with whom she would shortly have to deal? That she wanted—no, desperately *needed!*—to be on neutral turf for what they had to discuss.

"Trust me, Harry?" she said.

Through sheer luck they found a vacated, waterfront table halfway down, under a peaked awning of a café-bar called The Illiad, and took a seat. The jolly crowd, plied with cocktails, clashed with her emotional burden.

The proprietress, a good-humored Australian in her early fifties, cheerfully provided a cocktail menu.

Harry took one look at it, frowned at elaborate drinks with names like Ivory Jo-Jo's, West Indies Flying Yellow Bird, and Bep's Cocktail—not to mention Helen of Troy—and decided upon a whisky straight, no ice.

Miranda chose Homer's Delight—one part vodka, one half Advocaat, plus grenadine, triple sec, and whipped cream topped with a glacé cherry, hoping that the mixture was just the right combination to provide liquid courage.

While they waited, they could hear, above the noise of the partying crowd, the ropes and lines of the docked yachts creaking; they watched the masts of the sailboats gently swaying as a large tour boat departed for one of the myriad beaches, caught a scene from a large flatscreen television through the glass sliding doors of a sleek, aerodynamically designed motor yacht that looked like an inflated athletic shoe—a giant white Nike, perhaps, or maybe a futuristic Reebok. They made small talk until the drinks arrived, and when they did, Harry instantly downed a large swallow of his whisky. Miranda didn't bother with the straw, just took a huge sip, then licked off her whipped cream moustache with the tip of her tongue, unaware of the daub of white decorating the tip of her nose.

Harry reached across and affectionately wiped it off with his finger.

"Har—"

"Mir—"

They both spoke at the same time, and laughed nervously.

"You're all tense," he observed quietly. "Is it because of me?"

"Oh, Harry." She attempted a smile, but it came off rather sickly. "I *want* to tell you all that's happened, but I can't. Not yet."

There it was again. Another variation of "*later.*"

"From the looks of it," he said, indicating her various bandages and Band-Aids "I take it you've been through a lot."

You have no idea, she thought, and then, taking a deep breath, plunged on ahead. "Harry, about our engagement—"

"I noticed you're not wearing the ring," he said quietly, leaning toward her. "If it's about that bimbo Tiffany Pfeiffer and my Blackberry, I can assure you—"

"No. Oh, God no. Harry, it isn't that." She flicked her fingers as if ridding herself of a pesky fly. "It's—"

She lowered her eyes to her tall glass, frowning at the maraschino cherry floating on whipped cream halfway down. It was like a child's melted ice cream sundae, and she suddenly lost her taste for it and pushed it aside. Then she raised her eyes and met his gaze directly.

"It's that I *do* love you, Harry. I really *do.*"

"I hear a 'but' in there somewhere." He knocked back another quarter glassful of whisky. "Let me guess. But you're not '*in love*' with me. That is what you were going to say, isn't it?"

She nodded guiltily, a flicker of pain crossing her face. "I have the ring right here, in my pocket."

"Oh, *Christ,* Miranda! I don't give a rat's ass about the damn ring!"

"I know you don't."

"Why don't you keep it?"

"No." She shook her head violently. "That would be wrong. Convention requires that I return it."

He had to chuckle. "Since when did convention ever enter your equation?"

"Call it baggage. My mother would spin in her grave if I didn't return it. Some—" her fingers fluttered in midair, like birds about to take wing "—some things need to be properly observed."

She half-rose, dug the ring out of her pocket, sat back down, and reached across the little table and pressed it into his hand. The big Tiffany solitaire glittered in the sun. An unpleasant thought pecked at her. She could just imagine The Witch examining it through his loupe, hear that garbled frog's croak of a voice reeling off the four C's—color, cut, clarity, carats. The very thought made her shudder and she quickly closed Harry's fingers around it. From an adjoining table, a fresh round of exotic drinks arrived, bringing on a round of applause and loud expressions of cheer.

Harry sighed with anguish. "So you've finally made up your mind."

"Yes." She nodded soberly.

"Is there somebody else? Mr. Muscle, perhaps?"

For a moment, Miranda didn't make the connection. "Mr. *who?*"

"You know, the big guy. Back there at Albatross."

A visual image of Big Mike flashed fleetingly through her mind. "You mean Big Mike?" She laughed. "Don't be silly, Harry. He and I've barely met, and he's been a surly bastard from the get-go. There's something big and evil I've stumbled across, and that I can't talk about just yet. But yes, Big Mike did save my life. I owe him that. But forget him. This isn't about Big Mike. It's about us two, Harry. Our relationship. All I know is that you—" she sighed and pinched her nose at the hackneyed way she was putting it, but couldn't conjure up a better way to phrase it "—well, you deserve better than me."

"Aw, come on. That's hogwash, and you know it!"

Her voice was soft. "Face it, Harry. We've had some good times. Even great times. I want us always to be friends."

"Friends!" he said bitterly. Now it was his turn to smile grimly. "Isn't that just another way of saying 'Get lost'?"

"No." Miranda shook her head adamantly and her voice was firm. "I mean it. I really do." A slight smile suddenly crossed her lips.

"What's so funny?" he demanded.

"It just occurred to me that at least your mother will be relieved. I know she never really approved of me."

"Well, I can't deny the fact that Mother did try to persuade me not to marry you. But her opinion never made an ounce of difference to me."

"I know that, Harry," she said quietly, "which is just one more reason why I *do* love you. And look on the bright side. At least we won't both be subjected to those awful family gatherings at the 'WASPs' Nest'."

He tilted his head and frowned. "The 'WASPs' Nest'?" he parroted, obviously clueless as to what she was referring to.

"Oh." She cringed slightly. "Sorry. But that's how I always thought of their house in Kennebunkport."

Suddenly he threw back his head and laughed. "By God, Man . . .

I mean, Miranda! You are something else, you know that? You really hit the nail on the head with that one. Damn. Now I'll never be able to think of that rambling old house as anything else." He shook his head. "The 'WASPs' Nest.' That's a good one."

It was then that he happened to glance past her.

"Holy shit!" he exclaimed. "What is that?"

She twisted around to look. Big and shiny and unmistakable, the *Olympia II* had just nosed into the harbor, and was in the process of berthing lengthwise, with arrogant superiority, at the precise spot where she had first seen it dock, at the quay right beside Albatross, between the small, swift, gray vessels of the Greek Coast Guard.

"Oh, that," she said. "It's the Liapsis yacht."

He raised his eyebrows. "You mean *the* Liapsises?"

"Yes, of course." She nodded. "I had dinner with Yannis and his wife and son, among others, just the other evening."

"You're kidding! I've got a business meeting with Yannis Liapsis scheduled, which is how I managed to get here when I did. Jeepers creepers! You do move in high circles."

"Get real, Harry. It wasn't because of me. It was Jan Kofski. The gallery owner? He's apparently visiting them, and introduced me. They have a private island near here. But enough about them. We're talking about *us,* Harry. Now, will you allow us to remain friends, or not?"

He sighed heavily. "How can I help it? You know the answer is yes."

She sought his hand and squeezed it. "I honestly believe," she said huskily, "that we're better suited as friends than as an old, bickering married couple."

He read the sincerity in her eyes and swallowed. "I'll always be there if you need me, Miranda. You can count on it. Just so long as you promise that if I ever have kids, you'll be at the top of the godmother list."

She was astonished. "You mean it, Harry? Honestly?"

"'Heart crossed and hope to die'," he quoted.

Relief flooded through her, and her eyes grew moist. "You've got yourself a deal, Harris Milford Palmer."

"And I'll hold you to it," he warned. "Now here, before we both get all misty-eyed and can't see, take these."

He held out the sheaf of papers.

"I won't accept them unless we're still friends," she warned him.

"We won't be," he countered, "if you don't take these."

Miranda accepted them graciously and idly flipped through the pages of GlobaLux International's major corporate investors. Three different offshore companies with innocuous-sounding names jumped off a page at her.

"Oh, shit," she groaned weakly, letting the pages flutter back in place. She rubbed her forehead. "Oh, Harry."

"What is it?" He was leaning forward with concern.

"I have to get back to Albatross right away."

"Sure. No problem. I'll get the check and walk you back."

"No." She shook her head vehemently. "For the time being, at least until after you've concluded your business meeting with the Liapsises, I suggest you're best off not being seen with me."

"But why? I don't understand."

"Because," Miranda said, nearly upsetting her chair in her hurry to get up, "I don't want to screw up any deal you might be in the process of making."

She leaned down and quickly kissed his cheek.

"Let's talk again," she said, "before you leave Samos. But only after your business here is done."

He stared at her in bafflement.

"Trust me, Harry," she whispered, giving him a swift embrace before limping off as quickly as her sprained ankle would allow.

Big Mike was waiting for her, printout in hand, just outside the crenelated entrance to Albatross, leaning against one of the stucco pillars topped with big, round, frosted glass globes. Seeing his intensely somber expression, Miranda immediately went on the offensive.

"Look, I'm sorry," she said wearily. "I know it took longer than anticipated."

Beyond the sun-dappled greenery of Albatross' garden, the side thrusters of the *Olympia II* had pushed the giant yacht gently against the quay, its great white hull protected by round medicine-ball-size fenders at regular intervals, its hydraulic gangway already lowered. No one had disembarked, but Miranda could see the shadowy figures of crew members in white moving about the main and sundecks.

"It isn't that," Big Mike said grimly. "It's what I downloaded from your e-mail. From your friend, Mara."

"From your expression, I'm almost afraid to look." She cast him a strange glance. "Mike? Should I be?"

"It sure as hell shattered me," he replied, then sagged visibly, as if he were a balloon that had been punctured and needed the pillar to prop itself up as it shrank. "Christ almighty, I'd never have believed it," he whispered fiercely. "Not in a million years! Hell, I still don't *want* to believe it!"

"Why?" she persisted. "What did she find out?"

"Here." He thrust the message at her, the paper crumpled and moist from here he'd been clutching it. "Read it for yourself."

She took it and scanned the message, then frowned. "The provenance for all of the artifacts I asked about at Kofski's lists a 'Mrs. Norbert Kimmelmann'." She cast him a puzzled glance. "Am I supposed to know who she is?"

"No. But the trouble is, *I* do. She's visited here for the last few summers."

"So who *is* she?"

"Are you ready for this?"

The bitterness in his tone forewarned her. "At this point, no," she said wearily. "I'm not ready for anything more. But you might as well hit me with it anyway. Things can't be any worse than they already are, can they?"

He shut his eyes and slammed a fist against the stucco, scraping his knuckles. "Try the Prof's sister-in-law," he said hoarsely.

Miranda blurted: "What?" Her voice was shocked, and she nearly stumbled while standing upright. It was like a blow to her stomach, and she too now slumped against one of the pillars. "You can't be serious! Tell me you're playing a practical joke on me, Mike. Please."

But Big Mike could only shake his head. "If only I were."

She was suddenly aware of the cicadas shrilling from the trees as if chorusing the accusation. Muffled by the greenery, other sounds intruded upon her shock: the chug-chug-chug of a pleasure cruiser leaving the harbor; the clashing music, frivolous shrieks, and bursts of ouzo-boozo laughter carried by the breeze from the tavernas, cafés, and bars lining the waterfront. Miranda found herself envying those people their carefree, unencumbered lives, their ability to let off steam and, with a passion, focus all their energies upon one thing, and one thing alone—partying away during an untroubled holiday far from the stresses and strains of their everyday lives.

And here she'd come, all the way from Manhattan, hoping to leave stress and strain behind, to work at an archeological dig at long last—and what had happened? Instead of digging and sifting, she'd found herself buried smack dab in a fine can of worms. Embroiled in a cauldron of mystery, violence, conspiracy, and deceit.

All of which were the last things she'd expected.

"It's all so obvious *now!*" Big Mike raged quietly to himself. "Suddenly all those little pieces are falling into place. I don't want to believe it, but it's clear that the cream of our finds had to have been personally chosen by the Prof. And that those damn juggling Tatoulis Brothers and their sister, who were supposed to *protect* the site—what a joke!—tossed them from across one side of the fence to the other. And then that monster of a caricature, The Witch, transported them off to Athens, and on to Frau Kimmelmann!"

"Maybe . . . maybe there's more than one Mrs. Norbert Kimmelmann?" Miranda suggested, her voice weak with false hope.

"From Dortmund?" Big Mike shook his head savagely. "No. No fucking way. Jesus H.! And here I've been since the beginning—the very *beginning!*" He clenched his fists and futilely hammered them against his thighs. "How *blind* could I have been?"

"It's not your fault, Mike," Miranda said softly.

"Isn't it?" He turned on her savagely. "I've had blinders on!"

"No, you haven't. How could you ever have known that Professor Hirsch's sister-in-law was the recipient of the missing pieces? It took Mara to discover that. You've got to stop blaming yourself."

He heaved a massive breath, letting it out like the snort of a bull. "I should at least have guessed about the Tatoulises being involved."

"No, Mike," she said flatly. "Don't you see? You were too close. Why should you have even suspected them? You didn't have the information. The question now is, how do you suggest we proceed? We really don't have any choice but to deal with this matter."

Big Mike rubbed his chin, then snapped at her in what he knew, and she understood, was an attempt to lob the ball into her court. "What I need is your input, Miranda. How do *you* think we should tackle this God-awful mess? I need your decision. Christ! To think the Prof of all people being involved in the smuggling of antiquities! It just blows me away!"

Miranda sighed. "Me, too. But I owe him so much! My Ph.D., for example. My job at Jan Kofski's, for another." Her voice grew hushed and pained. "He's always been my hero."

"Yeah. Same at this end. I owe him, too. Big time. Which makes this all the harder."

There was a lengthy silence and a shared sense of guilt and indebtedness, not to mention a feeling of necessary collusion between herself and Big Mike. And he, she sensed, though suddenly stripped of his blinders, wasn't ready to throw Professor Hirsch to the wolves.

Nor was she. Her mind whirled, swirled, swarmed with possible scenarios like summer gnats. "Maybe," she asked softly, "there's a chance, flimsy as it might be, to keep him out of the smuggling end of it, and save his reputation? So long as we confront him first, lay our cards on the table, and see if he's willing to cooperate? Before we talk to anyone else?"

He stared at her. "How? Isn't it a little late for that? I've spent all bloody morning and most of the afternoon protecting us—just so nobody tries to kill us again!"

"Our insurance, as you called it," she said tightly.

"Yeah." Big Mike nodded, his face lengthening. "I've already contacted all the major newspapers and magazines and television stations. They'll be descending upon us like locusts in the morning. I've scheduled a press conference for tomorrow afternoon to show off Hera. First person I called was my contact at *Kathimerini.* He's on his way out here as we speak."

He added grimly, "Hell, he might have arrived already."

"And what, precisely," she inquired, "did you tell him?"

"The same thing I told all the others. *Le Figaro, France Soir,* the *Frankfurter Allgemeine, The New York Times,* among others. Plus magazines. Television stations. All the major museums. The National in Athens, the Pergamon in Berlin, the British, the Met in New York, the Getty—" He waved a weary hand. "Everyone I could think of."

"And what did you tell them?"

"That the Site at Ancient Asprodavos has made a major archeological discovery. That we've discovered the top half of Hera. Only I didn't give them our names as the discoverers. Don't kill me for that."

"Don't worry, I won't. In other words, we can still protect Wald and his reputation?"

"If we credit him with the discovery, I think so. Yeah." He scratched his head. "Think you can deal with that?"

"Can you?" she countered softly.

He looked down at the ground and kicked at a pebble. Then he looked up and nodded. "Much as I hate to, yeah. But the Prof's got to be willing to face the press and make an official statement. One *we* write up. And he'll have to follow our script to the letter."

There was a long moment of silence. When Miranda broke it, her voice was quiet. "I'm amenable."

"It means not entering the history books."

"So?" She shrugged. "It was never my intention to become a celebrity."

He could only shake his head. "You're one in a billion, Miranda, you know that?"

"Me? Don't make me laugh. You're the one who's worked wonders, especially for a guy who hasn't slept all night or all day, climbed a cliff, saved a damsel-in-distress, faced off dogs, been stabbed by a crazed Medea—"

"Hey, we're in Greece, remember? Land of myths and legends. Besides, that was the easy part. It was all that phoning and faxing and e-mailing that nearly did me in. Which," he smiled widely with satisfaction, "is why *they're* here."

He half-turned and poked a thumb in the direction of the distant round table, where The Witch and his wife had entertained the Liapsises and their party only yesterday? Or had it been the day before? Her mind was a jumbled blur; too much had happened in too short a period of time, and she had totally lost track of hours and days.

"Do you have any idea just who those people are?" he asked.

She peered past his shoulder toward the table, half-shielded by cascading bougainvillea and ancient, gnarled olive trees and palms.

"How could I know them, other than Apos and Captain Pispas?"

"Well, the man with the square face and that little gray curtain of a moustache? That's Andreas Yannides. He's Mr. *Malakas*'"—he mispronounced Apostolos' last name purposely as a venomous curse "—big boss. None other than the Greek Minister of Culture himself."

"You're kidding!" Her mouth dropped open.

"Nope, I'm serious. He hopped on the first flight out here from Athens. And that heavy man with silver hair and red complexion?"

"You mean the one sitting next to that pipsqueak Pispas?"

"Yeah. That's Manolis Kardalis, the local Prefect of Police. You don't think I'd trust Pispas as far as I can throw him, do you?"

"Goodness, but you *have* been a busy little bee," she said, wonder in her voice. "And I assume the Liapsis yacht's arrival is no accident either, but your doing?"

"Uh-huh." He grinned, showing teeth. "After all, their foundation has a vested interest in this, as they're among our major contributors at Asprodavos. I also requested that if they're still hosting their guests, the Kofskis and the Vassilakises, we'd appreciate their presence as well. Theodoros Vassilakis, if you'll recall, is Greece's very own Foreign Minister."

"I remember. The one in charge of stamping out the smuggling of human cargo into this country."

"As well as being Despina Mitropoulou's half brother," he added dryly.

"And *are* the Kofskis and Vassilakises still aboard?"

"We lucked out. They are."

It was almost too much to absorb all at once. Miranda's head was spinning. "And The Witch and his wife?"

"I specifically requested that they be omitted."

She felt a wave of relief. She wasn't sure how she'd have reacted to The Witch's presence.

"So how do you suggest we proceed, Mike? I gather you've given it a lot of thought."

"I have. First we need to talk with the Prof. Then we confer with certain parties. Split them up, tackling one issue at a time, starting with The Witch's part in smuggling human cargo. Oh. Did I mention that Providence is smiling upon us?"

"As a matter of fact, you haven't."

It just so happens that one of the *Meltemi*s, either the *I* or the *II,* I'm not sure which, has docked at Vathi this morning. That'll simplify things a lot. Prefect Kardalis and Mr. Vassilakis will be able to swipe that second boarding pass, the fake one with some stranger's picture on it, through that little gadget as proof of the method The Witch and his cohorts used. So we'll be needing it. Time for you to dig it up from wherever you buried it."

It was her turn to grin. "No need to. I have it right here," she said, smugly patting her pocket.

"So where *did* you hide it?"

"Where nobody would suspect. In plain sight, right on the shelf above my bunk in the ladies' dorm."

"Clever cookie. Just like *The Purloined Letter.*"

"I destroyed my own the other night. Burned it in that outdoor grill over there when no one was looking. Slipped it through the grating onto the coals right between some octopus and a huge fish."

He laughed. "I imagine the burning, melting plastic must have imparted an extra-special flavor. Remind me to ask Eleni whether or not the octopus and fish were especially praised!"

"Oh, and one more thing, Mike. You haven't read what Harry's hacker managed to get hold of."

She thrust the sheaf of printout she was holding into his hand.

"That's a partial list of some of the offshore corporations with major interests in GlobaLux, including the names of the clients *behind* the accounts. I suggest you look on page three."

She waited for him to flip through the printout.

"Notice three certain corporations and who owns them?"

"Ho-ly shit!" He stared at her. "The Liapsis Family Trust! Oh, but does this ever give us extra ammunition! I hope you gave your Harry a huge kiss for this."

"Well, I did give my *ex*-fiancé—" she emphasized the "ex-" "—a friendly little peck on the cheek. Now then, I'm pretty weary after all we've been through. What do you say we get on with it, Mike, and get this nightmare over and done with?"

"Yeah," he said, suddenly energized by the printout. "Time to go slay some dragons!"

He started to turn, but she tugged at his sleeve. "Dragons?" she said.

"Yeah. What about them?"

"They're mediaeval. We're in Greece, remember?"

They smiled at each other.

"Right," he corrected. "How could I forget? Time to go slay some Gorgons, Harpies, and a Minotaur."

It was midday.

Three days had passed but the worst of the madness was finally over. The press that had descended in droves had left, the dynamiting across the chasm had halted, and the bulldozers and earth-moving equipment had slunk away from the site of GlobaLux's "traditional island village" resort, where work had been indefinitely halted. Only a giant yellow crane remained, waiting to hoist Hera from Arion's cavernous workshop.

The other archeologists were indoors, having their siestas and waiting for the worst of the intense heat to abate.

Miranda and Big Mike were seated in one of the tarpaulin-tented work areas, where the chain-link fence at the chasm where the natural bridge had collapsed was in the process of being dismantled, while a second work crew had begun extending a length of chain-link to expand the Site at Ancient Asprodavos to include the entire area where the resort would now never be built.

Once again, Apollo's chariot blazed across a hot, cloudless sky of perfect blue, drenching schist and volcanic rock and thorny scrub, and casting purple shadows. The sea glittered calmly with its brilliant sequins, and a gull glided overhead. In this silence, it was possible to hear the wavelets lapping the pebble beach far below.

Miranda, one arm enfolding her knees tucked up under her chin, put out a hand and Big Mike instantly took it and held it gently. For a few minutes longer, they sat there in the shade, gazing toward the series of promontories jutting their great, sloping green humps downward into the sea.

From somewhere behind them came the disrupting sound of sturdy shoes and brisk hiking boots, of familiar voices raised vigorously and gaining in intensity as they approached.

"I say! There she is! *Hul*-lo there!" hailed a chorus.

"Yoo-hoo, Miranda! *Mi . . . ran . . . da!*" trilled Madge Blessing's distinctive Mid-western voice.

Miranda turned around, not believing her ears—or her eyes. Descending upon her and Big Mike, with raw-faced, sinewy Don striding in the lead, came the four nurses in their "Pediatric Oncology Unit" T-shirts, all talking excitedly at once, with Em and Fan helping along a wilting Madge, who instead of fanning herself with her wide-brimmed straw hat was now waving it back and forth in great arcs while hopping up and down.

"Hiding again, are you?" called out plump, jolly Em.

"We warned you we'd be visiting Samos once the cruise was over," Don joined in.

"And it was over sooner than expected!" Fan said breathlessly.

"We were on Amorgos when the *Meltemi II* was *confiscated!*" added Soph. "By the authorities!"

"So we hopped on the next ferry, and here we are!" Madge burbled, spreading her arms wide before beginning to fan herself.

"Who *are* they?" Big Mike whispered, letting go of Miranda's hand as they both scrambled to their feet.

"Friends," Miranda smiled broadly. "Now be nice. If it weren't for Madge, I'd never have been aboard the *Meltemi II,* never have discovered the immigrant smuggling. And we'd never have discovered Hera. Or . . ."

But before Miranda could say, "and I'd never have discovered you" she was immediately engulfed in warm, multitudinous embraces. Dozing lizards scattered, scales glinting in the sun, and the gull banked out to sea.

Madge's embrace was the warmest and heartiest. "Oh, my dear!

It's so *good* to see you! How we missed you!" Then she stood back. "Goodness! Why, you're more covered with Band-Aids and bandages and bruises than the last time I saw you! What adventures *have* you been up to now?" Her eyes twinkled mischievously. "You simply *must* tell me! I have this feeling that all those things we've been reading and seeing on television about this great statue being discovered, and all this immigrant smuggling business, somehow involved you? Am I right?"

Miranda smiled. "Don't worry. I'll fill you in on it personally."

"Oh, *good!* I do so love mysteries!"

Meanwhile Don's stern eyes were taking stock of Big Mike. "Strong, solid, muscular." She nodded brisk approval. "Strapping outdoorsy type."

Miranda introduced him all around.

"Goodness!" Madge exclaimed again, clasping her hands happily. "And thank heavens that that horrid Chara person stayed here when we sailed and someone else took over the cruise director position. You haven't run into her, by any chance, have you? Whatever on earth has happened to her?"

Miranda glanced at the chasm where the natural bridge had been, made eye contact with Big Mike, and a silent communication passed between them.

"Who knows?" she said breezily, with a shrug, for both had decided that some bodies, like some stories, were best left buried. "Now, I think all you ladies could use some refreshment. What do you say we all hop in a Jeep and Mike will drive us into Pythagoria. I know just the place for us to catch up on things."

"Oh!" Madge exclaimed. "You mean that lovely Albatross place?"

Miranda caught Big Mike's glance. "Oh, Albatross is never open until dinner. But I can think of a much more *fun* place for now. It's called The Iliad, and it's rowdy and noisy and serves the most marvelous cocktails. Plus—" this for the quartet of nurses "—the proprietress is from Down Under. New Zealand, if I'm not mistaken. Or is it Australia?"

Their chattering dimmed as their feet raised small clouds of dust as they left. Slowly, the lizards crawled back out from hiding in shady cracks and crevasses. The seagull returned, floating on the air currents.

Don looked back over her shoulders, surveying the distant green promontories. "Promising spot for hiking," she declared, with a brisk nod.

Big Mike took Miranda's hand and squeezed it. "Promising spot for anything," he whispered.

She exchanged a secret smile and returned his squeeze. *Promising, yes,* she thought, her eyes alight—for all Greek dramas did not, necessarily, have to end in tragedy.

[CHAPTER FORTY EIGHT]

Pythagoria, Samos

KATHIMERINI
English Edition

ATHENS, FRIDAY, SEPTEMBER 12, 2008

Shares of Mitropoulos Holdings Plunge

Millionaire arrested on charges of immigrant trafficking and antiquities smuggling

Nikos Mitropoulos, the majority stockholder of a holding company, which belongs to a group listed on the Athens stock market, and that included the now defunct Oracle Cruise Line, Golden Fleece Jewelry shops, 17 pottery factories, including several in Piraeus and on the islands of Samos and Paros, as well as countless souvenir shops throughout the Aegean and Ionian seas was arrested and charged with illegal human trafficking as well as the smuggling of antiquities out of the country.

Athens Prefect Pambos Roussopoulos said yesterday that an on-going investigation had uncovered the plot, which apparently had been going on for years, but declined to comment on what evidence the case had been cracked.

"This is a major victory in the stamping out of bringing human cargo into Greece and the entire European Union," said Theodoros Vassilakis, the Foreign Ministry's general secretary for Greece in Washington, D.C., speaking from his home in the Athens suburb of Kifissia.

In June, lawmakers from the European Union voted 369–197 to allow undocumented migrants to be held in detention centers for up to 18 months.

Also charged as an accessory was Chara Zouboulakis, 32, of the city of Arta in Epirus, Mr. Mitropoulos' close associate and one of three "cruise directors" aboard Oracle Cruise Lines' vessels. There is an outstanding warrant for her arrest, but she has yet to be located.

Despina Mitropoulos, Mr. Mitropoulos' wife, was on a flight to Brazil with their children at the time of her husband's arrest, and was unavailable for comment.

[CHAPTER FORTY NINE]

New York City

WEEKEND Arts
The New York Times

FRIDAY, OCTOBER 19, 2008

A Goddess Rises from Antiquity:
The Discovery of the Greek "Mona Lisa"

By Landon Ridgefield Jr.
and Wendy Skrebnevski

ATHENS, Greece—"It is the find of the century," crowed Andreas Yannides, the Greek Minister of Culture, during the unveiling, adding with a smile, "Of course, the century is still young and Greece is full of as-yet undiscovered treasures."

As the battles over cultural patrimony rage between the world's great museums and their countries of origin, a major archeological discovery on the Greek island of Samos has suddenly taken center stage—and in a starring, scenery-chewing role, no less.

Like a grand dame of ages past, who believed one's name should never appear in print unless it was the announcement of a birth or a death, the recovery of the top half of a long sought-after statue of the Greek goddess, Hera, has no scandal attached to her. No battles over looted treasures and their return. No lawsuits. No antiquities curators on trial. Not yet, at least.

The almost 9-foot-tall, top-half of the marble statue, remarkably intact, was "found on Greek soil and shall remain on Greek soil," Mr. Yannides announced firmly at the news conference on Wednesday.

Recovered by a team of archeologists led by Professor Waldemar Hirsch, Ph.D. of The Site at Ancient Asprodavos, the statue, dating back to 522 B.C., ranks among the all-time great discoveries of antiquity. And she is exquisite. Carved of pale gray Samian marble with its trademark bluish striations, and wearing a serene expression with the very faintest of smiles, she is already being called "the Mona Lisa of Antiquity."

There is one catch, however. The bottom half of the statue, which had apparently been cracked in two during an earthquake, was recovered from a cavern on Samos in 1942 by Dr. Professor Friedrich Hammerschlag of what was then called the Reichsmuseum in Berlin. Subsequently it occupied the place of honor in the courtyard at Karinhall, Hermann Göring's infamous hunting lodge, a notorious repository of some of the greatest art treasures ever looted from museums and private collections during the Nazi occupation of Europe.

Professor Hammerschlag died during its transport, and the location of the cavern had since been lost. At present, the bottom half of Hera resides in the Pergamon Museum in Berlin. At least for now

"But not for long. We are already engaged in serious negotiations with the Pergamon for the return of the bottom half," Mr. Yannides said, carefully avoiding the word 'looted.' "The top and bottom of Hera must be reunited, and will be."

The unveiling was attended by a weary-looking Professor Hirsch, flanked by two of his former students, Miranda Kalli of Manhattan and Michalis "Big Mike" Savides, a Greek-American who hails from Tarpon Springs, Florida.

Professor Hirsch attributes the credit for the discovery to Ms. Kalli and Mr. Savides. But Ms. Kalli, who has spent several years as an associate at the recently closed Jan Kofski

Gallery on Madison Avenue, declared that finding the statue was purely accidental. "If anyone is responsible for this find it's Professor Hirsch," she said firmly. "He has been instrumental in the creation of the dig in the first place. In truth, Mr. Savides and I were trespassing on an adjoining property outside the archeological site. If we hadn't fallen into the cavern, the top half of Hera might never have been recovered."

Mr. Savides, a man of few words, concurs. "It was pure happenstance and sheer luck."

The adjoining property in question, owned by a Swiss hotel consortium, has meanwhile been purchased by the Liapsis Foundation for an undisclosed sum. Reached by telephone, a spokesperson for Mr. Yannis Liapsis, Thanos Spyridakis, acknowledged the sale and verified that the title to the property has since been given to the Greek Ministry of Culture as a gift to the people. "The Liapsis family have been firm supporters of the Site at Ancient Asprodavos from the very start," he said.

When asked whether the statue would be displayed at the Liapsis-endowed museum in Athens, known as The Liapsis Collection of Ancient Art, or whether it would end up at the Archeological Museum on Samos, he said that both locations are under consideration.

During the news conference, Professor Hirsch also announced his retirement as director of what is known as The Site at Ancient Asprodavos. Citing ill health and weariness, he said that he is recommending Ms. Kalli and Mr. Savides to step into his shoes as co-directors. "It is time for a younger generation to take command. I cannot think of two more dedicated professionals."

Incidentally, Ms. Kalli and Mr. Savides were recently married in a quiet civil ceremony. The bride is keeping her maiden name.

"Is it any wonder," Mr. Yannides said, "that the goddess appears to be smiling?"